CARRIE SLEP
her body, like the
her thoughts stopp
the next.

Slowly, slowly, the   began to form within
her calm world, taking on harder edges, emerging
from the fro
She saw a pa
toward the c
a patch, a st
for grass on
from the Ta
that surrounded her home.

The stain inched forward toward the tree line
that marked the boundary of their estate and there
it stopped for the moment. When it began to move
again, the memory flooded back. It was as green
as the
throu
Car
Kashi
draw
burni
came
realiz
then.
feel th
praye
and h

Lisanne Norman

DARK NADIR

A *Sholan Alliance* Novel

DAW BOOKS, INC.
DONALD A. WOLLHEIM, FOUNDER
375 Hudson Street, New York, NY 10014

ELIZABETH R. WOLLHEIM
SHEILA E. GILBERT
PUBLISHERS

First Printing, March 1999
4   5   6   7   8   9

DAW TRADEMARK REGISTERED
U.S. PAT. OFF. AND FOREIGN COUNTRIES
—MARCA REGISTRADA
HECHO EN U.S.A.

PRINTED IN THE U.S.A.

This book is for Judith Faul Dumont, who is one of the very few people who can journey to Shola with me when I'm writing. Her help and support over the years have been tremendous as well as great fun.

It's also for her husband Chris, a very talented Game Master who's helped me solve a tricky problem or three over the years. Thank you both very much.

A few special thanks are in order, as usual.

To James Chorlton, aka Merlin, and Helen Lofting for letting me consult them on matters as diverse as the composition of space fleets and designing starships to tactics and very dirty tricks—and rescuing my computer when it crashes!

To John Van Stry for information on rearing large felines.

To Josh for his knowledge of military trauma medicine and ballistics.

Thanks also to the many friends who've sat and brainstormed with me at conventions—Sherrie, Keith, and Pauline to name only three.

And finally, thanks to Mike Gilbert for his drawings of my aliens which truly inspired me when I came to write about them.

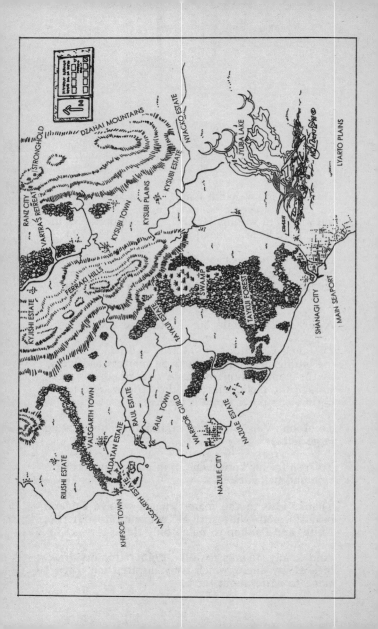

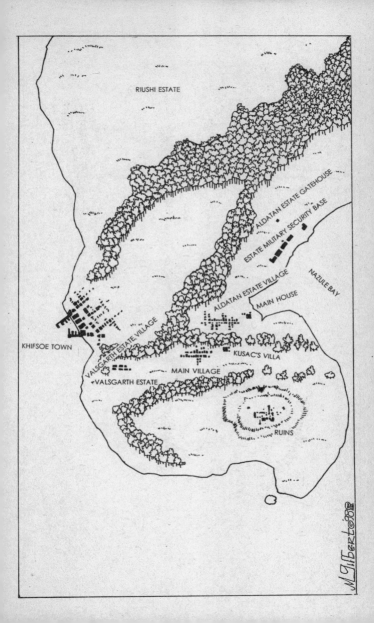

PROLOGUE

NO sooner had the young Sumaan pilot, Ashay, landed the shuttle back at the *Hkariyash* than he was ordered to return to the U'Churian vessel, the *Rryuk's Profit*.

"They have need of the Human medications on board their shuttle," said Captain Kishasayzar, speaking to him in their own language over the comm. "Carrie Aldatan has been seriously injured. Place yourself under Captain Tirak's orders for now. Their vessel may need protection until this fighting stops."

"As you command, Captain," replied Ashay, regretfully eyeing the groups of guerrillas and Bradogan's troops still engaged in sporadic fighting around the port gateways. "Do you not need protection?" he asked hopefully, lowering his long neck until his head was level with the view screen.

"Negative. Like all other Traders, we're keeping to ourselves. This is an internal matter now that they are no longer targeting us."

With a sigh, Ashay lifted off and headed down to where the *Profit* was berthed. The news of Carrie's injury saddened him. He'd liked the small Human female.

"Shuttle *Venture* to *Rryuk's Profit*," he said, toggling the comm unit. "Permission to land for protective duties. Requested medical supplies on board but need your crew to unload."

"*Profit* to *Venture*, permission granted. Our people will be waiting for you," came the reply.

The next half hour saw a nonstop procession of personnel carrying supplies from the shuttle to the sick bay. Jo, the Human female, supervised the proceedings, rushing between the two locations, relaying what little news there was on Carrie's condition to Ashay to pass on to their companions on the *Hkariyash*. As soon as the transfer was completed, Captain Tirak ordered Ashay to clear the landing pad and return to his own ship.

In the sick bay, as he worked frantically on the unconscious Carrie, Kaid was vaguely aware of the sounds of the ramp retracting and the hatches closing as the *Profit* began to ready herself for takeoff. They'd reach their rendezvous in two weeks. Only two weeks, half the normal time, but it would be too long for Carrie unless she was put in one of the *Profit*'s cryogenic units.

From the moment he realized she'd been injured in the fight with the spaceport officials, he'd locked his feelings behind a wall. The life of this fragile Human female, and that of her partner Kusac, lay in his hands. Kusac: her Leska, his sword-brother—together the three of them were the first Human and Sholan En'Shalla Triad, bound telepathically to each other. Without them, he was incomplete.

He fastened off the dressing, touching his fingertips briefly to her flesh. Still too hot. The drugs should have brought her temperature down by now. For an instant, he felt curiously disembodied as he saw his dark-furred hand against her pale skin. With a wrench, he pulled himself back. There was no more he could do; she would only deteriorate if he waited any longer. She needed surgery, and she couldn't get that until they reached their rendezvous. Sighing, he carefully disconnected the drip from the cannula and picked her up, carrying her over to the far side of the room where two of the cryo units stood open and waiting. Placing her on the contoured mattress, he stepped back. He'd done all he could. The rest was up to the U'Churian medic, Mrowbay. Now it was time to treat his sword-brother.

Kusac sat watching him on one of the adjacent beds. For a wonder, he'd managed to remain conscious despite suffering the full measure of her pain through their Link. The *Venture*'s basic medikit lay open on the bed beside him. He'd dosed himself with an analgesic, but Kaid knew he hadn't taken nearly enough. He looked bad. Against the blackness of his pelt, the skin surrounding his nose and eyes was deathly pale and his ears were lying back, invisible among his hair. The mental link Kusac and Carrie had meant he would also have to travel in cryo.

"Kusac, let me give you the premed now," he said, reaching for the hypoderm from the medikit.

His friend's amber eyes, though dulled with pain, held his steadily. "No, Kaid. I want to be aware of her till the last. I'll wait till Mrowbay's done."

Reluctantly he laid the hypoderm down and sat beside his sword-brother. "She'll be fine—you both will. Two weeks, then we'll have the facilities and surgeons of the *M'Zekko* to treat her."

Kusac nodded slowly. "Wake me first. I don't want her coming out of cryo and not sensing me immediately."

"When you're ready," Mrowbay said finally, looking round at Kusac.

After giving Kusac his shot, Kaid helped him to his feet, supporting him as they walked slowly over to the second unit.

Kaid, I know you're blocking us out now, sent Kusac, *but later, if you sense her pain, for the Gods' sake, don't try to cope. Use the third cryo chamber. Let T'Chebbi watch us. She's got Jo and Rezac to call on if she needs help. Vartra can't have meant the U'Churians when he spoke of you making a pact with the Liege of Hell.*

Stop worrying about me and my visions, I'm fine, Kaid reassured, helping him climb into the unit. *Just rest.* Lowering his mental barriers, he reached in, touching his friend's hand. Already the premed had taken effect and he could sense Kusac drifting toward unconsciousness.

"Two weeks, Kaid." Kusac's voice was barely audible and Kaid had to lean forward to hear him. "Find out what Tirak was up to in that time. I'll want to know."

CHAPTER 1

Day 1

CRYO, the long night without end, the cold from between the stars. Heartbeat and breathing decelerate as the chill gradually seeps deep into flesh and bones, robbing them of warmth, of movement. Thoughts slow, messages no longer being sent to limbs and organs as the mind pulls itself back, retreating from the bitter cold till all that remains is a tiny spark of consciousness poised between life and death. Cryo sleep, the temporary death, where nothing stirs, no breath, no thought—no dreams.

With Nayash, his pilot, recovering from a wounded flank, Captain Tirak had asked Kaid to help out on the bridge during takeoff. Now that they were under way, Kaid needed to check up on his people. The mess area where they were waiting was adjacent to the sick bay, but inexorably his feet led him back there. Saying he was checking up on Zashou would fool no one, least of all himself, but he had to see them once more—had to know that Carrie and Kusac were all right. He'd grown so used to their presences within his mind that their absence left him feeling unsettled. These feelings were so foreign to him that it was with relief he saw that Zashou was still asleep. It was hard enough for him to cope without having to explain it to someone else.

It was Carrie's unit he went to first. He looked through the cover, feeling instantly protective of her. She looked as if Khuushoi, Goddess of Winter, had embraced her, turning her flesh as pale as the snow on the Dzahai Mountains. Memories of taking Carrie there to visit his home sprang into his mind. It was there, once he'd fully accepted his place in their lives as their third, that he and Carrie had finally become lovers.

Through the pale cream fabric of her shift, the blood-stained dressing across her belly and side showed up starkly. Instinctively his mind reached out for hers, pushing aside the barriers behind which he'd been hiding. He could sense nothing. His hand shook slightly as his fingertips brushed the surface of the unit, caressing it as if it were her he touched. Mrowbay had spread her long blonde hair carefully on the pillow. He remembered how soft it felt, so unlike his own Sholan hair. Then he sensed the U'Churian captain watching him from the doorway.

"Mrowbay says she's stable," said Captain Tirak, "and safe. But you know that since you treated her. Excuse my curiosity, but you obviously care very deeply for her. Are you and her mate related? Brothers, perhaps? I know they're a mind-linked pair."

"Brothers. Yes," Kaid replied distractedly as a prescient fear he'd never known before swept through him. Turning to look at Tirak, he did a double take, thinking for a brief moment he saw Kusac standing there. The outward physical similarities between their species were uncanny. Pushing his fear aside with an effort, he retreated again behind his mental shields. "Her mother died in cryo when her family journeyed to their colony world."

Tirak made a sympathetic noise, his mouth creasing in a Humanlike grimace. "A tragedy, but it couldn't happen on the *Profit*, believe me. Any disruption of the cryo system is instantly reported by the computer. The units even have an integral backup system, capable of lifesupport in space in the event of a disaster. They can be launched automatically from the bridge, or manually from in here." He pointed to the wall behind the units.

A very Human scream, long and drawn out, sounded from outside the open door.

Gun instantly in his hand, Kaid leaped past Tirak and was in the corridor before it stopped.

"False alarm, Captain." Sheeowl's voice on the ship's comm echoed throughout the deck. "Was only Kate. She just met her first Cabbaran."

In the center of the corridor, standing almost upright on its haunches, was indeed a Cabbaran. Kaid recognized it instantly from the description Captain Kishasayzar had given them. Kate stood facing the alien, her body frozen in horror.

"We have more passengers, Annuur." Tirak spoke calmly to the Cabbaran. "Badly injured ones. That's why the change in destination."

As Annuur turned slowly to face them, Kaid understood Kate's reaction. Standing just short of four feet tall, the being before him was unlike any he'd seen before. Obviously a quadruped, and certainly vegetarian, his long, yellow incisors were just visible behind an almost prehensile upper lip. Forward facing eyes regarded him steadily from beneath a narrow stiff crest of dark hair that ran the length of his skull and down his neck. The same hair was spread out in a ruff across his shoulders and again over his flanks. The sandy body fur had been shaved from the sides of his face and shoulder so that the intricately colored tattoos could be clearly seen.

The lip quivered and Kaid heard him begin to chitter. A flat, mechanical voice started to speak in U'Churian.

"Nourishment dispensers empty," Annuur's translator intoned. "Is breach of contract, Captain."

"See to it, Sheeowl," Tirak ordered the crew female hovering beside the frightened girl. "Take Kate to the mess first. My apologies, Annuur. As I said, we had injured to see to and needed to depart from Jalna quickly. There was no need for you to leave avionics, you could have used the comm—or were you just curious about our guests?"

The ruff of fur across the Cabbaran's shoulders bushed out for a moment before settling again. Annuur's teeth made a clicking noise and his top lip curled expressively. A sharp burst of sound followed. The translator remained silent.

"Captain." Nayash, the white dressing over his wounded thigh vivid against his long, black pelt, now stood where Kate and Sheeowl had been. He raised an arm and flung something through the air to Tirak who caught it deftly.

"You won't need your weapon," Tirak said quietly in an aside to Kaid as he stepped past him. "This is Annuur, leader of our Cabbaran navigation sept. All right, you opportunist," he said, his tone becoming lighter. "One pack— and only one—to make up for your discomfort." He held his hand, palm open, out toward the Cabbaran. In it lay a brightly decorated tubular container.

The mobile lip curled upward in disdain. "Your insult remains," intoned the translator.

Tirak gestured to Kaid to join him. Holstering his gun, he did so.

"This is Kaid, the leader of our guests."

The whiskers on either side of Annuur's nose twitched as he leaned forward and sniffed audibly at Kaid. "One of those you kept in cryo." He turned his attention back to Tirak, giving Kaid a clear view of the exotic tattoos.

The hand that reached out to take the captain's bribe was spatulate in shape, with four fingers tipped by broad, horny claws. Almost delicately, the fingers closed around the tube and removed it.

"Candy. A children's treat back on Home," Tirak said softly to Kaid. "They can't get enough of the stuff. Comes in useful now and then."

Kaid noticed that Annuur wore a multi-pocketed utility belt not unlike the one the Sholan Forces used, save that the Cabbaran's was held in place by shoulder straps. It was into one of these pockets that Annuur placed his tube.

"Maybe talk later," he said, lowering his upper body to the ground before sedately trotting past them and down the corridor to the main access elevator.

"Time *we* talked," said Kaid, his voice grim. He wanted to know what Tirak had been doing with a mixed Leska pair not only on board his ship, but held in cryo until a couple of hours ago.

"The rest of your people are next door in the mess waiting for you," said Tirak, gesturing in the same direction the Cabbaran had taken. "When you're satisfied they're safe, one of my crew will escort you to my office so we can talk."

Remaining near the closed doorway, Kaid looked over at T'Chebbi. "Report," he said, in the highland patois that they'd both grown up using.

"All rescued personnel save Zashou seem healthy but undernourished—want them checked up in sick bay because of laalquoi levels in food they ate on Jalna. Younglings were waiting on Keiss for transport to Shola when were kidnapped by a Valtegan officer. Killed him, but cost them their captain and damaged the scouter. Were found by Ambassador Taira's ship. Tirak rescued them from Taira at Tuushu Station—where we're going. He put them in cryo while on Jalna to stop us contacting them telepathically."

Kaid moved into the center of the room. Kate was about Carrie's height, her pleasant round face framed by a mass of short mid-brown curls. The male, Taynar, was barely older than her. He'd obviously inherited the warm gray-brown pelt coloring of his family. "What did the Chemerians want?" he asked, though he could make bets on what the answer would be.

"Why should we tell you?" demanded Kate. "You're one of them, a U'Churian."

Kaid glanced at T'Chebbi who raised a sardonic eye ridge in reply.

"I haven't told them," she said, reverting to lowland Sholan like Kaid.

We're Sholan, he sent to the girl and her Leska. *Posing as U'Churians. We were sent to rescue you.*

Taynar hissed his disbelief as Kaid joined them at the dining table. "Telepaths can't fight."

"He's your bond-brother," snapped T'Chebbi. "Show a Clan elder proper respect!"

"My bond-brother?" Taynar was startled into sitting up. "How? My sister died years ago!"

"So your father would have you believe," said Kaid. "Khemu died only a few months ago, bonded to me. Our son lives on the Valsgarth estate. Like us, he's a member of the En'Shalla Aldatan Clan now."

"Your son? But how . . ."

"The Chemerians wanted a mixed Leska pair for themselves," interrupted Kate. "Taira said he'd met Carrie and Kusac on the *Khalossa.*"

Kaid nodded. As he'd thought. Ambassador Taira had shown an unhealthy interest in his Triad partners while on board the *Khalossa.* Opportunity had presented itself, and Taira was not one to let it slip by. "How did Tirak get involved?" He watched the female's jaw tighten as she lifted her chin defiantly.

"I made him," she said shortly, gray eyes flashing. "We thought they were Sholans at first."

He raised his eye ridges in respect. "No wonder they

were so wary of telepaths. I presume you gave them their mental blocks."

"I was as much to blame as Kate," interrupted Taynar sullenly. "He promised to return us to Shola. I thought it a fair price."

Kaid ignored the challenge in the youth's voice. Faced with few alternatives, they'd had little option but to agree to Tirak's demand. "No one is faulting you," he said. "You handled a difficult situation very well." He turned his attention to the other side of the room where Rezac sat. This was his first real opportunity to meet the male, who, despite being half his age, was his father.

They weren't that alike, he thought, surveying the younger male. How could Jaisa have seen a resemblance? There were superficial similarities, true, but they were just that. They both had the distinctive broader and lower set ears of the highland Clans, and the brown pelt, but. . . .

"Are you related?" asked Jo suddenly, looking from one to the other. "You look very alike."

"Hardly," snapped Rezac. "I'm from his far past! Fifteen hundred years ago to be exact."

Kaid could feel T'Chebbi's gaze burning into him as she waited for his answer. "Highland Clans always tended to breed among their own. It's a possibility," he said, trying to avoid her scathing look. He touched the edges of Rezac's mind with his, instantly aware of the link between him and Jo. "You've formed a Triad," he said, surprised, glancing back at the dark-haired Human female.

Jo flushed and looked away.

"You know about these links?" Rezac's antagonism was quiet for now in his desire to learn more.

"We have two mixed Leska Triads back on the estate."

"That's why you can fight," said Taynar. "I knew telepaths with a Human Leska were able to fight, but I hadn't realized it affected the Triads as well."

He was getting drawn in deeper than he wanted here, but there was no point in dodging the issue. A simple answer would do for now. "That's so," he admitted.

"With Carrie and Kusac?" asked Jo, concern in her voice. "How awful for you. You must be feeling pretty bad right now with both of them in cryo."

"What are these Triads?" demanded Rezac impatiently. "What causes them?"

"The bonds began forming after the Cataclysm for a mixture of reasons. For the better protection of small breeding groups of Talented, and because of Vartra's work with genetics. You and Zashou were one of the original enhanced Leska pairs, so it's not surprising you should form a Triad once you'd been exposed to Vartra's modern virus."

"Our Link is the result of Vartra's work?" asked Jo.

"Not the original work Rezac was involved with," said Kaid. "It's due to his genetic manipulations after you were taken by the Valtegans."

"You know, your talk is full of wrong-spoors," said Rezac, an edge of ice in his voice. "You might fool your own people with all this speculation about what Vartra did, but I lived then. I *knew* him! How could he possibly have done anything that would link Human and Sholan DNA?"

A small, purring chuckle from Taynar broke the tension.

"I've just realized what it was about you that seemed familiar," the youth said to Kaid. "You're the Triad that went back to the times of Vartra, aren't you? You met with the God. That's why you're En'Shalla."

Rezac laughed out loud at this, but there was no humor in his laughter. "You expect me to believe that? Just because this isn't my time doesn't make me an idiot!"

Abruptly, Kaid got to his feet. He'd heard enough. There might be a blood tie between him and Rezac, but that was all. This male was as unlike him as anyone could be. What could he possibly have in common with this arrogant and undisciplined young male who had fathered him so very long ago?

"I was able to tell Vartra that you and Zashou were safe and alive in our time," he said. "Zylisha was worried for her sister. The news put her mind at rest. You might tell Zashou that when you see her next. And that Vartra and her sister life-bonded." He turned aside from the Sholan to look at the Human beside him. "Jo, I have to join Captain Tirak now. I'll debrief you on your mission after I've spoken to him. You're in charge till I return." He gestured to T'Chebbi to join him as he began to walk toward the door.

A chair scraped on the floor. "I want to know what's

going on, too," said Rezac, the belligerence back in full measure.

"You'll remain here till I return," Kaid said unequivocally, coming to a stop and turning to look at him. "The situation with Tirak is delicate and requires a knowledge of current Alliance politics."

"I know a hell of a lot more about the Valtegans than you do!"

"That's of no consequence at the moment. Your information is fifteen hundred years out of date, Rezac, and has nothing to do with this. Stay here with the other civilians."

"Don't order me about! I've as much right to be involved as you," the young male snarled, tail lashing from side to side as he unconsciously lowered his body into a crouch.

T'Chebbi's hand closed briefly on Kaid's wrist. "I'll stay," she said quietly.

Kaid flicked an ear in reluctant agreement. "Sit down, Rezac," he ordered. "You want my credentials? I'm in charge of this mission, and cleared by Sholan High Command for First Contact negotiations. You're just another civilian as far as I'm concerned. T'Chebbi will stay with you." He stalked over to the door, slapping his hand on the air lock mechanism. When it opened, he strode out into the corridor where Manesh, Tirak's security officer, stood waiting for him.

T'Chebbi moved smoothly to block the door as it closed. "Suggest you relax, make some drinks, experiment with food, and get to know each other," she said to the small group. "Ship not big, these quarters even smaller. Will take us two weeks to reach rendezvous. Better if we get on with each other."

"And just who the hell are you to be taking over?" demanded Rezac, striding over to confront her.

"Sister T'Chebbi of the Brotherhood of Vartra, member of the En'Shalla Aldatan Clan," she replied, keeping her tone even.

"A priestess," he sneered. "You think you can stop me? Go ahead and use the gun, then!"

"Rezac," said Jo warningly as he moved to push T'Chebbi aside. "That's not a good idea. I told you things are different now. The Brotherhood is a Warrior elite, not just a religious Order. They're specialist fighters. Kaid and T'Chebbi are Carrie's and Kusac's bodyguards. Friends. We can trust them. They came to rescue us, didn't they?"

T'Chebbi watched him hesitate. "Art of warrior is to know when to fight," she said quietly. "And whom. Not now, on alien vessel, with injured comrades. Are you a warrior, or just a fighter?"

As Kaid settled himself in the chair indicated, he watched Tirak pull the tab on the container he was holding.

"A hot drink," Tirak said, offering it to him. "The one your colleague Carrie enjoyed in the inn. Didn't think you'd want a fermented one yet."

Kaid accepted it, tasting the beverage cautiously. Not too bad—a bit sweet for his taste, but drinkable, and certainly preferable to alcohol. Right now he needed the energy the sweetener in it would give him. He waited, sipping the drink, knowing Tirak's first questions would tell him how much he knew, or had guessed, about them.

"So, what species do the two hairless females belong to? Human or Solnian?" the U'Churian asked after a moment or two. "And are your species dependent on each other? Do you come from the same world?"

"They're Humans. Tell me, Captain, why is a military ship and its crew posing as traders in this sector?"

Tirak feigned surprise. "Posing? You have us wrong, Kaid. I'll admit our craft is a decommissioned military one, but we are just what we seem, traders."

Kaid shrugged, a very U'Churian gesture, and putting his drink down, got to his feet. "Thank you for your hospitality, Captain Tirak, but I think I should check in again on the Sholan female in your sick bay," he said. "She was asleep when I was last there."

"You can't push me aside like that!" exclaimed Tirak, ears flicking forward. "I put myself and my crew on the line for you—Nayash was injured in the fight at the spaceport! I let your people come on board, fetch medical supplies for the injured females, let another of them join us—I deserve answers, dammit! I want to know what's going on!"

Schooling his face into a look he knew the other would interpret as one of surprise and confusion, Kaid hesitated. "Going on? I know as much about what happened planet-side as you do, Captain Tirak. My people were caught up with yours when Bradogan attacked us."

Tirak's face froze. "Don't take me for a fool, Kaid. You came here with members of two unknown alien species on a rescue mission. Kusac may look like us, but he's no U'Churian—his link to the Human female proves he's as Sholan as Taynar! Then there are the others in your little group! And I have severe doubts about which species you belong to, especially since you admitted to being his brother! Do I have to go on?"

"All you need to know is that we must rendezvous with an alien vessel at the Chemerian home world."

"Alien to whom? Us? Or you Sholans? Don't try my patience or you might find my hospitality is suddenly withdrawn," Tirak snarled, baring his teeth. "Your position is far from strong. You have perhaps one able-bodied companion, the rest are civilians suffering from malnutrition and exhaustion."

"Don't threaten me," said Kaid quietly. "I could take the information I want straight from your mind, despite the primitive blocks the younglings gave you. Instead, I do you the courtesy of asking."

Tirak's low rumble of anger began to build. With an obvious effort, he remained seated as the mane of black hair rose around his face.

"Brawling like troopers is hardly appropriate for people of our rank," Kaid said, his voice now deathly quiet. "First Contact is better left to the diplomats of the *Rhijissoh* when they reach Jalna, it's too delicate a matter to be argued over with mere traders." He turned and walked toward the door.

"Wait!" The growl was gone from Tirak's voice and his hair had begun to settle around his shoulders again. "You say a ship goes to Jalna to make First Contact?"

"It's not your concern, Captain," said Kaid, keeping his back to the U'Churian as he rested his hand against the bulkhead. "By your own admission, you are, after all, only a trader." He afforded him a glance over his shoulder.

"How do I know this isn't another lie?"

Again Kaid shrugged. "Confirmation will be waiting at our rendezvous."

Tirak's snarl almost drowned his words. "May Kathan

himself damn you! Drugs! That's why we're here! Because of an illegal drugs trade!"

Kaid had to widen his ears to catch the words within the snarled reply. He took a couple of paces back toward the desk and waited.

"Drugs that turn the users psychotic and violent for days after they've used them—drugs that only started appearing a few years ago."

Kaid returned to his chair. "And you think the Chemerians are involved."

"Some," admitted Tirak. The knuckles on the hand that held his drink showed white through his pelt and the can had begun to buckle slightly. This was his only outward sign of anger now. "Your turn. Why were your people on Jalna?"

Kaid regarded him thoughtfully. What to tell him? His Triad was empowered to commence Contact negotiations if it proved necessary, so perhaps the truth was best. "Two Valtegan shuttles landed here several months ago. One crashed outside the port after dropping off an object, the other landed to sell four Sholans in exchange for supplies and spares. We sent a team, consisting of three Humans, to locate the crashed vehicle and discover what it had left behind. They went missing. Our mission was to rescue not only them, but the original four Sholans."

"The Valtegans." Tirak sat back in his chair. "What's your quarrel with them?"

"All life on two colony worlds wiped out," said Kaid grimly. "Millions of Sholans dead. We don't know why, we don't know how, and worst of all, we don't know where they come from. We didn't even know they existed until then."

"Kate and Taynar said as much," murmured Tirak. "We didn't place much credence on it, though. Seems we were wrong."

"With a weapon like that, they're a threat to all species. That's why we were following up on the crashed vessel— in the hope we'd find something to give us a clue about where their home world is. They subjugated Keiss, the world the Humans had colonized, without destroying them, and used them as slaves, but the Valtegans we captured there died rather than communicate with us. They were ferocious warriors. It was literally kill or be killed with them. We destroyed them all, save for one ship."

"The one that came to Jalna."

Kaid inclined his head in an affirmative gesture. "We knew nothing about Jalna—or about the species who trade here—until the Chemerians told us the Valtegan ship had been sighted."

Tirak began scratching his ear thoughtfully. "A Valtegan ship calls here every fifty years or so, but they come only to take samples of crops and food animals. One left just before this craft you mention arrived. What the Jalnians get in return, my people were unable to find out. The Chemerians have trading agreements with you?"

"More," said Kaid, his tone reflecting his feelings toward their two-faced allies. "Treaties for our mutual defense that are several hundred years old. We represent an Alliance of five species."

The U'Churian's jaw fell open in shock. "By Kathan's beard! The double-dealing . . ."

"Conniving, tree-climbing little bastards," Kaid finished for him.

A slow grin split Tirak's face. He leaned forward to edge Kaid's abandoned drink closer to him. "As you say. Against you, their duplicity goes further than with us. We've only been dealing with them for about fifty years. The young couple, we found them on Tuushu Station. They had just discovered they were the prisoners, not the guests of Ambassador Taira Khebo and they—persuaded—us to rescue them."

"So they told me. There are strict laws governing the use of telepathy among our kind and they broke them. You have my government's apology on their behalf."

"Yet your people broke the same laws." There was a hardness in Tirak's voice.

"Sometimes it's necessary for certain individuals to be empowered to operate outside the law." Kaid's voice was a gentle purr. "But you know that, don't you—Captain?"

Tirak chose not to respond and Kaid knew he'd made his point.

"The Chemerians implied that beyond their own colonies, we were their only market," the U'Churian continued instead.

"I suspect," said Kaid, picking up his drink, "that we will

discover some of our latest imports are goods obtained from Jalna and your—Free Traders Alliance?"

"Free Traders' Council," corrected the captain, relaxing back into his chair. "Then we will have to draft trade agreements and more with this Sholan vessel."

Kaid finished his drink and set the empty container down on the table between them. "I would say that negotiations have already started, wouldn't you, Captain Tirak?"

"What family are you from?" ventured Taynar, looking over at Rezac. "I know you're from the highlands like me."

Rezac glowered at the youngling. He was still high on adrenaline from the fight at the spaceport, and worse: with his Leska mind-mate Zashou sedated in sick bay, his Link to Jo had reasserted itself, demanding their unfinished business be concluded. He was frustrated almost beyond endurance on both counts.

Jo's hand closed on his arm. *He's only making conversation, trying to be friendly. He's terrified, just like his Leska.*

He clenched his hand into a fist, forcing his claws into the flesh of his palms in an effort not to respond to her touch. *I know. I'm trying, dammit, but you know what's wrong with me—with us!* Unable to completely suppress it, a shudder of pleasure at her touch ran through him. "Dzaedoh," he said through clenched teeth. "Likely you'll not have heard of us."

"Noni's kin?" the youth said in surprise.

T'Chebbi moved over to sit opposite Rezac and Jo. "Link day?" she asked sympathetically. "Are rooms made ready for us through the door." She jerked an ear to her right. "Go, take one now. See to your own needs. You put it off long enough." When he hesitated, she added, "That's an order, Warrior. I don't need what you and your third are broadcasting. Neither does anyone else."

Relief flooded through him. He could see to their Link needs without feeling he was neglecting what he saw as his duty. It was good not to be the one with the final responsibility for once. He got to his feet, urging Jo to accompany him.

Giyesh was waiting in the corridor outside. She directed them to a cabin opposite the medic's office. As the door closed behind them, Rezac relaxed the control he'd been fighting so hard to maintain. Reaching for Jo, he circled her waist with one arm, stroking the dark hair that crowned her head with his other hand. Breathing in her scent, he began to purr as their minds started to merge.

"Ah, you feel it too," he whispered in her ear as his tongue gently rasped against her jawline. "After the battle, the need to pair with one you love, to know you are both still alive. Zashou despised that in me."

"She's not a Warrior," Jo murmured, turning her face so their lips met, her fingers already beginning to unfasten the belt that held his tunic at the waist.

His tail flicked around her legs, holding them close against his. "You Humans are not so unlike us," he purred.

* * *

With a start and a cry, Kaid woke, Carrie's name on his lips as he sat bolt upright in bed. He shivered, chilled to the bone despite his sweat-soaked pelt.

T'Chebbi loomed over him with an extra blanket. "Bad dreams again?" she asked.

He took it gratefully, wrapping it round his shoulders for the time being. "More," he said, clenching his teeth to stop them from chattering. He looked around the dimly lit cabin. "Where's Giyesh?"

T'Chebbi shrugged. "Maybe still on duty."

"I dreamed I was in cryo, and I could sense her there."

"Carrie?" T'Chebbi sat down beside him, her nose creasing in worry as she flicked her long gray-brown plait over her shoulder. "That's not possible. Cryo is a nothingness. Drugs make you sleep first, you don't even feel the cold. Then you wake, and it's over."

He looked up, catching her gaze with his. "I was somewhere else, T'Chebbi, somewhere deadly cold—and she was there. I usually feel warmth from our crystal, but it's been cold since we put her in cryo. Until now." His hand emerged from the blanket, holding out the crystal he always wore. "Feel it."

Leaning forward, she touched it gingerly with her forefinger. With an exclamation of shock, she pulled her hand sharply away.

He let the crystal fall back within the blanket, smiling

wryly. "You felt it—too warm for just my body heat, isn't it?"

"You told me Carrie sensed her mother dying in cryo. Is it possible that the Talented stay aware? That they don't sleep?"

"Never heard of it happening. It could be a Human trait," he replied.

She grunted. "What was the dream?"

"Only what I told you. Just being in this bitterly cold place and sensing Carrie and her fear. The sooner we get to Tuushu Station, the better. She's terrified of cryo, T'Chebbi."

"She's safe asleep," she said, her tone soothing as she touched his face briefly. "Can I get you anything? A hot drink? You should try to sleep again."

"Nothing, thank you," he said automatically, then hesitated. He wasn't fooling either of them. "Join me. I'd like your company. Who's on sentry duty in the mess?"

"Taynar and Kate. Slept long enough in cryo, they said. Tallis is on graveyard shift."

"Should have left him on the *Hkariyash*," he grumbled, glad to be dealing with more familiar issues as she slipped into the bed beside him. "He's more trouble than all the others put together. He's done nothing but complain since he came on board." Pulling the blanket from his shoulders, he leaned over to drop it on the floor. T'Chebbi snagged it from him.

"We use this," she said, spreading it over him. "You feel like you been in cryo. We can manage Tallis. His mind is sickened after what the Valtegans did to him. He needs help more than anything."

He lay down, grateful for her warmth and company; it was helping dissipate the frozen images of his nightmare. As his shivering stopped, he could feel her soundless purr.

"You only had to ask if you wanted to join me," he said awkwardly. "You have the right—you are my Companion." He was finding it difficult to cope with his need for her company and the desire for Carrie's he was walling away.

"Sleep," she said, wrapping her arm across his chest and tucking her nose under his chin.

* * *

It had come as a shock to Jeran to find himself on Giy-esh's ship, almost as big a shock as it had to her, judging from her expression when they came face-to-face in the landing bay. Later, she'd managed to see him alone for long enough to arrange this meeting in the unused mess on the second deck. Sitting there at the main table, nursing a hot drink, he wondered why he'd come.

A shadow fell across the table and he looked up to see her standing in the doorway.

"I hoped you'd be here," she said, closing the air lock door behind her.

"I hadn't expected to see you again," he said awkwardly.

"Neither had I." She joined him at the table, sitting down opposite him. "This is rather embarrassing for both of us."

He frowned. "Why? Only you and I know what happened that night."

Giyesh looked away. "Not exactly," she murmured. "The captain overheard me talking to our medic."

"Your medic?"

"We rescued the young ones, Taynar and Kate," she said, her voice low. "Mrowbay thought he was an immature male. I told him likely he wasn't."

"You only came to spy on me?" He'd thought there had been more between them than that. A common attraction, a need for company that night at least.

"No! I came to talk to you, yes, to find out what I could about your people, but the rest . . . That was real."

"So all your crew know about us? What did you do? Go into details? Tell them how desperate I was for female company?" he asked angrily.

"I said nothing to them, I swear I didn't! Look, I didn't have to tell you this," she said defensively. "It was rather obvious that we'd slept with each other when I stayed away all night."

"So now it's my fault for keeping you with me?" He put his cup down with a thump.

"I didn't say that," she said, reaching out to touch his clenched hand. "I stayed with you because I wanted to, because you were so lonely."

"I didn't want your pity then, or now," he growled, snatching his hand away. "And I didn't need to be made a figure of fun among your crew. They must be laughing themselves sick every time they see me!"

"I didn't mean it that way, Jeran, and they're not laughing at you," she said. "You don't understand. Our ships, we're all family, all related. It's *me* the crew are laughing at, for getting caught by an alien. The captain, my uncle, he's mad at me!"

"Caught? How caught?" That surprised him, diverting his anger.

She shook her head, sending the mane of black hair swaying round her shoulders. "It's not important," she said. "But no one's laughing at you, honestly."

"I want to know. You've discussed personal matters about me with your medic, and your crew's laughing at my expense, too, whether you want to admit it or not. You owe me something in return."

There was a hunted look in her eyes as she obviously searched for some answer to give him. "I'm of an age where I should have chosen a mate, but I haven't," she said finally.

He narrowed his eyes as he looked at her. She was being less than honest with him, he knew that. Not lying, but near to it. "I'm the first? Is that it?"

She pushed the chair back, got abruptly to her feet, and headed for the exit. "Forget it, Jeran. It was a mistake meeting with you. I just didn't want you thinking it was you the crew were laughing at."

"Wait!" he said, leaping up to stop her. He caught up with her at the air lock, grasping her by the arm. "You're not leaving without telling me why this is so amusing to your people."

"You're not U'Churian, and not a soldier," she said.

"So what?"

"I told you. I was expected to choose my first partner and didn't. Instead I asked to see the worlds outside our own, then I'd choose. This is my first mission."

She was making no attempt to leave, even though she could probably get free quite easily. Releasing her arm, he reached for her mane of hair, taking hold of a lock that lay on her shoulder. "So why are we here? You didn't get me to come here just to tell me this."

"How would you know?" she countered, then stopped, blue eyes widening. "Unless you're a telepath?"

"No, I'm not." It was a mane, he realized, quite unlike Sholan hair. The night she'd come to him in the warehouse where he was imprisoned on Jalna, they'd talked, then one thing had rapidly led to another. They'd had no expectation of seeing each other again, so hadn't wasted time on irrelevancies. Matters were slightly different now. She obviously wanted to see him again, or she wouldn't have suggested this meeting. He stood aside, gesturing to the table. "Stay for a little while. Tell me more about yourself and your people."

Warily, she returned to the table, waiting till he sat down. "What do you want to know?"

"You say you're all family on this ship. Are you all related, all soldiers?"

She nodded. "Our unit of the family lives on Home, but the largest one is on the *Rryuk* itself. We learned long ago during our civil wars that having Family in space meant your name would never die, no matter what happened on Home."

He thought about this for a moment. "Who lives on the *Rryuk?* Just the soldiers?"

"No, everyone. Children, too. How else could we be self-sustaining?"

"Space cities," he murmured, watching her. He'd not realized just how blue her eyes seemed against her dark pelt. They matched her tunic. But then, the only light in the warehouse had come in from the spaceport outside through the small, reinforced window above the door. "How do you stop the inbreeding? We have a clan system similar to yours, but we're free to bond with those outside our Guild."

"Guild?" She wrinkled her nose as she spoke.

"Professions, like your soldiers."

"We can choose from the males on any of the Family's ships, or even Home itself. There's not just the Rryuks, but the other lesser families who are allied to us and officially bear our name."

"Are you training as a soldier now?"

She smiled, her sideways grin showing off her white teeth. He remembered her smile because the first time he'd seen it, he'd thought it a warning, as it would have been with his people. "No, I was brought up as one. I began training as soon as I could walk. We females only stay home till we've had our first infant, then we go into service on one of the smaller craft till it's time to breed again, if we wish."

Breeding cycles, again very different. "But you chose not to do this."

She nodded. "It angered my parents that I didn't want to enrich the Family before taking service on the *Profit,* but the elders said I had leave to go if I wished."

"And your uncle is one of the old-fashioned types, that's why he's angry with you for getting 'caught' by me. The others are amused because they've been around long enough to see the funny side."

She nodded again, setting the silver-colored ring in her right ear swaying.

"What's Home like? With all those Families it must be pretty crowded."

"Fairly. Lots of cities. When a male marries into the Family, we add a room onto the settlement until there's no more space, then a group starts up a new settlement. We have a colony world now, and many younger people are setting up there rather than on Home or in space."

"You marry for life then." Her scent was bringing back more memories of their night together. Pairing with her had been like he imagined pairing with a feral would be— from her there'd been no inhibitions, no holding back. Surely she couldn't mean he was her first lover?

"No, only for two or three seasons, then we choose again. It makes sure there is always new blood in the Family. What about your people? Do you have only one wife?"

"No. We take out bonding contracts for either three or five years if we wish to share our cubs," he said. "Otherwise we have as many lovers as we wish. Our females can choose when they want to have cubs, they don't have seasons, apart from their first."

"Your way is quite different," she said, her voice trailing off slightly. "Relationships outside our marriages aren't tolerated."

"What about between them, or before?" he asked, sliding across the intervening seat till he was sitting beside her.

She wanted him, he could feel it, that's why she'd suggested they meet here. The attraction between them was pure lust, nothing more—yet.

"Between is all right," she said softly, turning to face him as he slid his arm across her shoulders, urging her closer. "But not before. That's forbidden."

"So you and I have broken quite a few rules between us." His tongue flicked across her cheek while he traced a gentle finger down her throat, continuing over her tunic to her chest. He let his hand linger briefly on her small breasts before moving lower, coming to rest on her hip. Beneath her ship's uniform, he could feel the braided cord that held up the loincloth she wore. Everything about her excited him, from her exotic alien scent to the long, dark pelt that covered her body.

"Yes," she said, but her voice was barely a whisper as she leaned against him. "I'd like to break them again, but not here."

"Where then?" he asked, voice rough as he began to lick her ear.

"Two cabins up from here, there's an empty guest one. If I go first," she said, holding his face as her lips touched his, "and you follow in a minute . . . It has a privacy lock."

He returned the kiss purposefully, his teeth catching gently at her lip as, reluctantly, he released her. "Go now, before I get too carried away. I won't be far behind you."

* * *

Father Lijou sat with Guardian Dhaika in the other's lounge at Vartra's Retreat. They were drinking c'shar. The years had been kind to the elderly Sholan, he thought, watching the spring afternoon sun catch the reddish glints that still showed in the other's dark hair and pelt.

"You seriously believe that it's Brynne Stevens' Triad we want, not Kaid's?"

Lijou tried to ignore the tone of stark incredulity in Dhaika's voice. "I do. I've thought it since Kaid returned to Stronghold after seeing Vartra here." He had the satisfaction of seeing the faint gathering of Dhaika's eye ridges that betrayed his discomfort at being reminded of the incident.

"That was unexpected. Did Kaid ever say what it was the God wanted?"

"No, but the change in him was marked. It would appear that in the end, Vartra's will corresponds to Ghyakulla's. As I said, I believe Noni is wrong. Brynne Stevens will be the Human bound to our world with his Triad, not Carrie Aldatan."

"Brynne's lack of cooperation over that Derwent character isn't exactly conducive to trust in such a delicate matter as unity between our species," murmured Dhaika. "He's not what I'd call the epitome of a well-adjusted Human within a mixed Leska relationship."

"The Gods choose whom They want, Dhaika, you know that. They see into a person's soul. With all our Talents, that's beyond us."

"I know that." The slightly acerbic tone was moderated immediately. "So what is it you're suggesting?"

Lijou extended the claws on his right hand and gently tapped the arm of his chair. "Noni has a blind spot where Kaid is concerned. She's letting what she wants to happen blind her to other possibilities. I think it's time we—pursued—more viable options."

"I'm as unhappy with the way she tracks downwind of the Council of Guardians as you are, but to actually work against her. . . ."

"Not against her," corrected Lijou. "For Shola, Dhaika. Look at it this way. The Aldatan En'Shalla Triad is the motivating force behind the changes on our world. They've had to fight for their freedom, and it's been hard won. They can't change what they are, become people of peace, tied into the land, raising cubs. For one, the military won't let them. We need—Ghyakulla needs—a Triad that will do that. In Vanna Kyjishi and Garras Janagu, we have that. Look at the way they've both settled into managing the Clan and estate while Kusac and Carrie are away. Physician Kyjishi's expecting a second cub, Garras' this time. And Brynne has calmed down, too. None of those tempestuous relationships with other females any more—in fact, apart from their Link days, he's been celibate. Not only is he studying how to use his Talent at the Shrine, but since he had that vision from Ghyakulla, he's become more interested in the religious side. He's really Brotherhood priestly material, Dhaika. We should encourage this. We'd be fools not to. Think of it as listening to the Goddess rather than as working against Noni."

"I hear you, but you haven't convinced me."

Lijou leaned forward and helped himself to one of the tiny savory pastries on the low table in front of him. He knew better; Dhaika would take very little more convincing. He was all but his now. "Shall we agree that if he comes to either of us and asks for further instruction, then it's a clear sign that Ghyakulla has called him?" He popped the tidbit into his mouth.

Dhaika regarded him thoughtfully before replying. "If he comes of his own free will, then I will tutor him in the ways of the Goddess, and Her consort, Vartra. You've just been newly appointed as a Guardian, Lijou, so understand me well when I say I have no wish to Challenge Noni or the other females on our Council. . . ."

"Nor have I," interrupted Lijou. "I'm as aware as you that as two of the only three male Guardians we're outnumbered before we begin. But I am weary of the fact that in every level of our society there are political factions that serve only to advance their own view of how things should be. Free debate has been stifled for too long. We've become trapped in a quagmire of our own making, Dhaika, and we must break free if we're to keep the superiority we now hold within the Alliance. I can't help but feel there are desperate times ahead of us."

The Guardian stirred in his seat. "I thought matters had improved since Esken's power had been broken."

"They have, and even more so since he retired three weeks ago, but we need to evolve, Dhaika! As a society, we've been stagnant for too long. Growth and change are what we need, even if that change cuts us like a polar wind! But it's not just that that concerns me. We've still got the threat of the Valtegans hanging over our heads."

Dhaika sighed, reaching for his drink. "Fear has always been an unpleasant bedfellow. No news of the escaped Valtegan?"

"Kezule? None. A sustained search of the Taykui Forest margins has turned up nothing, now they're spreading the net farther. General Raiban would like to hold us at Stronghold responsible, but her people were on duty that night." He didn't want to get drawn deeper into this discussion. The media weren't aware of the escape of Kezule and Keeza Lassah, the Sholan female incarcerated with him as a spy. That there were two psychopaths loose in their continent's major game forest was a circumstance that deeply humiliated both the Brotherhood and the Forces. He made an effort to return to the original discussion.

"About Brynne Stevens," he began.

"I have said that if he comes to either of us of his own free will, with no prompting, then I will train him as our Order dictates," interrupted Dhaika.

"Even in dream-walking?" He pushed his point home.

"Yes, even that—if I believe Ghyakulla has called him!"

Lijou let his breath out in a gentle huff. "Thank you, Dhaika. All I'm asking is that we don't close our eyes to what could be in front of us."

"Maybe you're right," said Dhaika. "My position here as Guardian is to ensure that those called to the Brotherhood by Vartra or His Companion, Ghyakulla, receive the proper religious instruction in our mysteries. It's time Ghyakulla was allowed to call those She chooses, regardless of our esteemed matriarchs' personal wishes and their perceived political implications."

Lijou could hear a touch of enthusiasm creeping into Dhaika's voice. At last! It had been an uphill struggle convincing the older male. Though he could see to the normal instruction of their Order, the advanced religious studies were Dhaika's provenance, and that included dream-walking. He was only just beginning to realize how much more he had to learn about that psychic art.

He inclined his head in agreement, as much to hide the small smile as to show respect for the other. "You're absolutely right, Guardian Dhaika. It's time for us to listen to the deities once more."

* * *

Like a silent shadow, Ashay padded alongside Quin as they made their way through the spaceport gates toward the hotel. Though the heavy fighting was over, it was still not safe for any of the four Humans on Jalna to walk alone through the spaceport area. Ashay was the perfect escort.

No one in their right mind would argue with a Sumaan. Six feet tall to the shoulder, plus another foot for the mobile neck and its attached head, the reptilian Sumaan were formidable mercenaries. Heavily muscled hind legs and a tail almost as thick as his torso gave Ashay a bulkiness that belied his agility, speed and immense strength. As they passed through the checkpoint, the young Sumaan's neck curved downward, bringing his head on a level with the guard's. Lips pulled back from the tombstone teeth as he smiled his greeting.

Catching the guard's shudder as the youngster passed through, Quin smiled to himself. He could understand the Jalnian's reaction. He'd felt the same until he'd gotten to know Captain Kishasayzar and his crew.

There had been a lot of rapid changes, he noted as he approached the inner fenced area where the hotel and the tower that had been Lord Bradogan's stood. The guards waved them through without challenging them: the crew of the *Hkariyash* were well known to Tarolyn's men by now.

Port workers were still piling rubbish from the deceased Lord's dwelling onto the smoldering bonfire in front of the tower. Its acrid smoke coiled lazily up into the heat-blanched sky. Everyone had known what kind of man Bradogan was, but the new Port Lord hadn't been prepared for the sight that met his eyes in the basement cells. Treating several of Bradogan's prisoners had been beyond Jalna's primitive medical skills, and Tarolyn had needed to ask for help from those species still berthed in the port. He'd then refused to enter the keep again until it had been gutted and all trace of its former owner erased.

It was the Humans who'd been able to offer the most aid, as they were physiologically closest to the Jalnians. Quin had just come from checking on their patients at the makeshift infirmary that had been set up in one of the warehouses. As well as those who had been subjected to Bradogan's idea of hospitality, several Jalnians were being treated for energy weapon burns and a variety of sword and knife wounds sustained during the pitched battle in the port the day before.

Tarolyn, flanked by his faithful bodyguards, was holding court in the main foyer of the hotel. Seeing Quin enter, he dismissed the assorted crowd of alien traders and their Jalnian agents that had been clamoring for his attention, and gestured at him to approach. As the traders and agents moved aside, Quin could see Conrad sitting at the end of Tarolyn's table. Like himself, he'd reverted to using the black fatigues that were the Humans' Warrior Guild uniform.

"Get him a seat," the Lord ordered one of his guards as the Human approached. "And a drink for them both," he added to Conrad. "The heat outside is enough to scorch even the Sumaan's hide. How are your patients today, Quin?"

"Improving," Quin said, taking off the black baseball-like cap that protected his balding head from the sun. Gratefully, he accepted the glasses of water that his colleague slid across the table to him. He handed one to Ashay, who then ambled off to sit with the guards, and drained the second himself. "Another couple of days and all but five of them will be able to go home. I'd like the physician on the *Rhijissoh* to examine three of those, though. Their medics have more sophisticated equipment than us and will be able to analyze your species so we know exactly what drugs we can use. All I can do at the moment is make them as comfortable as possible." He'd already decided not to mention that at least one was unlikely to survive the day.

Railin Tarolyn narrowed his eyes as he listened to Quin. "So why didn't your Sholan friends wait for this ship?"

"Carrie was too badly injured, Lord Tarolyn," began Conrad.

"I asked him," Railin interrupted, continuing to look at Quin as he took the proffered chair and sat down opposite the Lord.

"It's exactly as he said. Her injuries were so severe that the *Rhijissoh* couldn't have dealt with her properly. They scanned her on the *Profit* and we now know the bullet is lodged against her spine. On its way in, it hit one of her ribs and splinters of bone have caused tissue and organ damage. The *Rhijissoh* simply doesn't have the specialized surgical facilities necessary for operating on a Human so badly injured. If she'd been Sholan," he shrugged. "Far better to stabilize her in the *Profit* cryo facilities, then get her to the rendezvous ship as quickly as possible."

Railin grunted. "Let me know how she fares. What of the Sholan woman who lost her child?"

"Zashou's comfortable. They're building her strength up with Sholan protein drinks until they're sure the poison from the Jalnian food is out of her system," said Quin, refilling his glass from a jug on the table.

"A tragedy," said Railin. "But the child was better dead than living so malformed. I had not thought it possible that the poison in our soil could do that. But she's young, there's plenty of time for more children. I've decided to leave security matters at the port as they are for now. People know where they are, know what to expect. Better to make my changes gradually, there'll be chaos otherwise. How long before this ship of yours arrives?"

"Another three days," said Conrad. "When they do, they'll be sending down a Contact team in a shuttle. I've been asked to request quarters for them close by your own."

"They can stay in a suite of rooms here," said Railin, pulling his pipe and smoking herb from his belt pouch. He glanced up at Conrad. "Who are they coming to talk to? Us, or our alien customers?"

"All those species who want to talk to them," said Quin. "Including yourselves."

Railin tamped the smoking herb down in the pipe bowl with the end of his small belt knife. As he reached for his flint box, Conrad pulled a lighter from his pocket and flicked it, letting it burn for a moment before handing it to Railin.

"Please keep it," he said as the Lord turned the object thoughtfully over in his hand before igniting his smoking herb with it.

So begins their throwaway society, sent Quin.

No need to be so cynical, replied Conrad.

"Thank you," Railin said, placing it on the table beside his pouch. "An interesting little toy."

"We've many more like this in the Alliance," said Conrad quietly. *And before you jump down my throat, I've been authorized to give him a few . . . inducements.*

"Yesterday, you and Quin offered to bring me some supplies from Galrayn in your scouter. I think we'd all eat more easily if we know the food is uncontaminated. I've had a list prepared for you." Railin slid the piece of parchment across the table toward Quin. "It may mean two trips, but I think you'd agree fresh meat and vegetables are worth the time it'll take. And if you could also bring my cook," his genial face lit up at the thought, "then I can promise you a meal second to none."

Conrad looked across at Quin. "Sounds fine to me." Turning back to Railin, he said, "I've been authorized to let you have a communications device for your estate, to enable you to speak instantly with your steward from anywhere on Jalna. The Alliance negotiators know it's vital that you remain in touch with your people for the duration of their visit, and are prepared to do what they can to facilitate this."

Railin puffed gently on his pipe, releasing a small cloud of aromatic smoke. "Very good of them, considering they need me more than I need them. What makes this Alliance of yours so sure that the other species will want them here?"

"I'm afraid I can't comment on that, Lord Tarolyn," said Conrad. "We're not actually part of the negotiating team. We've merely been asked to remain here to act as envoys for them. But I will say that two of the Alliance species already trade here—the Chemerians and the Sumaan."

"You have everyone at a disadvantage for the time being, Lord Tarolyn," said Quin, picking his words carefully. "But may I respectfully suggest that you tread carefully and don't overplay your hand? If you make demands that could be considered unreasonable, then there is nothing to stop the traders from combining to build a space station."

The new Port Lord raised a bushy eyebrow. "I think not. I may be just a dirt-sider to you, but I've some idea of the cost of such an undertaking, in people and time if not money."

He's sharp, no doubt about that, sent Quin. *Nobody's fool.* "With three more species to divide the cost among them, I don't think that's going to be a major consideration. What you really want is help with the environment, isn't it? You want your people free of this madness that comes from the land. Bradogan played on it, used it to his advantage to control the goods coming onto Jalna."

Railin narrowed his eyes. "I want it understood that Jalnians are not violent by nature. The cause of it is our poisoned soil and not all of us are tainted by it. With help, those who are can be freed. We could then take our rightful place in space with the rest of you."

"You have one major point in your favor," said Conrad. "The Sholans, who are the senior partner in the Alliance, have no love for the Chemerians, and it was the Chemerians who branded you as an unstable species. The Sholan government may well be prepared to back your request for aid with both the Free Traders and the Alliance to pay back the Chemerians for withholding information concerning the existence of the Free Traders."

"And the Chemerians?" asked Railin.

"Will say nothing, having been exposed as untrustworthy to both the Free Traders and the Alliance by having kept silent about the existence of both groups."

"I only want what is right and fair for my people. The technology you all possess would help us rise above what we are and become more. It isn't as if we have nothing to offer in return."

"You have your location for one," murmured Quin.

"Location?"

"Jump points are rare," explained Conrad. "That's why Jalna is so important to the Free Traders. It's a point where they can most easily converge for trade. It's a little farther for the Alliance, but still economically viable, I would think."

"For people not concerned with negotiating, your words are very much to the point, and in our favor," murmured Railin. "Why?"

"You're not so dissimilar from us," said Quin, shifting in his chair. "Our friends' time as Killian's guests reminded us of the basics of life—a safe place to live, good food, and our health." *If the Jalnians are accepted,* he sent to Conrad, *it advances Earth's arguments to become full Alliance members rather than associates.*

"Talking of which," said Railin, looking toward the foyer desk. "I see that damned manager is standing around doing nothing. It's past midday, time we had something substantial to eat and drink. You can tell me about this communications device of yours before you leave for Galrayn."

* * *

Naira and Zsyzoi were on the inland detail, working their way outward toward the margins of the Taykui Forest where they'd meet up with their opposite members. The cold wind ruffled Naira's hair, making him shiver.

"We're not going to find him," he muttered to his sword-sister. "He's long gone by now—and he knows our world."

"Only the desert area near Chezy and the Kysubi plains, and they've changed a hell of a lot since his day," said Zsyzoi quietly, edging forward slowly as she scanned her surroundings through the IR visor. "We have to keep looking. Now shut up, I can hear you complain anytime."

"How'd he get out anyway? You manage to pick up any gossip yet?"

"Naira, be quiet! At this rate, they'll hear us long before we hear them," she hissed angrily before coming to an abrupt stop and rounding on him. "Or is that the point of all your chatter?"

"Of course not!" he replied, stung by her accusation. "How could you . . ."

A dark shape launched itself toward them from the branch of a nearby tree. They separated, one to either side, diving for cover as the creature leaped beyond them, landing deep in the undergrowth.

Zsyzoi was already on her feet, tracking its passage as it headed deeper into the forest. She let out a string of expletives as she relaxed and began to brush the debris from the forest floor off her clothing and pelt. "Another four-legger," she said with disgust.

"Are you sure?" Naira asked, scrambling to his feet and peering in the direction of the still swaying vegetation.

"Sure," she confirmed. "Only the ferals move like that, we can't. Come on, we've still got another four hours before we're through for the night."

She suppressed her elation as she crashed through the ground cover, heading deeper into the night. She might have escaped the hunters this time, but they'd surprised her, cut her off from her den and forced her to move on before she was ready. Speed was what she needed now, to put distance between them and her. Running till she could go no farther, she collapsed to the ground, sides heaving, gasping for air.

Gradually her breathing slowed and the ache in her lungs eased. In its wake came the dull, dragging pain of her injuries. Whimpering, she curled up, hugging her belly and straining to lick at the still-weeping slashes on her flank.

They were deep, and the fluid they wept was bitter, making her feel sick and light-headed again. Only hunger had driven her from the safety of her den in the first place. It was a miracle she'd managed to escape the hunters at all in her weakened condition.

She had to keep moving, find shelter and food before morning left her exposed to the light. Still whimpering softly, she uncurled and staggered to her feet.

On board the *Rryuk's Profit,* a level on one of the cryo units fluctuated. The computer registered it, initiating a first-level diagnostic check on the system.

On Shola, Brynne stirred in his sleep, muttering incoherently before settling again to dream of moonlit forests.

In Vartra's temple at Stronghold, Lijou crumbled the incense into the brazier on the God's right. His mind was wandering, and not, for once, fully on his task. He was thinking of Kaid, what it must have been like for him to go back in time and meet the God, Vartra, in the flesh.

"Disbelief," said a voice in his ear as a strong grip closed on his forearm. "The first time is always the worst," it continued conversationally.

Around him, the temple seemed to darken and swirl. Lijou made a mewling noise and tried to pull back.

"So you're the new Guardian. And Tallinu's mentor."

Lijou was suddenly very afraid. The hand grasping his arm was real; the claws were sharp and beginning to prick into his flesh. It was none of the Brothers, he knew the smell of each one and all he could smell now was the scent of the nung tree. He peered through the dim, flickering light at the figure beside him but the face was hidden in deep shadow.

"Who are you?" he asked, hearing the tremor in his voice.

A gentle laugh. "You shouldn't need to ask," the voice chided. "How could I neglect you, the head of the En'Shalla Order? I have work for you, Father Lijou. I see your esteemed matriarchs neglected to tell you that participating in the ritual of dream-walking made it possible for me to reach you easily."

Half an hour later, Lijou stumbled from the temple, blinking rapidly in the brighter lights of the entrance hall. The night watch were at his side instantly, only to be dispatched by him for his co-Guild Master. Instead they sent for L'Seuli, who fetched Master Rhyaz.

"He gave you this?" asked Rhyaz. Stunned, he stood looking at the metal disk L'Seuli had put into his palm.

"Yes, Master," said L'Seuli. "I recognized it immediately."

"Take me to him."

When they stopped outside the watch ready room, Rhyaz looked again at the coin in his hand. "Tell me once more how he said he got it."

"He said the God gave it to him. How *did* he get the Brotherhood Sigil, Master Rhyaz?"

"I hope I'm about to find out, L'Seuli," Rhyaz answered as he placed his hand on the door, ready to push it open. "I keep this in the safe. No one has access to it but me. It's the original sigil, minted when our Order was founded."

CHAPTER 2

Day 2

KAID'S sleep continued disturbed, bringing memories forgotten for months to the surface.

"You!" said Kaid angrily, fists clenching at his sides as he stopped. "You dared to use the Goddess to bring me here!" Kaid was speechless with rage as he watched Vartra set down the scythe he'd been sharpening.

"Oh, it was real," the God said, taking him by the arm and drawing him toward the cottage. "The crystal in the rock face, everything. It was Ghyakulla's doing, not mine. She wanted us to talk."

"I've nothing to say to you!" Furiously he resisted.

"Maybe not," said Vartra, "but I do have things to say to you. Do you know where you are, how you got here?"

"Dhaika led me."

"Not quite. Ghyakulla did. You're dream-walking, in the realms of the Entities."

That caught his attention. "Entities? I thought there were only Gods."

Once more, Vartra tugged him gently onward. This time he didn't resist.

"There are no Gods and Goddesses, Tallinu, only Entities," he said, stopping in front of the cottage door and opening it. He stepped aside, waiting for Kaid to enter.

Automatically, Kaid scanned the main room, assessing the exits, looking for potential traps and threats, but the room couldn't have been simpler. It was a typical highland cottage, not unlike Noni's. On his right, a large kitchen range was set into the outer wall, sharing the flue with the small smithy on the other side. A table with four chairs stood in the center of the room. There were three doors, but only one looked like it led out of the room, probably to the rest of the house.

"I hadn't expected you to be living so simply," he said, lacing his voice with heavy sarcasm as he entered. "Where's the lab? All the scientific and medical equipment?"

"There is none," said Vartra, moving past him to sit at the table. "Those days are long gone, Tallinu. I fulfill a different role now."

Kaid grunted his disbelief. "You said there are no Gods, only Entities."

"I did. Won't you sit with me? We only have a short time."

"I'll stand for now." He couldn't sit at the same table as this person who'd betrayed him and abused his mind and body. "What is it you want with me? Get it over with, Vartra. I've more important things to do with my life than waste it here!"

"Still so angry. Yet I did my best to warn you. It isn't easy for me to come to you the way I did the night you took ill with the fever."

Despite his best efforts to stop them, Kaid could feel his ears begin to lie back in shock. It hadn't been a fever dream, it had been real. Feeling suddenly dizzy, he held onto a chair back for support.

"It was you? You were there, in my rooms?"

"Didn't I just say so? Sit down, Tallinu."

Vartra's voice was persuasive, and, still reeling mentally from the shock of discovering the visitation had been real, he sat.

"Every hunter is in his turn the hunted, Tallinu. What I did in the past when I still lived, had to be done. If I hadn't, you'd still be under the heels of the Valtegans. I was driven as much as you are, only I've been honest with you about it. The Entities don't have to reveal themselves or their plans to anyone."

There was that word again. "What do you mean, Entities?"

"A living concept, or archetype, that one uses to understand the forces of nature that govern our world."

He tried to absorb it. "It's the same as a God."

Vartra flicked an ear in a negative. "Entities *are* the forces they represent. Gods and Goddesses are personifications of those forces."

Kaid frowned, feeling the anger returning. "There's no difference, Vartra. You're playing semantics with me again."

"No. It's important that you understand the difference. Gods don't just represent a force of nature, we imbue them with older powers, make of them magical beings."

Kaid shifted uncomfortably, remembering a conversation with Noni about Gods and worshipers.

"Yes, worshipers maintain their Gods with the power of their prayers. Most Gods were folk heroes once, their very essence kept alive by those who believed in them."

"Like you. So how do you fit in, Vartra, except as a God?"

Vartra began to laugh, gently and self-mockingly. It was a laugh Kaid had heard many times in his mind.

"Stop it!" he snapped, hands clenching where they lay on the table.

"The Cataclysm changed many things, Tallinu. Many of the old Gods were swept away, many were forgotten as new ones sprang up. I was one of the new ones, taking over from one called Varza, a warrior who'd set aside his weapons to show that though there's a time to fight, there's also a time for peace. The people replaced him with me, refused to let me pass on to the next life. I became, for them, the conceptualization of peace after battle, of positive change, and law and order. I was the embodiment of the genesis of the new telepaths: the son of the Green Goddess, Her protector, and Her consort. Now do you see the differences?"

What he was saying had a ring of the familiar about it. It was what Noni had said to him. As he began to feel uncomfortable, his anger started to wane.

A purr of pleasure. "You do understand! It's the next stage in your spiritual development, Tallinu. Without understanding this, you cannot go forward."

"Very well. There are only Entities," said Kaid

abruptly. "What has this to do with me? Why did you call me here? To tell me you're more powerful than any God?" Even he could hear the trace of bitterness in his voice.

"So you could dream-walk, Tallinu. There are those among the Guardians who'd prevent you from learning this skill."

"Guardians?" He frowned, ignoring for now the negative comment. He'd not heard the title before except when applied to Guardian Dhaika as head of the Retreat.

"Wheels within wheels, Tallinu," said Vartra, getting up from the table to fetch the two beakers and jug that stood on the dresser behind him. Returning, he placed them on the table and sat down. "The Guardians are people who are one with our land, who guard and monitor the whole of our planet."

"How many more layers are there controlling us?" demanded Kaid. "Why have we at Stronghold never heard of them?"

"Those who need to know are aware of them, never fear. And now, like the few others who are permitted to dream-walk to our realms, so are you."

Mind working furiously, Kaid forced himself to lean back in his chair, letting his hands relax again. Sunlight from a side window dappled Vartra's tunic, making it appear first dark gray, then black as it almost merged into his tan pelt where he sat in the shadows. Compared to the person he'd met in the Fire Margins, this Vartra looked fitter and had gained weight and muscle. No longer did he appear the aesthetic Doctor of genetics, now he looked the part of the God—or Entity.

"Varza was from the plains, just as I am," Vartra said quietly. "We became one Entity."

"Why would I need to dream-walk? And why would anyone want to prevent me from doing it?" Guardians, protecting the soil of their world: it had the guildmark of the ravings of the Human mystic, Derwent, yet this was coming from Vartra.

Vartra leaned forward. "If you're called by an Entity, given permission to enter their realm, then you have power, Tallinu. The power to speak to them, to learn from them—to negotiate with them and change the way things might otherwise be. As Ghyakulla negotiated with me to bring you here."

His unease grew as he remembered that physically he wasn't in a highland cottage, he was actually meditating in the temple of Ghyakulla at Vartra's Retreat, deep in the heart of the Dzahai Mountains. "Where's here exactly?"

"It's a stepping stone," Vartra said, reaching for the jug. "A starting point, where one such as you begins your journey."

Kaid felt his temper rising again. It always came down to this: more work for Vartra. "I've done enough for you," he said warningly, the rumble of anger obvious in his voice. "You've used me once too often, Vartra. It ends here."

"You came here of your own free will," Vartra pointed out as he poured water from the jug into both beakers. "Into my realm, and my home. Your choice."

Kaid made a derisory noise. "So what? It means nothing to me. You tricked me into believing Ghyakulla had called me."

"She did," Vartra reminded him, picking up one of the beakers and taking a sip. "She called you because She knows what I need of you."

His anger finally dispelled his unease. He slammed his open palm violently against the top of the table, making the jug and the remaining beaker jump and shake. "What is it now, Vartra? You've taken everything from me, even my faith in you!"

"I was driven to do what I did during my life, Tallinu, by forces higher than myself. If I hadn't, it would never have been possible for you to have met Kusac, or Carrie, your Human lover."

With a wordless roar of anger, Kaid's hands closed, claws gouging deep tracks in the surface of the wooden table. "I knew it was your doing! Is there nothing in my life you haven't shaped with your meddling?"

"You forget yourself, Tallinu." Vartra's tone was icy as he regarded him unflinchingly. "You chose to come back to my time, to leave the blood of your Human lover with me. Without that, none of this would have been possible. You and Kusac shaped your own futures, used your own free will. I merely—enhanced the options. Did I interfere when you tried to burn down my temple?"

That hit him like a shower of cold water.

"You thought I didn't know?" Vartra flicked his ears in a negative as he put down his beaker. "Foolish, Tallinu. You know better than that. I didn't cause your Triad, that I swear, nor your love for this Human."

This time, Kaid could read compassion in the other's eyes. He looked away, not wanting to see it.

"Just as you've been guided by dreams and visions, so was I. We both serve Shola and Ghyakulla, Tallinu." He stopped for a moment before continuing. "You ask what I want. I'll tell you. To free Sholans from the threat of the Valtegans forever."

Kaid looked up at him again. Vartra's eyes had taken on a luminous quality that filled him with dread. It had been easy till now to forget that this was no ordinary male he was dealing with.

"If the Valtegans return, Tallinu, Shola will be lost forever, its land polluted by them, its people enslaved till they have no will to break free. That must not happen. You and the En'Shallans are the key to preventing it. That is what I want, Tallinu, nothing less! When it's done, then we can all rest in peace."

"Why should I believe you? You used me, told Jaisa to steal from my body and bear my cub!"

"Not me, Tallinu," Vartra said softly, picking his beaker up again to take another sip from it. "Not me. Vartra the geneticist did that. I'm no longer the same male. He died fifteen hundred years ago."

"You're the same person! No one can change that much!"

"Am I? Tell me, Tallinu the Brother, the priest and killer, what place in the life of one such as you does a fragile, hairless alien female hold?" Vartra's voice was growing louder. "You, once second in command in the Claws, the most feared of the Packs on the streets of Ranz, their top killer—the Brotherhood's best Special Operative at hunting down and killing rogue telepaths: what place has any female in your life, let alone one

who poses a threat to your whole species? One who's
responsible for altering the best of the few telepaths
Shola possesses till they're infertile with their own kind?
Tell me now that *you* haven't changed!"

Kaid's anger and anguish had built in equal portions.
There was no denying the truth of what Vartra was
saying. "You made it happen!" he roared, pushing his
seat back and springing to his feet, tail lashing angrily
from side to side, ears plastered flat against his skull.

"I did?" It was said very quietly. Vartra leaned back
in his seat, brown eyes looking up unconcerned at him.
"How so? You did that yourself as a child. I watched it
happening during the long drive to Stronghold. How
could I make a cub barely three years old become sexually attracted to a female so alien and unlike his own
kind? You know the answer to that as well as I do. Why
do you have to question what you feel for her? Why
can't you just enjoy having her as your lover and third
now you've finally achieved what you longed for?"

"Because I need to know what's real, dammit!" he
swore, clenching his hands till his claws pricked his
palms. "You pull me about like a cub's toy, Vartra, as
if I'm there for your whims and your use! I'm not! I have
needs of my own!" Uncertainty and insecurity as well
as anger threatened to overwhelm him. "I've visited too
many dream worlds, Vartra, I don't need yours! I need
to know what's true, what's real!" He needed to know
that what he felt for Carrie was his, not engineered by
the male—be he God or Entity—who sat before him.

"Sit down, Tallinu. I brought you here to do just that.
And to tell you what I need you to do now."

"I refuse. If I have the free will you say I have, you
can't make me," he snapped, fighting to slow his breathing and prevent the mist of rage from forming before
his eyes.

"Sit down, Tallinu." The voice was even quieter now,
persuasive. "I will offer a compromise, then. A deal, if
you like."

"What do you offer?" Kaid asked through clenched
teeth.

"I promise I will never again call you back to the time
of the Cataclysm."

He snorted in disgust. "And what use is that? You already know whether or not you've done it again! That's using your foreknowledge, not making a concession!"

"Sit." Vartra waited, looking up expectantly at him till Kaid reluctantly sat down. "We're outside time for now, Tallinu. The past, the present, all are one for this moment. What we decide now will happen, this I promise you. I have never lied to you, no matter what else you think you can accuse me of. I will not return you to the past. You have my word on that."

Automatically Kaid began reciting his litanies, calming his mind while measuring Vartra up with all the senses he possessed. This was the time for clear thought. Dispassionately, he looked back over his encounters with Him. He spoke the truth. Whether as God or mortal, Vartra had not lied to him. It mattered little what Vartra wanted him to do, if he could use it to buy the peace of mind he desperately needed. "I want more," he said at length. "No interference between me and my Triad partners. We'll find our way, or not, on our own."

Vartra raised an eye ridge. "My Triad, Tallinu? You accept it now?"

"It exists. I have to deal with it, no matter how or why it formed. I want no more interference between the three of us."

"We need your Triad to work, Tallinu. You must be welded together as one, able to support each other."

He could hear a note of uncertainty in the other for the first time. "No interference, Vartra," he said coldly. "And I'll father no cubs with her."

"Some things are not dependent on me, Tallinu," Vartra murmured, mouth opening in a faint grin. "That rather depends on your actions, doesn't it? Cubs are Ghyakulla's gift to us all."

"You know exactly what I mean," Kaid growled. "No confusing me, sending me fevers or visions so that I lose my senses when I'm with her."

"Do you think I did all that? You give me more credit than I'm due. Agreed, on one condition."

"No conditions, Vartra. This is my deal with you, remember?"

"One. You work at this Triad, Tallinu. No taking the easy option and letting it die. You work at it. You owe me that much at least by the oaths you swore to me when you paired with her the first time, and at the cub's Validation. What was it? *I'll do anything you ask, only let this be real.*"

Kaid regarded him impassively. "I have never been foresworn in my life. I have no intention of going back on my oaths now."

"Yet you leveled similar accusations against me. I want to hear you swear that you will work at this Triad of yours."

"I swear." A low growl accompanied his oath. "Tell me what you want me to do, then we can get this over with."

Vartra pushed the other beaker toward him. "Drink," he said. "You must be thirsty by now."

Kaid hesitated. He still didn't completely trust Vartra.

Again the other gestured to the beaker. "It's safe. I'm drinking it."

He picked it up, sniffing the contents suspiciously. "It's water," he said, surprised.

"Of course."

Cautiously, he sipped it, making sure it was indeed water before taking a longer drink.

"I need you to lay aside your mistrust of me, Tallinu, and finish the healing you began at Noni's. I know how much you suffered, not only at the hands of Fyak, but also Ghezu. But you're En'Shalla now, the Brotherhood and all of Shola look to your Triad as the public face of our Order."

Kaid continued to sip at his drink. He was finding it suddenly hot and airless in the room; the palms of his hands were becoming filmed with sweat. He leaned forward, straining to catch Vartra's every word as the God's voice became fainter.

"I need you all to be strong, stronger than you've ever been before, because for the sake of Shola, to beat the Valtegans, you will need to make a pact with the Liege of Hell Himself. Be prepared, Tallinu, for it may cost you your life, or that of one you hold dear."

He jerked in bed, shouting out in fear as he came instantly awake.

"What is it?" demanded T'Chebbi from beside him.

"A dream," he said, shuddering as he passed his hands over his brows, pushing his ears flat against his hair. The dream memory held him still in claws of steel as it dragged him back, even though awake, to relive the last portion.

"This is what I know, Tallinu, what you may have to face. I wish I had more to show you, but so far from Shola, we Entities hold little sway."

Hands bound behind him, he was being dragged toward a large window that gave onto the room next door. The hand holding his scruff pulled his head painfully back, claws gouging his flesh as he was hauled to a stop.

"Look, even now they betray you in this act of reproduction!"

He looked, seeing enough to know that one of the two figures in the bed was Carrie. The other—was Sholan, that was all he could tell. He turned his head aside, saying nothing.

A hiss of anger from his captor and he was flung against the transparent screen, his face pressed painfully against the cool surface.

"You'll watch till I say otherwise! That is your mate, linked mentally to you! Would you die for them now? You're a bigger fool than I thought!"

He shuddered again as the vision finally left him.

"More cryo nightmares?" T'Chebbi asked sympathetically.

"Yes." He'd told no one about this vision from Vartra, managed to hide it even from Kusac and Carrie when they had been intimately linked. Then the potential danger had seemed distant, avoidable. Now, out here in the dark between the worlds, with Carrie and Kusac both lying in cryo units, he wasn't so sure anymore.

The memories were fading so fast he couldn't visualize them enough to remember any more details. It was the first time they had recurred since Vartra had shown them to

him all those months before. Why should they come to his
sleeping mind now?

T'Chebbi's hand touched his arm, and with an effort, he
turned to look at her. He tried to force a smile to his face
in a reassurance he couldn't give himself.

"I'm fine now," he said, sliding back down under the
cover. He closed his eyes, focusing his mind, trying to recall
the scene, desperate for any clue that would answer the
questions it had generated.

T'Chebbi remained sitting up. "I don't like this, Kaid.
Something is wrong."

He raised himself back up on one elbow. "You sense
danger?" All Brotherhood members had a gift, hers was
the foreknowledge of approaching danger.

"Yes. No—I'm not sure, Kaid," she said, clutching her
arms across her chest. "Not yet, maybe not at all, but
there's something out there. Something and nothing."

Vartra had said as much. He lay back, staring up at
the ceiling, remembering the words that had followed the
vision. He'd still been groggy from the water he'd been
given.

> "The water is from Ghyakulla's fountain, Tallinu. The
> purest you'll ever taste. It opens the inner eye that lets
> us see what may be. You needed to take it to see the
> vision. Darkness is gathering between the stars, threat-
> ening the lifeblood of Shola. All that stands between us
> and it is your Triad."

"Who told you that?"

T'Chebbi's voice made him jump. He hadn't realized
he'd spoken aloud. "Vartra. It was a warning." He turned
toward her, pulling her down beside him. "Tell me if the
feeling of danger grows stronger. You're sure it isn't here
now? Because of Carrie's injury and us being on the
U'Churian ship?"

"The warning would have come sooner. This one is just
beginning."

"Yet you sensed nothing before the fight at the spaceport." It was a statement, not a recrimination.

"Maybe because there was no serious danger to her once
she was put in cryo."

"Maybe." He wasn't convinced. Tirak was honest enough in his intent to take them to their rendezvous, but he felt that any species that trusted another to navigate their military ships was worthy of suspicion. Their current situation involved two unknown variables—the U'Churians and the Cabbarans.

"What is it the Cabbarans do that's so different?" T'Chebbi asked sleepily as she curled up against his side.

Recently she'd shown a knack of following his thoughts that would have disturbed him if everything else around him wasn't so volatile. "They can navigate during jump, allowing them to do two jumps in one flight. That's why we can reach Tuushu Station so quickly."

"How?" She was instantly awake. "And why only two jumps?"

"Tirak says it's a natural ability, a skill they use when planet healing and one they found useful when they got into space. As for only doing two jumps, they can't make a hull for their craft that is strong enough to withstand the stresses caused by the time it would take to jump a greater combined distance."

"They have a psi talent?"

"Sounds like it, but they're not telepathic, I checked. It may just be a convenient lie to mask their technology. Tirak was certainly keeping something back when he told me."

"Think of the military advantage that would give us over the Valtegans when we do find them."

"I have. That's why I requested the interview with Annuur."

"And?"

"And if his sept is only a commercial one, then I'm a jegget. Tirak's mission was military, he admitted it. If this were an Alliance undertaking, Annuur would have an equal rank with the captain—if we used another species to navigate for us." Talking about this was preventing him from thinking about the remainder of his meeting with Vartra.

"So what did you do?" she prompted, nipping his jaw in frustration at the delay. "Don't spin this out!"

"Made a formal application for Treaty talks to begin between the Cabbarans and the Alliance on Jalna," he said, grabbing her chin to prevent her nipping him again. "I also spoke to Captain Kisha, as you call him, with instructions on how to contact the Cabbaran home world." He released her.

"Two new allies. The Alliance will be formidable when we do meet the Valtegans."

"Three if you count the TeLaxaud, but first we have to find them. They trade only rarely at Jalna, and there's no one who knows how to contact them."

"Curious, considering they helped build the port."

"It happens that way with people, why not with a species?"

"So what woke you?"

He bit back the answer just in time. She'd nearly caught him by switching the topic so abruptly. "I told you, a dream of danger. Now sleep," he said, reaching out to kill the night-light.

Sleep took some time in coming, and when it did, it was laced with more of the memories he'd tried to avoid.

"Before the effects of Ghyakulla's water wear off, as a measure of my good faith, Tallinu, I can show you the answer to one question," Vartra had said. "What, from the future, do you wish to know?"

He'd been light-headed and not thinking too clearly then. Foremost in his mind was his determination not to share his cubs with her, or anyone. An image had begun to form almost immediately, one he'd seen before.

The room seemed to lurch and he was looking at the newborn cub in Noni's arms, unsure what to do or say.

"She's yours, Tallinu," the familiar old voice said. "Your daughter. Take her from me, for Vartra's sake! Let her know you accept your child!"

He reached down to take the child from her, holding the little one awkwardly in his arms.

She gave a soft mewl, mind and hands reaching out for him. He offered her a finger and she took it, holding onto him firmly as she began to purr. He was totally unprepared for the flood of emotions that rushed through him as he stroked the tiny brown-furred hand. Gathering her closer, he laid his face against her tiny head, taking in her scent, bonding to her. Suddenly, this cub he'd tried so hard to avoid conceiving because of his love for her mother, was even more precious.

"A daughter," he said, looking over to where she lay, exhausted from the birth. "We share a daughter."

Light, streaming in from the small window in Noni's main room, blinded him.

"I know," she said, her voice tired but holding a purr beneath the words.

Still dazzled, he moved his head in an effort to see her clearly. As he blinked, his vision cleared—and the image was gone.

* * *

Day 3

General Kezule, Chosen of the God-King, Emperor Q'emgo'h, stirred, took a deep breath, and was instantly awake and squatting at the mouth of his lair. Peering through the bushes that concealed the entrance, he scanned down the slope in front of him toward the margins of the Taykui Forest. It was dawn. He blinked once, slowly, lashless green lids closing over his large eyes. Forked tongue flicked out, tasting the air for any Sholan scent, no matter how old. Nothing. The air was clean.

He relaxed, sitting back on the pile of grasses he'd made his bed while he slept in his laalgo trance; not to heal, but to pass the time until it was safe for him to venture out into the forest once more.

For perhaps fifteen minutes he sat there, constantly surveying the countryside, watching for anything that might betray the presence of Sholan hunters. He'd had a near miss a couple of days ago. They'd been out in force, their soldiers quartering the last three miles at the edges of the forest, obviously determined that if he tried to make a break for the plains, they'd catch him. He'd concealed himself in the tree canopy, and only the fact that they'd disturbed a pack of wild felines with young cubs to defend had saved him from discovery. The soldiers had had to scatter for safety themselves, several of the slower ones getting badly mauled in the ensuing chaos.

A flock of birds rose suddenly, squawking and bickering,

making him tense, but it was only a carnivore after a meal. He relaxed again, continuing to watch.

The trances served another purpose. When in that state, there was no chance his would-be captors could pick up his thoughts with their telepaths, and he could save the power cell in his wrist unit. Thinking of that reminded him to switch it on. He'd taken it from the Sholan he'd found in the hut by the swamp at the beginning of this journey. He gave a hiss of amusement as he remembered him. After the treatment he'd received from the Sholans while in captivity, the groveling terror of the male had soothed his ego—briefly. Fear of not doing one's duty was one thing, but the abject terror displayed by the Sholan was that of an incompetent officer waiting for his underlings to turn on him and rend him to pieces. There was no dignity in witnessing either, especially as he couldn't afford to let him live. Scuttling the swamp vehicle had saddened him; he'd enjoyed using it.

He checked the unit, making sure it was still emitting the signal that would prevent them from sensing his mind. It had been relatively easy to do. If they'd known in his time what the Sholan telepaths had been capable of, this disaster would never have befallen his people and they would still be in their rightful role as overlords of this world.

Sighing, he reached for the other comm, activating one of the news nets. Fifteen minutes later, he'd learned nothing much of interest and his stomach was growling with hunger. It was time to venture out and hunt. Pity he'd had to leave the female: her scent had helped mask his for the short while she'd been with him. He frowned, remembering her fear of him. That had angered him beyond reason at the time. He'd never abused her, why hadn't she trusted him? All he had intended was to cleanse his own system and fulfil his obligation to her by releasing her from the compulsion his bite had caused. He'd wanted to mate with her as little as she'd wanted it, but it was the only way to neutralize the chemicals his teeth had injected into her. There had been no pleasure in it for him. It was yet another of the indignities their captivity had imposed on him, and for that, those who'd brought him to this time would suffer!

When he reached their estate, then he'd begin to redress

the balance—once they'd returned them all to his time. What they had done to him would be nothing to the sweet revenge he'd take on them!

He took a deep breath, forcing himself to remain calm. Anger was good, but not yet. Later, when he had the Human female and the two male Sholans to vent it on— and maybe that hatchling of theirs, too. Time now to hunt, eat, and move cautiously onward to the Valsgarth estate.

                              *   *   *

Kaid walked down the corridor leading from the bridge to the cabin he and T'Chebbi shared with Giyesh. They'd all found themselves sharing quarters with crew members, undoubtedly so Tirak's people could keep an eye on them. Around him, like a heartbeat, he could hear the ever-present sound of the ship's engines. Another day, Tirak had said, then they'd be at jump point. It was taking them only three days to reach the requisite velocity. They must be traveling faster than the Alliance craft could, but Tirak was keeping those details to himself. Perhaps the Cabbarans had other technology that no one was speaking about.

As Kaid approached the doorway to his assigned cabin, he pushed those thoughts to the back of his mind and pressed the lock. Giyesh was off at her post and everyone was waiting, crowded into the limited space. He could feel their curiosity as he crossed over to the chair left vacant for him. He let his gaze linger on Kate and Taynar, the young Leska pair. They sat close together, Kate obviously still overwhelmed by recent events.

"I've been speaking to Captain Kishasayzar on Jalna," he said, taking his seat. "The *Rhijissoh* is expected there within the next four days and all is going as planned for the proposed Contact talks. Railin is now firmly entrenched in his position as the new Port Lord."

"What about Killian? Did he cause any trouble over our escape?" asked Jo. "And what about the laser gun we left behind?"

Kaid's mouth opened in a faint grin. "The laser blew the minute Killian's men tried to move it, taking out the whole wall of his barn. He had some idea of using it on the port once he realized Railin had taken you there. It took Ashay showing off his shuttle piloting skills again to make Killian calm down enough to sit at the table with Railin and the others to form a ruling council for Jalna. I think they'll do well."

"What's this meeting all about?" Rezac demanded suddenly. "We've been on board for two days now and you've told us damned little about what's going on here. I think we're due an explanation."

"It's time we had a debriefing," Kaid agreed quietly. "Before I begin, I want to remind you we are guests on this craft. Treaty negotiations have begun, and due to the unique circumstances we all find ourselves in, an interim agreement has been signed. We are allied with both the U'Churians and the Cabbarans. I expect you to behave accordingly." Again, he glanced around the room, ignoring the slightly raised eye ridge from T'Chebbi. She'd understand he couldn't have briefed her sooner.

"I'm assuming no one knows anything here, so I'll start from the beginning. Two Valtegan shuttles landed on Jalna some six or so months ago. One landed outside the Port, then crashed on takeoff, the other touched down to sell the four Sholan prisoners it carried and to buy supplies. Jo's party were sent to Jalna at the request of the Chemerians to find out about the first Valtegan craft, the one that crashed. Since Jalna is in what the Chemerians consider their home territory, until now all other Alliance members have been unaware of its existence." He turned to look at the three rescued Sholans, noting how Tesha and Jeran exchanged glances, keeping their eyes averted from Tallis, who sat slightly apart.

"We were sent by the Alliance to find you three. The Chemerians refused to authorize a rescue mission for you until our team was ready. I won't go into the whys of it. . . ."

"I think you should," interrupted Tallis. "I, for one, want to know why we weren't more important than some damned crashed ship!"

"Yeah, I'm rather curious about that myself," said Rezac from where he sprawled on one of the beds. "Not that I'm complaining, because it meant we were released from the stasis cube. . . ."

"*You* were in that cube?" Jeran's tone was astonished. "*You* were the holy relic they hauled off onto Jalna?"

Tesha's laughter had a note of hysteria to it. "You were what kept us alive! If it hadn't been for that damned cube, the crew would have torn us apart!"

Kaid looked from one to the other. "The Valtegans worshiped the cube?"

Jeran reached for Tesha's arm, shaking it gently. "Tesha, it's over now. We're free." He looked up at Kaid. "Yes. It was the only thing they hated and feared more than us. They chained us in there because only the priest J'koshuk, and their captain, M'ezozakk, dared enter the cargo area they called the shrine room."

A sound from Rezac's direction drew Kaid's attention. Rezac was sitting upright now, all trace of bored indifference gone.

"They were afraid of you?"

"Modern-day Valtegans are afraid of us, Rezac. You know about Keiss from your link with Jo, so you'll know that when we met them there, they'd make suicide attacks rather than face capture by us."

"What's this talk of modern Valtegans?" asked Jeran. "Are there other kinds?"

"I told you, but you didn't listen to me," said Taynar. "They—Kaid and the two in cryo—went back in time to the Fire Margins. They must have met Valtegans back then." His voice was hushed as he said the last few words. "You did, didn't you? Oh, Gods! There were Valtegans back on Shola then! That's why Vartra's a God! He saved us from them!"

Kaid briefly shut his eyes, then opened them to catch T'Chebbi's gaze across the room. Now what did he tell them?

"Damned right there were!" said Rezac forcefully. "That's my time, my world! We were Vartra's first enhanced telepaths. We led the rebellion against them, and won!"

As conversations spontaneously broke out, Kaid could feel the group beginning to fragment into its different factions of loyalties. He needed to bring them together now, once and for all.

"Enough!" he said, raising his voice to a command pitch. All conversation stopped, and eyes turned again to him.

"There are no Valtegans on Shola now," he said. "Rezac's right. They're gone, and it was the telepaths who did it." Having gotten their attention, he moderated his tone a little. "The first team were sent to find out what they could from the crashed ship, because we still don't know where their home world is. The Chemerians controlled access to this sector, we couldn't come without their consent and they only consented because they wanted the Valtegan craft investigated. Once the first trip was made, matters changed."

He grinned, a toothy, Human grin that made even Jo shiver, he noticed. "With our visit, we now hold the upper hand. The Chemerians' duplicity has been proved beyond doubt. They were playing the Free Traders off against the Alliance, keeping knowledge of them and the trading world of Jalna to themselves. Even those Sumaan employed by them were prohibited from talking about Jalna. No longer."

"I can tell you why they were afraid of you," said Rezac, sitting back against the bed head. "Racial memory. The survivors would have programmed their descendants to respond to us as a threat."

"Racial memory?" T'Chebbi spoke for the first time.

"Yes. They never forget anything of importance. They pass it down from generation to generation."

"How?" asked Kaid. Such unilateral species fear of an enemy such as the Military Forces on Keiss had met in the Valtegans could only really be accounted for by just such a system.

"The females and the drones. They croon over their eggs, licking and handling them until they're ready to hatch, then they go feral again. If they aren't separated in time, they'll destroy the hatchlings as they emerge. I saw it happen once."

Even with his shields up, Kaid could feel the horror of the memory that Rezac still carried. He glanced at Jo, seeing her get up and move over to the youth's side, reaching out to touch him comfortingly. Rezac accepted her gesture gratefully, taking hold of her hand. For all his brashness, it seemed his father was learning to cope with needing a female better than he was.

"How?" he asked again.

"In their saliva or something," Rezac said. "I don't know for sure, but it's a fair guess."

"How do the females get the memories in the first place if they're kept in breeding areas?" asked Tesha.

"The drones look after them. I presume they're given the memories by the warrior caste to pass on to the females."

"Drones? What drones?" asked T'Chebbi before he could.

"They have three sexes. The androgynous drones are the most passive and they fulfill the domestic roles our females do in Sholan society. They're a light brown, not green like the other two sexes."

T'Chebbi gave a snort of amusement from her position opposite the door. "You got surprise coming when we get home if females in your time like that!"

Kaid frowned at her before returning his attention to Rezac. "We know nothing of the drones. Tell us more."

"They were unimportant," said Rezac with a shrug of indifference. "Asexual servants, general domestics, they looked after the females and were used by the males for sex, not reproduction. They went in with the guards to retrieve the eggs before they hatched." His ears visibly lowered as he shuddered.

"Why were you shown a hatching?" asked Kaid. He had to probe the memory now, had to learn what he could about their enemy.

Rezac looked up at him, catching his gaze. "They showed us what would happen to us if Zashou ever turned down the Emperor's advances again," he said bleakly. "Food for the hatchlings."

Bright and clear, the scene burned itself into Kaid's mind, merging with what he'd seen so long ago when under the influence of the Valtegan drug la'quo that Ghezu had given him. Images of ravenous young, clawing and snapping at each other in their desperate hunger, filled his mind. Shutting his eyes, he shook his head to dispel them.

"Enough! I've seen them for myself!" he said, his voice raw. "Tell me how you came to be in the cube."

"Once the rebellion in the palace had begun, they forgot us. We ran, heading for the breeding room to release the females to cause even more confusion, but we took a wrong turn and met a patrol. They chased us into a lab area, and we knew nothing more until Jo, Kris, and Davies awakened us on Jalna."

"It was a weapons lab. They must have been testing a containment unit or something," said Zashou.

"We were lucky," said Rezac, his hand tightening around Jo's. "Even if we've come forward in time to face them again, we were lucky."

"Jalna and the laalquoi," said Kaid quietly, aware that there would be many more nightmares for Rezac and Zashou to relive before they were done. "What's the connection?"

"They use the plant as a dietary staple, the hardened resin and a narcotic made from the plant to control the females as well as several of the slave races," said Rezac. "They were beginning to farm it on Shola when we were taken. They must have done the same on Jalna."

"For the Jalnians even now to have one stone for each person is massive farming," said T'Chebbi. "More like they used world as farm."

"Jalna is lightly populated when compared to most colony worlds," said Kaid. "Could the plant have been native there?"

"No, it's a Valtegan plant," said Rezac. "About the only vegetation they do eat. It gives them chemicals and stuff they can't produce themselves. They must have introduced it to Jalna. They had four worlds of their own, Kaid, plus the Gods know how many slave worlds. We saw at least two other species on K'oish'ik."

Kaid repeated the word. "K'oish'ik." At last they had a name for the world that had spawned the Valtegans. He caught Rezac's gaze this time. "Any like these?" he asked, visualizing first a Chemerian, then a Touiban. "Or this?" Lastly, a Sumaan.

Rezac blinked and sat back abruptly in shock, banging his head on the wall behind him. Jo gave a small cry of pain and put her hands to her temples.

"You shouldn't be able to do that! No one can get through my shielding!" exclaimed Rezac, shocked.

"Were there any like them?" Kaid wasn't interested in Rezac's bruised ego: the shields had been almost nonexistent as far as he was concerned. He needed to know if the other Alliance species had ever been part of the Valtegans' empire. An ability to force a mental contact had its uses.

"None," Rezac growled angrily. "Nor any like the Jalni-

ans or Humans! But you've no right to force a contact on
me like that. Dammit, you could have asked! It affected Jo
as well!''

"I hope you don't intend to do the same to the rest of
us," said Taynar stiffly. "Brotherhood member or not,
you're breaking the laws in violating the mental privacy of
another being.''

Kaid could hear the quaver of fear in the lad's voice and
regretted his hastiness in dealing with Rezac. "You did the
same to Tirak," he reminded Taynar.

"War breaks rules," said T'Chebbi. "Know from experience, need to catch you when memory fresh. If asked, you
start thinking, memory fades.''

As Rezac subsided, Kaid glanced past him at her,
twitching the tip of an ear in recognition that he owed her.

"It's not something I do often," said Kaid.

"Four worlds of Valtegans!" said Jeran quietly. "The
odds are almost impossible. We saw the fleet that came to
our world, Kaid. It was massive. How can we possibly defend ourselves against them even if we have gained another
three allies? Rezac and those like him may have done it
once, but there's so few high level telepaths, and we've lost
all those on Khyaal and Szurtha!''

"They did it with fewer in Rezac's time," said Kaid
automatically.

"They weren't afraid of us then," said Zashou, the beads
in her many braids chiming as she pushed them back.

Kaid hardly heard her as Vartra's words echoed in his
mind. *To beat the Valtegans, you'll need to make a pact with
the Liege of Hell Himself.* He looked at T'Chebbi, wondering again if he'd already committed Shola and themselves
to just such a pact by signing the interim treaties with Tirak
and Annuur. Then he saw her move her hand fractionally,
signaling a negative. She might not yet know the details of
the treaty, but she knew danger, and was letting him know
that she still sensed nothing concrete.

He pushed aside his unease. Hardly begun, this journey
was already too full of portents and visions and feelings of
danger. The world of awakened psychic senses was still too
new to him; he wished he'd had longer to come to terms
with it. Suddenly, acutely, he missed Carrie; he longed for
the presence of her mind, calming and reassuring. And

Kusac, who'd become the brother he'd never had—he, who'd needed no one for so long, felt more isolated than he had in Ghezu's prison. Instinctively, his hand reached for the crystal at his neck as he pushed the loneliness aside. There was work to do, he must focus on that.

Taking a breath to steady himself, he looked at the small group of survivors from the massacre. "Jeran, despite what they did at Khyaal and Szurtha, I believe the Valtegans are not after us," he said. "In the past, they were driven from Shola, as you say. But in our time, they were driven from Keiss by us and the Humans, and with no reprisals. They left Jalna, too, perhaps before they originally came to Shola. Something more important to them than us or empire building seems to have their full attention for the moment."

"And when they look elsewhere?" demanded Tallis, his narrow face looking more pinched than usual as he frowned. "What then, Kaid?"

"Then we will meet them with a force made up of not only the Alliance, but the Free Traders," said Kaid calmly. "Remember that they still call in at Jalna. The Free Traders may one day have as much reason to fear them as we do. Rezac, Jo, why do you think they left Jalna?"

"Same reason we had to, I assume," said Rezac. "They poisoned the soil, turned the natives too violent to handle. They might even have been affected by it themselves."

"Perhaps we can fashion some of that plant from Jalna into a Valtegan specific weapon—a chemical weapon," said Kate.

"Weapons of that type should be banned by all our worlds," objected Zashou. "To use something like that would be barbaric!"

Around his shoulders, Jeran's sand-colored hair began to rise. "So is destroying all life on two worlds. When facing an enemy so dedicated to eradicating us as a species, I'm sorry, but I'll use anything that comes to hand!"

"The decision wouldn't be ours anyway," said Kaid. A thought occurred to him. "Kate, Taynar, how many of your ship's navigation charts did the Valtegan officer who kidnapped you see?"

"Some," Taynar said. "Jeezah, our pilot, managed to wipe the majority of the charts before he realized what she was doing, but we did use one of the outer sector ones showing the jump points. He was definitely heading for a friendly base."

"Then we know a Valtegan base is reachable from the Chemerian homeworld," said Kaid quietly. "Rezac, did you ever see star charts, either yourself or through one of your telepathic contacts?"

"No. We weren't interested in the location of craft or worlds except for wanting to know where the rest of the fleet was. Our people took over the bridges and used the craft as weapons within the fleet to destroy them, get them fighting against each other."

"You did a commendable job. Then unless they've been collecting the salvage, there should be graveyards of dead ships floating around. And as far as we're aware, no Alliance member has ever come across them," murmured Kaid, thinking of the four Brotherhood outposts and the craft found there two hundred and fifty years ago.

"What about the Free Traders?" asked T'Chebbi. "Maybe they find what we haven't."

"Worth asking Tirak," agreed Kaid. "But the Chemerians might be more useful. Since they've kept this," he indicated the whole ship with a sweep of his arm, "from us, what else have they concealed? Tirak said his people are only allowed to approach Tuushu Station on one, specific, guarded route. They don't have free access to the Chemerian system. They're just as secretive with the Free Traders as they are with us."

"I want to know why the Valtegans visit Jalna every fifty years to take soil and plant samples," said Jeran.

"To see when it's free of poison," said T'Chebbi. "Then they can come back."

Rezac shifted uneasily. "But why leave the other species alone, let them trade there? It doesn't make sense. They have to control and dominate wherever they go. This is so unlike them."

"They had four worlds. Perhaps these ones from another world," said T'Chebbi. "Perhaps still fighting each other."

"Or the original slave worlds," suggested Zashou.

"Could be either," said Kaid. "If they lost their tech level as we did, perhaps their Empire was split. They could have just rediscovered each other and be fighting among themselves for dominance. It would explain the lack of interest in finding our home world."

"But why destroy our two colonies?" asked Tesha.

"The best theory so far is that they formed part of a corridor in space that ends at Keiss," said Kaid. "Unfortunately, projecting it in the opposite direction hasn't led to anything interesting. When you look at a holo map of those sectors of space, it becomes more obvious. Khyaal and Szurtha were just in their way, nothing more."

"Figures," growled Rezac. "It's the kind of thing they would do. Destroy what they couldn't use in case it was a threat to them."

"Doesn't explain Jalna, though," said T'Chebbi.

Kaid's attention began to drift. They could speculate all they wanted, but the hard fact was none of them knew anything for sure. He scratched unconsciously at his throat: he felt uncomfortable, itchy. The longer pelt was beginning to irritate him more now than before, but the lab's potions would remain effective for several weeks yet, both in his black coloring and the length of his pelt. Showers were fine, but what he needed was a good brushing to get rid of some of the denser, inner fur. It had been well over a week since either he or T'Chebbi had had time for such luxuries.

Carrie slept the sleep of winter, her body, like the ground, lying rimed with frost, her thoughts stopped between one impulse and the next. No one dreams in cryo.

Slowly, slowly, the images began to form within her calm world, taking on harder edges, emerging from the frozen mists that seemed to surround her. She saw a patchwork of forests and plains, leading toward the coast, a coast she knew well. Wait. There was a patch, a stain on the land: a greenness too bright for grass or forest. Almost iridescent, it crept away from the Taykui Hills, migrating toward the forest that surrounded her home. In her mind, she frowned, brows furrowing as she watched and tried to remember where she'd seen such a color before. But thoughts came slowly in this world of cold mists.

The stain inched forward toward the tree line that marked the boundary of their estate and there it stopped for the moment while she fought against the insidious chill, trying to remember. When it began to move again, the memory flooded back. It was as green as the drug la'quo that Kezule had used to travel through time!

She could hear the sound of her cub crying. Kashini! She'd left her daughter alone! Hard on its heels came the memory of her own mother in cryo on the outward trip to Keiss, the trip that had cost so many lives.

"Mother! Don't leave me!" she'd cried out to the silence of the sleeping ship.

She'd tried to move, to scream—anything to draw attention to herself, let them know her mother needed their help as she relived her first cryo nightmare. Terror flooded through her as she realized she was just as powerless, just as trapped as before—and just as aware of the threat to her daughter as she'd been of the danger to her mother those many years ago.

Pain lanced through her, burning, searing pain in her right side as she became aware of the distant sound of a klaxon. The realization she was in a cryo chamber came to her then, shocking and terrifying her more if it were possible. Then common sense took over: they must be waking her, how else could she feel the pain of her wound? Let them be quick, she prayed as she pushed the fear back. They had to know that Kezule was loose and heading for her daughter!

The klaxon roused Mrowbay from his desk. Leaping to his feet, he ran for the cryo units, yelling out a command for the alarm to cease, demanding a report from the medical computer.

"Life signs of patient in unit one fluctuating above acceptable limit," the electronic voice intoned. "Recommend increasing anaesthetic and coolant levels."

"Implement," snapped the medic, punching a sequence out on the control panel of Carrie's unit to review the errant readings.

Perception blurred and slowed as the frozen mists began to rise around her again. Not waking her at all, they were making her sleep! In desperation, she reached out with her mind for Kaid. He was her Third, mentally Linked to her and Kusac, he'd sense what was happening and intervene to help her!

*   *   *

Moments before the klaxon sounded, Kaid stiffened, reaching for the crystal at his throat—not the large one that linked him with Carrie, but the smaller one in the center of his Triad pendant. He knew instantly something was wrong with her.

"T'Chebbi, take over," he said, rising to his feet and walking to the door. "I have to attend to something."

In the passageway, he broke into a run. Mrowbay looked up from Carrie's unit as he entered the sick bay, claws skidding on the floor as he came to an abrupt stop beside him.

"What's up?" Kaid demanded of the large U'Churian without preamble as he peered through the transparent cover at the sleeping Human. "And don't tell me, nothing, I know better. I sensed her." He put his hand on the unit, spreading his fingers, willing himself to feel her mind once more within his.

"You can't have," said Mrowbay, hitting the final keys before looking up at him. "I know you're concerned for her, but no one can be aware of anything in cryo. It's impossible."

"Not for her. She's done it before. Tell me what happened."

"Nothing. Just some minor fluctuations in the levels of . . ."

"Wake her," interrupted Kaid. "She's aware, that's why your levels are out. She'll be terrified. Wake her."

"I can't. I've just increased the depth of her sleep," objected Mrowbay. "If I tried, she'd die, Kaid. The shock to her system would be too great."

Already he could feel his pendant cooling, the nebulous almost-contact with her fading. The medic was right. To wake her now without the proper medical care would kill her. "She's aware, Mrowbay," he said more calmly. "If we can't wake her, then put her deeper so we know she's really sleeping."

"What you claim is impossible, Kaid," said the U'Churian, taking Kaid by the arm in an effort to urge him away from the unit. "I know my equipment, and I've had a Human female in cryo before. Kate said nothing about dreams when she came out."

Kaid clenched his feet, claws gripping the floor covering as he refused to be moved. "And I know Carrie. Her memories are mine, Mrowbay. She was aware in cryo. Put her deeper. If we can't wake her long enough to calm her fears, then put her deeper."

"Do as he asks," said a voice from the doorway. "If he says he senses her mind, then he's right. Do it on our responsibility," said Rezac. "We know the workings of our Leskas' minds as well as you know your equipment."

Kaid glanced over at him from beneath lowered brows, unsure whether to be glad of the intrusion.

"Very well," sighed the beleaguered medic, turning back to the unit. "But on your heads be it."

Rezac remained where he was till Mrowbay had finished and returned to his office. Then he joined Kaid by Carrie's unit.

"Tell me about the Triads," he said. "How close does the link to your third grow?"

"I'm not the one to ask," said Kaid, moving away from him. "In a few days we'll be on the *M'Zekko*. There'll be a mentor there who can tell you what you need to know."

"I don't want theory. You're a member of the first Triad. You've got the personal experience," said Rezac, grasping him by the arm.

Kaid could sense Rezac's concern, the need the younger male had had to help him, and his confusion as to why it should be so important to him to do it. He was trying to conceal it beneath the request for information on the Triads, but he could feel the truth of it. As difficult as his position was, Rezac's was worse. While he, as the son, could try to ignore their biological relationship, Rezac, as his father, obviously could not. On some strange, subconscious level, he was aware of the relationship.

It surged through him then, a feeling from Rezac akin to what he felt when he touched his own son, Dzaka. With his free hand, he carefully disengaged himself from Rezac's grasp.

"Thank you for your support. I can tell you very little about the En'Shalla Triads. There are too few of us and our relationships are too new for any of us to know what is normal."

"You must be able to tell me something! Is it like a

Leska Link? Are there Link days?" He spread his hands
in a plea for help. "I still sense nothing from Zashou, and
as for Jo . . ." He stopped in mid-sentence, ears dipping in
the Sholan equivalent of a shrug. "What do I do, Kaid?
She's my soul's mate, yet I still love Zashou. She was my
first love, my own kind, the one I wanted above all others,
even if she hates me except during our Link time."

Kaid's mouth widened slightly in a sardonic Human
smile. He understood only too well, except Carrie, Kusac,
and T'Chebbi were tied in his impossible dreams.

"You love them each as well as you can," he said, reaching out to touch the other's shoulder comfortingly. "Love
them for their own worth, don't compare them or how you
feel about each of them. And thank the Gods for Their
double gift!"

"But what of Link days?"

Kaid lifted his shoulders in the Human shrug. "It depends on how closely you're Linked to Jo."

"She's always there. I haven't been able to sense Zashou
since she lost our cub. It's as if Jo's replaced her." He was
unable to stop his ears from lying flat in distress.

"It'll take some time for Zashou to recover," Kaid said
awkwardly, remembering how Carrie had been after she'd
lost her first child. He didn't want to talk about himself
and Carrie, and especially not to this brash young male.
Then he forced himself to remember that this time, Rezac
was not being brash, was not pushing himself forward, but
was instead asking for help.

"We don't have Link days," he continued slowly. "We're
gradually drawn to each other—we know when it's our
time. A Triad is more than that. It's a legal marriage between the three of us. The cubs Carrie has belong to us
all."

"And now? With them both in cryo? How do you cope?"

Kaid stiffened, closing down the light rapport he'd permitted between himself and—his father. "I wait," he said
shortly, and began to move out into the corridor. "I've told
you all I know. At Valsgarth, our Clan estate, you'll learn
the rest."

* * *

"We've found nothing," said Raiban in disgust. "My people can't even tell me if Kezule's still in the Taykui Forest or not!"

"Then you'll have to spread the search wider still," said Rhyaz calmly, regarding the General of Military Intelligence on his comm screen. She looked tired and harassed, as well she might under the circumstances. "He's not likely to want to remain hidden in the forest. He'll have some destination in mind by now."

"Obviously," she snapped. "It's where he's likely to head for that's got me worried."

Rhyaz raised an eye ridge. "Where's that?"

"Lhygo Spaceport, of course! He'll want to get off-world, find out where the others of his kind are."

"I think not, General. If I read him right, he'll not do that."

"Oh, and where d'you think he'll go? Back to Chezy and the ancient Valtegan hatching ground?"

"Perhaps. It's more likely than the spaceport."

"You're not exactly being helpful Rhyaz."

"May I remind you, General, that after your people let Kezule escape, you personally refused us entry to the facility at Shanagi? If I remember rightly, you said. . . ."

"I know what I said, dammit! That was in the heat of the moment," she said tartly. "If I'm going to spread our net wider, we'll need the Brotherhood's help. I'm not prepared to advise we lessen our defense commitment to track down one Valtegan when we face a larger threat from them in space."

Rhyaz inclined his head. "The Brotherhood is more than willing to help you, General. What about Keeza Lassah?"

Raiban gestured briefly. "They found her shredded clothing, covered in her blood, and traces of his. She's dead, Rhyaz."

"You found her body?"

"Don't need to. If he didn't eat her, then one of the feral cats did. And by the way, it was General Naika's staff who were on duty when Kezule escaped."

"Ah, then we're no longer being held responsible? That's good to know. Thank you for telling me, General." He held his peace on the issue of Keeza. Brotherhood personnel were already looking for her; he wanted her alive and that meant kept out of Raiban's claws. As far as he was concerned, she wasn't dead until he saw her corpse.

Raiban growled gently. "I want your people guarding the spaceport, Master Rhyaz," she said. "Every passenger has to be checked, every piece of luggage and cargo large enough for Kezule to conceal himself in, and every vehicle not only guarded from the moment it lands, but searched immediately prior to takeoff."

"You're going to need an explanation for the newsvids, General. This is going to cause long delays and be very unpopular with everyone. And as I said, I think he's very unlikely to head for there. My bet is he'll make for the Valsgarth estate."

"Revenge? It might be the Brotherhood's way, but that male is a professional soldier, Rhyaz, a general! His priority will be to return to the nearest unit of his people."

He could hear the amusement in Raiban's voice and decided to ignore the insult. "Not revenge, a desire to return to his own time and reverse what has happened to his species' future on Shola. Security on the Aldatan and Valsgarth estates needs to be increased, General."

"There's enough people there already. In fact, I'm tempted to pull some out to help us catch Kezule. There hasn't been any threat to the mixed Leskas for a long time. If you want more soldiers, you'll have to use your own people, Rhyaz, if you've any left after deploying them at the spaceport. I expect them to be in position first thing tomorrow morning. Send me a list of the names and numbers you're sending and I'll have them added to the Forces payroll. Good day, Rhyaz."

As soon as the screen blanked, Rhyaz turned to his aide, L'Seuli. "She's right, we won't have the personnel on Shola to spare. Once you've drawn up Raiban's list and issued orders for those concerned, check the active roster and see who we can recall without arousing suspicion."

"Are you sure he'll head for there, Master Rhyaz?"

"No, but it's more likely than the spaceport."

"What about Chezy? Kezule took Fyak back to his time from there. He might be able to use the same method to take himself back."

"I've already got a small unit there, just in case."

* * *

As Brynne approached Stronghold, the winds caught the small aircar, buffeting it from side to side as he attempted to descend toward the outer walls.

"Control to approaching 'car. Ident codes required for permission to land." The voice filled the tiny vehicle, its highland burr obvious even to him.

"I don't have any," said Brynne. Until this moment, he'd had no doubts about making this journey. "Do I need one? I'm from Valsgarth estate. Do I really need one?" He was having his work cut out to control the vehicle in the strong crosswinds.

"Name?" The voice, relaxed before, was suddenly crisp.

"Brynne Stevens."

"We have no notification from Valsgarth that you're expected."

"I'm not," he said, hauling on the semicircular control bar as the craft suddenly began to drop toward the walls at an alarming rate. "Look, I've never been here before, and I'm having a devil of a job flying this 'car right now. . . ."

A second voice cut him short. "Concentrate on your flying, Mr. Stevens. We're having the central courtyard cleared for you. Land as soon as you can. Remain in your vehicle, you'll be met."

He sounded angry, Brynne thought as he glanced briefly out of the side window. Damn. That's all he needed, to start off on the wrong foot. Below, figures were running out of the gatehouse toward the groups of students in the courtyard.

Embarrassment flooded through him and he was glad the aircar didn't have a vid unit. Maybe arriving unannounced like this was the worst thing he could do, but at least they hadn't refused him permission to land.

He was met by one of the black-robed Brothers, who, with punctilious formality, escorted him to Father Lijou's office. This was the first time he'd had any real dealings with the Head Priest and, as the older Sholan rose to his feet and came out from behind his desk to greet him, he was subjected to the priest's piercing gaze.

"Mister Stevens," Lijou said, extending his hand toward him, palm uppermost. "An unexpected pleasure, indeed. This is your first visit to Stronghold, I believe."

Brynne touched fingertips in the brief, formal telepath's greeting. "Yes, my first." He should have asked Garras to make an appointment, he just knew he should have. As he followed Father Lijou over to the less formal seats, he prayed that he wouldn't be sent back to the estate because he'd ignored protocol.

"Then we must let you see round Stronghold," said Lijou. "But tell me, what brings you here? And so unexpectedly." The last was said with an under-purr of amusement. "Landing here is a specialized skill. Your arrival caused quite a stir."

Brynne noticed irrelevancies, like the broad gray streaks that framed the Father's dark-pelted face. When Lijou's mouth opened in a slight smile, he looked down at his hands. "I didn't mean to put the wind under everyone's tails," he muttered, part defensively, part embarrassed.

"An interesting way to put it," said Lijou. "It looked rather more like the wind was under your tail. Now, what brings you to our hallowed halls?"

"I don't know." Brynne looked up at him. "I hoped you'd be able to tell me. The need to come here has been growing for weeks now."

"Our Gods indeed have long arms, Brynne Stevens. You're the first of the Humans to be called by Them, but doubtless not the last. As a member of the En'Shalla Clan, you're automatically a member of the Brotherhood. However, I think it's time you swore to our Creed and became a properly initiated member. You need to start your training with us." The Head Priest got to his feet. "I advise you to tell your Leska that you'll be based here for the foreseeable future, Brother Brynne."

"He's been sworn in?" asked Master Rhyaz.

"I did it immediately. I have twinned him with Jurrel. They're collecting his basic kit from housekeeping at present. And, yes, first thing tomorrow, he'll be taught how to handle that aircar of his properly," Lijou smiled.

Rhyaz nodded. "I thought we'd lose him the way the winds caught that 'car of his. It's most unsuitable, merely a runabout for the cities. He should be allocated something more robust in future."

"Doubtless that will be one of the first things Garras does when he next returns to the estate," said Lijou. "I'm dividing Brynne's training between ourselves and Dhaika at the Retreat. We have plans for this Human."

"Oh?" Rhyaz' tone was one of polite curiosity.

Lijou shook his head. "Religious matters, Rhyaz, nothing that you need concern yourself with as yet."

The other flicked an ear in compliance. "What of Vartra?" he asked cautiously. "Have your meditations and prayers elicited anything more about His warning?"

"I'd have told you immediately," Lijou replied, a pained expression crossing his face. "I understand the significance of being handed the Guild coin, Rhyaz. Whatever the nature of this task He has for us is, so far, He's keeping it to Himself. What did you do with the coin He gave me?"

"Put it back in the vault where it belongs. I've also done as He said and put all our people in the field on alert. They're to report any dreams or visions of the God immediately, either to yourself or to me. I can't help but wonder if this isn't all connected to Kezule's escape."

"Who knows but the God?" sighed Lijou. His thoughts turned toward the three people still missing. "What of Kezule, Keeza Lassah, and the Human, Derwent? Have the searchers found anything at all yet?"

"Nothing but the bloodstained remains of her clothing," said Rhyaz. "Raiban thinks it likely Kezule killed her and something—or someone—carried her body off and ate her."

"Then she's dead," sighed Lijou, getting up from the chair.

"I'd prefer a body before pronouncing her dead," temporized Rhyaz. "The Taykui Forest is vast, we've only covered a fraction of it. Kezule could still be out there, dug in deep in some cave, doing his hibernation trick till he thinks our guard is down. Our telepaths can't sense a trace of any of them. I have a feeling we're not going to find them, they're going to find us when they're good and ready. The same applies to Derwent."

"What about calling in the Sumaan? They have ways of

tracking their own people that might work well with a species as similar as the Valtegans."

"And admit we've secretly been holding a Valtegan? I
think not, Lijou."

"Just a suggestion," said Lijou, making for the door. He
stopped, hand on the lever. "Rhyaz, if we have to recall all
the Brothers because of this warning from Vartra, and contact the Instructors, how many people do we actually
have?"

"Enough," said the warrior leader grimly. "Let's just
pray it doesn't come to that. Part of our strength is that
our numbers and resources are unknown."

CHAPTER 3

NONI was not happy. As she pottered about her kitchen making the batter for her pan-fried cakes for first meal, she muttered and cursed under her breath. There was a light rap at the door, and Teusi entered.

"Good morning, Noni. May the sun shine on you."

She grunted as she began to pour the mixture into the hot pan. "Some chance of that. I need you to set up the back room again, lad. We got company coming."

"Oh? When? And who?" he asked, taking his coat off and hanging it on the wall hook near the door.

"How the devil should I know? I'm nobody, after all. Just an old female here to do the Gods' bidding! You'd think I was running an Accommodation Guildhouse the way They send me lodgers!"

The batter hissed and spat for a moment or two as she tilted the pan, coating its base with the golden liquid.

Teusi took the kettle from the hob to the faucet to fill it. "A vision, is it, Noni?" he asked quietly as he turned on the tap.

"Of course a vision! What d'you think—I got one of them comm units plugged directly into Their realms?" She snorted her disgust. "As to who and when, you think They're going to be so obliging as to tell me that? You wait till your time comes, youngling! I'm lucky to get any kind of warning at all!"

"I'll start now," he said, returning to the stove with the filled kettle.

"After first meal's soon enough," said Noni gruffly, regretting taking her temper out on him. Teusi was a good lad, a fine apprentice. No substitute for Tallinu, but then she'd known from the day the Brothers had brought him back from Ranz that he'd not succeed her. His path was one she'd not have willingly trod at any stage in her life.

"Eat first, then we'll see to it together," she said, lifting the skillet from the hob to flip the cake over.

*   *   *

It had been a confusing day, thought Brynne, as he followed Jurrel out of the Shrine of Ghyakulla, back into the Temple of Vartra. He was overwhelmed by it all, he realized as he walked between the huge supporting pillars into the main aisle.

Ahead of him stood the huge statue of the seated God, a glowing brazier held between His hands. He hesitated, then took a step forward. Jurrel's hand, dark pelt almost invisible against the black robe he now wore, held him back.

"You forgot the incense," the Sholan said quietly. "Always the God is due our respect."

Brynne could feel the blood rush to his face as he quickly turned away to take a piece of incense from the container by the nearest brazier.

"It's easily done," Jurrel said, picking a piece himself to crumble over the glowing coals. "Especially when there is so much to remember."

Brynne looked up at the statue, blinking as the light from the God's crystal eyes reflected into his face. "Ghyan taught me better," he said, stepping back quickly as the perfumed smoke surrounded him.

"Allow yourself to occasionally forget and make mistakes, Brynne Stevens," said a new voice from behind them.

Jurrel bowed to the God before turning round. "Tutor Kha'Qwa."

Brynne found himself face to face with the Head Priest's titian-pelted life-mate. He quickly inclined his head to one side, echoing Jurrel's greeting.

Surprisingly, she linked her arm through his and led him down the aisle toward the entrance. "We shall go to the west wing senior common room, Jurrel," she said over her shoulder. "You can go ahead and make sure it's empty for us."

"Yes, Tutor," murmured Jurrel, dipping his head again before hurrying off to do her bidding.

Kha'Qwa leaned heavily on his arm. "We'll follow at a more sedate pace and take the elevator up." She smiled at him, her green eyes sparkling in amusement at his obvious confusion. "I'm not inclined to walk too far these days. How is your little one? Marak, isn't it?"

Brynne had been trying not to notice her obvious pregnancy. "He's fine. They say he's doing well for his age," he mumbled, unsure how to address the Guild Master's wife. Wasn't there some unspoken code about heavily pregnant females remaining on their estates? Worries chased each other around inside his head.

The hand on his arm tightened, claws unsheathing only enough to prick the fabric of his robe sleeve before retracting. "I am on my estate," she said gently, an amused purr underlying her voice. "The Brotherhood is my home, Brynne, as it is yours now. Apart from you En'Shallans, we renounce all family ties when we join. And there are no prohibitions on where we females can go when pregnant, it's just that many prefer to stay home. Carrying and sharing a cub with the one you love is a joyful time to be experienced with one's family." She stopped at the heavy doors leading out into the main entrance. "It's also not that easy to walk upright when carrying this weight," she laughed, patting her belly.

"I've still a lot to remember, and to learn."

"That's why you came to us," she agreed, waiting for him to open the door. "But the first thing you should know is that there is no time limit on your learning. Each of us progresses at his or her own rate within the religious side of the Order. This is not like one of your Terran colleges. No exams to sit, tests to take. We, and you, will know when you're ready to advance. We've twinned you with Jurrel because he's just returned from a tour of duty on Keiss, so he's had experience with your species. Normal rules can hardly be applied to you since you've reached maturity, so you're free to leave Stronghold for the delights of the local villages during your leisure time. All we ask is that you take Jurrel with you. Humans are still a novelty in these parts." She stopped at the elevator door, leaning against him more heavily now.

"Jurrel says I'll be learning warrior skills, too."

"Of course. We believe that body and mind are one entity."

The elevator doors slid apart with a tiny hiss of compressed air.

"I'm sure you'll find many of the answers you seek here, Brynne," she said, as they stepped inside.

* * *

"I think it most unfair that the Clan Lord didn't choose a mate for you this year," complained the young female sitting at Kitra's left. "He's treating you differently just because he's your father."

"She's the youngest in our year," T'Chya pointed out, taking the last fruit pastry from the plate in the center of their table. "At least we know the worst now, Kitra has to wait. It's not as if any bonding ceremonies will be held before the year's out anyway."

Kitra sat quietly, chewing her food, well aware that both her friends were right. Because of her age, her father had, indeed, yielded to intense pressure from her mother to postpone a betrothal until the following year.

"I still think it's unfair, and so does my father," said Chisoe. "He's complaining to the Clan Lord today."

"That's only because you're jealous of Kitra," said T'Chya. "You'd hoped to get one of the Brothers for yourself instead of a telepath."

"Not true! I don't think Kitra has a Companion anyway! I think he's just her bodyguard and she's making it all up."

"You talk such rubbish, Chisoe," said Ghaysa, stretching as she began to push her chair back from the table.

"Then she should prove it! What's it like having a mind-dead lover, Kitra?" demanded Chisoe, rounding on her. "Do you get bored? Is he rough because he can't know what pleases you?" she taunted, flicking her ears forward aggressively.

Kitra swallowed the mouthful so hurriedly she almost choked on it. "He's not mind-dead, we can sense each other easily! And he's the gentlest person I know!"

"My proof comes from her own mouth!" said Chisoe

triumphantly. "She's lying! How can a non-telepath sense anything, or a trained killer be gentle with any female?"

"You think you know everything, don't you?" said Kitra angrily. "Well, you don't! The Brothers have their own Talents and Dzaka's as sensitive as any telepath! He chose me to be his Companion!"

"Way I heard it, you chose him, Kitra," said Ghaysa. "I'm not saying I agree with Chisoe, but you must admit it looks peculiar, going outside our own kind for your first lover, and now you're choosing to stay with him. Aren't you carrying being different too far? You don't have to copy Taizia and Kusac, you know."

Kitra got to her feet. "Fine friends you are," she said, fighting to slow her breathing and prevent her sight narrowing on the other females around the table. "You accuse me of lying and being incapable of making my own mind up, while mocking my choice at the same time!" She stormed out of the refectory, pushing her way past the other students.

It was so unfair! She was caught between two worlds—the adult one of Dzaka and her self-imposed responsibilities for her young niece, Kashini, and the world of the Telepath Guild, where she was considered little more than a kitling. Not just that, but even Dzaka thought her too young to make any commitment to him and refused to be seen with her outside the estate!

Tears filled her eyes, and as she began to lope down the corridor toward the main door, she didn't see the Human female who neatly sidestepped into her path.

The collision was abrupt and would have sent her reeling if strong hands hadn't gripped her firmly by the shoulders.

"Careful there! You need to watch where you're going, young woman!" said a voice she recognized. "Wait a moment, it's Kitra, isn't it?"

She dashed a hand across her eyes, blinking furiously till she could see Ruth, praying the other hadn't seen her tears. She glanced around, but there was no escape and the female still held her by one shoulder. Behind her, she could hear her name being called by Ghaysa.

"Hello, Ruth. You'll have to excuse me, but . . ." she began hurriedly, trying to pull away.

Ruth turned and, slipping an arm across her shoulders,

drew her on toward the outer door. "Don't tell me you're playing hooky from lessons, too! What luck! C'mon, I know just the place to go!"

Inexorably, she was drawn out into the grounds in Ruth's wake.

"I come to the Guild several times a week for lessons," said her companion as they walked briskly to the outer gates. "It's not easy for me to go back to school after so long running my own life, you know, and every now and then it gets to be too much for me."

Stunned until now, Kitra found her voice as she realized they were approaching the gatekeeper. She hung back, knowing he'd stop them.

"Not a problem. You just watch me," whispered Ruth.

She made no attempt to slow down, and barely nodded in his direction, then they were out in the street, free and clear.

"But how did you . . . You're not allowed to leave . . ."

"I'm En'Shalla, and an adult, and if I behave as if I've a right to leave, why should he question me?" She stopped to give Kitra an impulsive hug before taking her by the hand and dragging her on down the street through the midday shoppers. "That's the trick, you know. Looking as if you've every right to be doing what you're doing."

She stopped suddenly outside an inn, pushing the door open. Before Kitra could find her voice to object, they were settled in a small booth away from prying eyes and ears.

"Order what you want," said Ruth as the attendant came over. "My treat for giving me your company."

Kitra stammered out an order for coffee, which Ruth echoed, then added a request for a plate of cold cuts of spiced meats.

"You've had to go back to school?" Kitra asked as soon as they were alone. She had to ask because it sounded so unlikely. No adult went back to school! "Why? Don't you feel as if they're taking your adult status away, making you a cub again?"

Ruth reached across the table to touch her hand. "I go back because there's so much I want to learn, Kitra, and I cope because of that. When I go home, I'm in charge of my own life."

"Father has sent me back to stay at the Guild," she said,

blinking as her eyes began to fill once more. "I don't have that option." She looked away, wishing she was anywhere else, wishing she could control her tears like an adult.

"It must be worse for you," said Ruth sympathetically, "especially after running your brother's house. Why don't you ask to be allowed to commute to the Guild instead?"

She flicked her ears back in a negative gesture, not daring to shake her head lest the tears spill over. "Father says I must come back because of his position as Clan Lord. Taizia has the excuse of Khayla to look after, I've none."

"Then why not get Dzaka to ask for quarters in the guest house a couple of nights a week? It would at least give you some time together away from your classmates."

That did it. The tears, despite furious blinking, spilled down her cheeks, and she snatched her hand away from Ruth's. Hands covering her face, she tried to explain. "Dzaka won't . . . He'll not acknowledge—me—outside the estate." It was difficult to talk when her throat was so tight.

Suddenly she found herself enveloped by Ruth, her ribs almost cracking with the fierceness of the Human's hug. "That no-good, fair weather. . . ."

"No!" she said, pushing against Ruth's encircling arms. "You don't understand, it isn't like that!"

"It had better not be," said the older woman grimly, releasing her and sitting back.

"He's just afraid for me, afraid it would harm my reputation. That other males wouldn't approach me because he's a Brother." She scrubbed at her eyes, determined that Ruth not think badly of him.

"What's this about other males? Does he want to share you?"

"No, but . . ."

"Then is he tired of you?"

"I don't think so . . ." She barely had time to form one answer before Ruth had fired another question at her.

"Does he love you?"

"Of course!" Then she realized that in all the time they'd been together, she couldn't actually remember him saying those words. "I assume he does."

"So it's a commitment he's afraid of."

"He says I should get to know other males before deciding on a life-mate."

"Do *you* love him?" Ruth regarded her carefully.

"Oh, yes," said Kitra, ears lying back a little despite her efforts to not betray her feelings. "I knew it was him I wanted from the first night. I can sense him, Ruth, and he does love me, even if he can't say so."

A discreet knock on the side of their booth heralded the arrival of their drinks.

Ruth had decided what she was going to do long before she delivered Kitra back to the Guild. On her return to the estate, she went to the villa in search of Dzaka.

By the time she'd finished talking to him, he had come to the conclusion that redheaded Sholans and Humans had a lot in common and was thinking fondly of his school days at Stronghold. Never had he been given such a dressing-down, even from Kaid, after the worst of his escapades. He was surprised at just how many Sholan swear words and phrases Ruth knew how to use.

"You've reduced her to the level of a child, Dzaka, in the eyes of her classmates at the Guild! If you thought she was so young, why did you let this go beyond the first night? Why string her along if you don't love her?"

"I do love her!" he retorted, stung by the accusation. "I asked her to be my Companion, didn't I? That's a commitment!" His tail hung low, brushing against the backs of his legs, and his ears were flat against his skull in embarrassment. This was almost as unbearable as his interview with Carrie and Rhyasha, Kitra's mother, had been. For an empath like himself, being exposed to Ruth's contempt for him and concern for Kitra was a grueling experience.

"That means nothing when it's kept from the rest of her world."

"I'm only trying to do what's best for both of us! The Clan Lord would never consent to any kind of bonding while she's so young and inexperienced. She has to meet other males. . . ."

"Experience be damned! You just want the best of both worlds! Her and your freedom!"

"Not true!"

"Then prove it." Ruth's voice was suddenly quiet. "Go to the Guild and spend the night with her at the guest house. Go as her lover, her Companion. Show those jealous little jeggets that your female is no child, that she's worthy of the love of one of the Brothers. And go in your Brotherhood uniform!"

"What?" Her last comment had thrown him. "Why?"

"Because they're saying she's lying. That you're merely her keeper, her bodyguard."

Dzaka began to growl without realizing it. "They call her a liar?"

Ruth nodded. "They fantasize about attracting a Warrior or a Brother, but tell Kitra she's so young no one would look at her twice. They're making her life miserable, Dzaka."

"You're right," he said abruptly, getting to his feet. "I wasn't aware this was happening. I'll go to the Guild."

She waited till he reached the door. "Dzaka, if you stop at the kitchen, Zhala will have a basket of Kitra's favorite foods ready for you to take with you."

He grinned at her then. "You're a conniving she-jegget yourself, Ruth. So what should I wear? This robe, or my grays?"

"Oh, the grays, definitely. You're visibly armed and look so much more dangerous. The other females will be mad with jealousy!"

"Is that what attracted you to Rulla?" he asked innocently. He made a hurried exit as a cushion sailed through the air toward him.

From the moment he'd arrived at the Telepath Guild, he'd been noticed. As he made his way through the front doors, the Warriors on duty there snapped to attention and their officer came over to him.

"Good evening, Brother. No trouble I hope." His eye ridges met in a concerned frown.

"Nothing. Merely a social visit," said Dzaka. Mindful of Ruth's browbeating, he forced himself to continue. "I'm here to see my Companion."

The officer's eye ridges disappeared in surprise but he said nothing, merely nodded then rejoined his fellow guards.

Dzaka continued past them to the office, where he was subjected to more of the same stark curiosity when he requested overnight accommodation for himself and Liegena

Kitra Aldatan. It was granted, of course, and they directed him to the classroom where her last lesson was about to finish.

Strengthening his mental shields, he headed off to wait for her. As the bell signaling the end of lessons began to ring, the students came surging out of the classrooms, slowing as they saw him lounging against the wall. This was going to be the truly difficult part. He was not one to show his emotions publicly; it was not the Brotherhood way, nor his.

"You're wearing purple," said a voice at his elbow.

Turning his head, he found himself looking down at a young female.

"Only telepaths can wear purple," she continued.

"And the Brotherhood," he replied. "We're En'Shalla, talented like you." He could sense Kitra now and turned back to look at the classroom.

She looked smaller than he remembered, standing there in the doorway, dwarfed by some of the larger females around her. Even shielded, he could always sense her to some degree, and now he could feel her confusion at his presence.

"Excuse me," he said, pushing himself away from the wall to go over to her.

"I see your bodyguard's checking up on you, Kitra," said one of the females beside her.

Kitra ignored her. "Dzaka, there's nothing wrong at the villa is there?" she asked, concern on her face.

"Nothing," he said, reaching out to touch her hair and breathe in her scent. "I missed you, that's all." It was true, and he was surprised at how easy it had been to say it. He let his hand slip down to circle her throat in an intimate gesture of affection.

She tilted her head, resting her cheek against his arm and smiled up uncertainly at him. "It's good to see you."

The gesture was wonderfully familiar and suddenly he forgot the reserve and training that made him suppress his emotions. The others ceased to exist; there were only the two of them. He swept her close with his other arm, bending down to nuzzle her cheek and jaw.

"I hope you're free till morning," he murmured in her ear. "I made plans for us."

She returned the embrace, and the glow of pleasure he felt from her made Ruth's chastisement worthwhile.

"What have you arranged?" she asked.

"The guest house. Zhala packed some food for us."

"You're teasing me!" she said, looking up at him as he drew her away from the classroom. "No, you're not, I can sense it! This isn't because of Ruth, is it? Because there was no need. . . ."

"Maybe at first, but not now," he said. "You should have told me what was happening, how you felt. You're my Companion, Kitra, and I want to be with you, on Valsgarth estate and here in the Telepath Guild." He began to cover her face in tiny bites and licks, ending with a kiss.

There was the sound of someone clearing their throat, then a voice said, "Excuse me, Brother Dzaka."

Guiltily, they broke apart and turned to face Guild Master Sorli.

"I don't think the corridor is quite the place for such an enthusiastic greeting. We try to discourage the students from such behavior in public. Perhaps Kitra could show you the gardens, or one of the smaller common rooms?"

As Kitra clutched his arm in distress, Dzaka once more wished the floor would open up for him, until he saw a twitch of amusement at the side of the Guild Master's mouth.

"Better still, why not just take her to the guest house?" Sorli continued quietly. "Your rooms should be ready by now. And, Dzaka, it's nice to see you visiting Kitra. She's been a little low in spirits lately."

"Yes, Master Sorli," he murmured, edging toward the door again, Kitra's hand clasped firmly and reassuringly in his. "We were just leaving."

As fast as politeness allowed, they made their way out into the courtyard. Once there, Kitra began to laugh.

"What's so funny?" he asked, glancing at her as they headed over to where he'd parked the aircar.

"You. You should have seen yourself when Sorli came up behind us like that!"

"You were just as embarrassed," he pointed out. "And left with as little dignity as me."

She began to run, dragging him after her, her steps almost small bounds of sheer pleasure. "But what was best," she said, stopping at the side of his aircar, "What was really best, was T'Chya, Chisoe, and Ghaysa! I could feel them hating me when they saw you waiting there."

He looked round at her as he opened the hatch. Eyes sparkling with mischief, her unbound hair caught by a slight breeze, he hadn't seen her so happy in weeks—since midwinter in fact. "It really mattered that much?"

"I know it shouldn't have," she said, her eyes clouding over. "But they were *enjoying* mocking me!"

"*Us*, not you," he corrected her. He wanted to see her face light up again, wanted to feel her joy—hadn't realized how unhappy she'd been over the past month or two. Then she was filling his arms again, as all the feelings he'd tried so hard to hold back because of her age and his uncertainty over any future they could have, refused to be repressed any longer.

"I've missed you so much," he said, before gently taking hold of her ear with his teeth.

"You said that."

"More than I knew till now."

"You didn't say that before," she purred, reaching up to stroke his neck with gentle fingertips.

"And I love you." He felt her mind and her body suddenly become still. "I don't know why it took me so long to say it." He'd let go of her ear and was nibbling his way across her cheek.

Her hands took hold of the hair at either side of his neck and she pulled his face gently round to kiss him. "I know you do, Dzaka Arrazo."

Her mind touched his, filling him with her need for him. He pulled back with an effort, suddenly vulnerable to the attention they were attracting.

"It's your uniform," Kitra grinned. "Brothers are always considered distant, beyond normal emotions—and very dangerous."

He reached in to grab the container of food Zhala had given him, then sealed the aircar again. "This one certainly will be if we don't get away from here," he growled. "It's like a wave of curiosity! I can feel every one of them." He hustled her toward the guest house. "I don't suppose it's got dampers, has it?"

"Of course," said Kitra archly. "We can't let non-telepaths affect our tranquillity, can we?"

Later that night as they finally turned to the food that Zhala had packed, Kitra broached the subject of their future yet again.

"Mother's given us a year, Dzaka, that's all, then Father will have to choose a husband for me."

"We knew that would happen," he said quietly, reaching for his mug of wine.

"I don't want it to happen. We love each other, why should I have to life-bond to someone else? It doesn't make sense, Dzaka. Will you stand with me on this, ask for us to be married?"

He hesitated a moment before answering her. "I can't, Kitra. Nothing's really changed. We'd be told to wait until you're older, until you've seen more of life, have a career. And that I'm not a suitable life-mate for you. I'm gene-altered, there would be no cubs for us. There's more to the future for you than just finding a life-mate. No matter what happens, we can always remain Companions. No one can take that away from us."

"I want more! I don't care about cubs! I want you, not someone chosen by my father and approved by the Clan Council!" she said, taking the mug away from him and setting it on the night table, forcing him to pay attention to her. "People on the estate have a choice, why shouldn't we? Lots of people my age—and older—are complaining about it, now we realize there's an alternative. Only those who are Grade One and Two telepaths and from the main Clan families have to put up with arranged marriages, no one else! Why should we be so different?"

"You know why," he said, reaching out for her, but she avoided him. "Don't let's argue and spoil tonight. Let's enjoy what we have now."

She felt angry and cheated by his reaction. "If it was up to me, I'd fight for you," she grumbled, nevertheless allowing him to soothe her.

"When the circumstances are right, I'll fight anyone who tries to keep us apart," he said, and she could hear a hard note creep into his voice. "But not now. It's too soon. We could lose it all if we fight them now."

* * *

Day 4

The Brotherhood meditation lamp was said to be the
oldest on Shola, one that had belonged to the first Temple
of Vartra. There was reason to believe that claim now,
thought Brynne, remembering that it was here in Stronghold that the person Vartra had carried out his most
important work, that of binding the Humans and Sholans
together.

Unbidden, a comparison between the lamp and some of
the Victorian relics in a dingy old bric-a-brac shop back
home in Norwich sprang unflatteringly to mind. He smiled
to himself, then hurriedly suppressed it. This was the
temple's most valued lamp, and it was a real honor for him
to be included in the evening's senior students' meditation
class. Even Jurrel had been nonplussed at the invitation.
Taller than most, slim and rangy, the midnight-pelted Sholan and he were becoming fast friends. An able teacher,
Jurrel had a fine understanding of the differences between
life here and the freedom Brynne was used to on the estate.

"So Father Lijou believes that because of the memory
transfers, you'll be able to join in this session?" his companion asked quietly as they settled themselves on the densely
padded prayer mats.

"That's what he says. I need to use the skills to activate
the acquired memories of them."

Jurrel grunted. "Makes sense. They've never done this
before. Not enough of us have any dependable telepathic
talent, though."

"We wait only upon your convenience," interrupted the
tutor, with gentle sarcasm.

This time, it was much easier for him to let down his
mental shields and link to the tutor. Joining with the others
to become a part of the group consciousness was not so
easy. He knew the solution, but balked at taking it, at con-
sciously letting go of his Humanity to access his Sholan self.

Don't relinquish your Humanity, came the tutor's thought,
*just accept your Sholan side. Embrace it, let it carry you into
our shared meditation.*

Ghyan did this for me before, he objected.

You must join us unaided. It is the Brotherhood way, came Vriuzu's implacable reply.

He tried, but his Sholan side was what he was most afraid of: it was the beast within him—it was what he was drawn to in Vanna. He'd fought against it, repressed it out of fear, so that now it was almost impossible for him to access it.

It is what enhances your Leska Link.

Tomorrow was his Link day with Vanna. He'd have to return to the estate, leave Stronghold!

Despite his closed eyes, the temple seemed to lurch around him, and suddenly, his mind was open and beginning to merge with those around him.

The onslaught on his senses was so sudden and overwhelming that he really began to panic. He wasn't one person, but ten, with all their individual emotions and responses. Immediately, he felt the steadying presence of Father Lijou.

You're doing well, Brynne Stevens, the Head Priest sent, using a private link. *This is how a meditation circle for those with Talents or gifts should be. This is the reality of your Sholan self. It is what and who you are. Use those senses, they are really yours, not just borrowed from your Leska.*

He could recognize them all by scent now, especially Jurrel; hear their breathing, and sense their curiosity about him, the first of the Humans to visit Stronghold as a student. It was as if a door to another world had suddenly opened for him.

It was always there, sent Father Lijou. *Only your fear kept the door closed.*

Not just me, Derwent! He told me to be afraid, that to succumb to the Sholan way was to lose my path, to give in to the base senses that we Humans had evolved beyond! He was furious, but mainly with himself for trusting a man who knew nothing about the Sholans.

He had the gift of Glamour, sent Father Lijou. *In his company, the ridiculous seemed credible. We all have our Ghezus or Derwents. In the end, you recognized him for what he was, that's what matters. I will leave you to your studies now.* With that, the presence withdrew.

Lijou's link gone, he didn't realize he was now part of the group again. To sense so much, yet be rational and not driven by the Link's compulsion to mate, felt so strange. Then he felt the amusement of the group at his thoughts and would have retreated from them in embarrassment had the tutor not prevented him.

Let's use some of that rationality to proceed with the lesson. "Focus on my voice," he said.

Brynne listened to the soothing voice slowly build a picture of a woodland scene in their collective mind. So real was it that he could smell the loamy soil and hear the bird-calls. Caught by the reality, he let his attention drift as he looked around him. A movement in the bushes claimed his attention; a wild jegget. Intrigued, he followed it off the path—and with a gut-wrenching lurch, he was in the deep forest, running for his life.

Through the bushes he crashed, branches whipping him about the face and shoulders, the uneven ground making his footing precarious. The sounds of his pursuers were loud—three of them at least. He had to reach the cave and safety.

The trees were thinning out. Ahead now he could see the rock face with the fissure that led to his hideout. They were gaining on him—the noises were louder, he could hear their labored breathing—or was it his own? He knew that even when he reached the ledge, it would take him precious seconds to squeeze through the split, seconds that from the sounds of the crashing behind him he didn't have. He gathered himself, risking all in one leap, praying that he hadn't misjudged it in his weakened condition.

Too low! He was too low! Hands and feet scrabbled for purchase on the crumbling surface as he propelled himself up onto the ledge and staggered toward the fissure. Sharp projections tore at his flesh as he forced himself through the narrow gap. He heard the lead feral land on the ledge in a flurry of loose stones, then its rank breath enveloped him as its jaws gaped wide, snapping shut just as he fell into the chamber beyond.

Shaking with shock and fear, he forced himself to crawl farther into the darkness, trying not to hear his pursuers snarl and yowl their anger and frustration at being balked of their prey. Terror made him forgetful of his surroundings and the low roof met his head with a resounding crack. Nausea and giddiness engulfed him as he passed out.

*   *   *

Someone was calling his name, he realized through the throbbing headache. He needed to move, to get deeper into the cave, farther from the ferals. Then he realized where he was—Stronghold. At the edges of his mind, he could dimly sense Vanna, demanding to know what was happening.

"This is what Ghyan said happened at the Shrine," said Lijou, watching Jurrel help the prostrate Human into a sitting position. "How long was he unconscious?"

"Only a few minutes," said the tutor. "It was uncanny, Father. One moment he was with us, his mind joined to ours, the next he was gone."

"He's been touched by the Gods. This is work for Guardian Dhaika, not us."

"I wonder what it's like to feel a God's hand on your shoulder."

"Terrifying," said Lijou, closing his eyes momentarily in remembrance of the encounter. "Truly terrifying. Believe me, you don't want to experience it. Take them to their room, question Brynne gently, and report to me when you know what he experienced. Remember, this is even newer for him because he's Human." As he spoke, Vriuzu sent to him, letting him know that Physician Vanna Kyjishi was on the comm demanding to know what had happened to her Leska. "Tomorrow, I'll take him to the Retreat."

Confused and worried, Brynne used the fact that he needed to return to the estate that night because of his Link day with Vanna to avoid visiting Guardian Dhaika. It wasn't strictly true, he could have left tomorrow, but after hoping he'd find the answers he needed at Stronghold, to learn that he had to go to Vartra's Retreat instead was too much.

As he took off from the courtyard, battling the crosswinds posed little difficulty.

"Not bad. Amazing the difference two days make," said Jurrel quietly from the seat beside him. "Some of the Brothers and Sisters never get the knack of takeoff and landing here."

Jurrel was his insurance that he made the trip home safely. After the incident in the temple earlier, no one wanted to take the risk of him flying back alone. If he should pass out during the flight . . . He shuddered. It didn't bear thinking about. Jurrel was also a reminder of just how different he was becoming. Briefly he wondered if this was how Kaid had felt when he'd begun to experience his visions.

"Do you want to talk about what you experienced?" asked Jurrel.

Brynne glanced at him. "You're too good a sensitive," he said. "I told everyone all there was to tell yesterday. It was like the last time. Just an animal in the forest."

He found these experiences more disturbing than the vision of a future event would have been. It was as if what was happening to him now was merely reinforcing what he and Derwent had been working on—trying to get him centered, or grounded, in the very soil of Shola.

"Be one with the earth," Derwent had said constantly. *"Feel Him surround you, feel the life within. The rocks are His bones, the soil His flesh. It's their God, Vartra, incarnate."*

But he couldn't feel it. Try as he might, he could feel no link, no empathy with this alien world—until the visions started. That was the truly frightening part. Now he could feel all that Derwent had been talking about, except it wasn't a maleness he sensed, it was an indisputably female presence.

He needed to get back home, talk to Ghyan, whom he knew he could trust, see what the priest made of all this. Sure, he'd been the one to suggest going to Stronghold, but he didn't really know anyone there. He couldn't be sure he could trust them. It was possible that they, like the Telepath Guild, had no real interest in him, only wanted to know what Derwent and he had been up to.

* * *

That morning, Kaid needed the heat from the shower to dispel the chill in his bones. It was like this whenever he slept. Somehow, the link between him and Carrie had reestablished itself in a new form. Despite her being in cryo, when he slept, the natural barriers between them must be lowering enough for her mind to touch his. Even when there were no dreams about her, his body and mind were still tuned in to Carrie's.

He flattened his ears, lifting his head upward under the spray of hot water, trying to wash away the memories of a restless night. T'Chebbi was still asleep, having been on watch during the early hours of the morning. Despite the interim treaty he'd made with the U'Churians and the Cabbarans—it only needed the final signatures of their appointed leaders—Kaid felt it wiser not to relax their guard too much. Tallis' behavior was reason enough. Several times he'd been caught snooping around areas out of bounds to them as visitors on the *Profit*. Still, in a few hours they'd reach the jump point. After that, it would only be ten days until they'd be on a Sholan destroyer, with medical aid for Carrie and Kusac—and Tallis. That male was definitely becoming more psychotic as the days passed.

Kaid was finishing his first meal when Manesh entered the communal mess room.

"Captain Tirak would like you to join him on the bridge," she said.

"What's up?" asked Taynar from the leisure comp unit by the doorway.

"Nothing to worry about, taiban," said Manesh, reaching out to pat him on the head.

Taynar bristled. "Don't call me that! I told you, I'm not a child, even if your kind are at my age!"

Kaid suppressed a grin as he followed the U'Churian security officer out into the corridor. "Bad age for him, being still a youngling but with the responsibility of an adult because of his Human Leska."

"On our world, he wouldn't be allowed that responsibility," said Manesh, stopping at the hatchway through to the bridge section.

"Leska Links aren't subject to age," said Kaid mildly, stepping through into the corridor beyond. "They come at the whim of the Gods, striking without warning. Taynar had no say in this Link with Kate. Were it not for that, he'd not be exposed to the responsibility either."

"Just as you had no say with Kusac and Carrie, eh?" Manesh asked, drawing level with him again.

Kaid caught the sideways look and knew she was fishing

for information. "Just so," he murmured, waiting for the
other to precede him onto the small bridge.

He stopped dead at the sight that met his eyes. Floating
on the view screen against the backdrop of stars was a craft
that was all too familiar in design. He could feel his pelt
rising and he began to growl softly.

"We got a distress call from this ship, Kaid," said Tirak,
turning his chair round to look at him. "It's not one we
recognize. Is it one from . . . You know it?"

Kaid stepped forward, resting his hands on the back of
Giyesh's chair. He studied the image carefully, checking for
the identifying marks and features that typified the Valtegan ships they'd encountered at Keiss. But there had
been only one like this—the one that had escaped them.
From the blunt, swept back angular nose to the stocky hull
bristling with sensors, there was nothing elegant about this
craft. It was built for one purpose only—conquest.

"Valtegans from Keiss," he snarled.

"Out here, in Jalna's system? Are you sure?"

"Positive, even though they've removed the markings."
He pointed to the streak of darkness on the side. "That's
where we hit it as it went into jump near Keiss' moon. It's
the one that sold our people on Jalna. Get us out of here,
Tirak, it's a trap!" He clenched his hands on the chair back,
feeling his claws puncture the covering.

Tirak swung back to his displays, grabbing for a headset.
"Full speed, Nayash. Get us out of here. Annuur, jump
coordinates, now! Def Level One, Manesh."

"But the distress call," said Giyesh, her dark face creasing in concern. "They're still transmitting, and it's in Jalnian Port patois!"

"Relay it to Jalna," snapped Tirak, hands flying over his
controls. An alarm began to blare out and Kaid heard the
sound of several dull explosions vibrate throughout the
hull.

Manesh swung her seat around, diving for the floor hatch
behind Tirak's post. Flinging it open, she dropped down
out of sight. Sayuk likewise leaped to his feet, heading off
the bridge past Kaid at a run.

"If the signal's genuine, they can deal with it," Tirak
continued as they began to accelerate away from the Val-

tegan craft. "Kaid, get your military personnel up here and the rest stowed in their cabins under the safety restraints."

"Anything else?" he asked.

"Turrets deployed, Captain," reported Sheeowl as Mrowbay rushed in and flung himself into the seat vacated by Manesh. "Ventral turret on-line. Awaiting signal from Sayuk."

"Stand ready to support the gunners, Kaid," said Tirak, adjusting his headset.

"Dorsal turret on-line. Batteries armed and ready," said Mrowbay from the weapons console.

Kaid turned and ran for the mess, his mind automatically reaching out ahead of him to check that his people were there.

"What's happening?" demanded Rezac as he rounded the doorway. "What were those explosions?"

"Are we under attack?" said Taynar.

"Return to your rooms and secure yourselves for acceleration," said Kaid calmly, looking for T'Chebbi. She'd obviously just awakened and was still finishing adjusting her clothing. "We face possible hostile action, but this is a military vessel." He turned to Rezac. "You and Jo remain with me," he said, then looked at the others' anxious faces. "The explosions were Tirak blowing off the hatch covers hiding the ship's weapons turrets. We're not under attack yet, and might not be."

"But . . ." began Taynar.

"Move," said T'Chebbi, grabbing the youth by the arm and hustling him out the doorway. "No time to argue!"

When they'd gone, he looked over at T'Chebbi, who shrugged as she adjusted her weapons belt before tucking her plait over her shoulder.

"Tirak answered a distress call," he said quietly, moving closer to them. "When he got within viewing distance, he called me. It's a Valtegan cruiser."

T'Chebbi began to curse. "Should have known! All those warnings and I never . . ."

"Enough, T'Chebbi. No time for recriminations. Maybe it's a genuine distress call, we don't know yet."

Rezac began to growl. "Want me to check?" he asked. "I can reach that far mentally."

"No," said Kaid. "Valtegans in our time go into a killing frenzy if they feel a Sholan mind. Whatever you do, don't use your Talent on them, ever. Now, let's go. Tirak wants us up on the bridge. Can you operate a weapons array if you need to?" he asked Rezac.

"Try me," he said grimly.

"If the call is genuine, then there's nothing to fear."

"There's everything to fear," said Tesha's quiet voice as she came back into the mess. "You've never had dealings with these people. I have." She was trembling, with ears flat to her head, tail drooping to the floor.

"So have I," said Rezac. "Captivity can be survived. They aren't mindless. They operate on rules, rigid codes of behavior. Every other species is subordinate to them, of no value except as slaves. If you can accept that and obey them, you can survive. We did."

"The ones you knew were different, they didn't fear us! They didn't even give us a chance to learn their language, Rezac!" She was becoming hysterical, her voice rising in terror.

Rezac moved closer, reaching out to touch her face. "You can cope, Tesha," he said quietly. "Someone who could survive a Jalnian whorehouse can survive this. It may not be the same ship, and even if it is, there's more of us this time, a force to be reckoned with. It won't be so easy for them to bully all of us."

Kaid watched in surprise as Rezac drew her close until she was leaning against him. Then his hand slipped round to cup the back of her head. What was he doing? He'd never seen this sensitive side of him before, except with Jo in the few days when Zashou was still in the sick bay. He'd assumed that was just their Link; it appeared he was wrong.

Tesha's trembling gradually stilled as Rezac held her. "You need to rest, Tesha," he whispered. "Go and join the others. Let T'Chebbi take you."

T'Chebbi moved smoothly over to the young female, looping her arm around her shoulders as Rezac let her go. "Is no danger yet," she said soothingly. "May not be." She began to draw her out into the corridor.

As her voice faded, Rezac asked, "What are our chances, Kaid? I assume that's the same ship that took Tesha's people and had our stasis unit on board."

"Not good," he said softly. "We're outgunned and outnumbered. Our only chance is to outrun them. What did you do to Tesha?"

Rezac shrugged, looking away. "It's nothing. One of the tricks we developed during the time before we were taken by the Valtegans. I had to calm her. Her panic would have infected the others."

"Impressive."

Back on the bridge, the ship-to-ship speaker was relaying the incoming message. Mangled Jalnian Port patois, its meaning almost lost in the sibilant pronunciation, filled the room.

"This is *M'ijikk*. Surrender, or we open fire."

"Short and to the point," murmured Sheeowl.

"Annuur, we need to jump now!" Tirak's tone was urgent.

"Not enough speed. Kill us to engage jump now," came the reply.

"Still can't raise Jalna, Captain. They must be blocking our long-range transmissions," said Giyesh.

"Open a channel to them," ordered Tirak, gesturing at the screen.

"Channel open."

"This is *Rryuk's Profit,* U'Churian vessel of the Free Traders. You have violated the laws of this region by sending out a false distress signal. Your demand for our surrender is an act of piracy and aggression, and will be met with force."

"Rezac, can you reach Jalna mentally?" asked Kaid quietly.

He shook his head. "I haven't been able to reach far since we contacted Carrie when we woke. Maybe the drug, maybe the long sleep."

"Keep trying. You never know when the ability will come back." Kaid returned his attention to the conversation. Focused on it, he was not expecting the Human hand that touched him surreptitiously on the arm. As he looked round, Jo turned her back to Rezac and put her finger to her lips, jerking her head toward the corridor.

Torn between what was happening and her, he reined in his irritation. It had to be important for her to drag him away. Still listening for the reply from the *M'ijikk,* he took a couple of slow steps backward and waited for her to join him.

"I know that voice, Kaid," she whispered, keeping her eyes on Rezac, who, like everyone else, was waiting for the Valtegan craft's reply. "He was the Overlord of Keiss, one of those with a taste for Terran women. He may remember me. If he does, you'll have to watch out for Rezac." A shudder ran through her and her face creased in remembered pain. "What happens to the others if a Third dies?"

She had his full attention now. "Don't even think about it, Jo. While there's life, there's hope." Reaching out, he touched her cheek comfortingly with his hand. He could feel her fear, but she wasn't telling him everything. There was something else she was holding back, something that frightened her more, but there was no time to pursue it now. Later, if there was a later for them.

She nodded, blinking quickly to prevent tears forming. "Just watch Rezac, please." She began to move away from him, then stopped. "Elise, Carrie's twin. She went to him too. He'll think she's her sister."

"What?" Shock washed through him.

"He'll see Elise in Carrie," she repeated before returning to the bridge.

How long he stood there, he'd no idea. It wasn't till T'Chebbi joined him that he seemed to get back his ability to think clearly.

"Something wrong?" she asked in Highland, grabbing hold of him as the ship lurched suddenly. "Saw you talking to Jo."

"Dealt with," he said briefly, steadying himself against the bulkhead. "What's happening?"

"They repeated their demands. Sheeowl just fired the maneuver jets in an effort to get up to jump speed. Kaid, this Valtegan isn't bluffing."

"I know. Jo recognized him. He's M'ezozakk, the Overlord of Keiss."

T'Chebbi hissed her anger. "Then he does know Jeran, Tesha, and Tallis."

"More. He knows Jo, and knew Carrie's twin, Elise," he said grimly, before moving past her back onto the bridge. His priorities were clear: to get out word of this marauding Valtegan craft, and to get them, if possible, back to Shola.

"Incoming fire," Nayash was saying. "Impact in ten seconds. Brace yourselves."

They barely had time to grasp the grab rails lining the bulkhead before the craft lurched violently to the port side in an effort to evade the missile. The increased g forces plastered them against the wall. Nayash began to count. At zero, the ship was rocked by an explosion.

"Aft section hit, starboard side. Possible minor hull breach in workshop area. Section has been sealed," said Sheeowl calmly.

Kaid focused on Tirak. Dropping his shields completely, he began to monitor the bridge crew with all his senses. This was the skill that had kept him one step ahead throughout his life: it was easier now that he understood exactly what he was doing. He was surprised, therefore, to find Rezac already there, listening to the surface thoughts of those in the room. So far, in the present crisis, the younger male's mental presence had gone undetected.

He relaxed into his task, letting his mind push past the barriers Kate and Taynar had erected for the U'Churians, until he'd formed a light connection to each of them, a mental web with himself at the center. Tirak and Rezac were the ones he intended to monitor most closely.

The headset Tirak kept touching was linked through the computer to all the bridge and gunnery controls, allowing him to be constantly updated on their current condition. A touch to the sensor pads located in the side piece that lay across his cheek, and he could see their displays on his secondary screen.

While Rezac was anxious to fight, to strike his first blow against their ancient enemy in this new time, Tirak knew better. Like Kaid, he saw the inevitability of their destruction or capture. Escape was impossible. They were underpowered compared to the larger Valtegan cruiser which, even now, was beginning to loom larger in the view screen. Tirak couldn't allow the *Profit* to fall into enemy hands, and his honor dictated he would stay with his ship to make sure it didn't. All that remained for him to decide was whether to give his crew and guests the choice of surrender or death, or make that decision himself.

Another explosion rocked the *Profit,* this time on the starboard side. The lights flickered then died. Tirak's mind was made up, his decision taken for him by this latest hit. He had to do it now while he still could, when the emergency power came on.

As the lights came up again, Tirak's hand began to move toward the destruct control. Kaid felt Rezac's realization of what was about to happen surge through him.

He clamped his hand round Rezac's arm, using his extended claws to create enough pain to break the younger male's concentration. It was Tirak, however, who cried out in agony, ripping his headset off before collapsing in his seat.

"Captain down," Kaid said calmly, releasing Rezac. "Jo, you and Rezac take him to sick bay."

"Where did that hit come from?" he heard Giyesh say as Rezac rounded on him.

What the hell did you do that for? Have you any idea what. . . .

You were too obvious. When he came round, Tirak would have known it was you.

He was about to blow us up! If it hadn't been for that lucky. . . .

Luck? Kaid's mental tone was pure ice. "See to the captain, Rezac," he repeated, deliberately turning his back on him. Rezac was delaying him. He had urgent matters of his own to see to.

"Assuming control of the bridge," said Sheeowl, the trace of a tremor in her voice. "Routing the captain's console through mine."

M'ezozakk's voice filled the bridge again. "You try my patience with your futile attempts to outrun me. Surrender now, or my next shots will destroy you."

"Unless you want to die, I would surrender," said Kaid quietly. "Alive, there's much we can do to frustrate whatever plans they have. If we're destroyed, he might go after another craft, this time a genuine trader."

His exchange with Rezac had shattered the mental web, but he no longer needed it. He knew Sheeowl's mental pattern, could easily give her a gentle nudge in the right direction if it was needed.

She hesitated, turning to look at Nayash and Giyesh on her left, then back to Mrowbay, Kaid, and T'Chebbi.

"It would be selfish to wish a grand death at the expense

of others," said Nayash. "Kaid's right. If they don't have us, they will go after easier prey. Surrender, Sheeowl."

"Death is so final," was Mrowbay's quiet contribution.

"Do it now!" said Giyesh frantically. "Before he changes his mind!"

Sheeowl turned back to her console. "Open a channel, Giyesh," she said heavily.

Kaid looked at T'Chebbi. "Stay here," he said in an undertone. "You know the drill if they don't. See that nothing of any use to the Valtegans remains on the computer. Conceal only what we need."

He turned and ran down the corridor to the sick bay, hoping he hadn't left it too late. If debris from the hit to the aft section had been propelled too far from their craft, then his plan would fail and he'd be sentencing them to death. He passed Rezac and Jo, ignoring their startled exclamations.

He went straight to the cryo units, scanning the controls, trying to remember what Mrowbay had told him. He felt sick to the pit of his stomach at what he was about to do, but it was their only chance of survival. Behind him he heard Rezac and Jo enter.

CHAPTER 4

"WHAT did you do to Tirak?" asked Jo, helping Rezac manhandle the unconscious captain onto a bed. "What are we supposed to treat him for? Surely he's not bad enough to need a cryo unit?"

"He's fine," said Kaid shortly. "I just knocked him out mentally. If he starts coming round, give him a light sedative. We need him out cold till after the Valtegans board. Rezac'll tell you why."

His fingers fumbled the sequence the first time, and cursing, he leaned against Carrie's unit, taking a few deep breaths to steady himself.

"What're you doing over there?" demanded Rezac. "You shouldn't be interfering with those!"

Calmer now, he began again more slowly, getting the sequencing right. This time, the prelaunch light came on. With a small explosive bang, the umbilicals disengaged and fell to the floor as heavy protective shields slid over the transparent cover. Slowly the unit began to move away from him toward the bulkhead. He started on Kusac's unit.

He sensed Rezac about to rush him and stopped, pulling out his gun and rounding on him. "Don't interfere, Rezac," he warned. "This is not your concern. They're my Triad. I'm running out of time. Stay back, or I'll use this."

"Leave him, Rezac," said Jo, holding onto him.

"What do you know about this, Jo? What the hell's going on here? Why has no one told me?"

Keeping an eye on Rezac, Kaid finished punching in the sequence. Kusac's unit began to move forward to join Carrie's.

Take the third unit, he sent to Jo. *A premed will put you out almost instantly, the unit will automatically do the rest, even after it's launched.*

Jo threw him a terrified look and shook her head. *Tesha's more frightened than me.*

You're more at risk, and more valuable alive.

No.

Kaid nodded, and stepped up to the bulkhead where the final launch controls were situated. A sudden fear that he was doing the wrong thing swamped him. He pushed it aside. No time for doubts or second thoughts now.

He hit the hatch activator. The bulkhead hissed back, hydraulic motors engaging the two units in the launch tubes. As the hatch closed again, sealing them in, he leaned against the wall, watching the amber light, waiting for it to begin pulsing.

"I hope you know what the hell you're doing, Kaid. You may be in charge, but by the Gods, you assume too much responsibility!" said Rezac angrily.

"You think I want to kill them?" he demanded. "No one is dearer to me than them, Rezac! They are my life!"

The light blinked at him. He reached up and hit it, watching the green one come on. It was done now, for better or for worse. The hull vibrated as the units were expelled from the ship into the darkness of space.

May the Gods protect you, he prayed, closing his eyes briefly. *And forgive me.* He hadn't even had time to say his farewells, to look at them one last time.

He felt exhausted, but there was still so much to do. Rousing himself, Kaid sent to Jo. *You need to warn Rezac that M'ezozakk may recognize you.*

He hadn't felt this empty when he'd put them into cryo. Then there had at least been hope. Now the odds on his Leska partners surviving were stacking up against them.

I can't!

You must. If you don't, I will. When she didn't reply, he stood up and reholstered his gun, looking pointedly at Rezac.

"I can't believe that you'd do something as stupid as this! You sent them out there to die, Kaid! To get blown up by the Valtegans—or worse, to drift until the power supply runs out!"

"Gods, I'll be glad when you've finally grown up enough to use that brain of yours!" Kaid snapped back.

"Shut up, both of you!" said Jo angrily. "You make a

great pair, each as bad as the other! Kaid, why didn't you just tell him why you did it? It would have been the sensible thing to do!"

"I'm not answerable to him or anyone!" Kaid snarled.

"I'd swear you could be brothers, you're both so damned arrogant, independent, and determined to be responsible for everything!" She turned on Rezac. "As for you, did you stop to think just how long they'd have survived once the Valtegans found them? Or do you think they'd be altruistic enough to wake them and heal Carrie? You know them better than that!"

Rezac glowered angrily at her. "Are they even designed for survival in space? The debris from the explosion is floating around us out there! How does he know it won't damage the units?"

"I don't know," said Kaid, shocked into an icy calm by Jo's unwitting recognition of their family relationship. "It's a risk I have to take. That debris is their camouflage."

"Of course they're equipped for space," said Jo. "The units were sitting in launch cradles. Forget about them for now, Rezac. We've got larger problems."

"What? What could possibly be worse than the situation we're in?" he demanded.

"The captain of the Valtegan ship knows me," she said quietly, looking away from him.

The angry swaying of Rezac's tail stopped abruptly and his jaw dropped open in shock.

"He's General M'ezozakk. He was the Overlord of Keiss, commander of the permanent garrison that was there until your people came to liberate us," Jo continued.

"He brought your stasis cube to Jalna," added Kaid.

Rezac found his voice. "He's one of the ones you had to pair with for the resistance."

She nodded, looking up at him now. "I think he'll recognize me. If he does, it won't take him long to work out I was a spy."

"You're right. We have a worse problem," he whispered, feeling behind him for a bed to sit on.

"Carrie's identical twin, Elise, worked there with Jo," said Kaid. "M'ezozakk had her tortured to death. With Carrie gone, Jo's got a better chance of not being recognized."

"I didn't realize he'd recognize Carrie." He reached out for Jo, holding her tightly.

"You didn't want to," said Kaid. "You see your own arrogance in everyone but yourself. Stop fighting me, Rezac. I'm not your enemy."

"You're dismissing him too easily, Kaid," said Jo, stroking her lover's head. "He knows the Valtegans better than anyone, better than I do. Yes, he's young and hot-headed, but you two need to work together if we're going to survive this."

Rezac looked over to him. "What about the last cryo unit, Kaid? Could we put Jo in it and leave her here?"

"And risk M'ezozakk blowing up the ship once he has us?" asked Kaid.

"We could launch it like the others! There's time, surely?"

"I suggested it and she refused."

"Damned right I did!" exclaimed Jo. "I'm not the only one he'll recognize. How could I protect myself yet leave Tesha and the others to cope?"

"Let's hope he doesn't remember you," said Kaid. "We have to return to the bridge. If M'ezozakk does recognize her, Rezac, for Vartra's sake, contain yourself. If you don't, you'll put all our lives at risk, including hers. We don't know what happens to a Third when the Leska pair dies, and from what Jeran's told us, M'ezozakk would delight in killing you. I'll get T'Chebbi to break the news to Jeran's group that we're surrendering."

Tesha and Jeran had said little when they'd been told the news. Tallis, however, began to rant and rave. "Why don't you stand and fight? You're Brotherhood, or so you say," he snarled, rounding on T'Chebbi. "This is the coward's way out!"

"Not," said T'Chebbi firmly. "We fight, we die. Is simple. And next ship from Jalna gets taken instead."

"So what? You think I care? It's those damned U'Churians! If they'd gotten their act together, we could've escaped! There's got to be some guns on this damned ship somewhere! That's it! We could pretend to surrender and . . ."

"Shut up, Tallis," said T'Chebbi in disgust, turning away from him. "Their ship is twice our size, more crew than us."

Tallis lunged out and grabbed her by the arm, swinging her around. "You're selling us into slavery! You don't know what these people are like!"

T'Chebbi's hand closed on his. A quick flip and he was sprawling on the floor. "Enough!" she roared at him. "Is done! Get down to vehicle deck with others, now!"

He'd gone, muttering and cursing all the way, but when the Valtegans actually came through the hatch, he fell silent and slipped to the back of the group, hoping to remain unnoticed.

This was T'Chebbi's first encounter with Valtegans. Narrowing her eyes, she began to study the nearest one. Topping six feet tall, and dressed in khaki fatigues, he was humanoid in appearance. Green-skinned, his round, hairless head had a forehead that unlike a Human one sloped straight down to become the nose. Eyes were large and yellowish in color, and lashless. His ears were small and set low against his skull, the bottom edge of them level with the slightly V-shaped upper lip. Three-fingered hands with an opposable thumb gripped the rifle firmly, knuckles showing a lighter color. Like her, he had claws, but large, nonretractile ones. A commotion from behind her made her tear her gaze away and turn round just as the soldier became aware of her curiosity.

As M'ezozakk's carmine-robed torturer came through the hatch, with a howl of anger and rage, Tesha propelled herself at him.

"Tesha!" yelled Jeran in horror, stepping forward instinctively to stop her. Kaid's hand clamped over his, pulling him close to his side and holding him there. "No!" he hissed. "Be still! It's her choice."

She didn't get far. An energy bolt hit her full in the chest, knocking her from her feet and flinging her backward into their midst. As they scattered to avoid her, Kate gave a tiny cry and crumpled to the ground. Rezac bent down and lifted her up as the rest of them regrouped.

Kaid kept his hold on Jeran. "Don't look," he said, keeping his voice low. "They're hoping for an excuse to kill all of us. Don't give it to them."

Jeran swallowed hard and nodded, once, but his body remained stiff and unyielding in Kaid's grasp.

"Get them into the *M'ijikk*," said the officer in charge, lowering his gun. "I want no more casualties. I'll flay the first one to fire a shot!"

* * *

"You tell him," said J'koshuk. "It's not my job. You're the First Officer, and in charge of this detail."

Mzayb'ik regarded him with naked hate. "I saved your life in there! One day, J'koshuk . . ."

"You'll what?" asked the priest, folding his arms across his carmine robes. "Our Church is strong, Mzayb'ik. Since we fled Keiss rather than return to M'zull, I have been surrounded by heresy. We should have returned to expiate our disgrace in an honorable death. We did not. As first officer, you are as guilty as the general for making that decision. A charge of heresy laid against you, even should you disprove it, would hardly further your career."

"What career? As you said, we have no home!" hissed the other. "Unless the general's plan succeeds, we're dead now, living on borrowed time!"

"The auguries predicted success . . ."

"The auguries!" spat Mzayb'ik, tongue flicking out angrily. "You tailor them to suit the general's wishes! You lick his eggs as willingly as would any drone!"

Skin flushing a darker green in anger, J'koshuk turned away, ostensibly to watch the four Cabbarans being escorted into the turbo lift to the upper levels. "I suggest you don't keep him waiting any longer for the news. It will not improve with delay," he said coldly.

With a final hiss of anger, Mzayb'ik stalked off to the vehicle dispatch office to make his call.

M'ezozakk's face filled the small vid screen. "Well? Have you got them secured in the cargo holds yet? Are the Cabbarans on their way up to the brig?"

"Yes, General. All went smoothly. As we thought, the craft was U'Churian. Their captain suffered a minor concussion but is coming round now. The four Cabbaran navigators are on their way up even as we speak." He hesitated. There was no way of knowing how General M'ezozakk would react.

"What is it, Mzayb'ik? Don't keep me waiting."

"There are Sholans on board. We got back three of the ones we sold on Jalna, but one died in a suicide charge on the priest," he said in a rush. "And we have Humans. Two females. What do you want us to do with them?"

Speechless for once, M'ezozakk stared out of the screen at him.

"General? What shall we do with them? The scent of the Sholans is affecting my troops badly, especially since the female got shot."

"I'm on my way down." The screen darkened abruptly.

Mzayb'ik returned to the main loading area where the air lock between the two craft was being sealed. Twenty of his soldiers ringed the small group of aliens who had come off the U'Churian craft. Even inside the office, he'd been able to smell their volatile mood, and the scent of the Sholans.

It was the scent more than the sight of them that made his skin feel slick with sweat and triggered his desire to destroy them in the most primitive, physical way. He fought against it, knowing that, though joining his men in ripping the Sholans limb from limb might satisfy his primal urges, he would have to face the wrath of his general afterward, and nothing was worth that. At least M'ezozakk had said nothing about the dead one—yet.

J'koshuk intercepted him again on his way across to the captives. "And what did our good general have to say?"

"He's coming down," said Mzayb'ik, continuing to walk, making the priest trot to keep up with him. He stopped just outside the ring of soldiers and rounded on him. "I won't forget this, J'koshuk," he said quietly, eyes narrowing as he stared at him. "One slip, one mistake, and you're mine!"

J'koshuk shrugged and smiled, showing his razor sharp teeth in a wide grin. "I don't make mistakes." He held the final sibilant in a prolonged hiss.

Mzayb'ik snarled and pushed his way through his men till he faced the motley group of aliens. He wished he could have gauged the general's mood better, but that one was too good at keeping his reactions to himself. He looked at the females. It had been a long time since they'd seen Humans—or females. They looked almost like people, if lesser creatures could even be called people. At least they weren't covered in hair like the U'Churians and the Sholans.

The smaller one looked scared. He took a step closer, breathing deeply to check, then berated himself mentally. Of course she was scared! What other emotion could she feel in the presence of her obvious superiors? He tried to make eye contact with her, but like the other, she kept her head down, looking only at the ground.

A stir from behind alerted him to the arrival of General M'ezozakk. He turned round to greet him, steeling his expression and suppressing his anxiety, hoping that he was exuding the correct scent signals.

M'ezozakk stopped beside him and scanned the group.

"They've been searched and I've separated them into species," said Mzayb'ik. "Nine U'Churians, two Human females, and five Sholans, including two of those we had before."

"I can count," said M'ezozakk testily, moving closer to the U'Churians. "Which one is Captain?" he asked in bad Port patois.

Tirak, pushing away Mrowbay's support, stepped forward. "Me. I take it you're the commander of this craft. What is the meaning of this piracy? You have no right to perpetrate an act of war on peaceful traders."

M'ezozakk stared at him, blinking once, slowly. "Why are you transporting these creatures?" he asked, indicating the others. "What purpose is behind this?"

"Profit," said Tirak. "They're passengers who paid us to be taken off Jalna."

"To where?"

Tirak stared back at him. "What business is it of yours? To my world, if you must know. They had nowhere else to go."

M'ezozakk looked consideringly at him, then with frightening speed, backhanded him across the face. "You lie. They have a world to go to."

Tirak staggered against Mrowbay, putting his hand to his face as he clutched at the medic to regain his balance.

"Never lie to me again," said M'ezozakk, turning away from him and walking toward the Sholans.

He stopped in front of Tallis, reaching out to grasp him by the tunic and pull him closer. "We meet again. You didn't like Jalna?"

Tallis began to whimper in terror.

"Where were you going? Not home, we destroyed it." He shook him briefly and Tallis began to babble incoherently. With a hiss of disgust, M'ezozakk flung him back. "A coward. You're useless. You'd tell me anything you thought would please me," he said in disgust. He looked at the rest of them.

"A new one. Where from?" he demanded, hand snaking out to grasp Taynar by the throat.

Terrified, Taynar hung limp within his grasp. He looked frantically at Rezac, then over to the U'Churians. "Keiss."

M'ezozakk grunted then released him, pushing him aside and turning to Zashou. "A female," he said, then glanced over at the Humans. "Three." Frowning, he breathed deeply, then began to advance on them.

"You, I know," he said in Valtegan, stopping in front of Jo. Reaching out, he took hold of the hair that now just touched her shoulders. "It's been a long time. You're the one I sent for many times on Keiss." His hand curled round her throat, non-retracting claws overlapping as he circled it. "What brings you so far from your world? Not a desire for my company, I'm sure. What are you Humans plotting this time, I wonder?" He forced her chin up till she was looking at him.

Behind him, Rezac stirred, beginning to growl low in his throat. M'ezozakk ignored him.

"Answer me!" he said, giving her a small shake. "How is it you and the Sholans are here at Jalna in the company of these traders?"

Jo put her hand up to cover M'ezozakk's and smiled. "We came to rescue the Sholans, General, nothing more. Our ship was damaged on landing so we chartered Captain Tirak's. I had not thought to see you again," she said in his language.

M'ezozakk watched her face carefully, reading her scent signals. She was afraid, but then her fear was pleasant, had always added spice to their encounters at the base. "We will talk more," he said, relaxing his grip, letting his hand slide down her throat to her shoulder. "Renew our closeness." He rubbed his thumb gently across her throat, his forked tongue flicking out to touch her cheek.

This time the commotion behind him could not be ignored. He swung round, glaring at the scuffle within the Sholan group. One of the males was having to be subdued by his own people.

"Bring him here," he ordered, closing his hand over Jo's shoulder till his claws began to penetrate her clothing.

Rezac was dragged, struggling, before him. The reason was instantly obvious to him: they carried each other's scent. What he had assumed was due to her traveling in close proximity with the Sholans was actually caused by their relationship with each other.

"Ah, you've been mating with this one." M'ezozakk was prepared to be amused. "A strange choice, but then, I see none of your own males among this group."

"Leave her alone," snarled Rezac, struggling within the grip of the two soldiers.

M'ezozakk felt Jo stiffen. "Have you an affection for this animal?" He reached for her arm, pulling back her sleeve. "I must ensure your interest in him dies," he said, raising it to his mouth. "I would not want you distracted." He bit down deeply on her forearm, making her scream out in pain and shock.

"No, not that!" howled Rezac in Valtegan, his struggles becoming more frantic as Joe tried to pull away from M'ezozakk. Abruptly, the fight went out of him and with a whimper, he sagged against the soldiers, an agonized look on his face.

Releasing Jo, M'ezozakk thrust her at J'koshuk. "See she's quartered in the room opposite mine. Guard her well: the drug works faster on Humans."

"Yes, General," murmured the priest, gesturing for two soldiers to escort her above.

M'ezozakk switched his attention to Rezac. "Put the U'Churians in the main hold for the time being, and the Sholans in the other. J'koshuk, he's yours," he said, indicating Rezac. "I want information from him. He speaks Valtegan, I want to know where he learned it, and what these Humans are up to."

"Yes, General."

"The other Human?" ventured Mzayb'ik.

"Put her with the U'Churians for now," said M'ezozakk, turning and heading for the turbo lift in the wake of Jo and her escort. "I want to speak to the Cabbarans." He stopped, and turned to look at his two officers. "And I want no more mistakes. No deaths unless I order them, is that understood? Don't get carried away with your calling, J'koshuk. You'll get your chance to play with him after I have my information!"

As the guards moved to separate them, Kaid stirred, about to step forward. Tirak grabbed him, holding him back. "No!" he hissed. "Let them think you're U'Churians. You're more use to your people with us than with them!"

When he hesitated, T'Chebbi spoke. "He's right. Look how few guard us in comparison to our people."

The opportunity was gone as half a dozen soldiers began to herd them toward the cargo hold at the rear of the ship.

T'Chebbi sat with Kate, talking to her, holding her, trying to get some response from her other than a low, repetitive whimpering. But the teenager was too deeply in shock. Being separated from Taynar hadn't helped.

The rest of them crouched in a silent group on the bare metal deck. Eventually Tirak spoke.

"What did M'ezozakk do to Jo? Why did he bite her?"

"Zashou says it's a mating thing, to bind a female to that particular male. Their teeth secrete a chemical which they inject with their bite," said Kaid. "It makes the female violently aggressive and protective of the male who's bitten her, fighting off any other male who approaches her. He did it partly to goad Rezac."

"It worked," said Sheeowl.

T'Chebbi came over. "I can do nothing with her," she sighed, squatting down beside Kaid. "Can you reach Rezac? Is there anything you can do to help him?"

Kaid nodded. "I can reach him, and could help deaden the pain, but to what purpose?" he asked heavily. "When I sleep, he'll bear the full brunt of it himself and that'll be worse for him." He only prayed that he'd inherited his strength and determination from his father and that Rezac would survive. "I've done what I can for Zashou. Luckily, their Link is still dormant. She's sleeping for now."

"You can't just leave him to cope alone!" said Giyesh.

"Believe me, he doesn't want me inside his mind right now," said Kaid. "I've been where he is. He doesn't need a witness to his suffering, and that's all I'd be."

"What about Jo?" asked Manesh.

"I can't reach her."

"Isn't there a danger these Valtegans will pick up your telepathy?" asked Tirak.

"No, they're not able to sense it themselves, and these ones know nothing about either Sholan or Human telepaths," he said, resting his head on his forearms.

"How's Jeran?" asked Giyesh, reaching out to touch him. "Can you tell him I'm concerned for him, that he's to take care?"

Kaid nodded.

"It was the Cabbarans they wanted all along," said Tirak, resting back against the bulkhead. "Why?"

"I'll hazard a guess," said Sheeowl. "Their navigational skills. They've been to Jalna, they know what the Cabbarans can do, and they want a team for themselves. Could they be lost, unable to find their way back home?"

"Possibly," said Kaid. "More likely it's to aid their war effort. Keiss was used as an R and R world for their troops. We know very little about them, not even who they're fighting."

"So the rest of us are superfluous. What do we do?" asked Tirak. "Sit here and rot while we wait for this M'ezozakk to kill us all?"

"We make sure we give them false information about our species, information that will aid our people against them," said Kaid. "And we wait for an opportunity to escape, or to be rescued."

"You're wonderfully optimistic," said Giyesh, a note of hysteria in her voice. "Look around you, Kaid! I couldn't get a distress signal sent out before we were taken, and we're sealed in this cargo hold!"

"Pull yourself together, Giyesh," snapped Sheeowl. "You knew this mission could be dangerous when you chose to come with us."

"We're in the vehicle bay," said T'Chebbi. "A shuttle

stands outside, and the *Profit* is only a short walk away
through the docking port."

"It might as well be on Jalna!"

"We only need one person to escape for as long as it
takes to send a coded message to Jalna," said Kaid. "Till
then, we play it cooperatively and stay alive."

"Our people start looking for us soon," added T'Chebbi.
"Yours, too."

"How soon?" asked Sayuk.

"Seven, perhaps eight days. Maybe sooner," said Kaid.
"Then they'll come looking for us. And they'll find the
cryo units."

"If the Valtegans don't find them first," said Manesh
quietly.

*   *   *

Rhyasha Aldatan closed the nursery suite door behind
her and made her way along the balcony to the guest suite
where Dr. Jack Reynolds and his Companion Jiszoe were
staying. As she collapsed tiredly into the comfort of the
bowl-shaped easy chair, the Human physician rose and
went to the dispenser unit, returning with a gently steaming
mug for her.

She accepted it, sniffing curiously at the brown liquid.
"Kashini's finally fallen asleep," she said, taking a cautious
sip. "I've never known a cub to behave like that before—
and the noise she was making!"

"It's her Human side," said Jack, lowering his tall,
slightly portly frame into his seat. "All Human babies cry
like that."

"Are you sure there's nothing wrong with her?" she
asked the doctor. "It started so suddenly, Dzaka said. I
can't believe it was just a bad dream as her nurse says."

"Dzaka's empathic talent has proved most reliable and
useful at the medical center and elsewhere, Clan Leader,"
Jiszoe said quietly. "Jack relies on him a great deal, even
when we have telepathic nurses and medics on duty. If he
says it was just a dream, then that's what it is. I'd trust his,
and Kitra's, opinions."

"Kashini was certainly extremely distressed when I arrived," said the older female, taking another mouthful. "This is nice," she said, indicating the mug. "What is it?'

"A chocolate derivative drink," said Jack. "Something to help you rest. I assure you, Rhyasha, there is nothing wrong with your granddaughter. You have my word on it. May I suggest that we all go back to bed? Morning has gotten far too close."

"It's good advice," said Miosh, leaning forward to pat her friend's hand. "We've got a full day ahead of us tomorrow, with the vet coming to check the breeding stock."

"And he always arrives early," sighed Rhyasha as she finished her drink. Putting the mug down on the low table, she got to her feet. Hesitating at the door, she said, "You'll call me if anything . . ."

"Nothing will happen except that little madam will wake up at the crack of dawn, as bright and breezy as usual," said Miosh, opening the door and drawing her through it.

"You didn't tell your mother everything," said Dzaka as Kitra collapsed in an exhausted heap in the central depression of their bed.

"What good would it have done?" she asked tiredly. "Whatever it was, it's happened and been dealt with, for good or ill. What we have to decide now is what we do about it."

"We need to get word to their rendezvous ship." He climbed onto the bed, curling himself round his young Companion and slipping an arm under her neck. "Tell them we're sure my father and your brother and bond-sister are in trouble."

"How, though, without panicking Mother and Father? And who's going to believe us when I say I picked this information up from a cub only three months old?"

"Father Lijou," he said, wrapping his other arm across her waist. "He has the contacts."

"Good thinking," she murmured, reaching out to run her fingers through the long, brindled fur on his chest. "You can contact him in an hour or so when we've had some sleep. I don't know what we'd have done without you, you're so good with Kashini."

He rested his chin on the top of her head. "I did very little. I'm afraid it hasn't been a good weekend."

"Not true. You're a natural father, Dzaka. You must really miss your own family."

Nnya, and his son, Khyaz, killed by the Valtegans on Szurtha. A wave of sadness swept through him and his arms tightened around Kitra, needing her warmth, her life, her nearness. He loved her more than he dared tell her. Everything about his beautiful young Companion marked her as beyond his reach. The youngest child of the main Aldatan Clan family, one of the strongest telepathic bloodlines on Shola, her future was not in a marriage to a gene-altered Brother like himself who couldn't even share his cubs with her.

"Though I'll always grieve for their passing, it's you I'm with now. You gave me back what I thought I'd lost when they died—my life," he said.

A gentle purr began to vibrate through her body. "They're placing bets, the Brothers and Sisters on the estate, that we'll life-bond before the year's out."

He grunted. He'd been aware of the betting for some time and had studiously ignored it—as he was trying to ignore her.

"What would you say if I asked you now?" Her voice was drowsy, on the verge of sleep.

"There's time enough ahead of us, Kitra. The year's just begun. We have now, let it be enough," he said, searching for an ear in the cloud of tight, blonde curls, then, when he found it, gently licking its tip. "You might meet someone else you like more."

"So might you, and I don't want that to happen." Her voice became suddenly more alert. "Dzaka, will you . . ."

He tilted her face up to his. "Don't ask me now, Kitra," he said forcefully. "You're only fourteen, in your first year as an adult. I'd have to say no, and I don't want to. You can't choose a life-mate when you've only known one male. Anyway, your father will likely choose one for you."

"I don't need to know anyone else. I know who I want, just as my mother did."

He made an exasperated noise. Vartra knew he wanted her as his life-mate, but now was too soon to tell her it was impossible. Even if they'd been genetically compatible, her father, Lord over all the Telepath Clans, would definitely refuse them because she was so young and inexperienced.

"You said if I asked now. What if I left it? Then you would say yes? Is that what you mean?"

"When you've seen more of life, know what you really want, then we'll talk about it," he temporized.

"How long, Dzaka?" she asked, nose wrinkling. "A year—two?"

For him, an empath, her intensity was a palpable force that was becoming more uncomfortable for him by the minute. He did the only thing he could, diverted her.

* * *

Day 5

Early the next day, Dzaka headed out to Stronghold. Father Lijou listened to Dzaka's story in silence. He took his time replying. This would need careful handling.

"I understand your Companion's fears, Dzaka," he began.

"Mine, too, Father Lijou," interrupted Dzaka.

". . . and yours," he amended, with an inner sigh. "But you have to realize I need more than this to start an alert."

"An inquiry, then. Find out what the situation is with them."

"We're expecting a report shortly. Clan Lord Aldatan is in communication with the *Rhijissoh* in his capacity as head of Alien Relations. If anything's wrong with his son and bond-daughter, believe me, he'll be the first to be informed. And if, as you fear, it's already happened and been dealt with, there's little we can do anyway."

"They can get there sooner and be ready for any medical emergency."

"The *Rhijissoh* is always ready for emergencies. It's a class Y recon ship, prepared for anything. Meaning no disrespect to your Companion, Dzaka, you have to remember she's just out of childhood . . ."

"Females mature earlier, Father Lijou," said Dzaka stiffly. "And her lack of years doesn't affect my judgment of the situation."

"You're an empath, not a telepath. Did you consider that her emotions might have colored even your perception, which at the moment is far from impartial?"

"Are you saying my judgment is flawed, Father?"

Vartra save me from self-righteous young males, Lijou thought with another sigh. "No, I am merely saying it's natural for you to be affected by Liegena Kitra's distress for her brother and bond-sister. And your own fears for your father."

"The distress was Kashini's," reminded Dzaka.

This was going nowhere fast. Lijou got to his feet, bringing the interview to an abrupt end. "I will do what I can, Brother Dzaka, but I will not alarm the Clan Lord or the *Rhijissoh* without good cause. Now, you will have to excuse me, I left a meeting to speak to you."

"For that, I thank you, Father Lijou," said Dzaka with stiff formality as he got up. "Should Kitra and I sense any more from Kashini, I will pass on your words of comfort to my Companion and my niece."

"You forget yourself, Brother Dzaka." It was his turn to be sharp. "You are only consolidating my opinion with this attitude. I suggest you retire to the temple for the next two hours and pray to Vartra to clear your thoughts so you can view the matter more dispassionately."

Dzaka threw him a smoldering glance before bowing his head in obedience. Silently, the young priest left the room, closing the door carefully behind him. The final click of the lock sounded loudly in the silence.

Muttering oaths and imprecations, Lijou left his office through the door to his private quarters, heading for the bedroom where his life-mate Kha'Qwa, now with only eight weeks to go in her pregnancy, was lying resting.

The drapes were partially closed, keeping out the brightness of the late spring day so she could doze.

"Kha'Qwa, are you awake?" he asked, hesitating in the doorway.

"I am now," she said. "Even with my psi gifts on the wane, I could sense you two. Take him seriously, Lijou. Remember Carrie finished her last weeks of pregnancy in four days while they were in the Fire Margins, and as a result, Kashini was born a fully awakened telepath. And how else would a cub Kashini's age communicate her fear? Tell Rhyaz what Dzaka said, even if you speak to no one else. Remember, you wanted Dzaka to get more involved with life again. Now he is."

"What if they're wrong?"
"What if they're right?"

* * *

While the priest stood a short distance away talking to the guards, irrelevant thoughts buzzed around like insects in Rezac's brain. He let them. They prevented him from reaching out psychically to try and blast the priest's mind. He'd lost track of time. He thought there had been a point when he'd been left alone for some time—a sleep period for them, perhaps, but there'd been no rest possible for him. The hard leather cuffs that held him to the wall bit deeply into his throat and wrists as his legs began to buckle under him.

He jerked upright again, gasping for breath as the sudden movement sent agony through his side. He knew he had at least one broken rib, maybe more. His legs began to tremble under his weight again and he tried to force them as straight as they would go, damning both his weakness and his stupidity at getting himself into this situation.

They know nothing about telepaths, either Sholan or Human, Kaid had sent to him as he'd been dragged off. *They're psychotic about destroying us. They must not find out Shola exists.*

Help Jo and Zashou, was all he'd had the chance to send as they fastened him to the wall in one of the empty cargo holds. The Gods alone knew how many hours—or days—ago that had been.

"Soften him up," J'koshuk had ordered the guards, then stood back and watched while he was beaten nearly senseless. Then he'd taken over and the real pain and the questions began.

Kaid had been right about their attitude toward Sholans. He'd never had such brutality directed at him before. On K'oish'ik, he and Zashou had been the favored pets of the Emperor Q'emgo'h. They'd been roughly handled, but nothing like this. But then, in those days when his telepathic Talent had first been enhanced, all that was necessary was to expose him, or any of them, to the pain of other people. They experienced it as if it was their own, and it had them bent double, retching in seconds. His Link with Jo had reversed that for both him and Zashou, but everything had its price and now he was paying.

The collar round his neck was bolted to the wall behind him, preventing him from resting even during this respite. As his head sagged down once more, it cut into the underside of his jaw, forcing him to lift his chin again. He peered across at his torturers from under swollen eye ridges, straining his ears forward, trying to catch what they were saying. They were too far away.

He thought of his mates. What would this do to them? What were they suffering? Jo, hurt by M'ezozakk in the past and now in his power again—his creature now that he'd bitten her. If only he hadn't cried out, it would never have happened. And Zashou. Fragile and sensitive, not a fighter at all. Thank all the Gods that their Link was still dormant. He clenched his hands, moaning in despair, realizing that his own foolish actions had brought this down on all three of them.

His jaw was suddenly grasped, claws cutting into the soft underside.

"The general is disposed to believe that the female taught you our language," said the priest. "And that she and you came to rescue those on Jalna. But I do not."

He was caught with no other logical explanation to give him. How could he tell the priest he'd been trapped inside the stasis cube they'd worshiped as a holy object? That it was actually a device from their far past in which he and his Leska had been imprisoned? Anger replaced despair as he realized this priest enjoyed what he was doing. Nothing he could say would make any difference now that M'ezozakk had the answers he needed. He'd been sentenced to death.

"May your God-King curse you for all eternity!" he snarled. "May he curse you till your very shadow shrinks from you in fear!"

As the blows began to rain down on him again, he had the satisfaction of seeing the color drain from J'koshuk's face. Then, as fresh agony exploded in his side, darkness finally claimed him.

* * *

Day 6

"Clan Lord Aldatan!"

Tired and hungry, Konis decided to keep walking. He'd missed second meal because of yet another "crisis" in his department, and was determined that nothing would stop him from going to the senior staff mess for the midafternoon break.

"Clan Lord Aldatan!" The voice was louder, more insistent.

Cursing under his breath, he stopped and waited. The young male halted beside him, still breathing heavily as he handed him a flimsy piece of paper. "Message just came through from Jalna. Knew you'd want it immediately."

Frowning, Konis took it from him.

Another cry, its tone anxious and urgent, rang out through the busy corridor. "Shayza, no! It's not for the Clan Lord!"

Konis heard the sound of clawed feet skidding on the decorative tiled floor, then Hanaz, Governor Nesul's aide, came to a stop beside him. His hand reached for the message, attempting to twitch it from Konis' grasp before he could read it.

"Your pardon, Master Konis, this is not an AlRel matter," he said. "It's intended for General Raiban and Masters Rhyaz and Lijou."

"Not for Master Konis?" said Shayza blankly. "But it concerns . . ."

"I know what it concerns," snapped Hanaz sharply. When Konis didn't respond to him, he spoke again, this time his tone gentler. "Master Konis?"

Konis finally looked up at him, releasing the document. Suddenly the high-ceilinged palace corridor seemed airless and cramped to him. As his surroundings began to darken, he felt Hanaz grasp him supportively round the waist.

"Fetch Master Lijou. He's with the Governor," said Hanaz. "We'll be in the Summer Office."

Konis felt the grip on him tighten as he was turned around.

"Master Konis, I'm sorry you found out this way, but you cannot collapse here," Hanaz said quietly. "The Summer Office is only a few yards away. I'll help you."

Konis made a small noise of agreement, clutching Ha-

naz's arm as they began to walk. It seemed an age before
they stopped in front of a door flanked by two armed Warriors. At Hanaz's gesture, one stepped forward to open it
for them.

"We're expecting Father Lijou," the Governor's aide said
as they entered. "Admit no one else without my permission."

As the door closed behind them, Konis found his
strength again, and straightening up, turned on Hanaz.
"Why was that message going to be withheld from me?"
he asked.

Hanaz urged him on toward the seats in the center of the
room. "To prevent you reacting like this, Master Konis," he
said gently. "The message means nothing more than what it
says: your son and his companions failed to contact Captain
Kishasayzar as scheduled thirty-nine hours ago. It does not
mean that anything has happened to them."

Feeling a chair against the back of his legs, Konis sat
down abruptly. "When would I have been informed?" he
demanded.

"When they arrived at Tuushu Station, or when we knew
for certain they were missing."

"Their transmission is over a day late and they aren't
replying to subsequent messages! I'd call that missing!"

"I really couldn't comment, Master Konis. It's outside
my field of expertise, that's why I've sent for Master Lijou.
The Brotherhood deals with such matters daily. Meanwhile,
can I get you something? A glass of water perhaps?"

"I don't want any water," Konis muttered. "I'm hungry,
that's all. I haven't had time to turn around, let alone eat,
since I left home this morning."

"Some food can be brought here for you. What would
you like?"

"Good news of my son and bond-daughter, Hanaz," he
said, leaning back exhaustedly and closing his eyes. "That's
all I want right now."

The door opened and he sensed Lijou entering. The faint
noise of his footfalls and his long robes brushing the carpeted floor sounded unnaturally loud to Konis.

"Is this just a routine message, Lijou?" he asked. "Don't
lie to me, I'd rather know the worst."

"I wouldn't lie to you, Konis," said Lijou as the Head
Priest sat on the chair next to his. "Yes, a report like this

is standard procedure when a team misses a scheduled transmission or meeting by a six day. As to whether this message means more, no one could say right now. It's honestly too early to tell."

Konis opened his eyes to look the other straight in the face. "When would you have told me?"

Lijou reached out to touch Konis' knee briefly. "When I knew what had happened. They're not expected at Tuushu for two weeks. Until that deadline passed, or we received a message from them during jump, I'd have said nothing to alarm you."

"Two weeks," said Konis in a hushed voice. "We'll have to wait two weeks till we know what's happened to them?"

"That's why we don't tell the families at this point." Lijou's tone was sympathetic. "You mustn't speak of this to anyone else, Konis. Not Rhyasha, nor Kaid's son, Dzaka. No one must hear about this until we're sure. It's a U'Churian vessel that's missing, not one of ours. That makes the situation more complex."

"What were they doing on a U'Churian ship? I thought they were with the Sumaan." He was finding it difficult to keep his thoughts straight.

"We don't have word on that yet," said Lijou. "Likely there's some simple explanation."

"Like what? I know from the treaty negotiations that the U'Churians are not as advanced as we are. What would make them leave Jalna on their ship?"

"Something as simple as a systems failure on the *Hkariyash* could account for it, Konis. The same for the lack of communication with the *Profit*," said Lijou soothingly. "There's no reason yet to assume the worst."

"What are you going to do about it? Are we looking for them yet?"

"Rhyaz is talking to Raiban now. Believe me, we will be searching for them, Konis. If nothing else, we're aware that how we conduct this matter will impact on the way both the U'Churians and the Cabbarans view us as allies."

"I must be kept informed, Lijou. I can cope if I know what I'm facing. It's not knowing that's frightening."

"I will keep you informed," promised Lijou as the door opened again and Hanaz entered carrying a tray of sliced meats, bread and hot c'shar. "Hanaz told me you hadn't eaten since this morning. Do you mind if I join you? Like you, I haven't had time to stop for a meal."

"It would turn to dust in my mouth right now," said Konis.

"You must eat, my friend," said Lijou as Hanaz put the tray down on the low table beside them. "Many people saw you nearly pass out from lack of food."

Konis stared at him. "For a telepath, you've become too good at lying, Lijou. I want your word that you'll keep me informed. Dammit, it's my son and bond-daughter that are missing out there!"

"You have my word, Konis. As soon as we have any definite news, I will tell you. I care about your son and his Triad too, you know. Now please, my friend, you must try to eat something."

"I haven't time," he muttered, trying to get up. "The Governor's waiting for me."

Lijou gently prevented him. "That can wait. The Governor has put your meeting off until tomorrow."

Konis looked up sharply at him. "If you want this to remain confidential, Lijou, that's the worst thing you could do. My meeting with the Governor must go ahead as scheduled."

Lijou hesitated, obviously unsure how to counter his logic.

Konis reached for the plate of food. "I'll eat something, if it'll make you happy, but my meeting *will* go ahead."

"This is neither the time nor the place, Azkuu," said Konis angrily as he gathered the papers for his meeting with Governor Nesul. He was annoyed. Azkuu had come from downwind and effectively trapped him in the AlRel office. "Clan matters aren't pressing, these new treaties with the Free Traders are."

"You're Clan Lord, too, Konis," she growled. "If the duties are becoming too much for you, then you should pass them over to someone else."

"Don't be ridiculous," said Konis, looking up at the older female. "When have I ever neglected Clan duties?"

"You want a list? I'll give it to you, then. Over your son and the Human, and your daughter Taizia. Now you're doing it with Kitra. It reeks of partisanship, Konis."

Anger surged through him. His son and Carrie were missing, perhaps dead, and here was this narrow-minded female complaining about their bonding! "You leave my son and bond-daughter out of this, Azkuu. As for Taizia and the other telepaths involved in the Brotherhood breeding program, those orders came from the highest level, nothing to do with me!"

"Way I heard it, Konis, Taizia got herself pregnant by this Brother and forced your hand."

Konis straightened up, allowing his ears to rotate sideward and begin to fold down in a display of his anger. "You overstep the bounds of familiarity, Azkuu," he said coldly. "My daughter was free to make a bonding contract of her choice at that time. That it was later endorsed by the military directive is their good fortune. Now, if you'll excuse me, I've pressing business to attend to."

"You'll hear me out first, Konis. You know me well enough to know I'm not saying this out of malice, but others aren't speaking so kindly. This latest crop of betrothals has the young ones demanding they be given a say in the choice of their future life-mates! And the older ones are muttering, too. We can't afford a rebellion. Vartra knows you're busy enough now without having to bring down that rhakla! You want my advice?"

"No, frankly, I don't, but doubtless I'm going to get it anyway."

Azkuu glowered back at him. "You're right, you're getting it. Get that last daughter of yours life-bonded as soon as possible, and I do mean bonded. If you're seen to uphold our traditions with her, it'll go a long way to quieting the other Clan Leaders, who in turn will see their offspring do as they're told. It's only the ceremony they want. No one expects her to bear cubs yet."

"She's too young to be life-bonded, Azkuu. Next year is soon enough."

"You're not listening to me, are you? Kitra is old enough, you know that as well as I. You've become too alien, Konis, too changed by the goings-on of your son and his En'Shallans for the majority of the Clan Leaders. If you don't act now over Kitra, you're going to have trouble, not only in the Clan Council but in the Guild!"

"I told you my decision, Azkuu."

Azkuu sighed. "I tried the easy way, Konis, but your intractability has forced my hand. This is an official request from the Clan Council. Choose a life-mate for Kitra now, or face a vote of censure at the next meeting in three weeks' time. I'm sorry, but you left me with no choice."

Konis was too stunned to answer as Azkuu turned and left. Then anger really took hold of him. How dare they question his judgment, Challenge him like this! Become too alien, had he? Raiban's words echoed in his mind. *Once you step outside the groundling's rules, you can never go back.*

She was right, but it was the rules that needed changing, not him! With the inclusion of the Brotherhood, their genetic pool of Talented was much larger, there wasn't the need for the stringent genetic checks to make sure each individual in a potential couple was from a different family tree. And that was only taking the Brothers currently based on Shola into account. How many more of them there were, only Lijou and Rhyaz as joint Guild Masters knew. Now he had an argument for relaxing the system of choosing life-mates for the most Talented telepaths. Change was easier to force from within an organization, but what could he do in three weeks?

The door chime sounded, making him start, but it was only Hanaz, Nesul's aide.

"The Governor's ready for you now, Master Konis," he said quietly.

Konis pulled his thoughts back to the more pressing business at hand and followed Hanaz out.

*   *   *

"Azkuu said what?" demanded Rhyasha that evening, disbelieving her own ears as she leaped up from her chair to pace round the lounge.

"Kitra must be betrothed and life-bonded within the next three weeks," repeated Konis, trying not to wince at his mate's outraged tone.

"And you told her what she could do, didn't you?" When he didn't answer, she rounded on him. "Didn't you?"

"Actually, I said nothing," he replied, beating a retreat

behind his desk. "She said the request was official, from the Council as a whole."

Rhyasha stopped pacing and regarded him silently.

"Now that we have the Brothers, there's no need for arranged bondings if the candidates are allowed to choose from a group of previously screened partners. We can change it, Rhyasha. We need to."

"But not in three weeks, not for Kitra."

"No," he admitted, looking away as he sat down at his desk and activated his comm. "Not in time for Kitra. I've got a list of possible young males from among the Telepath Clans," he added hurriedly. "Help me choose one for her, Rhyasha." He hoped she'd hear the plea in his voice and not fight him over the inevitability of this.

"You're prepared to sacrifice our youngest daughter. Have you learned nothing over the past year, Konis?"

"Of course I have, but in fairness, they have a valid point, Rhyasha. Two of our three children have made unconventional marriages. As Clan Lord, I should set an example. A vote of censure at this time could cost me my position as head of the Council," he said, stung by her attack. "I can change things, force them to accept the Brothers as mates for their sons and daughters, if I stay in charge."

"Choose whom you want, it makes no difference to Kitra or me," she said abruptly, turning her back on him and heading for the door. She stopped and looked back over her shoulder at him. "But, Konis, you can tell Kitra and Dzaka yourself."

When summoned to Konis' office, Dzaka accepted the news as impassively as one would expect from one of the Brotherhood.

"When?" was all he'd asked.

"Within three weeks," replied Konis, obviously relieved by the younger male's response. "It's politics, Dzaka, not personal. I wish for Kitra's sake it could be otherwise. The Clans are demanding she have a traditional Telepath Clan life-mate."

"I understand, Clan Lord." It came as no shock to him: he'd expected it for some time now. "We were together two nights ago. You'll need to . . ."

"There's no need," said Konis hastily. "I know you're gene-altered. The betrothal is only a formality for now, but I will have to ask you not to be alone with her again. In a year or two, when she's provided an heir for her new clan, it's up to you . . ." He tailed off into silence. "I do wish it were otherwise. She's going to take it badly."

Dzaka sensed Kitra approaching and turned toward the door as it was flung wide. She stalked in, tail swaying in a lazy arc, ears spread wide and forward, every line of her body ready for a fight.

Ignoring her father, she looked only at him. "Well? What do you have to say about this?"

"We must do as the Clan Lord asks," he murmured. "It's no more than I said would happen."

Her scorn washed round him as her ears began to fold in anger. "That's it? That's all you have to say? What we feel for each other means nothing to you?"

There was no reply he could give her. Nothing could change their circumstances.

"I'd expected more from you," she said scathingly. "I thought Brothers fought for their friends and what they believed in."

He shifted uncomfortably, trying to keep his own emotions in check. "Your father is right. I tried to tell you."

"Kitra," began Konis.

She turned on him. "Leave it, Father, lest I say something you'll regret," she growled before spinning round and stalking out, tail rigid and fur extended.

There was nothing more to be said, so Dzaka left, heading back to the estate, to the house that Vanna and Garras shared. Though he'd been expecting this, it had still taken him by surprise and a part of his mind couldn't believe it had finally happened—especially after their last night together.

Vanna's friendly voice called out to him as he stood on the doorstep, telling him she'd be with him in a moment, and to go in and wait for her in the kitchen. He pushed open the back door and sat down at the table. He couldn't face going back to the villa yet—didn't dare in case Kitra was there, collecting her things from his room. It had taken more strength than she'd ever know to say nothing to her father when everything he wanted in life was her.

Sitting there, wrapped in his misery, he wasn't aware of Vanna entering until her hand touched his shoulder.

"I just heard. I'm sorry, Dzaka," she said quietly.

He said nothing, just leaned forward on the table, resting his head on his forearms.

"Dammit, he has as good a lineage as any in the Seventeen Clans!" said Garras angrily when he heard the news. "Both parents were telepaths, and we know his grandfather Rezac was!"

"But Dzaka isn't," said Vanna.

"The female Kusac was betrothed to wasn't."

"Dzaka can't claim both parents were telepaths unless he publically reveals the fact that Kaid is one."

"Most folk have worked that one out for themselves," Garras snorted. "And he's En'Shalla! He has every legitimate right to ask for her as his mate."

"No, he hasn't. Dzaka's one of our gene-altered Brothers. He and Kitra aren't fertile with each other. Believe me, Garras, I went through each of those ideas with Dzaka. He had no choice but to accept Konis' decision."

Garras sighed noisily and picked up his mug of c'shar. "So what's he going to do now?"

"He's gone back to the villa to continue watching Kashini."

He shook his head. "Damned shame. They were good for each other. About time the Clans changed the arranged life-bondings to a system like ours that gives the young ones a choice."

"That can only happen if Konis stays Clan Lord—which brings us full circle."

Garras took a swig from his mug. "Ah, well. At least once the bonding ceremony is over, they can be together again."

"Not even then, Garras. Konis forbade it for a year or two, and Kitra was so enraged that Dzaka refused to stand up to her father, that I doubt she'll have anything to do with him now."

"Well, he's one of our Clan. I have the right to speak for Dzaka in this matter since Kusac and Carrie are away, and I intend to do so!"

*   *   *

Jo couldn't afford to be afraid. The scent of her fear had always excited M'ezozakk, made him difficult to control. Those times she hadn't been able to suppress it, she'd suffered her worst injuries from him. Then, at least, she'd had access to Human medics afterward. This time, she was alone. Worse, in trying to help her, Rezac had been taken. *Never get yourself noticed by a Valtegan officer.* The warning echoed through her mind. And she and Rezac, therefore their whole Triad, had been noticed.

Another bout of shivering wracked her and she pulled the cover off the bed to wrap around her shoulders. She was losing the battle against fear, she realized. The slightest sound from outside filled her with an icy dread. Her head hurt with a dull throbbing that dominated her senses: her limbs and joints ached with the fever that she knew was building. One moment she was drenched in sweat, the next, icy cold. And her arm felt hot and swollen, difficult to move. She didn't dare look at it.

The arrival of the medic with an armed escort a short while ago had sent her retreating to this far corner of the bed. Something was seriously wrong, she realized.

"What did he do to me?" she'd asked unsteadily as the medic examined her. "Why did he bite me?"

"He was setting you apart, preventing the other males from approaching you."

She winced as he carefully touched a soft, sterile probe to the puncture wounds. "You're here."

He said nothing, merely took his sample and left.

*   *   *

M'ezozakk followed the medic into the room he'd assigned to Jo. "You'd better be right," he said, tongue flicking out angrily. "If you've disturbed me from my sleep for nothing . . ." He didn't bother finishing the sentence.

Jo sat cowering on the farthest corner of the bed, clothing darkened by sweat, her face slick with it. Against her chest she cradled her injured arm.

M'ezozakk sensed instantly what the medic had meant but he still had to see it for himself. He stalked into the room, his booted feet making no sound on the carpeted floor. Ignoring her cry of fear, he grasped hold of her and hauled her into the center of the bed. Her forearm was red and swollen, the puncture wounds oozing a dark, greenish-yellow substance.

"I haven't treated it yet," said the medic.

M'ezozakk bared his teeth, his loud hiss one of pure rage. "You deceived me!" He flung her back, causing her to hit the wall violently. "You deceived me!" He rounded on the medic and soldiers. "Get this piece of trash out of here," he snarled, his voice suddenly deceptively quiet.

"Where do I put her?" asked the medic. "When the fever passes, she'll turn on every male that approaches her."

"Put her in with the Sholans," he said, pushing them aside angrily as he turned to leave. Then he stopped. "No. Take her down to J'koshuk. Have her restrained till he's finished, then loose her on her mate. Let *her* finish him off!" He laughed. "A fitting end for both of them!"

* * *

"Kaid! Kaid!" Someone was shaking him.

He struggled up into a sitting position, recognizing T'Chebbi's scent in the darkness. "What is it?" he asked, rubbing the sleep from his eyes. He shivered, chilled to the bone by the coldness of the deck beneath him.

"Be afraid, Kaid," she whispered, clutching his hand and moving closer. "Be very afraid. It's come."

"What? Where?" He could feel her trembling against him and wrapped his free arm around her.

"Danger. Here—all around us. I've never felt it so strongly before," she whimpered.

In the distance, a klaxon began to sound, then a blinding glow filled the room, lighting it up for a brief moment. Darkness returned, and with it, oblivion.

A low-pitched klaxon began to echo through the ship: one sharp burst, one long. Startled, J'koshuk let Rezac's limp head fall against the restraint collar. He looked over to the four guards lounging at the back of the hold, guarding the heavily bound female.

"Check it out," he ordered. A proximity alert this far

out from the Jalnian shipping routes? J'koshuk turned back
to the unconscious Sholan as the lights began to flicker and
fade before plunging the small hold into darkness. Within
seconds, the emergency lighting came on, its faint, reddish
glow making giant shadows leap across the bulkheads.

This was worrying. The Sholan could wait, this warranted
his personal attention. He began to stride toward the exit
when, abruptly, even those lights went out.

Slowly, the giant ship hovering below the *M'ijikk* and the
Profit emerged from its chameleon shields. As the main
landing bay doors folded back, an eerie glow suffused the
two smaller craft. They began to move, being drawn downward into the belly of the ship until they had disappeared
from sight. Even before the doors had closed, the craft
shimmered briefly, then it, too, was gone.

His head hurt, that was J'koshuk's first realization,
closely followed by the fact he could see a glow beyond his
closed eyelids. A tremor ran through him and he realized
he'd been lying on the deck for some time. J'koshuk flicked
his tongue across his dry and parched lips, tasting the air.
The scent of fear was there, but it was old, more than two
hours old. He'd been unconscious, but why? And how?

The sound of the door sliding back drew his attention.
He opened his eyes. Four pairs of armor-clad legs entered
and marched in step toward him, forming a wall in front
of him when they stopped. A terrible certainty began to
form in his mind, then, beyond the legs, he saw the flick
of a gray robe.

A sound not unlike those Rezac had made a short time
ago, escaped him. He shut his eyes again.

"You are awake. You will stand and do as you are told,"
said the flat tones of a translator.

He cowered where he was, incapable of moving, praying
that this was all some terrible nightmare, until he heard
footsteps. With a strangled sound, he leaped to his feet,
swaying a little with dizziness and renewed pain from his
aching head. He took a deep breath, flicking his tongue out
again. Nothing. No scent, no taste from them. He opened
his eyelids a fraction. What he saw defied belief.

"You are our captives," the voice from behind the soldiers said in the same flat, impersonal tones. "Your ship is ours. You are ours. An interface with those on this ship is required. I have chosen you."

J'koshuk concentrated on trying to breathe and to break the paralysis that seemed to have possessed his mind and his limbs.

"Look at me."

He couldn't. Briefly he wondered if this was how his captives felt when facing him. Agony lanced through his body, taking the strength from his limbs. He collapsed to the deck, writhing. As suddenly as it came, the pain was gone. He lay where he'd fallen, gasping for air, instinctively looking up at the source of his torment. Four weapons were trained on him.

A strange sensation began to solidify in the pit of his stomach, flooding through him. Fear. A movement from the robed figure as it stepped forward drew his eyes away from the weapons.

"An interpreter is needed. It will be you. You will obey our orders without question or you will suffer pain. Is that understood?"

J'koshuk nodded his head, tongue flicking out again in a futile attempt to moisten his lips. Still no scent, not even from the robes. It was unnatural. How, in all the names of the Holy Ones, had they boarded the *M'ijikk?*

"Answer me!"

"Yes," he croaked, trying to swallow. He felt a constriction around his throat and put his hand up to investigate. A solid band of metal, with no hinge or clasp, now circled his neck.

"The collar ensures your obedience. It inflicts pain when you disobey. You will go now and release the one you were questioning. A medic will come to treat him. You will help. You will accompany him onto our ship and when he wakes, tell him what you've been told. Do not harm him any further."

With that, the tall, robed figure turned away.

"Wait! Who are you? What do I call you?"

The alien turned to face him again, the faceplate in its helmet glinting in the harsh light.

It said nothing for the space of several heartbeats. "Primes. We are the Primes. You will address me as Seniormost."

CHAPTER 5

Day 7

THE next day, Konis called in at the Telepath Guild to talk to Sorli about his troubles with the Clan Council and Kitra.

"We have a common problem, then," said Sorli, as his mate, Mayoi, finished handing their drinks to them then departed, shepherding out the student who had carried the tray of refreshments for her.

"We have?" asked Konis, surprised. He was grateful he didn't have to dissemble with this Guild Master as he had with the previous one.

"Only a small proportion of students in the Guild are from the leading Clan families, so the issue of arranged bondings isn't a major one. However, at this Guildhouse, we're unique in being so close to your son's estate. And on his estate live the mixed Leskas, who, no matter what position they held in their birth family, are able to choose, or not choose, their own life-mate. This is making the Sholan Leska pairs here, who don't have that luxury, dissatisfied, and they're demanding the same freedom."

"Just like the Clan heirs," agreed Konis morosely, taking a sip of his c'shar. "How can I be accused of failing in my duty as Leader of the Sixteen Telepath Clans because two of my children have made unconventional matches? What in Vartra's name was I supposed to do? Kusac and Carrie took matters into their own hands, and as for Taizia, no decision can be reached on her future until her contract with Meral expires and we know if their child is Talented or not!"

"Seventeen," Sorli corrected him gently, holding out the plate of pastries Mayoi had brought.

"Eh? Oh, yes, I mean Seventeen Clans. Keep forgetting Kusac's got his own Clan now."

"Perhaps it's time we looked at the whole issue of arranged bondings," said Sorli. "Do you feel they actually work?"

Konis shifted in his seat, taking one of the pastries. "Well, most of them seem to work well enough, but you can never . . ."

"No, not that. Do they actually achieve the results we want? Has the birth rate of Talented cubs gone up because of our genetic pairings?"

Konis' eyes narrowed slightly. Was Sorli on the same trail as himself? "Actually, no. Not according to the records of the past fifty or so years. There have been more Talents from among the contract bondings, even allowing for the fact they represent the larger proportion of the telepath population. I have been looking into the whole matter for some time, Sorli, and I believe my son was right. We need an injection of new blood into the main Clan families. We're becoming too inbred." He braced himself for the argument against his stance.

Sorli said nothing for a minute as he took another bite of his pastry. "My conclusion, too. It's time for a change, Konis. But how do we accomplish it against the conservatism of the other Clan Leaders?"

Surprised, Konis' mouth fell open as he stared at Sorli.

"Do shut your mouth, my friend, lest I accuse you of catching flies," Sorli said, his tone gently teasing.

Konis shut his mouth with a snap.

"I don't know why you look so surprised. I always said the winds of change were sweeping our world. Why should I then be ignoring them?"

"I'm used to Esken," Konis said.

"Ah, well. You'll find my tenure quite different, I assure you. Now, you didn't come here without a proposal to put forward. I'd like to hear it."

Konis relaxed a little. With Esken, he'd never had the feeling they were part of the same team, working toward a common goal. He'd always had his own agenda and power ploys that advanced himself, usually to the detriment of others. Sorli was something of an unknown quantity, only because it wasn't in Esken's nature to let anyone under him in his Guild shine. Already some of the rigid protocol, dating back a hundred years or more, that Esken had been so fond of, had been dropped in favor of a more relaxed system. It augured well for the future, if it continued. This matter would certainly test the new Guild Master's attitudes and outlook.

"There will be resistance from the Clan Leaders to change of any type," he said. "So we have to move gradually and in stages. New blood is desperately needed, but we'll have that with the inclusion of the Brotherhood in the contract bondings. That's been a large enough chunk for the older leaders to swallow as it is. We can't look to extend their inclusion in main family life-bondings for some time yet. What I can do is, instead of matching names on my lists, make the list available to the Clan Leaders and give them the right to choose their child's future husband or wife."

"Is it workable, though? What if one person should be chosen twice? We can't have them haggling like merchants over mates. And how will the younglings be able to choose among those from the other continents, those they've never met?"

"There is that, of course," Konis agreed, reaching for his mug. "The other main option is to arrange social functions, perhaps here, or possibly at the Governor's palace, at which they can meet. Kusac set up a similar system for potential mixed Leskas before he left for Jalna."

Sorli nodded. "I know. The military endorsed his request for tests to be done on our students and we transferred those he subsequently requested over to his estate. How is his system working?"

"Very well," said Konis. "Among the new pairs there's been a higher proportion happy with their Leskas and less trauma over adjusting to the Link as a result. I'd say it was definitely an improvement."

Sorli leaned back in his seat, steepling his fingertips together thoughtfully. "I'm pleased, of course, but I wonder if our implementation of it wouldn't be a step too far for our ultraconservative Clan Council. Perhaps we need to observe Kusac's system for a little longer. After all, it's only been a few weeks. I do, think, however, that making the list available to the Clan Leaders for them to choose from is a step in the right direction. If they feel they have a say, it'll go a long way toward dissipating their censure of you."

"I don't care a damn about their censure," growled Konis. "I've got larger worries at home. You have no idea what I'm having to put up with from Rhyasha!"

Sorli grinned openly at this, letting his hands fall back into his lap. "A female of great strength is your Clan Leader, Konis. I don't envy you. You're caught between a rock and a hard place right now."

"Tell me about it. They all take after their mother, even Kitra!"

Sorli raised an eye ridge. "Oh, I'd say it was about equal, Konis. You're well matched, you and Rhyasha. Both strong willed and determined. It's easy for us males to undervalue ourselves."

"I always thought they got their strength from their mother," Konis murmured, surprised.

"There's a lot of you in that son of yours. I watched him grow over the years, and knew he would finally leave the hunt to go off by himself."

"Seems everyone but me knew that."

"When the younglings are your own, it's easy to be too close to the problem to see it. Implementing the list will have to wait till the next half year now. It'll be useful then, but it won't do anything to alleviate your current problem, I'm afraid."

"No, it won't," Konis sighed. "You know, Sorli, I'm almost minded to resign from my position right now and let Kitra choose her Companion as a mate! Being told I'm shirking my responsibilities is beyond endurance."

"Appearances are what they go by, Konis. You and I know differently, but they don't want to see the larger picture. All they want is to be sure their own predictable lives aren't disrupted by strange new ideas. And you have to admit, they don't come stranger than these Links with the Humans."

Konis made a grumble of annoyed agreement.

"Tell me, Konis, how are our friends at Stronghold going to make themselves more available for potential mates? Have you discussed it with Father Lijou?"

"They can't. The nature of the Brotherhood is to be inconspicuous. It's more a matter of if one of the Brothers or Sisters wishes to bond with a telepath, they now have the legal right to do so."

"So they won't become part of the breeding program."

It was Konis' turn to smile. "You think so? I'd say that they have their own program, wouldn't you? How else could they ensure their gifts continued?"

"Possible, but I've never heard of cubs up at Stronghold." Sorli sounded skeptical.

"With villages nearby, there's no lack of foster families," pointed out Konis. "And what of Dzaka? He had a wife and child on Szurtha. I'll warrant there are more of them than we know. We're seeing only what they want us to see of their numbers."

Sorli looked acutely uncomfortable. "I hope you're not right."

"I'm speculating, Sorli," said Konis. "Think of them as a Clan, like our Warriors. We've never had any trouble from the Warrior Guild. The Brotherhood have never been a threat to Shola, the reverse in fact, and they've been around since the Cataclysm. Why should we suddenly fear Stronghold?"

"We won't always have leaders like Father Lijou and Master Rhyaz," murmured Sorli.

"Even when Ghezu was in power, they kept very much to themselves."

"True," he sighed. "Perhaps I worry too much."

"Nothing has happened to make us afraid of them, Sorli. I'm sorry I drew your attention to them. I really do think you are fretting needlessly."

"I'll take your word for it, Konis. After all, you've had more dealings with the Brothers than the Telepath Guild."

Konis picked up the slight innuendo but said nothing.

"What do you intend to do about Kitra?" asked Sorli, changing the subject.

"I've chosen a life-mate for her," he sighed. "Ashok Chazoun."

Sorli frowned, obviously trying to place him. "Wasn't he the one whose betrothed died a couple of years ago? Some aircar accident, if I remember. Very sad."

"That's the one," nodded Konis. "His family wanted him

to have time to get over the tragedy. They're in favor of the match."

"Surely he's a little old for her, Konis? He's nearing thirty now, if memory serves me. Twice her age. He's surely not going to be happy with a life-mate of Kitra's youth."

"He's younger than Dzaka, and they've agreed to an early marriage. Have you any idea how difficult it was for me to arrange this to suit our Council's time scale?" he said, anger creeping into his tone.

"I meant no criticism. It must be hard for you to be both Clan Lord and father in this matter. What about Rhyasha? Is she pleased with the match?"

"She'll have nothing to do with it, won't even discuss it with me. Neither will Kitra. I'm an outcast in my own home, Sorli," he said resignedly.

Sorli regarded him speculatively. "It's a pity Kaid is away. When do they return?"

"We've no word yet, I'm afraid, but then they aren't due to make contact for a day or two yet. Why?" The lie didn't trip easily from his tongue.

"As an Arrazo, Dzaka's from a telepath family on one side. With Kaid home, his father could tell the Council of his own Talent. Kitra would have a sound reason for requesting him as a life-mate."

Konis raised an eye ridge at him. "When did you find out about Kaid?" he asked quietly. "That information is classified, only known to a few within my son's Clan."

"I helped train him when I was at Stronghold. He's as gifted as any Level One telepath, and given his son is a powerful empath. . . ."

"How do you know that?" demanded Konis.

"I asked Father Lijou for his records," said Sorli.

"It makes no difference," said Konis brusquely. "Dzaka, like his father, is gene-altered, and the information on Kaid's telepath status can't be made public. The Council want a traditional mate for my daughter, one from the Clans. They'd never accept Dzaka."

"But he's En'Shalla, and they're a Clan now," Sorli reminded him.

"It makes no difference, I tell you!" Konis said harshly. "I cannot do anything! Don't you think I would if I could? Do you think I've learned nothing since Kusac arrived on

Shola with his alien Leska? Maybe if Dzaka, or Kaid if he were here, were to plead his cause with the Clan Leaders, they might agree to it, but Dzaka won't! I've gone into it from every angle, Sorli!"

"All of you have my sympathy, Konis. Kitra and Dzaka are so good for each other. I wish there was a way I could help them and you."

"Nothing short of a miracle will help them," muttered Konis, trying to keep his thoughts away from the missing U'Churian ship and her crew lest Sorli pick them up. "And it has to happen in the next three weeks!"

* * *

Kaid came to with a start. He could sense the alien presences immediately, and without thinking, reached mentally for them before even opening his eyes. Nothing. There was a blankness, a space where he should have sensed at least a living entity. No scent either. The only sounds he could hear were the slight ones caused by the movement of body armor. The Valtegans hadn't worn body armor.

He lay where he'd fallen, sprawled on the deck, aware of T'Chebbi still within his arms. She was awake and lying just as still. He remembered a klaxon, and a blinding light.

Slowly, he opened his eyes. Three soldiers were guarding the entrance to their hold. His eyes widened in shock as he took in the dark body armor and the slick faceplates on the helmets. The longer he attempted to look at them, the more difficult it was not to turn his head away. The sensation of nausea the sight of them generated didn't do much to help his dull headache.

He felt T'Chebbi's finger tapping his hand in Brotherhood code. *Do you see them?*

Yes, he replied. There was nothing to be gained by remaining where they were. He tapped T'Chebbi's wrist in warning and releasing her, began to sit up.

Looking slowly round the room, he saw nearly everyone was there, his own people included. Apart from the Cabbarans, the only ones missing were Rezac and Jo. Most of them were awake: only Taynar, Zashou, and Kate remained unconscious. Coincidence, or was he the first of the telepaths to wake? He tapped T'Chebbi's wrist again, asking her.

Affected telepaths for longer. Just woke myself.

Movements from his left made him look round to see Tirak sliding cautiously across the floor toward him.

"They've been standing there like that for the last half hour," he said quietly. "Don't know who they are. Never even heard of anyone remotely like them. Aren't strong on conversation, either."

The hold door slid open and they fell silent. A figure, wearing a gray tabard over the body armor, entered. Following him were three more guards and the priest, J'koshuk.

Gray-robe stopped a few meters into the hold. "This ship has been taken. It, and you, are now ours. You will accompany my guards to your new quarters. Attempt to escape and you will be shot. Disobey and you will be shot. Waken the sleepers. You leave now."

"So, the pirates have been outdone. At least this new lot are even-handed," murmured Tirak as they got to their feet.

Glad of the excuse to do something, Kaid and T'Chebbi began to rouse the sleeping telepaths.

"Wait!" Kaid called as he saw gray-robe turning to leave. "Our navigators and two of our number are missing! Where are they?"

The robed one didn't even acknowledge him.

"We think they're working their way through the ship," said Tirak. "That they haven't gotten to Jo, Rezac, or the Cabbarans yet. Jo and Rezac were also the only ones hurt."

"That priest knows, though," said Zashou, heading purposefully toward where J'koshuk stood with the guards.

"No," said Kaid, grabbing her. "Tirak's right. Now isn't the time. Later, when we know they haven't gone on ahead of us."

Zashou looked hopefully at him. "Do you think that's possible? Can you reach him?'

Kaid tried and shook his head. "Nothing."

One of the guards stepped forward, waving his weapon toward the exit. "We leave now," said his translator.

As they filed out of M'ezozakk's ship, they found themselves emerging into a large landing bay on a par with the main vehicle deck of the *Khalossa*. As they cleared the *M'ijikk*, to their left, beyond a wall of soldiers, they could see the *Profit* and numerous smaller craft. On their other side, M'ezozakk and his crew stood by an elevator under heavy guard. As they passed them, Taynar and Kate crowded closer to him for reassurance.

Can you feel it? Zashou sent to Kaid. *Can you feel the Valtegans?*

He could, and he had to strengthen his shields to block out the psychotic fear and hatred that they were projecting at the Sholans.

It's like an insanity, he sent. *It's universal with the ones in our time, a response they have no control over.*

A missile flew through the air toward them. Instinctively, Kaid pulled Zashou aside as the object, a metal belt buckle, was vaporized in midair by a vigilant guard.

Retribution was equally swift. The beams from ten rifles strafed the group of Valtegans, dropping them instantly to the deck, where they writhed and shrieked in agony.

"An object lesson to us all," said Tirak soberly as their guards urged them to proceed to the rear of the hangar where an elevator stood waiting for them.

There they were split into two groups, Tirak's party being taken up first. Kaid used the time to look back at the Valtegans. Those already on their feet again were being loaded into the elevator nearest the *M'ijikk*. The General was one of the first to be taken. Of the carmine-robed priest, there was no sign.

T'Chebbi dug him in the ribs. "The lift comes."

Herded on by their six guards, they'd barely time to turn around before the cage door clanged shut, closing them in. The smell of the air had changed, taken on an aseptic quality now that they'd moved beyond the stench of fuel and grease. Still no other scents—no sweat, no fear, nothing but the smells of his companions. He found that disturbing. The memory of their efforts to bring the first Valtegan captive to the *Khalossa* came sharply to mind. They'd made just such an effort to keep the ship free of their scents in order to prevent him from going catatonic with fear. But these people were doing nothing to allay their fears, quite the reverse in fact.

He forced himself to look at the guard opposite, keeping

his eyes away from the helmet. Taller than him by several inches, the guard's armored body appeared stocky. The legs were straight, unlike his, ending in flat, booted feet. Extra protection, circled by a utility belt, covered the groin and hips. Arms ended in four-digit opposable hands, encased, like the joints of the suit, in a flexible scale of the same dense black. As the lift began to slow, he moved his gaze up to the helmet.

Broad based, it seemed to grow out of the soldier's shoulders and chest, making sideways movement of the head seem at worst impossible, at best, awkward. A translator grille was placed where one would expect a mouth to be, with slight depressions that might be auditory pickups to either side. But it was the visor that fascinated and repelled him. Black, iridescent, it wrapped almost completely around the head, taking on a spectacle shape above the translator grille—and it was impossible to look at it without feeling his gorge rise. The moment he looked away, the nausea began to retreat. He realized there was no lack of mobility and vision within that helmet, and no compromise on safety either.

Beyond the guard, Kaid could see Tirak's group waiting. The soldier he'd been studying turned aside to unlatch the gate and hold it open for them to leave. The aseptic smell was far more pungent now.

Zashou clutched at Kaid's arm. "Antiseptics! Do you think they've found Rezac and Jo? Could they be treating them?" There was hope in her eyes.

"Possibly," he said as they were led through a small door to their right into a corridor. He was only partly listening to her, his attention was focused on their surroundings, trying to find any point of reference to give him a clue as to the nature of their captors, and memorizing their route.

The corridor was long and featureless with an automatically triggered air lock every hundred meters. They passed only one door on his right, but several on the left. The lack of doors made him think it likely that the medical area backed onto this corridor. Darker patches on the right-hand doors showed that signs had recently been removed—for their benefit.

Lighting was slightly more subdued than they were used

to, but the walls and the floor covering were blandly utilitarian in color.

Tirak slowed down, falling back a little to join him. "Could these be the people the Valtegans are fighting?" he asked quietly. "Their treatment of us is almost hospitable by comparison."

Kaid grunted noncommittally, glancing around him as they came to a junction and rounded the corner to their right. A couple of hundred meters away, a closed air lock cut off his view. They were isolated from the rest of the ship. No risks were being taken with them. Before he could reply, the leading guard halted at an open doorway and gestured them in. Slumped in a padded chair was a very subdued Rezac, his neck and wrists encased in bandages. He stirred as they entered, hands gripping the chair arms, but he didn't look up.

Kaid pushed through the others as they clustered just inside the doorway, reluctant to go any farther into the room. "T'Chebbi, check the place out," he ordered, gesturing at their new quarters as he made straight for Rezac.

"Help her," said Tirak to his crew. "Rest of you stay here."

"You were right, Kaid. I blew it," Rezac said, his voice hoarse and low. The effort of talking was obviously costing him dearly. "I've risked my whole Triad. Sorry, Zashou." His voice tailed off. Then, "Is Jo with you?"

"No. We'd hoped she was here by now," said Kaid as he squatted down in front of him. "You were afraid for her," he said quietly. "It's understandable, given her past history with M'ezozakk." Behind them, the door slid shut and he could hear T'Chebbi organizing the search.

"You don't understand, Jo was in the hold with me at the end," Rezac said, finally looking up at him.

Kaid winced when he saw the state of his father's face. Sealant glistened on cuts across swollen eye ridges and cheeks, dried blood matted his hair and pelt, stained his clothing. Anger rose in Kaid, and a surge of protectiveness that shocked him. He reached out, touching gentle fingertips to his father's neck in compassion. "He did a good job on you."

Rezac flinched away from him, a strange look in his eyes. Zashou was not so restrained. Crying out, she rushed over to them, jolting the chair in her distress, making Rezac moan.

Kaid fended away her questing hands, capturing them in his. "He's been treated, Zashou. He'll recover. It looks worse than it is."

"When a Valtegan bites a female," Rezac continued doggedly, licking his cracked lips, "his teeth inject something like a poison. It changes them, makes them violent toward any other male. They use it on their females to ensure they won't mate with anyone else. And there's only one way to neutralize the poison."

A strangled cry made them turn round. The door had obviously opened again as Tirak had J'koshuk by the arm. "He knows where Jo is, don't you, Priest?"

"I don't know where she is!" the Valtegan said, spilling the bundle of clothing he'd been carrying. "It's as the Sholan said, she was in the hold with me before they came."

Kaid rose and in one fluid move, pushed Tirak aside and grasped J'koshuk by the throat.

"Why? Why did M'ezozakk send her back?"

But it was Rezac who answered. "It went wrong. M'ezozakk's bite really poisoned her. He sent her back to kill me when the priest had finished. She's dying, Kaid. I need to see her before . . ." He stopped, unable to go on.

The noise had brought three guards into the room, rifles leveled at them. "Release the Interface," one ordered. "He is not to be touched."

"Where is the female?" demanded Kaid, advancing toward them, dragging J'koshuk with him by the throat. "We know she's dying. He has a right to see her before she does!"

"Release the Interface," repeated the guard, powering his gun up.

Abruptly, Kaid released the priest, taking a step back. "He's free. Just bring us the female. She has a right to die with her own people."

The lead guard hesitated as J'koshuk ducked between the other two and scuttled from the room. "She will be returned presently," he said, stepping back as the door slid closed.

Kaid ran to the door but it was already locked. "Dammit!" he snarled, pounding it with his fist. His decision to surrender was costing them all too much. First Tesha's life, now Jo's. What would her death do to Rezac and Zashou? And what of his Triad, of Carrie and Kusac? He rested his head against the surface. Nothing had been gained, and their prospects were even worse now than they'd been with the Valtegans.

He felt a hand on his shoulder, smelled T'Chebbi's scent. "This caring, it hurts too much," he whispered, clenching his fists in helpless frustration.

"I know." She tightened her hand on his shoulder. "But we got work to do." Bending down, she began to pick up the scattered garments that the priest had been holding.

The suite turned out to have five sleeping rooms off the main gathering area. Showers and toilet facilities were adjacent to the inner rooms. Heavy carpets covered the floors and each bedroom was equipped with several deep sleeping pads and blankets.

"Obviously they like living close," observed Giyesh as she and Jeran returned to the lounge.

"Not necessarily. They could sleep in shifts," said Sheeowl.

Kaid had just finished searching the sanitary facilities when Rezac called him over.

"You didn't ask me what I told them," he said quietly as Kaid squatted in front of him again.

"I didn't need to," replied Kaid. "You told them as little as possible. I knew you wouldn't let us, or yourself, down."

"Not a second time."

Kaid rested his hand on Rezac's leg. "Were our positions reversed, I can't swear I wouldn't have reacted the same way." He tightened his grip briefly before moving away. "Try and rest for now."

"Is clean," said T'Chebbi, coming over to join him. She'd been checking the main room and was the last to finish. "Getting beaten up like that must be a family trait," she said quietly to him. "Haven't seen anything so bad since we got you back from Ghezu and Dzaka got worked over on the estate because of Kitra."

Kaid shot her a fulminating look before sitting down on the nearest couch. "Short of dismantling the lighting units and the air-conditioning, there are no surveillance devices to be found," he said to Tirak.

"Big change from the cargo hold," said Giyesh. "I think they were expecting us. They knew exactly how many of us there are because the number of beds matches. Apart from the Cabbarans."

"Still prisoners. Door is sealed, we can't leave," reminded T'Chebbi, finding herself a seat.

"Impressions of our hosts?" asked Kaid, looking around the room as people began to settle on the chairs and couches.

"Their suits aren't atmospheric," said Mrowbay. "They aren't fitted with breathing tanks, and the air's enough like what we breathe to rule that out."

"Their translator spoke Sholan," said Jeran, taking a seat beside Giyesh.

"I noticed that," said Zashou, returning from fetching a drink of water for Rezac from one of the bathing rooms. "Why our language when there are as many U'Churians? Seems very odd."

"Everything about this is odd," said Tirak.

"Could any of you look at their helmets without feeling sick, or was it just me?" asked Kate, sitting on a hard chair at the long dining table.

"Not you," said T'Chebbi positively. "I felt it too."

"I wonder if that's a side effect or the purpose of the visors," said Kaid. "The suits are certainly combat worthy. We could learn a lesson or two from them."

"The helmet's ingenious," said Manesh. "Won't help us if we jump one of them, though. Be like trying to open a steel can with no opener or knife."

"Primes, the priest called them," said Rezac. "Seniormost, the one in gray." He stopped, catching his breath in obvious pain. "J'koshuk, the priest, he helped the medic that treated me. They have collars that inflict pain. He wears one. If we don't obey, they'll put them on us." He paused again. "He was told to warn us."

"Well, now we see their claws," said Tirak.

Kaid noticed Zashou put her hand up instinctively to her neck. "They haven't collared us yet," he said reassuringly.

"There's no food dispenser, no water apart from in the

sanitary facilities," said Taynar morosely. "I hope they plan to feed us."

"No nibbles," agreed Mrowbay sorrowfully.

This lightened the air a little, making them all smile.

"No scent, no mental presence. It's as if they aren't there," said Kaid. "Are they actually alive?"

"You mean artificial beings?" Tirak asked thoughtfully. "It's possible. They call that Valtegan their interface. I don't know how they managed to take us captive, but their technology is certainly more advanced than ours."

"And ours," agreed Kaid.

"They were expecting us," repeated Giyesh. "Even down to the number of beds. Sixteen."

"Strange beds. Like beanbags back on Keiss," said Kate. "And the furniture, it's like ours, not for people with tails like you."

"You can tell that by looking at their suits," said Tallis scathingly.

"Not necessarily. They could have them tucked down one leg or have short tails! What're your space suits like?"

Kaid couldn't stop his mouth opening in a slight grin. "She's got you there, Tallis."

"Some of our soldiers have their tails amputated as a mark of their dedication," said Tirak.

All the Sholan stared at him in horror, but it was Zashou who spoke. "How could they cut off a limb?"

"Eh?" Tirak looked confused. "You use your tails?"

"For balance, and more," said Jeran. "We still hunt on fours, don't you?"

"Wrong shape of legs," said Giyesh, patting him on the thigh, grinning ingenuously and flicking her ears. "We came from trees, not the plains like you."

Kaid caught a faint sound from outside. "Quiet," he warned, getting to his feet as the door began to slide back, admitting two guards. They stood, one to each side of the doorway, covering their group with rifles as a floating stretcher was brought in. Following it was a shorter figure in the gray tabard.

"Your companion is returned," it said. "She will need caring for."

Kaid moved quickly over to the floater. "How long?" he asked.

"She will recover in a few days. The poison was very advanced. It will take some time to clear from her system, but she and the child will survive. Her medication is here." He gestured to one of the guards and Kaid was handed a pack containing several ampoules and a pressure hypo. "Give her a dose every thirteen hours."

"Recover?" echoed Kaid.

"Child?" said Rezac, trying to get up.

"You must remove her from the floater," continued the mechanical voice. "She needs rest. We would have wished to keep her longer, but it was decided the distress it caused her injured mate would not aid his recovery."

"Put her here," said Jeran, moving the low table so the way to the hurriedly vacated couch was clear.

Throwing the pack to T'Chebbi, Kaid gently lifted the unconscious Jo and carried her to the couch, laying her carefully down.

"The rest of my crew, where are they?" asked Tirak.

"They are housed nearby. Do not concern yourself. Food will be brought shortly by our interface. You will not harm him again or punishment for all will follow. Is this understood?"

"We understand all right," said T'Chebbi with a growl as the soldiers and their leader left.

Rezac was trying to stumble over to the couch. Seeing him, Kaid held out a supporting arm, helping him sit down beside her. She lay still, her face pale against the silver blanket in which she was wrapped. One arm, a cannula and drug pack attached, was draped across her chest. Her hair was damp and she was wearing clean clothing.

Kaid moved back, gesturing to the others to give them some privacy. He hadn't realized she was pregnant, but he should have expected it, given their new Link. Equally obviously, it had been news to Rezac. Another complication to add to the many they faced. At least she and the cub would live. This was what she'd been concealing from him on the *Profit*.

As Rezac's hand closed on Jo's, she began to stir.

"Jo," was all he could say.

Her eyes flickered open and she frowned, trying to focus on him. "Rezac?"

"Here. How do you feel?"

"Better, but not good," she said, turning her head to look around her. "Kaid. We're all here?"

"All," he said.

She nodded, looking back to Rezac. "You're hurt," she said, puling her hand away from his to reach up and touch his face.

He winced and she looked again at his hand. "Oh, Rezac, what did he do to you?" she asked, her voice barely a whisper.

"It's nothing, my own fault," he said. "I shouldn't have called out like I did, but I couldn't let him bite you."

A look of panic crossed her face. "The bite! I'll turn on you, Rezac, on all of you! He told me I would! You're not safe with me here!" She began to move, trying to sit up.

"No, not now," he said, leaning forward slightly to cup her face in his hand. "They've reversed it, Jo. You're going to be all right, believe me."

T'Chebbi was handing out the fresh clothing J'koshuk had brought. She came over to Kaid with his. "They knew she's pregnant by Rezac," she whispered.

He nodded, putting his finger to his lips. "Later," he mouthed.

Kaid carried Jo into the middle sleeping room, placing her carefully in one of the strange beds, pulling another over for Rezac and seeing him bedded down beside her, then he left them alone.

"Why didn't you tell me you're carrying our cub?" Rezac asked, his hand caressing her face. "He'll be fine," he hurriedly assured her. "They said he was fine."

"He?" she asked, holding his other hand carefully.

He blinked, realizing that he'd given a sex to their child. "You said he."

"I just sense it," he said. "Why did you keep this to yourself? Are you ashamed? Do you wish you hadn't conceived?" He tried to keep his voice even, not let her hear his concern.

"No, Rezac, never that. I would have told you when we reached safety. I was just so afraid for us, and for . . . him."

He nodded. That he could understand. Had he known she was pregnant, his fears for her would have been even worse. Leaning forward, he gently licked her cheek, changing it to a kiss when she turned her face to meet his.

I love you, he sent, wincing as he hurt his bruised face on hers.

What will become of us, Rezac? Soon I'll be in no state to escape, even if we get the chance. How can we bring a child into this captivity?

I don't know, Jo, but we're together, among friends. We'll survive, never doubt that!

"The bite went wrong because she was pregnant," said Zashou, joining T'Chebbi at the dining table. "It's a miracle they were able to reverse it. Gods, what a mess!" She pushed a hand through her blonde braids. "Pregnant and captive. She must be terrified."

"How do you feel about it Zashou?" asked T'Chebbi. "Can you cope, having lost your own cub so recently?"

"My cub was born dead, malformed because of the laalquoi in our food on Jalna. It should never have been conceived," she said. "Jo's good for Rezac in a way I could never be." She sighed, looking down at her hands, examining the claw tips. "We were ill-fated from the start. I wish he'd met her before me."

T'Chebbi snorted derisively. "Liar! You love him as much, you just refuse to admit it to anyone, even yourself."

Zashou's ears laid back angrily. "You've no right to say that!"

"Is truth. I feel it. Why not admit it?"

"He has Jo now," she said stiffly.

"Needs you both. Loves you both as much," T'Chebbi said quietly.

"How would you know?" she demanded.

"I'm at the edge of a Triad. I don't even have as much as you."

"And Kaid's besotted with Carrie," snapped back Zashou. "Have you no pride?"

"More than you. I admit my need, and I know Kaid needs me as much as her. Don't be a fool, Zashou. Not too late to tell him how you feel. No disgrace to do it even now. Our situation similar, only Kaid met Carrie before me."

"You were at the Brotherhood together before she even met Kusac! Or was it when he went back in time?"

"He saw her in visions from the God," said T'Chebbi, breaking eye contact. "Rezac's not beneath you. His family is as good as yours."

"You don't know anything about him!" she said angrily. "You and Kaid are equals! It was never that way between us!"

"You sold yourself to keep the family going—married money," pointed out T'Chebbi. "Rezac has too much pride to do that."

Zashou began to growl low in her throat. "Why are you so damned concerned about Rezac? What's it to you? Unless," she stopped, ears pricking forward. "Unless you know something I don't know about Rezac. Is Kaid his father? Is that what happened when they went back in time?"

T'Chebbi looked up, catching sight of Tallis hovering nearby, realizing she'd said too much. She forced a laugh. "They didn't go back that far. Arrived only days before your rebellion struck, told you that already." She got to her feet. "Look at the size of our prison, Zashou. We got to get along. We don't need you and Rezac fighting all the time. Sort yourself out now. Come to terms with what happened. Gods, it's been how long? Two years at least!"

"I had a life before him, T'Chebbi! A husband, a family . . ." she began.

T'Chebbi leaned forward till her nose almost touched the other female's. "Had Valtegan overlords! Had living in fear as a telepath! You blame Rezac for troubles he didn't cause!" She pulled back and stalked off to the other side of the room where Kaid and Tirak sat deep in conversation.

The damage had been done, though, and as she tumbled ideas over in her head, Zashou wondered if they'd gone back twice because they got it wrong the first time. A shadow fell across her and she realized Tallis had settled down opposite her.

"It must have been a shock for you, that news about Jo," he said, his tone ingratiating. "Now everyone's rallying round them, just because they got injured through their own stupidity. They're making you look like the jealous one. You have my sympathy, Zashou."

She couldn't believe she was hearing this! How dared he say that! She spat a few choice swear words at him, then told him to remove himself before she saw him off. With extreme satisfaction, she watched his ears flatten backward in acute embarrassment as he slid from the seat and beat a retreat to the other, smaller table.

Then she stopped smiling as she realized that if someone like him was scenting her vulnerability, then her relationship with Rezac was a matter for common gossip. T'Chebbi was right. In this close a community, there were no secrets, and if she didn't want to remain an object of ridicule, she'd have to rectify it now. She slid her head down onto the tabletop, resting it on her forearms. Why had it gone wrong? T'Chebbi had been right again, she had liked Rezac at the start. Even *he* knew that because she couldn't hide it from him on their Link days. If only it hadn't been for their damned Link, they might have had a chance at a lasting relationship. She'd never loved Shanka Valsgarth, her husband. It had been nothing more than a marriage of convenience. His money for her family's social position.

She felt a hand on her shoulder and turned her head to see Kaid.

"Would you like to go and lie down?" he asked. "Tirak and I've been allocating rooms. We put you in the inner one on the right with Manesh and Mrowbay. Thought you'd be happier with some female company at least. We need to keep the middle room free for those with Link days." He hesitated, eyes darkening briefly in a pain she could feel at the memories the phrase engendered. "Jo and Rezac are in there just now. We have two days before Kate and Taynar need it. We'll have space in our room then. I'll leave it up to you three to decide who sleeps where."

"Why are you so protective of him, Kaid?" she asked, too emotionally and physically exhausted to care any more. "Are you his father? Did you go back too soon?"

Kaid looked startled. "Of course not. What gave you that idea?"

"You're so alike. Jo noticed it."

"You've got an active imagination," he said, moving away.

She watched him as he walked back to the table. There was something about him, something in the way he moved, held himself, that reminded her so strongly of Rezac—but she was too tired to think it through. Sleep sounded like a wonderful idea. She pushed herself up from the table and made her way through to the room she'd been allocated.

Lifting off the folded cover first, she flopped down into the giant pillow-shaped bed. Almost instantly, it molded itself to her shape with a fluidity that was quite unnerving. And it was warm against her pelt, almost as if it was alive. She was too damned tired to even care if it ate her while she slept. At least she'd know nothing about it and it would mean an end to her troubles.

* * *

J'koshuk stood at the back of the room watching the wide screen. He had to peer around the group of three gray-robed figures, but he could see enough to know he wanted to remain where he was, at the back, and hopefully inconspicuous. They were watching the crew of the *M'ijikk*. They had been placed in a large, sparsely furnished open room. A dozen tables and benches were all the comforts they had. At one end, a partition had just been drawn back, revealing the cages of their food animals. The doors were triggered open and the terrified animals leaped out and scattered among the Valtegans.

After the initial stunned reaction, chaos quickly followed as people dived in every direction in an effort to catch them. J'koshuk groaned inwardly as he watched the partition close, preventing them from recaging the creatures. Didn't the Primes realize what they were doing? The presence of the Sholans had set everyone's aggression level sky high, then they'd been taken captive without the opportunity to retaliate. Now this. It wouldn't be long before so much fresh blood and raw meat would send his people over the edge. Then they'd turn on each other.

A calmness descended on him as he realized the Primes knew exactly what they were doing. What better way to reduce the number of captives and make sure those they retained were the best of their kind? One island of relative calm remained; those surrounding the general.

It was silent—neither the robed ones nor the guards were communicating verbally between themselves in a way he could hear, and no sound penetrated from the room beyond. It was a stark contrast to the scene they were watching and sent a chill through him.

A hand closed on his arm and he yelped in shock. It was the guard beside him. Silently he followed one of the gray ones out into the corridor, then into a room opposite.

"These are your quarters. When you are not required, you will stay here. Your collar monitors your movements at all times. When we need you, there will be a pulse against your neck like this."

Against his throat, he felt a sudden firm pressure that was gone almost instantly.

"The door will be opened and you will be able to leave. You will come to the room we just left. Do you understand?"

"Yes."

"If you prove dependable and worthy of trust, you will be allowed the freedom to leave this room when you finish performing your daily tasks. If you transgress, you will be punished and your freedom revoked. Should you transgress a second time, you will join the next culling. Is that understood?"

"Yes," he croaked, his mouth suddenly dry with fear.

"A nourishment unit is supplied. You will eat and drink what is provided. There will be no more raw food. This is a designated rest period. You will eat and sleep for the next ten hours." With that, he was left alone, the door sealed and locked.

The suite was large, meant for six if the number of bed units was an accurate guide. There were two main rooms—a lounging area and the sleeping one, as well as bathing facilities. He found a small pile of leisure items—games and reading material—from the *M'ijikk* in one of the beds, and a change of his own clothing. He'd been expected, like the Sholans.

His stomach growled, reminding him it was many hours since he'd last eaten, and he went to investigate the nourishment unit. He'd gone beyond fear now, and was working on autopilot.

The unit had been relabeled in his own language, just as when he'd been alone with them, his captors had communicated with him in Valtegan. The food, however, was alien and cooked, and included items labeled: *Meat with green plants; Meat with liquid and green plants 1; sweet, sweet with liquid 1.* Drinks were no better. He chose meat without liquid and a drink of plain water.

The food arrived hot and steaming gently. The smell turned his stomach, but mindful of the warning of his host, he took it over to the table and began to cut it up with the provided cutlery. The knife was so soft that it barely sliced through the meat and the pronged thing he gave up on, using his fingers instead. At least the meat was still pink inside and hadn't been cooked all the way through.

It lay in his stomach like an inert lump, making him feel bloated and uncomfortable. The water did little to help digest it and he got up to investigate the unit again. Perhaps there was something listed that would ease his discomfort. He staggered a little, catching hold of a chair back to keep his balance. He felt weak. This cooked food just didn't agree with him.

Trial and error produced a brew that though warm, had a vaguely familiar taste to it. As the warmth spread through him, it began to ease the pain in his belly. He headed toward one of the padded chairs this time, lowering himself into it with relief. Eating cooked food might give him a pain in the gut, but if it kept him from the culling he'd just witnessed, then it was a small price to pay. He took a large mouthful of the drink, his thoughts turning to Mzayb'ik, wondering how he'd fared. Had he been one of those who'd stood by the general? Likely. Mzayb'ik wasn't a true opportunist like him. He had too much of a sense of loyalty, which got you nowhere at the end of the day. Lifting the small bowl, J'koshuk took another sip of what he assumed was an herbal tea, then rested his head against the back of the chair and yawned. All he had to do was follow their rules—for now at least. There had to be a chance for advancement if the Primes intended to keep them all captive. Whatever their ultimate purpose and destination, he would do well to be indispensable long before they arrived at it. It was what his caste were best at, after all. Surviving.

*   *   *

"The Cabbarans won't like this," said Sheeowl, pushing her food about her plate with the bendable fork. "It's mostly meat, and half raw!"

"They'll like the vegetables, though," said Giyesh. "Nice and crunchy."

"Mine's all right," said Kate. "You need to change the settings, that's all. I put them on high and the meat's cooked right through."

"Could be worse, could be raw meat," observed T'Chebbi, munching contentedly on her meal. "Wonder what they gave the Valtegans."

"You realize that the food could be drugged," said Tirak, eyeing a chunk of meat he'd finally managed to impale on his fork.

Kaid had already finished. "I know," he said. "That's why I'm not eating much and only drinking water from the faucet. Even if it is, we don't exactly have an option, but we'll have an idea of what it does."

"At least they gave us our own food and drink replicator," said Jeran.

"I think I'll follow your example," said Tirak, pushing his half finished meal aside.

"Nothing is free. It's the price they'll ask for all this that worries me," muttered Tallis.

"There's no point in worrying about that now," said Tirak, getting up from the table. "I'm convinced that these are the Valtegans' enemy. Kaid, a word if you will."

Kaid joined him on the couch farthest from the others.

"We need to work together on this. My priority is escaping. What's yours?" asked Tirak.

"The same, or getting a message out to my people telling them what happened."

Tirak nodded. "So far, so good. Have you any thoughts on how we'll accomplish this?"

"None yet. We're not far from the flight deck, that's a plus. The corridors were deserted but we don't know where in their daily cycle we are. It could be their night for all we know."

"It might have been deserted, but you can be sure they've got us and the corridors under surveillance. They know too damned much about us for my liking."

"I wonder if they found out about us before they took the *M'ijikk*, or after. They could have been pacing it, waiting for an opportunity to attack."

"Some attack! Not a shot fired, we were all out cold on

the deck!" snorted Tirak. "They must have been on top of us by the time that alarm went off. Why didn't M'ezozakk spot it? Not much you can do to defend yourself against that type of technology. And how the hell did they get our craft into their hangar?"

"Possibly some kind of beam, maybe magnetic. We've certainly nothing like it. If we do get back to your ship, we'll have that to contend with when we try to escape. But our first step is to get out of these rooms, and stay out long enough to board the *Profit.* For that we need some of those suits, enough of them to look like a party of guards escorting the prisoners."

"They wouldn't be taking them back down to the flight deck."

"Perhaps they want information from the ship's computer, or if I'm right and the elevator's next to their sick bay, maybe they're escorting them there for a medical."

"Rezac had medical attention. Perhaps he remembers where he was taken," Tirak observed. "Jo's unlikely to have been aware of anything much."

Kaid shook his head. "He said something about a medic treating him in the hold. I don't think he'll be able to tell us much."

"Worth a try. So for now, we observe."

"We observe their routines, listen to noise levels outside, and look for opportunities to escape. We let them relax, think we're afraid to try anything. One day, they're bound to make that one slip of attention that'll give us our opportunity to escape."

"Agreed. Tell me, Kaid. Why d'you launch the cryo units?"

"M'ezozakk would have recognized them from Keiss," he said. "It was their best chance for survival."

"And now? Will you tell these aliens they're out there?"

"I can't. We don't know how safe we are. At least out there, they have a good chance of getting picked up by our people when they come looking for us."

"Let's hope you're right," said Tirak, getting up.

Kaid leaned against the back of the seat and closed his eyes. He wanted to sleep, to forget the happenings of the past few hours for a little time at least.

* * *

Brynne had been told to report to Vartra's Retreat when his Link day with Vanna was over. He was discovering it was quite different from Stronghold. Its emphasis was on the religious side and though there was a gym, it was not part of his schedule. He was taking a private condensed course on the cults of Vartra and Ghyakulla and religious meditation techniques. Interesting as it was, it had more of the feel of history lessons about it than anything else.

His time was divided between there and Stronghold, where the physical side of his training continued, mainly with Jurrel as a tutor and sparring partner. His meetings with Kha'Qwa were part of his schedule, but as to what their purpose was, he wasn't certain. Discussions on social studies and current events were mainly what they talked about. But he did enjoy his visits with her.

The need for Link days with Vanna was diminishing as her pregnancy advanced, so he was free to stay longer. This, coupled with the fact that it was difficult for him to remain isolated from the Sholan community because it was all there was, meant he was having to make the effort to fit in for the first time.

"Is this actually a religious establishment?" he asked of Jurrel as they made their way from the refectory to one of the smaller common rooms.

Jurrel gave him a curious look. "Tell me how you think it should be," he said.

"I always associated retreats with people getting away from it, taking a break from the outside world—no comm units, no broadcasts and newsvids, just peace and quiet and prayer.

"We have that, but of course," he said with a slow, open-mouthed smile, "we don't disturb them."

"What about the priests or priestesses coming here to shut out the outside world totally and just pray or study?"

"There are those," Jurrel agreed. "But they tend to live at shrines and come here only for study. We have a wonderful library of ancient texts and prophecies."

"What about the self-denial? The living in poverty, working the land, and so on?"

"Oh, we have people who do that, too, but not in our Order unless they've retired. The Brotherhood dues you pay also go to the upkeep of land where we can retire when we're no longer able for active service either as a priest or a warrior. Remember, Brynne, that Vartra is a God of Warriors, too. As for asceticism, why not enjoy good food? One can always fast if need be." He stopped, holding Brynne back at the door to the lounge. "It would be easier for you if you stopped trying to find a Terran comparison for everything when one doesn't always exist. Just be one with us, enjoy our world." He let him go and pushed the door open. "And our good food," he grinned, mouth opening widely.

The beast was exhausted, they'd have to make a stop. Clenching his fists in the crest of hair down its spine, he jerked back sharply, causing it to lift its neck and snort. Its headlong flight began to slow gradually and by the time it was walking, sides heaving and sweating, he was able to bring it to a halt. Sliding down, he kept one hand firmly wound in the mane.

Leaning heavily on his mount, he continued limping toward the distant mountains. There hadn't been any sign of pursuit yet. The false trail he'd cast must have worked. Now it was time to find a safe place for them to hide out for a day or two so he could rest up and let his wounds heal a little more.

He winced as his foot turned on a stone, pulling at the swelling on his leg. He'd have to clean it again when they stopped. No matter what he did, he just couldn't seem to get out all the poison. A couple of days and it was as bad as before. Worse, if he was being honest with himself. The swelling kept growing larger and his fever was barely kept in check by the plants he'd eaten and chewed up to use as a poultice. Living rough and having to be constantly on the move didn't help at all.

Water wasn't far off, he could smell it now. Having grown up in the city, he knew nothing about herbs and plants, but somehow he'd known instinctively what to look for. He tried to think of home, but it sent a sharp pain through his head. Shaking it, he stumbled on. Didn't do to think about the past. The future mattered now, getting up into the mountains so he could find that place he kept seeing in his dreams. The place with the sweet smelling tree.

He'd have to hunt for food for both of them. The beast was so domesticated it wouldn't know how to go about finding prey in the wild. Suddenly he found himself falling as a root grabbed at his foot. The ground rushed up to meet him, knocking the breath from his lungs as he measured his length. How long he lay there, he'd no idea but gradually was aware of the beast tugging at his hair, lipping at his face with a tongue that felt like a piece of thick, wet sandpaper.

"Yeah, I'm awake again," he mumbled, trying to push himself up, but he was too weak to stand this time. He lay there, smelling the dampness in the soil, feeling the chill air on his pelt, wondering if he'd finally reached the end of his endurance. The beast snorted and nosed something wet and bloody into his face.

"What the . . ." He put out a hand to investigate and found the carcass of a fish. He began to laugh.

He was being shaken quite forcefully, Brynne realized as he surfaced from sleep. "What the hell are you doing?" he mumbled, flailing at the hands. "Get off me, Jurrel!"

The shaking stopped and he pushed himself up from the tangle of soaking sheets. His hair was plastered damply across his face and eyes. Reaching up, he pushed it aside then scrubbed at his beard and mustache. Jurrel was squatting on the bed near his feet.

"Woke you again, huh? Sorry," he mumbled, beginning to unwrap himself from his damp bedding. "What was I doing this time?"

"Laughing. Don't tell me, you were watching performing jeggets," said Jurrel dryly. "I think you owe me a decent explanation this time, Brynne. And don't tell me you just saw animals because I don't believe you!"

"I told you, it's nothing," he said, getting up and heading for the bathing room.

Jurrel launched himself off the bed, grabbing him by the arm. Brynne pulled away angrily. "Don't touch me!" he said, his voice almost a snarl. "I'm a telepath, I can't stand to be touched when this happens!"

Jurrel took a step backward, hands held outstretched to show he meant no threat. "Brynne, you have to talk about it. You can't let this keep on happening without telling someone! You need help."

"I need a shower," Brynne retorted, continuing into the bathing room. He stepped into the cubicle and turned on the water. He wanted to be left alone, nothing more, but Jurrel always stuck with him like he'd been glued on. *They* might be afraid something would happen to him during one of these visions, but each one scared the crap out of him.

Sighing, he reached out for the container of soap. It wasn't there. Dashing the water from his eyes, he continued to fumble on the small shelf where it usually lived.

"I have it," said Jurrel quietly from behind him. "I left it out when I showered earlier. Would you like me to help? If you won't talk, then perhaps I can relax you by washing you."

Human reactions fought with Sholan ones as, water sluicing down his body, he stared at Jurrel. He didn't know how to respond. He'd shared showers before, but not with males of either species—not this intimately. He snatched the bottle from Jurrel's hand. "I'll do it myself," he snapped, turning his back pointedly on him as his world suddenly exploded into a room of blinding lights, white tiles, pain, and someone else's absolute terror.

His head hurt and when he tried to move, he felt sick.

"Be still," said Jurrel's calm voice from beside his ear. "You fell and hit your head."

"My side," he mumbled, trying to move his hand down to feel himself. "I hurt it, too."

"Your side is fine. I caught you. You hit your head on the wall as you fell."

"Must see," he said, forcing his head off the tiled floor. The room swayed and spun around him and he had to swallow hard to stop himself from throwing up. He felt himself being supported into a sitting position.

"You're as obstinate as any Sholan," Jurrel complained, wrapping a towel around his shoulders as Brynne looked down at his side.

"Nothing!" he said in shock, pulling at his naked flesh. "Not a mark!"

"I did tell you," his companion said quietly, beginning to rub him gently with the towel.

"I felt it, Jurrel—a burning pain in my side, just over the ribs." He looked up at him, confused.

"What did you see?"

"A room, lights and—tiles," he said, glancing down at the tiled floor beneath him.

"Visions are strange things. Some are just snatches of scenes you never see any more of, some are events that might be happening, or might be to come in the future. Sometimes you never know what they are," he said, putting a hand under Brynne's chin and turning his face so he could look into his eyes. "Follow my finger."

Shivering, he did as he was asked, then clutched the large towel closer. Jurrel got up and went for another.

"You've got a mild concussion, no more. We have people who know how to make sense of visions. If you'll tell no one what you see, how can we help you?"

"What is it with this world? This kind of thing doesn't happen back on Earth," he said as Jurrel helped him stand. Nausea swept through him again and he had to clutch at the Sholan to stop himself from falling over.

"How do you know? Until we came, your people didn't even believe in telepathy and your gift was considered a freak and unstable," he said calmly, leading him back through to the bedroom and sitting him down on his own bed.

Leaving him there, he went for Brynne's toweling robe and helped him into it, tying the belt round his waist before pulling the covers over him.

"I'm going to fetch fresh sheets," he said, turning to leave.

"It's a journey," said Brynne, lying back against the pillows that smelled acutely of damp Jurrel. "I'm seeing someone on a journey."

Jurrel squatted down on the floor beside him. "Who? Do you know who it is?"

"No. In the dreams it's always happening to me."

"Can you tell where you're going?"

"There was forest at first, now it's plains. I always travel at night to avoid being caught. I had a riding beast this time."

"Is it sequential? Do you pick up where you leave off?"

"No. I've traveled in between each dream. In this one I'd stolen the beast perhaps the day before. I'm injured, I know that."

"In the side?"

"Yes, but the worst one is on my leg. I have a fever."

"Can you recognize any of the landscape?"

Brynne began to shake his head then moaned as he regretted it. Jurrel reached out to touch his forehead, brushing aside the forelock that had fallen across his eyes.

"No, I can't, but then I've not traveled much around Shola on foot. I'm Sholan," he added, his eyes catching Jurrel's. "That much I'm sure of. But the pain in my side had nothing to do with that, I know it didn't. That's something completely different."

Jurrel's hand stroked his forehead again. "It could be a vision of when this traveler finally gets the medical help he needs. Maybe he's reaching out mentally and you're picking it up."

"I don't know, Jurrel. I just wish the visions would stop," he said tiredly, closing his eyes. "I can't go on like this. I'm a danger to myself." He was remembering other dreams he'd had, about being cold and floating in an empty darkness.

"That's why I'm here," said Jurrel quietly, continuing to stroke his forehead and smooth his wet hair away from his face. "We'll go and see Guardian Dhaika tomorrow and tell him about this."

The touch was soothing, made the nausea retreat. Right now he didn't care that the hand was male, just that it was comforting. Sholan males were something of an enigma to him anyway, lacking some of the masculine qualities he was used to, yet having the gracefulness he associated with femininity. Some of them sent out all the wrong signals, as if they were a third, as yet uncharted sex all of their own.

"There are more," he said, beginning to relax under Jurrel's touch. "The room I saw was part of them, but they don't make sense. Fear, there's always a sense of fear. I don't want to go to Dhaika yet. I haven't enough to tell him that sounds believable."

"It's your choice, but please, keep talking to me about them. There's no need to shut everyone out. Between us we might discover what they mean. You've not had an easy time since you came to Shola. First a Leska Link, then these visions. It must have been incredibly lonely. You need friends, people you can turn to. I can be here for you if you wish."

"What's your Talent, then?" he murmured, noticing the stroking had stopped. He was relieved to be able to talk to someone at last about the dreams, someone who wasn't going to ridicule him. "Empathy?"

"Among other things," Jurrel agreed, getting to his feet.

* * *

Rhyaz sat down on the chair beside Lijou's desk. "The *Rhijissoh*'s reached Jalna," he said.

Lijou looked up from his work. "I heard. I take it we're in full communication with that world now."

Rhyaz flicked an ear in assent. "Yes. Just finished speaking to Captain Kishasayzar and the four Human agents we left there."

"So we now have up-to-date news on the situation there. Good. About time. Relaying it through the Sumaan ship took far too long. What news is there on the *Profit*?"

Rhyaz picked up the crystal paperweight on Lijou's desk and began toying with it. "Contact negotiations have started, and the Cabbaran and U'Churian delegates are arriving in a few days to endorse the temporary agreement that Kaid reached with them on board the *Rryuk's Profit*."

"Be careful of that, Rhyaz, it's an antique," warned Lijou. What was it with this paperweight? Everyone seemed to need to pick it up and handle it for some reason. He remembered the last time had been when Ghezu. . . .

"The news is bad." Rhyaz put the crystal down with a thump that made Lijou wince, even as he realized that his mind was suddenly going off into irrelevancies. He knew he didn't want to hear this news.

"Still no word from the *Profit*, and Kaid neglected to tell us that Carrie was seriously injured."

Lijou picked up the paperweight, finding comfort in the smooth surface. "How badly?"

"Bullet lodged against her spine, an archaic Jalnian one with a soft tip. It's serious. She needed specialized surgery, that's why they put her in cryo on the U'Churian ship."

"Then Kusac's in one, too. And they've been missing for

three days," said Lijou slowly, trying to take it in. He roused himself. "What are Raiban and Chuz going to do?"

"I had words with them. As of now, *Rryuk's Profit* is officially listed as missing. A search has been implemented along their last known route. The U'Churian delegates' ship is due at Jalna in two days. They plan to join us in the search, same with the Cabbarans they'll be bringing with them. If the *Profit* is there, we'll find it, Lijou. Could be nothing more than a comm breakdown. They might still turn up on schedule at Tuushu in four days' time."

"It takes longer than four days for them to get there," said Lijou. "I know, I read the reports. They aren't officially due there for another seven days."

"The *Profit* can get there faster because of their Cabbaran navigators. They've got . . ."

"I read that report, too," interrupted Lijou. How was he going to break this news to Konis? It had been bad enough when the message at the palace had been given to him by mistake, but now he had problems enough with that younger daughter of his. And Rhyasha. It would break her heart to lose them both. "Don't try to convince me you believe it's a comm or engine failure. You wouldn't be insisting on a search now if you did."

"We've got one of our own ships posted near the jump point at Tuushu. When they emerge, we'll see them. We can't afford to lose them, Lijou," said Rhyaz quietly. "There's also the fact that they're aboard the ship of two new allies to be taken into consideration. That was my lever with the High Council. We can't let any of the species that trade at Jalna think we're slow to respond to one of their missing ships at this stage in our treaty talks."

Lijou nodded. "When do I tell Konis and Rhyasha?"

"Can you delay it? No need to worry them any sooner than we need to. As you say, we've seven days before we need to tell them."

In his hands, the crystal suddenly seemed icy cold, and its chill went straight to his heart. He put it down just as hurriedly as Rhyaz had done. "You realize this could be what Vartra's warning was about. Not them, but why they've gone missing."

"I'm already working on that assumption. All our people in the field have been contacted and put on alert. I'd be doubting the sanity of following the vision you had, but there's no way I can rationalize that coin you gave me."

Lijou shivered. "Don't remind me," he murmured. "I've been visiting the temple more often than usual, hoping for an answer, another vision, even another visitation, dammit! But nothing! It's as if Vartra has left us to get on with it!"

"What about any of our other visionaries?"

"Nothing. No, wait. Dzaka came to me two days ago with a tale of Kashini screaming in fear for most of the night. He said he and Kitra had the distinct feeling she knew her mother and father were in danger. I dismissed it as pure fancy. Seems I might have been a little too quick in my assessment."

"Contact Dzaka. See if he or Kitra have picked up anything more. And make sure every vision or dream, no matter how trivial or unrelated it may seem, is reported to you."

Lijou nodded. "Is there anything else I can do?"

"You're doing plenty as it is by using the priesthood to pass on messages to our people," said Rhyaz, getting up. "This remains between ourselves for now, Lijou. Chuz and Raiban don't exactly want it common knowledge either. Let's see where we are when the U'Churians arrive."

CHAPTER 6

Day 8

A yowl of terror had Kaid leaping from his bed before he even realized he was awake. In his haste, he stumbled, his blanket caught round his legs. Cursing, he bent to free himself, flinging it behind him as he raced into their common lounge. He passed Mrowbay sitting slumped asleep on the couch but more important matters claimed him. The shriek sounded again, and this time he knew which room to go to. The middle door was open as, T'Chebbi now behind him, he headed into Rezac's and Jo's room.

Zashou was crouched beside the two beds, keening.

Reaching down, he hauled her to her feet. "What is it?" he demanded, shaking her. "Stop that damned racket, Zashou! You're not helping anyone, and I can't hear myself think!"

She continued to howl, oblivious to his presence. He shook her again, and when she still didn't respond, he slapped her, a hard, stinging blow that made her gasp and put her hand to her face in shock.

"You hit me," she faltered.

"Damned right I did! Now, what's happened?"

She pointed at the empty beds. "They're gone," she whimpered. "I came in to talk to Rezac, and they were gone!"

Pushing her aside, Kaid joined T'Chebbi, who was already kneeling on the floor examining one of the empty beds.

Pulling the cover off the other, he found what he was looking for. A red stain on the sheet at chest height. "Blood. His wounds were bleeding again." He let the cover fall back and stood up.

"He's dead!" Zashou wailed. "They've taken him because he's dead!"

"Enough," snapped Kaid, pushing past her and the group that had materialized around them. "If he were dead, you'd be as well, you know that!" He headed back to the lounge, reaching out mentally for either of the two missing people, and encountered a barrier he couldn't penetrate. "What the hell?" he muttered, then Tirak claimed his attention.

"I heard Zashou. Who's missing?" the U'Churian demanded, clutching at the blanket he'd wrapped around himself for modesty.

"Rezac and Jo. They're not with any of you?" asked Kaid, trying to catch the eyes of the circle of half-dressed U'Churians and Humans. He felt a flash of annoyance, then remembered their nudity taboos. They'd soon lose them, living in such close quarters.

A chorus of negatives answered him.

"Not in the sanitary facilities either," said T'Chebbi.

"Have you seen these?" asked Taynar, holding a wrist comm out to him. "Our stuff. It's been returned."

Automatically, Kaid took it from him.

"They've been here while we slept!" said Zashou hysterically, pointing to the pile of assorted personal possessions that lay on the low table beside Taynar. "How could they come in here and take two people from their beds without us even knowing? What kind of beings *are* they?"

"I was on guard," said Mrowbay quietly. "I don't remember seeing anyone."

"Were asleep when I came through," said T'Chebbi.

All eyes turned on the helpless Mrowbay. He shrugged, ears flattening briefly. "I don't understand it," he said. "I wasn't even tired."

"He's not to blame," said Kaid. "His sleep couldn't have been natural. To take two people out of here without waking any of us is virtually impossible."

"Why? Why have they taken them?" demanded the distraught Zashou.

"Is obvious," said T'Chebbi, looking through the pile of possessions on the table. "His wounds were bleeding, and she's pregnant. Maybe something happened to her in the night, too."

"I know what they were doing, damn him!" said Zashou hysterically. "That's all Rezac's good for, fathering cubs!"

"Why not?" countered T'Chebbi, looking up at her. "You don't want him or his cubs. Why should he waste himself on you?"

"Enough, both of you!" Kaid roared, losing his temper. "Zashou, don't be so damned stupid! Neither of them was in a state to do anything last night except sleep! T'Chebbi, leave her alone. Am I the only one to see the real implications here?"

"How'd they know they needed medical attention?" asked Mrowbay.

Kaid rounded on him. "Right! They must have some kind of monitoring devices on them. Dammit, I should have thought to search them both!"

"I'd not have thought of it either," said Tirak. "They were in such a bad way, who'd have wanted to disturb them with a search?"

"Not the point," said Kaid, sitting down. "I should have."

Manesh indicated the pile on the table. "No, it's my responsibility. I'm the security officer. Everything they give us, including all of this, we should now consider suspect."

"They'll be clean," said Sheeowl quietly. "When they can knock out our watch and possibly the rest of us as well, come in and remove two injured people without waking us, they don't need to plant devices in our wrist comms."

"She's right," said Tirak, hoisting his blanket more securely around himself.

"I'll check them anyway," Manesh said firmly, holding her hand out for Kaid's wrist comm.

"What now?" asked Tallis. "What do you intend to do to protect us? We're civilians, not part of your military forces. We have a right to protection. Who're they going to take next?"

Kaid sighed. "We'll put two people on watch tonight. It's unlikely they'll take anyone else, Tallis. Rezac and Jo obviously needed medical attention, that's why they're gone."

"There's some books and vids among this lot," said Sayuk, who'd been looking through the pile. "No use without a vid unit, though."

"Like that?" asked Taynar, pointing to a squat object sitting in what had been one of the vacant niches in the far wall.

"Like that," she agreed, looking over at it. "It's ours, from the *Profit.*" Her tone was frankly incredulous.

Tirak sat down in the nearest seat. "I don't understand this. Why keep us prisoners yet provide us with all the comforts of home?"

"Boredom increases the need to try to escape," said Kaid. "This makes us hope the Primes will get around to releasing us if we cooperate with them."

"You don't know that they won't," countered Tallis. "They've not questioned any of us, not offered us any violence. They may well let us go."

"You were the one demanding to be protected a moment ago," said Manesh. "Now you think they're harmless. Make up your mind, Tallis!"

"Stop ordering me about! Who do you think you are? I don't have to do what you tell me! I'm Sholan, not U'Churian!" His tail was beginning to lash from side to side angrily.

"Stow it, Tallis," said Kaid sharply. "We're in this together. As you said, you're a civilian. You'll do what you're told and like it."

As Sheeowl had predicted, their belongings were clean. Lighting and heating they already had access to, but now that they could keep track of time, they felt more in control of their environment. The door to the corridor outside let in only faint sounds, but they were able to hear when people were passing by.

At first, Tirak kept his crew close and alert, but as the hours passed and they remained undisturbed, he allowed them to relax, realizing they'd be burned out long before the need for action came, if it ever did.

As their day wore on, Kaid watched with a detached interest as the two crews formed social groupings. It gave him something to do other than worry about the continued absence of Rezac and Jo and the fact that mentally, he couldn't reach beyond their suite. The return of his wrist comm had given him cause for concern because his, unlike those of the other Sholans who wore one, was fitted with a personal psychic damper which was still working. Although the feel of the mental barrier wasn't the same, he wished he could be sure that the reason he couldn't penetrate beyond the walls of their suite had nothing to do with the Primes finding the device.

As they began to settle after their last meal of the day, he noted Giyesh and Jeran finally move quietly off to a corner of the lounge on their own. He knew of their night together on Jalna and had seen them meeting for odd stolen hours together on the *Profit*. Sensing Tirak about to interfere, Kaid reached across the table to touch the other's hand, flicking his ear in a negative before he realized the captain wouldn't understand the Sholan gesture.

"Leave them," he said quietly. "They strengthen each other. He needs her even if she doesn't need him. He's been through a lot recently, and just lost two of his companions. They're not undermining any discipline, quite the reverse. They're showing the rest of us we can work together."

Before Tirak had time to reply, the door slid open and J'koshuk entered. Instantly, Kaid was up and moving toward him. As the door slid shut, his hands closed around the Valtegan's throat, slamming him against it.

"Where are they?" he demanded, ears laid sideways and lips drawn back from his teeth in a snarl of extreme rage.

"Who?" hissed J'koshuk, clawed hands scrabbling at Kaid's forearms, his voice barely audible because of the pressure on his throat. "No one is missing!"

Shifting his grip, Kaid was surprised to feel metal under his hands. Hooking the fingers of his left hand round the band, he hauled the priest into the center of the room. A quick glance told him all he needed to know about it for the moment.

"Two of us are gone! Where are they? When will they be returned?" he demanded, shaking him by the collar.

"They're back," wheezed J'koshuk, trying to keep his voice calm as he clutched at Kaid for support. "They were only gone for a few hours."

"Liar!" shrieked Zashou, bearing down on them, claws outstretched. "We've spent the day watching and waiting!"

Kaid fended her off until T'Chebbi ran over and grabbed hold of her, then he hauled J'koshuk closer. "Where are they?" he asked again, staring into the other's bulbous green eyes.

The priest flinched and looked away. "I watched them being returned myself not thirty minutes ago."

Kaid felt a cold knot of fear grip his lower belly. "Check it out, T'Chebbi," he said calmly. Suddenly, he was afraid to discover J'koshuk was telling the truth. The seconds stretched interminably as he waited for her to return.

"They're back. Are sleeping," she said.

Zashou whimpered in fear, then Kaid heard a dull thump as she hit the ground.

"Fainted," said T'Chebbi in disgust.

Knowing her as he did, Kaid could hear the note of uncertainty in her voice that the others would miss. He returned his attention to the priest, smelling the stench of his fear. "You're their creature, their servant. What manner of beings are the Primes? What did they do to my people? Why did they take them?" he demanded.

"They were taken to the medical unit for treatment. Beyond that, I know nothing, not even what the Primes look like!"

"You're running their errands! You must know more than that!"

"I'm a captive like you. I do just that, run their errands, under guard. I've been sent to check on the male."

"You caused his condition!" snarled Kaid, giving him another shake.

"They know that," said the priest quietly when he'd stopped. "Now release me and let me do my job. If I were you, I'd not earn their displeasure. It isn't me they'll punish."

Kaid snarled his anger but released him. Something was wrong about this priest. He followed him, watching J'koshuk as he checked Rezac's dressings, felt his pulse. Obviously satisfied, J'koshuk turned to leave, and found Kaid blocking his way.

"What about her?" He indicated Jo.

"I wasn't instructed to check her."

"Where did you get your medical training in Sholan physiology?"

J'koshuk looked startled. "What do you mean?"

"Where did your sudden concern for us come from,

J'koshuk? You hate us as a species, want nothing more than to destroy us. What changed?"

"I don't know what you're talking about. I do what the Primes order me to do," he blustered, but Kaid could see his protruberant eyes widening in fear.

"You hadn't noticed, had you? What have they done to you, J'koshuk? What price are you paying for being their messenger? Get out of here, and don't bother coming back. Tell your masters you're not welcome."

"I have no choice," J'koshuk said, his face turning a sickly yellowish hue as the color drained from it. The scent of his fear grew stronger, pervaded the room. "I must do as they order me."

Kaid stood aside. "Then don't return here without information for me," he said quietly. "I want to know what the Primes want with us, and if any of your people have gone missing."

J'koshuk edged past him into the main room. As he did, the door hissed open to reveal armed guards, rifles pointed at him.

"Do not intimidate the Interface," the translator intoned as J'koshuk fled to safety.

They woke Jo and Rezac, and though mindful of the fact they were injured, searched them thoroughly for any monitoring devices. They found nothing. Neither of them had any memory of even leaving the room, and only the fact that Rezac had fresh dressings and Jo's cannula had been removed, convinced them that anything at all had happened. That night, no one wanted to go to the bedrooms. They preferred to remain together in the lounge.

* * *

Day 9

The next day, J'koshuk awoke to a pulsing in his collar—his alarm call. Flinging his clothes on, he quickly headed for the food dispenser and chose some eggs and the warm herbal drink he'd had the night before. He didn't relish facing a day with stomach problems. He'd barely finished when the soldiers arrived for him.

They led him to a room up the corridor, away from his own and the Sholan quarters. As soon as he entered it, he could feel the pigment drain from his face. Walls and floor were tiled in white, a color he knew showed up the brightness of blood to devastating effect. The lighting was bright but could be intensified by moving the large circular units standing a short distance away. It reminded him too forcefully of his office in Geshader, on Keiss.

In the center stood a chair with a rack of surgical implements close beside it. The chair was different, more comfortable than his interrogation chair had been, padded in an easily cleaned seamless fabric, but it reclined from upright to a full bed size, with attached anchorage points for wrists and ankles as well as neck. And at the neck was a series of wired contacts that he knew instantly fixed onto collars like his. It might also look like a medical room, but he didn't need the old scent of Valtegan fear to tell him its last purpose had been for interrogation.

An armored glove closed with a viselike grip on his shoulder, propelling him into the room. He knew his options—he went quietly, or he suffered pain and went anyway. Pulling away, he found he was released instantly. Walking over to the chair, he sat down, noticing somewhere deep in his mind that it fit him easily. The guards stayed where they were and he realized with surprise, they had no intention of fastening him down.

The minutes passed and it grew more difficult to avoid staring at the instruments on the rack. He concentrated on looking around the room again, examining it, looking for the subtle differences. It was spacious compared to his room in Geshader, and a palace compared to the cargo hold on the *M'ijikk*. He smelled antiseptic in the air, overlying the strengthening scent of fear he knew was his own. Four sealed body-sized units backed onto the far wall. Above them were monitor screens. Maybe it doubled as an emergency medical room. It certainly wasn't the main one he'd accompanied the unconscious Rezac to.

The heavy sound of approaching feet made him turn to look over his shoulder. Two of the Seniormost Primes. He quickly turned back, hoping they hadn't noticed him, but it was impossible to tell under those helmets.

They came round in front of him, arms hanging easily at their sides.

"We will question you now. You are our Interface, one who will move freely among the captives if you prove your honesty. We do not expect lies. If you lie, we will know it and one of the guards will punish you. They have been adjusted to have no compunctions about inflicting pain. They will stop only when ordered. Is that understood?"

J'koshuk blinked rapidly, unable to stop his fear sphincters releasing their scent. They *adjusted* their own kind? What was behind those visors? What manner of beings were they?

"Why did you take the ship called *Rryuk's Profit*?" asked the flat, mechanical voice.

"For the navigators, the Cabbarans," he said quickly. Keeping information from the Primes wouldn't help him. There were several among the bridge crew who could tell them this.

"Why?"

The voice seemed to come slightly from one side this time, but he couldn't be sure. It unsettled him, not knowing which one he was talking to.

"We were disgraced at home and couldn't return without facing our execution. We hoped the navigators would buy us our lives."

"What value have these aliens to your kind?"

"They can navigate during jumps."

"The nature of your disgrace?"

He turned his head slightly, looking from one to the other. Which one had spoken? "We lost our Rest and Recuperation world to the Sholans when they answered a distress call from the Humans."

Silence, while they obviously conferred with each other. Then, "How did you learn of Jalna?"

"From a small trading ship we captured some time ago."

"What took you to Jalna? You have not been seen there before."

"Our ship had been damaged in escaping from Keiss and needed repairs. We knew we could sell the four Sholans there for the supplies we needed. That's where we saw and heard about the Cabbarans."

"If they defeated you on Keiss, how were you able to take these Sholans?"

J'koshuk twitched. He'd been hoping they wouldn't ask. "Our Commander of Forces called us to take part in a military mission."

"Its nature?"

"I don't know. I am only the priest, not included in bridge briefings unless summoned by the Captain." He couldn't stop his tongue from flicking out nervously.

From the neck down a tidal wave of pain washed through him, setting every nerve on fire, making his body twitch uncontrollably. It seemed to go on and on, then just as suddenly, it stopped.

He lay panting in the chair, barely able to open his eyes or think coherently.

"You lie." The mechanical tones were devoid of inflection.

"I don't," he whimpered. "We followed orders, placed ourselves in a formation around the Sholan worlds. That's all I know."

A guard stepped forward, and taking him by a handful of his robes, lifted him up and slammed him into the back of the chair.

"I don't know!" J'koshuk said frantically, clawing at the armored glove. "All I know is that we destroyed every living thing on both worlds!"

The guard released him, letting him fall back to the seat.

"Where did the weapon come from?" he was asked after a moment or two of silence.

"I don't know," he said, gripping the arms of the chair, bracing himself for more pain. "It wasn't on our craft. Only General M'ezozakk would know."

"You did more than trade at Jalna. You left something behind. What was it?"

He looked from one to the other in shock, trying desperately to remember what they'd done there. How did the Primes know so much about them? "The Holy Object!" he said in a rush. "We sent it down to protect it from the authorities on M'zull in case they wouldn't accept us back. We hoped one day to retrieve it."

"Describe it."

"A large cube. It hurt to look at it." This was something

he did know about and he could hear himself beginning to babble in his urgency to tell them about it before they turned on his collar again. "Light seemed to bend round it and it felt strange to the touch. It wasn't heavy—moved easily, as if floating. It's been worshipped in the General's family for generations."

Silence fell while they considered his answer.

"What is the location of this Human world?" he was asked at length.

He could taste the sudden rank smell of his fear strongly now. He clenched his hands tightly round the arms of the chair, claws indenting the semi-rigid surface. "It's not my job. I'm only a priest who interrogates those the Church considers heretics. I'm not trained as a navigator."

Again the silence. He'd never before experienced such terror. Though his body was shaking, another part of him was sitting back, analyzing what they were doing that was so effective.

"The food. Do you cope with it? It is nutritional for your kind." The question shocked him with its incongruity.

Briefly he wondered whether to lie, then decided against it. "It hurts my stomach. I need freshly killed meat, eaten raw, not cooked."

"There are settings that control the amount of heat applied to the food. You can choose one that barely cooks it."

"But it isn't raw!"

"Accustom yourself to it. There is no reason why you cannot. Your stomach is capable of processing it." The reply was said almost before he'd finished talking.

"You have work to do shortly, using your particular skills. You will choose one of your crew to interrogate. The guards will aid you. Return to your quarters and clean yourself." Both Primes turned away from him and began to walk away.

"Me?"

"You question our decision?"

He could almost hear the implication in the flat, inflectionless voice. "No," he said hurriedly, getting out of the seat before they changed their minds. Why did they want him to question his fellow crew members? Then he supplied his own answer, because he obviously knew them better.

As the guards escorted him back to his rooms, he realized that to return him to his quarters like this, the Primes were capable of smelling his scents. So the suits were two-way, they concealed his abductors' natures, not protected them. He put this to the back of his mind to consider later, when he had more such small facts.

* * *

Mara had only just collapsed into a chair at the long trestle table when she heard a footfall behind her. Smothering a sigh, she waited for the inevitable words. They didn't come, instead the steps stopped and she felt a hand on her shoulder. Looking up, she saw Greg standing over her.

"You did a good job explaining to Toueesut why he wasn't invited to the Sholan funerals yesterday," he said, passing her a cup of coffee. "Can I join you?"

"Sure," she said, taking the mug from him. "How'd you know I wanted a coffee?"

He slid onto the seat opposite her, putting his own coffee on the table before handing her a sandwich. He leaned closer, almost whispering in her ear. "Dealing with our Touiban colleagues still gives me a headache. You've no idea how grateful everyone is that they've taken to you. Leaves me free to get on with our own work rather than mediating between our species. I've a proposition to put to you," he said, sitting back and taking a sip of his drink. "I've been talking to Dzaka. We've a space on the team, and he says you're free to take us up on any offer of employment we want to make. Are you interested in formalizing what you've been doing with us? And getting paid for it?" He grinned, looking at her over the top of his glasses.

Mara took a bite out of her sandwich, looking consideringly at him. In his mid-thirties, he was considered young for the position of team leader here at the monastery site, but any objections from the Earth delegation had been overridden by the Clan Lord as head of Alien Relations. The Humans had wanted Greg, the Sholans wanted him, and the Touibans were ecstatic to see the back of their previous team leader. End of discussion.

"I know you don't need to worry about money, being a member of the En'Shalla Clan, but . . ." he began.

"Oh, it's not that," she said, interrupting him. "I like what I'm doing now. I don't know if I'd want to be told where to go and what to do."

He shook his head in a quick, negative gesture. "Nothing like that," he reassured her hastily. "You'd carry on doing what you're doing now. It just makes it, well, official. With your Leska Link to Josh, you know everything he does about archaeology—it's like having two of him now." He realized how she might interpret that and began to cover his tracks. "Not that I mean you don't have your own flair and patience, you do, it's just that . . ."

Mara grinned and reached out to touch his hand where it lay on the table. "It's all right. I do know what you mean," she said.

"Uh. I suppose you do, being a telepath," he mumbled, running a hand through his thinning sandy hair to hide his embarrassment. "Well? Are you interested?" he returned doggedly to his original point.

She took another bite of her sandwich. "Master Konis wants me recruited to AlRel in the fall."

"What about till then? You might be able to do both. You'd continue to get hands-on experience with our Touibans," he wheedled, making his pale blue eyes wide and innocent. "At least think seriously about it. See what Josh says."

She couldn't help but laugh at his humor. "Josh says I should accept, but . . ."

"Then it's done," he said, sitting back satisfied. "May I be the first to officially welcome you to the team?"

"It isn't that easy!" she exclaimed, slightly rattled at being bulldozed into the position. Within her mind, she could feel Josh sending soothing and congratulatory thoughts. "You already asked Josh about this!" she said. "Has this been set up between the two of you?"

"Not at all," said Greg, suddenly very much the professional. "You're genuinely being offered a position on the team. The fact that if we don't have you, then we have to accept whoever HQ sends has nothing to do with it. You were unanimously elected to the post."

Conflicting emotions were running through her now.

Some of the surprise and pleasure she'd felt had evaporated. Sandwich discarded on the table, she began to get to her feet when a familiar trilling and gentle scent wafted over her. She shut her eyes and groaned softly.

"Is trouble? We watch from farther away so no intruding into your business, but concern makes me need to approach." The familiar fluting tones of the Touiban Speaker, Toueesut, sounded from behind her. "Happiness there should be at being part of this great digging and finding of ancient artifacts. Talent you have in plenty for the job, and ability to focus on what is important. You are the ideal Human for the position."

"Everyone's been consulted apart from me," she said, letting herself fall back into her seat.

"I said it was unanimous," said Greg placidly.

"Who's behind all this? Is it Vanna, suggesting it as therapeutic for me?" she demanded, not sure whether to be offended or not.

"Vanna has nothing to do with it. And we can't afford to have someone working for us who isn't pulling their own weight," said Greg. "This site is still the most complete one on Shola, the most important. None of us would be here if HQ had any inkling exactly what is buried here. Only the fact it's on En'Shalla territory has prevented all of us from being replaced. They'd love to get us winkled out of here and their top experts in—not just for the site, but because they'd be able to put some anthropologists and others in the team and spy on you all!"

"So you're using me to keep the boogeyman away."

Not true, sent Josh. *The person who suggested it was Master Konis himself as soon as Garras showed him the request to send a new team member out here. Why look anywhere but among our own when we have you, and you have all my knowledge at your fingertips?*

It's not mine! It's not for me, it's for the estate! she replied.

"It is that we are bothering you too much, that we make too many demands on your person?" asked Toueesut, his bristly chin wriggling in concern as he fairly bounced around from foot to foot behind her.

In the distance, she could hear the distressed trilling of

his swarm mates. As she turned, she saw them swirling round each other in an intricate dance.

"No, no," she said placatingly, touching him on the sleeve of his brightly embroidered jacket. "It's nothing you've done. You know I'm happy to help you at any time."

"Then why you distress all with your confusion over accepting this position?" he asked, catching hold of her hands, beginning to almost massage them with his callused, leathery fingers.

She'd never gotten this close to one of the little people before and now that they were touching, she could feel his thoughts and emotions, was aware of how soft and fragile he felt she was. His hands held hers firmly yet they were never still, the thumbs rubbing over the back of her hands, the fingers doing dances of their own across her palms and digits. She marveled at how hands that had essentially evolved for supporting themselves against the ground and rocky outcrops in order to walk upright could be so flexible at manipulating almost microscopic electrical components. How could these beings be the comm tech experts of the Alliance?

"It is us who requested you be made a permanent member of our working community, so that the high level of peace and efficiency could be maintained," he said, enveloping her in sweet scents of every kind until she was almost choking. "We are those responsible for being selfish enough to want you to continue smoothing matters between the discordant ones and ourselves. It is your music that sounds so sweetly in our minds when you are here." He stopped, even to the point of standing still and holding her hands tightly between his own.

"Stay," he said. "It would sadden the swarms if you did not. Is it selfish to want to work with those who create harmony in our lives on a world alien to us both? You bring a touch of home to us."

Astonished by them for the second time, Mara could only blurt out, "But why? Why me? I've done nothing special for you!"

Toueesut put his head to one side, brown eyes twinkling at her from their dark sockets, the bristles around nose and chin suddenly pointing forward as he concentrated totally on her. "But you have," he trilled softly as behind him the other eleven Touibans made a harmonious accompaniment to his voice. "I told you. Your mind-music sounds sweeter than any others here."

Mara Ryan, came the thoughts of Konis Aldatan in her mind, *Have you any idea of the breakthrough you've made with these people? If you dare turn that position down. . . .*

"I'll take it," she said hurriedly, though she knew well that Master Konis had only been half-joking. "I'll do what you want, work with the team."

Those were the last words she got out for the next five minutes, as twelve deliriously happy Touibans descended on her, pulling her to her feet and twirling and whirling her round with them until she had to beg them to let her go lest she fall down with giddiness.

From the lab, Dzaka watched the remarkable display dispassionately. At his side, Josh stood, mouth agape, experiencing it as immediately as Mara. When she was eventually returned to her seat at the table, he spoke to Dzaka.

"How unusual is this kind of behavior?"

"Unique," said Dzaka, looking away and continuing with his cataloging. "Interaction with other species is normally strictly confined to business. They prefer to interface with us through a telepath, and tend to live in Valsgarth rather than any other city. Master Konis could tell you more if you're interested, or one of the AlRel staff living on the estate."

"He already has," said Josh, watching the two groups of Touibans returning to the lab, chattering and trilling as they went. "Toueesut said he liked her *mind-music,* and Master Konis has just called it a breakthrough."

Dzaka grunted in surprise, interested despite himself. "I always thought they had a level of awareness akin to our psi talents. They've been employed at Stronghold before now, and never demanded a telepath from us. I take it she decided to accept the post."

"Yes."

"She needed a direction, now she has it. She's already paid the Touibans back in full for their support of you both against Pam Southgate."

"So that's partly why they asked for Pam to be removed

from the team. We could never figure out why," Josh said thoughtfully.

Dzaka looked up at the bearded Human. "If they sensed her mind, then they'll also know yours," he said. "Even more so now you're Leska Linked."

Josh shrugged, dark eyebrows disappearing beneath his sandy hair in embarrassment. "Yeah, it's weird being the only Human Leska pair. I wish Zhyaf hadn't died, but it was no life for Mara being Linked to him. Look, I'm sorry things are bad between you and Kitra."

"Kitra decided there's no longer anything between us," he said, concentrating on copying the data from the notebook into the comp unit.

"I didn't realize things were that bad. Everyone's saying this bonding is just a political one."

"It's political," he agreed, "but no less real because of that."

"You should have asked for her yourself."

"I couldn't. She has to marry within the Clans to pass on the telepath bloodlines," he said shortly. Why the hell did everyone feel the need to give him advice he couldn't take?

"We're a Clan," Josh pointed out as he went back to his work. "And your parents were telepaths. Everyone knows Kaid is or he couldn't be Kusac's and Carrie's Third."

"Everyone might know it, but it isn't written in the records, and I'm not about to tell Master Konis officially. It's for my father to reveal his Talent, not me."

"Dzaka," he began.

"You know nothing about our family," said Dzaka, his anger boiling briefly to the surface as he glared at the Human. "My father had to conceal our relationship even from me until a few months ago because he feared for my life at the hands of Ghezu! Do you think I'd betray him for anything?"

"I didn't mean it like that," stammered Josh. "You're right. I know nothing about your family. I should have kept my mouth shut."

The fire went out of Dzaka's eyes and he sighed, breaking eye contact. "No, I should apologize. I know you're like all the others, only concerned for us. I'm gene-altered, like you. I can't give her the cubs the Clan Council demands. There is nothing I can do but accept the Clan Lord's decision."

"Is there anything we can do? You really love each other, don't you? Mara could take a message to her if you want."

"I gave my word to Master Konis not to communicate with her until after the bonding, and Kitra's made it plain she wants nothing to do with me because of that. It's over between us, Josh. I've had to accept it, so will everyone else." He'd finally said it, and as he did, he could feel it take form, a reality all its own. Logic was one thing, feelings and emotions were another. He felt the coldness he'd known when he heard of the death of his wife and cub begin to creep once more into his heart. This was the last time he'd let himself care so deeply for another person. "It's over."

* * *

Day 10

Snow and ice covered everything, turning the false dawn into a pale blue wonderland. Before Carrie's face hung the tendrils of some plant; caught and encased in ice, they glittered and sparkled in what little light there was. They chimed hollowly as they swayed gently against each other in the faint breeze.

She became aware of the cold then—a cold so bitter it almost burned, enough to freeze the dead.

"Not in my realm," a voice purred in her ear. "My snows insulate the ground, keep it warm, letting the life within sleep and gather strength to face the heat of the new year. Like you, my soft, furless Sholan." A cool tongue tip touched her cheek, caressing it briefly.

Carrie whimpered. She could feel a furred body pressed against her, an arm laid across her shoulders, but she herself was unable to move.

"You're safe while you sleep within my arms, little one, but your Warrior will not fare so well. I grant you this last look at him before you wake."

A silver-pelted arm reached past her, parting the frozen fronds till she could see Kusac lying sleeping within a bank of snow. Only his head remained visible. Fear leaped into her heart at the sight of him.

"Hush, little one! He rests safe for the moment," Khuushoi said softly, her breath cold upon Carrie's cheek as she held her closer. "It's been so long since anyone visited me here. Dreamers like you are rare."

Coldness, not warmth, spread from Khuushoi's body to hers. Carrie tried to move, to reach out for Kusac, but she was held still within the embrace of the Goddess of Winter.

"There is no need for fear." Khuushoi's tone was amused. "Those kissed by Winter cannot wake till the appointed time. Your company has brought me pleasure, eased my loneliness. In return, heed me well, I have a warning for you. Prepare yourself for a time when you may have to choose between him and your child. When that time comes, choose wisely, little Human."

Once more, the cool tongue caressed her cheek as around her, the light began to fade.

* * *

Everyone had been exhausted by sitting up the night before, so Kaid's job was made easier for him. He needed to get a night watch routine established to give them all an anchor, something they could feel secure about and in control of in this alien environment.

Rezac was almost fit again, his injuries from the beating having healed at a rate consistent with using an accelerated drug like Fastheal. Even his broken ribs were paining him less. Jo was better too, but still tired and lethargic, although she'd made the effort to get up and join them during their afternoon. With fourteen of them able-bodied, watches through the night weren't a problem.

A deck of cards had been included with their possessions. Now the watch had something legitimate to do to keep them alert when they weren't making the half-hourly patrols to each of the five sleeping rooms. Kaid had elected to do the last two hour stint along with Tallis and Sheeowl.

He and T'Chebbi were sharing a room with Kate and Taynar. He'd decided to take the younglings in with them so they could keep an eye on them and make sure they were adapting to their loss of mental privacy and increased dependency on each other. He needn't have worried. They were as unconcerned as young jeggets when it came time to retire. Oh, they had their odd spats and rows during the day like any couple, but at night, matters between them were fine. One less worry, thank Vartra.

Sleep didn't come easily for him, and when he finally drifted off, he found himself locked in a cycle of nightmares about being pursued remorselessly by shadows that, when he finally gained the courage and desperation to face them, proved only to be images of himself.

The last dream was different. He lay entombed in darkness, floating weightlessly above the world. A feather-softness touched his cheek, but he couldn't turn his head to see what it was. It came again and this time he knew it was the gentle lick of a tongue. But it was cold, so cold it almost burned.

Remember Winter's kiss. He heard the words whispered in his ear, then the gentle flick of the tongue as the darkness was shattered by the flare of a brilliant light shining directly into his eyes. Suddenly, he couldn't breathe. Chest heaving, he tried to fill his lungs with air as he gasped in pain, tears streaming down his cheeks.

He jolted himself awake, shaking violently with fear or cold, he couldn't tell which. From the pod beside him, T'Chebbi reached out a comforting hand, running it across his damp pelt. Groggy and disoriented, he pulled her closer, taking comfort from her warmth against his chilled hide. Before he knew it, she had joined him under his blankets and was covering him with tiny bites.

Within minutes, her skillful fingers and tongue had roused him to fever pitch, then kept him there for longer than he could bear. There was nothing subtle about their pairing, it was both wild and furtive, leaving him as exhausted as she'd planned.

Someone was shaking him violently awake and, unusually for him, he responded sluggishly, unable to bring his eyes to focus on the face hanging over his. His left arm hurt and he'd a crick in his neck from peering up at the visitor. Trying to move, he became aware of T'Chebbi still lying partly under him.

Mumbling an apology, he rolled onto his side and sat up, shaking his head to clear it.

"Kate and Taynar are gone," said Jeran urgently. "It's taken me ages to wake you. You were both out cold."

Kaid peered over toward the other pair of sleeping pods. He was right, they were empty.

"Did either of you see or hear anything?" asked Manesh from her position by the door.

Kaid ran his hands through his hair, pushing it back from his face. "Nothing. How long have they been gone?"

Jeran shrugged as he sat back on his heels. "It's the twenty-third hour now. We came on at the twentieth and don't remember doing a patrol."

"Everyone else is awake. You were the most difficult to rouse," said Manesh.

"Figures," said T'Chebbi, sitting up and rubbing her shoulder. "You don't usually fall asleep on me like that. Gods, but you're heavy, Kaid."

Jeran tried to cover his snort of amusement, Manesh didn't bother. "Rezac and Jo were alone when they were taken," she said. "Whatever was done to us, if anything, they must have done double to you two."

"Makes sense," agreed T'Chebbi, wriggling herself free of Kaid's legs in an effort to get up.

Aware of his need for modesty in the presence of the U'Churian female, Kaid grabbed for the cover and wrapped himself in it before he scrambled to his feet and headed for the two empty beds.

"Searched them already," said Manesh. "Nothing. The taibans are young and healthy. What reason had the Primes to take them? That's what's frightening everyone."

"They're a Human and Sholan pair, like Rezac and Jo," said Jeran. "Mixed species. Who's going to be next? Giyesh and me?"

"Stop talking like that," said T'Chebbi sharply as she joined Kaid. "You'll start a panic for no reason. Could be they're doing health checks on us all."

"One hell of a way to get us to go to the doctor," he said with a shaky laugh. "Maybe we should tell them we've got several of our own here."

Kaid lifted the bottom sheet, smelling it briefly before reaching for the one on the other bed.

"Something?" asked T'Chebbi.

He caught her eyes as he shook his head. "I don't smell any drugs, but they might have no odor I can detect now." He threw the sheet back on the bed and got up. "Give me a minute to get dressed," he said.

Manesh and Jeran disappeared, closing the door behind them.

"What did you scent?" she asked, her voice barely above a whisper as he went back to his bed to get his clothes.

"Later," he said. "We have the others to calm down first."

Tallis literally pounced on him as they entered the lounge. "What the hell's going on, Kaid? First Rezac and Jo, now these two, and without even waking you! How are they getting in and out of the rooms? Who's going to be next?"

"Sit down, Tallis," he said, fending him off as he walked farther into the room before perching on the padded arm of one of the couches. "I'm as much in the dark as anyone else, but we'll not achieve anything if we let ourselves panic." Their fear filled the room like a miasma.

Tallis had followed him, tail tip lashing agitatedly from side to side beneath the hem of his robe. "I demand you . . ."

"Shut up, Tallis!" roared Rezac, getting to his feet and glaring at the older male. "I'm sick to death of your whining and complaining!"

"That's enough, Rezac," said Kaid mildly. "The brutal truth is we're captives and there's nothing we can do to stop these Primes from doing whatever they want with us. I suggest we all get used to that idea right now, then we can look at the more positive aspects of our situation."

"Positive aspects?" exclaimed Tallis. "What positive aspects?"

"T'Chebbi, escort Tallis to his room," said Kaid. "It's obvious no one else is going to get a chance to speak while he remains here."

She got to her feet, ears flattening to the side as she looked Tallis' way. He backed off hurriedly toward one of the dining tables, grabbing a hard chair and lowering himself onto it. "I'll shut up," he muttered.

Kaid gestured briefly to T'Chebbi, and, flicking her long plait over her shoulder, she resumed her seat.

"Rezac and Jo were taken because they needed medical attention," Kaid continued. "They were returned unharmed. That's positive. However, that wasn't the case as far as we know with Kate and Taynar. Unless you know of any medical reasons, Mrowbay?"

The U'Churian medic shook his head. "None. They were both healthy as far as my limited knowledge of your species could tell. Perhaps they're just curious as to why two obviously different species choose to be a couple."

"Could be. Kate and Jo are also the only Humans among us. That, or the fact they're telepaths, could have been more of a deciding factor."

"Maybe they just needed healthy specimen of each so they can treat Jo and Rezac more effectively," said T'Chebbi thoughtfully. "A benchmark."

"Could be as simple as that," agreed Mrowbay. "Taking us when we're unconscious is a way of ensuring we can't escape or cause trouble."

Kaid glanced at Mrowbay. "Good point."

"Maybe they can't treat us wearing those suits," said Jo. "They're probably only three feet tall and as fragile as a twig! No contest against even us thin-skinned Humans."

Nice one, Kaid sent to her as around him, a few smiles and chuckles broke out.

"They could be isolation suits as well as armor," said Jeran. "We might be able to cross infect each other with common illnesses. After all, we breathe the same kind of air and eat similar food."

"We can't assume that," interrupted Tirak. "The air we're breathing and that's in the corridor out there, has been scrubbed till it smells of nothing."

"The captain's right." Kaid gestured round the lounge. "Just because the furnishings, gravity, food, and air are all compatible with life-forms like us doesn't mean that the Primes are even organic. We have no idea of the size of the vessel we're on, or even if we're on a vessel. We could have been kept sedated in the hold of the *M'ijikk* for days."

"Don't say that. You're frightening me," said Zashou, clutching her arms across her chest.

"We need to face our situation honestly if we're ever

going to get out of here," said Jo. "I think it's unlikely they're constructs, but it is a possibility."

"Just like the three foot tall twigs," grinned T'Chebbi.

"As I said, none of us have yet been offered any physical violence," said Kaid. "And they're well capable of it. We saw their demonstration as we left the *M'ijikk*. Quite the opposite in fact. Rezac's and Jo's injuries were treated, they've kept us all together when they could have separated us—apart from the Cabbarans, that is. Let us control our heating and lighting, and our food."

"And given us our own clothing and entertainments from the *Profit*," added Sheeowl.

"We've no proof as yet that taking Kate and Taynar is an unfriendly act," pointed out Sayuk.

"I'd call it downright unfriendly," growled Manesh. "No matter how comfortable a prison is, it's still a prison. Removing someone from their bed at night without permission is kidnapping."

"We don't know enough to reach any real conclusions," said Tirak grimly. "What we need more than anything else is information."

Kaid nodded. "Agreed. We need to keep studying the Primes and their guards. Watch how they move, their speech patterns, how they place themselves at the doorway when they come here. Most of us have military backgrounds, we know the drill. Look for their weak points, then we can start planning an escape."

"And what do we civilians do?" asked Zashou.

"You're a telepath. Keep probing at them, see if you can get through to their minds. If you can, find out anything at all," said Kaid. He glanced at Rezac. "Which reminds me, I need to speak to both of you about your psi abilities."

"When?"

"Now. I think we've covered about everything we can for the moment." He looked around the room again, making sure he made eye contact with each of them in turn. "There's still several hours of sleep left. I, for one, am going back to bed. I suggest you do the same. Sitting up all night won't do any good, it'll only wear us out."

There was a general stirring and murmuring as people began to get up and wander off to their rooms.

"We'd better include you, Jo," said Kaid as she began to rise. "You know what Rezac knows."

As they made for the middle room, Kaid snagged T'Chebbi and drew her with him, tapping a message on her wrist with his fingers as he did, letting her know he needed her analytical skills.

The minute they were settled on the beds, Kaid began to talk in the Highland patois. "My bet is this is a fairly standard suite, therefore there's likely another the same backing onto us. I'm sure we're under constant surveillance. There might even be concealed entrances on the back walls." He indicated the one behind them. "We'll keep our talk to a minimum. Spend some time with T'Chebbi, Rezac. I want her to teach you how to communicate with us in the Brotherhood touch code. It's simple and efficient, and open gestures are easily missed by non-Brothers. Keep it low-key. I don't want the Primes noticing what you're doing." He sensed the other's surprise at being included, then a touch of regret that it hadn't been a show of trust in him instead of common sense.

"Agreed," said Rezac quietly, resting his arms on his knees.

"Why not use thought?" asked Jo, struggling with the new language which for her was still an acquired skill.

"They've a damper field on outside this room," said Rezac before Kaid could answer. "They either know we're capable of telepathy and don't want us to read them, or they're telepathic themselves. Which ties in with them taking Kate and Taynar because of their abilities."

"I'm going to be next," said Zashou, a note of panic in her voice. "I just know I am!"

"Anyone could be next, Zashou," said Kaid sternly, "or no one. The Primes might be able to monitor our mind talk, but they can't know this patois. It's archaic and only used by the Brothers in this form nowadays."

"How did the Primes learn Sholan?" asked Jo.

"From Valtegan databases. Must have had one, considering *M'ijikk* was M'ezozakk's own ship," said T'Chebbi.

"In the interests of keeping this talk short, what do you want to know about our psi abilities?" asked Rezac.

"What they are and how powerful. When we went back to the Margins, we saw Jaisa do things we'd never even considered possible. The nearest I've seen to that level of gift has been in unstable telepaths, and they usually ended up having to be terminated."

Zashou looked at him, amber eyes widening in shock. "Terminated? You killed telepaths?"

"It was what the law dictated," said Kaid. "When a telepath with a wild Talent went out of control, they had to be contained. Up until recently, the Telepath Guild would request that the Brotherhood capture and terminate them. We couldn't allow someone who was mentally unbalanced and, for instance, had the ability to kill using the power of his mind, to roam free on Shola."

"The Telepath Guild ordered the deaths of their own? What kind of world has Shola become?" Zashou looked from Kaid to T'Chebbi. "I don't want to be part of a society that lives like that!"

"Shola's a good world, but as I said, that ruling's changed now. Those with wild Talents are still captured by us, but now we're free to recruit them if we can, and if we can't, they're contained and handed over to a tribunal to decide their fate. Some of our best people, and our few telepaths, were once mentally unstable because they couldn't control their Talents. We've always collected those who could fight yet still retained some of the psi gifts of the telepaths—gifts thought not worth including in the Guild's breeding program. We saved the lives we could, Zashou. But we were talking of your abilities, not ours."

"So the current Telepath Guild recognizes only telepathic ability," said Rezac.

"Until recently, yes. But now we've met the Humans, the Guild has become aware of those other talents we've been harvesting for so long. They're beginning to adopt our training methods and actually educate those thought to have too little a gift."

"Vartra was only working on enhancing telepathy," Rezac admitted, "but we all had several other abilities that were actually usable. We didn't look on them as separate skills, though. When we changed, it was more like all our senses expanded, some more than others. Vartra had us experiment, see what we could do, then got us to chart the results and compare them with data from the other resistance cells where telepaths were in hiding. I remember

Jaisa was good at generating movement within objects, literally shaking them apart."

"I saw her do that to an iron grille that blocked our way up through the storm drains into the temple on the plains," said Kaid.

Rezac nodded. "That was one of her little tricks. We just approached every situation and looked at as many ways to solve it as possible. If we couldn't do it by conventional means, we used our minds."

"How did you overcome the Valtegans and start the Cataclysm?" asked T'Chebbi.

Kaid noticed Rezac glance at Zashou before answering. This was obviously something that had added to the rift between them.

"Goran captured Valtegans for us to experiment on. It took some time, but eventually we learned how to read their minds. I found I could force a contact with them and make them do what I wanted. We could control them, operate their bodies for a short time. Useful if you wanted a guard at his post to turn aside and not notice you, or to open a gate for you. They have a Challenge system something like ours, so it was easy to subvert them, fill their minds with hate for their superiors till they turned on them."

"It was contemptible," said Zashou, eyes flashing with anger. "They treated the captured Valtegans like animals!"

She's empathic, too? Kaid sent to Rezac, using a tight channel only he'd receive.

How'd you guess? Rezac sighed. "Once we were taken by them to K'oish'ik, their home world, we used the same tactics to set up our rebellion. That involved working with the other captive species, persuading them to join our cause, and using them as the fighters since we were unable to fight ourselves. There were a few of us who could communicate over interplanetary distances. We formed the network to keep everyone in touch. When we were ready, we attacked simultaneously, Sholan telepaths and the alien slaves."

"When you were brought out of stasis, you sent telepathically to us on Shola. Why couldn't you send for help from Jalna before the poisons in the soil affected you?" Kaid asked.

"They were weak and ill for several days," said Jo. "They were lucky to have survived for so long, Kaid. And we had our orders. Wait for our contact to communicate with us in a month's time. When she didn't, we couldn't know that communication with anyone else was impossible because we were broadcasting on a wavelength no one else was listening to."

"What about now?" he asked. "Surely with your enhanced talent you can get through this barrier."

Rezac shook his head. "No way. I've tried other mental frequencies as well, but I just don't have the power."

T'Chebbi stirred. "What about combining your talents, linking minds first, then trying?"

"Zashou's mind is still silent. I can only hear Jo."

"And that for only a few more weeks," murmured T'Chebbi.

"Excuse me?" said Jo. "What do you mean by that?"

"The cub," said Kaid. "It needs to develop separately from you and it can't if you're Linked with Rezac. Your Talent will fade by the twelfth to fourteenth week and not return till he's born. That's what happened to Vanna."

"Can you tell me how long this pregnancy will last?" she asked, skin flushing pink with embarrassment. "None of us knows anything about Sholan childbirth."

"I helped deliver Carrie's cub," Kaid said, trying to distance himself from the memories. Talking about her was difficult, brought his anguish to the surface. "She should have gone for twenty-four weeks as Vanna did, but time traveling accelerated her pregnancy."

"I just remembered. Zashou affected the Valtegans' eggs," said Rezac suddenly, keeping his eyes on Kaid and steadfastly not looking at his mate. "Once they had gotten used to us, we were free to walk around certain areas of the palace. In the days before our attack, several times we made our way to the royal harem and hatchery. There's a trick we found to magnify our ability rather than just combine it. We'd use it so we had the power to affect their eggs and their females by making them sterile."

"You could manipulate cells? Can you show me how to do it?" Kaid demanded as endless possibilities raced through his mind.

"Rezac," said Zashou warningly. Suddenly they were all aware of her extreme displeasure.

"It's a Leska thing," Rezac said doggedly, refusing to be silenced by her disapproval, either mental or verbal. "We had to be pairing to trigger it."

"The gestalt! It has to be the gestalt," said Kaid.

"Gestalt?" Rezac had obviously never heard the term before.

"It's like a force that's beyond you, and it's triggered by strong emotions," Kaid explained. "It just suddenly snaps into being and floods through you. It's difficult to control, though, and we've not found a practical use for it."

"Carrie's eyes changed first time," reminded T'Chebbi. "Cellular manipulation."

"How do you know about it?" demanded Rezac. "You don't have a Leska."

"We have a full three-way Link," said Kaid. He corrected himself quietly. "Had."

A small silence that no one knew how to fill followed.

"So theoretically, Jo, Zashou, and I together might be able to generate enough power to break through the barrier," said Rezac finally. "Do you know of a way to trigger this gestalt that doesn't involve mating?" he asked Kaid carefully.

"Carrie did it once, but she collapsed immediately afterward. Her Talent and Link were new to her, though. They considered the gestalt too unstable to experiment with. I hope it is possible, because if so, it'd be one hell of a lot easier for you just to link minds in public when the Primes come to the door, rather than having to be off in another room waiting for a signal from one of us."

"I won't do it," said Zashou, her tone one of barely controlled fury. "I absolutely refuse!"

"I wouldn't go a bundle on it either," said Jo, eyeing Rezac warily.

Diplomatically, Rezac said nothing.

"Is a way round it," said T'Chebbi. "Include Kaid and you have four."

Zashou got to her feet, tail lashing from side to side as she projected the full measure of her scorn and anger. "This conversation is finished," she said.

"What's the problem?" T'Chebbi asked her, perplexed

by her reaction. "This could free us all. You want to stay here?"

Kaid got to his feet. "Leave it, T'Chebbi. The morals back in their times were very different from ours. Same applies to Jo. We modern Sholans are the odd ones out here."

"You all had other lovers, not like this is first love. I don't see a problem," she grumbled as she rose. "Think about it," she said sternly to Zashou, before looking over to Jo. "We fight with weapons at hand. This could be a powerful weapon."

They returned to their room, Kaid sealing the door behind them with relief. The last part of the conversation had gone in an unexpected direction and he was glad to escape from it. He didn't blame the two females because he didn't know if he'd be prepared to involve himself either.

"At least it woke Zashou up mentally," said T'Chebbi. "Even I felt her!"

"There is that," Kaid agreed. "And we know now how Carrie managed to change her eyes. Just think of the untapped potential in the gestalt, T'Chebbi!"

"You got to control it first," she reminded him as she began to get undressed again. "Now tell me what you were smelling on the sheets."

"Kate and Taynar were new Leskas on their way to Shola when they got kidnapped by the Valtegan on Keiss," he said, unbuckling his belt. "I don't think they had the special contraceptive implants available on Keiss then."

"You think she's pregnant? Surely she'd have said something. Taynar would. He'd be so proud we'd never hear the end of it."

"I recognized the scent, T'Chebbi. No one else would except Rezac or Kusac." He stopped, mind blanking for a moment. So much of his life had been bound up with them that he found it impossible to avoid mentioning them several times a day. It made coping with their loss almost impossible.

"Taynar's young, too young to be aware if even a female Sholan was pregnant, let alone his Human Leska. Kate's certainly got the Talent to conceal it from him if she wanted to. Then again, she's young enough that she might not realize she was pregnant. Having discovered Human females with Sholan partners can conceive, the Primes will certainly be curious to find out if she has. It's the only other possible common factor."

T'Chebbi stuffed her hand into her mouth to stop the mewl of horror escaping. "What are they keeping us for? As breeding animals?"

"That's what worries me," he said, stripping off his tunic. "I assume you have an implant."

"Yes, immediately after . . ." She faltered to a stop, looking away from him.

"After what?" he asked a moment later.

"Immediately after I knew I was genetically compatible," she said, concentrating on meticulously folding up her tunic.

"That's not what you meant to say." He could feel his pulse begin to quicken as she mentally retreated from him. She moved away from him but he reached out to stop her.

"You were pregnant, weren't you?" he said, his voice deathly quiet as he continued to hold her by the arm.

"I didn't know we were compatible," she whispered, keeping her eyes away from his.

"Why didn't you tell me?"

"You were leaving for Stronghold."

Relief flooded through him. The vision had been false. It had only shown the possibility, not the actuality of a cub. He pulled her close, wrapping his arms around her and resting his chin on top of her head. "You should have told me. It was Vartra's damned genetic fix," he said. "I changed you as we paired. Is that why you didn't come to see me off?"

"I couldn't. I was still deciding what to do. It was my problem, my choice, not yours. I knew you didn't want to share your cubs with anyone."

"You should have told me," he repeated as she moved away from him. "Yes, it was your choice, but I'd have been with you if you'd wanted me there."

"It was nothing, Kaid. I terminated two days later. Vanna was good to me, asked me no questions."

"I wouldn't have let you be alone unless you wanted to be, that's all. It was my fault, not yours. If it happens again, you tell me."

"It won't. Unless we choose it to," she said, placing her tunic on a drawer unit against the far wall. "I'm not Jaisa."

He said nothing this time, ashamed that he was glad she'd chosen to terminate. "I know you're not Jaisa. We're Companions, with responsibilities for each other," he said quietly.

"Yeah, well, let's leave it now. Is over. Wasn't what either of us wanted, even without a mission coming up."

He had to respect her wishes. "We should try to sleep, T'Chebbi. There's no point in staying awake waiting for them to return Kate and Taynar. They won't be brought back tonight, I can guarantee that."

She returned, climbing into her sleeping pod and pulling the cover up. She lay silent for a moment. "If Kate is pregnant, happened after Mrowbay examined her, otherwise he'd have said tonight. Can only be a very few weeks pregnant. Want me to ask Jo, see if Kate's spoken to her?"

He turned off the light before coming back and easing himself down into his own bed. "No, leave it. I don't want Jo worried. You can ask Kate a few questions when she's returned." Reaching out, he touched her shoulder. "Thank you for earlier," he said quietly.

She turned her head and grinned at him. "What for? Was what I wanted too. Least I know it wasn't me that caused you to fall asleep as it got interesting!"

* * *

Kezule had reason to be grateful for his excellent memory as he spread out the map he'd gotten just over a month ago from the swamp skimmer. The Sholan pilot had had detailed maps of his own territory, but only the most general ones of the southwest area for which he was heading. The God-King be praised that he'd had the foresight to call up the map on the aircar before he and the female had abandoned it. With the aid of the pilot's stylus, he'd been able to add in features he'd remembered from the comm map to this one. By his reckoning, he was about halfway to his goal.

He'd kept close to the foothills where the ground was more even, traveling only at night to avoid capture. It was less risky than crossing the open plains, even though with his ability to control many of his autonomic body functions, he could present no more heat source than the average medium-sized scavenger. Though he lost time by keeping his temperature low and being less mobile, he saved it by not having to run for cover every time a vehicle passed overhead.

From the air traffic he'd observed since leaving the forest, the search for him was still concentrated there. That meant his ploy with the remains of the skimmer and the pilot had worked and they'd assumed one of the sharp-toothed swamp reptiles had been responsible.

He studied the map, comparing the distance he'd already traveled with that still remaining before he needed to leave the safety of the hills and head cross-country to the telepath town of Valsgarth. Another four days if he was lucky, six or seven if the rain continued, he thought, brushing stray droplets of water off the map. He'd need all his wits about him then to avoid being picked up by them. He could only pray his modifications to the telepath's wrist unit continued to blank his mental signature.

The wind had changed direction and was blowing rain into the opening of his cave. Folding up the map, he stuffed it into a pocket and moved back from the opening. Cave! He hissed his derision. It was barely more than a crack in the rock face, but it afforded him cover from the day's light and the persistent drizzling rain.

He could feel the stiffness in his joints as he hunkered down on his heels, wrapping his damp woolen robe more closely against his legs and feet. He was definitely getting too old to be out in the field, his Emperor had been right to retire him from the front line and give him an easier posting. A justified reward, He'd said. Maybe, but he hadn't liked it any better for that. Guardian to the hatchling princes wasn't what he'd looked for, though many another would have welcomed it. He sighed, wishing for darkness when he could move on and look for a larger hideout to shelter in till the rains stopped. He might even be able to light a fire, dry out his clothes, and rest in more comfort than this damp animal hole provided.

His inner clock reminded him it was about time for one of the regular news items on the information net. He turned the wrist comm on, finding he'd missed the first couple of minutes. He listened to the same tedious round of stories. Spring flooding here, a shipping accident there, a robbery, a guildhouse—whatever that was—reopening after being partly demolished in a tribal war in the desert region, and the funerals of bodies found at an archaeological site on the Valsgarth estate.

That caught his attention and he sat up, putting the comm unit to his ear to hear it better.

"Funerals were held yesterday for the remains of the ancestral bodies found in the lower chamber of the archaeological site in the hillside under the ruined monastery of Vartra. In two separate ceremonies, the ten Sholans and fifteen Valtegans were cremated. Guild Master Father Lijou Kzaelan officiated for the Sholans, and Sister Tokui Mayasu, Head Priestess of the Green Goddess cult led a short service for the Valtegans. The Sholan ashes will be scattered over the Valsgarth and Aldatan estates as they are believed to be those of founder members of those clans. Valtegan ashes will be scattered in Nazule Bay. Parents are once again advised to be alert for the distinctive bright green la'quo stones. In reality they are a dangerous resinous drug. Should you find any, please hand them in to your Clan Leader or Guild Master."

Kezule hissed in anger. Ashes! They had *burned* the corpses, not buried them decently in the ground! Worse, their final resting place would be at the bottom of some bay! Shola had been a backwater world fifteen hundred years ago, and it was no better now, no matter what technological advances had been made!

So incensed was he that he almost missed the run through of the headlines as the program drew to a close.

"Trade treaties have been signed with three member species of the Council of Free Traders at Jalna. These historic documents have brought two new species into the Alliance—the U'Churians and the Cabbarans. The Jalnians join Terra as Associate members. The fourth species, the Te-Laxaud, have not yet been contacted, but it is hoped they will soon join the talks."

He switched the unit off in disgust. So they'd formed an alliance with other species, had they? It wouldn't help them once he returned to the past. All this would be undone when he and his unit weathered out the Cataclysm in the mountains as he'd planned. But this time, he'd go back earlier, take all the eggs—keep his wife, too—and set up his own dynasty to rule this world till they could contact K'oish'ik again and reestablish the God-King's rule on Shola.

Slowly it penetrated through his cold-fogged brain that if a treaty had been signed, those he hunted would soon be home. He wanted to be on their estate before they returned in order to spy out the land and find a safe hideaway. Then he could plan his kidnap of them.

Once more, there had been no mention of his escape. Their authorities obviously intended to keep it secret. He allowed himself a sardonic smile. It wouldn't do to frighten the natives by letting them know that one of their ancient enemies, a more dangerous predator than any they'd met before, walked their world freely, would it?

He began to shiver and turned his thoughts back to more mundane considerations. Time to deal with the chill seeping into his bones from the damp clothing and the even damper weather. Slowing his breathing, he settled down to wait for dusk, staring out through the unceasing curtain of rain at the hazy alien landscape beyond.

CHAPTER 7

T'CHEBBI roused Kaid some time later. "They're back," she said, keeping her voice low. "Kate and Taynar. They're sleeping now. Had to knock Kate out, went hysterical. Taynar was out cold anyway. I checked them over thoroughly. Tiny wounds where blood and tissue samples been taken—had to look real hard for them on Taynar because of his pelt—but nothing else I can find. If Kate was pregnant, she's not now. Checked for a contraceptive implant when no one looking, but was no sign she'd been given one."

"How come I slept through all this?"

"Found them in the central room, one we use for Leskas. Left them there."

He scrubbed at his face with his hands before sitting up. He felt sticky and uncomfortable, needed a shower. He glanced at his wrist comm. Fifth hour. "You should have awakened me," he said, hauling himself up and searching for his tunic.

"You needed the rest," said T'Chebbi with a shrug, handing it to him. "Only found them half an hour ago."

"Anyone else know they're back?"

"Yes, everyone. Mrowbay double-checked them."

He pulled his tunic on, bending down to pick up his belt, then combed through his hair with his fingers.

"How are the others taking it?"

"Subdued," she said.

Heads looked up from what they were doing as he entered. He could have sliced the underlying tension with a knife. Nodding, he made for the food dispenser set into the far wall.

Tirak joined him. "Thank Kathan the Primes didn't keep them long," he said quietly.

"It was long enough," said Kaid, punching in his choice of eggs and vegetables. "They're a mixed Leska pair, that worries me."

"Perhaps they can tell us what the Primes wanted when they wake."

"We can ask them," said Kaid, picking up his plate and pressing a pad for a drink. "Better, I'll get the information myself telepathically from Taynar. He's been trained to use his talent, Kate hasn't yet. That way I can experience what he did."

Tirak narrowed his eyes. "Why didn't you do that with Rezac and Jo?"

"They're sick, Taynar and Kate aren't," he said shortly. He hadn't wanted to get that close to his father's mind, but he couldn't tell Tirak that.

"Get Zashou to tell you, then. If I understand your family groupings, she's a wife of his too, and a telepath."

"I can now she's mentally up and running again," he agreed, picking up the glass and moving aside for the captain.

After he'd eaten, he took Zashou aside as Tirak had suggested and asked her what she'd picked up from Jo and Rezac of the night they went missing.

"Nothing," she said. "They've no memory of it that I'm aware of." She fixed him with a hard look. "They have their privacy, Kaid. I don't infringe on it. Frankly, I don't want to. I'm glad he's found someone to divert his passion away from me."

"You're being too hard on him, Zashou. Ease up a little. You're as difficult for him to live with as he is for you."

Her amber eyes regarded him thoughtfully. "Why do you always want a reason to excuse him?"

"I don't, I feel equally for you both. It's not a pretty situation for either of you, to be Linked to someone so diametrically opposed to your individual principles."

"There's a mystery between you two, Kaid, and I'll solve it, believe me. He finds the need to keep defending you. I think we've all enough jeggets in our barn without you two starting an affair."

He'd not risen to her obvious bait. "If they remember anything, ask them to tell me, please."

When Kate and Taynar came round, he and T'Chebbi were there to reassure them. Kaid wished they had their medikit because Kate could have done with some kind of sedative. Remembering what Rezac had done with Tesha, he tried the same with Kate, gently linking to her mind and trying to calm her panic. It wasn't as easy as he'd thought and made Kate somewhat drowsy, but at least she was better able to cope, and so was Taynar.

With Taynar's permission, he linked to him and relived their experience. The memories were confusing, fragments of images and sensory input. It would take a lot of teasing through to make sense of them, and though he knew the skills, he lacked any experience using them. He'd have to do it the Brotherhood way.

He asked for the small table to be left empty so he could work. At first he thought he was having difficulty focusing on Taynar's memories, then he realized that this wasn't so. There was something else happening. Other images were intruding, trying to dominate his mind. He began reciting the litanies one after the other, using them to block these thoughts that were not his or Kate and Taynar's, but they were strong, and determined to dominate him.

The lights overhead had been so bright, their glare bleaching out every detail of the surroundings.

With an effort, he pushed his thoughts back to the words he was quietly reciting.

A sudden bright flash, accompanied by a pulsing sensation filled his mind. It was so clear, so real. Shocked, he jerked upright in his chair, looking round the room for its source. It came again: the flare of light, the pulse. Then again. He gasped for air, suddenly finding it almost impossible to breathe. Roaring filled his ears as the pulse throbbed once, twice, three times more. Pain lanced through his side, paralyzing him with its severity. Against his chest, the crystal he never removed flared so hot it seared him.

His body rigid with agony, he began to slide from the chair. All he could hear was the quickening beat of a heart, all he could see were the helmets of the Primes watching him as he struggled for every breath.

A strangled mewl escaped him as he and the chair hit the floor with a crash. He felt himself being lifted and carried, unable to tell which was his reality as he continued to fight for each breath. *This is what death's like,* he thought as his body suddenly relaxed and the vision faded.

The relief was short-lived, and fresh pain coursed through him. Doubling up, he clutched at his side and abdomen, keening his agony, taking his breaths when he could. Never had he experienced pain like this, not in Fyak's lair, nor in Ghezu's prison.

Faces and voices came and went but they meant nothing as the unremitting pain tore through him. After what felt like an eternity, it began to ease. He lay there panting, poised for the next wave, but it never came. Lassitude spread through him and he realized he'd finally been given a powerful analgesic.

When he came round, T'Chebbi's scent enveloped him. Gradually he realized he was lying on his side with his head cradled in her lap. The crystal lay against his arm. It was no longer even warm.

"They brought our medikit," she was telling him. "I gave you a shot. What happened?"

"Not me—a vision," he croaked. His throat was raw from crying out, but deep inside him, a tiny flame of hope had been kindled. It was so tiny, so faint and fragile, he dared not even look at it. "Let me sleep, T'Chebbi. I'll talk later."

"You sure you're all right? Could find nothing wrong with you but I've never seen anyone in such pain."

He could hear the fear and concern in her voice, feel it in her mind. He wrapped his free hand around hers and gently squeezed. "Sure."

*　*　*

Yesterday had been a strange day for J'koshuk. He'd continued to be assigned members of his crew to question, and the sessions had been routine. One look at the four Prime guards in the questioning room, and the sight of him, was enough for most of them. Everything had come spilling out, more than the Primes wanted, but less information than they needed. He'd been bored by it all as he enjoyed having to pry information from unwilling captives. The gossip value of what he was hearing, however, finally piqued his interest and he began to try developing more subtle methods of persuading them to talk than the threat of personal violence. He found this was also a heady experience, though not quite as pleasurable.

But yesterday, he'd been suddenly stopped and returned to his quarters for the night. In the corridor, he'd passed a group of three guards heading for the Sholans' quarters. Today they wanted him to see the Cabbarans. They were having problems with them. They refused to eat or some such thing.

"You will interface with the Cabbarans," the Prime seated at the desk was telling him. "Discover why they refuse to cooperate with us. For the last three days they do not eat, do not talk. They fail to thrive. This is unacceptable. You will find out why and arrange a solution."

"They're only creatures, not even lesser beings," said J'koshuk. "Why bother with them? Let them die, they're of no value."

Almost before he'd finished talking, pain lanced down his spine, felling him to the floor. He screamed and writhed there for several long seconds before it stopped. The relief was instant and, shaking, he got to his feet. Resentment boiled inside him. Who were they to treat a priest of the God-King like this? When he got his chance . . . He schooled his expression to blankness as he faced the Prime again.

"You have no value to us if you do not obey. Go to the Cabbarans and deal with the situation as you have been ordered."

"Yes, Seniormost," he said quietly, inclining his head.

The Cabbaran accommodation had obviously not been living quarters. It was a large room, empty apart from a screen which had been erected across one corner, and the mandatory floor level sleeping units. At first, he couldn't see them, but as he ventured farther into the room, he saw they were in the beds. A long, pointed head lifted itself from the depths of the nearest bed. Large forward-facing

eyes regarded him balefully as the pointed ears were rotated, openings facing him.

J'koshuk stopped. He hadn't had the opportunity to look
at them closely when they'd been herded onto the *M'ijikk*.
The head was topped by a crest of hair that disappeared
down the creature's back. As it raised itself higher on its
front legs—arms, he didn't know or care which—he could
see the brightly colored tattoos on cheek and shoulder.

"Send messenger now? No good. Take away. Where our
crew? Want join them. We are Free Traders. Have rights
if captive!"

J'koshuk was taken aback at the speech. If he'd thought
about it, he'd have realized they could obviously communicate, but to hear words, albeit translated by a machine like
the Primes used, issuing from the mouths of what appeared
to be creatures, shocked him.

"Impossible," he said, playing it safe. "The Primes demand to know why you refuse to eat."

"Take us to our crew, then we eat. If not, die. Is simple.
No more talk." He put his head down on the edge of the
bed and closed his eyes

"You start eating, then we talk," said J'koshuk, folding
his hands in the sleeves of his robe.

The minutes ticked by as he waited for the Cabbaran to
reply. It was obvious he had no intention of doing so.
J'koshuk sighed. Negotiation was not his strong point, not
his caste's calling. Force would get him nowhere in this
situation as they were obviously quite prepared to die
rather than cooperate. Or were they?

He turned to one of the guards. "I wish you to pretend
to kill one of them," he said in a voice so low he hoped
the Prime could still hear him.

There was no response, no movement, nothing from the
black-suited being that towered over him.

Praying to the spirits of all the God-Kings since the dawn
of time, he stalked over to the sleeping units, crimson robes
billowing out behind him in what he hoped was an intim-
idating manner. He stopped beside the bed next to the one
who'd spoken, and pointed down at the inhabitant.

"Take him," he said to the guard.

As the Prime moved forward, the only sound was that
of his footfalls as he drew closer to the Cabbarans.

The speaker cracked open an eyelid, J'koshuk noticed.

Bending down, the guard's hand scooped up the Cabbaran, holding him by the loose flesh at the back of his neck. He squealed once, then hung limply in the guard's grasp, eyes dull, obviously waiting for his end.

"You will eat or this one dies," said J'koshuk.

"He can eat if he wants. I do not," replied the speaker, shutting his eye again.

J'koshuk swung round to glare at the one the guard held. "Are you going to eat now?" he demanded.

"Not eat," said the voice from the translator.

"Kill it," said J'koshuk.

The guard released his rifle to pull a pistol from the side of his belt. Putting it to the middle of the Cabbaran's back, he activated it. The Cabbaran stiffened, then went limp again in his grasp. The Prime threw him to the floor, and J'koshuk prayed he wasn't really dead.

"And the next one," he said.

The guard took a couple of steps and reached for the next Cabbaran. The speaker remained motionless, not even opening an eye this time.

"Do I have to order the death of another before you'll agree to eat?" demanded J'koshuk, reaching down to pull one of the speaker's ears.

"Choose your own path," the translator said. "We chose ours. You cannot force us."

Furious, J'koshuk let it go and signaled the guard to drop the Cabbaran unharmed. Now what? "If I take you to see your crew, will you eat?" he asked desperately, aware that he'd lost any chance of having the upper hand by saying this.

"All of us go, and we stay there, not in this medical room."

J'koshuk heard the door opening and looked round to see a Seniormost enter.

"Take them," he ordered. "New quarters will be prepared adjacent to your crew. You will eat, or you will die."

The speaker pushed himself up on his forearms again. "Can't walk. Too weak," his translator said.

"Carry them," ordered the Seniormost, leaving.

Two more guards moved forward to pick up a Cabbaran

each. They turned to face J'koshuk. It was obvious they were waiting for him.

Hissing quietly with anger, he bent down to pick the speaker up. He staggered slightly under the weight, nostrils shrinking at the smell. The indignity of being forced to carry a lesser creature was greater than that of having pain inflicted on his person! Stiff with rage, he followed the lead guard into the corridor. They only had a few yards to walk, the Cabbarans had been in the block next to the others from the *Profit*, separated only by a corridor.

Kaid had just awakened as the door opened to admit the strange cavalcade of guards and supine Cabbarans. The U'Churians sprang instantly to their feet when they saw their crewmates.

J'koshuk pushed to the front. "Where do you want them put?" he hissed, not bothering to conceal his anger and contempt for beings who tolerated four-legged creatures among their crew.

Kaid began to sit up but Tirak's hand was on his shoulder, holding him still. "In the bedroom to your left," the captain said.

They waited where they were, covered by one guard as the first and J'koshuk deposited their live burdens in the room. Once they'd returned, the other two went.

J'koshuk, mindful of his orders, stopped long enough to snarl at them, "See they eat. They've refused food for three days." Then he was gone.

"Mrowbay, see to them," ordered Tirak. "Sheeowl, get water. Giyesh, find something on the menu they can eat." He looked down at Kaid.

Before he could speak, Kaid called T'Chebbi over. "Help them all you can," he said.

Nodding briefly, she followed the others.

Tirak sat down on the arm of the couch beside him. The haunted look had gone from around his eyes. "We've a chance now," he said quietly. "I knew they'd do this, it's what I was waiting for."

Kaid was lost. The drugs were still in his system and he wasn't exactly capable of thinking coherently yet.

"Cabbaran navigators are indentured to their crew,"

Tirak explained. "We have a contractual obligation to each other. They are part of our Family." He saw Kaid's confusion. "It's the way they work their contracts. Just take my word for it," he added. "We need them as navigators if we're to escape."

"T'Chebbi and I doctored the Nav systems on the *Profit*," Kaid said. "We can get us to a safe place with what we hid before wiping the logs."

Tirak's ears flicked briefly. "You *were* busy while I was out cold."

"There was work to do," replied Kaid, meeting his gaze. "The integrity of your ship to protect. We helped Sheeowl."

"I know you did. Where are you planning to go if we get out of here?"

"It's your ship, Tirak. But I know a safe place where we can defend ourselves if necessary. At an outpost remote from our home world, and yours."

Tirak nodded. "How far?"

"Where's here?" shrugged Kaid. "Two jumps from where we were. With your navigators, a week?"

"Less, if pushed, and we would be. Say three days, but it's dangerous."

"We send a message as we jump, hope they follow us not it. At least we die trying. Anything's better than this."

"Agreed. Your outpost, our navigators." He stopped to look up as Sheeowl approached them.

"Mrowbay says they'll be fine. Annuur made sure they all drank enough. Says he wants to talk to you."

"Excuse me," said Tirak, getting up.

Jo ambled over and sat down beside him. "I've just been doing some calculations," she said quietly. "You tell me how Kate has avoided getting pregnant in the fourteen and some weeks she's been off Keiss. I didn't last that long and I had an implant."

"Lucky?"

She looked across at him. "No one gets that lucky, Kaid."

"Sterile? Or he is."

"Yeah? What's the odds on that?"

"Unlikely," he admitted. "Have you any reason for asking?"

"Not without worrying Kate."

"Where's the medikit?"

"In your room. Why?"

"Do you know if there was a miniscan in it? Did T'Chebbi use one on me?"

"Yes, she did. Would that tell us what we need to know?"

"Don't know. It's set for field missions, not domestic."

"Except a mission with Leskas in it involves domestic issues," said Jo.

He flicked an ear in assent. "Try it if you get the chance without arousing her suspicions. Make sure you do it covertly. We're being monitored. I want to keep that unit."

She nodded. "How are you, by the way? You had us all very worried for a while."

"I'm fine now," he said, leaning back against the couch arm. "Groggy, but fine."

"What was it?"

"Don't know. Maybe a trapped nerve or something."

She gave him a long look. "The disappearances are only happening to us, not the U'Churians."

"I know. We're working on it. Trust me."

She nodded slowly and reached out to touch his blanket-covered leg. "I do. You take care." She got up and ambled out of the room.

* * *

Commander Lyaka of the Alliance vessel *Rhijissoh,* stood waiting in the main docking bay for the arrival of the shuttle from the U'Churian vessel *Vranshan.*

"Ten days from Home to here is pretty good time, Commander," remarked his assistant, Jiosha. "We can't match that. Takes us three weeks in military craft."

Lyaka grunted as he watched the field that covered the bay entrance begin to change color for the approaching shuttle.

"Only the private barques can go faster . . ."

"Stop rambling, Jiosha," he growled impatiently. "I want you scanning those U'Churians from the moment they arrive, not making pointless noises to me!"

"I'm already doing that, Commander," she said quietly,

clasping her hands across the front of her purple telepath's robe. "There was a point to what I was saying. Their Captain Thaylan is wondering about the *Rhijissoh*'s capabilities. He's aware our vessels are somewhat slower."

"Who's with him on the shuttle?"

"I'm aware of seven people, Commander. Three of them are, I presume, Cabbarans."

"Anything more you can tell me?"

She turned an impassive brown-eyed gaze on him. "I will need to spend some time in their company before I can do more than pick up the most basic of thoughts, Commander."

"Your Guild told me you were the best at working with alien minds."

"I am one of the best, but these are two new species," she said stiffly. "I will have to learn how they think. Then, Commander, I can sit at the edges of their minds and just absorb their stray, surface thoughts. I don't think you appreciate the amount of work that is involved."

Lyaka could see the shuttle now, just beyond the pale blue curtain of the force field. "I appreciate your job is as complex as any, Jiosha, but I need to know that these people are dealing honestly with us if we're going to combine our forces to look for the *Rryuk's Profit*. I don't want them using the opportunity to avail themselves of our technology."

"Then use their ships, Commander."

"Not practical. We need the instant communications they lack."

"You need their speed, and their navigators, from what I understand. And for that, you need their ships, too."

He growled softly. "Who briefed you?" he demanded.

She turned an innocent look on him this time. "Why, you did, Commander."

"I told you nothing of . . ." He stopped, eye ridges meeting as he scowled at the small dark-furred telepath. "You read me!"

"I cannot be responsible for what you're thinking in my presence, Commander. It does seem to me that a combination including their ships and our comm equipment would be best. I suggest you make that your first trade offer—in return for information concerning the Cabbaran navigation system."

Lyaka turned his attention back to the approaching shuttle as it penetrated the *Rhijissoh*'s barrier. "You would do well to concentrate on your own duties, Jiosha. Make sure our guests aren't planning anything that would compromise our security." He'd never come across a telepath quite so ready to voice her own recommendations. In his experience, and he'd worked with a good many, an opinion had to be forced out of them.

"As you wish, Commander. May I remind you that I will also be protecting the interests of the U'Churian and Cabbaran people against similar infringements of their security? The Telepath Guild does not involve itself in any kind of espionage work."

"I'm aware that telepaths are neutral, Jiosha," said Lyaka, watching the shuttle maneuver to its designated landing area. "Khyno, Vaszha, go and greet our visitors, if you please."

Lieutenant Khyno, sub-Lieutenant Vaszha at her side, both resplendent in formal dress uniform, proceeded to approach the craft, stopping only a few meters from the hatch.

"You will attach yourself to our visitors as their liaison," Lyaka said to Jiosha. "Escort them to their quarters after our initial discussions, take them to the senior lounge set aside for them and their diplomatic party to dine in, and show them around the permitted areas of the *Rhijissoh* should they ask for a tour. I presume you've acquainted yourself with these areas?"

"Yes, Commander," she murmured. "Do I accompany them on their search, too?"

"That is your primary function. We will each be using our own craft," he said, turning to glance at her once more. "However, as you surmised," the word was said with heavy sarcasm, "there will, indeed, be one joint craft. You will be on it."

The hatch was opening now, and the first of the U'Churian military delegation was stepping out, closely followed by his two companions. Despite the fact he'd seen the images recorded by the *Hkariyash,* the similarity between them and his own people astonished Lyaka.

Averaging the same height as themselves, the U'Churians were all dark-pelted. Dressed in mid-thigh length blue tunics bearing an emblem over the right shoulder, each one

carried a sidearm fastened to his or her belt. Khyno and
Vaszha moved forward to greet them.

"You'd think we came from the same stock, wouldn't
you?" said Jiosha quietly. "But notice, their legs are
straight, and their mouth and nose slightly more pronounced than ours."

Lyaka narrowed his eyes a little to see better. At this
distance, and with their longer black pelts, it was difficult
to see the details clearly. "Enough like us to be distant
cousins," he murmured, seeing what she was talking about
as the party moved away from the ramp to allow the quad-
rupedal Cabbarans to emerge. Briefly he wondered if they
were the navigators.

"This group aren't a navigation unit," said Jiosha
abruptly. "Navigators travel in septs of four. The
agreements between them and the U'Churians makes them
effectively Family members."

"Family?"

"The species data sent by the *Vranshan* an hour ago said
that each profession has six or so leading Families and all
members of that profession belong to one of them. The
Cabbarans become quite literally Family members of the
ship on which they work," she said. "Your aide likely didn't
have the opportunity to brief you, Commander, since you
were greeting the Ambassadors when the information
arrived."

Lyaka didn't have the time to reply as the small party
drew closer. He was continuing to be impressed with her
efficiency, however. Normally telepaths weren't interested
enough in work of a military nature to be as fully up to
date as Jiosha obviously was.

Khyno stopped and indicated the leading U'Churian.
"This is Captain Thaylan, Commander Lyaka. And Lieu-
tenants Rryal and Hannak," she said, indicating them in
turn. "This is Cheerow, Mimkee, and Duchurr, the Cabar-
ran military delegates."

"Captain Thaylan, welcome to the *Rhijissoh*," said
Lyaka, bowing his head in greeting. This is Jiosha Dzahai,
who will be helping you during your stay with us."

As he spoke, the three Cabbarans rose up to a sitting
position, leaning forward to sniff audibly at the commander
and the telepath with their long, mobile snouts.

The translator device on the lead Cabbaran's belt burst into life. "Commander's telepath. How follow thoughts alien to you?"

Lyaka caught Jiosha's startled expression, then saw her mouth open in a slight smile.

"With difficulty, Delegate, and not without help from yourselves."

"All tele-paths wear this color?" asked Captain Thaylan, touching Jiosha's robe. His voice was a deep rumble, the Sholan, though understandable, not quite correctly pronounced.

"By law they must," said Lyaka. "It is an offense to read a sentient's thoughts without their permission, therefore telepaths must advertise their profession at all times."

"Mental privacy is highly valued, Captain Thaylan," said Jiosha, inclining her head toward him.

"Report from Captain Tirak said this," he nodded. "Good knowing he was given the truth."

"If you'd like to accompany us, Captain," said Lyaka, turning slightly to indicate the air lock behind him. "I have refreshments laid out for you. We can update you on the measures we've taken so far to locate the *Rryuk's Profit*. May I say your command of our language is excellent."

"Sent to us by *Profit* when interim treaty signed."

Lyaka waited a moment for the Cabbarans to resume their normal walking stance before leading the way out of the landing bay.

"If you wish, Captain, I can increase your knowledge of our language," said Jiosha as she fell into step on the large U'Churian's other side. "We call it a skill transfer. It would also help me to understand your own language. I match my mind with yours and send you the understanding of Sholan."

The slightly smaller officer behind him spoke rapidly to her captain in their own language.

"Tirak said ask for this," Thaylan nodded. "What news have you?"

"Of the *Profit*?" asked Lyaka, stepping into the corridor and waiting for his guests. "Not good, I'm afraid. We found some debris only a few hours ago. I'm having it brought in for you to inspect. However, there wasn't enough to account for the whole ship. There's a possibility that she's still sound enough to have continued her journey. The damage could be due to meteoric impact and account for her lack of communication."

"Four ships already dis-patched during jump to search route," Thaylan said. "Look for fuel traces, see if *Profit* dropped out."

"You launched craft during jump?"

Thaylan's mouth widened in a Human style grin. "You cannot? We not so be-hind you as you think!"

Lyaka glanced at Jiosha, wondering how the U'Churian had known their rating of their tech level. She arched an eye ridge in surprise at him. It seemed this Captain Tirak was quite astute.

Thaylan put a large pawlike hand on his shoulder, grinning almost from ear to ear. "Your Jiosha give us Sholan language. We pre-pared. Tirak warn us. Got drugs for headache. Then we talk trade. Want co-munication in jump from you. Maybe give you help on hull con-struction. Need it before nav-i-gation, yes?"

Yes, thought Lyaka, *this Tirak has briefed Thaylan well— too well!*

* * *

Day 12

"So you're Vanna's Human," said Noni, eyeing the young man up and down. "At least she got a decent sized one, not like Tallinu."

Started pale blue eyes peered out from under shoulder length, wavy brown hair. They flicked across Noni's face, assessing her even as she assessed him.

"Could almost be Sholan with all that hair over your face. What you call it?" she demanded.

"A beard and mustache," he said, grinning. He liked her immediately.

"So I'm an irascible old crone, am I?" she asked, much to his dismay. "We'll have less of the old, if you please. "Teusi!"

"I know," sighed her assistant. "Take Jurrel to the store. You do realize it's raining, don't you, Noni? We'll get soaked walking to the village and back."

"Take the aircar then, and not the store, go to the inn. We might be a while. You, sit," she said, pointing a claw at Brynne. "I don't suppose . . ."

He grinned again and reached into his robe pocket, pulling out a bag of ground coffee. "I was told you liked this. This one's from Earth."

She nodded her thanks as she took it from him and began reading the packaging. "Damned outlandish script! Why don't they write it in a civilized language like Sholan," she grumbled.

"Look at the back," Brynne said. "Way down near the bottom. It's one of the coffees exported specifically for Shola."

She glanced across the table at him from under lowered eye ridges. "So it is. Thank you for your consideration, Brynne Stevens. It'll be interesting to taste the difference between this and the kind I usually get."

Brynne shrugged, hearing the door behind him close as the other two males went out. "I take it Teusi goes out to the store a lot."

"Depends on who's visiting. He's my apprentice, some things he's not ready to know yet. Jurrel said you wanted to talk about visions and dreams you think you've been having. Said Dhaika sent you off with a cuff round the ears about a week ago, telling you not to bother him or Father Lijou again with such rubbish. What makes you think you got anything worth me hearing?"

"The fact I'm sitting here talking to you," he said, watching her lift a jug of coffee and start pouring it into the first of the two mugs.

"Don't do yourself any favors, boy, I'm just curious." She handed him a mug then poured her own drink, leaving him to add what sweetener and whitener he wished from the pots on the table. "Yes, you can light one of your smoking sticks. Use the dish beside you for the ash. I've a fancy to see this strange Human habit for myself."

Floored, he was left with nothing to say as he reached for the shallow pottery dish at his side of the table.

"What else do you know about me?" he asked, fishing his tobacco tin and lighter out of his pocket.

"You don't really expect me to answer that, now, do you?" She took a sip from her mug. "So you were the pupil of the Derwent person that ran off from Valsgarth. The fake mystic who tried to teach our younglings that religion and telepathy went together, and our world is a male entity—Vartra in fact." She snorted loudly in derision. "He's a typical Terran patriarch from what I hear. No wonder he disliked Shola! We're a matriarchal world, we just let our males think otherwise."

Brynne choked on his coffee.

"You don't believe me? Who d'you think runs the Clans, my lad?" she asked, raising an eye ridge. "That's where our roots are. All the rest is commerce. Let the males play with it, we got enough females there to keep 'em on track, too."

"But many senior positions are held by males."

"Seem's the word, lad. Yes, it goes to the best person for the job, but if the best's a male, then look to the female beside him. Much easier to keep things on track from alongside your mate than out in front."

He looked disbelievingly at her. "Stronghold." He opened his tin and began rolling a cigarette.

"Kha'Qwa has a rather different kind of mate," she said thoughtfully. "That Lijou, he's more like us. Tallinu was the one I had hopes for, but his path lay elsewhere. Teusi, now, he's a good apprentice. He'll do well if he sticks it out with me. Maybe you're one of the different ones, too. Being Talented helps. Gives you an appreciation of your female side. But then, we Sholans are more balanced than you Humans when it comes to that. Once the males get past thirty, they settle down some. They're mostly past the drives to sire a family on the first pretty female they meet. You Human males never seem to get past it."

"How many Humans have you met, Noni?" he asked, putting his cigarette to his lips and flicking open his lighter. "I heard I'm only the second." He inhaled deeply, waiting for her answer.

Her brown eyes twinkled at him over the top of her mug. "I don't have to leave here to meet Humans, lad. Nor do they need to come here to visit me."

He frowned. What on earth was she talking about? How could she meet people without actually meeting them? Did she mean she talked to them on the comm? And he was like Tallinu and Teusi? He shook his head, confused. He couldn't make sense of what she was saying.

Noni's mouth opened in a gentle smile as she continued to sip her coffee. He had potential, right enough. She could use him, but not yet. When he was ready, he'd hear what she was saying clear enough.

"In all Derwent's mishmash of ideas, he did get one or two things right," she said. "At least you got through the barriers he put up about your Sholan side, lad, or you wouldn't be here. Now, tell me about those dreams of yours."

When he'd left, Noni called the Temple of Ghyakulla in Ghyasha.

"Rhuna, what can I do for you?" the Head Priestess asked.

"Looking tired, Tokui," Noni said, noticing the lowered eye ridges and darker green of the Sister's eyes.

"Setting up these colleges for our priesthood is hard work, Noni. No one is getting enough sleep these days. Almost overnight I'm expected to train up some twenty senior acolytes to the standard of priests and priestesses to cope with it. If they were Talented, it would be so much easier."

"Everyone's in the same den, Tokui. I sympathize with you, believe me."

Sister Tokui reached up to tuck a wayward lock of golden-flecked, brown hair behind her ear. "You didn't contact me to offer sympathy, Noni. I really am busy. Please make your point."

"We need to meet tonight," she said. "At the temple. You contact the other Guardians."

"Tonight?" Tokui's ears dropped in surprise before hurriedly righting themselves. "What's so important that we have to meet tonight?"

"That's what the meeting's about," said Noni.

"Noni, be reasonable! We all need more notice than this! I've got meetings scheduled . . ."

"Then cancel them or send a deputy," interrupted Noni. "Seventeenth hour, usual place."

"Noni! You can't do this!"

"Just have," she said with satisfaction and cut her comm connection.

Ghyasha was the town midway between the Kysubi and Lyarto Plains, the heartland of Shola's grainfields and almost the center of the Kaeshala continent. It was the perfect place for the Green Goddess cult's main temple, though that was disputed by the one in the Ferraki Hills, it being the older of the two. As with other Sholan towns and cities, Ghyasha existed to support the temple and the acolytes who lived and worked there. It was the place where mothers took their cubs to be blessed as newborns, where farmers went for help with their herds when all else had failed, and the center for the old folk remedies that the Guild of Medics frowned on. More, it was the core religious support for the majority of Sholan females of all ages. And it was where the Guardians met.

Teusi accompanied Noni into the antechamber of the meeting room before leaving her to join the other aides in the refectory. As she entered the chamber, she scanned the seats, spotting Lijou instantly. Hobbling over to his side of the semicircle of chairs, she glared pointedly at the male sitting next to him.

Rhio sighed and got to his feet. "Speak to you later, Lijou," he said, moving over to an empty seat at the other end.

Lijou stood, offering his arm to her. She accepted his help, even though she didn't need it, and sat down. Didn't do any harm for them to think she was more frail than she actually was. Gave her another edge over them.

"Noni, what the devil was so important you had to drag us all out on such short notice?" demanded Keaal, tapping her foot impatiently on the floor.

"Don't you try to rile me before the meeting's begun, Keaal, because you won't," she said. "Who're we waiting for?"

"Tulla," said Lijou. "Storm over the desert delayed her. She's coming in to land now."

Noni gave him an appraising glance. "You're pretty good, not many can send and receive that far. But then, you should be. If I remember right, weren't you the second choice for Clan Lord?"

He smiled gently. "You know I was, just as you knew where Tulla is," he replied equally quietly.

"How's that lifemate of yours doing?" she asked, changing the subject. "When's your cub due?"

"Less than seven weeks now," he said. "Kha'Qwa's going to ask you to be the birther. She's determined to have our cub at Stronghold rather than in the hospital."

"I intended to be there anyway," she said. "I'll come see her tomorrow to organize things well in advance. How's the nursery going? Finished it yet?"

Lijou's ears flicked back in embarrassment. "Not yet. Kha'Qwa keeps nagging me to take her to Shanagi to choose furniture and things, but I'm not so sure. I'm afraid it's tempting fate."

Noni looked sharply at him, a look he thankfully missed. "Don't you go taking her anywhere, Master Lijou," she said, poking him gently in the ribs with her index finger. "She's too far on to go traipsing out to Shanagi. You get those merchants to come out to you! They'll jump at the chance, believe me. Get to see inside the most secret place on Kaeshala, if not Shola itself? You'll have to fight 'em off!"

Lijou laughed. "A good reason to keep them away, Noni. Rhyaz would have my hide if he could hear you!"

"That's as may be. It isn't his mate that's having a cub. All you do is get the stores to use the comm link to show you round their place so Kha'Qwa can choose. Then you send someone out to fetch the crib and whatnot that she thinks she wants so she can see it in the comfort of the nursery. Only need a couple of the store's attendants, no more, and your own folk to bring 'em and take 'em back. No security breached, is there?"

"I suppose not," he admitted.

"You tell Rhyaz I said you were to do it. If he wants to argue, tell him to come and see me and we'll discuss old times."

The door opened and a breathless Tulla scurried over to the last vacant chair. "Sorry I'm late, everyone, but there was a storm over the pass and we had to fly round it."

"Get on with it, then, Noni," said Keaal. "We're all here, waiting breath-bated to find out why you dragged us out tonight."

"Wait your turn, Keaal," Noni snapped. "Tokui's in charge tonight."

Sister Tokui waved her hand tiredly in Noni's direction. "Carry on, Noni. You called the meeting."

"I want some information first," she said, fixing her glare on Dhaika. "I want to know why Dhaika's been ignoring the decision of this Council and not passing on information concerning visions and dreams."

Startled, Dhaika looked over at her. "What're you talking about, Noni? I pass on anything relevant. I always have."

"Ah, but who decides what's relevant?"

"I do, of course."

"Well, you've messed up this time, you old fool! Where'd you get the brains to dismiss the visions that Human Brynne's been having? From one of your students?"

"Brynne? He's come to you with his dreams and you think they're visions?" He shook his head. "It's you that's got no brains if you believe his ramblings, Noni."

Beside her, Noni felt Lijou stiffen slightly. So he knew more about this than he was letting on, did he?

"What's this all about?" demanded Keaal, looking from one to the other. "What dreams? What visions?"

"It's nothing," said Dhaika defensively. "Noni's gotten it all out of proportion. If she'd bothered to contact me first, I could have explained it to her and we could have avoided this meeting."

"Explain it now!"

"Someone better had," said Tokui impatiently. "This is also my concern."

"There's nothing to explain. He's having vivid dreams, that's all. The kind that every new student gets at some time or another. And he's Human, which means what he's learning makes even less sense to him. It's his subconscious adjusting to our ways, that's all. Until recently, he'd had hardly any formal training as a telepath. He'd shut off his Sholan side, the part of him that he's inherited from his Leska. Now he's having vivid dreams."

"You said that already," said Miosh. "I disagree with you about Brynne. I know him a little, I've seen him around our estate, talked to him a few times. He's not one given to flights of fancy. The opposite, in fact. He's the kind that'd turn his back on anything that seemed mystical. Remember that it was Ghyan, our priest, who advised him to go to Stronghold because of the nature of what he was seeing. He believed it to be more than him finally coming to terms with his altered state of awareness."

"More to the point, what are his dreams about?" asked Tokui.

"Nothing worth hauling us across Kaeshala at this time of night for!" said Dhaika.

"Oh, I'd say that visions of someone running through the forest and avoiding a hunt were worth passing on to the rest of us," said Noni lazily, mouth open in a slight smile. "Wouldn't you? Especially considering *who* we have loose on Shola. Namely that Valtegan general and the Derwent male." Now she felt a very positive reaction from Lijou.

She turned her head to look at him. "You didn't think we knew nothing about Kezule, did you?" She arched an eye ridge at him before looking back to Dhaika. "There's more, isn't there, Dhaika? Dreams of a creeping danger threatening Shola, of a darkness waiting out beyond our world. I'd say they were good enough to pass on, wouldn't you?"

"I want to know why you ignored Stronghold's directive as well as the Council one," said Lijou grimly. "You know why we sent him to you. He's been with you for over a week and you haven't seen fit to inform me of any of this? Dammit, we're supposed to be working together for the same ends here, the safety of our world! You forget in the isolation of the Retreat that out there in space are the beings who murdered millions of Sholans without a second thought! Anything that touches on them must be reported to me!"

"I don't think they are visions! I see them as the product of a fertile imagination and an alien mind trying to adapt to our ways! Why would the Entity speak to him, a Human, when we have so many more Talented people of our own?"

"Gods, you disgust me!" said Keaal. "I'm not fully at ease with a Human learning our religions and becoming a priest, but even I don't see why Ghyakulla shouldn't choose him to send Her messages through. They're part of our world now, Dhaika, their nature changed by our people as much as they've changed ours. There's no excuse for that kind of prejudice!"

"I'm not prejudiced, just skeptical!" exclaimed the beleaguered guardian. "How do you know they're true visions and not what I say they are? How many of you would have decided differently in my place?"

"How come you know all this, Noni?" asked Lijou. "What brought it to your attention?"

"Don't you go blaming Brynne for not coming to you, Lijou. Dhaika told him not to bother you with his 'hallucinations,' " said Noni. "Jurrel had the good sense to bring him to me. If he hadn't, we'd still be in the dark about it. Sensible lad, that Jurrel."

"Thank Vartra he did," said Lijou, turning back to Dhaika. "Had you not kept this information to yourself, I could have told you that we've had confirmation of his visions," said Lijou. "I lacked the information I now have to tell the Council more. Dammit, Dhaika, I cannot make sense of what our visionaries see if I only have half the picture!"

"What information do you have for us?" asked Sister Tokui.

Lijou looked over at Miosh, then Noni. "This must go no further for now," he said quietly. "I'm sorry to have to break the news to you like this. The ship carrying the Aldatans and Tallinu has been reported missing. A scheduled transmission they should have made before entering jump is now ten days overdue. A search was mounted as soon as we heard, but so far, we've found no trace of them."

Stunned silence greeted the news.

"Missing?" echoed Rhio. "What happened? Has there been an accident?"

"We don't know," said Lijou. "They were on a U'Churian vessel because it had the cryogenic facilities our trading ship lacked. The U'Churians' technology lags behind ours, but not significantly enough to have put their lives at risk by traveling on the vessel."

"They could have forgotten, had a transmitter failure even," said Miosh, her voice hushed. "Maybe they're in jump already."

"That's what we're hoping, but frankly, we couldn't take the risk of waiting to see if they arrived at their rendezvous.

With the treaty just having been signed between the Alliance and the Free Traders, we needed to show our new allies that we take our responsibilities to all our member species seriously."

"Why did they need cryogenic facilities, Lijou?" asked Noni quietly.

"Carrie Aldatan was seriously wounded. They had to rush her to the medical facilities on the rendezvous ship. We don't plan to tell the family until every effort has been made to trace them."

Noni was still trying to absorb this first piece of news but something made her catch Lijou's eye. "We'll have the rest, if you please, Master Lijou," she said, surprised at how gruff her voice sounded. She grasped the head of her walking stick more tightly. It was something solid and familiar in this nightmare she'd suddenly been thrown into.

"I've been warned by Vartra Himself that there is a threat to Shola from space. It's quite possible that our missing ship is the beginning of something far more sinister. The Brotherhood is preparing now. Rhyaz is speaking to the Governor tomorrow."

"It seems I was very wrong about Brynne's visions," said Dhaika, his voice barely audible.

"Dzaka came to me nine days ago with a tale of the cub Kashini crying inconsolably one night, and transmitting to him and Kitra a deep fear for her parents. I thought it impossible in a cub so young."

"I remember the night," said Miosh, voice trembling. "I was with Rhyasha. Kashini was beyond comforting for hours. Then suddenly, she stopped and just fell asleep."

"Dzaka told me that they felt that whatever was happening was over," said Lijou. "I should have paid more attention to him. He wanted us to start searching for them then. We all need to be less judgmental about what we hear, less afraid of seeming gullible to each other," he said, looking round the semicircle of Guardians.

"You should have told us earlier about the missing Aldatans," said Keaal, tail moving jerkily to show her displeasure.

"Why? It wasn't concerned with visions as far as the Brotherhood was aware," said Lijou. "If I'd had news of these latest visions of Brynne's sooner, I would have told you. In him we have another visionary on a level with Kaid

Tallinu. I want him trained and taught to dream-walk as soon as possible. That way, the Entities can speak directly to him. He obviously has a role to play in our future. He's part of our world, called by our Green Goddess Herself."

"No," said Noni, anger rising in her. She fought to keep it from her voice and thoughts. "His Triad is not the one that will link us all, not the one we need to have in this Council so we can learn about the Humans. And Tallinu was never taught to dream-walk. It never held him back. What need has Brynne of it?"

Dhaika shifted uncomfortably in his seat. "He wasn't taught, but Vartra took him to His realm during a meditation session at the Retreat several months ago."

"Why was I not told of this?" she demanded, knuckles whitening on her stick in an effort to hold back the explosion of rage. "You know my concerns for him! I should have been informed."

"It was a matter personal to him and the Entity," said Dhaika stiffly. "You know I don't breach confidentiality unless there is a sound reason to do so."

"How do you know there isn't a greater purpose behind Brynne's Triad?" countered Lijou, leaning closer to her. "You're so sure it's Tallinu's that you're blinding yourself to the choice of the Goddess!"

"They were not the first. Tallinu's is. The first Triad, and the Aldatans were the first mixed Leska pair," she said in a tone that Challenged any argument.

"Lijou still has a valid point," said Rhio.

"He has no point at all. Brynne is the only one of his Triad to have visions. In Tallinu's, all three of them have seen. We need to wait and see how Brynne and his partners develop before we agree on taking the drastic step of training him further."

"With respect to your family, Miosh," said Tulla gently, "we may have no choice if the Aldatans remain lost. All we may have is Brynne's Triad."

"We don't need to decide now," said Noni firmly. "More mixed pairs are forming almost daily, aren't they, Miosh?"

Miosh inclined her head affirmatively as she put a hand up to her eyes to rub at the tears forming in them.

"We wait," said Noni. "Actions taken in haste are worse than no action. I say we do nothing for now."

"Teaching someone to dream-walk is not a decision to make lightly," said Sister Tokui, letting her tail rise and fall lazily on the seat beside her. "There's the danger to the person themselves. To visit the realms of the Entities isn't easy or safe, even for the most experienced of us. To get lost there is to die. To cause harm to a person or animal that lives there is to die. We don't yet know enough about these Humans, whether altered by a Leska Link to one of us or not. I would have to agree with Noni. We should wait."

"Why not teach him?" asked Keaal, looking round the group. "What better way to find out about them than in the realms? There's no room for pretense. You're stripped down to your soul. I say teach him, if he agrees to it, knowing the dangers."

Tokui looked at Miosh. "What do you say?" she asked gently.

"We may have lost one Triad. We can't afford to lose another," she said, rubbing futilely at her damp cheeks. "We must wait."

"Wait," said Tulla.

"I say let him choose," said Rhio.

"Rhaid, you've said nothing so far."

Rhaid roused herself and looked over to Sister Tokui. "I've faced evil, Tokui. I know what imprisonment is like. If the Valtegans come, that's what we'll all face. I say we offer to teach him. He'll know what's at stake as well as we do. His people lived under the talons of the Valtegans on Keiss and are as much at risk from them as we are. He should be the one to choose, not us."

"Dhaika, yours is the casting vote," said Tokui.

"He'll say wait," snorted Lijou, getting to his feet and beginning to pace in front of the semicircle of chairs. "You're blinding yourselves to what really matters here. This isn't just about our cozy little world, there're millions of stars out there, millions of worlds! We live in an interstellar community, for Vartra's sake! Humans, Sholans, and the rest of our Alliance, we're at war with aliens determined to wipe us out! We need to develop every edge we can get, not put it off because of our own petty politics! I thought this Council of Guardians would be different, have a greater insight into life because we were all telepaths! But you're no better than the World Council at Shanagi!"

"Lijou, you're new to our Council so I'll excuse your outburst this time," said Tokui coldly. "Sit down. The meeting's not over yet."

Lijou glowered angrily around the room before returning to his chair.

"Dhaika, your vote," said Tokui.

"Wait," he said.

"Then the majority decision is to wait. In the interim, I would suggest that since you obviously have a visionary on your hands, Dhaika, you accelerate his learning program. The sooner he's equipped to cope with these visions, the better for us all. And, Dhaika," she said, fixing a hard look on him, "Next time he comes to you with any kind of dream or vision, you will report it immediately, not only to the Brotherhood, but to me personally. Is that understood? Fail to do so and we will have you replaced at the Retreat."

Dhaika inclined his head.

"Don't underestimate the Humans. This has been a lesson to us all, one the Telepath Guild learned, and so should we. Is your business with us concluded, Noni?" Sister Tokui asked.

"Yes, except to remind you I need to be kept informed of any visions, too." She tried to focus on the positive aspects of the meeting. She'd gotten what she wanted. There had been a danger they'd want Brynne taught to dreamwalk and that would not have suited her purposes. But the news that Tallinu as well as the Aldatans was missing was a blow indeed, one that she couldn't think about until she got home. His work had always been dangerous and the chance he'd not survive each mission had always been there, but to have death loom so close barely six months ago and now this, was more than she could take.

"Noni," she heard someone saying. "Are you all right? I've spoken to you three times."

"Eh?" She looked up to see Lijou bending over her.

"Are you all right?" he asked. "I'm sorry you and Miosh had to hear the news this way, but I had no choice."

"I'm fine," she said tartly. "You go see to Miosh. I've

got Teusi with me. I'll call you tomorrow," she said, levering herself up out of the chair by leaning on her stick.

"Are you sure? Sister Tokui's with her."

"I'm fine, I tell you! Now stop fretting over me," she said, pushing him aside. "You just see you contact me immediately you have any news of them, you hear me?"

"Of course I will, you know that."

"Right. Good night to you, then," she said, beginning to walk toward the door.

"Good night, Noni."

Lijou could see Dhaika eyeing him warily as he waited for him in the parking area outside the temple precincts.

"What do you want, Lijou?" Dhaika asked, stopping, "I'm in no mood for any more recriminations."

"We had an agreement, Dhaika," said Lijou angrily. "You said you'd teach Brynne to dream-walk if you believed Ghyakulla had called him. You purposely ignored those visions of his to avoid doing that. Worse, you told my student not to come to me with them!"

"I did not. I truly believed they were his overactive imagination."

"Don't wrong-spoor me, Dhaika! It comes down to the fact that you're afraid of Noni, doesn't it?"

"Don't be ridiculous!" Dhaika blustered.

"What's so difficult about saying no to her?"

"Have you ever said no to her?"

"I did in there."

"You disagreed with her, that's different. Your time'll come, and when it does, you won't find it so easy as you think to say no."

Lijou ruthlessly suppressed a few uncomfortable memories of encounters with Noni. "Are you reneging on our agreement?" he demanded.

Dhaika glanced round him furtively. "She'll hear you. She's still around here somewhere."

"Oh, in Vartra's name, Dhaika, stop worrying about *her*!" Lijou snapped. "I've got us shielded! Do you take me for a fool? Now, are you going to teach Brynne or not?"

"What if she finds out, or the others? What if something goes wrong for him?"

"I was there every time you were teaching him, wasn't I? Do you think I'd let anything happen to him?"

"You're new to dream-walking yourself, Lijou. When I agreed to do it, only Noni had said no. It's another thing to go against a majority Council vote, especially when I also voted no."

"Shola's at stake here, Dhaika! Not the ruling of the Guardians, our whole species! Get a backbone and start thinking for yourself!"

Dhaika stiffened, ears flicking forward. "I've made my decision," he said, sidestepping the Head Priest. "Unless you're prepared to pull rank on me and order me to do it, I'll bid you good night."

Furious, Lijou turned to watch Guardian Dhaika board his aircar before heading back to his own.

Noni sent Teusi home for the night as soon as he dropped her at her cottage. She'd remained silent during the trip, wanting no chatter, no matter how well intentioned. She went in, closing her door behind her and reaching for the light sensor. A hand covered hers, preventing her.

"You're a fool, old one," said a familiar male voice in her ear.

"How so?" she countered, trying not to let her fear be heard.

"You meddle too much this time. Let this matter take its own course."

"I do no more than I was chosen by the Entities to do," she countered.

"Not this time. I've been sent to warn you that in this matter the pledge between us has been set aside."

"Then the price must be paid."

"You'd barter at this time? When Shola herself is at stake?" The voice grew louder, the hand tightening around hers.

"It's part of the pledge," she said, forcing herself to remain calm.

She heard His low growl of anger, then abruptly the hand and the presence were gone, leaving behind it the gentle scent of nung blossom and an echo of laughter.

The price will be paid in full, never fear.

"I didn't say what I wanted!"

When was it ever anything but Tallinu's safety? He's the child you never had, Old One! But this time, you'll get more than you bargained for.

* * *

Oblivious to the furor surrounding him, Brynne had chosen to spend the evening in one of the meditation rooms at the Retreat. His visit to Noni's had left him almost more confused than before. For the first time he had the room to himself, as Jurrel had decided to exercise in the gym.

He lit the taper with his lighter, then leaned forward to touch it to each of the oil wicks in turn. That done, he passed his hand over the light sensor beside him, keeping it there till the room was lit only by the warm glow cast by the lamp. Giant shadow images of the petals and stamen of the lamp flickered on the plain walls, yet the atmosphere they created was welcoming, peaceful even.

Once more he leaned forward, this time to crumble incense on the hot charcoal at the heart of the lamp. Heavily scented clouds of smoke billowed round him then slowly drifted ceilingward, wafted there by the heat of the flames. Focusing on the flames, he rested his hand in his lap and began to recite the litanies, each one in turn, letting them guide him deeper and deeper away from the everyday world.

A faint noise caught his attention but try as he might, it wouldn't be ignored. He found himself straining to hear it better. Part of his mind was aware that the nature of the shadows had changed, that they were not so pleasing: they didn't flow across the walls as before, now there was a spiky, jagged quality about them. The sound was becoming clearer too, resolving itself into a monotonous chant. Flames flared, lighting up the room briefly as the shadows leaped and jerked in huge shapes that covered the ceiling in darkness. He heard the wind blowing through the trees, felt it against his face, moving his hair, as the shape on the other side of the fire resolved itself.

Though the face was much leaner, and the eyes now burned from dark sockets, he knew Derwent instantly.

"Did you think you'd be free of me that easily?" Derwent asked mockingly. "You made a pledge to me, Brynne. I won't let you forget that. It's time for me to redeem it."

Brynne sat motionless. He wasn't here, he couldn't be. This campfire out in the forest wasn't real, it couldn't be. He *knew* he was in the Retreat, yet every sense, augmented by his Link to Vanna, told him otherwise. He could smell the woodsmoke, scent the moisture on the air and the damp earth on which he sat. He heard the wind not only in the trees, but stirring the grass around him. To his left, a jegget stopped suddenly, sitting up to watch this strange, alien spectacle. He could hear its tail flicking gently against the stalks of grass as it wondered what to do. Even its thoughts were open to him, but not those of the man opposite.

"This is real," Derwent said. "As reality goes. I used the link I established with you for training to call you here."

"Where is here?" he heard himself ask, surprised at how calm his voice sounded.

Derwent's face clouded over as he frowned, but his eyes sparkled feverishly in the light cast by the twin moons.

"Aduan and Agalimi," said Brynne in answer to the unspoken thought.

"It took me weeks to calculate the right phases so I could work this spell," said Derwent, relaxing again. "So much easier when there's only one moon. It matters little now." He waved his hand in an airy, benign gesture. "You're here."

"Where is here?" Brynne repeated.

Derwent picked up a stick and poked at the fire, sending showers of sparks leaping up into the night. "Depends what you want to call it. Some say the dreaming land, others dreamtime. I call it the plains. You're in my world now, Brynne Stevens. The world of the guiders of souls. It's our path in this life." He looked across the flames at him, holding his gaze with his piercing pale eyes.

"I need your help, Brynne," said Derwent, his voice gentle and persuasive. "I want sanctuary so I can stay on Shola. We have work to do on this world. They've turned their backs on the true nature of their gods and it's up to us to be their salvation. We have a mission here."

Derwent sounded so reasonable, so sane, Brynne found himself thinking. Of course he must help him, he owed it to him. "What do you want me to do?" he heard himself ask.

"I need you to come to me, lead me up to Stronghold. There I can get sanctuary, if you ask it for me."

"How will I find you?" He felt as if the words were being squeezed from him against his will. He had no wish to help Derwent. Why was he agreeing to do so?

"You've been to the plains before with me. I brought you here the night I initiated you as a shaman. Remember?"

He tried, but the memory, if memory it really was, was hazy, lost in time. Initiated? He didn't remember anything like that.

"Reach out your hand to me, Brynne," Derwent said, holding his across the fire toward him. "Take my hand. I'll remind you."

He hesitated even as he felt his arm moving of its own volition. *No!* Something deep inside him screamed. *No! I don't want to be involved! I won't help you!*

"Your hand." The voice was growing authoritative now, insisting he obey.

He watched helplessly as he stretched his hand across the flames toward Derwent. Sudden pain shot through his leg and, instinctively, he yelled out and pulled back from the fire. Clutched by its scruff, in his other hand he held the offending mammal.

The fire exploded in light and sparks, blinding him, making him shield his eyes with one arm and tuck the jegget close against his chest with the other as he flung himself backward to safety.

A hand touched him and he pulled back, ready to fight.

"Not necessary." He could hear the purr of amusement in the Sholan voice. "You're safe now. You Humans are almost as troublesome as some of my people."

He opened his eyes and looked around him. Night, the forest, the fire and Derwent, all were gone. In his arms, the jegget struggled. He clutched it more tightly.

The male squatting in front of him reached out to caress the jegget's head briefly before holding his hand out to help him up.

"Who are you?" asked Brynne, refusing to accept it.

"Now you're learning," said the male with a satisfied nod. "But there's no need to fear my touch." He extended his hand another couple of inches.

Cautiously, Brynne accepted it and let himself be helped

off the ground. "I've seen you before," he said suddenly. "I know your face." He looked him over, noting the gray tunic and the pouched belt round his waist. He was well muscled, likely one of the Brothers come to his aid.

"Perhaps," the other admitted, mouth opening in a grin. "I've come to show you the way back."

"Where am I? What the hell happened to me? Where's Derwent?"

His new companion began to walk along the path toward a wooden door. He stopped and waited for Brynne to join him. "Where are you? Well, I rather think you should work that one out for yourself, but I'll give you a clue," he said, reaching into a pouch on his belt. He held out his closed fist to Brynne.

Again, he hesitated.

"You really have learned that one, haven't you," he purred in pleasure. "Take it, there's no hidden danger from what I'm giving you."

Brynne held his palm out to receive the object. "A coin?" He looked up at the male in surprise.

"Show it to Dhaika and say the owner gave it to you to keep. Remember that part, Brynne Stevens, that the coin is yours. It will work for no one else."

"Work?" asked Brynne, looking at the triple spiral pattern on its face. Then he realized the male had started walking again and ran to catch up. "What do you mean, work?"

"Watch carefully the route you take to get home and remember it well. When you wish to visit me again, take the same route. I will be waiting for you. Have this coin, it'll open the door. Tell Dhaika he is to teach you to dream-walk."

"But . . ."

"Tell him what I said." The voice was firm. "As for Derwent, there is a link between you, but the realms of this world are now barred to him. He'll not call you there again. However, he will remain a danger to you until that link has been severed. You must tell Master Lijou about it. He'll know what to do." He touched the door and it swung open to reveal darkness outside.

"Thank you," said Brynne, stepping outside. "But . . ." The door had closed silently behind him, revealing on its face the same triple spiral pattern as the coin. But in its heart was a blue-white faceted crystal.

Unsure what to do next, Brynne looked around. It was pitch black here, not a glimmer of moonlight even. Then he saw a point of green light approaching him. The closer it got, the larger it grew, and he knew this was his path home. In his arms, the jegget whimpered, reminding him he still held it. He looked round hurriedly but there was nowhere suitable to put it down.

"Looks like you and me've got to ride this one out together," he muttered, bracing himself.

Remember the route, a voice echoed in his head as the green light surrounded him and swept him away.

Cradled within it, he was carried along faster and faster until he found himself suddenly deposited at an archway. Beyond it, he could see the familiar glow of the meditation lamp and the gently flickering shadows on the walls.

"Reckon this is our stop, girl," he said, stepping through it. Abruptly, he found himself back in the meditation room with the scent of nung tree incense heavy in the air. A figure opposite him stirred, his shadow becoming separate from the rest.

"You were gone for a long time," said Jurrel quietly. "Where were you?"

"I wish I could tell you," said Brynne, blinking and putting up his hand to rub his eyes. A movement on his lap drew his instant attention. Curled up on his black robe lay a sleeping jegget. "Oh, Gods," he moaned, shutting his eyes momentarily as fear clutched his vitals. He opened his hand and looked at the coin he held. "It was true. It really happened." He turned the coin over to find the symbol of the Brotherhood.

Jurrel leaned forward. "Vartra's bones! Who gave you a Guild coin?"

"I'd rather not say," said Brynne faintly. "Do you think Father Lijou would mind being disturbed right now?"

"Not when he sees that coin," said Jurrel. "We'll use the comm in my room. I know it's secure."

"No, I need to go to Stronghold tonight," said Brynne, staggering to his feet, the jegget clutched firmly to his chest.

* * *

When Lijou arrived back from the meeting, Rhyaz was sitting inside the lobby waiting for him.

"Dhaika won't honor our agreement," he said shortly, stopping long enough to hand his cloak to his aide. "The council voted not to teach him. We need to be autonomous, Rhyaz! I will not have this happening again!"

"We are virtually autonomous, Lijou," said Rhyaz, taking him by the arm to guide him upstairs.

"Not when it comes to dream-walking!" He resisted. "I want to go into the temple."

"Very well," said Rhyaz, changing direction to accompany him. "You have the skill, Lijou. We don't need Dhaika."

"I'm too new at it to teach anyone. I need time and practice to perfect it for myself before I can even think of showing anyone else how to do it! I couldn't make them see that the fate of Shola could hang on us having Brynne trained and ready! No, don't come with me. I need time to get rid of my temper," he said, pushing the heavy door open. "I'll see you shortly."

Rhyaz nodded and waited till his co-leader had gone in before turning to Lijou's aide, Yaszho. He raised a questioning eye ridge.

"He's not pleased," Yaszho ventured. "He was silent for the whole journey."

Rhyaz nodded and dismissed him with a wave of his hand. A noise from outside drew his attention. An aircar so late? Frowning, he strolled into the duty room to see for himself who was landing.

"Jurrel and Brynne, Master Rhyaz," said the Brother on duty at the comm.

"Indeed," he murmured as he headed back into the lobby again. What, or who, had brought them here on the heels of the meeting?

"Master Rhyaz," murmured Jurrel as they entered.

"Do you know where Father Lijou is?" asked Brynne. "I need to see him."

"Is it urgent? He's in the temple at the moment." Was that a jegget the Human was carrying?

"You don't mind me bringing her in, do you?" asked Brynne. "I need her to show Father Lijou."

"They're vermin, you know," said Rhyaz, looking in surprise at the small mammal. He'd never seen one up this close before. Mainly white, her nose and ear tips were a soft, dark brown in color. Small black eyes glittered up at him as she surveyed him with as much curiosity. "They can't survive naturally this high in the mountains. If it gets loose and it's pregnant, we'll be overrun with them come autumn. It would be better if you left her with the guards."

"Oh, she isn't pregnant," assured Brynne. "And she seems quite tame. Maybe she was someone's pet."

"Pet?"

"An animal you keep as a companion to talk to and stroke," explained Brynne. "But being furred, I don't suppose a furry critter has that much appeal for you."

"You keep animals in your homes?" This astonished him.

"I guess you don't have pets, then. She won't get loose, I promise. I need to show her to Father Lijou."

Rhyaz sighed. It was late and he didn't have any interest in prolonging this discussion. "If you plan to keep her, you'll have to have her in a container that she can't escape from," he said.

Brynne turned to Jurrel, who sighed. "I'll see what I can find. I guess we'll need stuff for her to eat and drink as well."

Brynne flashed a smile of thanks and headed for the temple doors. As he walked down the main aisle toward the statue, he couldn't see the priest anywhere. The light from the braziers drew his gaze.

"Vartra's bones," he whispered, feeling the color drain from his face as he realized just who he'd been talking to that night. "It was Him!"

"What was him?" asked a voice he recognized as the Head Priest's.

He turned to find Lijou standing between the pillars on his left. "I saw Him tonight!" he said, pointing incredulously at the statue.

"Vartra? You saw Vartra?" Disbelievingly, Lijou came closer. "What are you holding?"

"A jegget. She came back with me. I was called somewhere by Derwent and He, the God, rescued me. He gave me a coin to show Dhaika and told me that you should sever the link between me and Derwent." It all poured out in a rush that probably didn't make much sense, Brynne realized, watching the various movements of Lijou's ears and eye ridges for telltale signs of his emotions. There were a lot.

Lijou took him by the arm and led him off to the side chapel of Ghyakulla. Once they were sitting, he said, "Start at the beginning."

By the end of his tale, Lijou was holding the coin in his hand and watching as the jegget sniffed her way cautiously round the small indoor garden. He smiled, then he began to laugh, loudly. When he stopped, he patted Brynne on the back.

"You keep your jegget with the blessing of Vartra, and me!" he said. "She's rather special. Anyone bothers you about her, tell them she's been granted sanctuary here by me. A pet, eh? I wonder if Kha'Qwa would like one. She's been a little low lately."

CHAPTER 8

Day 13

NOTHING was said about his failure with the Cabbarans. J'koshuk knew it was a failure because obviously the Primes had been trying to keep the navigators separate from the rest of the crew. For three days he'd continued interrogating the members of his crew brought to him by the Primes. Then on the fourth, he was taken to the room where he'd viewed the culling, over a week ago now.

They passed a gurney being towed down the corridor toward the medical section. He stopped dead, recognizing his old rival Mzayb'ik lying there, his head heavily bandaged.

"What . . ." he began.

"It is not your concern," said the guard, pushing him on.

A shiver ran down his spine. He would have argued, wanting to know more about his rival, but he remembered what the Seniormost had said about the guards and their tendency to overreact.

Two things were immediately obvious to him. Of the crew of nearly eighty, barely half remained in a room that was now laid out like a hospital ward. All present sat or lay on treatment beds staring vacantly into space. The second was a flash of floating drapery as a door at the far end of this room closed. The shock of the scene before him rendered him speechless and he could only stand and stare disbelievingly.

Three Seniormost were present, one of them wearing a gold tabard over the dark body armor. Was this their general? He *knew* they were looking at and discussing him. How, he'd no idea, but he knew.

The smaller gray-clad Prime and the one in gold left, accompanied by two heavily armed guards.

"I am giving you more freedom," said one of the remaining Primes. He pointed to a table in front of him. "Wear this communicator at all times. You will report to this area when it shows the eighth hour after midnight. You will take your designated prisoners, one at a time, to the interrogation room. Violence will not be used unless absolutely necessary. You will extract the information we want verbally, if possible. Do you understand?"

"Yes, Seniormost."

"These males each carry an implant in their head. If it is damaged, they may terminate. This is to be avoided."

"Yes, Seniormost," he chanted, then the words actually registered in his brain. Implants?

"Failure to comply will result in severe punishment being inflicted on you. Do not make it more expedient to implant you with one of our control devices."

He paled at the words, icy fingers of fear running down his spine. "Yes, Seniormost," he whispered. His obedient reply was no meaningless chorus this time.

"You may not approach any closed air lock door. This sector is sealed off from the rest of our ship. Any attempt to move out of this area will be punishable by instant death. Your collar has a locator in it. Your movements are constantly tracked. We do not need to find you to kill you."

A guard came forward to hand him a small comp reader. J'koshuk's hand trembled as he took it.

"The questions we want answered are on this. Do not lose it. The sessions will be monitored, as will your progress. Do not fail to achieve the results we expect."

"I won't," he said fervently.

"Take the communicator," said the Prime, pointing to a small table in front of them.

He stepped closer to the viewing window to pick up the clip-on wrist unit. Glancing up, he looked through the window. He could see what the Prime was talking about now. Fixed to the head of each of his people was a small, dark object, barely an inch across. Instinctively, he put his hand up to his own head, feeling the smooth dome of his skull, just to be sure.

* * *

Day 14

The next day, Master Sorli's wife, Mayoi, waited for Kitra Aldatan to arrive with a mixture of feelings. Personally, she felt a great deal of sympathy for the youngling. Kitra had seen her brother and elder sister make unconventional matches of love, and now she was being offered up as the sacrifice to Clan customs in an arranged match. It was particularly sad since she had already formed an obviously deep attachment with one of the Brothers on the home estate. However, as life-mate of the Telepath Guild Master, her own duty was clear. She must uphold the Clan laws, and Kitra's behavior, though not exactly breaking them, was certainly crushing them underfoot.

A knock on the door, and the young female entered.

She's so like her mother, Mayoi thought, watching her walk across to the desk, tail swaying insolently, an unconcerned air on her face. *Rhyasha was just as self-possessed when we were that age! She's not going to be easy to deal with.*

"Sit down, Kitra," she said, indicating the formal chair beside the desk. "I regret having to speak to you like this, but I've had a complaint about your behavior from the Chazoun Clan."

Kitra frowned, nose wrinkling slightly. "What have the Chazoun Clan to do with how I behave?"

Yes, she was going to be difficult. "Your betrothed is Ashok Chazoun," she reminded her gently.

Kitra's frown vanished and her mouth opened in a smile. "So he is. I'd forgotten."

Mayoi ignored it. There was no point fighting that battle when Kitra obviously wanted it so much. "Your betrothal and wedding are only a week away, Kitra. You should be planning for that, not visiting the males' dormitory after your curfew."

"The curfew is for younglings, Mistress Mayoi," she said, playing with the end of a lock of her hair. "Since I'm to be married like an eighteen year old in just over a week's time, why should I observe a curfew set for younger females?"

"Because you aren't eighteen, Kitra. And even if you were, you should not be visiting the young males at any time of night. You're lucky your father hasn't chosen to have you chaperoned!" She was beginning to lose her patience, which was exactly what Kitra wanted. "If I find you out of your room after curfew again, I'll appoint a chaperone myself."

Kitra looked at her with wide-eyed surprise. "Are you afraid I'll get myself pregnant to avoid this life-bonding?"

Mayoi softened again. "No, Kitra, I don't think anyone would believe you capable of such a selfish and foolish act. But your behavior is embarrassing for Ashok and his family. They're not to blame for your situation. It's not fair to take it out on them."

"It's not fair of the Clan Council to demand I marry this early either!" she retorted, standing up. "Is that all, Mistress Mayoi? As you said, it's past my bedtime."

She sighed. What was the point? The Council were mad to try to impose this match on such a spirited youngling. "Yes, you can go, but be warned. I meant what I said, Kitra!"

She was gone in a flash, leaving the door wide open behind her. Mayoi sighed. She'd tell the Chazouns she'd spoken to her, but she'd also remind them Kitra was barely more than a cub and they needed to be patient with her. Sorli and Master Konis were right, the Clan laws needed changing, and quickly.

* * *

"The Betrothal ceremony will not be held here," said Rhyasha with finality.

Konis paced in front of her desk. "It has to be held here, Rhyasha! I'm her father and the Clan Lord!"

"Then hold it in your office in Shanagi, but it will not happen here! I thought you'd learned better after we nearly lost both Kusac and Carrie, but it seems I was wrong. You should be standing up to that council of old aunties and refusing to allow Kitra to marry at her age!"

He turned on her angrily. "I can't! The laws need to be changed, and I cannot do that unless I'm Clan Lord! You know that pack are so conventional they'd vote me out with no discussion needed if I'd refused."

"So you'd rather sacrifice our youngest daughter," she said, sitting back in her chair and regarding him coldly. "I don't understand your behavior, Konis. If you really intend to go ahead with this betrothal, then as Clan Leader, I refuse to offer you our hospitality. No."

"You'd do that?" he asked, shocked. "You'd use your rank over me like this?"

"Yes."

"You're pushing me into a corner, Rhyasha. Don't do this," he pleaded, placing his hands on the desk and leaning toward her.

"Where do you think Kitra is right now? Your decision will not only give her a life-mate she doesn't want, but has already lost her her Companion!"

"Kitra ended that relationship . . ."

"When you ordered Dzaka not to see her till after the bonding and he obeyed you," she finished.

Konis had the grace to admit his error. "All right, I agree I said that. But Kitra's Betrothal must be held here. Rhyasha, don't fight me over this. I don't need a confrontation with you. I've a lot of stress at work right now with these treaty talks."

"The Chazouns can host it just as easily. In fact, there's no need for a Betrothal ceremony at all. Kitra's below the legal age to sign it. Just call Ashok and his parents into your office and get them to witness your signature for her! Then all you have to worry about is getting her to the temple the next day. As for your work, what stress? Kusac and Kaid did the preliminary groundwork. All your department has to do is get High Command to decide on the military clauses and add them to the treaty!"

He realized he'd said more than he should and tried to focus on his original point. "Are you saying you won't even sign the Betrothal contract?"

"Damned right I won't! I don't agree to this at all! I should have stood up more for Kusac, and I'm not making the same mistake this time. If you want your daughter bonded like this, you can sign all the papers yourself."

"Think of how this will look," he pleaded. "It'll cause a scandal! As her Clan Leader, you *must* sign."

"My signature isn't necessary. As Clan Lord and my husband you outrank me on this issue, so I'm exercising my right to register my disapproval. I wouldn't sell *my* daughter to maintain *my* position on that council if it stooped to blackmailing me, and neither should you!"

"Why do you have to turn this into a battle, Rhyasha?" She should be supporting him at this time, even if she didn't know what it was that was preying on his mind. After all their years together, she should *know* he needed her understanding right now.

"You started it when you agreed to their demands! What will it be next, Konis? Have you thought of that? Blackmailers never stop after the first time. They like the feeling of power too much. I'd make sure your position as Clan Lord is worth sacrificing your family for, and the price you're likely to go on paying for as long as you hold it. And I'm not just referring to the breach between you and Kitra." She stood up. "Now, if you will excuse me, Clan Lord, I have pressing estate work to see to," she said with cold formality.

With a snarl of rage, Konis stormed out.

* * *

A new supply of sealed packs of Cabbaran food from the *Profit* were discovered in the middle bedroom.

"I hate the way they seem to walk through walls," muttered Tallis, watching as Mrowbay and Sayuk piled the beds in one corner of the lounge.

"It gives me the shivers," said Kate. "They know so much about us all—our food, medicine, everything."

"They could get some of that from the medical computer in our sick bay," said Giyesh. "Mrowbay kept files. I don't think they were wiped."

Kate looked at her gratefully. "It's still frightening."

"Almost as frightening as going back in time," said Tallis carefully.

"Going back in time?" asked Giyesh. "No one can do that."

"Kaid did," said Tallis. "Along with the two in cryo. Kate said she heard about it on a newsvid on Keiss."

Kate nodded an affirmative to the U'Churian female.

"They did. It was on the 'vid because it was some religious rite. They got to set up a new Clan because they succeeded. They're En'Shalla now, beyond the laws governing Shola."

"That's a little hard to believe," said Giyesh skeptically. "Perhaps it's meant as a kind of allegory."

"There is such a rite," insisted Tallis. "What did the 'vid say exactly?"

"That they'd gone back to the time of the Cataclysm," Kate said, putting a segment of fruit from the bowl in her mouth and continuing to talk around it. "Apparently the disaster was caused by a Valtegan starship crashing into the smaller moon and sending chunks of debris falling to the surface of Shola. Tidal waves, firestorms, nuclear winter—that kind of thing. The 'vid reporters were more interested in that than anything else. Said we should all cooperate in the drive to uncover Shola's history, which had been lost for so long. They've got archaeologists from Earth doing excavations and suchlike all over Shola."

"Did Kaid and the others bring anything back with them?" Tallis asked carefully.

"Don't know," Kate shrugged. "I didn't hear any mention of it. Why don't you ask Kaid? He was there, after all."

"I don't think our esteemed leader likes me," said Tallis, mouth twisting in a slight grimace. "I think he resents any telepath since his partners went into cryo."

"I've never had a problem talking to him."

"You're not a Sholan telepath. He's certainly got very little time for Rezac, not much for Zashou, and as for Taynar," he shrugged. "Well, he's only a youngling."

Kate frowned.

"You're seeing insults where there's none," said Giyesh. "He's your leader. Like our captain, he's other matters on his mind right now, which is as it should be. Our safety depends on their decisions."

Tallis toyed with a piece of skin from Kate's fruit. "Maybe you're right," he conceded. "It's been hard for him with his lovers in cryo. He's probably finding it difficult to keep his mind on anything much right now."

Giyesh made a small noise of anger. "What's this all about, Tallis? You trying to make us doubt him? It's our job to support our leaders, not undermine them, and especially not in front of young ones."

Tallis tossed the rind onto the table and sat back in his chair. "I'm a civilian, Giyesh. Kaid isn't my leader. I didn't elect him, nor did any of us but T'Chebbi. Even your captain defers to him at times."

A shadow fell over the table. Tallis looked up to see Rezac and Jeran standing beside him.

"Thought we'd join you," said Rezac, sitting down next to him as Jeran took up the offer of part of Giyesh's seat. "Jeran says you're up to your old tricks again, Tallis. I'm giving you a friendly warning—this time."

Tallis could hear and feel the almost soundless growl of displeasure from the telepath. "You the morale officer now, Rezac? Listening in to what everyone says? You're breaking Guild rules, you know. Mental privacy and all that. I'm entitled to my thoughts."

"I'm a civilian too, Tallis. But as for your guild system, it doesn't apply to me. Stop trying to play your little political games right now. We need to be united, and that's difficult enough when we're not all of the same species. We don't need you undermining Kaid or anyone else."

Tallis got to his feet. "I don't like your implications, Rezac. I was merely being friendly, which is more than can be said for you or Kaid." He stalked off to the other side of the room.

Rezac turned to Kate. "Jeran says Tallis was a supervisor at the mining corporation where they worked. He enjoyed snooping on all the employees, reporting any infringements, no matter how small. They reckon he used his Talent to find out what they were up to. I'd think twice before trusting anything he said."

Kate looked from him to Jeran.

He nodded. "You had to watch everything you thought and said when he was around. No one liked him. When the Valtegans took us, it was better for us to forget that, to start fresh. All we had was each other. Even then, he avoided pulling his weight. Left it to Miroshi to do anything that involved using telepathy."

Giyesh growled in annoyance. "I bet he used his ability to make what he said sound more believable too!"

"Probably," agreed Rezac. "He picked on you, Kate, because you have less experience, you'd be easier to influence."

"I'm not a child," she said, finding her voice. "You're right. He was beginning to sound believable. But why? Why bother? What does he gain by doing that?"

"Amusement," said Jeran. "Someone like him, with no friends, has to create situations where he feels important and noticed, even if it's dislike."

"It was more than that," said Giyesh thoughtfully as Jeran moved round to take Tallis' vacant seat. "He was also after information."

"About what?" asked Rezac.

"Going back in time." She looked strangely at him. "Did they really do that?"

Rezac nodded. "Kaid said so."

"You came from that time, didn't you? Did what he say sound true?"

So Tirak had told his crew. "Yes, he knew things that only someone who was there could have known," he agreed. "He described people and places I knew. That knowledge couldn't have lasted for fifteen hundred years. What was Tallis interested in about the past?"

"He was asking if they brought anything back with them."

"Kezule." He'd said it before he could stop himself.

"Who?" asked Jeran, frowning.

Rezac shook his head. "Forget it. It's just a name, nothing more. The important thing is to keep an eye on Tallis, make sure he doesn't try that trick on anyone else." He was thinking fast now, had to. He couldn't be sure Tallis hadn't heard him. Better to let Kaid know about it now than have him find out later.

"Not just for Kaid's sake," said Kate. "He was having a go at Captain Tirak as well."

"Keep not just an eye on him then, keep a mental ear out for anything subversive." He pushed himself up from the table. "I'm going to let Kaid know what he was up to."

"Kezule?" said Kaid. He'd been making a quick visit to the Cabbarans with Tirak and had missed the interchange. "What makes you think he's interested in him?"

"I told you, he was asking if you'd brought anything back from the past."

"But to think he meant Kezule is a rather long leap, Rezac," said Kaid, leaning against the drawer unit.

"You asked me about him at your briefing on the *Profit*," reminded Rezac, sitting down on his bed. "He's obviously been thinking about the whole issue. Now that I have, it seems obvious to me, too. Did you bring this general back with you?"

There is no reason not to tell him. Might even help if he thought he was being trusted with inside information. "Yes, we did. He's at Shanagi being questioned. They're studying him, trying to find out all they can about his species. This isn't common knowledge, you realize."

Rezac gave him a scathing look. "Don't take me for a fool, Kaid," he said. "I might be younger than you, but I've been around. I've had some experience of leadership."

"I know." Now that they were alone, his curiosity was getting the better of him. "What were you doing in Ranz?"

"Why?" asked Rezac, narrowing his eyes suspiciously.

Kaid shrugged. "Just curious," he said, watching the other's tail tip begin to flick gently. He didn't want to talk about it, obviously. "I wondered why you went there when you lived in the western peninsula."

"I came from Ranz," he said. "My parents owned a general store. I got picked up by the University telepath program. They offered me a chance to get an education and training in my psi abilities, so I took it."

"And the packs?" He knew he was pushing, but he wanted to know.

"What do you know about the packs?" The tail was no longer moving gently, it was an agitated twitch.

"Goran said you were involved with them when the program picked you up." It wasn't strictly true, but he wasn't going to tell Rezac he'd had a vision of him working out with Goran in the gym under the monastery. He could sense the younger male considering his answer, wondering whether to tell him the truth or not.

"Why's it so important to know?" he asked.

"I was in Ranz for several years myself," said Kaid. "With the Claws."

"You?" There was stark incredulity in his voice. "You were with the Claws? You read me, damn you!"

"No," said Kaid. "Ask T'Chebbi. She knows. I was Second. The Brotherhood picked me up and took me to Stronghold." He noticed the other's tail tip lay still now.

"I was with the Claws, too," Rezac admitted. "You couldn't refuse the University recruitment drive. Once they'd spotted me, I had to go. Telepaths of my ability were rare, they said, and offered to move my whole family. So we sold up and went. It was a chance to escape, to start again."

"That's what Zashou can't forgive, your past."

Rezac nodded. "Look, the Claws, they wanted me. They threatened my family to make me join. I tried to stay out, but they started trashing the store. Even then, it wasn't till they took my sister that I agreed."

"No one told me you had a sister." Was it possible he wasn't Rezac's son, but his sister's?

"My family wanted nothing to do with me," he said quietly. "Never spoke to me again after I joined the Claws. They were ashamed and afraid of me. What about you?"

Kaid hesitated. "I was a foundling. I left home for Ranz and fell in with the Claws, that's all."

"You must have been good to become Second."

He shrugged. "The Brotherhood got my past officially erased on the condition I stayed with them. It seemed like a good deal."

"Strange how similiar our past is," murmured Rezac. "At least Carrie didn't hate you for it, like Zashou does me. At least, I presume she didn't."

"No, she'd no problem with that." Rezac's story had shaken him. There was a similarity between them after all, a bizarre one. What were the odds against both of them, so far apart in time, ending up with the same pack? "We'd better return to the lounge," he said. "Don't want the others worrying because we stay away too long." He had to ask this last question. "Did you have someone in Ranz? A Companion?"

"There was someone once, yes, but I had to finish it when the Claws started trying to recruit me. Once I was the Claws' telepath, I was a target for the other packs. They protected my family, but in return, I was one of them, expected to choose one of the pack females. I wasn't exactly a safe person to know back then. Why?"

"Just curious."

*   *   *

That night, Kaid dreamed of home—a strange dream, crazy and disjointed as most dreams were. Elements of Rezac's story wound their way in and out of his own memories of the Claws for a while. Then they became more focused and he saw his son, Dzaka, keeping watch in the nursery at the villa. Saw him argue with Jack when the doctor came to check on Kashini, then storm out, leaving the Human alone with the child. Mara was working out with Garras' other students in the Warrior's exercise hall—and coming along well, by the look of it. Vanna seemed fine, her pregnancy advancing well as she greeted Brynne and another male from Stronghold.

His thoughts kept returning to his son, though. Dzaka should be with the cub: she was the vulnerable one. In his dream, he tried to reach out to him, to tell him this, but each time he failed. He was about to give up when he saw Dzaka's ears flatten against his skull as slowly he turned round and looked straight at him.

At last! *Guard Kashini well. There's danger approaching,* he sent.

Dzaka's nose wrinkled and his brow creased. He seemed to be peering at him, almost as if he was trying to focus on what he saw.

"Carrie?"

Day 17

Shock at hearing her name fragmented the images, making him feel as if he was spinning endlessly in space. He was aware of voices, could feel himself being touched. It made him feel unclean, nauseous, and with a strangled growl, he pulled away from the hands that grasped him. His stomach began to spasm and he broke out in a cold sweat. Confused and ill, he knew there was a danger of choking if he vomited. As he pushed himself up on one arm, the voices stopped fading in and out and became distinct.

"Get him the bowl from the table," he heard T'Chebbi say.

He was with his own, then. No longer protesting, he allowed himself to be touched and pulled into a sitting position. Opening his eyes, he found everything blurred. He blinked, trying to clear his sight, and felt the bowl thrust onto his lap. Suddenly light-headed and cold, he grabbed for it.

"Kaid. Kaid." The voice had become insistent.

He was lying on his back again. Opening his eyes, he looked up at the face swimming above him. T'Chebbi.

"Do you want to sit up?"

Of course he did! Lie here like some beached sea creature? But all that came out was a groan. He let himself once more be slowly pulled into a sitting position, realizing he felt better this time.

"Kaid, you were gone. Do you remember anything?" she asked.

Beyond her he could see Jo and Rezac, concerned looks on their faces.

"Gone where?" he asked, shocked to hear how rough his voice sounded. He swallowed, discovering his throat hurt.

"They took you, like they did the others. Do you remember anything at all?"

This was so confusing. They were mistaken, surely. "I was dreaming," he said hoarsely. "Of home, of Carrie." He ran a shaking hand across his folded back ears. A cup of water appeared. Taking it, he emptied it in one go. He'd been thirsty.

"You were gone for two days. Don't you remember?"

Everything was so vague. "Why do I feel so ill?" he asked. "I told you, I was asleep, dreaming of Carrie—no, not of her, I *was* Carrie!"

T'Chebbi looked briefly at Jo. "Carrie's gone, so is Kusac. We think they're dead, Kaid, that's why you've been so ill. Was like Link deprivation, Rezac says."

Memory returned in stark clarity then. They were dead, and by his hand. "I only remember the dream," he said, his voice hushed as he realized he had to face that possibility.

He sent them away, then lay there, staring at the ceiling, wondering why Dzaka had thought he was Carrie. Could this dream have been one of Carrie's in cryo? Or was it just that Dzaka had recognized her in his mental pattern? Whatever the reason, it had brought the whole question of his Triad partners' survival only too vividly to his attention.

He loved them both—how could he not? They had become his touchstone for what was bright and full of promise for the future, a future of the kind he'd never thought to have for himself. They'd gotten into his heart from almost the first with their courage and determination to stay together and to overcome the odds they knew were stacked against them. It was the little things, a word here, a gesture there that came back to him now, tearing at his heart.

He turned over, burying his face in the sheet beneath him and let the memories he'd blocked return. Vartra had been right about the cost of this venture—it had cost him not one but both of his Triad.

He'd put Kusac through hell during his first few days at Stronghold before accepting that the younger male wouldn't be put off, no matter what was thrown at him. He'd even submitted to being a warm body for inexpert students to practice massage techniques on. It had been, mentally and physically, a painful experience, one Kusac had never had to face before in his sheltered life as a telepath.

The relationship that had been forced on him with Kusac had made him face his own past in a way that his relationship with Garras never had. He'd been the junior sword-brother then, but with Kusac, he'd been senior and had to take responsibility for him. In doing that, he'd been able to come to terms with who and what he was, and accept his own telepathic talent.

He remembered the comfort he'd felt knowing Kusac lay beside him during those nights at Stronghold when he'd doubted his own sanity; remembered the set of his friend's ears, the tilt of his head when puzzled, how his nose would wrinkle in thought—and being teased with a gentle, shared humor for the first time in his life. He missed Kusac's quiet strength at his side. And even before this intimacy, Kusac had trusted him enough to ask him be his third, become one with him and Carrie.

He tensed, anticipating the grief for her, but it wasn't enough. He could have howled it to the moons, it was so deep and pained him so much. It filled every part of his being till there was room for nothing else. He clenched his hands in the bedding, claws puncturing through the fabric into the filling as his tears flowed. The loss of them both was unbearable.

He remembered her scent, the silken feel of her blonde hair as he ran his fingers through it. Her skin, covered in a pale, soft down that was almost invisible. He ached to hold her one more time, to hear her voice, see her smile, feel her touch. He had to believe there was still a chance they were alive, that the warming of the crystal four days ago had been her stirring in cryo.

He wept till he was empty and exhausted, then he walled his grief and fear for them away deep inside and got up. His eyes felt gritty and his head was thick and heavy, but it would pass. He would make it pass.

He showered, finding sore spots on his back and at the sides of his head. Momentarily he wondered about them, then remembered Jo had said he'd been taken by the Primes. He froze, leaning against the cubicle wall. He searched his memory, remembering nothing beyond being afraid of being touched, then realizing it was T'Chebbi and the others. If he had been afraid, it was because he'd been aware, on a subliminal level, of being examined by the Primes.

He searched his body thoroughly then, looking for any other wounds or tender areas, remembering the time Vartra had called him back to the past. The thought of lying helpless and unconscious, being examined intimately for two days bothered him profoundly. He found nothing, but he wasn't reassured. His only comfort was that they'd returned him apparently unharmed.

Showered, his pelt brushed till it was free of loose hair, he dressed and joined the others in the main room. They were eating—he had smelled food, then. Nodding to those who looked up, he strolled over to the food dispenser and chose a meal. Overcoming his instinct to sit alone, he went over to the smaller table where T'Chebbi sat with Rezac, Zashou, and Jo. Because of his wrist psi damper, he was only faintly aware of their concern. Without it, he'd have found being with anyone unbearable right now.

Talk stopped as he sat down. After a minute or two, he glanced up at Rezac. "I'm fine, thanks," he said in Highland, then looked at T'Chebbi. "You coped well, and, no, it won't be a repeat of Stronghold. Now can we please carry on as normal? You said I was gone for two days. How long was I ill?"

"Most of today," said Jo, spooning some food into her mouth. "We'd almost given up on you being returned. Do you remember anything?"

"Only that I didn't want to be touched until I realized it was T'Chebbi and you," he said. "I take it you checked me over when you found me."

"Not at first," said Rezac, pushing the remains of his food around his plate with the fork. "We had to wait until the worst of your sickness was over."

"We needed Rezac's help because you fought so hard. Too much for me and Jo. Had to keep it among our own," said T'Chebbi quietly, moving her plate aside.

"You did fine," he reassured her. "Thank you, Rezac, Jo."

"We found the usual small wounds on your back where samples had been taken, but on you, they'd healed. There were scars," said Zashou.

Kaid glanced up at her, then back to T'Chebbi.

"Had to tell her," she said. "Didn't realize she was looking on your back."

Zashou got abruptly to her feet and left.

"That one is getting on my . . ." T'Chebbi continued, but Kaid cut her short.

"Leave it alone, T'Chebbi. She's no worse than Khemu was. She couldn't cope either. It takes a strong female to live with one of us. It's not her fault. Did you find anything else?"

T'Chebbi sighed. "Think not, but difficult to tell with all that scarring. Scanner said nothing but traces of drugs."

"We found new marks," said Jo. "On your forehead and temples. Some kind of gel that they hadn't wiped off properly. I'd say they'd done some kind of scan of your brain."

"Or some experiment," he said quietly, heart beating faster as he realized his sickness could have had nothing to do with his Triad partners. "They definitely know we're telepaths, that's why we're being targeted."

"Zashou's running so scared she's sleeping with us, and I mean *with* us," said Rezac worriedly. "You should have known her before all this. She was so different from what she is now. She lives in constant terror of what's going to happen next."

"She was like this on the *Profit*," said T'Chebbi.

"We've had over three years of this level of fear," said Rezac quietly. "No breaks, only fear. The time in stasis for us wasn't even as long as a night's sleep. One minute we were running from the palace guard, the next we were on Jalna with you."

"Hadn't thought of it like that," admitted T'Chebbi. "Look, I have this problem with females like her. I know I have. Can't help it. They do nothing but mewl, never try to help out."

"Don't underestimate her, T'Chebbi. She pulled her weight, too," said Rezac, looking over to where Zashou sat with Sheeowl.

"Why two days for you and only one for us?" asked Jo. "Was it because you took ill when you were there?"

"Possibly. How did they bring me back?" Kaid asked, taking another mouthful of the meat.

"Heard a noise from the room, rushed in, and you were back," said T'Chebbi. "You were conscious, but only just, and trying to get up. They'd left drugs for you, all neatly labeled with pictures showing the dosage and what they were for."

"Before you ask, they were printed and smelled of nothing," said Rezac.

Kaid looked appraisingly at him. "You'll make a Brother yet. So I was conscious when you found me." He poured himself a drink from the jug on the table. "You said Link deprivation. I don't think so, but it's possible. As you say, it could have started while I was with the Primes."

"They returned you when they thought you were stable," nodded Jo. "Makes sense."

"I said it was *like* Link deprivation," amended Rezac. "In its final stages, and far more violent than anything I experienced."

He nodded. It wasn't what he'd hoped to hear, but it could equally have been caused by them experimenting with his psi talents. However, he didn't want to alarm the others any more than they already were. "Could you identify the drugs?"

"It's only a miniscan. Can't give that much info, even

with Sholan drugs," reminded T'Chebbi. "Just showed analgesics and anesthetics, and a couple unidentifiable alien chemicals."

"No psi suppressants?"

"None that we could tell, and the stuff they left for you was to stop you vomiting and sedate you. We don't even have any psi drugs in the medikit. They took 'em out."

"Yet they left me my wrist comm," he said thoughtfully. "Why that and not the drugs?"

"They can take the comm away from you instantly?" suggested Rezac.

"That makes sense, but what doesn't is why they're interested in us, why they took the *M'ijikk* in the first place. No Alliance member ever conducted a First Contact like this. It defies common sense. Their behavior toward us is no basis on which to form any relationship that depends on trust."

"Maybe that's not what they want," said T'Chebbi. "Maybe they're just curious, or checking out the opposition if they decide to start empire building in this sector."

Kaid pushed his plate away. He'd had enough. His stomach was still unsettled. "I need to talk to Tirak." He began to rise but Rezac beat him to it.

"I'll go. You rest," he said.

As Kaid watched him walk across to the captain, T'Chebbi rose and began collecting their plates to return them to the dispenser.

"He feels an affinity with you," said Jo. "Especially now."

Kaid looked questioningly at her. "Now?"

"Your talk a couple of days ago, and because he saw your scars. People have to earn Rezac's respect. They don't get it for free."

He shrugged. "My own fault. I walked into a trap. Not exactly something to be proud of."

"Not the way T'Chebbi told it."

"She's biased," he said, making his tone light. "We go back a long way."

*   *   *

Brynne had spent less time at the Retreat recently, and when he was told to report to Ghyakulla's Shrine in the temple, he was surprised to find Guardian Dhaika there with Father Lijou.

"I've been telling Guardian Dhaika about your coin," said Lijou. "Would you mind showing it to him?"

"Sure," said Brynne, fishing inside his robe for it. The coin now hung from a silver chain round his neck. He held it out for the Guardian to see.

Being careful not to touch it, Dhaika examined the spiral-decorated face. "I've seen enough," he said.

"Well?" Lijou asked of him as Brynne let the coin drop against his robe.

"I've come to teach you to dream-walk," said Dhaika. "Father Lijou is going to help me."

Puzzled, Brynne sensed an undercurrent of animosity between the two males. "I'm not so sure I want to," he said hesitantly. "The whole business with Derwent has kind of freaked me out."

Dhaika stirred, drawing Brynne's gaze to him. Without even trying, he could sense the glow of self-righteousness from him.

"He's not ready. I told you that, Lijou, whether or not the God wants him."

"Dhaika," said Lijou warningly. "The choice is yours, of course, Brynne. I told you dream-walking isn't without its dangers, but Derwent is not one of them. I dealt with that as you know. However, you have a personal invitation to visit the realms. That in itself confers a protection."

So Dhaika didn't want him to go, and Lijou did, but wasn't putting pressure on him. His mind was suddenly made up. "What do I do?" he asked.

Vartra had been right, he did recognize the route, though the colored light that took him there was different. Two ancient gnarled fruit trees formed an archway over a wooden door. In the center of it was carved the triple spiral with the crystal set in its heart. He reached out to touch one of the trees, taking himself a pace closer to the entrance. Beneath his fingers, the bark felt as rough as any tree he'd ever touched. Turning his attention to the door, he tried to remember what Dhaika had said about opening it.

"Place your hand on the carving and the door will open," he'd said.

Brynne took the chain on which he wore the coin off, comparing the two images. He wasn't quite ready to go in yet, despite the fact that the being on the other side of the door had rescued him from Derwent's schemes. He was curious, though, and almost without realizing it, his hand went out to touch the carving. The door swung open.

"Oh, what the hell," he muttered, stepping through. "How bad can it be after Derwent?"

He found himself on a path among the trees. On his left, a small stream tumbled over a stony bed, gurgling and chuckling as it headed farther into the forest. Sunlight flickered through the leaf canopy overhead. The scent of summer blossoms was in the air, and around him he could hear the gentle buzzing of pollen-gathering insects.

Slipping the chain back over his head, he began to walk, finding the path sloped slightly downward, meandering its way through the trees till he came at last to a small clearing. In it he saw a figure he recognized from the night before. Clad in the same gray tunic, Vartra sat on a fallen tree trunk.

"Now you know how to get here on your own," Vartra said. "Though you came through my doorway, this is part of Ghyakulla's realm. She's allowed me to meet you here."

"Why?" Brynne asked, stopping in front of him. Vartra looked so real, not like something in a vision at all. He could see every detail, almost count the hairs on his pelt had he the time and inclination.

"It is real. You are here, it's just a different reality from the one you normally inhabit. Sit with me."

Brynne moved past him to perch on the log. "Why did you want to see me again? Couldn't you have said what you wanted that night?"

"You wouldn't have taken it in then. It was something of a shock to you to come face to face with Derwent like you did."

"You're telling me," he said with an involuntary shudder. "Where is he now?"

"Oh, he's carrying on with his journey," said Vartra. "Enough of him. What I need to say is important, so listen well."

* * *

Brynne rubbed his eyes, finding the light in the shrine very dim in comparison to the sunlight in the clearing.

"Well come back," said Lijou quietly.

He looked around, saw Lijou, and knew Dhaika had left.

"He's returned to the Retreat," said Lijou. "He'd done what was needed. I watched over you."

"It's real," he blurted out, clambering to his feet. "He's real!"

"Yes, He is. Rather a shock to realize that, isn't it? I had a feeling Vartra would be there. Ghyakulla rarely has any physical contact with us. The fact She used Her realm for your meeting shows that Vartra speaks for Her. What did He have to say to you?"

Brynne's eyes glazed over slightly. "We need to keep faith with those we trust. It didn't seem to make much sense. He said that circumstances will make us want to doubt them, but we mustn't."

"So much of what we sense is taken on faith," said the priest quietly. "Including our belief in each other."

"What does it mean?" asked Brynne.

"Exactly what He said it did. We must trust those we do trust. We're facing a time of trial when our beliefs will be stretched to the utmost, Brynne. Dhaika refused to listen to me when I said we needed you trained as quickly as possible. He couldn't believe that Vartra had told me this. Now the God has taken it into his own hands to make sure you get the training you need. Trust. Dhaika refused to trust me, and the Gods."

"What's about to happen, Father Lijou? Is what I've been experiencing part of it?"

Lijou roused himself and got to his feet. "It may well be," he said briskly. "Vartra gave us our own coin and told us to ready ourselves, Brynne, so we are. All the visions you've had form part of the picture, but where the danger will come from, we don't yet know. That's why we need you trained. Tallinu was perhaps the best of our visionaries, but he's no longer with us. You show great promise. Let's hope we find the answers we need through you."

He felt his heart sink. "So I'm going to keep on having these dreams and visions?"

"I hope so," Lijou said, putting his hand briefly on Brynne's shoulder. "Now, don't worry, you'll get used to it. Tallinu did. It's your calling."

Brynne grunted. He wasn't so sure he wanted to get used to it. It was damned upsetting and inconvenient to keep waking up in a cold sweat because of some vivid dream in which he actually was the person rather than an observer. And no matter what Father Lijou said, there was the fear he'd meet Derwent again.

Lijou's hand closed comfortingly on his shoulder. "The link between you and Derwent is severed, Brynne. You'll not meet him when you're dream-walking, I guarantee that. From the first I've made sure there were those close to you who could help and protect you, and I have personally monitored your training. Do you think I would let any harm come to you?"

"I suppose you're right," he admitted. "What you're saying is not that different from what Derwent saw as my future."

"As a guider of souls?"

"Something like that," he said vaguely. "It certainly had to do with walking realms and dreaming."

"It's coming up for second meal now. Why don't you get something to eat and take some time off to rest? You and Jurrel can return to the Retreat tomorrow. No need for you to head back today. You'll absorb what you've learned better if you rest for a while immediately afterward. Sleeping is even better."

"I am tired," he admitted, letting the priest turn him toward the doorway. "And hungry."

"Using one's Talent tends to make you hungry," agreed Lijou.

* * *

Day 19

"She's causing havoc among the older males, Konis," said Sorli. "Six days ago Mayoi warned her if she broke curfew again, we'd appoint a chaperone. Granted she hasn't done that, but she's gotten herself a reputation among the students for being very available, shall we say. Ashok Chazoun is refusing to have anything to do with her, and wants the betrothal called off. Frankly, I don't blame him."

Konis continued to look out over the Guild grounds. "What does his father say?"

"He's prepared to keep the contract if you exercise some control over Kitra. The life-bonding can take place as planned once she's been medically examined to prove she's not pregnant. After the ceremony, they want her sent to their Clan estate until she's provided them with an heir."

"Unacceptable," he growled.

"You can't blame them, Konis. They want to be sure their Clan's heir is Ashok's cub," said Sorli gently. "Why didn't you keep her at home until she was bonded? Or appoint a chaperone? She might not have gotten so out of hand if you had."

"If I had, she'd have run away, Sorli," he said, turning to face him. "Forcing her into this bonding has caused enough of a breach between me and my family."

"I'm sorry we had to send her home, but you see my problem. She's disrupting the whole Guild. Keep her on the estate till she's safely bonding."

"She's fourteen, Sorli. She's losing her youth to this family. It'll be a year at least till she can return here, you know that, and that's only if they allow her to return. At her age she has only the legal rights her family allow her, and that will be the Chazouns."

"You arranged the match with them. If you had your doubts, you should have chosen someone else."

"When I arranged this match, it was on the understanding the bonding would be in name only. Now they want an heir immediately! That's not acceptable as far as I'm concerned."

"What do you intend to do?"

"Resign," he said grimly, heading for the door. "This has gone beyond what is reasonable."

Rhyasha flung herself across the door to Kitra's room. "Don't you even think of touching her," she said. "You've no one but yourself to blame, Konis. You said she needed to get more experience!"

"Dammit, Rhyasha, stop being so melodramatic! I'm not

going to touch her!" he said tersely. "What do you take me for?"

"What are you going to do?" she asked, relaxing a little and letting her arms drop to her sides.

"Talk to her. You can come with me if you don't believe me."

"You be kind to her now," she warned. "She's been told by the Guild what the Chazouns expect of her and she's taken it very badly. She's still in shock. So am I."

Kitra sat hunched up in a chair near the bed. She looked up as they came in, but said nothing.

Konis sat down on the bed as close to her as possible. "Kitra, I've canceled the Betrothal. It's not going to happen," he said. "I'm not agreeing to their demands. It's over, kitling."

She looked up at him, the short pelt on her face streaked by dried tears. "You canceled it?"

He nodded. "There's to be no bonding. If you want Dzaka, you have him. I'll even take you to the temple now and sign the life-bonding contract between you."

She stared at him, unable to take in what he said.

"Did you hear me, kitling?" he asked gently, reaching out to take her hand. "I said I'd take you to the temple to . . ."

"It's too late," she said. "It's over between us. He wouldn't have me anyway."

"Of course he'd have you," said Rhyasha, almost as stunned by what her life-mate had said as Kitra was.

She shook her head. "I asked him. He said I was too young, would still be even in a year. And I don't want him any more," she said with finality.

Rhyasha shot a fulminating glance at Konis. *See what you've done? It's too late to undo it now!*

"Think it over, Kitra," said Konis, squeezing her hand gently. "I'll talk to him if you want. Take a chance, do it now. Today. Just in case the new Clan Lord decides to make another contract for you."

"What new Clan Lord?" demanded Rhyasha sharply.

He looked up at her. "I resigned. You were right. They can't be allowed to blackmail me like this. You and Kitra aren't worth sacrificing for them."

Rhyasha sat down beside him. "You resigned?"

"What was I supposed to do? Agree to the Chazouns' outrageous demands? I had no other choice, Rhyasha."

"You resigned because of me?" said Kitra in a small voice.

He turned back to his daughter. "I had to, kitling. I should never have agreed to the Council's demands in the first place. Now, please think this over. I'll talk to Dzaka . . ."

"No! I told you, it's too late," she said, wrenching her hand away from his and running from the room.

Konis started to get up but his wife held him back. "Let her go. She needs to cope with this her own way," she said. "You really resigned?"

"I sent letters to all the Council members. I've named Rhaid as my successor. She's unlikely to support Kitra's early bonding, but having made such a mess of it up till now, I wanted to be sure that Kitra got the chance to life-bond to Dzaka."

"It might well be too late, Konis. She's distraught because he didn't stand up for her. You should have put Dzaka forward as her husband and damned the Council."

"I couldn't, Rhyasha. He's gene-altered. There's no way he'd have been an acceptable life-mate for her."

"Are you sure this is what you want? You could call their bluff and face them at the Council meeting, rather than go the whole way and resign. I'd be there to support you."

"Thank you," he said, touched. "But I've done it now, and I don't regret it. Have you ever heard anything like those demands? It was supposed to be a bonding in name only till she was eighteen!"

"I know. It makes me just as angry," she said, leaning against him. "I'm proud of you, Konis."

"I'm not," he sighed. "I hope Kitra won't do anything silly. I think I'll alert Ni'Zulhu and ask him to keep an eye on her," he said.

"Already done, Master Konis," said Ni'Zulhu from the military base by the gatehouse into the estates. "We were alerted by Mnesu, her bodyguard, when he saw her leaving. She's on her way to the Valsgarth estate."

"Thank you," he said. "Let me know where she goes, please."

"My bet is she'll head for Ruth's," said the security chief. "She's been there a few times—most of the younglings visit Ruth in times of trouble. If she's gone off in a state, she'll be wanting to talk to someone right now," he offered.

"Let me know anyway."

"Will do, Master Konis."

* * *

Day 23

He crawled painfully into the heart of the bush, collapsing before he could turn round to conceal his entrance. Lying there panting, he could no longer keep his head up and let it drop to rest on his arms. He was tired, deathly tired of running and hiding, of being dragged by some strange compulsion to this mountainside.

Gradually his panting subsided, leaving him just exhausted. His leg throbbed, a dull ache that he'd grown used to. Thoughts began to fade in and out as he drifted toward sleep or unconsciousness, he didn't care which.

The smell of blood was sharp in the air. He sniffed, lifting his head, looking for its source. Dawn was not far off, he was vulnerable now. A figure, no more than a silhouette, stood between him and the false light. He rolled over, pushing himself up till he was on his feet.

A raised arm came down toward him. "Stupid female, no need for this."

There was only one blow, but it was enough. He fell to the ground again, head reeling, almost unconscious. Female? He was female? Confused, stunned by the blow, she lay there unable to move.

At the Retreat, Brynne lay paralyzed, caught in her dream memory as she relived the incident.

Deep in the Prime ship, Kaid was similarly held, but for him the dream was laced with his own dark childhood memo-

ries—memories that had been dealt with long ago when he'd
first been taken to Stronghold as an unwilling recruit.

> The ground shook as the male landed on his knees
> beside her. Razor sharp claws grasped hold of her,
> penetrating her hide and ripping her clothing from her.
> Holding her fast, already naked and erect, he loomed
> over her.
> Whimpering, she tried to push him aside, but he
> was larger, stronger, and determined. Pinned to the
> ground as she was, still she fought him, feet lashing
> out as she thrashed from side to side, consciousness
> fading in and out with sheer terror. In desperation,
> she pulled her legs up, readying herself for a final
> attempt at a stomach-gouging kick.
> He lunged forward, his weight pinning her in an all
> too convenient position. Her cry of anguish as she
> realized her mistake quickly turned to a howl of
> agony.

Kaid woke with a gasp and a start. He lay there, heart
pounding, listening to the quiet breathing of the other three
people in the room, wondering what had triggered such a
dark dream. It had been many years since he'd been
haunted by them. Killing his foster-father, Nuddoh
M'Zushi, had been what had driven him from Dzahai village to Ranz and the Claws, made on outlaw of him. It had
been why the Brotherhood, urged on by Noni, had sought
him out.

He remembered those days, when Father Jyarti, then
Head Priest, and Noni had helped him to come to terms
with his early years. The death of Nuddoh had brought to
light all that had happened to him and the others in
M'Zushi's care, and none of those involved in his case had
blamed him for finally turning on his tormentor. But this
dream had been subtly different, enough so to make him
wonder if it had, indeed, been a dream at all.

He yawned, putting it from his mind for now, and turned
over, reaching out for T'Chebbi. It had been dark enough
that he needed to feel the presence of one he cared for
beside him.

*   *   *

At Vartra's Retreat, Brynne woke to find Jurrel leaning over him. Instinctively, he punched out at him, trying to leap from the bed. His fist was caught and held by the Sholan's larger hand and he went sprawling on his face, held in a body lock till he realized the dream was over.

"Take it easy," said Jurrel, slowly letting him go. "I heard you cry out, that's why I came in. I thought the last week had been too quiet. What was it this time?"

Brynne moved his face out of the covers and lay there shuddering. "I was attacked. I thought it was you. With the light behind you . . ."

"I get the picture," said Jurrel, sitting on the edge of the bed. "Was it the same person again?"

"No. Maybe. I don't want to talk about it." How could he explain he'd experienced someone's memories of rape as intimately if he'd been the victim?

He began to push himself up, realizing he felt bruised and sore everywhere. He shuddered again, realizing the dream had been far too real. Jurrel's steadying hand was there to help him, but he had to fight the impulse to shrink from his touch. Sholans confused him, both sexes sending him the same signals, both equally attractive. It had gotten worse since Jurrel's partner Banner had arrived.

"I'm fine," he said sharply.

Jurrel released him. "Father Lijou will want to know about it."

He slid between the covers, glad of the nightclothes he wore. "It wasn't important, only someone else's memory. It wasn't actually happening like the others," he said, leaning back against the bed head. "Someone nearby dreaming, that's all." That he did believe, even though this one had been different. It had been the same person, of that he was positive, but there had also been a brief trace of something else—a masculine presence that had never been there before.

"Do you want me to stay?" asked Jurrel.

"No. Go back to Banner." He could hear how sharp his tone sounded even to him. It wasn't Jurrel's fault he was finding it difficult to accept the arrival of the other's sword-brother. "I'm sorry. I thought the dreams were over, that's all," he forced himself to say, aware of his friend's hurt feelings but unable to say more.

When Jurrel had left, he lay down and closed his eyes, wishing he knew what the nature of the attraction he sensed between them was. If he knew that, he might know how he wanted to respond. He'd had no such problem back on Earth, but here, among this sensuous, lithe-limbed, furred species, he was lost. He had no male Sholan bench-mark to tell him what an appropriate response to these feelings was. This latest dream had made it worse, had turned the whole situation on its head and made a nightmare out of it.

Afraid to sleep again, he got up and pulled on his robe, heading along the corridor to the common room, where he knew he'd be able to get a hot drink. He sat down at the table, warming his hands on the mug before rolling himself a cigarette and lighting it. It tasted good, going a long way to calm his jangled nerves. Then he sensed Jurrel approaching.

What now? he thought, ignoring him and picking up his mug to take a drink. He almost leaped out of his seat in shock as he felt gentle fingers touching his neck.

"You're tense. I can't leave you like this," said Jurrel as he began to knead him. "You'll never get back to sleep."

"I'm all right, I told you," he said, trying to pull away. "You know not to touch me! Go back to Banner."

"Strengthen your shields, that's what the other telepaths do." The grip tightened, determined not to let him go this time. "It was Banner's suggestion I come back. Put your mug down and lean against the chair. Let your arms go limp."

He did as he was asked, but kept hold of his cigarette as Jurrel's thumbs probed the knotted muscles. It was helping, he had to admit, though Jurrel was being none too gentle.

"Who taught you this?"

"Human massage? I worked with some Terrans during my last tour of duty," he said, beginning to work on the lower section of Brynne's neck, where it joined his shoulders.

He stiffened, but the touch was strictly professional as the Sholan eased the taut muscles and tendons.

"Relax. You're making it ten times more difficult for me. And lose the cigarette. You're not smoking it anyway."

He did, and tried to relax, finding it possible if he shut his eyes and forgot who was behind him. The fingers moved, slipping inside his robe, beginning to work on his spine.

"See? That's better, isn't it?" the voice purred gently in his ear. "Relax into it. Don't think of anything."

The pressure was more gentle now, lulling him with the rhythmic movements. Waves of tiredness lapped through him.

"You're trying too hard, Brynne. Trying to fit in won't work. All you need to do is be yourself," said Jurrel, his voice quiet, his touch almost a caress as his hands slipped over Brynne's shoulders. "You've been fighting your Sholan side for too long. Just be yourself."

"I don't know who I am here," he murmured, leaning back against Jurrel.

CHAPTER 9

Day 24

COME morning, despite all Jurrel's attempts to persuade him, Brynne refused to speak to Father Lijou about the dream. When Banner joined them for first meal, he added his voice to his Companion's.

"He needs to know."

Brynne looked across the table at him. He'd only met Banner briefly the day before, but now that he saw them together, he could tell that though both were dark-pelted, it was Banner who was actually black. Blue eyes, brighter than any he'd seen yet on a Sholan, regarded him steadily from beneath short, curling hair.

"I know it's not easy," continued the older male, "but Father Lijou must know this person is female. If you can't speak to him, why not talk to Tutor Kha'Qwa?"

His voice was deeper, too, thought Brynne, before catching the gentle amusement in his eyes. He looked down quickly at his food. "I can't," he said, feeling the blood rush to his face.

"Then I'll tell her," Banner said unperturbed.

"You wouldn't!" He looked up, shocked at the betrayal of his confidence.

"One of us must. I can't see any problem. You were a conduit for the dream, nothing more. Why should you feel somehow responsible that you experienced it?"

"It's what you are," said Jurrel. "Maybe in sharing her nightmare you helped her come to terms with it. Did you think of that?"

Brynne looked helplessly from one to the other. He'd never been in a situation like this before. "You don't understand. Somehow, I intruded on her memory. That in itself was like a rape."

"No," said Jurrel, leaning forward impulsively to touch his hand. "Her dreams found you several weeks ago. This was just one of many. If anyone has intruded, it's her."

Careful not to offend, Brynne moved his hand away. Touch, for him, was another way of receiving subliminal messages, and right now, he couldn't cope with Jurrel's.

"Seems we need to learn more about telepaths, Jurrel." Banner's voice held a rumble of laughter beneath it. He got to his feet. "It's decided, then. This takes precedence over your classes. I'll tell the porter and meet you outside with an aircar in five minutes."

"I didn't say I'd go," said Brynne, watching the broad-shouldered Sholan head for the refectory door.

"But you will," said Jurrel, starting to gather their plates. "Won't you?"

He got up to help, needing to say something to him on a personal level but unsure how to put it.

"About last night," prompted Jurrel as they walked over to put the plates away. When Brynne said nothing, he continued. "We're friends, Brynne, think of it that way. You needed my company. We're each free to be with whom we want. Think Sholan, not Human. If you'd like my company again, ask me." He grinned, reaching out to flick a finger briefly across the side of Brynne's neck, a gesture both intimate and affectionate. "Or I might ask you."

* * *

"Noni, the 'car's here," said Teusi, standing at the doorway to the back bedroom. "They've taken them to the education hall in the village."

"Damned younglings out on a lark," she muttered, giving a final twitch to the coverlet on the bed. "Reckon I'll be sleeping in here tonight. You stay close to me, lad. We'll find the one we want there, lay you odds on it," she said, making her way over to join him.

"I wouldn't bet against you, Noni, you know that," grinned Teusi. "I'd lose nearly every time."

"Nearly, eh? Only nearly? Cheek of you!" she said, waving her stick at him and pretending to scowl.

He laughed and preceded her to the door, stopping to pick up the case in which she kept her first aid potions and balms.

"They got caught by the crosswinds up near Stronghold," said Leohl, the village elder, as she escorted Noni to the room where the makeshift beds lay. Behind them, three younglings followed as helpers.

Noni glanced at the table to her right where two bodies shrouded by white sheets lay. "Lost two," she observed.

"Tragic, it was," murmured Leohl as she opened the door for Noni. "It was meant to carry four and they had six in it. These two weren't strapped in. When the aircar hit the ground, they were thrown out of the broken canopy. Dead when we found them, I'm afraid." She gave a gentle purr of sadness. "So young."

"So drunk, probably," Noni sighed. "Ah, well. Summer's here without a doubt. They won't be the last this season. Anyone we know?"

"Thankfully no. The craft was registered to a hire firm in Ranz. The Protectors are on their way over to question the survivors. They'll be here shortly."

Noni approached the first bed, glancing over the unconscious female, assessing her injuries. Moving closer, she checked her pulse and eyes. "She needs to see the Stronghold physician when he gets here. Clean and dress those wounds in the meantime and keep her covered," she ordered one of the youths following them.

She made her way to the next, a male this time, lying there moaning. Blood oozed sluggishly from a cut on his head and his forearm was gashed. "He'll need that arm seen to before I can stitch it. Clean him up, lass. I'll be back."

"Have you found the one you're looking for, Noni?" Teusi asked in an undervoice as Noni assessed the third and fourth victims.

"No, lad, and that surprises me. I was sure I'd find her here."

"Her?"

"Did I say her?" She looked up at him, mouth open in a faint smile. "Then it's a female we'll be expecting."

*   *   *

Doggedly, with no idea of where she was actually headed, she kept pushing herself onward, no longer even caring about the force that drove her so mercilessly. No longer able to support herself on her injured leg, she staggered through the tall bracken on three limbs.

The scents of civilization assaulted her nose and she realized she was nearing a settlement. One smell stood out from the others, its faint scent hauntingly familiar. She stopped, raising her head above the undergrowth in an effort to track its source. This was the trail she'd been following all along.

The breeze changed direction, carrying within it the smell of stale ale and cooking, but not a trace of her scent. With a low whimper of distress, she risked sitting up, breaking her cover. She *had* to find the nung tree! The perfume came to her again, as the breeze once more wafted from her right. Turning her head, she saw the cottage, and the tree standing in the garden. Even from this distance, the pale flowers stood out like stars in the night sky against the dark green foliage.

Falling back to the ground, she began to lope unevenly toward the house. Nearly there, then it would be over and she'd be safe.

As Teusi brought the aircar down to land on the hard pad next to her cottage, she turned to look out the side window, ears swiveling forward.

"She's here, Teusi. The one day in the week I go out expecting to find her, and she comes to me," she said in disgust. "Figures, doesn't it?"

"Here?" he echoed, turning off the engine. "Where?"

"How should I know, lad? I've only just arrived back, same as you. Leave my bag for now. You go look round for her, I'll get the house opened up and a kettle on to boil."

"You got a prowler!" shouted Nunza, bustling up the roadway toward him as Teusi opened the gate.

Hurry, lad! Leave Nunza to me. Take our visitor in the back way, I don't want that interfering old busybody sticking her nose into this business! sent Noni.

With a flick of his tail to indicate he'd heard her, Teusi headed round the side of the house at a run.

As Nunza put her hand on the latch, Noni emerged from the aircar. "Get your hand off my gate, Nunza," she said. "If we got a prowler, Teusi'll handle it."

"He'll need a hand, Noni. A prowler's a danger to everyone. I called the Protectors. They'll be here soon. He should wait for them."

"Interfering old fool! I'm expecting someone," said Noni, pushing her aside and opening the gate. "Likely it's her you saw."

"Didn't know you were expecting anyone."

"Why should you know my business?" demanded Noni, shutting the gate firmly.

"Who you expecting?" Nunza asked, sidling along her side of the fence, trying to peer down the path which Teusi had taken.

"No one *you* know! Now get you on home and mind your own business, Nunza! I got things to do, family to welcome," she snapped, turning her back on the gossip and heading for her front door.

"Strange visitor that tries to stay hidden and sneak up on your back garden!"

"Maybe she's just trying to avoid prying folk like you!" Noni shut her door with a resounding bang. Inside now, she made her way toward the back bedroom and the door out into the rear garden.

Teusi was bending over a still form lying at the foot of the nung tree. "She's hurt, Noni," he said, looking up at her. "I think it's safe to move her, though."

"Think isn't good enough, lad. You have to know. Moving her could cause worse injuries if you don't know what's broken."

"It is safe to move her," he said, rolling her onto her back and sliding his arms under her. "She's got a wound on her right thigh. Looks like she's had it some time. It's badly swollen and infected."

"Take her in and put her on my bed. We'll see to her there."

"Wonder what caused that," Noni muttered as she gently swabbed the last of the muck and poison out of her patient's thigh wound. "Not a knife, or a fall."

"She's got other small cuts on her head and face," said

Teusi as he fastened off the thread he'd used to stitch the small wound on her arm. "And on her lower back. I'd say she's either been in a fight, or more likely, been beaten up."

Noni grunted as she began to rinse out the now clean wound. "You seen her feet? And hands? Cut and bruised like I've rarely seen before. She's been traveling and living rough for some time. Still got a low-level fever."

Teusi moved round to check the hands and feet for himself. "You're right. How can you be sure she's the one we're waiting for, Noni?"

She looked up at him, eyes twinkling, nose creasing as her mouth opened in a slight smile. "I know, lad. Trust me. It's a feeling you get, a certainty in here." She reached out and tapped his forehead between the eyes. "A rightness of the moment. You'll know when it happens to you the first time."

"What's so special about her?" he asked, collecting his bowl and taking it to the sink to wash out.

"No idea, lad. Not my business to know that," she replied, watching in approval as he refilled it with fresh herbal antiseptic then went to treat their patient's feet. "She'll need to rest up in bed a couple of days at least. Those feet aren't taking her anywhere far in that state."

Keeza woke gradually, aware first of the soft surface beneath her, then the lightness of the cover that lay over her. It smelled sweet, of flowers. If this was a dream, she didn't want it to end. She couldn't remember when her last night in a real bed had been.

"Get the soup for her now, Teusi. She's awake," she heard an elderly voice say. "No need to fear us, lass. Whatever you're running from won't catch you here."

The smell of soup filled the air, making her stomach grumble loudly.

"Aye, I reckon you are hungry," laughed the old one. "We were able to count each of your ribs."

The voice sounded friendly. She opened her eyes, looking around. The first thing she saw was Teusi advancing toward her, a bowl of soup balanced on a tray. Instinct made her cringe back but he stopped dead, coming no closer.

"I won't harm you. I've got food. You need to eat, build up your strength so you'll heal," he said.

Heal? Her leg! She moved it experimentally. It hurt, but the pain felt good, not like the tight, dull throbbing she'd grown used to.

He took a step, drawing her attention back to him. He was younger than she was, barely twenty, she realized. Round, low set ears were framed by mid-brown hair. Green eyes looked seriously at her from under slightly drawn eye ridges. She could sense his concern that he didn't frighten her, especially after the beating she'd obviously suffered. He knew!

Panic flooded through her and she shrank back onto the pillows, painfully drawing her legs up and pulling her arms free of the cover. Before she could do more, she felt her mind grasped and held firmly.

Don't be a fool, lass! If we meant you harm, why would we treat your wounds and feed you? The thought was scathing and acerbic.

She looked at the old one finally, seeing the face she knew she would. It was just like the dreams, right down to the long snow white plait that lay over her shoulder. "I know you!" she blurted out.

"Aye, and I know you, lass," said Noni. "Seen you a few times, I have. You've been sent here to me. Now stop being a fool and drink that soup. Teusi here isn't interested in you. He's got himself a young female in the village that he's playing jeggets with!"

"Noni!" exclaimed Teusi, ears flattening to his skull in acute embarrassment.

"Where am I?" Keeza asked.

"At Noni's, just outside Dzahai village. Teusi, give her the damned soup before it congeals!"

Teusi approached her and held out the tray.

Cautiously, she took it from him. Her stomach growled again as she straightened her legs and placed the tray on her lap. She was starving and this was hot, cooked food, not raw flesh. She sat there, unable to touch it.

"Eat," said Noni.

Ignoring the spoon, she picked up the bowl and began to drink greedily.

"I reckon she's well enough to finish off the stew we had," she heard Noni say. "Go fetch it, lad."

A bowl of stew was placed on the tray. She stopped drinking to look at the stew, then back to the soup, unsure what to do in the face of such a choice.

"Stew's hot. Finish the soup first," advised Noni. "And use the spoon for it. I don't want you choking on the meat."

She glanced up fearfully, then sensed the attempt at humor behind the old one's remark.

You're a telepath, then.

"No," she said, putting the empty soup bowl down.

Then what are you?

Tentatively she reached for the second bowl, looking over to Noni for permission. Having got it, mindful of her instructions, she picked up the spoon. "I'm . . ." She stopped, a stricken look on her face. "I don't know what I am," she whispered, ears lying flat. "I can't remember."

"It'll come back, never fear," Noni said reassuringly. "Your memory's just missing for a few days, that's all. What they call you? Do you remember that?"

As she spooned up the stew, almost gulping it down in case they changed their minds about letting her have it, she searched for a name. "I don't have one."

"Got to call you something," said Noni. "Can't keep saying *Hey you!* can we? How about we call you Ghaysa? How does that sound to you?"

"Ghaysa," she said, putting the spoon down to lick the inside of the bowl. It sounded right, had something of a familiar feel to it. "I'm Ghaysa."

"Take her tray away, Teusi, and give our guest this mug of water to drink. Ghaysa, you sleep now. Got a lot of healing to do."

She drank it and lay back on the sweet-smelling pillows feeling drowsy. Sleep she did, surfacing only once, briefly, as she heard Noni's angry voice.

"You calling me a liar? I tell you, she's my second cousin twice removed's child, Ghaysa. Had an accident on her way here. Knocked her memory clean into next year, it has!"

"Rhuna, you know we've got to talk to her."

"Not while she's sick, you don't! What could she possibly tell you anyway? She isn't a prowler and wasn't anywhere

near that aircar crash, so how could she know what caused
it? You go back and ask the younglings that were in it what
happened, and leave us law-abiding folks alone!"

A loud sigh. "I'll tell the commander, Rhuna, but I'll be
back tomorrow. You could save us all a lot of bother if
you let me question her now."

"Can't. She's had a potion to break her fever and help
her sleep," Noni said shortly. "Now, good day to you!"

She heard the door slam as she drifted off to sleep again.

* * *

"There seem to be two distinct dreams or visions,
Brynne," said Kha'Qwa thoughtfully, studying the Human
in the chair opposite her. "Those that have to do with this
female, and another that involves what sounds like a medical area."

"That was our thought," nodded Jurrel.

Kha'Qwa glanced at him before looking back to Brynne.
"It's good you had someone to talk them through with,"
she said. "I'm sorry Father Lijou isn't here to talk to you,
but I know he'll be grateful for you bringing what was
undoubtedly a very difficult experience to us. I think you're
unnaturally susceptible to others' minds at the moment because of your new awareness of our people and religion.
Once you progress a little further with your training, it
should die down. Very few of our visionaries, and we have
more than most because of the nature of the Brotherhood
training, have so many experiences in so short a time. Most
can go for months, even years, without being aware of anything out of the ordinary."

"I'm glad to hear it," said Brynne with relief. "You've
no idea how bad it can get."

"I can imagine," she said sympathetically. "Do you know
what this female looks like?" She asked the question casu-
ally, hoping not to alert him to her interest.

"Darkish, I think," he said, brow creasing as he obviously
tried to remember. "Sort of all colors—brown, and gold,
and sort of orangy, with white as well. Longer-furred than
most of you," he added.

"Striking coloration," she said. "As I said, I'll pass the
information on to Father Lijou when he returns."

"There's trouble at the estate, isn't there?" said Brynne quietly, catching her eye for the first time.

Startled, she looked away. "Now why would you think that?" she asked, keeping her tone light. Damn! She might be mind-dead right now, but he was hypersensitive!

"I've been picking that up too. Flashes of danger to Carrie and Kusac. What's happened?"

"Nothing at all," she said, beginning to get to her feet. "Not everything you sense at this time will be accurate, or even traceable if it is, Brynne. Some of our gifts aren't an exact science the way telepathy is."

Brynne rose as well. "They're my Clan, Mistress Kha'Qwa. I have a right to know. Maybe knowing will help me pinpoint some of the feelings and dreams."

She was caught, and she knew it. "Their ship is missing," she said. "Father Lijou is with their family now."

"How long?"

"Nearly three weeks. They've been searching for them since the third day. That's when we discovered they were missing. So far, there's been no trace either at the Jalnian end or Tuushu Station."

Brynne stood there, too stunned to speak.

"Dark news, indeed," said Jurrel. "They'll be calling off the search soon. It's unusual for it to go on so long."

"They were on a U'Churian craft with a crew of Cabbaran navigators," said Kwa'Qwa. "Both species are involved with the Forces in the search, and we have even managed to place one of our telepaths on a jointly operated ship. When there is news, we will hear it, believe me. Every possible stone is being turned in our attempts to find them."

"Let's pray they turn up," said Jurrel.

As soon as they'd gone, Kha'Qwa went to the comm on her mate's desk, calling up the file she knew he had on the missing female, Keeza Lassah. Two pictures stared out at her from the screen, one taken as a convict, another while still with the Consortias, before joining the Shanagi project.

"It's her," she murmured. "It has to be her!"

* * *

The past four days had been chaotic for Konis. He'd given up taking calls and had them all routed to his secretary to deal with. They were all about the same matter—his resignation as Clan Lord. He felt beleaguered. To top it all off, Kitra refused to return to the Guild and he hadn't the heart to make her. Thankfully, Sorli had been understanding and had spoken to Ghyan so their priest could continue her instruction on the estate. Now this!

"You have to make a decision soon, Konis," Rhyasha was saying. "I've had to cut myself off, too. When they can't get you on the comm, they're asking for me. I've been told you even refuse to speak to Governor Nesul."

"Later, Rhyasha," he said, sitting down in the informal area near her. "Lijou's on his way up."

"Lijou? I didn't know you were expecting him."

"I'm not. He arrived at the gatehouse asking to see me."

"Doesn't sound like Lijou," she said.

A scratch at the door, then it opened. "Guild Master Lijou," said Che'Quul, letting the Head Priest enter.

"Unexpected though it is, it's nice to see you, Lijou," said Rhyasha, standing up to greet him. "Do you have private business?"

"No, I wanted to talk to you both," he said, coming over to join them.

Behind him came Miosh, carrying a tray with glasses and a bottle of spirits.

Konis glanced up, frowning as Miosh placed the drinks on the table between the chairs.

"Bit early for that, Miosh," Rhyasha said.

Miosh backed away and began to leave.

"You've news for us, Lijou," said Konis abruptly. "Don't try to sweeten it. It's about Carrie and Kusac, isn't it?"

"I'm afraid so," said Lijou, taking the nearest chair. "Their ship's officially been declared missing. They were due to make a scheduled transmission before entering jump some three weeks ago. It wasn't made. We hoped it was because of a transmitter failure and that they'd already jumped, but they haven't yet turned up at their rendezvous."

Konis sat and stared at him. He couldn't be hearing this. It was impossible. He had been convincing himself that Kusac and Carrie were fine ever since he'd seen the note about their missing ship. But now it was all too real, now that they were being officially informed—now that Rhyasha knew, too. At least Lijou hadn't revealed to Rhyasha that he'd known about the crisis almost from the start. Time seemed to slow down and he heard Lijou's voice as if it was far away.

"Immediately we heard about the lack of communication, we, the U'Churians, and the Cabbarans, implemented a search for them. We've found some wreckage, definitely from the *Profit*, but not enough to cripple the ship. That only proves they had an accident of some kind, nothing more."

"That's good," he heard Rhyasha say in hushed tones. "Tell me that's good!"

"It's not bad, Rhyasha," Lijou said, leaning forward to pour two drinks. "It means there's still hope. They could have broken down and had to leave jump, may be sitting somewhere between the two worlds. They weren't on their own craft, they were on a U'Churian one." He pressed a glass into her limp grasp, then turned to hand one to Konis.

Automatically, Konis accepted it, taking the neat spirit down in one gulp. He recognized the taste instantly. Arris.

Lijou nodded. "You need it," he said compassionately. "We're doing everything we can, believe me. Both us and the Forces. We've combined with the U'Churians on one of their craft and it's currently traveling through jump on the same route in the hope they can find them. Don't give up hope, we haven't."

"How long . . . ?" Rhyasha began, then stopped, unable to finish.

"Nearly a week overdue."

"They've been missing three weeks?" said Rhyasha, still clutching her drink. "Why weren't we told sooner?" There was a note of hysteria in her voice. Then she looked at Konis. "You knew," she said. "That was the stress at work, wasn't it? Why didn't you tell me?"

"I told him not to because it was still early," said Lijou. "Konis found out by accident, Rhyasha. I didn't want either of you worried needlessly in case they turned up safely." He leaned forward to urge the hand holding the glass up to her mouth. "Take it, Rhyasha. It'll help," he said gently.

"Nothing but finding them will help," she said tightly. "Why were they on a U'Churian ship, Lijou?"

"Carrie was seriously injured on Jalna. She was hit by a projectile, a bullet, which is lodged against her spine. They needed to put her into cryo facilities to keep her alive."

"Dear Goddess!" she whispered.

"Why didn't they wait? The *Rhijissoh* could have treated her when it arrived," said Konis. "Why leave Jalna with them both in cryo?"

"There could be many reasons. Maybe they couldn't stabilize her enough for the wait," said Lijou, again urging Rhyasha to drink. This time, she did.

"Who else is missing with them?" asked Konis, finding his voice.

"All the rescued ones, as well as Kaid and T'Chebbi."

"Their families must be told."

"They are being," said Lijou, turning his attention back to him. "Except for Dzaka. With your permission, I'll speak to him myself."

Rhyasha's glass fell to the floor. It hit the tiles, cracking into myriad pieces as she suddenly stood up. "Excuse me," she said, turning and walking through the open doors into the garden beyond.

"Thank you for telling us personally," said Konis, getting to his feet. He gestured toward the garden. "I have to be with her . . . You understand."

Lijou rose. "Of course. I can't tell you how sorry I am to bring such bad news to you, Konis. You know how much I've prayed it was only a communications failure. I'll let you know the minute we hear anything more."

Konis nodded vaguely. He'd already dismissed the priest's presence from his mind.

Lijou left the main house, having stopped briefy to apprise Che'Quul of the situation. While he was there, Taizia and Kitra burst in through the main entrance. Distraught, they made straight for him.

"This can't be true, Father Lijou," said Taizia. "There must be some mistake."

"I'm afraid not, Liegena," he said, reaching for her hand. "We might still find them. Don't give up hope yet, we haven't."

"Mother needs us," said Kitra, tugging at her older sister's arm. "Excuse us, Father Lijou. And thank you for coming with the news yourself."

He nodded, watching as the two sisters hurried across the ornamental inner garden to disappear into the lounge. Sighing, he climbed into his aircar. This was the part of his job he hated. It was never easy to give the news of a possible death to a family, but when they happened to be your friends, it was doubly difficult.

He took Garras with him when he went to speak to Dzaka.

"Return to Stronghold with me," he said abruptly, aware Dzaka was still coming to terms with the loss of Kitra. "Kha'Qwa would be pleased to have your company for a few days."

"I have work to do here," Dzaka replied evenly. "Thank you for your concern and the invitation, Father Lijou."

"I think you should come back with me," said Garras quietly. "Take an hour or two off, Dzaka. You won't be operating at maximum efficiency if you don't take some time off to cope with this now, you know that."

Dzaka hesitated. "There's no replacement for me until third meal. I'll come over then if I may."

"We'll expect you," said Garras, clasping his hand to Dzaka's cheek in an affectionate gesture.

"If you need us, Dzaka, call," Lijou said, getting up to leave. "I like to think of myself as a friend of your father's. Anything I can do to help you, I will, gladly."

"Just keep me informed of any news, please," was all Dzaka said.

* * *

The Primes eventually arranged an extra sleeping area for the Cabbarans. A door suddenly appeared in the back wall of the middle bedroom, allowing access to another room which had been fitted out to suit their vegetarian allies. Annuur moved his people into it once Kaid had checked it thoroughly for any weaknesses in construction that might give them a way to break out of their quarters. Predictably, there were none.

It had been quiet for the past week. No one had gone missing and they'd been undisturbed by the Primes. Tirak was pushing Kaid to formulate some kind of escape plan but he was resisting. They didn't even know what was outside the rooms, let alone where on the ship or space station they were. And they had no weapons, not to mention there were nineteen of them from four different species.

"It just makes it more of a challenge," said Tirak, exasperated.

Kaid raised an eye ridge at him. "Uh huh," was all he said.

The door opened, drawing all their attention to the arrival of J'koshuk and four Prime guards. The Valtegan stood at the door, surveying those present.

"What do you want?" Kaid asked, not bothering to disguise his dislike. "I thought I told you to stay away from us."

"I remember our conversation," hissed J'koshuk. "However, I don't intend to enter your prison. I'm here at the request of the Seniormost to take one of you for questioning." He pulled his lips back in a grin that showed off his many needle sharp teeth. "I'd choose you, but we got all we needed from you already."

"You're lying," said Kaid, hiding his shock. "If you had there'd be no need to question us further."

"Corroboration." The word was drawn out. J'koshuk gestured the leading two guards into the room.

"You will remain in your seats," intoned the translator as they advanced.

J'koshuk pointed to Jeran. "That one. Time I renewed more old friendships."

One of the guards began to move to the table where the young male sat while the other covered him.

Jeran got to his feet, ears plastered flat to his skull in obvious fear, looking over to Kaid for reassurance.

"Just answer the questions," said Kaid. "You've got nothing to hide."

"Wait! Take me!" said Tallis, jumping up. "I can help you, tell you what they've been talking about!"

Rezac lunged at him but he side-stepped, moving hurriedly toward the door. "Kezule! They have a general from the past . . ."

Kaid moved swiftly, leaping to his feet and managing to collide with Tallis. In the confusion, he tripped him up. The snap as he broke Tallis' neck was barely audible. Trying to support the limp body, Kaid looked up at J'koshuk.

"I'm afraid he's hurt himself."

At a signal from the Valtegan, the two guards moved to investigate. A blow from the lead one sent Kaid flying and, by the time he'd scrambled to his feet, Tallis' body had been scooped up and taken to the doorway.

J'koshuk looked unblinkingly at Kaid. "I will take the one I chose."

In Vartra's name, lad, use your eyes out there! sent Kaid. *Tell them what you need to, you've nothing to hide. Getting back safely is your priority.*

As he passed him, Jeran's ears raised fractionally to let him know he'd picked up the message.

"This one is dead," said the guard holding Tallis once the door had closed.

J'koshuk wasn't surprised. He was convinced it had been no accident, but then, killing a treacherous underling in such circumstances was an acceptable practice among his people. How the Primes would view it was another matter. As they made their way to the interrogation room, the guard carrying the body abruptly left them.

The Sholan he'd chosen was so afraid he was barely able to walk. J'koshuk snorted, amused. It would be interesting to see what he had to say for himself now that they could actually communicate with each other. Then he remembered waking up understanding Sholan. A shiver ran through him. He didn't want to think about how he'd acquired that skill. Reflexively, he passed his hand over his head, knowing even as he did, it was still smooth. He had nightmares about waking up with one of those devices implanted in his skull.

The Sholan was incapable of getting into the chair, the guards had to lift him in. The restraints were clamped round his wrists and ankles, anchoring him firmly. He sat there, eyes closed, shaking as if in the grip of a fever.

"Violence is not permitted," reminded the guard as he stepped back to his position by the doorway.

J'koshuk frowned. He thought he'd be free to interpret the situation as he had with his own kind.

"Your name," he hissed angrily, walking round to stand beside the chair.

"Jeran." He opened his eyes, trying to twist his head round in an effort to see him.

"Why were you on the U'Churians' vessel?"

"Going home." He took a deep breath, obviously trying to relax.

"They came to find you? I think not," said J'koshuk, moving round so Jeran could see him. He put his hand over the other's arm, letting him see the length of his claws, and their sharpness. "You're nothing to them, as worthless as the one they killed." He flexed his hand, letting the claws touch the Sholan's pelt and prick through to the flesh. "I remember you." He leaned closer. "Just as I remember the others. Where are they now? Like the one who tried to give me information. Dead. I'd say your rescuers don't look after you well enough if you keep dying. Maybe you're next."

He moved out of sight again, making sure his footfalls were audible as he walked round the back of the chair.

"Why did they really come to Jalna?" he demanded, suddenly appearing at Jeran's other side.

Jeran looked him straight in the face. "You haven't got what you want from Kaid, have you? You wouldn't be questioning me otherwise."

Without thinking, J'koshuk's hand reached for the controls on the seat, depressing the one that administered pain through the restraints. As Jeran howled in agony, body arching upward, a similar surge of pain hit him.

The voices from the translator sounded faint but Jeran could just make them out.

"A tolerance has been acquired by the priest. We need to increase the drug inhibitors. His attitude is still not acceptable."

"See to it. Return the Sholan."

He felt a sting at his neck, then the restraints were released. Coolness swept through his inflamed nerves, dulling the pain. A moment later, head swimming, he was hauled to his feet. Swaying, hardly able to see, he was half-carried along one corridor then down another, back to their quarters.

By the time the guards stopped outside the door and pressed the entrance panel, he was beginning to recover his senses. The door slid open, and he saw their lounge.

Kaid was already on his feet, glowering at them, tail swaying in short, angry movements.

Before he could say anything, Jeran straightened. "I can stand," he said, attempting to pull himself free.

He was released, and slightly unsteadily, he walked into the suite, the door hissing closed behind him. He turned and placed his hand over a portion of wall next to the door, leaning on it as much for support as to identify it.

"The lock's behind there," he said.

Giyesh reached him before Kaid could, flinging her arms round him, making small noises of distress.

"Well done," said the Highlander approvingly, reaching out to support him. "Could you identify anything in the corridors, like elevators or access panels? How many Primes did you see out there?"

"Never mind that!" said Giyesh, outraged. "How are you? Did they hurt you? What did they do to you?"

Embarrassed, Jeran tried to disentangle himself. "I'm fine. No need to make a fuss," he muttered.

"Giyesh!" said Captain Tirak warningly. "Contain yourself! I should never have agreed to allow you to come on this mission! I apologize, Kaid. She's young. Normally females aren't involved in missions until after their first mating, but I was asked to make an exception in her case."

T'Chebbi came over with a fork and began to scratch the wall carefully around Jeran's hand.

Kaid had released Jeran and was waiting for T'Chebbi to finish. "Her reaction is quite understandable, Tirak, given J'koshuk's treatment of Rezac."

"Can move now," T'Chebbi said, stepping aside.

Giyesh backed away, a frown creasing her black nose till T'Chebbi touched her arm.

"Needs to report now," she said. "Before he forgets. You know that. Leave Kaid to debrief him, then he's yours again."

Kaid led him to the nearest table, grabbing a comp pad

and stylus from Rezac on the way. "Draw it," he said, handing them to Jeran once they'd sat down.

"We're here," Jeran said, looking at the sketch they already had on the page. "So this room is where they interrogated me," he said, marking it with the stylus. "Looks like a medical area. They had a kind of chair with restraints on it." He looked up at Kaid, unaware that the other could read the echo of remembered pain in his eyes. "J'koshuk can control it, put some nerve stimulator through the restraints."

"What's the room like?" asked Kaid. "Tiled?"

Jeran nodded. "White tiles everywhere. Like I said, it looked like the medical unit in our mining base. All shining steel and white tiles. Bright lights, too," he added, looking back at the rough map. "There's a corridor there. Just caught a glimpse of it," he said, drawing one in just below their suite. "I didn't see any Primes other than those who took me." He pushed the comp toward Kaid.

"There was one other thing, but I might have imagined it," he said hesitantly. "I wasn't gone long, right? One of the guards told J'koshuk not to use violence on me, but he did. I don't remember much after the nerve thing hit me, but as I was coming round, I saw J'koshuk on the floor thrashing around. I think they did the same to him. That's when I heard the voices."

Kaid looked briefly at Rezac and Tirak. "What voices?"

"Prime ones, through the translators. Said something about tolerances and inhibitors. That his attitude was unacceptable. I think they meant J'koshuk."

"Why talk to each other?" asked Tirak. "They haven't before. Even Annuur and his crew noticed that. I thought they used communicators in their helmets unless they were talking to us."

"I think there was someone else there. Someone not in a suit." Jeran looked from one to the other, shrugging his shoulders. "I got given a shot to stop the pain. I'm still feeling light-headed, so I can't be sure."

"What type of scent?" asked Kaid.

He shook his head. "Can't describe it. Alien's the only word."

"What's the nearest to it?" demanded Rezac.

"You're asking the impossible," said Kaid. "Some scents

just are alien. He hasn't had our exposure to other species. Did they finish the session because J'koshuk used the neural device on you?"

"I presume so."

"Any explanation, apology even?"

"Nothing. Just a shot and then they brought me back."

Kaid lifted the comp pad and sat back in his chair. "They're being very careful with us," he said. "Not wanting to hurt us, even to the point of punishing J'koshuk for doing it. Why? Is it a blind for something else? It doesn't exactly fit in with kidnapping us from our rooms the way they've been doing."

"J'koshuk seemed different," said Jeran, sure of his ground this time. "He was more like his old self. More aggressive toward me. And I couldn't smell fear until after the Primes zapped him."

Kaid sat up again, frowning. "Maybe it's not us the Primes are interested in. Maybe it's the Valtegans. It would explain the conversation you heard. J'koshuk certainly did become less aggressive and more afraid of us."

"I remember you telling him," nodded Tirak.

"No wonder they're interested in us," said Rezac. "Attitude alteration fits right in our skill band. Hell, if they'd told me what they wanted, I'd have volunteered to help them! Those lizards are the biggest threat going. They just absorb and enslave every species they meet!"

"Except for ours," said Jeran quietly. "They decided to destroy us."

"After last time, they knew we posed their biggest threat," said Kaid. "We still don't know what the Primes plan to do with us. Jeran, what was J'koshuk asking you about?"

"Why you went to Jalna. I don't think he's gotten any information from you, Kaid. Why ask me if he had? Whatever the reason for taking you telepaths, it wasn't to question you."

"Interesting J'koshuk took you," said Rezac. "They haven't gone near Zashou, or Tallis." He stopped, looking at Kaid.

"I had to kill him," said Kaid shortly. "He was prepared to sell what he knew to J'koshuk for protection. We can't afford a traitor in our midst, and he proved himself to be one."

Jeran could feel the blood draining from his face, making him feel even more dizzy. "Dead? I thought he'd fallen like you said."

Tirak began to growl low in his throat.

"He was one of us," said Rezac, his voice hardening. "Ours to deal with. He threatened the safety of all of us, not just this time, but by trying to spread panic and undermining you and Kaid to the others. He was warned."

"What if it had been one of my people?" asked Tirak.

Jeran watched as Kaid looked at Tirak. "Unlikely, given the nature of your mission. You might have a couple of young crew members, but I reckon you handpicked them all. Tallis was a civilian."

"You just killed someone!" said Jeran, trying to keep his voice low. "Like you'd stamp on a bug!"

"Be quiet," said Kaid harshly. "He *was* a bug. The kind that preys on others' misfortunes. He didn't need to try and buy immunity from the Primes at our expense. He was prepared to tell them everything he'd heard us talking about. You heard him say that himself."

Jeran subsided unhappily, aware of the truth in what Kaid said.

"He's right," Tirak said abruptly. "Tallis was a threat to us all. Had I been close enough, I'd have done the same."

"Our job is to protect you," said Kaid. "Tallis hasn't been completely sane since we rescued him. Even then he was trying to force us to abandon you in favor of getting him out of Bradogan's Keep immediately."

Barely conscious, J'koshuk felt a hand grasp his collar, pulling his head up till he was almost choking. He coughed, sending spasms of pain through his chest. He tried to lift his arms but he was still paralyzed.

Thin fingers fumbled at the back of his neck as an alien scent enveloped him. He sneezed violently. Abruptly, both fingers and scent vanished and he was left to fall back against the floor, banging his head on the tiles beneath him.

"You were warned. You will be returned to your quarters till we've decided what to do with you," said the impersonal tones of the translator.

He shrieked in pain as his arms were grasped and he was dragged to an upright position.

From the corridor outside they heard the faint sounds of someone screaming. Jeran looked toward the door and shivered. "J'koshuk," he said.

* * *

Day 26

Kitra hesitated outside the door to the shrine room before entering. It had been two days since they'd heard the dreadful news about her brother and Carrie, and since then, her father had virtually taken up residence in the household shrine. He'd done it before, when Carrie had been wounded during the Challenge. She went over to sit on the stone bench beside him.

"Father, you must speak to the Governor," she said softly, reaching out to touch his hand. "He's been trying to reach you for days."

"I've no heart for it, Kitra," he sighed, letting his fingers curl round hers. "I just want your brother and Carrie home safely."

"The treaty is in danger," said Kitra. "If you let it founder, then what they worked to set up will die. You can't do that to their memory."

He looked up, eyes glowing in the candlelight. "They aren't dead yet!" he said fiercely.

"Then why shut yourself in here?" she countered. "Please, Father, see Governor Nesul and Father Lijou. They've been waiting in your study for hours."

"I told Ni'Zulhu not to admit them to the estate!" he said angrily. "What right had he to ignore me?"

"Father Lijou says there is too much at stake. He really is sorry to have to disturb you," she added. "I could feel him. He's very distressed himself, not just over my brother and Carrie, but about Kaid as well."

"Konis," said a voice from the corridor outside. "Words can't express what I want to say, but we need you, my friend."

He looked up, seeing Lijou. "You'd intrude on me even here?"

Lijou inclined his head at the rebuke. "I can help, it's what we are taught to do as priests," he said quietly.

"I don't want your mental sedatives, Lijou," he growled. "No one messes with my mind! I'll work this through myself."

"But you aren't," said Lijou, his gentle criticism obvious even to Kitra. "You're neglecting Rhyasha as well as your work."

Keeping a hold on his daughter's hand, he got to his feet. "You reminding me of my duties?" he asked. "I'd be worse than useless right now, Lijou, you know that."

"You're wrong. The fact that your family is missing will aid our efforts to conclude this treaty."

"Use my grief to take unfair advantage of our future allies? You worry me, Lijou. Your ethics are no better than the Brotherhood's!"

"I am the Brotherhood, as are your son and bond-daughter," replied the priest calmly. "You would be showing our new allies that we're the same as them. That we care for our children and want to protect them from the harshness of the universe. And remind them that we are treating their missing ones the same as our own. That's not misusing your grief, my friend."

Kitra tightened her hand round her father's. "You must. It's what they would want," she said.

Konis looked down at her, remembering she was there.

"Your daughter is right," said Lijou. "You have a bright young adult there."

"I have," he said, letting her hand go to put his arm round her shoulders. "I wish I'd realized it sooner. Very well, Lijou, I'll talk to you and Nesul, but Kitra comes with me. I'll let her guide me."

"Out of the question," said Konis sharply. "Rhaid will lead the Council as well as me."

"You must head the Clans, Father," said Kitra quietly from his side. "If they hadn't put pressure on you over me, you'd not have realized what was going on. Most of the Council respect you. Look at the number of calls we've had."

"You're the only one with the breadth of vision to know the changes we need to make to survive in this new interstellar community," said Lijou.

"And the courage to implement them," added Nesul.

"Rhaid can do that."

"Rhaid has overcompensated," said Lijou carefully, "since her time as Fyak's captive. She would return the Clans to the old ways, with males unable to hold office at all."

"Nonsense. She'll come around. That's temporary, I assure you. She just needs a firm hand to guide her."

"And who would guide her if she was Clan Lord?" asked Lijou. "She'd make an able second, granted, but not Lord."

"Not my concern."

"It is, or have you forgotten that young daughter of yours?" asked Nesul, flicking an ear toward Kitra. "I have kitlings, too. I'd not want Rhaid choosing life-mates for them or deciding the course of their lives."

"You'll not let it rest till I agree, will you?"

"We can't force you, Konis," began Lijou.

"But we can make it damned uncomfortable for you," added Nesul.

Konis growled. "I'll not do it, unless . . ."

"Anything," said Nesul. "The Council has authorized me to agree to your demands, within reason."

"I want Azkuu and her little pack replaced. I'll not sit at the Council table with those who blackmailed me."

"Agreed," said Nesul.

"Rhaid will be my acting Second. I want time with my family—what's left of it," he said bleakly, reaching for Kitra's hand again.

"Understandable. Agreed."

"My policy changes will be backed up by the law and made effective immediately. No more delaying and tracking upwind so as not to offend this Clan or that."

Nesul sighed. "Very well."

"Finally, I want backing on this matter with the Arrazo Clan. It's been put off too long. I don't care if Naeul's youngest is missing, so is my son. Naeul will be indicted for illegally incarcerating his daughter Khemu, falsifying records of her death, his treatment of her cub, Dzaka, and for denying him his birthright by keeping his parents apart."

Beside him, Kitra stirred.

"That was something we hoped to deal with quietly," said Nesul.

"I will not," said Konis, his tone hard. "This way, Dzaka will have the right to life-bond to whom he chooses, En'Shalla Clan or one of the original Sixteen."

Nesul shook his head. "I don't think . . ."

"Agreed," said Lijou. "You will do it, Nesul. We all need the support of the Clans. The Arrazo family may be liked in the lowlands, but up by Stronghold, it's another matter. You need the support of the Brotherhood and the Highlanders, too."

"You push a hard bargain," sighed Nesul. "Very well."

"Today," said Konis, getting up and going to his desk. Opening a drawer, he pulled out a sheaf of papers. He returned, handing it to Nesul. "The case against Naeul Arrazo has been ready for months. Send it to the Protectors today, or the deal is off."

Nesul took them from him and stood up. "Today," he said, a growl of displeasure in his voice. "I take it that means you retract your resignation."

Konis nodded as he sat down. "I'll stay," he said, closing his eyes and lying back in his chair. "Now go. I'll be at the palace tomorrow. You have my word."

He sat there, listening to them leave, feeling a sudden weight on his lap as Kitra climbed up and wrapped her arms round his neck.

"By tomorrow, you could have your Brother your way, kitling," he said quietly. "Think again about it."

* * *

Kezule remained silent within his hiding place in the heart of the undergrowth some hundred yards from the entrance to the estate. It was definitely the one he wanted. Security like this would not have been out of place at the Emperor's palace. All day he'd watched traffic come and go. Only two vehicles had been allowed to fly straight in; the rest had landed outside the gates where the passengers had debarked while the vehicle was checked and guarded before they were allowed to reenter. He presumed that within the right-hand building their identities and appointments were verified.

Beyond the high wire perimeter lay a group of temporary buildings inhabited by their military. From there came the guards. Patrols seemed to follow no set time as far as he'd been able to discern. There were aerial checks, too, the vehicles flying out over the peninsula and remaining there for several hours. From his analysis of the hardware on the roof of the gatehouse, they also had satellite surveillance.

The estate was also home to Humans and their young, judging from those he saw playing up near the guards' quarters. These beings knew nothing about bringing up young, he thought derisively. To let them run free like this when they should be receiving instruction, learning duty and loyalty, was tantamount to the adults signing their own death warrants. When they grew up there would be no respect for their elders, nothing to stop them turning on them at the first sign of weakness. He wondered then what they considered weakness. Among his own kind, living with another species, treating them as equals, was the kind of weak concept the intellectuals would play with. It was as well no one paid them much attention—at least in his day.

The Emperor—may His memory be revered for all time—had loved His intellectuals, but it had been His warrior caste who had protected Him, advanced His empire, and crushed His enemies, and He never forgot that, for all the ramblings of the other castes.

The dampness caused by the cooling of the air had made the ground underneath him wet, drawing his thoughts back to the here and now. He moved carefully, tugging his robe under himself till he lay on more of it. When the night had reached its height, then he'd move on, deeper into the forest ahead of him. Time spent checking out the security around the estate would not be wasted. He'd only have one chance to get in undetected.

A noise from the gatehouse caught his attention. Night was falling and the lights were being turned on, illuminating the land both inside and outside the gatehouse. As it spilled over, almost touching his patch of dense undergrowth, he heard an alarm blare out. Soldiers spilled from the buildings to gather in lines by the gate.

Hissing his anger, he began to back off hurriedly as rumbling voices shattered the stillness. Had he been discovered? What had given him away? Out of direct sight now, still keeping low, he twisted around, trying to remember which way the fallen tree lay. He'd seen it on his way here, checked it out as a possible lair in the event of pursuit, never dreaming he'd actually need it. Quickening his heartbeat, he triggered the hormones needed for speed and aggression, then checked the unit on his wrist. The screen was turned off. Cursing, he activated it again. He must have knocked it while adjusting the robe. It had only been moments, but it was long enough for one of their telepaths to pick him up. Diving deeper into the forest, he searched frantically for his own scent trail to follow back to the tree, realizing as he did, that if he could follow it, so could they.

It was faint, but he found it. Getting his bearings, he veered to his right then leaped for the nearest tree. Clawed feet bit deep into the bark some ten feet above the ground as his hands grasped the thick limb overhead.

As he pulled himself up, he risked a glance behind. His night vision rendered the scene as a surreal landscape of reds and blues. In the midst of it, he could see the heat mass of the Sholans heading toward him. Up in the tree canopy, he could hide his scent from them. Keeping one hand on the branch to steady himself, he scrambled along the limb to where it crossed another. He leaped again, clinging to the swaying branch with all four sets of claws, praying it was strong enough to bear his weight. Speed would help. The less time he spent on each branch, the less chance his weight would snap it.

Hauling his robe up through the tie belt, he crabbed along as fast as he could, trying to ignore the swaying, looking for another thick limb in the adjacent tree. Down this time. He gauged the drop, then spreading his arms wide, jumped, landing splayed across its width. Scrambling up, he ran along it till he came to the next overlap.

He managed to cover some six hundred yards like this before he was forced to drop to the ground. No matter, it had broken his trail. It wouldn't be so easy for them to pick up his scent now. Bearing left, he compensated for the drift from his course. The Sholans were not far behind, he could just hear them in the distance.

Trusting his dark robe and the night would give him enough cover, he sprinted through the trees for the small clearing he knew lay ahead. Just beyond it lay the fallen tree. Heart pounding, breath getting more ragged, he dodged round thornbushes, knowing that to get snagged by one would leave traces of his presence. So far, they didn't know he was here, they only suspected. He misjudged the distance, overshooting the clearing and running headfirst into a mass of outstretched roots.

Dazed, he staggered back, putting his hand to his face. Momentarily blinded, he could hear labored breathing— was it his own, or a pursuer's? Panic filled him. Feeling his way along the roots with his other hand, he dashed the sleeve of his robe across his eyes, wiping the blood from his face. His feet suddenly gave under him and he fell, sliding down into the pit at the base of the tree. Biting back a cry of shock, he scrabbled around, searching in the soft earth for the small side cavity he'd seen during the day.

It lay under the center of the upturned rooted crown— a hole that went in some five feet till it was blocked by the remains of a broken taproot. Squirming in, he scrabbled with his claws at the soft earth, digging around the remaining roots. The soil came away easily, filling the hole around him as he dug deeper among the mass of roots. Within minutes, he'd carved out enough to fill the original hole and make himself a small chamber large enough to curl up in.

Taking handfuls of the damp soil, he smeared it over his face, head, and the sleeves of his robe in an effort to hide his scent, and the smell of blood. Tugging his hood over his head, he let it droop down over his eyes. Above him, a tangle of roots provided enough air for him to breathe while still concealing him. He lay still now, quieting his breathing.

Soft footballs and the sound of hushed voices approached his clearing. Eyes slitted almost shut so no moonlight or torch could reflect off them, he waited. The footsteps came closer, sounding more like a beast's than those of a Sholan. Then he saw it, looming over his hideout.

A large paw came down square on the net of roots above him and stayed there, claws extending for a better grip.

"I was sure I heard something," a voice muttered. The

paw moved, sending a small shower of earth down onto his hood.

Kezule had to fight the urge to sneeze.

"You're imagining things," said a second voice. "This clearing's too open—nowhere to hide. Come on, we've fallen behind the others."

"In a minute," said the first voice.

The whole tree vibrated to each of its four steps, then it stopped for the space of several heartbeats before leaping to the ground. "You're right. Let's go."

Hardly daring to breathe, he lay there, listening to their receding footsteps. No wonder they'd made such good time following him. He'd completely forgotten Sholans had the ability to travel on four legs like beasts.

As the minutes passed, he began to breathe more easily, then risked moving enough to knock the dirt from his hood. He'd wait a few hours yet before venturing out. With any luck, they'd put the incident down to the imagination of the telepath.

* * *

Without warning, it happened again. First the sensation of suffocating, then the heartbeat. Kaid lay there, claws extending into the bedding underneath him as he fought for each breath, unable to move or cry out for help. With each beat, an image was blazoned into his mind. With each beat, the image changed, evolved, till he realized he was watching an embryo grow. With the realization came the pain, the cessation of the visions, and the paralysis. They heard him then.

The Primes came for him this time. T'Chebbi and the others would have prevented them, but Kaid knew he had to go.

"No," he whispered, barely able to talk. "Let them take me, T'Chebbi. I need to find out what this is."

She grasped his hand. "You come back, hear me?" she said fiercely.

"I will."

By the time they had him on the floater and in the corridor, their drug had begun to work. Exhausted, he lay there, gradually becoming aware again of his surroundings. The floater was being guided by two Valtegans dressed in the uniform of M'ezozakk's crew. Like the priest, they wore collars. Ahead of them paced the gray-robed Seniormost. Kaid tried to reach out mentally for them but he was far too weak and the drug had affected his ability to concentrate. Cursing, he suddenly felt the crystal begin to warm against his chest. He reached for it, clutching it tightly in his hand, praying.

As they guided him into a large examination room, a flash of memory returned. He'd been here before. The aseptic smell he'd noticed when they were first brought on board filled the air. Subdued lighting made the room seem dim. He turned his head, seeing the examination table and treatment unit to which they were obviously heading.

The floater was moored over the table, then gradually lowered till it was locked in place. The two Valtegans moved away and stood a few meters distant—passive, quiet, unlike any Valtegans he'd seen before. The Seniormost switched on an overhead light, instantly blinding him. More memories—of this light, of insect faces and long hands that prodded and probed, of masks that reflected the light back into his eyes.

Within his mind, the heartbeat pulsed again and again, becoming faster. This time the image was of a cub, a cub he recognized as Kashini. With each beat, the image grew older, until it was Kashini as he'd last seen her. By now the heartbeat matched his own, throbbing through him as it intensified and quickened, giving him the same sense of urgency and danger it possessed.

He moaned, shaking his head in an effort to be free of it. It was too demanding, too overwhelming in its intensity for him to make sense of it: all he could do was endure.

"Why are you in pain?"

He heard the Seniormost's voice but could see only the cub in her crib, sleeping. The image was continuous now, filling his vision as if he were actually there.

The question was repeated.

Others clustered around him, shadowy figures he couldn't quite make out.

"You must answer us."

Why wouldn't they leave him alone? Couldn't they realize he had to watch, had to find out why he was seeing this—where the danger lay? Gray-brindled hands came into view, grasped the cub, lifting her up and holding her close. Dzaka? What was happening to his son and Kashini?

"Readout indicates mental contact with another," he heard the mechanical translator say. "Terminate this portion of the experiment. He will not communicate with us while this continues."

"No!" he yelled, gripping the sides of the floater. A moment more, that's all he needed!

Hands were laid on him, holding him still as he thrashed around trying to avoid them. In his head, the images continued as Dzaka dashed from the room, running downstairs before coming to a halt at a door.

He felt the sting of a hypo and the vision ceased abruptly.

"It's done," he heard a distant voice say.

"No!" He fought them more fiercely as he was catapulted back to his own reality. "What have you done? What have you terminated?" He could feel the drug begin to course through him, turning his limbs leaden and useless, restricting his thoughts until he was mentally trapped within his own skull. It had been an earlier vision from a different viewpoint, he realized. Before they'd left Shola for Jalna, he'd seen Dzaka burst into the kitchen, holding Kashini protectively in his arm. Now the horror of the vision was complete. His son and Kashini were in danger, and he could do nothing.

His chin was grasped and turned till he faced the Seniormost. There were two of them, this one taller than the other. He'd never seen two before, he thought irrelevantly.

"Why are you in pain? Who are you linked to?"

Against his chest, the crystal pulsed. He knew without a shadow of doubt that Carrie was alive.

CHAPTER 10

Day 26

"ARE you linked to a Human female?" the taller Seniormost holding Kaid asked. "You must answer."

He licked lips that were dry and cracked with a tongue not much better. "Why?" he croaked. "Why should I tell you?"

"We have one such. She had been healed, but she does not thrive. We need to know why. Are you the reason?"

So they had her. That explained a great deal. He blinked, and wished he could think straight, but the drug had left him dizzy and confused. "Yes. She was injured. Was there another, a male like me?"

"We found only her. How is it your link is different from the others with Human partners? You have been apart for sixteen days, yet only now do you suffer."

They hadn't found Kusac? How long had she been awake? "I must see her," he said abruptly, interrupting the Seniormost.

The hand round his jaw tightened, the armored glove pressing into his flesh, reminding him of its strength and his weakness. "You must tell us what we wish to know."

"It's not the same for all of us," he said, praying they'd believe him. "How long has she been out of cryo?"

"This is not your concern. You are here to answer our questions."

"I must be with her!"

"That is for her partner. You inferred the missing one is her partner."

"We both are. I can help, if you take me to her! I have medical knowledge of her species!" He was getting frantic now, trying to reach out to her, but his mind was as paralyzed as his body. The pulse had to have been her—the image her knowledge of the danger facing Kashini. They'd been linked in some strange way for days if only he'd realized!

"You cannot mentally reach her unless we permit it. Do not bother attempting. Why were you in pain?"

He closed his eyes. Delaying them by lying could only harm her. "I felt her pain," he said. "Where she was wounded by the bullet." As he said it, an awful thought occurred to him. His reactions to her pain had been as intense as those of a Leska partner.

"You are of different species. Explain this."

"It happens to some of us," he said, numbed by the shock of his realization. "Our minds meet and link for life. There are three of us."

"This must be studied. You will rest for now." The Seniormost released him and began to turn away.

"I must see her!"

"Perhaps when you've rested." He gestured with his hand and the smaller one came forward to place a fresh hypo against his neck.

Tiredness began to spread through him, making his sight and mind blur. He fought to keep his eyes open. "I need to be with her! If she's out of cryo, she could die without my physical presence!"

"That is not your concern. She has survived till now. She is not in any immediate danger."

Consciousness faded, but not his fear that he'd wake back in their prison, alone.

* * *

Long, thin fingers gave the device a final adjustment before rearranging his patient's dark hair and replacing the tool in the tray at the side of the treatment bed. Large, dual-lensed eyes looked up at the gray-robed Prime.

"Adjusted now implant is. Properly to work more data needs it. Intended not for species Sholan. Understand this. Likely problems be," said the translator. Beneath it, the voice was low-pitched and slightly rough, vibrating like a musical string being stroked by a bow. "Wake him you can now."

"Understood," said the tall Seniormost.

*   *   *

The Primes obviously considered leaving him in his room for two days his punishment as, later that day, they came for him, taking him to the interrogation room once more. J'koshuk had spent the days trying to think of anything that would improve their opinion of him, make him have value in their eyes. The thought of being implanted like the others filled him with terror.

"You are to be given one last chance. I want information from this one," said the Prime, indicating the dark-pelted Sholan sitting quietly in the chair. "You will concentrate on him for now. Do not harm him physically. He was awakened and implanted three days ago. Pain may be used, but with discretion. You have five days, no longer." He handed him a reader. "These are the questions I want answered. Your wrist unit includes controls for his collar. This Prime will show you how to utilize them." He indicated a white-robed Prime standing nearby.

"I've seen that female in the stasis room before," J'koshuk said as the Seniormost turned to leave.

He stopped, and waited.

J'koshuk flicked his tongue across his lips. "She was on Keiss, at our recreation city. Unless she has a double, she should be dead. When we discovered she was a spy, General M'ezozakk gave her to me to interrogate, then have terminated."

"Undoubtedly she has a double. Have you see this male before?" The gloved hand pointed to Kusac.

He shook his head. "There were no Sholans on Keiss when we left."

"You will question this Kusac about Kezule. We are interested in him."

Kezule. That had been the name the one called Tallis had called out before he was killed. He'd forgotten about that. He inclined his head, then added Kezule's name to the list of questions. "I may do what I want to him, within reason?" he asked, wanting to be sure. From the list, he saw they thought Kusac was her mate. Whether or not he was, he could certainly solve the problem of the female's identity, and that right now was his own priority. "These Sholans are almost as difficult to get information from as my own people."

"Within reason," agreed the Prime. "Just get us the answers we wish."

* * *

Noni and Teusi moved her into the back bedroom that evening.

"Don't know how you kept going, girl," said Noni, watching from the doorway as Teusi helped the female they'd named Ghaysa limp over to the big bed. "Thank the good Goddess you knew what herbs to take."

"Luck," she muttered, sitting on the edge of the bed once he'd drawn the covers back. Lifting her legs in was easier than she'd thought it would be. Her right leg had much of its mobility back now that the swelling was finally subsiding.

The bed was cool, and as soft and fresh-smelling as the other had been. She lay back, pulling the covers over her and let herself drift off to sleep again.

Morning brought with it a scent she recognized from her dreams.

"The nung tree in the garden," said Teusi in answer to her question when he brought her first meal. "Noni says you're to rest up today. You can use her bed during the day if you want."

"Maybe later," she'd said, tucking into the cooked eggs and meat.

She'd slept again, till almost evening, waking in time to go through to the main room for the last meal of the day.

"You remembered anything yet?" asked Noni, handing her a mug of coffee when she'd finished. "Try that. Human drink and very nice."

It was good. "No, nothing yet."

"What about the accident?"

She wrinkled her nose, looking up at Noni. "Accident?"

"An aircar crashed a couple of miles away," said Noni.

She thought about it for a moment. "I don't remember any crash."

"Ah, well. You just tell the Protector that when he comes tomorrow."

Panic welled up inside her. She might have lost her memory, but she instinctively knew she didn't want to have anything at all to do with the Protectors. "Why do they want to see me?"

"They think you witnessed the crash. Just routine, nothing to worry about. Where did you come from? North, or up from the southern lowlands?"

"Lowlands," she said automatically, then froze.

"See? It'll come back on its own, so don't you fret," said Noni comfortingly.

"I'm not worrying," she forced herself to say with a sinking feeling. Like a faucet leaking, suddenly bits of memories were beginning to return. Like making damned sure the Protectorate didn't see her. She'd have to leave tonight. But for where? She'd thought if she found the old one and the tree she'd be safe.

Vartra's Retreat! It wasn't far away, she realized. They could grant her sanctuary there. She could go into retreat, work for them, maybe in their gardens growing things. After living off the land for so many weeks, she could surely do that.

She stood up, faking a large yawn. "I think I'll turn in now. I'm still tired."

Noni nodded. "Sleep well, youngling."

On her way past the old female, she stopped to hug her impulsively. "Thank you," she whispered, then fled to the rear bedroom.

Noni sat there contemplating her mug, wondering what this female could possibly have done to make her need sanctuary. She sighed, taking a mouthful of coffee, wondering if this— Ghaysa—was the one in Brynne's dreams. She'd done what had been asked of her, taken the female in, then sent her on to the Retreat. At least the carefully planted mental suggestion hadn't been noticed. Finishing her drink, she wondered if she'd ever find out what the purpose had been to this, or would she just disappear behind Dhaika's walls for the rest of her life? Not every encounter had an ending these days.

* * *

"Josh, what do I do about the Touibans?" repeated Mara, grasping hold of the newspaper her mate was reading and tugging it away from him.

"Hey! Don't do that," he protested. "These papers cost a lot to import, Mara."

"You're not listening to me," she said. "And the paper's over three weeks old anyway."

"You tell him," said Ruth, ladling the last of the mushrooms onto the girl's plate. Putting the spoon back in her pan, she took hold of the offending paper, whisked it away from him and headed back into the inner kitchen carrying it.

"Oi! That's not fair," he protested. "It's only just arrived! I haven't finished it yet!"

"Not at my table you don't," Ruth's reply drifted back. "Just because you have a Link with Mara doesn't mean you give up talking to her."

"You're ganging up on me," he complained, picking up his mug as Mara sniggered at him.

"I was asking you a serious question. What do I do about the Touibans' request to join our Clan?"

Josh sat up in his chair, spluttering over his coffee. "You didn't tell me about that," he said. "I know you took them for the tour around the estate today, but you said nothing about that. And I didn't pick it up from you, either."

"No, I kept it to myself, trying to work out why they wanted to join our Clan."

"This is one for Master Konis," he said. "They really asked if they could join us?"

She nodded. "I thought I'd misheard them, but I hadn't. Anyway, I've got to see them tomorrow and give them some kind of answer. And I can't disturb Master Konis or Rhyasha at this time."

"You could contact Falma. He's Konis' aide," suggested Josh.

"Go straight to Rhyasha, my dear," said Ruth, reemerging with her own food. "Don't be put off by the situation. With her son and bond-daughter missing, I'll bet she'd welcome any diversion right now. Master Konis went back to work today, so she's been on her own. And there's Kitra. Involve her if you can. She could certainly do with something to keep her busy. Besides," she smiled slightly, "Dzaka still does a tour up there now and then. Who knows what might happen if we present them with an opportunity?"

"I'll see what I can do, but it might not involve me at all," said Mara, spearing her mushrooms with her fork. She felt really sorry for the young Sholan girl. The last few weeks had not been kind to her.

"Why on earth would they want to join us?" repeated Josh. "I mean, surely they'd want to go home? What do they think they'd gain?"

"Knowledge. They're motivated by knowledge." Mara popped the mushrooms into her mouth.

"I know that, but . . ." He shook his head. "Alien motives. Who can figure 'em?" he grinned, reaching out to tousle Daira's ears.

Ruth's fosterling grinned up at him. "You're the aliens here," he purred.

"Finish up your meal, then go take your shower," said Ruth, looking in his direction. "You and Mandy have got classes with Ghyan over at the Shrine tomorrow."

"You're not sending Mandy for her shower," he objected, getting slowly to his feet.

"She's older, but she'll be following you shortly," said Ruth. "Go on, no dawdling now."

He trailed off, tail hung low, ears flattened, looking dejected.

"I'll bring you a cookie with milk if you're in bed in half an hour," said Josh, taking pity on him.

Magically, the tail lifted and he scurried off.

"He gets spoiled too much by those living here," said Ruth.

"He's all right," said Josh.

"The Touibans," reminded Mara.

"Call Rhyasha in an hour," said Ruth. "After we've cleaned up here."

Mara's call resulted in her being asked up to the main house. She was ushered into the lounge where Rhyasha and Konis waited for her.

The greetings over, and drinks dispensed, she was asked to explain what had happened. As she told them of the day's events, Konis began to nod.

"This is more than I could have hoped for," he said. "If we're understanding them correctly, then what they really want is permission to bring their whole swarm here and start up a new hive on Shola."

"A hive?" echoed Rhyasha. "They won't let our Cultural Evaluation teams enter the hives." She saw Mara's confused look and began to explain. "Touiban swarms include their females, but they never leave the hives. We've only ever interacted with groups of males."

"I thought they had cities and towns like us."

"They do," nodded Konis, "but the hives are at the heart, and we're not allowed there. This would give us an unprecedented opportunity to study their whole culture for the first time. And all thanks to you and Josh. You're to be commended, my dear. You've achieved what none of us have been able to do in several hundred years."

"I did nothing special," she murmured, overwhelmed by the praise.

"Nonsense," said Rhyasha. "You've taken the time and trouble to be genuinely interested in them. They've obviously appreciated it."

"It's not just me, it's all of us, otherwise they wouldn't want to be part of our community."

"True, but it was you, personally, they took to. I'd love to handle this, Rhyasha, but I've got too much to do over at Shanagi with this treaty and the Clans. Can you see them tomorrow? With Mara, of course. Find out exactly what it is they want and make the necessary arrangements."

"Of course, but I'm not the one best suited to this, you realize," she said. "My knowledge of the Touibans isn't great."

"Kusac will straighten out any loose ends when they return."

"Konis . . ."

"He *will* return," stated Konis firmly, ending the conversation.

*   *   *

Day 27

"Even if she is Keeza, what can we do?" Lijou asked Kha'Qwa as he escorted her to the waiting aircar. "If she's evaded all the searches so far, then what makes you think we're going to find her now? She'll be found when she wants to be found, as will Kezule. We're powerless till that moment. Besides, I think she's dead, eaten by him."

Kha'Qwa shivered, her claw tips pricking his arm through the fabric of his robe. "Don't talk like that! Rhyaz thinks she's alive."

"He likes bodies," he began, then stopped, remembering his life-mate's increased sensitivity to these subjects so near the end of her pregnancy. "Sorry. Didn't mean it."

They stopped at the steps up to the vehicle.

"You tell Noni I was asking for her," he said. "I wish you'd agree to go to Shanagi's medical center. Much as I trust Noni, I want you to have the best treatment. There's still time for you to change your mind."

"I am getting the best," she said, leaning forward to rub his cheek with hers. "Look, there's Brynne now, with Jurrel and Banner." She pointed across the courtyard to where the three males were walking. "I knew Jurrel would be good for him. See, they're laughing. When did you see him laugh before, or allow another to touch him?" she added as Jurrel draped an affectionate arm across Brynne's shoulders and drew his attention to a small group sitting on a grassy mound at the side of the wall.

"So complex, these Humans," murmured Lijou, watching as the three joined the others. "Too many inhibitions, and it takes them so long to lose them."

"Brynne was a special case. The day he set down on Shola, he Linked to Vanna. He had no chance to get to know us as a species before being tied in an unbreakable relationship. At least this one is of his choosing."

"You try to twin people too often," Lijou said affectionately. "Just watch you don't get it wrong one day."

"I have a good success rate," she purred, nuzzling him under his chin. "I chose you for me, after all."

"I know, and I'm glad you did," he said, tilting his chin up and enjoying the caress. "As a mere priest, I'd never have had the nerve to approach a warrior like you otherwise."

"Mere priest indeed! In you, strength and compassion go hand in hand," she said, moving back from him and turning toward the aircar. "I must go. Noni's expecting me."

"Take care," he said.

* * *

She'd reached the Retreat by the time dawn's light hit the horizon. The land was rugged around the temple, built as it was into the side of the mountain. There'd be many more caves and crevices like this in which she could hide. It was cold, though, this high up. The plains had been warmer, but the couple of days at the old one's house had given her her strength and most of her health back.

The fever was gone, and the wound on her thigh was beginning to knit at last. She leaned forward, fingering the dressing. Suddenly she was back there in the forest with him, feeling his hands holding her tightly about the thighs as he pulled her closer. She struggled, whimpering with fear as she tried to scrabble backward away from him. The hands tightened, claws penetrating her hide, cutting her almost to the bone as he tried to mount her.

Pain lanced through her leg, breaking the trance, returning her to the present. She'd managed to sink her claws into the wound, she realized, watching tiny pinpricks of blood welling up through the dressing. That was what had brought her back.

She shivered, wrapping the blanket she'd stolen from Noni round her. It wasn't her way to repay kindness with theft, but she'd had no choice. The taste of civilized life had softened her: she could no longer face living that rough again.

There'd been more memories, of blood spraying around a white room, coating the walls till it dripped from them in lazy, red runnels. She felt sick at the thought of it. Is that what *he'd* done to the others before taking her as a captive? She shuddered again, glad she'd escaped with her life.

And others, of a male in robes edged with purple. A telepath. She tried to remember more, focusing on him. They'd landed in a clearing. Her captor had been angry with the telepath, she remembered that. He'd hit him, hard, just like he'd hit her many times. Reflexively, she put her hand to her head, feeling old scars and still tender spots. No, not like he'd hit her, because he'd killed the telepath, then taken his spare clothing.

Her head hurt now, with so much remembering. She lay

down, wanting to sleep. Her feet hurt too. She wondered again why she was here as she began to drift off to sleep.

* * *

When Kaid came to, he found himself not back with the others as he'd feared, but in another, smaller room. Hunger growled deep in his belly. They'd kept him drugged for some time. He moved, discovering he was free to climb out of the bed on which he lay and move around the room. This bed was high, totally unlike the ones in their living quarters. And there was no discernible door—all the walls seemed the same until he approached one and it began to de-opaque, giving him a view into the next room.

Carrie lay supported on a cradle, bathed in an eerie blue glow from a force field of some kind. As he watched, two gray-robed Primes, followed by one in white, came into view and began to work with the console by her head. Were they the same two he'd seen? One did look to be smaller. The glow surrounding Carrie started to flicker and fade. Around his neck, the crystal began to warm and in his mind, he felt the now familiar pulse. This time there was no pain, no difficulty breathing, only the pulse.

He felt her scream begin to build in his mind long before her mouth opened and she started to whimper.

Against his chest, the crystal felt as if it was incandescent. He pounded on the wall, desperate to attract her attention—or theirs. Then he remembered what he was, what they shared, and reached mentally for her. Like a swimmer afraid of drowning, his mind was seized and almost submerged by hers. Incoherent terror rushed through him, threatening to take him down with her. He needed all the strength of his mental disciplines to fight back and contain her, and he knew he couldn't hold her for long. He continued beating on the wall, shouting to the Primes, even though he knew it was futile.

"Leave her! Let me wake her! You're risking her sanity doing this!" Even as he cried out, the field around her darkened and her scream began to fade, as did her presence in his mind.

He sagged against the wall in relief. They'd heard him and realized what was happening to her. Now he could try

to take in the fact that she really was alive. Against all
odds, she was alive! His vision blurred and he put up a
hand to his eyes, surprised to find them damp with tears.
A movement from the room caught his attention as the
smaller Prime turned toward him. Against his shoulder, the
wall seemed to quiver, then move. Staggering back, he
watched the section he'd been leaning against begin to
slide open.

Hesitantly, he stepped into the room. It was cold, the air
chill on his unclothed pelt.

"You will wake her," said the translator. "You will then
take her to your room. Food will be left for you. See that
she eats. We will question her later." He turned and began
to walk from the room.

"Not if I can help it," he murmured before approaching
the remaining Primes at the console, and Carrie.

She was thin, painfully thin, her cheeks hollowed, her
eyelids shadowed.

"What have you done to her?" he demanded, moving
closer, anger trying to force back the sudden fear that she
might yet die.

"We healed her, but she does not thrive. We told you
this. Do not touch her till I tell you it is safe."

Again the light faded, but this time it dimmed more
quickly around her head and upper torso. The white-robed
one stepped forward and put a hypo to her neck just as
she began to stir. The tension left her body and she went
limp, head rolling toward him as the drug took effect.

"She will sleep for a short time, then wake. Take her
and go."

He hesitated, afraid of what would happen to them when
he touched her, afraid it was what he wanted.

"Take her."

He moved forward, picking her up in his arms, cradling
her close against his chest. In his mind, her presence began
to grow, but only to the level it had been before. He sighed
with relief. Maybe he'd been wrong about their Link.

He breathed in her scent, smelling the alien drugs that
still clung to her skin, and more. Eyes blazing, he looked
up at them. "You've removed her contraceptive implant,"
he snarled.

"She is your mate. What need had she of such chemicals? They interfered with our treatment."

"Take your mate and leave," said the gray. "Be thankful we found her."

Tightening his grip on her, he backed off, almost stumbling in his haste to leave the stasis room. His mind was reeling with the implications of what they'd done. The opening slid shut behind him, opaquing the wall again until they were alone. Carefully, he laid her on the bed, pulling the cover over her, his hand lingering on her cheek. It was like a physical pain to stop touching her, but he had to.

Food, in insulated bowls, had already been left on the night table. They obviously expected her to wake very shortly. He went over to the far wall and squatted down, leaning back against it. Right now, he needed to think. She was there, in his mind again, a part of him that he couldn't ignore. He'd gone from thinking her dead to this; he should be ecstatic, but he wasn't, because no matter what the Primes said, he knew why they'd removed her implant. They wanted her pregnant, like Jo.

His anger rose again. They had to escape as soon as possible, no matter the cost. The Primes had no intention of freeing them, he was sure of it now, and he had no intention of letting them breed his people like slaves. They were being treated like experimental animals! How could he pair with Carrie and make her pregnant under these circumstances—and how would she survive the lack of Kusac if he didn't?

In his mind, he could almost hear Vartra's sardonic laugh.

"Some things are not dependent on me, Tallinu. That rather depends on your actions, doesn't it? Cubs are Ghyakulla's gift to us all."

The memory triggered more, like a string of beads that had come undone and were tumbling free. His obsession with Carrie had been his alone, no one had gifted it to him. Vartra had told him that. He knew now that the pulse, or heartbeat he'd heard had been his memory of the long, drugged trip from the monastery to Stronghold when, as a three year old, he'd lain with his head on Carrie's belly, listening to the heartbeat of her unborn cub, Kashini. That was when his desire for Carrie had been forged. With unforgiving clarity, he faced the fact that it was then he'd decided the next cub she carried in her belly would be his.

His head began to pound and he lowered it to rest on his forearms. Now he'd never have the opportunity to ask her himself. If she had any chance of life with Kusac dead or missing, he had to step into his sword-brother's place, and she *would* become pregnant. How could he do that to either of them? He loved them both too much for that.

Through the pounding in his head, his thoughts turned back to Carrie's current condition.

She should have started to wake by now, surely. Tiredly, he got to his feet and went over to check on her. She looked so frail that it caught at his breath. Even as he touched her for reassurance, he felt the pulse of his headache change, felt the swirling power of the gestalt begin to slowly build.

He'd have recoiled in fear if Carrie hadn't stirred and grasped his hand. Their eyes met, and as they did, so did their minds.

Senses expanded, and as his heartbeat increased with the pounding of the pulse that echoed through them both now, her scent, more potent than any aphrodisiac, overwhelmed him.

She knew everything. "You want to share your cubs with me." Her voice was quiet, rougher than he remembered.

He'd nowhere to hide any longer, not even from himself. "Yes," he whispered, though it tore him apart to admit it to her. "I'm not Kusac, Carrie. I'm not trying to replace him, but I don't want to be second . . ."

Her hand tightened on his. "Never that, Tallinu," she whispered, shifting her head so she could look up at him. "Kusac will always be my passion, but you're my rock, my stability from the first. I love you for that."

"I can't father another bastard cub, Carrie. I can't do that to us!" But he let her urge him closer till their lips touched and he felt the Link compulsion start to build.

It wouldn't be. The Triad's registered at the temple. We're life-mates, too.

We didn't make vows, didn't share our blood.

She bit down hard on his lip, making him yelp and pull free at the sudden pain. *Bite me,* she sent.

I can't! Distracted, he touched a finger to his lip, feeling it begin to swell.

She lifted his hand to her mouth, closing her lips round the fingertip, purposely triggering his claw. He tried to pull it free, but the claw caught, cutting her. Then she released him.

"Kiss me!"

He did, tasting their blood as it mingled on their tongues and lips.

Now we're of one blood, she sent.

We're of one blood, he agreed, trembling as the pulse grew stronger before exploding in a surge of energy they knew was the gestalt. Already their minds were merging, becoming one. He hadn't much time left he realized, seizing control of the gestalt and trying to hold onto his own identity.

Will you share this cub with me, Carrie? he sent, not trusting his voice.

Yes, and others, Tallinu.

Moving the cover aside, he eased himself onto the bed beside her. Seeing her move, about to turn round, he caught her shoulder, holding her back.

"Not this time," he said hoarsely, as he knelt. "I want to see you, watch your face."

Looming over her, he untied her sleeping wrap, pushing it aside as he drew trembling hands down her ribs. He felt the bullet scar and stopped, checking it with gentle fingers. There was barely a trace of the life-threatening wound. Whatever the Primes had done, they'd saved her life, and for that he was grateful.

He kissed the soft flesh of her belly, caressing it before drawing the gentle tip of his tongue across her as he reached for her hips. Leaning forward, ready to join with her, ready to let go of the tenuous control he had on the gestalt and their Link, he stopped, afraid he was taking advantage of Kusac's absence.

"We need each other to live," she whispered, her hand closing on his arm. "En'Shalla. Let it happen, Tallinu."

He let go. The beat pulsed once more, sending fire coruscating through bodies and minds as they were swept up together. There was no *him,* only *them* as he simultaneously felt himself moving within her and experienced her flesh being penetrated by his. It was too much, too intense: they had to stop, but couldn't. They became one entity, swirling in a sea of shared sensations.

Just as it seemed they could bear no more, the explosion of relief came and he was himself again, clutching her shuddering body against his. He caught his breath, supporting her as he lowered them to the bed. There was no need for words, she was there, in his consciousness, part of the fabric of his mind.

He felt her retreat a little from him, start building a shield he'd never sensed before, knowing instantly that it was the means she and Kusac used to give themselves mental privacy. He felt her wave of sadness that she quickly suppressed.

Do the same, she sent. *Set it where you will, then you're in control of how much of your thoughts I know.*

The sheer amount of information passing between them confused and fascinated him. He knew from moment to moment how she felt, what she was thinking.

Not yet, he sent, sliding his hand across her belly as he watched her from half-closed eyes. "I'll know when," he whispered, remembering the vision of their daughter's birth. Now he could see the mother's face, and it was Carrie's. "I've feared and wanted this for so long." Then his hand tightened briefly and he released her only to take her into his arms, kissing and caressing her.

It's done. We'll find Kusac, Carrie. I won't stop till we do, believe me. I'm getting us off this ship as soon as possible. Our daughter will not be born into captivity, I swear.

* * *

Hands bound behind him, Kusac was dragged by J'koshuk toward a large window that gave onto the room next door. The hand holding his scruff pulled his head painfully back, claws gouging his flesh as he was hauled to a stop.

"Look, even now they betray you in this act of reproduction!"

He looked, seeing enough to know that one of the two figures in the bed was Carrie. She was alive, then. He supposed he was glad but he felt nothing. The other—was Sholan, that was all he could tell. He turned his head aside, feeling divorced from everything around him. He had felt this way since they'd awakened him. He didn't even try to reach for her mentally, he knew the pain it caused him because of the collar.

A hiss of anger from his captor and he was flung against the transparent screen. Painfully, his face was pressed against the cool surface. He tried to look away. J'koshuk's hand slid under the metal collar round his neck and gripped it, holding him there.

"You'll watch till I say otherwise! That is your mate, linked mentally to you! Would you die for them now? You're a bigger fool than I thought!"

Kusac closed his eyes. It had to be Kaid. He was the only one other than himself who could keep her alive. At least they had each other. Vaguely, he wondered why he still lived.

"Say something!" hissed the enraged Valtegan.

He chose to ignore the command. He could never tell whether an answer or silence was expected. Either at the wrong time would bring the same punishment. Somewhere, deep inside, where the drugs and their device hadn't yet reached, he ached to be with them.

How could he ignore what was going on before his eyes? J'koshuk was angry beyond measure with his captive. He'd expected some reaction. If one of his people had witnessed such a betrayal, he'd have torn the window down in an effort to reach the male and kill him!

He raised his hand to hit him, then remembered the Prime's directive and lowered it, letting the Sholan go. Reaching for his wrist unit, he activated the control once, holding it down for the space of two counts.

The male fell heavily to his knees before crumpling to the floor.

That wasn't the effect it had had before. J'koshuk was about to press it again when the white-robed Prime behind him stepped forward and grasped his hand, preventing him.

"You have overused it. It is ineffective for now. He has become numbed by the pain. Return him to his cell."

"You do it," snapped J'koshuk, taking a risk. He needed to know what his status was, if he had standing among them. This white-robed Prime was obviously of lesser rank than the grays. "I've his answers to process for the Seniormost. I haven't the time to do your job."

There was the usual short silence, then: "I will return him," said the Prime, motioning J'koshuk to one side with his pistol.

Satisfied, he moved. Now he had an idea of where he stood. He left the room, heading back up the corridor that flanked the medical section till he reached the junction leading to the interrogation room on his left, the captives from the *M'ijikk* and his own quarters on the right. Activating the lock, he went in, going to the nourishment unit to fetch himself a drink.

He settled himself at the desk, opening the drawer to take out some paper and a stylus. Putting his reader down, he sat back, letting his anger dissipate. So far, he'd given the Primes most of the answers they'd requested. Some had been beyond him as his captives didn't have that information themselves. He sipped the herbal drink, picking up his last summary of information from the Valtegan captives. A picture was beginning, very slowly, to emerge, and he wanted to understand it. Understanding would give him an advantage, and an advantage would lead to consolidating his position here. He might still be a prisoner, but he was at least the most valued and trusted one. He aimed to keep it that way.

The Primes had no interest whatsoever, as far as he could discern, in the U'Churians and the Cabbarans other than keeping them alive. Why they would want to keep such evil smelling mammals as the Cabbarans alive was beyond him. He'd have let them die. They were only mouths to feed, and bodies to guard. They contributed nothing, not even information.

A thought occurred to him. Perhaps he was not privy to all that went on. It was true he'd not been aware of the two from the cryo units until he'd followed the guards down to the stasis room several days ago. Well, they had told him he was free to go where he wished within the proscribed area. Obviously it was to their advantage if he knew his way around.

He hadn't recognized her at first because he knew he'd had her killed on Keiss. She'd been another that had frustrated him beyond measure. Do what he could to her, she refused to talk, had laughed in his face, no less! The pain he'd inflicted on her was calculated to have a Valtegan screaming for mercy, yet she'd laughed.

He shifted uncomfortably, leaning forward for his papers. Had she been that different that she'd cheated death? Had she come back now to haunt him? The male had proved to be as difficult, though he had felt the pain, of that he was sure. He smiled to himself. The rest of his crew might have mocked him because of his caste, but no longer. They now knew personally just how much pleasure he could derive from his work. There was a skill to it, in playing with a person, inflicting just enough pain to induce the right kind of fear so he spoke the truth. Too much and they said anything just to stop the pain. But apply it carefully, and over several days, and you could make the most difficult subject tell you his deepest secrets. Unless it was that damned Human female and her mate!

He scowled, creasing his forehead. The dark-furred mate— what had the Seniormost said his name was? He looked at the reader, scrolling back to the beginning of the session. Kusac. That was it. He'd refused to speak about the female at all. He'd had to give up in the end. Even on the other questions, it had taken some time before he'd told him anything of use. Still, he liked to soften his prisoners up first, so the day had not been a total failure.

He took another mouthful of his drink, feeling more relaxed now as he finished going through what he'd learned from his former crew. The weapon that they'd used on the two planets of Sholans seemed to interest the Primes greatly, but he'd been able to find out very little about it and its origins. However, that didn't mean they knew nothing. His former senior crew members had not been made available to him. Obviously the Primes had conducted their own interrogations, leaving the bulk of his people to him.

He had discovered that as they had taken up their positions round the first world, a shuttle had docked with them, and a package had been handed to one of the senior officers. It had been taken to the engineering area, and given to the head officer to install on their ship. After the second planet, it had been uninstalled and collected again.

He remembered the reconnaissance patrol they'd flown

several hours after they'd used it. The devastation had shocked them all. Sensor readings had been double—no, triple—checked, but remained the same. No life had been left on either world. He shuddered at the memory. War was one thing, annihilation on this scale was a threat to them all. Should such a weapon fall into J'kirtikkian hands, they could suffer the same fate. No matter the reason, Valtegan should not use such a weapon against Valtegan.

Not being of a technical caste himself, the rest of the data concerning the device had meant nothing to him and he'd merely passed it on verbatim. A request to have it explained had gotten him nowhere; he'd been ignored.

Following closely on this interest in the mystery weapon, was their concern over the war they were fighting in and around the J'kirtikk sector. Outside of the command crew, he was the only person who was aware that the enemy they fought was their own kind.

They'd asked him how it had come about, but he couldn't really tell them. For as long as he'd been alive, this war had existed, with sporadic border engagements on each side as they'd almost taken it in turns to try pushing through into the other's territory. It hadn't been going on for just his lifetime, but for many generations before him as well. It was their mission in life, to reunite the two worlds, weld them once more into an empire under the God-King, Emperor M'iok'kul. Which was only right. They should be united under one God. Anything less was blasphemy, which was his domain.

The Primes wanted to know the state of the war, the weapons used, where encounters took place, how often, and if there were any subject worlds. That had surprised him. Why should they wish to rule inferior beings? They were dirt beneath the heels of the Valtegan people, not even true people, unworthy of notice—except for the females.

He thought again of the Human female. They'd not had much success keeping her out of stasis until they brought the other Sholan male in. Yes, they'd healed her, but later, when they tried to reduce the drugs, she'd started to scream and could not be stopped. So back she went into stasis, but in a reduced field he'd heard one of them say, so she could heal. Now she'd been wakened successfully, and they'd rewarded the Sholan male for doing it. But why *him*—the one who'd attacked and threatened their Interface, namely himself? If anyone deserved rewarding with female company, it was he, J'koshuk, for getting all the information they'd wanted.

It had been a long time since he'd been allowed access to the drones. M'ezozakk, burn his memory, had forbidden him to go near them after he'd failed to get the four Sholan captives to talk. M'ezozakk had said abstinence became a priest. He hissed low and angrily at the memory. He had the same urges as the rest of the bridge crew, and the enforced celibacy had almost tempted him to drink at the common crew water fountains to suppress it, but he was of high caste, to abuse his system with those chemicals was beneath him.

He'd been given the Human female once on Keiss, as a reward for uncovering a plot by four patients in the infirmary to steal the Human females for a night. He snorted at the memory. The soldiers had thought to test their new-found health on the females, interpreting their rising male chemical levels as the need to rut! Her skin had been softer than that of drones, he remembered. More responsive, too. The scent of her fear had acted like a strong aphrodisiac. It wasn't often one of his caste got to be with a true female. Since they were larger than the males, and definitely violent, it took a strong male to even think of approaching the breeding room, let alone enter it. Besides, he knew the females had to be drugged into submission and there was always the risk it would wear off too soon. Not exactly an invigorating experience.

They'd taken a J'kirtikkian craft once, with breeding females on board. He preferred drones—or Humans. He sighed, attempting to overcome his increasingly lustful thoughts by releasing the opposite, calmative chemicals, aware that he'd let his imagination roam into areas best left alone. He downed some more of his drink, feeling its soothing coolness spread through him, helping him regain his equilibrium.

Picking up the reader and stylus, he started to scribble notes from it onto the paper, beginning his report for the Seniormost.

* * *

Day 29

There had been something of a stir at the Retreat over the last two days. Food had been missing from the main kitchens, and no culprit could be found. Windows were shut, the door locked, but still the food went missing. Brynne's jegget was the prime suspect despite his protestations that she'd been locked in the room with him each night.

Guardian Dhaika had called him into his office, complaining bitterly, but had stopped just short of ordering him to get rid of her. Incensed, Brynne headed out into the grounds with her, letting her off the fine leash he'd fashioned for her to wear while indoors. He wasn't taking the chance of her being mistaken for a wild jegget and being treated as vermin only fit to be killed.

At first she'd poked around in the grass, finding cricketlike insects to eat, then, disturbing a small rodent, she'd scampered off in pursuit of it.

"Belle!" he called, getting to his feet as he saw the flick of her tail disappear over the grassy knoll ahead of him. "Come back here!" He reinforced it with a mental command, but the jegget, usually obliging, was intent on the hunt, reverting to her wild nature for now.

Cursing, he followed her, seeing the flick of her sable-tipped tail rise above clumps of grasses every now and then. He followed her down the hillside till he'd lost sight of the Retreat. He was in wild country now, not quite sure of where to go.

A faint sound drew his attention. He listened, trying to identify it, and when he couldn't, he reached out for it with his mind. He recognized the feel instantly and backed off. Derwent—and someone else. Cautiously, he hunkered down amid the long grass, wishing he wasn't wearing his black robe. He stood out like a sore-thumb against the green landscape.

He waited, hearing the noise again. It was the sound of feet trying to get a grip on stony ground and it was coming from around the bluff ahead of him. Remembering his training, he lay down in the grass and began to wriggle slowly closer. He heard a muffled cry, then the sound of someone falling. Again he reached out with his mind, this

time for the other person and was shocked to recognize
her, too. It was the female who had disturbed his sleep so
many times over the last few weeks. What the hell was
Derwent doing to her? Then he remembered the last dream
he'd had. What if the rape hadn't yet happened? Anger
flared, for her, and for himself, that one person could so
violate another.

He'd reached the edge of the bluff now and could see
them clearly. Derwent had her by the wrists and was busy
binding them firmly with rope.

"I knew once I had her, you'd come to me, Brynne," he
said, not bothering to look at him. "Your precious Leska,
Vanna. How does it go?" he asked, pulling the rope tighter
till the female whimpered in fear and pain. "When I hurt
her, do you feel her pain? If I kill her, do you die?" Finished, he hauled her round in the gravel to look in
Brynne's direction.

He knew it wasn't Vanna, but Derwent thought it was,
despite the fact that the two females were nothing alike.
Brynne stood up slowly, wishing he hadn't come alone.

"What do you want, Derwent? You know that's not
Vanna. Let her go. It's me you really want," he said, beginning to walk toward them.

"Stay right there," warned Derwent, pulling a knife out
and placing it against her throat. "I want sanctuary, and
she'll buy it for me, won't she? Unless you want me to cut
off one of her pretty little ears?"

As Derwent glanced away from him long enough to
move the knife to her ear, the female locked eyes with him.
He could feel her fear as acutely as if it were his, read the
plea in her eyes. The fear of rape was in her mind, too.

Rage surged through him, a rage like he'd never felt
before. Snarling, he launched himself at Derwent. Strength
he didn't know he possessed propelled him forward, knocking the other to the ground. As his hands closed round
Derwent's throat, his vision narrowed down to nothing,
until he felt a hand on his shoulder.

"Brynne, he's dead. You killed him. Let go now."

The red mist began to clear and gradually his sight returned. He shuddered, feeling Jurrel unclenching his hands
from Derwent's throat and helping him to his feet.

"She's safe. We cut her loose."

He looked over to where she sat whimpering, Banner watching over her.

He went over to them, crouching down in front of her. Ears plastered to her skull, brown eyes huge with fear, she stared up at him.

"Are you all right?" he asked, reaching out to touch her nicked ear. He could feel the self-control it took for her to keep it still, letting him examine it. It was barely more than a scratch.

"She won't talk," said Banner. "What happened? Who was the Human?"

"Derwent," said Brynne shortly, letting her go. "He's wanted for evading deportation." He looked up at his two friends. "She's coming back with me."

"The Protectorate will want to interview her about his attack."

"No!" he said, even before he felt her flash of fear. "No. She wasn't here. Derwent attacked me. She's not involved, understand?"

A chittering by his feet drew his attention away from them. He bent down to pick up Belle. "She's coming back with me," he said more quietly.

"She's the one from the dreams," said Jurrel. "Isn't she? Him, too."

Brynne nodded, standing up and holding his hand out to her. Hesitantly, she took it, allowing him to help her to her feet. "No one's to know she's here," he said, catching the glance that passed between the two Sholan males. "I have my reasons," he said to Jurrel. "Please. Trust me."

Jurrel flicked an ear in agreement, taking Belle from him as he held the jegget out.

Brynne began to unfasten his robe, taking it off to reveal the T-shirt and jeans he wore underneath. "The dreams, finding her here, it isn't just a coincidence." He held out the robe to her. "What's your name?" he asked gently.

"Ghaysa," she said, her voice barely audible as she accepted it from him. She stood there, letting it hang from her hand, her eyes never leaving his face, obviously in shock.

"We're taking you to the Retreat," said Brynne, "but you need to put the robe on. You'll be safe with me, I swear it."

She nodded slowly, beginning to put an arm into one sleeve.

He looked up at Jurrel and Banner. "You'll help me get her in?"

"Of course," said Jurrel, stroking the jegget.

"For now at least," agreed Banner. "Belle fetched us. If it hadn't been for her, we wouldn't have known where to find you. That in itself is strange."

"I wasn't soon enough," said Brynne, taking hold of Ghaysa's limp hand. "I didn't think Derwent could get this far without being picked up."

He stepped between her and Derwent's body as they passed it, trying to shield her from the sight of it. God knows, he didn't want to see it again himself, but beyond that, he felt nothing, not anger nor regret at killing the man who'd once been just about his only friend on Shola.

Getting her into the Retreat was easy: they just walked in. No one would think to stop the Brothers and a Sister. They left her in Brynne's room, with the jegget for company, locking the door behind them as they went to Guardian Dhaika's office to report Derwent's death.

The Protectors let Brynne leave first, but kept Banner and Jurrel for further questions as it was obvious they'd been more aware of what had happened than Brynne. They said he'd gone kzu-shu, into a warrior's red-mist trance, where nothing exists but the prey. Given the fact that Derwent had nearly caused Brynne's death by keeping him and his Leska apart when he'd been seriously ill, and the older male's attack on him, it had been understandable, said the chief Protector.

Brynne returned to his room to find Ghaysa curled up asleep in the center of his bed. This was the first chance he'd really had to look at her. A mane of hair of just about every conceivable Sholan color—brown, gold, ginger, and white—lay on the bed surrounding her head like a corona. Her pelt was the same glorious mix of colors. Hand reaching out to touch her hair, he sat down beside her.

She woke suddenly, eyes flying open to stare up at him. Fear began to fill them and he moved back, holding his hands up so she could see he didn't intend to harm her.

"You were running," he said quietly. "Through the forest. Then you stole a riding beast. It brought you a fish."

She stared at him, then whispered, "How do you know?"

"I shared your dreams," he said. "They came to me, I didn't look for them, Ghaysa. The male hurt you. Your thigh." He looked down, seeing the bandaged leg through the overlap of the robe. "His claws cut you."

"You saw that too?" She shut her eyes.

"Only when you remembered it," he said. "But nothing since then. Why? Why should I sense you so strongly?"

She looked at the robe she wore, touching the purple trim on it. "You're a Human telepath."

He could hear the fear in her voice. "That's why you're safe with me."

"You're in danger."

He frowned. "Me? Why should I be in danger?"

She flicked an ear in a negative. "Not just you. Telepaths. But I can't remember why."

Now he was confused. "Your memory will return," he said gently, not knowing what else to say. "You've been through so much, it's no wonder you don't want to remember it right now. How long were you Derwent's captive?"

"The Human? Only a short time."

"I thought he was the one in the dream." If not Derwent, then who? It hadn't been a Sholan male, of that he was positive, even though the male in the dream had been mostly in shadow.

"No," she said slowly. "Not the Human. Someone else." She frowned, her hand going instinctively to her bandaged thigh. "The Human didn't harm me like that."

Relief flooded through him. He'd not been too late, then. He heard a scratch at the door and went to answer it. It was Banner, carrying a bundle of clothes.

"From one of the Sisters. I noticed Ghaysa's were torn. She can't keep your robe." He hesitated, putting a hand up to scratch behind his ear. "What do you plan to do about her? She can't stay here indefinitely, nor come to Stronghold with us. Not even bond-mates are allowed to do that. Have you managed to find out anything about her yet?"

"Nothing. She's really lost her memory, though. What-

ever happened, it's terrified her." He sighed. "We've another couple of days here before I'm due back at the estate.
I could take her with me. She'd be safe there, surely." Then
he remembered her warning. "Jurrel's coming with me, why
don't you come, too?" If danger did threaten, and he
wasn't convinced it did, he'd rather have Banner with them
as well. "Where is Jurrel?"

"It's second meal. He's gone to get food for us all. She
looks like she could do with a few decent meals." He hesitated. "I'll think about coming with you. Jurrel might prefer
me not to."

This time, Brynne didn't try to avoid the amusement in
the other's eyes and voice. "You're just as welcome as Jurrel. You're his Companion."

"Don't undervalue yourself, Brynne," he said. "You matter to Jurrel, too." He touched him lightly on the arm.
"Now, do I have to stand out here, or can I come in? I
also brought some fresh dressings for Ghaysa's leg."

Showered, her bandages replaced with fresh ones, and
dressed in decent female clothing, Ghaysa began to relax a
little. They couldn't possibly mean her any harm. Hadn't
they kept the Protectors away from her?

She found the Human intriguing. So like her own kind,
yet different at the same time. They greeted her in a
friendly way when she finally joined them on the floor
round the plates of food. After helping her to generous
portions, they continued talking among themselves. The
two Sholans were telling stories of their time on the Humans' planet, Keiss.

"I've never been there," said Brynne. "I came direct
from Earth."

"Now there's a world I'd like to visit," said Jurrel, waving the bone he'd been gnawing. "From all accounts it's
like Shola was back at the time of the Cataclysm."

"You wouldn't like it," said Brynne, feeding some scraps
of meat to Belle. "Fumes, smog, too many road vehicles.
And the mental noise!" He shook his head.

"No psi dampers?" asked Banner.

"They still don't really believe in our gifts," reminded
Jurrel.

"Nothing. You had to grin and get on with it," said

Brynne. "Night was best, when most folk were asleep, then you could have your mind to yourself again."

"So you like it here?" asked Banner, reaching for some more bread.

She could sense him considering his answer.

"Not at first," Brynne admitted. "My Leska Link with Vanna Kyjishi happened almost as soon as I set foot on this world. From then on, my life was decided. It's only now that I feel I've begun to get control of it again."

"Despite the dreams and visions?" asked Jurrel.

She felt the Human's eyes on her, and concentrated on her food.

"Yes. They've helped me save one person so far." He looked away, his attention back on his companions. "It's what I did on Earth. Helped find missing persons."

"You did? We do that, too," said Jurrel. "You should mention it to Tutor Kha'Qwa."

"You kill them," Ghaysa blurted out, shocking them to silence.

"You listen to too much gossip," said Banner, his voice a low rumble of reproval.

"What else is there?" she countered.

"The truth. Not everything we do is negative. Ghaysa," said Jurrel, passing her a glass of the fruit juice he'd just poured. "We do far more that is positive, only no one hears of it."

She snorted disbelievingly.

"You've had dealings with us before?" asked Jurrel.

An image flashed into her mind of a room and a tall figure, black-robed like them, standing with the sun behind him. She remembered weights at her wrists, and clenched her hands, claw tips pressing into her palms. The image faded. "No," she lied, aware that the Human had picked up something of it from her.

"Leave her, Jurrel," said Brynne lazily. "Her memory will come back in its own time."

He was protecting her from his fellow Brothers? Why would he do that for her, a total stranger?

Not quite, came back his thought. *You forget I know you through the dreams.*

"Whether or not she has, she can ask for sanctuary here," said Banner. "The merits of her case would be looked at dispassionately by Guardian Dhaika. It could be granted if she agreed to entering a closed order."

"I'm sure that's not necessary," said Brynne. "She's not a convict. It was Derwent she's been running from all along. He's been free for a couple of months now." He looked over at her again. "He thought she was my Leska, Vanna. And there was the rape. That was Derwent."

Banner made a noise as if he was clearing his throat. "If he had her captive, why let her go?"

"He left her for dead," said Brynne.

She'd told him it hadn't been the Human! Why was he lying like this for her? Yes, she'd been left, but not quite for dead. *He'd* known she was still alive.

"I told you, I need the chemical your body produces," he'd said, rising to his feet and reaching for his clothes. "Was as little pleasure in this act for me as you. Biting you made us dependent on each other. This sets us both free." He pulled the tunic over his head, looking down at where she lay bleeding on the ground. "Go. Get help for yourself. It's over for you. I go on alone now. Believe me, those responsible for making me use you like this will pay dearly."

He'd pulled on the robe then, belting it. "I regret wounding you," he said, hesitating. "You served me well, but you fought me. The error was yours. I have never injured you before, I did not intend to do so now. You should have trusted me to do what was best for both of us. Tell me your name. I wish to remember it."

"Ghaysa!" She was being shaken now. Moaning, she put her hand up to her head. It hurt. Remembering hurt more than she could bear.

She felt herself lifted and carried, then placed on the bed. The one called Banner looked at her eyes, felt her pulse.

"Shock," he said, pulling a cover over her. "She needs to be kept warm. We should go. If you need us, you know where we are."

"I'll call you," said the Human. His voice sounded close, then she felt the bed move as he sat beside her.

A gentle hand pushed her hair back, continuing the caress between her ears as she heard the plates and glasses being collected, then the door closing.

She could sense Brynne more strongly now, knew he was like the Brother who'd come for her, the one who'd stood against the light. He'd been fair with her. She felt herself begin to drift to sleep, knowing with him, she was safe.

Chapter 11

JURREL had dropped by to make sure all was well before retiring. They'd talked quietly for several minutes before Brynne had said what was really on his mind.

"I feel drawn to her," he said, leaning against the doorpost.

"You would be, you've shared so much of her suffering. I am, when I sense her through you."

"Through me?" How much had Jurrel picked up, he wondered, fear tightening the pit of his stomach.

Jurrel shrugged, putting his head to one side, mouth opening in a slow smile. "I pick up your emotions when I'm near you, and today, when you were sensing her . . ." He left the sentence unfinished.

"Being Talented is more complex than I thought," Brynne said, relieved.

"It's a world of the senses, which you have to experience to understand. You're aware of so much more that's going on around you than those without a gift. That's why you have to face yourself without fear, and be responsible for your own actions," said Jurrel. He hesitated, obviously unsure whether to continue. "You realize what happened this afternoon, don't you? You went kzu-shu. It's a Sholan thing. You've done what you were afraid to do, accessed your Sholan side fully. You can't go back now, can't block it off any more."

"I knew I couldn't go back the night we spent together," he said quietly. "I'm beginning to come to terms with myself."

"Don't look too deep," Jurrel said, smiling again. "You can get lost doing that. Vartra knows, Banner and I don't have an exclusive relationship, we've had female lovers, too, but this one . . ." He shook his head, obviously concerned. "We know nothing about her, except she's lost her memory."

"She's harmless," said Brynne. "Far more hurt than capable of hurting me. I trust her."

"You've touched her mind, you should know. Just be yourself, do what you think is right rather than what you think's expected of you."

"With you around to remind me, how can I forget?" Brynne countered, reaching out to clasp him briefly on the shoulder.

Jurrel put his hand up to cover Brynne's. "There's something else I must talk to you about. Is Ghaysa asleep?"

Puzzled, Brynne nodded.

"Have you ever killed before?" he asked in a low voice.

Shocked, Brynne would have pulled away from him, but Jurrel held onto his hand.

"I take it you haven't. Don't look so shocked, my friend. What do you think I'm training you to do in the gym at Stronghold? We're fighters, we kill to protect, not for the sport. We're not murderers."

"I know, but . . . I didn't think that . . ." he stammered.

"Calm down, Brynne. Look we can't talk here," he said, glancing up and down the corridor. "Can you leave her for a few minutes and come to our room? I'm sure Banner would watch her for you."

He hesitated, aware of how important Jurrel considered this. As far as he was concerned, he had no regrets over killing Derwent. After the stunt he'd pulled a few days ago, and the way he'd treated Ghaysa . . . Jurrel's grip on his hand tightened.

"We must talk, Brynne."

Brynne nodded and followed him down the corridor to their room.

Jurrel opened the door and called to Banner. "Would you mind watching Ghaysa for a while? I need to talk to Brynne."

"Sure," came the reply. He heard the bed creak. Banner came out wearing the short black Brotherhood tunic. "Take what time you need." He strolled down the corridor.

"Thanks." Jurrel stood aside for him to enter.

The room was identical to his, large enough for the usual double bed and two small night tables at either side of it, a couple of drawer units, and a chest at the foot of the bed. A desk, with the ubiquitous comm unit, stood against one wall.

Brynne perched on the edge of the chest, assuming Jurrel would join him there. He didn't, instead he chose to sit on the bed, making Brynne twist round to see him.

"You're going to tell me I shouldn't have killed Derwent, aren't you?" he asked defensively.

"No, I'm not going to do that. After all, I wasn't there, I don't know the dynamics of the situation. In the Brotherhood, you'll be taught to kill more efficiently than you would in any other military organization. If you take someone's life, you need to be sure it's never done lightly."

"It wasn't," said Brynne. "I know what was in his mind. He thought she was Vanna, my Leska, and was threatening my life."

"I know he was," said Jurrel quietly. "In normal circumstances, you'd not find yourself in a situation where the decision to kill was yours alone until nearing graduation, by which time you'd be emotionally as well as physically prepared for it. Today's happening was unfortunate."

"I don't have a problem with it."

"Not now, but you may later, Brynne. You killed Derwent with your bare hands. You saw his face, heard his last breath, even if you can't remember it now. At some point, that memory will come back and have to be dealt with."

Brynne had looked away uncomfortably as he'd spoken. Unbidden, the image of Derwent's face had, indeed, come to his mind, "I don't want to remember it," he said harshly, standing up. "The man was mad. If I hadn't come along, he planned to rape her. After sharing her memories of that, do you think I'd let him get the chance to do it again just to get sanctury at Stronghold?"

He pushed aside memories of times shared with Derwent, good times as well as bad. He did not want to remember any of it.

"I'm not criticizing your actions, Brynne, only offering my help if you find you need it. I'd be failing in my duty to you—and as a friend—if I didn't tell you this."

It was an awkward moment for him, poised between taking offense and the knowledge Jurrel was only saying this because he genuinely cared about him. He could see his friend's concern in the expression on his face and the set of his ears, as well as feel it.

"If I need help, I'll come to you," he said.

> She'd been pinned down in an alleyway, a blind end. There'd been cover, huge trash dumps overflowing with paper waste and cardboard packaging. She'd hidden there, picking them off with her pistol as they tried to rush the opening, but her ammunition charge was running out now.
>
> The sound of sirens split the night. The Protectors. They'd likely save her, but did she want that? To her right, something hit the ground with a hollow clatter then rolled a few feet before coming to rest. A gas canister. Already thick fumes were beginning to spill from it, pouring across the ground toward her. She put her gun down, knowing it was useless now. Better to be found without it in her hands, then at least they couldn't accuse her of resisting arrest along with everything else.
>
> She began to cough, eyes starting to stream as the fumes reached her. Powerless, she keeled over.

Awake now, she remembered the cell, smelling the stale air and hearing once more the creaking door. She recalled the scent of blood as he slit the throat of the medic, saw again how it had sprayed into the air and over the ceiling and walls; saw again the guard's face as he writhed in agony when she kept the stun gun trained on him. His death cry echoed in her mind.

Her dream had triggered Brynne's own nightmare. He saw his hands round Derwent's throat, throttling the life out of him, pressing tighter and tighter till his face became swollen, taking on a bluish tinge. He felt hands clutching at him, shaking him.

Whimpering, she reached out for Brynne, lying asleep on top of the bed beside her. "Make them stop," she whimpered. "Oh, Gods, make them stop! I don't want to remember any more!"

Groggily, trying to dispel his own nightmare, he pulled

her close, wrapping his arms around her as she shivered and whimpered, her hands clutching at him in terror.

More was coming back to her now. The flight from Shanagi, landing the aircar in the clearing in the forest. The telepath they'd taken as hostage. *He'd* killed him, then turned to her, thinking she was a telepath, too.

She scrambled from the bedding, crouching on all fours, beside herself with terror, not knowing whether to run or stay. "It wasn't me!" she whimpered. "I didn't mean to do it!"

She felt herself grasped firmly round the waist and pulled close. His arms went round her, containing her, holding her and her fear still; she smelled his scent, almost Sholan, yet different.

"Hush! You'll bring someone here," he said urgently, afraid it would rouse Jurrel. "You're broadcasting! You're safe."

Struggling against him, trapped within her own head, she knew she was only trying to run from herself. Her whimper deepened, becoming a howl, which was suddenly silenced as he covered her mouth with his.

Stop it, Keeza, she heard him say in her mind. *I'm here. You're safe, but you must keep quiet!*

Shocked, she became still, feeling his grip slacken slightly as his tongue hesitantly touched her lips.

It's a kiss, he sent in reply to her confused thoughts.

In her mind, his presence expanded, filling it till he pushed the fear back and she no longer felt alone. She could sense him now, feel the anger and anguish he'd experienced as he'd had to kill the male who'd attacked her earlier. He'd never taken a life before, and her nightmarish memories had caused him to relive it in details as horrific for him as those she'd just experienced.

He began to withdraw, releasing her, but she clung to him.

No, don't leave me! I don't want to be alone! He wanted her, needed her presence to push *his* memories back just as much as she needed him to do the same for her. She could feel it all in his mind.

His teeth caught gently at her lips, one hand coming up to cup the side of her face and caress it while the other began to stoke her back, fingers pushing through the long pile of her pelt.

She tugged at his clothes, frantic to have him, to make him want to stay with her despite the distress she'd caused him. Suddenly she stopped, realizing he'd said her name.

Yes, I know who you are, Keeza Lassah, he sent, catching hold of her hands.

Then you know . . .

I know who you are, he repeated, pulling his own clothes free and placing her hands against his bare chest. *It wasn't you who did those things. You didn't want to kill any more than I did. Neither of us had a choice.*

His kiss was deeper now, his tongue touching hers, his mind filling with his desire to have her. She shivered, this time with pleasure as her hands accepted his invitation and she began to stroke his chest. He had a pelt of sorts, but not a full one, not like hers. She'd never felt so much skin before—it was impossibly soft. In the semidarkness of the room, it was easy to forget he wasn't Sholan.

He was waiting for her, she realized, and hesitantly, unsure of what she'd find, she ventured lower, almost leaping back in shock as she discovered just how aroused he was.

It's all right, he sent. *I'd never force you. We can stop now if you wish.*

In answer, she let her hands slide over his hips, pressing him hard against her belly. Stroking his rear through the thin fabric of his shorts, it came as a surprise to find he hadn't even the vestige of a tail.

He moved against her, making a small, muffled noise of pleasure before drawing her down with him onto the bed. He released her only long enough to undress, then his arms were round her again.

He'd felt almost this smooth, came the unbidden comparison and she shied away from the memory, clutching Brynne closer. *But not as warm.* And Brynne was so warm against her body.

Hush, he sent, soothing her until she stopped shivering. Then, gently nibbling and biting her, he worked his way across her cheek and jaw to her chest, looking for, and finding, a nipple.

As his teeth closed softly on her, she whimpered, trying to remember to control her claws as she began to knead his shoulders. His free hand caressed her hip and uninjured thigh and her mind was filled again with his need to keep her safe, to protect her, and his desire to stay with her.

Why? Why should you want to help me? I've brought you nothing but nightmares.

You need me. No one has ever needed me like this before. He moved lower, nibbling and caressing his way across her belly and hips then the tops of her thighs while his fingers gently began to slide higher, teasing gentle moans of pleasure from her.

Everything was so new—him, what he was doing to her, the sensations she was experiencing. No male had treated her like this before. When he stopped and began to sit up, she reached for him anxiously.

Don't stop!

I'm not. He reached for the light beside him, letting its warm glow illuminate him before he leaned over her.

"I'll not have you afraid of me," he said gently, stroking her laid back ears and brushing her tousled hair away from her face.

Something long asleep within her awoke at that moment. She wanted this male, wanted to be with him always. Tears began to spill from her eyes as she realized how impossible it was because of her past.

No, he sent, stopping to wipe her tears. *I'll find a way, I swear I will!*

* * *

The moment he woke, Kaid knew he was alone and back in their prison. His mind was empty, not a trace of her. It was as if it had never happened.

His howl of rage and grief brought the others rushing from their rooms. Tirak would have entered, but T'Chebbi barred the way.

"No. Leave him," she said. "Even I'm not going in."

"What's wrong with him?" demanded Rezac, trying to push her aside. "He wasn't hurt when we found him, just drugged."

She resisted with a strength that surprised him. "Don't know," she said, but she had her own, private thoughts as she heard the sound of breaking furniture.

T'Chebbi remained where she was, not so much stopping anyone from going in as preventing Kaid from leaving if he should try. He needed to work this rage off, and she knew he was best left alone. There wasn't much to break in their room anyway.

When all had been quiet for some time, she risked opening the door and looking in. At first she couldn't see him amid the broken pieces of drawer units and shredded bedding. She ventured farther, letting the door close behind her. Then she saw him, crouched in a corner, his knees up to his chest, head hidden in his forearms.

"Kaid?" she said softly. When he didn't respond, she went closer, squatting down in front of him. Cuts on his hands and arms were oozing blood.

"Kaid?" Still no response. Reaching out, she gently shook him.

He looked up, eyes glazed with pain and swollen with crying. "Carrie's alive, T'Chebbi. They took me to her. We're Leska Linked now, but I can't sense her. She's gone again."

"Oh, Gods," she whispered, ears lying back in shock.

"And I made her pregnant. They're breeding us, T'Chebbi, and I can't do a damned thing to help her!"

"They'll have to bring you together again. Link days at least!"

"Will they?" he asked, voice bleak. "They healed her. She had a scar. How long did they have her out of cryo for that? And I didn't know, dammit!"

"But you did," she said gently, stroking his head as she knelt in front of him. "The pain attacks. That must have been when they woke her. You felt her pain."

He looked up at her. "You're right. I did." He was silent for a moment. "When they took me to her, our minds were pulled together by the gestalt. I had no choice but to pair with her, T'Chebbi. What could I have done? Tried to fight it and let her die?" He shook his head, letting it rest on his forearms again. "They didn't find Kusac, only her."

"They're able to control your minds? Stop you sensing each other?"

"They must be," he whispered, fresh tears beginning to fall. "I know I should be with her now and I'm not!"

She gathered him close, trying to comfort him, knowing

that even though he held her tightly in return, there was nothing anyone but Carrie could do for him.

He remained withdrawn until after the Primes had done their appearing and disappearing trick and replaced the ruined bedding and drawer units. Then his rage got the better of him again as he pounded the outer door, demanding they talk to him.

Tirak let him vent his fury for perhaps five minutes, then seeing T'Chebbi wasn't prepared to stop him, went over himself. Reaching out, he grabbed Kaid by the arm, holding it still. For a few moments, it was a battle of wills and strength, then Kaid dropped his gaze and relaxed.

"This is achieving nothing but unsettling the younger ones," said Tirak quietly. "Time we really started planning our escape. We have nearly enough information now."

"I'll not leave without her." Kaid's tone was hard and uncompromising.

"That goes without saying. Do you know where she is?" he asked, drawing Kaid with him toward the small table. A gesture from Tirak and those sitting there left hurriedly.

"I'm pretty sure."

Rezac joined them with the reader. When he seemed inclined to stay, Tirak glowered at him and he left, tail swaying angrily.

"You were conscious when you left here. Where did they take you?"

Kaid scrolled through their rough sketch, trying to focus his mind on it rather than Carrie. It took a lot of concentration because, careful that the Primes wouldn't recognize it for what it was, they'd concealed it within other doodles.

"Down here," he pointed to the lines that represented the corridor outside their suite. "Parallel to the one we came up when they brought us here. It's a cryo area, except they use some kind of stasis field technology. I think they use the room to put folk in stasis and bring them out. They're keeping her in a small room off the main one." He added the details to the sketch. "As Jeran said, this seems to be in their main medical area."

Tirak grunted. "At least we know they're not doing any fighting right now, despite the body armor. They couldn't afford to cut their medical facilities off from the rest of the craft otherwise."

"With the technology they used to get our craft on board, seems to me they don't need to do much fighting," said Kaid, his voice hard. "Which brings me to the point of what we do if the *Profit* isn't usable."

"We take whatever craft we can find, or die trying," said Tirak, equally grimly, catching his gaze. "They might be concentrating on your people now, but how long before they turn to mine? I have females on my crew, too. Death is preferable to this."

Kaid looked at him long and hard, then slowly nodded. "Agreed. If we don't make it, we'll see there're no survivors on either crew."

"Agreed. And see if we can take this monstrosity out with us, too," Tirak snarled.

* * *

J'koshuk slipped into the stasis room where he knew the tall Seniormost on duty would be monitoring the Human female. He could see her through the transparent screen, just beyond the Prime's control desk.

"Your lack of progress with your captive is disappointing," said the translator.

"He's trained, Seniormost, not as easy a subject as I'm used to," said J'koshuk.

"It was assumed that you were also trained in your profession."

"I am, but he might not have the knowledge you want. If he doesn't know the answers, he can't give them to me no matter what I do to him." He knew he was emitting some fear scent, but they must expect that, he reasoned. It didn't mean he was incompetent.

"I have some answers for you, but they make no sense. He keeps babbling about some God of his being responsible for the links with the Humans. The Kezule person is all tied up in that, too. I can't get anything that makes sense out of him on either subject."

The Seniormost stood, holding his hand out for the reader pad.

J'koshuk had found the male's ramblings more fascinating than he was letting on. Oh, he didn't believe the God rubbish, but he hadn't been aware that his people had once ruled the Sholan home world. That had come as a surprise to him. And it had been confirmed that as far as Kusac was aware, Kezule had been plucked from the past and brought forward to this time.

The Prime turned and inserted the comp into a slot in his desk, waiting a few seconds for the data to be downloaded, then returned the wiped unit to him.

"I will examine him later. Leave him for now. You may use this time as you wish. I will send for you when I need you."

He glanced at the window again. The female was in her usual place, lying in the bed. Every time he'd seen her, she was either sleeping or resting. No, he couldn't use the time as he wished, more was the pity. He'd still found nothing out about her except her name. Carrie. He'd driven the Sholan so hard that when he finally cried it out, it hadn't been in answer to his question, but as a plea for help. He snorted gently. How could one so fragile help anyone? She was worthless, useful for only one thing. Pleasure.

"Why do you remain?"

J'koshuk started. "I was waiting to see if you had any further instructions," he stammered as he turned to leave.

* * *

Moving had been agony, but Kusac refused to remain on the floor where J'koshuk had left him. Pulling himself up onto the bed had been the worst, as every nerve in his body jangled with echoes of the pain he'd endured. He collapsed on the bed, lying there exhausted and unable to think straight. Overhead, the light still glared down at him. He turned his head, closing his eyes in an effort to shut it out, wondering how long they'd let him alone this time.

He'd been deprived of sleep for what seemed like days. Every time he'd been on the verge of drifting off, two of the black-armored guards would come in and haul him out of bed, stand him in a corner and watch him, or make him walk round the bed till he could barely move. Then they'd leave him for a short time and it would start again. Sometimes it wasn't the guards, it was Valtegans, their clawed

hands gripping him hard and scratching his flesh, adding
more hurts to those already inflicted on him. Finally, the
one called J'koshuk had come, and the questions had
started again.

He'd no idea what had happened to them. All he knew
was that Carrie was safe and with Kaid, because he'd seen
them together. The priest had told him they were being
treated well. They had cooperated, unlike him. He had to
hold onto that thought, it was all he had.

The one emotion he'd been allowed was fear. What truly
frightened him was that his mind was silent. He could sense
nothing: not her, not Kaid, not the priest or the guards. He
knew about the implant on the side of his head, just below
his left ear. That he could sense, insinuating its way into
his thoughts, cutting him off from his world, from those he
loved, and from himself.

They knew about his Talent, knew he was part of a
Triad, the priest had told him that, but J'koshuk wanted to
know more. And much more about Carrie.

He'd refused to talk about her, giving her name only
when it was forced out of him by intense pain. He shivered,
remembering it. He'd tried to keep quiet, to tell them nothing and be worthy of his sword-brother, but in the end,
he'd had to speak, even though each word had been torn
from him.

He hadn't been prepared for a situation like this, how
could he have been? One minute he'd been in cryo, the
next he'd awakened to this nightmare. It made him realize
how unreal his world as a telepath had been. He'd protected Carrie and Kaid as much as possible, telling J'koshuk
only what he knew already. For the rest, the priest had
wanted to know how they could breed with the Humans
and why they'd gotten involved on Keiss. And with Kezule.

He'd let himself ramble then, talking about the God,
knowing they'd find it impossible to believe. He'd managed
to hide the fact it was he and his Triad partners who had
brought Kezule forward in time, though. If the Primes
thought it was others, they wouldn't expect him to know
how it had been done, wouldn't expect them to duplicate it.

His ears picked up the telltale sounds of someone outside. He'd gotten good at that by now. The door slid back,
admitting a Seniormost accompanied by two guards. Too

exhausted to move, he lay there, not even curious about what was coming next. Experience had taught him it could only be more pain.

* * *

Carrie knew Kaid was gone as soon she woke. There was an emptiness in her mind where he'd been, and an even larger one where Kusac should be. She began to weep then for his loss, praying to all the Gods she could think of that he was safe. Then she wept for her cub, the daughter on Shola who faced an unknown danger that she could do nothing to prevent; and for the new one growing inside her, hers and Kaid's, to be born into this nightmare of captivity.

Exhausted, she clutched the pillow that still carried his scent, burying her face in it, knowing he was her only hope, her life now. She lay like this throughout the day, not awake, yet not asleep. Guards came with food, their presence barely noticed by her.

Armored hands grasped her arms, pulling her from the bed, forcing her to stand beside it. With a cry of horror, she tried to wrench herself free, coming face to face with a Seniormost for the first time.

Six feet tall or more, he towered over her, dwarfing her by his bulk as well as height. The gray tabard, obviously worn as a badge of office, came down to mid-calf length, giving him the air of a medieval knight. Black and dark as the void of space the armor was, absorbing and reflecting no light. She looked higher, to the helmet, seeing the faceplate that covered most of its surface. It seemed to ripple and move even as she watched, making her feel sick to the pit of her stomach. Fragments of memories she wanted to forget began to stir within her subconscious. With a shudder of revulsion, she looked away.

"Release her," the translator said.

The guard let her go, stepping back to a position just behind the Seniormost.

"You do not eat. Why?" asked the Seniormost, pointing to the dish of untouched food.

She looked beyond him. The door was open but she could see another armed guard waiting there.

"The Seniormost asked a question," hissed the guard, moving closer.

Feeling the blood drain from her face, she took a step back. "You've taken my mate away. Why?" she countered.

The Seniormost let his arm fall back by his side. "He is not your mate. The missing one, also in a cryogenic unit, was your mate."

Kaid had been asked the same. "They're both my mates. We're a unit of three." She could sense nothing from either of them, and remembering the Valtegans back on Keiss, she didn't dare try.

"There are several pairs among your number, but no other threes. Why?"

She shrugged. "I don't know. Maybe they haven't met the right person to be their Third yet."

"Why do you not eat?"

"I want my mate. Take me to him, then I'll eat."

"You will eat first, then, perhaps, we will return him."

"No."

"You'd risk your life, and his offspring's, just to be with him?"

Her stomach tightened with fear. How could they possibly know? She pushed it aside. This had to be dealt with now, time to worry about that later.

"Yes, I will," she said firmly. They mustn't know how physically dependent on each other Leska pairs were.

"As you wish," the Seniormost said, then turned and left, the guard following him.

Stunned, she stood there for a moment, than sank down on the bed. He was going to let her starve herself? Maybe he didn't believe she would.

Her mouth watered as she smelled the food standing on the night table. She *was* hungry. Resolutely, she climbed back into bed, curling up with her back to the enticing smells and burying her face in the pillow. It helped, a little.

Kaid's scent came back to haunt her. She knew it was futile, but she reached out mentally for him, finding the same barrier as before. Remembering the Jalnian effect, she tried other mental frequencies but found nothing. Whatever they were using, it was thorough. They knew how to disable telepaths.

Her efforts had exhausted her more than she'd realized,

more than they should have. Then she remembered she'd had major surgery only two weeks before and spent much of the time since in stasis while they tried to heal her. Unbidden, earlier memories of waking in pain, seeing the bright lights and the white tiled ceiling overhead, then the helmets of the Primes as they bent over her, came back again. With an effort of will, she pushed them aside and began to recite the litanies Kaid had taught her. A gentle warmth began to spread through her limbs and gradually, as her drowsiness increased, she let herself drift off to sleep.

* * *

Deciding to leave for the estate a day earlier because of the risk of Keeza being discovered, Brynne's first stop after seeing his companions settled in his house was to visit Vanna and his son.

"He seems to know when you're here," said Vanna, as Brynne took the squirming bundle from her.

Excited mewls and squeaks greeted him as his son, now a hefty size, climbed up his chest to wrap his arms around his neck and nuzzle him. A small rough tongue began to lick him madly under the jaw.

He laughed, supporting the cub with one hand while he ruffled Marak's ears with the other. "And hello to you, too, young fellow! It's a good job I've got a beard, you'd be licking me raw otherwise!" He turned to look at Vanna. "How's our young lad been since my last visit?"

"He's into everything now he's mobile," she said, sitting down beside him. "He might still be unsteady on his legs but that doesn't stop him, I assure you! He and Kashini drive their nurses to distraction. Still, it's good that they've got each other to play with. How have you been?"

"Fine," he said. "I'm home for five days this time."

"That's longer than usual. Any special reason?"

"Yes," he said, making a grab for Marak as the cub tried to climb over his shoulder onto the back of the couch. He tried vainly to disengage him, but Marak clung on for dear life, refusing to be moved. "Vanna, can you help me here? He's got his claws caught and I can't get him down."

Laughing, she leaned across him to free their adventurous offspring and let Brynne lift him down onto his lap.

"What's the reason for the long visit, then?" she asked.

"I've met someone," he said, looking up at her. "Someone who's important to me."

"Jurrel? He's been here with you before, surely," she said raising an eye ridge.

Brynne met her curious stare this time, something he'd never been able to do before. "Does everyone know my private business?" he asked, keeping his tone light.

"Only those who care," she reassured him gently. "We want you to find your own place in our world, and someone to make you happy. So is it Jurrel?"

"Someone else," he said. "A female, though you're right, Jurrel is important to me, too."

The eye ridge arched higher. "Have you brought her with you?"

"She's with Jurrel and Banner right now. Banner is Jurrel's Companion and sword-brother."

She digested this for a moment, and he could sense her thinking that with him, nothing was straightforward. "Will I get to meet this female—what's she called, by the way? She must have a name. Where did you meet her?"

"Ghaysa, and I met her at Vartra's Retreat. Yes, but in a day or two, when I've sorted some things out here first," he said, letting Marak distract him from her penetrating gaze. Their link might be lessened while she was carrying Garras' child, but she was still too damned intuitive by far for his comfort right now. "You'll like her. She's not as strong as you. Much more vulnerable. She needs me, Vanna."

Vanna reached out to stroke his cheek. "I'm glad for you." Her eyes narrowed. "Was she the one in your nightmares? Are you still getting them? I've been really concerned about you, Brynne. They've been affecting me, and that upsets Marak."

"It's not something that I have any control over, Vanna. Tutor Kha'Qwa says it'll lessen after a while, that the intensity is because it's new to me," he said, letting his son chew gently on a finger. "I'm picking up things from all over the place. You know I wouldn't upset you and Marak if I could avoid it."

"Maybe getting involved with the religious side wasn't such a good idea after all."

"It got involved with me, if you remember."

She sighed. "I suppose you're right. So how's Jurrel taking the arrival of this female? Or Banner for that matter?"

"They're amused," he grinned, turning to touch his lips against her hand as she moved it away again. "Banner particularly. I think he sees me the same way he sees Jurrel, like an enthusiastic cub discovering the world for the first time."

She laughed again. "I think I'm going to like this Banner! I never quite saw you like that, Brynne, I must admit."

He nodded, stroking his son's back as the little one curled up, his purr becoming a slightly deeper buzz of pleasure. He could feel it, a warm, contentment that stemmed from having his mother and father together with him.

"He misses me," he said, surprised.

"Of course he does. You're his father. He cares for Garras, but he knows who his father is, Brynne."

"You did put up with a lot from me, didn't you? Yet you've never been anything but fair."

She shrugged his compliment off. "It was you who said it, Brynne. We had to make this Link between us work one way or another. Who knows? If you'd had some chance at an independent life on Shola before our Link formed, things might have been different, but it didn't happen that way. I'm happy now with Garras, and it looks like you've found someone, too. You've changed, you know. But you had to find out for yourself what you wanted from life here. No one could tell you what you needed to know."

"Enough of the serious stuff. Bring me up to date on what's been happening here. How are things?"

Her face clouded over. "Bad news, I'm afraid. I didn't want to tell you right away. Kusac's and Carrie's ship is missing. Been overdue now for nearly a month, and the searches have turned up nothing."

"I know. It's dreadful news. I was told a short while ago because some of my visions involved them," he said.

"You saw something?"

"Bits and pieces," he replied. "But I'm positive they're alive, somewhere."

"Somewhere?"

"I was seeing a white-tiled room, and experiencing an overwhelming feeling of terror. Bright lights, too," he added, eyes unfocusing briefly as he tried to call the images up before him. "Like the shower in my room at Stronghold."

"Have you spoken to Father Lijou about this?"

"He knows, but there's not been enough information in what I've seen to be of much help."

"Dzaka said he's felt Carrie's presence several times," she said thoughtfully. "I think you two should talk."

"I will," he said. "Strange he's picking up Carrie, though. I'd have thought it would be Kaid who'd try to contact him."

"You know Carrie was injured, don't you? They had to leave Jalna on a U'Churian ship because they had cryo facilities. She was too badly hurt to wait for the contact ship."

"That I wasn't told. I hope to God she's all right. If she's in cryo, it's even more strange that Dzaka should think he's sensing her. I know they're still alive, Vanna."

* * *

Rhyasha and Mara were taking the Touibans to their new quarters. It had taken a few days to adapt a house unit to their special needs, but now it was ready for them to move into. It had been decided the best place for them was next to the Brothers' accommodation. Luckily a house had been kept vacant beside theirs against just such a need.

Six excited Touibans were something to see. To be at the center of twelve of them was like riding a roller coaster as they swirled and danced round the two females in a state of high excitement. That morning, they'd had the Touibans' personal belongings moved from their temporary quarters in the medical building to their new home. Several villagers had been drafted to help the Touibans rearrange their furnishings as closely as possible to the way they'd been before. Now they wanted to show it off to those who'd made it all possible.

Though Mara had been involved in much of the work, she wasn't prepared for the sight that met her eyes.

The impression was of walking into a brightly colored pavilion tent. Jewel bright patterned draperies covered every wall and hung looped down from the ceilings. On the floor, plush rugs in similarly bright colors overlapped each other, creating a feeling of warmth and soft opulence. The already subdued lighting was even more diffuse for being above the tented ceilings.

Low tables and large, soft cushions were spread in the middle of the main room, while at the four corners stood taller tables bearing precariously placed bronze statuettes. Before each of them, sticks of incense and scented oils burned.

Oh, my goodness! sent Rhyasha. *Such opulence! How can they live among so many bright things!*

It's wonderful! Mara looked around, obviously in a daze, breathing in the scented air. *I've got to have my room done up like this! It's like desert tents back on Earth! You know, nomadic folk.*

That explains it. Several of the Touiban swarms are nomadic. This must be one of them. You have your room decorated like this if you want, child I'm glad you enjoy it, since you'll spend quite a bit of time here working with them! I'll stick to the archaeological dig, I think. Much calmer surroundings. This is so loud!

Isn't it just? Mara beamed at her. She turned to the anxious Toueesut. "It's absolutely wonderful. Is this what your homes look like?"

He nodded. "This is but a poor example of the decorative harmony we enjoy at home, but it will suffice for the moment. Now we have gained the kind permission not only of your ambassadors but our own to establish a small hive within the heart of your family, we can request much more finery. Such drabness is not conducive to the starting of a new life, and our ladies rightly expect far more glorious decorations than these."

"When will your ladies arrive?" asked Mara.

Toueesut released a scent that reminded her of a babbling stream on a hot summer's day. She looked closely at him, seeing his heavily mustached mouth split in a very Human grin. A trill of laughter surrounded her as the six who'd been hanging back while they had their tour of the premises, clustered round her.

"Our ladies are always with us, how could we be without their songs that touch the softer sides of us all?" asked Toueesut.

"Good gracious," said Rhyasha faintly, looking down at

the almost identical sea of whiskered faces. She glanced again at the five around the Speaker. "Why didn't we realize?"

"Because they usually work in sixes?" asked Mara quietly. "We must have one of the few full swarms on Shola."

"Indeed, we do. I wondered at the time when they asked to send twelve."

"Their scents, Rhyasha. I'm finding I get pictures in my mind when I smell them."

Toueesut nodded almost violently with enthusiasm. "Now you see and hear the music of the minds that we make use of among ourselves. Never have we spoken of this before, because never have we found that harmony of mind outside our hives."

A gentle perfume permeated the air, bringing images of cool springs welling from dry rocks to both Rhyasha and Mara.

Toueesut sighed gustily, making the stiff bristles round his nose quiver. It was echoed by all of them.

"We have worked many, many times with the Sholans, but it is only here we have heard a song of harmony of spirit and mind that is like enough to ours. We had thought ourselves alone capable of making such glorious music and it is a joy to all of us to know this is not so. We bless the Makers for bringing us to your Hive land and for letting us hear your songs."

"We're happy to be able to hear yours, too, Speaker," said Rhyasha, bowing toward him as the six females danced and wove their way back to their mates. "Which one of the lucky ladies is yours?"

He looked confused for a moment.

Rhyasha moved her hand toward the translator she wore tucked into a pocket in her belt.

This is why we need to carry translators, she sent to Mara.

"No need for mechanical speakings," he said, waving his hands expressively. "Only a misunderstanding that is natural on your part when you are not even knowing six of our number are our ladies. They are wives to us all as we are husbands to them, with each one of us having a unique tune to bring to our swarm."

"We have a lot to learn from you about your people,

Speaker. I hope you'll be willing to allow your swarm to help us."

"It is for the joy of sharing such knowledge that we wished to come together within your larger Hive. We hope you will be willing to share yourselves in just such a way with us."

"Of a certainty, Speaker," assured Rhyasha, watching while the six females disappeared—at least she assumed they were the females, since the Speaker and five others remained.

"We would be honored if you will be joining with us to celebrate the new beginnings of our small hive on your garden world. A meal has been prepared using the finest of ingredients and cooking it in the best traditional style." Toueesut indicated the low table, surrounded by cushions.

"We're the ones who'd be honored, Speaker," said Rhyasha, moving toward it. "I fear we may not be able to do the meal justice. Had we known, we wouldn't have eaten shortly before we came." *Grin and enjoy it, child,* she sent to Mara, *even if it tastes foul.*

Startled, Mara took her seat on one of the soft cushions, looking questioningly at Rhyasha. Toueesut sat between them, the other five males arranging themselves around the table, leaving spaces for their wives.

You don't know what they eat.

Her fears proved to be groundless as the six returned bearing plates, cutlery, and several large bowls of hot food. It smelled familiar, Rhyasha realized as the lids were lifted up and the bowls presented to her to help herself. As she spooned a reasonable-sized helping onto her plate, she recognized it. "Isn't this a Sholan dish?"

"But of course," beamed Toueesut. "Chiddoes stewed in red wine and sweet vegetables. What else would we serve our guests but food traditional to our new home?"

* * *

It was late afternoon before Brynne was able to go in search of Dzaka. He found him in the bathing area of the exercise hall. Meral was massaging a muscle he'd pulled while training.

"Hello, Dzaka, Meral. Can we talk?" he asked, walking over to the massage couch.

"I heard you were back," Dzaka said, looking up at him as Meral echoed Brynne's greeting.

"News gets around fast," said Brynne, pulling a chair over to the couch and sitting down.

Meral stopped working on his shoulder. "Shall I go?" he asked.

"No, don't stop," said Dzaka. "If you leave it now, the joint'll stiffen."

"Look, I'm sorry to bother you, but I need to know about the dreams you've had concerning Carrie, Kusac, or Kaid."

Dzaka frowned, eye ridges meeting. "How does what I've seen involve you?" His tone was sharp.

This was obviously not one of his better days, thought Brynne. "Brotherhood business," he said quietly. "I've also been seeing things. It's time we put them together, see what we have."

Dzaka put his head down on his forearms again. "Father Lijou's doing that. What need have we to duplicate it?"

"The need to know if we can help our friends and family," said Brynne, his voice taking on a hard edge. Self-pity was all very well, but not when lives were at stake.

He caught sight of a concerned look from Meral and wondered why.

"You bring discredit to Jurrel's teaching!" said Dzaka, lifting his head again, this time to glower at him. "Strengthen your shields or turn your psi damper up, dammit, you're broadcasting!"

Brynne stiffened, then reached for his damper, acknowledging the reprimand and the truth in what his senior said. "I apologize, Brother Dzaka," he said. "I was with Marak and forgot to turn it on again."

Meral leaned over the prone Sholan, speaking quietly in his ear, but Brynne caught it anyway.

"If you tense up like this, Brother Dzaka, then nothing I do will be of much use."

It was Meral's turn to be growled at. "Don't you Brother Dzaka me, you impudent cub!"

As the youth stood up and reached for the massage oil, he exchanged a meaningful glance with Brynne.

Relieved it wasn't just him, Brynne plowed on. "I've told Father Lijou what I've seen, but they're only glimpses of a room, nothing more. I thought perhaps if I told you about them, you might have seen something that would help to make sense of them. The bottom line is that I know they're still alive."

That got his attention. "What have you seen?" he demanded, sitting up.

Brynne told him of the tiled room and the bright lights, then the insubstantial dreams of coldness and fear.

"Like mine, something and nothing," Dzaka murmured when he'd done. "I've had the odd one about being chased through the forest. Ouch! Watch it, Meral!" he exclaimed, turning to look at his friend.

"It isn't as easy when you're sitting up," objected the young male. "Don't complain at me when it was you who said to carry on. I'm only doing what you asked."

Brynne was grateful for the interruption. He was sure his shock at knowing Dzaka had experienced Keeza's flight would have been only too plain on his face. When Dzaka turned back, he'd managed to compose himself again.

"I had a strange one a few nights ago. I was with Kashini in the nursery and I swear I saw Carrie, yet it also felt like my father. Very confusing," he said, shaking his head. "She was warning me of danger, I think."

"Who's in danger, though? Us or them? I think it's us, because why try to warn us otherwise?"

"Carrie was in cryo, Brynne. How could she warn us? And even if she weren't, she couldn't reach us over such a vast distance. It could have been just my own wishful thinking."

"I seem to remember hearing that it was Carrie who picked up Rezac's sending all the way from Jalna. And what better focus could she have than her daughter if she thought she was in danger?"

"How would she know anything about what was going on if she was in cryo?"

"I heard that Carrie dreams in cryo," said Meral, continuing to knead Dzaka's left shoulder. "Might be no more than gossip."

"Where d'you hear that?" asked Brynne.

"On the *Khalossa,* when I was first assigned to them as bodyguard. Heard it from a Human called Skai."

"Gossip," dismissed Dzaka. "Nothing more than gossip."

"I don't think so. Skai and she were both on that first crossing from Earth. As soon as they woke her, Carrie told them her mother had died. That was the beginning of the Humans' fear of her."

"I never heard of anyone either dreaming or being aware in cryo before," said Dzaka.

"She's Human, remember? Not a Sholan. Just because no Sholan has experienced it doesn't mean she didn't. Hell, this world has done weird things to me with all the visions I've been having! Whoever heard of anyone actually meeting a God, for God's sake!" said Brynne.

"You met a God?" Dzaka leaned forward intently, ignoring Meral's exasperated exclamation.

A chittering at the far side of the room, followed by raised voices, drew their attention.

" 'Scuse me," said Brynne, getting up hurriedly. He returned with Belle.

"Get that damned piece of vermin out of . . ." they heard as the door banged open. "Oh. Excuse me, Brother Dzaka, Brother Meral, but . . ."

Dzaka had caught sight of the jegget in Brynne's arms and now turned to meet the angry intruder. "Yes, Lasad?" he asked, raising an eye ridge.

"He's got a jegget in here!"

"Brother Brynne has, indeed, got a jegget. Full marks for noticing it," Dzaka said dryly. "Perhaps you also noticed that we're busy? Or don't your powers of perception stretch that far?"

"Yes, Brother Dzaka, but . . ."

"She's a gift from Vartra, and approved to live with me at Stronghold and the Retreat by Father Lijou himself," said Brynne. "I thought all Brothers had to acquaint themselves with the daily updates from Stronghold. Seems to me you forgot to do so over the last couple of days or you'd have been aware that." He stopped for a moment, picking up the other's thoughts. "And the Aldatan colors are red and black, not what I'm wearing. I'm a Brother like yourself."

Lasad's ears laid back in shame as he mumbled an apology and backed out hurriedly.

"See that the rest know about her," Brynne called out as a parting shot. When he resumed his seat, he could feel both Dzaka's and Meral's surprise and amusement.

"Seems that Stronghold suits you well," murmured Dzaka. "Where did you say this jegget came from?"

Brynne hesitated. He wasn't sure if he was supposed to talk about his dream-walks. He decided he needed to be honest with him. "I haven't told you this, you realize. Derwent called me to a dream world one night. Had it not been for Vartra, he'd have dominated my mind and made me take him to Stronghold."

Dzaka and Meral stared at him.

"It's what I was doing with Derwent," he said. "Going into other realities, entering dream worlds. He wanted me to join him in the forest and lead him to Stronghold."

"Vartra saved you?"

Brynne nodded. "Belle bit me at the crucial moment, then Vartra arrived and brought me back."

"I didn't know that was possible," said Meral.

"I think you're not supposed to know about it," said Brynne apologetically. "It's what happens when we have visions, as best as I can tell. We're somewhere else, outside time and space—a dream world."

"What did Vartra say?"

"To keep faith with those I trust," he said, looking up and locking eyes with him. "That's why I know they're alive," he said, stroking Belle's head as she purred and chirruped happily. "He also gave me a coin."

Dzaka jumped down from the massage couch. "We've work to do," he said briskly. "Ghyan keeps records of the dreams and visions from the estate. We're going to see him. What do you call her?" He stopped to scratch behind the jegget's ears. "She's rather cute."

"Belle. It means beautiful in my language."

"I'm coming with you," said Meral, recapping the oil and wiping his hands on a towel. "Wait for me."

Keeza couldn't believe the size of the house that Brynne lived in. While he went off to see his Leska and their son, Banner and Jurrel remained with her. They were content to leave her to her own devices so long as she remained within the building.

It was large compared to anywhere she'd lived, having a lounge, a den, and three bedrooms. The kitchen was so spacious it even had room for a table! As for the bathing room, it had both a bath and a shower. All this space for one person overwhelmed her.

She decided to try out the delights of a bath while the two males started cooking something for third meal.

"Keep an ear on Ghaysa, Jurrel," said Banner, going over to Brynne's desk and activating the comm. "I want to see what I can find out about her."

"He's my pupil, Banner. Unless I have good reasons, I won't go behind his back like this," he said, his tone carrying a low rumble of annoyance.

"You aren't, I am," said Banner, punching in a Brotherhood security clearance. "It's not Brynne I mistrust, it's Ghaysa. Damned convenient, this memory loss of hers."

"It's genuine, as are the times when Brynne picks up her returning memories."

"We'll see," he said, entering Ghaysa's description into his search of the Protectorate's data bank. "You said that in his dreams, she was running from something. Chances are she's escaped from some correction facility."

Jurrel continued to mutter his disapproval. "Even if you do find something, we still have the problem of there being a bond between them, one we'll not easily break, if at all."

"We'll face that problem when we have to. She's not on any wanted list. I'll have to go deeper into their files."

"You're trying to find proof to justify your suspicions. She's a telepath, probably a Level One like Brynne. She could be innocent of anything except running away from her bond-family."

"I've found something," Banner said. "An anomalous entry. A female called Keeza Lassah, executed five months ago. That's all the information there is. The rest is locked. Not even an image of her, or description of her crime." He looked over at Jurrel. "This has our mark on it, Jurrel."

"Now you're being ridiculous. If it was her, Stronghold would be looking for her, and we'd know about it."

"Not if her mission was known only to a few. And remember, we've been off-world for the last year." He turned back to the comm, beginning to enter a new destination. "If she was to be executed, then the newscasts must have carried her story."

"You're on the wrong trail. This is such a long shot, Banner, that it's not worth considering!"

"You think so?" he asked quietly. "Come and look at Brynne's Ghaysa, convicted of murdering a Pack Lord."

After her bath, Ghaysa joined Banner and Jurrel in the den. Immediately she sensed a difference in their attitude toward her. They concealed it well, but now they were wary of her, one of them keeping his eyes on her all the time.

When Brynne finally returned, it was with relief that she rose to greet him. As he put the jegget down and made his way over to her, Jurrel spoke up.

"Brynne, there's something you should know," he began.

"I know already," he said quietly, before giving Keeza a hug. "Leave it for now, please. We'll talk later." He could feel their concern at being put off, but all he could do was send reassuring thoughts in their direction with no guarantee of how well they could receive them. He hoped it was enough.

"I've some friends coming over later that I'd like you to meet," he said to Jurrel. "You too, Banner. He remembers you. Dzaka Arrazo, Kaid's son, and Meral, Taizia Aldatan's mate."

"Dzaka Arrazo? Are you sure? The Dzaka I knew wasn't an Arrazo, and he was only Kaid's foster son."

Brynne shook his head. "No, he's Kaid's true son, and his mother was Khemu Arrazo. Dzaka and I are combining our visions and dreams with those Father Ghyan has collected from the estate over the last few weeks. We want to see if we can pick up anything he and Father Lijou may have missed. I'd like your input, especially as you were with me when I had the dreams, Jurrel."

"Surely, but what about Ghaysa?"

"I've arranged something for Ghaysa to do," he said, steering her to the nearest chair. "Vanna's sister Sashti is here. She's a masseur, has her own business. You'll like her, Ghaysa. She's agreed to come over tonight to—as she puts it—spoil you rotten! All the works—a massage, oils, shower, everything. Does that sound good?"

Bewildered, she looked up at him.

"No, I don't think you need it. I think you'd like it after living rough for so long. Come on, humor me, please?"

"It sounds wonderful," she said, as vague memories of similar sessions came back to her. A house in Ranz, it had been, one she couldn't leave for some reason. Despite that, she remembered her stay there had not been unpleasant. It frustrated her, wanting to know more, yet fearing it at the same time. She wished she could remember only the good things.

Stop worrying, he sent. *Just stay upstairs with Sashti in case anyone recognizes you.*

What about Sashti?

She won't know you, trust me.

Sashti arrived just after they'd eaten third meal, and whisked Keeza upstairs, leaving time to talk before Dzaka and Meral arrived.

"I know she's Keeza Lassah," he said without preamble. "But I know she killed that Pack Lord for a good reason."

"The judge thought otherwise," said Jurrel. "I'm not saying I agree," he added, "just stating facts."

"She's dangerous, Brynne." Banner's voice was deep with concern. "There's more. The fact she's listed as dead means she was released into custody, and that can only be to one of two groups. Us, or the Forces' Intelligence. Whatever they wanted her for, she's escaped from them. If we try to dig deeper, we're going to draw attention to ourselves, and inevitably, her. Meanwhile, you particularly are at risk when you're alone with her."

"She wouldn't hurt me," he said. "You're not telling me anything I hadn't worked out for myself. Whatever she's done, she was used by powers that she couldn't refuse. Dammit, she's been treated abominably! And I want those responsible!"

"In doing that, you'll give her away," Jurrel reminded him. "Which is exactly what you want to avoid. She's been convicted of murder, Brynne, before she was recruited. We're all at risk here—the whole estate is. If she's frightened, there's no saying what she'll do, who she might kill.

You're playing with someone who's capable of going totally feral. I don't think you realize that."

"I know I trust her," he said calmly. "And I trust you. What are you going to do now you know?"

"Watch her carefully for now," said Jurrel.

Banner gave a rumble of disagreement. "We should turn her over to the authorities."

"What are you going to do?" repeated Brynne, looking at him.

"I haven't decided!" Banner said, exasperated.

"I need some time," said Brynne. "She's a telepath, and I think an unregistered one. That being the case, she needs to be tested for the altered genes. She'd have been in prison when they did the tests. They wouldn't have thought to check condemned criminals. Would it help any if she's like me? She'd be an En'Shallan then, subject only to Father Lijou."

"It wouldn't wipe out what she's done," said Banner.

"No, but given she's forgotten so much, perhaps if she agreed now to personality reprogramming, they'd pardon her. She had that choice before and turned it down," said Jurrel. "Now she's got Brynne, she might just change her mind."

"She'd not be Keeza any longer if they did that," objected Brynne. "I'm not surprised she turned it down."

"Depends what she's done in the meantime," said Banner. "They rarely use people like her for anything but suicide missions."

"If they did, then whatever she'd done would be part of the mission imperative," argued Jurrel. "I think if she agrees to reprogramming, it would go a long way to helping. The newsvids said nothing about her being a telepath. If she's a latent, just awakened, then being gene-altered wouldn't hurt either," he added.

The door chime sounded and Brynne got to his feet. "This'll have to wait. I appreciate you saying nothing for now at least."

Day 30

Ghyan's records proved to be unable to add anything to what Dzaka and Brynne had experienced. However, they did manage to drag more details out of Brynne concerning the room. The general consensus was that it was a medical area. When discussing Dzaka's experience of thinking he saw Carrie, they kept in mind that she'd traveled back in time, and that she'd picked up Rezac mentally when he sent from Jalna. It was possible that she'd been trying to warn them of danger yet to come, but equally possible she was just concerned about her child. The rest they put down to a forewarning of the ship going missing, and the cryo area in the U'Churian ship.

Brynne had offered to return the files to Ghyan the next day. He was up early, making an unscheduled call at the medical unit, then back home before leaving for the Shrine. When he arrived at the priest's office, he found Ghyan interested to hear about his studies at Stronghold.

Eventually, he got the chance to ask the questions he wanted. "On Earth, our priests make vows that anything revealed to them as a confession is never spoken of to anyone else. It's private and above the law. Is that the case with our Order?"

Ghyan looked consideringly at him. "There are special occasions when that's so," he agreed. "Are you wanting to discuss such a matter with me?"

"I might," said Brynne, "if I knew that it would remain private, no matter what it concerned."

"Something's troubling you deeply, isn't it? Obviously you're afraid of the action I may feel obliged to take once I know what this is about."

Brynne nodded.

"And am I right in saying you won't tell me unless you get those assurances?"

"Yes. I'm not asking for selfish reasons, Father. I want to help someone."

"Someone more scared than yourself? That would be very troubled indeed," Ghyan said, sitting back in his chair, watching him.

"It's not my story to tell, Father Ghyan. The person concerned trusts me."

"A vulnerable person?"

"One who's been badly mistreated. One who has no place to go to, no one to turn to but me."

"I can't withhold my help, Brynne. I'm not happy about

granting this anonymity to your friend. I dislike doing it when I have a feeling the matter is likely to involve the law. Is this person one of Vartra's followers?"

"I honestly don't know, Father Ghyan, but this person is one of us and comes under the God's protection."

"One of us? In what way?" His brows met in a frown.

"En'Shalla. A gene-altered telepath, and linked somehow psychically to me."

"You have proof? If I'm going to get involved with something that concerns the Protectorate, I need to be sure of the facts beforehand."

Brynne took a piece of paper out of his pocket and handed it to him. "The gene test result. Obviously it can belong only to the person concerned."

Ghyan took it from him and examined it. "Can I keep it?"

Brynne reached out to retrieve it. "I'm afraid not, Father. It's my proof for this person. I can't let it out of my possession."

Ghyan sighed. "Very well, you have my word that this will be a matter between ourselves and Vartra."

* * *

Kaid lay awake that night, able to rest his body but not his mind. He'd been gone almost three days this time, T'Chebbi said. The Primes had had enough opportunity to watch the pairs to know about their five day cycles and recognize he and Carrie had a mental bond. Thankfully, they'd let them remain together for their first Link day. And gave them another for good behavior, he added cynically.

He thought back to when he'd had the first of the pain attacks, now eighteen days ago. It should have been obvious to him even then, with the pain over the ribs, exactly where Carrie had been hit, what was happening. No, it hadn't been then. That had happened a day earlier, when he'd had difficulty breathing and first seen the bright lights.

Remember Winter's kiss. The words echoed in his mind again, as did the touch of a cold tongue. He shivered, remembering he'd thought Carrie looked as if she'd been touched by Khuushoi, Goddess of Winter, when he'd left her in cryo. Maybe she had. The thought unnerved him and he turned his mind away from it.

So twenty days ago, they must have transferred Carrie from cryo to their stasis field. Then, a day later, when he'd felt the most pain, they'd brought her out to operate on her wound. When she began to sicken because of Link deprivation, they must have had to return her to stasis, hoping a short period there would stabilize her. It hadn't, as he'd found out himself when they'd repeatedly tried to wake her. No wonder she'd looked so ill. It was a wonder she'd survived.

Psi dampers could affect Leska partners—he vaguely remembered tests Esken had run on Carrie and Kusac at the Telepath Guild—but they weren't able to prevent the demands on mind and body that the Link generated. With their minds isolated, their need to be together physically in the same place was even greater. He'd bet his life that the Primes hadn't taken that into consideration yet. Then he realized that his life did depend on them being reunited.

A coldness spread through him, chilling him to the bone. Whatever happened from now on, whether or not they found Kusac, he would still be Linked to her, their lives dependent on each other. It was not as comforting a thought as he'd once have thought it.

He rose early, glad to end the night that had brought him so little rest. Some sixth sense made him quietly check the other rooms. In the one next to his were two empty beds. Jo and Manesh were on watch. With their help, he checked the whole suite before rousing Tirak.

"What's up?" he asked. One look at Kaid with his fingers over his lips and he hauled on his tunic and followed him into the lounge.

"Two more are gone," said Kaid. "Giyesh and Jeran this time."

Tirak mouthed some colorful expletives. "Because they're of different species?"

Kaid nodded. "My guess is they want to see if your people are genetically compatible with us or the Humans."

"But they're not telepathic!" exclaimed Manesh.

"Jeran is capable of receiving mental communications," said Kaid, glancing over to her. "I suspect he's a sensitive who's been enhanced by the laalquoi in the food chain on Jalna."

"Dammit! We've got to get out of here, Kaid!" said Tirak.

"Agreed, but we wait until they and Carrie are returned."

* * *

Kezule had taken four days to work his way along the several miles of the landward estate perimeter. His recent brush with the Sholans had made him even more cautious, checking out and watching their security systems thoroughly. The boundary was deep within the forested area, and though a swath several feet wide had been cut back on either side of the fencing, he'd been able to travel unseen by using either the tree canopy or the dense ground cover.

For the upper section of the estate, by the main gatehouse, the fencing was eight feet tall in addition to the detector grid alarm system. Farther down the fifty-mile-long peninsula where he now was, the fencing had been reduced to a mere three feet to allow the free passage of wild animals. He'd tried lobbing a stone at the perimeter while some of the larger beasts leaped through, but an aircar had been there within minutes. Two armed soldiers, covered by a third in the vehicle, had gotten out and thoroughly inspected the area before leaving. Only the fact he'd used his natural coloration to conceal himself in the trees overhead had prevented his discovery.

His clothing bundled up on the branch beside him, he stayed there even after they'd left. In his mind, he reviewed what he knew about their security. Leaving aside the perimeter fencing, there was the detection field; aircar patrols at regular times; foot patrols round the perimeter at irregular intervals day and night, and satellite surveillance relayed directly to the gatehouse if the antennae on the gatehouse were anything to judge by. At the gatehouse itself, nearly all vehicles and occupants were checked physically by the soldiers for intruders—those that weren't flew straight over, having obviously transmitted some security code to the guards first.

That covered the land side of the estate. Looking across

the peninsula, he could see Nazule Bay shimmering in the distance. In his time, they'd used anti-personnel fields around their coastlines and major rivers. He saw no reason to assume that the Sholans were any different. Getting in would not be straightforward, but then he'd expected no less.

On his travels, he'd passed three alternative exits from the estate. Two were disused and chained closed. The third, however, was in daily use for access to the nearby coastal town of Khifsoe. He'd stayed there a day and night, hidden in the trees as he was now, observing groups of soldiers, some on foot, some in vehicles, passing through, presumably on leave. There'd been a checkpoint, too, but nowhere near as large as the one at the main entrance. Time to head back up there and look for any weak points. Even among his own troops at Khezy'ipik there had been those who would take unlicensed leave when off duty. He was sure these Sholans would be no different. Guarding an essentially safe compound led to boredom and the need to seek excitement elsewhere. That was achieved by beating the security system to go outside without permission.

Slinging his bundle over his shoulder, he began to move along the branch, ready to retrace his route. At least the weather was better now, more suited to his kind than the dampness he'd endured when he first escaped. Game, small and large, was plentiful, and so long as he took care to hunt wisely, he'd not draw attention to himself.

CHAPTER 12

Day 31

Giyesh could hear voices. They sounded faint and far away. She concentrated on them, becoming gradually more aware not only of what was being said, but of her surroundings.

Above her was a large expanse of whiteness. The ceiling, she realized. Trying to move, she found she couldn't. Her limbs felt dead, as if paralyzed. Strangely, she felt no fear. An unfamiliar scent was in the air. There was a dry mustiness about it.

She heard a low, vibrating hum, a buzzing almost, that was drowned out as a translator began rendering it into speech she could understand.

"Sensitivity has some this one. Mind level for speaking low."

"Can they work as a pair like the others?" Again the translator's electronic voice interpreted the words.

She was hearing Primes talking. There must be one in the room without his armor on!

"Female brain no speaking signals producing from."

"Then why do they associate intimately? What is the purpose?"

"How know I? My time waste you. M'zullians work mine is. Stupidity yours. Not helpful this."

"These ones need to be questioned further before they can be returned."

"Yourself do. Priest Interface unstable is. This told you I. Stability wanted then Interface implant. Not safe for Enlightened One close to be him."

"Not acceptable. I want to observe the effects of the new drug coupled with sleep programming."

"Monitoring for him constant required. Implant work.

Why change. M'zullians when near Sholans behave. Check weekly levels only. Problem priest is.''

"I've told you, the guards either over-react or fail to respond. We need them able to decide for themselves what level of aggression is appropriate."

A burst of static was the answer this time, then she heard the humming again as it and the scent came closer.

"Waking female is. Sedate further need I do."

Cool fingers touched her throat, parting her long pelt, and as something stung her neck, she jerked her head round. Large oval eyes, their lower lenses still whirling as they adjusted for close work, peered down at her from above a tiny mouth edged by two mandibles. She began to scream.

The first they knew of Giyesh's return was her scream. Kaid and Sheeowl, closely followed by Manesh, ran as far as door to her room, waiting there while her bunk mates quieted her.

"No Jeran," said Sheeowl, peering in.

"I saw one!" Giyesh shrieked, trying to push Sayuk away. "It has pincers on its face and huge, swirling black eyes! It had pincers on its face! Let me go! I've got to get out of here!" She heaved Sayuk aside and began racing for the door, eyes staring, pelt bushed out to twice its size.

Manesh leaped in front of her, trying to grab her but was sent spinning by a backhanded blow. She did manage to grab Giyesh's hand, but the hysterical female turned on her, claws extended. Kaid stepped in, delivering one well-aimed blow to the back of her neck. She crashed to the floor unconscious.

"T'Chebbi, medikit!" he called, bending down to scoop the unconscious female up.

"Thanks," said Manesh, rubbing her bruised cheek. "Didn't think she was capable of that."

"Terror can give you strength," said Kaid, carrying Giyesh to the door. He stopped, looking at the group of concerned faces blocking his way. "Move it!" he snarled. "You should be used to this by now!" He pushed them aside and made his way through to the lounge, putting Giyesh down on the nearest couch.

He looked up at Tirak as T'Chebbi handed him their

medikit. "She'll only be out for a few minutes," he said. "I'd like to give her a tranquilizer, if you've no objections. Our drugs won't harm her, and might just do some good."

Tirak nodded. "Can't leave her in this state. Reckon she saw one of them?"

"She certainly saw something," said Kaid, loading the hypo and placing it against Giyesh's neck. "Whether or not it was a Prime is another matter."

Sayuk and Manesh came limping in to join them.

"I'll treat Giyesh with a little more respect after this," said Sayuk sitting down. "If she's so scared of what she saw, why'd she want to leave the rest of us?"

"She didn't," said Rezac. "She was hysterical."

Kaid handed the hypo back to T'Chebbi then squatted on the floor beside her, waiting for Giyesh to wake.

"My food's still warm," said Zashou from her seat at the table. There was an audible tremor in her voice.

"Food?" said Kate, clutching Taynar's arm. "You're talking about food at a time like this?"

"How warm?" Kaid asked sharply. "Five minutes? Less?"

"Five," she said, looking over at him. "We've been out of it for five minutes."

"Check comm units," said Kaid, looking at his. "Anybody's not working?"

"I was using the rec unit," said Taynar, moving back to check it.

"What's the matter with you all?" Kate demanded, her voice becoming shrill. "Giyesh has come back alone and she's seen something awful and all you can talk about is food and comms and . . ."

"We're trying to find out what they do to us when they come in here, Kate," said Kaid gently. "This is the first time they've not picked their time carefully. Zashou was eating, and Taynar was using the rec unit. Usually we're all asleep, or at least resting."

"Game's still stopped," Taynar said, pressing the controls on the pad. "Frozen, in fact. Have to reset it."

"Electrical?" asked Tirak. "Right frequency could knock us out as well as the equipment."

A moan from Giyesh focused their attention back on her.

"Hold her legs, just in case," Kaid told T'Chebbi as he got a grip on her forearms, pressing them against the seat.

Giyesh moaned again, blinking up at him. "Kaid?" She tried to lift her arm and found it held down. "What are you doing?" she demanded. "I want to sit up!"

"How're you feeling?" he asked.

"My neck hurts. I want to rub it. What the hell do you think you're doing?" She struggled futilely against them, looking around wildly. She caught sight of Tirak a few feet away. "Captain! What's going on?"

"I think you can let her up now, Kaid," said Tirak. "You were taken by the Primes, Giyesh. When they returned you, you had a panic attack."

"You said you'd seen something. A face," reminded Kaid, still crouching near her.

She frowned, then a look of horror crossed her face. "I did! Whirling eyes and . . . pincers! They were talking, I heard them talking!" Her hands clenched the edge of the couch, knuckles showing through her dark pelt.

Kaid glanced up at Tirak. "How could you understand them?"

"They were using translators. I smelled one of them. It was out of its suit. It needed the translator so the other one could hear it." She looked round the sea of disbelieving faces. "I did hear them," she said belligerently.

"I'm sure you heard something." said Tirak calmly, sitting down on the arm of the couch. "What about the scent. What did it smell like?"

"Dry and stale. Kind of musty. Like nothing I've smelled before."

"Jeran mentioned a smell when J'koshuk took him," said Jo.

"Why would they use translators to talk to each other?" asked Mrowbay. "Even if one was out of its suit? They can hear us, can't they? Surely they'd use their own language."

"What about a universal translator in the room?" asked Zashou. "We came across something like it back on K'oish'ik."

"That's it," agreed Giyesh, pouncing on the idea. "That's got to be it! We're all speaking Sholan because you gave the knowledge of it to us, but I heard the Primes speaking U'Churian today!"

"What did they say, Giyesh?" asked Tirak.

"They're using implants on the Valtegans to change

them," she said. "But not on J'koshuk. On him they're using drugs. One said he's unstable and has to be watched."

Rezac snorted in disgust. "Tell me about it!"

"Change them how?" asked Kaid.

"The way they behave to you," she said. "I remembered it because it was so strange. Why should it matter to them how the Valtegans treat you Sholans?"

"Valtegans hate us so much, might be just using us as test case," said T'Chebbi.

"I saw Valtegans when they took me," said Kaid thoughtfully.

"Eh? It was the Prime guards that came for you," said Tirak, surprised.

"They towed my floater and waited in the stasis room. Their behavior was totally different from when we were on the *M'ijikk*. More docile. I didn't notice any implants."

"Weren't in much of a state to notice anything," said T'Chebbi. "You said J'koshuk was different too. Noticed it myself. Far less aggressive."

"Not when with us," said Annuur's translator, as the Cabbaran nosed his way through the others to Kaid's side. "Told you. Pretended to kill us one at a time."

"The J'koshuk I met would've killed you," said Rezac, leaning over the back of the couch to look down at the Cabbaran.

"We come back to my theory that maybe these are the ones the Valtegans are fighting," said Tirak.

"Why readjust the Valtegans, though?" asked Jo. "Doesn't make sense to waste all that effort on captives."

Annuur wrinkled his mobile lip expressively. "Aliens. Who guesses their motives?"

Kaid had to smile.

"Maybe they'll release them with a purpose. Like killing superiors when get back home," suggested T'Chebbi. "Fits in with possibility they at war with Primes."

"I'd have expected a more violent reaction from the Valtegans to the mere sight of them when we were taken off the *M'ijikk*," said Kaid, "considering how they behave toward us after fifteen hundred years!"

"Got a point there," T'Chebbi admitted, scratching her ear.

"One of the Primes said the implants had been designed

for the M'zullians," said Giyesh. "That J'koshuk isn't implanted. The other said he wanted to use new drugs on J'koshuk so that, unlike the guards, he could judge what level of aggression was needed in any situation. I think he meant the guards only follow orders, they can't decide what to do by themselves. He said the Enlightened One shouldn't be left with J'koshuk."

"That could describe what we've seen of the guards," agreed Tirak. "Enlightened One, eh? Sounds like they have someone important on board."

"They would have. What I've seen of their stasis and medical sections suggest they're equipped for a conflict," said Kaid, getting up. "This has given us even more questions and not one answer, I'm afraid. Did you overhear anything about why they've kept Jeran?"

"One said he was sensitive, the other wanted to know if we could work as a pair. We don't have the right brain patterns for telepathy, apparently. They wanted to ask us more questions before returning us, but I don't remember being asked anything."

"So why return you?" asked Zashou.

"They knew I was awake and could hear them. It was that face!" Giyesh shivered, clutching her arms about her chest. "Those huge eyes with the dark centers, and the pincers!"

"More likely it was your scream," snorted Mrowbay. "Enough to wake the dead it was!"

Kaid reached out to grip Giyesh's shoulder comfortingly. "There's no point in getting upset about it, Giyesh. Whoever they are, they've been here all along. So far, they haven't actually harmed us."

"They kept Carrie from you," she said quietly.

Kaid's ears dipped. "They may yet return her."

"At least we've an idea of how they get in and out of here without us knowing," said Jo. "Makes it less frightening."

"Not to me," said Zashou.

"Nor me," agreed Giyesh.

* * *

Brynne had asked Jurrel and Banner to let him have the afternoon alone in the house with Keeza.

"You want me to do what?" demanded a shocked Keeza. She got up and began to pace round the den, tail flicking in agitation. Stopping suddenly, she said, "Tell me again why this matters."

Brynne sighed and began again. This would make the third time. "I want you to bond with me," he said.

"That bit I do understand," she interrupted. "It's the next I don't."

"We're genetically compatible, which means we could have cubs with each other. Because of this . . ."

"That just isn't possible," she said, sitting down on the chair next to him. "You're Human, I'm not. How could we possibly share cubs?"

"Just take my word for it," he said, reaching across to take hold of her hand. It lay passive in his. "There are two Human and Sholan hybrid cubs on the estate already, one of them mine. I told you I went to visit my Leska and our son yesterday. You didn't doubt me then."

"I thought she was Human like you. It never occurred to me she was Sholan."

"I'm not asking you to have a cub, Keeza, only to go through a bonding ceremony with me. Because we could have cubs together, our priest, Ghyan, is willing to perform the ceremony, that's all. He knows who you are . . ."

He stopped as she tried to pull away from him with a cry of distress. "Keeza, stop panicking! He's a priest of Vartra, bound by his Order not to reveal confidential conversations with his congregation to anyone. It'll give you more security if you're my bond-mate. Make it more difficult for any authorities to take you off the estate."

"What's so special about this estate?"

"It's the En'Shalla estate. Three people walked the Fire Margins to win us—the mixed Leskas—the right to have our own Clan."

"I think I remember reading about it," she said vaguely. "But we're not Leskas."

"You're a telepath, and your genes are similar to everyone's here. If you marry me, you become En'Shalla, too. The Gods' will, Keeza, subject only to the Order of Vartra. Now do you understand?"

She nodded slowly, putting her hand up to tuck a shorter

lock of hair behind her ear. "How long a contract are you suggesting?"

Brynne watched her. He'd found himself trying to memorize her every little gesture. This was one of her most endearing. When she did that, she looked as if she was Kitra's age. "I've thought about this," he said, taking his time. "The only one that makes sense and gives you the protection you need, is a life-bonding." He felt her hand clench slightly within his and rushed on before she could say anything. "Before you object, once we've sorted this out, you needn't stay with me if you don't want to. You can think of it as a marriage of convenience if you prefer."

"You know nothing about me except what you've shared in my mind," she said quietly. "Most of my past life is a complete mystery even to me. I can't even remember what I've done since I was taken from the prison."

"Like you said, I've felt your mind. You're not a killer, Keeza. Whatever you did, you must have had good reasons. I trust you."

"You're a fool, Brynne," she said, looking him straight in the eyes. "You've read the reports. You know I worked my way into a Pack Lord's den then killed him. How d'you know I won't do the same to you?"

"Because I know you love me," he said, reaching out to pull her into the chair with him. "Just as you know I love you. I realize it's sudden, but my proposal is quite real—if you'll have me."

"How do we reach this shrine without me being seen?" she asked, returning his kiss as his lips brushed hers.

"I get Father Ghyan on the comm and ask him to come here. It's all arranged," he murmured. "But I don't need to call him just yet."

Sister Vaidou pressed a small sterile dressing over the cut on Brynne's palm, then turned to do the same for Keeza.

"It won't stick if your skin's wet," she said, getting ready to apply the dressing.

Hurriedly Keeza took her hand away from her mouth and wiped it along her thigh to dry it off. "It was bleeding," she said.

"You'll have gotten dirt in it now," said the Sister, checking that Keeza's palm was dry enough. Blood was welling again from the narrow cut that ran across the pad in the center of her hand. "It's meant to bleed. How else can you and Brynne share your blood?" She smiled as she applied the dressing. "This must have been a spring romance for you both. So sudden."

Keeza didn't quite know how to answer, then Brynne came to her rescue.

"Not so sudden, Vaidou," he said, standing behind his new wife and resting his hands on her hips. "We met mentally weeks ago." He shrugged, smiling. "Working here, you know how it is with telepaths. There's more than one way to get to know a person."

"Yes," said Vaidou uncertainly.

"Let's go and help Ghyan clear up," Brynne whispered in Keeza's ear, urging her past the Sister.

Ghyan was standing at the table he'd used for performing the bonding ceremony, packing away the very new estate register book and the ceremonial knife.

Brynne watched the priest's eyes narrow briefly, then widen in surprise as they approached him. "Can we help you?" he asked. "We can't thank you enough for doing this."

Ghyan took Keeza by the hand. "I'm done now. It's a pleasure to be able to help you. Did you know that years ago, Kusac and I were friends at the Guild?" he said. "I left for the temple at Valsgarth a couple of years before Kusac disappeared. No one was more surprised than me when he turned up here with his Carrie. I threw my lot in with him the night he asked me to marry him to his Human Leska."

"Kusac disappeared?" Brynne was confused.

"He was very different back then," said Ghyan, perching on the edge of the table. "Much quieter, a very conscientious student who had no idea how to relax. Then he ran off and joined the Forces, posing as a low-grade telepath. We didn't know what had become of him for a year. It wasn't till his message for help was picked up by the *Khalossa* that we found out he'd been shot down on Keiss by the Valtegans along with Vanna and Garras, and he'd met Carrie."

"I didn't realize he'd been in the military," said Brynne. "And you married them?"

Ghyan's mouth opened in a slow smile. "Yes, it was my pleasure to be able to perform my friend's life-bonding ceremony. He was betrothed to someone else, and unable by law to even enter into a short-term bonding contract because of that. It wasn't till he discovered Carrie was carrying their cub that he realized they had the right to marry. Their hybrid cub negated the betrothal contract, you see."

"I'd heard some of this," said Brynne, "Why are you telling us this? Not that I'm complaining, you understand."

Ghyan looked from one to the other. "Just letting you know you're not the first couple I've helped, that's all," he said lightly, patting Keeza's hand before letting it go. "I hope everything works out for you. If I can be of any more help, please don't hesitate to ask."

"Thank you, Father," said Brynne, aware of Keeza shrinking back against him. *What's wrong? I told you our secret's safe with Father Ghyan and Sister Vaidou.*

I know!

Then he realized what Father Ghyan had been alluding to. It rendered him speechless.

Ghyan caught his look and nodded, raising an eye ridge. "Ah. I see you've just found out the good news," he said, smiling again as he got down from the table and picked up his case. "It seems that more and more often these days, my wishes for a fruitful marriage are unnecessary."

There wasn't much Brynne could say until after the priest and his aide had left.

"Why?" he asked, coming back into the den. "Didn't you trust me enough? Did you feel a cub would make you safer?" Had she been even more manipulative than she'd suggested? Had he been fooled the way she'd fooled the Pack Lord?

She put her hands over her face and just sat there. "No! At first I didn't even think it was possible. Then, when I realized the truth, I thought it would please you. I was wrong, I had no right to make that choice alone."

He didn't know what to say. Suddenly his—their—world had been turned upside down, and the first small seed of doubt had been planted. Her distress was real, he could feel it, and it hurt him every bit as much as it hurt her. She'd trusted him completely, so why was he suddenly reluctant to do the same? Didn't this cub make her even more dependent on him? He hadn't feared for his physical safety because of her violent past, was he that afraid of her emotionally? Then he remembered what he and Vanna had gone through when they'd discovered she was pregnant, and began walking toward her.

"It's all right," he said, crouching down in front of her. Gently he tugged her hands away from her eyes. "Don't cry, Keeza. I know you didn't mean any harm." He kissed her palms, first the one with the cut where they'd mingled their blood during the ceremony, then the other.

"Blood is life. What better way to seal our marriage than to share a cub?" His voice sounded hollow as he said the words, as if he was hearing them spoken for the second time, and from very far away.

He felt a sudden weight on his shoulder, then a small, wet nose stuffed itself into his ear. Belle leaped from there down into Keeza's lap, stretching up to pat her face, making her smile and reach down to pet the jegget. As he watched them, a sound like a sigh echoed in his mind.

Each house in the village had a garden behind it. Brynne's was no different. Later in the evening, he found an opportunity to go for a walk with Jurrel and tell him what he'd done.

"Say something," said Brynne, exasperated and worried by the other's silence.

Jurrel turned to look at him. "What do you want me to say?"

"Anything you want."

"I don't think you know what you're doing," he said. "Worse, I don't think you know *why* you did it."

"That hurt," said Brynne.

"It's the truth, though. Why would you need my opinion if you're so sure of yourself?"

"You're my friend, and more. It matters."

Jurrel sighed, stopping by the bench. "Sit down," he said. "I can feel your tension so strongly it's affecting me."

Brynne sat. "I want to help her, Jurrel," he said as his friend began to knead his shoulders firmly.

"Do you? Or were you looking for an excuse to marry her? And if so, why should you need an excuse?"

"I didn't marry her to prove anything to myself, or anyone else!" he said, stung.

"Then what's the real reason? Be honest with yourself if not with me." Jurrel was working his way across Brynne's shoulder blades, making him wince. "You get these knots in the same places every time," he muttered. "Next time you're getting wound up, spare a thought for me. I'm the poor male who's got to undo it all."

Brynne sniggered briefly, then sobered up again. "You're going to laugh at me or call me an idiot," he said defensively.

"Try me."

He swung round on the bench to look at his friend. "Yes, I was looking for an excuse to marry her, because I fell in love with her."

"That's a good enough reason," Jurrel said, stepping across the bench to join him. "Feel better?"

Brynne rotated his shoulders and neck experimentally. "Lots, thanks."

"I still think you're out of your mind, though. Two days isn't long enough to know if you're suited to build a life together."

"Telepaths can't lie to each other when they mind-speak. I know all I need to know about her."

"Then what you've done is right for you. You'll certainly be more able to protect her as her life-mate."

"And she's pregnant," Brynne added.

Jurrel made a choking noise, then reached out and grabbed him by the ears, shaking his head. "Have you got insanity in your family?" he demanded.

"Hey! That hurts!" Brynne exclaimed, grabbing at his hands to stop him. "What did you do that for?"

"To shake some sense into you! How in Vartra's name did you persuade her to get pregnant? And why?" Jurrel let his ears go but Brynne held onto his hands.

"I didn't. She decided on her own. Just don't say anything, please. I've already said it all to myself. What worries me more is I don't want to have to choose between the two of you."

"Then don't," said Jurrel. "I'm not going to ask you to." He narrowed his eyes, searching Brynne's face. "I think perhaps you do know who you are after all, Brynne Stevens. When you make your mind up, you certainly do it fast!"

"Vanna taught me that you have to hold onto what's worth having or else you'll lose it," he said quietly.

"A wise female," said Jurrel, gripping Brynne's hands before removing his own. "We'd better get back in before Keeza starts worrying."

"She won't. She knows what we're talking about."

"Then she will worry," said Jurrel, getting up. "She must love you a great deal to commit herself to sharing a cub with you so soon."

Brynne said nothing as they walked back indoors.

* * *

The Seniormost had not harmed Kusac the day before, merely questioned him again about Vartra the God, Kezule, and the telepaths. It was almost a repetition of what J'koshuk had asked. He'd refused to answer him, refused to even confirm what he'd said to the priest. He left him alone eventually, sending in food and dimming the lights so Kusac could sleep.

Several hours later, he was awakened by being hauled from his bed by a Prime guard. As he staggered, reaching out to support himself against the bed, a blow struck him hard across the face. He yelped as much at the unexpectedness of it as at the pain. The guard pulled him into the center of the room, gripping him firmly by the upper arms. Kusac didn't struggle, there was no point. Against his back, the guard's armor was hard and cold. He could feel his heart begin to race as he tried to prepare himself for trouble.

"Are you awake now?" the priest asked in Sholan, standing in front of him. "Good. The Seniormost was most displeased that you refused to talk to him yesterday." J'koshuk smiled to show his many pointed teeth. "When he's displeased, I'm displeased."

Another blow hit him, this time on the other side of his face, rocking his head so hard he hit it on the armor behind him.

"You'll answer me though, because this time the pain can't be turned off. You'll have to live with every bruise and cut. And every time I come to question you, I'll add to them. Do we understand each other?"

Kusac looked at him silently. Yes, he understood, but he was damned if he'd answer him! He saw J'koshuk lifting his arm and closed his eyes, determined not to give the Valtegan the satisfaction of seeing him flinch.

It landed on the same side, making him gasp involuntarily as his head bounced off the guard's armor again. As he righted himself, he could feel his cheek swelling and his field of vision in that eye begin to shrink.

"You're new to this question and answer game, aren't you?" said J'koshuk, circling round them. "I can tell. I'll give you a few hints before we go any further."

Kusac's head ached and his face was throbbing, and J'koshuk had barely begun. He'd coped with pain before, used his Talent to block it, but he could feel nothing left of his abilities now. Kaid had taught him what to do in the event of capture, but then it had been academic, now it was only too real.

The footsteps stopped in front of him. His jaw was grasped from underneath and his head forced up so he was looking directly at J'koshuk. Razor sharp claws pricked the sides of his cheeks.

"One. Always look at me when I'm talking to you." He thrust Kusac's head away. "I like to know I have your full attention. Two. Always answer the easy questions. I can't stand sullen captives. Three. Don't give in too easily. I won't believe you." He moved closer, his forked tongue flicking out to stop millimeters from Kusac's face. Then it was gone. "I enjoy my work. It gives me pleasure to unlock my captive's deepest secrets and fears. Now, shall we begin again?"

His legs were trembling, he realized, forcing them straight then bracing them at the knee joint. It was a game, and he needed to make concessions if he was going to have any chance of surviving it.

"Yes." In his mind, he began to recite the litany to banish pain.

"You learn quickly," said J'koshuk. "Let's start with the female in the other cryogenic unit. Carrie."

* * *

Day 32

Giyesh woke with Jeran lying in the bed beside her. He was shocked to learn he'd been taken, and had no memory of being examined or questioned. Kaid pressed him hard, but to no avail. Then he called Rezac over to read the young male's mind.

"You're treating him like a criminal," objected Giyesh, taking the opportunity to return to her lover's side.

"Giyesh," warned Tirak from his seat nearby. "Don't interfere between Kaid and his people. You're making a fool of yourself over Jeran. You should never have been allowed to come on this mission. Why I let the elders talk me into taking you, I'll never know. You should be home looking after your first taiban now!"

Giyesh stiffened, moving closer to Jeran.

"It's all right, Giyesh, no one's forcing me to do anything," said Jeran quietly, stroking her knee.

Rezac took advantage of their conversation to say in a low voice, "Why aren't you doing it, Kaid?"

"No need for me to when you can," he replied. "You're more than capable from what I saw that day with Tesha."

Rezac's eyes narrowed, his eye ridges meeting. Kaid felt the gentle touch of the other's mind briefly against his and cursed to himself. He'd been hoping to conceal his condition for a while longer.

It's begun, hasn't it? Link deprivation. Do you know anything about it? sent Rezac.

Of course I do! I watched Carrie and Kusac go through it. I know what to expect.

Knowing it and experiencing it are very different. You're mentally and physically separated, that's the worst it could be. If they keep you apart, you've got another day at most before you go into a coma. Then you die. Tomorrow morning, I'm calling the Primes, unless either you're taken or she's returned.

No! You'll do nothing!

Then you'll both die. So will your cub. Is that what you want?

He glowered at Rezac, making an effort to strengthen his mental barriers. *You'd no business reading me!*

I didn't. Your shields are low and I couldn't help sense

the state you're in. We can't afford to lose you, Kaid. You're what's holding all of us together. Even Tirak looks to you as the leader.

Rezac was right, and he'd be failing in his duty if he didn't accept the offer of help. His father had an uncanny knack of knowing when something was wrong with him. He wondered if Dzaka thought the same of him. *Do it, then.*

I'll need to monitor you, Rezac warned him. *And tell the others if necessary.*

Kaid shut his eyes. He was deathly tired and ached all over. *No.*

It would be better to tell the Primes now. You're only going to get worse and there's nothing we can do to ease it.

You know I can't. To do that would be showing them our weakness. It's academic anyway. They don't come when we call them. He could feel the compassion in the other's thoughts. How could the Leskas live like this, tied so completely to another? He was so used to his freedom, his independence.

But no more loneliness. You've only had one Link day, sent Rezac. *You wait, it's worth it for that one day in five that's yours.*

He remembered saying something similar to Kusac. Now he would be finding out for himself. *Do what you have to,* he sent with a sigh.

You'll tell T'Chebbi? That one's like a feral when it comes to defending you.

He opened his eyes, smiling faintly. "I'll tell T'Chebbi."

"Tell me what?" she demanded from by his elbow.

See what I mean? sent Rezac with a slow grin.

"Go and read Jeran," said Kaid, pushing himself out of the chair. "I'll talk to T'Chebbi now."

"You got till midday tomorrow? That's all?" T'Chebbi asked, shocked.

He nodded, holding his arms open for her. She went to him, clutching him tightly as his arms closed round her and he rested his head against hers.

"I need you to understand how much I love you," he said, the words coming slowly, as if he was having difficulty saying them. "One day, you and I will share cubs, because

I don't compare you with Carrie, don't love either of you more than the other, just differently."

"I know," she whispered, clenching her hands in his still long pelt. "I know you don't. I love them and you that way, too." She could feel tears beginning to course down her cheeks and pushed away from him, scrubbing at her face. "Look at me, some warrior I am!"

"The best," he said, capturing her again. "I chose you to guard Carrie, didn't I?" He licked her tears away, making her laugh, and cry again. "I'm not that bad. Rezac's watching me, he'll not let me go into a coma."

"Wish it was me. I'd know how things were then, when to worry."

"Ask Rezac, he'll tell you. You have to trust him, T'Chebbi. I am, with my life."

"Should be me!"

"No, you're my Second. You have to lead for me, that's more important this time," he said, stroking her head, smoothing back her ears as if he was soothing a cub. "And ease off on Zashou, please. It hurts Rezac when you go for her. She can't help being afraid."

T'Chebbi stiffened slightly. "Where is she? Didn't see her in the lounge with everyone else."

"This would happen now," Kaid sighed. "With any luck she'll remember nothing when they return her."

"What do you want to bet she's hysterical?" grumbled T'Chebbi.

"Well, it'll be your problem, your chance to show her some patience. I won't be well enough to deal with it."

She could hear the sudden strain in his voice and looked up at him. His face was creased in pain. Instantly she reached for his hand, feeling the heat and the sweat as he began to sag against her. Grabbing him, she steered him over to his bed, helping him lie down.

"It's all right," he said, holding his belly. "It's part of it. Just a stomach cramp. It'll pass in a moment. Go see if you can find Zashou."

"I'll go find Rezac first," she said, getting up.

"Don't panic everyone about me, T'Chebbi," he whispered as she made her way to the door. "We don't need it."

Zashou proved to be there, still asleep in the room she shared with Jo and Rezac. Kaid rested for a while,

T'Chebbi keeping him company. Then, anxious not to worry any of the others because of his absence, when he felt a little better, he returned to the lounge. Rezac joined him, carrying an herbal drink.

"Try this, might help ease your stomach a little," he said quietly.

Kaid accepted it, finding it surprisingly pleasant. "What was going on between Giyesh and Tirak earlier?" he asked. Keeping his mind busy was better than the alternative.

"Tirak and his crew, they're all related, something like a mixture of the Guilds and Clans you say Shola has now. Females take a different husband every five years and are not supposed to see military service until after their first cub. Only Giyesh didn't fancy that and had her parents pull strings to allow her to come on this mission instead."

"How'd you find this out?"

"Been talking to Jeran. He's as taken with Giyesh as she is with him," Rezac said, looking over at the table where the couple were sitting. "Apparently she's running upwind of custom, and Tirak, over Jeran. She's not supposed to have lovers before her first mating is over. I think the Captain hoped she'd choose Nayash or Mrowbay, not one of us. Jeran says she'll be in trouble for it when she gets home."

"So they're a military family?"

"Yeah. All Rryuks, like the name of their ship. Only reason Tirak's let them be is because of us." He turned to look at Kaid. "Because we have lovers who are aliens."

"Less alien than a hell of a lot of Sholans I know," muttered Kaid.

Rezac grinned, ears flicking in amusement. "How right you are. You better figure out what you're going to tell Jeran when he comes and asks if he can stay with the *Profit*, not come home with us."

"I'm ahead of you on that," he said, face creasing slightly in pain. "What did you find out from Jeran?"

"Nothing. He was out cold the whole time. This can wait, Kaid."

Rezac was right. In his current state, he might inadvertently say more than he meant to about the Primes and their motives. "Carrie's going through this, isn't she?"

Rezac just nodded. "It's nearly third meal. Try to eat

something light, like eggs. Then go rest. T'Chebbi can watch you for now. I'll take over later."

"I don't think I can eat."

"Try something. Just eat what you can."

Kaid nodded and took another sip of his drink. He'd noticed lately that Rezac had been keeping an eye on everyone, acting like a Pack Second, keeping his hand on the pulse of the group. Especially himself. "I'll try," he said tiredly.

Rezac and Jo likewise retired early. Lying beside her, Rezac gently rubbed his hand across Jo's belly.

"Tell me how Kaid is," she asked.

Rezac rolled back into his own bed and stared up at the ceiling. "Not good," he admitted. "I'm not completely sure what's going on with him. This is what usually happens if you try to deny a Leska Link, not after the first pairing. But then, this is hardly a normal Link anyway. He said they once experienced a full three-way bond but apart from then, it's never been that active for him. They're all aware of each other during Link days, but he doesn't feel the compulsion strongly unless it's time for him to be with Carrie."

"What about when she was pregnant?"

"Weren't Linked then. The three-way thing happened when he and Kusac swore a sword-brother oath, he said. Probably his Link to her has activated to a full Leska one to save her because of Kusac being dead."

"Or missing," corrected Jo.

"More likely dead, I'm afraid. Anyway, I've created a minor link of my own to him, and I'm watching him carefully. That's why I want to sleep now, so I'm alert during the worst of it."

"How quickly could he go into a coma? Will you have enough warning?"

"Yes, if I'm physically with him. T'Chebbi's watching him now. He's at the vomiting stage."

Jo grimaced. "Sounds awful. Would that have happened to us if we hadn't . . ."

"But it didn't," he said, cutting her short. "You came to me and now we have a cub on the way." He reached out to caress her belly again. "I can feel it," he said suddenly.

"You can't possibly," Jo replied, feeling for herself. "I'm only nine weeks."

"Are you sure?" he asked, disappointed.

"Positive! It's far too small for that yet. You know, Zashou was right about that at least. You're like a cat with two tails over this cub."

He raised his head to look at her in surprise. "A cat with two tails? What an odd saying." He thought for a moment then grinned. "Still, say it again in a couple of day's time when this is over and I'm sure I can come up with something better than a second tail."

Jo grabbed her pillow and began to hit him with it.

* * *

Day 32

A second wasted day, thought J'koshuk, hissing angrily at the captive hanging limply in the guard's grasp. Oh, not wasted as far as the Seniormost was concerned, but certainly as far as he was. The Seniormost, after making him spend yesterday in his rooms with nothing to do, had given him an extra two days to question Kusac, and finally lifted the worst of the restrictions on what he could do to him. He'd gotten all the answers the Primes wanted now, and it still didn't make much sense, but making sense of it was the Seniormost's job, not his.

It was the Human that *he* wanted to hear about, and the damned Sholan still refused to tell him anything! He'd tormented him to the point where he'd say almost anything just to be left alone, which meant Kusac could tell the truth now and know it would be suspect. Lately, though, J'koshuk had noticed he'd developed a knack of telling when his captives were lying, so continuing wasn't a problem. Which was just as well, because he only had a few hours left in which to get the answers he wanted.

His own equipment from the *M'ijikk* had gotten him better results than the sophisticated pain collar of the Primes. Deep bruising that caused no surface wounds that the Primes could see was a great persuader. And the pain lasted.

Reaching behind him, he picked up the animal prod

again and put it under Kusac's chin, sending just enough of a current through it to make him jerk his head up. "One more time. You say you met the Humans on Keiss."

Kusac mumbled something indecipherable.

"I can't hear you."

"Yes." Still mumbled but at least he could hear it this time.

"You met this Human female on Keiss."

"No."

"Think again." Turning the power up to full, he touched the prod to Kusac's neck.

He jerked away from it, trying not to cry out. "Not Keiss!"

"Then where?"

"The second ship," he mumbled, head dropping again.

"You're lying. She was on Keiss before your people came, wasn't she?"

"No. On ship." He shook his head slowly for emphasis. "Why important?"

"You dare question me?" he demanded, about to hit him again. Then he stopped. It was always the same answers. A different approach was needed. Perhaps letting him know how much information about her he already had might break down his resistance. "She was on Keiss, wasn't she? More, she was in our city at Geshader."

"No."

Aiming above the guard's grip, he hit Kusac's arm hard with the prod and held it there for several seconds.

Unable to pull away from either the blow or the current as it surged through him, Kusac's body went rigid and he began to whimper—a low, involuntary sound.

That had gotten a better response. The combination of the blow and the charge might just work. J'koshuk removed the prod and Kusac sagged against the guard.

"She was at Geshader, wasn't she? Working as a spy."

"No!"

"She's in a room down the corridor. If you won't tell me, maybe I'll go ask her myself. Would you prefer that?"

Kusac straightened up and raised his head slowly, eyes narrowing as he looked at J'koshuk. "They won't let you near her or you wouldn't need to ask me."

Angrily, J'koshuk hit him again, aiming the prod high up

on the inside of Kusac's thigh near his groin and holding it there.

Howling in agony, Kusac fought to escape the prod, trying to wrench himself free from the guard. J'koshuk dodged, keeping up the pressure against his leg until suddenly, Kusac collapsed, gasping, "Not Carrie! Elise! Was Elise, her twin!"

Shocked, J'koshuk removed the prod and stepped back. "Twin? What's twin?" he demanded.

Each word was gasped out painfully as the guard hauled Kusac's limp body upright again. "Like her. Sister. Born at same time."

Two? Humans had multiple young? He had to be lying! Reaching out, he grasped him by the jaw, lifting his head up. Tears streaked the blood-matted, swollen face. But it was Kusac's eyes that told him that he'd at last gotten some of what he wanted. There was no fire left in them.

"The one I questioned was called Elise," J'koshuk said. "How like her sister is she?"

"Exact."

He remembered how the female had laughed in his face as he'd tortured her. No one had ever laughed before. More, she'd told him nothing. Never had that happened either. There wasn't a person living who couldn't be broken somehow—except him. Had it been the other—twin—that had been the spy? Had he gotten the wrong one? He dropped Kusac's head, losing interest in him.

"Leave him. I want to see the Human female." He began striding toward the door.

"No! Leave her alone! She wasn't the spy!" Kusac cried out as the guard pushed him aside and followed J'koshuk.

Staggering, his abused leg buckled under him, pitching him forward to sprawl on the floor. He lay there, unable to move as the door closed behind him. "No! Not Carrie!" he howled, clenching his hands and thumping them uselessly against the steel floor in despair.

* * *

"We're here, Commander," said Nara, putting her head round the door of the cramped common area on *Striker Two*.

L'Seuli grunted and uncurled himself from the narrow bed on which he'd been sleeping. Standing up, he tried to stretch his cramped limbs and tail.

"You should get some rest while you're here, Commander," she said sympathetically. "This is the fourth outpost you've been to in the last two weeks."

"It's also the last one, Nara," he yawned, running his hands across his short, sand-colored hair and scratching behind his ears vigorously. "I head home tomorrow."

"Captain Kheal is waiting on the flight deck. Said to tell you there's hot food waiting for you in his quarters."

L'Seuli's ears pricked up. "There is? Now that does sound good. What about you and Chima?" He tugged at the hem of his tunic before readjusting his jacket. His grays were still stiff and new, but he'd needed them to reflect his current rank during this mission.

"Crew rations," she said, making a face. "Still a hell of a lot better than the muck on board *Striker*."

He frowned, then changed his mind. "Anything is, Sister Nara. Let's get going, then."

Kheal was waiting for him just inside the exit. He stood to attention, saluting him. "Commander L'Seuli. Welcome to Haven."

L'Seuli returned the older male's salute. "At ease, Captain. My pilot tells me there's food waiting for us. After *Striker*'s rations, it's a welcome thought."

"I hope to make your visit here as pleasant as possible, Commander. This way, if you please," said Kheal, indicating the waiting elevator.

"How's work progressing?"

"Fair. The station had a skeleton crew, which we've assimilated. All the essentials were up and running, it's just been a question of expanding to accommodate a crew of sixty and five assault craft."

"You have everything you need?"

The elevator halted, door opening to let them out onto the second level. Again, Kheal let L'Seuli precede him.

"Yes, Commander. Is this your first visit to our outpost?" He stopped outside his office, opening the door for them.

"It is, but I have been fully briefed, Captain," he said, well aware the captain thought him too young for his rank. "The original asteroid was found here two hundred and fifty years ago during part of the Brotherhood's regular policing activities in this region after the Chemerian/Sholan wars. Charts discovered here led us to the other three outposts, and the conclusion that they formed part of an early warning system of unknown alien origin. Like the other three, it was abandoned and showed signs of a fierce conflict. In light of current discoveries, it's now thought to have belonged to the ancient Valtegans. Over the years, other asteroids have been excavated at each location, including this, our main one, and outfitted with parts salvaged from obsolete craft bought from the Forces. They now serve as our forward observation posts to protect Alliance space and thus Shola. How am I doing?" he asked, raising an eye ridge.

Kheal's ears dipped in embarrassment. "I was told your last assignment had been in the Ghuulgul Desert during the tribal rebellion. I assumed that . . ."

L'Seuli touched the flash of purple at the edge of his jacket. "Perhaps in fairness I should tell you that the purple on my uniform does reflect a telepathic ability, which was why I was picked for that mission. May I suggest, Brother Kheal, that we forget our current ranks and collaborate as equals on this matter? You obviously have more experience of this outpost than I have. The point of my mission is to see that Guild Master Rhyaz is as fully briefed as possible on your current state of readiness. I'd appreciate your assistance to do that."

Kheal's mouth opened in a half smile. "Certainly, Brother L'Seuli. We can inspect the facility as soon as we've eaten. Would you like to take a seat?" He gestured to his desk where plates and covered dishes of food sat.

Within a few minutes, L'Seuli was helping himself from one of the several large casserole dishes on the table.

"I don't suppose you've got any further orders for me, have you?" asked Kheal, helping himself to vegetables. "Something that would explain why we're suddenly increasing our presence in space?"

"Why do you think we're here?"

"Possibly because of some threat to Shola, possibly because of the new treaties."

"A reasonable hypothesis. I expect the troops are rife with speculation."

"And bets. It would be useful to have something concrete to tell them."

"I'm afraid I've no additional orders for you beyond remaining vigilant."

"I've been given two telepaths," said Kheal after munching in silence for a few minutes. "Brother Vriuzu from Stronghold, and Sister Jiosha from our guildhouse on Nalgalan."

"So Jiosha's been reassigned from Jalna," said L'Seuli, helping himself to more stew. "I wondered if she'd be posted here. We started training at Stronghold together."

"Why have we two when the other outposts have only one?" asked Kheal, doggedly pursuing his point "And why any at all? Normally they stay at the guildhouses to avoid recognition."

L'Seuli finished his mouthful. "How are you deploying them?"

"You're ignoring my question, Brother. Why?"

"Did you know Vartra's been seen in the temple at Stronghold? He's been visiting our Brothers and Sisters with visions again. You did receive the directive on reporting all such occurrences direct to Stronghold, didn't you?"

"Yes, we received it."

"Don't censor them. Send them all immediately, no matter how strange."

Kheal sat back in his chair. "Some idea of what we're watching or waiting for would be helpful."

L'Seuli rested his elbows on the desk, watching him. "All I can tell you at this moment, Captain, is that four of our people are missing, and have been for twenty-seven days. Three of them are an En-Shalla Leska Triad. We've found some debris but not a trace of their craft so far—no drive emissions even. They're out there somewhere, and it's possible a message from them might come at any time. This outpost is nearest to their last known position."

"Whatever's responsible for them being missing could be heading for Shola."

L'Seuli sat unmoving for a moment longer. "I did not say that, Captain Kheal," he said softly, then resumed his meal.

Almost word for word, he'd had the same conversation at each of the other three outposts, and each of their commanding officers had drawn the same conclusion. Inspecting the facility was almost a formality now he'd completed his main task.

* * *

The Clan Council meeting had been delayed by a week and they were sitting for the first time since Konis had withdrawn his resignation. As he looked round the chamber, he was pleased to note the wary looks on the faces of four of the newly appointed Clan Leaders. It wouldn't do any harm at all for them to remain cautious of him for the next few months. He would not let Azkuu's little power struggle be forgotten.

He tapped the table in front of him loudly with his stylus, waiting for the chattering to cease.

"Before we begin, there's some long overdue business I have to attend to," he said, picking up an official letter from the folder in front of him and getting to his feet. He walked round the table till he came to Naeul Arrazo, holding the document out to him.

"What's this?" demanded Naeul, taking it from him. "What're you planning now, Konis? Isn't it enough you've replaced four of the Council?"

Konis ignored his outburst. "My predecessor should have seen to this years ago, Naeul. He didn't, but the matter was brought to my attention and I'm dealing with it now."

Naeul had opened the letter and was reading it.

Konis looked at Falma, nodded once, then turned back to Naeul as his deputy opened the door and slipped out.

"That is your indictment for the crime of assault against your daughter Khemu Arrazo; for illegally imprisoning her on your estate; for falsely reporting her death to various officials, including the ruling Clan Lord; for failing to register the birth of your grandson, Dzaka Arrazo, and finally, when the cub was born, taking him from his mother and having him fostered, against her will, in your estate nursery. The Protectors are waiting for you, Naeul Arrazo." As he turned away to walk slowly back to his seat at the head of the table, the door opened and a senior Protector entered.

"Now look here," began Naeul, getting up and angrily starting toward Konis.

"You can argue your case with the judiciary, Liege," interrupted the officer, taking him firmly by the arm.

Rhyasha smiled a small smile to herself as she watched Naeul being led, protesting, from the room. The rest of the Council sat in stunned silence till the door shut behind them. It was satisfying to see them so rattled after what they'd allowed Azkuu and her little group to do, not only to Konis, but to Kitra. And finally, justice had been gained for Dzaka and his mother, Khemu. She hoped the poor female's soul would now be at peace.

"I remember that business with Khemu," said Lossa, the first to speak. "She was supposed to life-bond with my eldest. What happened, Konis?"

"Khemu Arrazo became pregnant and Naeul, fearing the scandal, told this Council that she'd died in a climbing accident," said Konis. "He refused to let her see the father and locked her up in her room till her cub was born." He stopped, looking over the Council members. "Naeul didn't stop at that, though. He took the infant from her and placed him in the estate nursery, then moved his daughter out of the main house into one opposite the nursery, imprisoning her there. As he grew older, Khemu could see and hear her son every day, but was never allowed to speak to him. Naeul made sure she never forgot the shame she'd brought to his family."

"Naeul did that?" exclaimed Khayle. "I'd never have thought it of him!"

"You were always a bit soft on Naeul, even as a youngling," said Mnae with a cackle. "Never looked twice at you, though."

"Just as well," snapped back Lossa. "How did you find out about this, Konis? What became of the cub? And why did she choose to become pregnant in the first place?"

"More important, who's the father?" asked Chaidda, his male voice deep among those of the females.

"The father didn't know about the cub till four years later," said Konis. "As luck would have it, Khemu managed not only to escape, but to take him with her. She left him outside the gates at Stronghold for his father to find."

Khas'ih Rakula began to laugh softly. "I know whose son he is. His father's the third in your son's Triad, isn't he, Konis? Dzaka is Kaid's son." She looked over to Gar-

ras. "One of your En'Shalla Clan. Father and son both, I'll
be bound. So the Brotherhood has had a telepath in its
midst all these years."

Garras said nothing for now, letting Konis continue
uninterrupted.

"You're right, Khas'ih," said Konis. "Kaid found the cub
and was able to foster him. He suspected who he was, but
had no proof. Using his friends among the Brothers, he
kept his ears alert for any word of Khemu Arrazo. When
he found out where she lived, he went to her. That's when
he found out the truth of what had happened. She's dead
now, of a wasting sickness, but they bonded before she
died. Dzaka has been entered in the records as her and
Kaid's legitimate son. He promised her he'd ensure Dzaka
got his legitimacy, as Khemu had already given him her
torc and knife. Today, the truth has come home to nest in
Naeul Arrazo's hall. May Vartra grant Khemu's soul peace
at last."

Murmurs of agreement went round the room.

"Wasn't Khemu his firstborn and heir?" asked Khayle.
"If memory serves me, she was. That makes Dzaka his
heir now."

"No," said Rhyasha. "Dzaka is an En'Shallan, a gene-
altered Brother with a psi gift. He's an Aldatan now."

"That's the one your Kitra wanted, wasn't it?" asked
Mnae, clicking her tongue disapprovingly. "Would never
have done, Rhyasha. No cubs, y'see."

"You didn't say why she chose to have his cub," said
Lossa. "We thought Khemu was pleased with our contract.
I find it all very confusing."

"If I may answer that, Clan Lord?" Garras asked, catching Konis' eye.

"Please," said Konis, relieved to be spared that answer.
"You were Kaid's sword-brother in those days, you knew
him better than anyone."

"As you said, Khas'ih Rakula, Kaid is a telepath, but
he'd suppressed it until he was with Khemu. He'd never
known another telepath before, and when their minds
touched . . ." He spread his hands expressively, leaving the
rest unsaid.

Chaidda gave a rumble of annoyance. "Too damned convenient," he said.

"Wasn't he one of the fosterlings with Nuddoh M'Zushi?" asked Mnae, tapping her stylus against her comp. "Big scandal about Nuddoh some thirty-odd years ago. Got himself killed, didn't he?"

Konis began to feel uncomfortable as he saw all eyes turn on him again. From the surprised look on Garras' face, he realized he couldn't pass this one over to him.

"Quite right," said Rhyasha smoothly. "He was found murdered, and thank Vartra he was! He'd been abusing the younglings in his care for years and no one knew a thing about it till then. Wouldn't you suppress your Talent if forced to live in circumstances like that?"

Mnae nodded. "Remember it well," she said. "Rhuna Dzaedoh got called in to help out. 'Course, didn't call himself Kaid back then, it was Tallinu. He was all set to become her apprentice then he up and left, just like that, the night Nuddoh was murdered. Was another three years before the Brothers found him and brought him back."

Konis could feel them scenting more of the scandal but was powerless to stop them now they were on the trail. Any attempt to do so would only make it worse.

"He killed Nuddoh?" asked Dzaio.

"It was never proved," said Rhyasha. "Charges against him were dropped. All that was a very long time ago, and it's his son, Dzaka, we're discussing."

Did he do it? Konis sent to his wife.

Of course he did! Wouldn't you if you found an adult male about to rape one of your fellow fosterlings? And he didn't just run off, he told Noni what he'd done before he left. He was in a bad way, too, according to the records.

How old was he?

Not much older than Kitra is now.

Had he been . . .

Sometimes, my dear, you are touchingly naive! she sent.

"What're you trying to tell us, Rhyasha? That Dzaka has as good a background as any of us here?" asked Khayle dryly.

"As far as I'm concerned, he has," she snapped back. "But no, I'm not. I'm reminding us all that this isn't the time or place for gossip!"

"Point taken," said Konis, seizing the opportunity. "A letter will be sent to the Arrazo Clan to invite Naeul's

successor to take over his place on the Council. My main
business today concerns the arranged marriages that our
heirs have to make as part of our breeding program."
While he was talking, he activated his comm unit, waiting
for the screen and keypad to raise itself from the concealed
recess in the table in front of him.

"If you'll look at your own comms, you'll be able to see
the data I've had assembled for you. Both graphs cover a
fifty-year span."

When everyone was ready, he continued. "As you can
see from the graph, despite our best efforts, the birthrate
of Talented cubs among the main Clan families is dropping." He looked up at them. "And before anyone asks,
yes, it takes into account those lost to the En'Shalla Clan.
So, our breeding program is no longer working. Now if you
look at this chart," he flipped to the next page, "you can
see that the intake at the Telepath Guildhouses on each
continent have gone up over the last fifty years. Which
leads me inevitably to the conclusion that we, in this room,
are breeding ourselves to the point of extinction." He
looked up again, taking advantage of the silence. "Either
we abandon the breeding program completely, or we must
introduce new blood into it."

"New blood?" exclaimed Lossa. "New blood? Do your
charts tell us how many of those telepaths outside the main
families are Grade Ones?"

"Almost as many as we've had recently," replied Konis.
"Our bloodlines have become too inbred. We must open
the program up if we want to survive."

"You're scare-mongering, Konis," said Chaidda. "Trying
to push through alien ideas under the guise of a crisis."

"You think so?" Konis's voice had an underlying purr
to it. "Out of forty-six cubs born to our generation here in
Kaeshala, our main continent, do you know how many were
either Grade One or Two Talents, Chaidda? Eight, that's
all. And six had no trainable Talent. Tell me now there
isn't a crisis! And remember, we've lost both Szurtha and
Khyaal. No telepaths from there to swell our numbers
any more."

Chaidda looked uncomfortable. "I thought there were
more than that," he said.

"I'll not have my younglings marrying outside our families," said Khayle firmly. "I don't hold with your new ideas, Konis. You're too ready to throw tradition to the winds these days."

"Depends what he's suggesting," said Mnae thoughtfully. "Cough it up, Konis. What you got for us?"

"I'd have thought better of you, Mnae," said Dzio, his eye ridges meeting in a frown. "You've always spoken up for the old ways."

"Seems to me the old ways aren't working right now," she said. "Been noticing that for myself lately." She reached for the jug of water in front of her and poured herself a glass. "Take this history thing, now, and all the Humans digging up Valtegan bones. Seems to me if we'd been able to talk more between the guilds, they might never have been needed. We'd have known our history all along. Guild secrets made us stronger in the past, but we have to become a community now, unless we want some of them new aliens that're joining the Alliance to take over our position at the head of the table. So tell us what you're suggesting, Konis." She raised the glass to her lips and took a sip.

It proved to be a long day, and one Konis had to fight hard to win, but win he did in the end. It was with relief he collapsed into his seat in the aircar he and Rhyasha were sharing with Garras.

Opening the locker beside him, he pulled out three containers of c'shar. Handing two to the others, he pulled the tab on his can, waiting for it to heat up before taking a sip.

"Gods, this tastes as foul as ever," he groaned as Mnesu took off.

"Still, it's over—till next time," sighed Rhyasha, leaning back against the seat, her can still unopened. "You got the changes pushed through, and backdated for those families that want their younglings to have a choice this time."

"I don't know how you cope," said Garras. "It would drive me mad doing this every two months!"

Konis looked over at him. "You'll get used to it," he said tiredly. "I'll be interested to see how Lijou intends to make eligible Brothers and Sisters available to our fragile Clan kitlings."

CHAPTER 13

It had taken Carrie a while to realize what was happening to her, but when the fever and the stomach cramps started, she knew. Would Kaid understand what it was? There were several people who could tell him. He'd find a way to get them together again, surely. If she called for the Primes and told them, they'd know their Achilles' heel. She had to let Kaid deal with it.

Sitting up, the covers wrapped around her, she tried to stay awake. With Kusac, she'd almost slept herself into the coma. Not this time, this time she was going to fight it. Nausea hit, making her run for the washbasin. She'd eaten nothing for nearly four days, so all it did was leave her throat and stomach feeling raw and painful.

Trembling, she returned to her bed just as the door opened. It was the Valtegan priest, and he was alone. She recognized him from Kaid's memories. The door closed behind him, sealing the guard outside.

"Come here," he ordered, his voice sharp and sibilant. "I wish to examine you."

"You're not supposed to be here," she said, releasing her hold on the covers so her hands were free. "Only the Primes are allowed in."

"Don't tell me what I can do. You're the captive, not me. Come here!"

"I'll call the guard." Under cover of the blankets, she began to slide her legs over the far side of the bed.

He came toward her, tongue flicking out, tasting the air, and her fear.

When she saw his skin begin to darken, she jumped to the floor, putting the bed between them. She knew the signs from the days when her sister worked in Geshader as a prostitute for the resistance. Too many times she'd seen what had gone on through Elise's eyes and experienced the pain and injuries they'd caused her while at the height of mating.

"You shouldn't be here," she repeated.

"Call out if you want," he said. "There's no one to hear you. The guard outside is mine. He does what I say."

With the speed of a striking snake, he lunged for her but she'd already moved. Hissing in anger, he came after her, catching her by the hair as she tried to dodge past him.

Screaming and clawing, she was jerked toward him. Her wrists grasped firmly in one of his hands, he took hold of her jaw in the other, pulling her face close. He started back in surprise as he saw her eyes. Vertical pupils—a hunter's eyes—glared back at him.

"Your eyes! Your sister didn't have eyes like those!"

She remembered him now! "I'm a mind-stealer, a telepath like the Sholans, J'koshuk," she said, voice roughened by fear and hate. "Touch me and you'll regret it. My sister laughed in your face, right until the moment she died. I'll do the same." Reaching out for his mind, she began to fill it with fear of her.

She didn't see the raised hand until too late. The blow stunned her, breaking her concentration. Dazed now, and weak from lack of food and the effects of Link deprivation, she could do nothing as he flung her down onto the bed.

"Your sister might have laughed at me, but you won't," he hissed, grasping hold of her sleeping robe.

Terror filled her, but on the edges of her mind, she felt the gestalt hovering. She reached for it, feeding it with all the energy she had left, and screamed for help.

Lying in his bed, terror exploded in Kaid's mind. He saw the hand descending, felt the blow to his face, and was suddenly caught up in the memory of the rape dream, watching as the male advanced on him again. He didn't need the warming of the crystal to tell him that this time, it was no dream.

His gasp of pain alerted T'Chebbi, who could only sit and watch in stunned horror as his cheek began to swell and a gash appeared on his forearm.

"Rezac!" she shouted, but the door burst open before she'd finished crying out.

Kaid gasped again, like a drowning man coming up for
air, then clutched at Rezac as he bent over him. "Help me
up!" The contact with Carrie had been brief, but it had
been enough to give him back some of the strength he'd
lost. He hauled on Rezac's arm, pulling himself into a sitting position.

Rezac caught Kaid's thought and nodded, helping him to
his feet. "I know," he said. "I felt it, too."

"What the hell are you doing?" demanded T'Chebbi.
"You're not going anywhere in that state! I sent for you
to help, Rezac, not make him worse!"

Kaid reached out and touched her face. "He is. I need
to call the Primes."

"You're not strong enough," said Rezac. "You'll collapse. Take some energy from me." He held out his hand.

Kaid looked at him, hesitating.

"You're wasting time," he said, grabbing Kaid's hand
himself.

The rush of energy made him briefly light-headed. He
staggered, to be caught by Rezac, then it was over. Turning,
he ran for the door, colliding with Manesh.

"There's an alarm going off outside," she said.

On the floor of his cell, Kusac felt the pull of the gestalt
as briefly, his mind was swept up with those of the other
two. As abruptly as it came, it was gone, but it left something behind. A glimmer of his Talent had returned. Not
much, but it was more than he'd had before. With it came
a cold fury that he knew could only be satisfied by killing
J'koshuk. In the distance, he heard the alarm begin to
sound.

Kaid hammered at the outer door, yelling for the Primes,
attempting to force his mind through the barrier to try and
contact Carrie again. T'Chebbi had come hurtling after him,
medikit at the ready to dress his wound, but it was ten
minutes before he'd accept that no one was coming and
gave up. Slumping against the wall, he finally let T'Chebbi
tend his wound.

"Just dress it," he said hoarsely.

She did as he asked. "What caused this?" she asked,
winding a bandage over the dressing.

"Later," said Rezac, touching her on the arm.

She turned her head to look up at him as behind them, the door opened. A Prime guard stood at the entrance, rifle held ready.

"The Seniormost wishes to see you," he said, pointing it at Kaid. "You will come with us."

Kaid got to his feet and stepped out into the corridor. Flanked by two guards, he was led down to the stasis room. A Seniormost and several more guards were waiting for him.

"I know my mate's been hurt. Take me to her now," he demanded.

"There has been an unfortunate incident."

"Just take me to her," he snarled, his hands clenching into fists at his sides.

"It was not due to us," the translator interrupted. "It was our Interface, the one called J'koshuk. He abused our trust and attacked the female. He has been punished."

A footfall from behind made him swing around but not before a hypo had been fired against his neck. It stung, and he resisted the impulse to rub it, reaching out for the Seniormost instead. He heard the sound of weapons being powered up and stopped dead, looking around the ring of guns trained on him.

"What the hell's going on?" he demanded, rounding on the Prime again. "Where is she? I want to see her!"

"It is for that you were brought," said the translator. The Seniormost indicated one of two doors in the opposite wall. "She is in there. You may take her with you. She was not thriving even before this incident. We intended her no harm."

"What?" He wasn't sure he'd heard right. He felt light-headed for a moment as their Link reestablished itself, then he knew what had happened. He'd been drugged, his Talent suppressed!

"Take her with you and return to your room."

Hesitantly, he began to walk toward the indicated door, then he ran. A low whimper of fear greeted him as he stepped inside. She was crouched in the far corner of the room, clutching a blanket.

She looked up, eyes filling with tears. "Tallinu?"

He was at her side instantly, lifting her up and wrapping what he could of the blanket around her.

"I have you now. You're coming with me." He turned and walked back to the stasis room, stopping in front of the Seniormost. "If I see J'koshuk again, he's dead. You understand?"

"You will not see him again," said a voice from behind him. "No harm was ever intended to you or any of your crew."

He turned, squinting to see the figure against the glare of the light. He thought he caught a flash of gold.

"Take your mate, Kaid. You and she will not be separated again, you have my word."

"Why are we here? Why haven't you released us?" he demanded.

An armored glove grasped his shoulder. "You will return now," said the translator as he was tugged around.

"Let us go! We've done nothing to warrant this treatment!" he shouted over his shoulder as they were led firmly from the room. "We were never your enemies!"

As he was let back into their suite, shocked exclamations greeted him. "T'Chebbi, get me the medikit," he said, pushing past everyone as he headed for their bedroom.

Once inside, he knelt down, placing Carrie carefully in his bed. She clung to her blanket when he tried to take it away.

"No! Leave me! I'm fine," she said fiercely. "I want to shower, that's all."

"Carrie, I need to see what he did to you," he said quietly. "I want to be sure your wounds are clean. Vartra knows what kind of infection you could catch." He knew she at least had an arm wound because he'd suffered it, too.

"No! I'm fine!"

The door opened and T'Chebbi came in, followed by Rezac.

Kaid frowned at him. "You're not needed, Rezac," he said, taking the kit from T'Chebbi.

"I can help her," Rezac said, coming over and squatting down a little distance from them. "Let me help, Kaid. I have more experience of this than you."

"What can you possibly . . . ." Kaid began.

"Listen to him," insisted T'Chebbi. "Go talk over there." She nodded toward the doorway.

Kaid's face froze, ears going into the sideward position of anger.

T'Chebbi leaned forward. "Talk," she insisted. "What's important here?"

Reluctantly, he got to his feet and accompanied Rezac to the door, keeping his eyes on Carrie all the while. "Well? Keep it short."

"I've helped Valtegan rape victims before, Kaid. I know what to do."

"What can you do that I can't?" he demanded.

"For a start, I'm not her mate. She doesn't want you to see her injuries. Don't forget Jo has gone through this. Between us, we can help her more than you can right now."

He stared at the younger male, saying nothing.

Rezac sighed. "Look, I know we've got a personality problem between us, but dammit, for once trust me! Let me get Jo."

"Leave him alone, Rezac, for the Gods' sake! He's got enough on his mind without you hovering round him," said Zashou from the hallway.

T'Chebbi exploded from the room, leaping up at Zashou and grabbing her by the neck of her tunic, pushing her back into the hallway. "Why you behave like this? Do you have to always be so jealous of Rezac? Some love yours is! Only thing between them is . . ."

"T'Chebbi, no!" Kaid called out angrily. "This isn't the time!"

She glowered at him over her shoulder. "Yes! No more *No, T'Chebbi!* You cause more trouble by saying nothing!" She turned back to Zashou, giving her a shake. "You want to know what's between them? I tell you, foolish kitling! Rezac is Kaid's father, that's what you sense!" She pushed Zashou back till she collided with the wall. "He's his father, and somehow Rezac senses it, that's why the bond. Now leave them and us alone!" Turning her back on her, she pushed past Kaid and Rezac, returning to Carrie's side.

"You're from the past, too?" Rezac asked, a dazed look on his face as pieces of the puzzle suddenly began to fall into place.

"I haven't got the time for this right now," said Kaid, turning away from him, but Rezac grabbed his arm.

"I need to know."

"Yes," he said, unwilling to look at him.

"That's why the questions about my past—about the female in Ranz."

"My mother died when I was two. A fever they said. I was sent to relatives and ended up with Vartra's people at the monastery."

"Vartra's fever," said Rezac in a numbed voice, his ears folding back in shock. "That's what killed her. She had psi abilities. We used the serum too soon, didn't know it wasn't stable enough. It killed a great many people."

"It was unstable because Vartra was using psi abilities he didn't know he had to bind the genes the way he wanted. Carrie noticed it. Her blood sample with our altered genes made it possible for him to correct the worst mistakes." Even though he hadn't known it, Vartra had shaped his life almost from the start.

"When you went back as an adult, you met your child-self."

Kaid nodded, still unwilling to catch his father's eyes. "I sent him—me—forward because I'd been brought up as a foundling in this time."

Rezac's ears righted themselves and he seemed to pull his scattered wits together. "Dzaedoh. That's my name, and yours, and explains the similarities between us. Hell, I'm just getting used to the idea of being a father. I don't need a son older than myself!"

Kaid looked up then. Noni's kin? He was Noni's kin? "You're a grandfather. I have a son. Dzaka. He's older than you are, too."

"Shit!" Rezac shook his head, grinning wryly. "I can see why you didn't want to tell me."

"T'Chebbi can see to me, Kaid," said Carrie from the other side of the room. "You and Rezac need to talk."

Kaid raised a questioning eye ridge at Rezac, who shook his head. "I'm through." He returned to her side, taking her face in both his hands, trying not to hurt her bruised cheek. "You'll follow my orders, Carrie. If you don't want me to help, you'll have Rezac and Jo. They can do more for you than I can right now. T'Chebbi can stay, if you wish."

She nodded, covering his hands with hers. "Stay close."

Leaning forward, he flicked his tongue gently across her cheek. "Of course. Where else would I be?"

He joined Rezac back at the door. "I'll fetch Jo, but remember, Carrie's pregnant, and we're only hours from our Link day," he said quietly.

Rezac reached out impulsively to touch Kaid's arm. "We'll be especially gentle with her," he promised.

Kaid sat outside the door in the corridor, feeling every touch as if it was happening to him. As each scratch was treated, he saw and felt not only the present pain, but the remembered pain of how it was inflicted. By the time Rezac came out, Kaid was fit to be tied.

"Did you have to be so rough?" he growled, but Rezac knew how to take him.

"I treated her like a newborn!" he protested. "Jo, too! Look, I can do more. I can make her forget it happened. It might be best for her."

"What does she say?"

Rezac sighed. "She says no."

"Then you have your answer. Are you done?"

"Yes, but, Kaid," he began, catching hold of him.

"What?" he asked, anxious to be with her.

"I know you said it's your Link day, but leave it as long as you can. Tomorrow would be best."

Kaid glowered at him, outraged. "What d'you think I am? Some thoughtless youngling?" he demanded.

"No, but you're new to Leska Links," he said candidly. "It isn't easy denying them for even an hour, let alone a day."

Kaid growled and shut the door firmly.

"How is she?" asked Tirak as soon as Jo and T'Chebbi rejoined the others in the main room.

"She'll be fine, physically" said Jo, as they headed over to the dispenser to get drinks. "I think they got to her pretty quickly. J'koshuk was known for his sadistic tendencies more than anything else."

"Mentally?"

Jo joined Tirak at his table. "She'll cope. Being strong-minded helps."

"Carrie's strong-minded for sure," agreed T'Chebbi as she sat down.

"And Kaid's wounds? Where did they come from?"

"Ah," said Jo, taking a sip of her drink and wondering how much to say. "Well, you could best describe them as sympathetic injuries. That isn't a normal occurrence even for us."

"Where's Rezac?" asked Sheeowl, looking around for him.

"Gone to see Zashou."

"Then all this time travel stuff really happened?"

"It happened, Captain," said T'Chebbi. "I was there when they left. Was their souls that went, their bodies remained. Got new bodies as they arrived in past."

Tirak stared at her.

"True," she insisted. "Was a religious ritual. Been done many times before. Except, they were the first to come back. Others just died."

Tirak made a noise deep in his throat. "Well, I hope she's all right. Damned shame they didn't find Kusac as well."

"I hope you're satisfied now," said Rezac, pacing back and forth in their room. "Thank the Gods neither I nor Kaid rose to your taunts. All you did was make yourself look extremely foolish."

"I know," she said quietly, examining her hands.

"T'Chebbi was right. You've made it quite clear you don't want me and wish our Link had never happened, so why must you keep following me around and intruding where you don't want to be in the first place? It's got to stop right now, Zashou."

"I'm sorry. I'll leave you alone."

He stopped in front of her. "You've gotten most of what you want now Jo's pregnant. My Link with her is stronger than ours, so you only need to have occasional Link days with me. Who knows? You may be lucky and our Links will stay as they are. You can have your own life, Zashou, like you always wanted. Just let me have mine."

"Yes, Rezac."

Surprised at her cooperative and subdued reaction, he

could only say, "Good," and leave before she changed her mind.

Once he'd gone, Zashou curled up unhappily in her bed. She wasn't used to rejection, and Rezac, for the first time since she'd met him, had just rejected her completely. She didn't like it, and didn't know how to deal with it. Why hadn't she listened to her own good advice when she'd first realized what she was doing?

* * *

Dzaka stirred. The noise had been faint but even in sleep he'd recognized it. Kashini. Still more asleep than awake, he staggered from his bed to her cot. When she saw him, she stood up unsteadily, her arms held out to him, and began to wail. Leaning down, he picked her up.

He knew that cry. He'd heard it the night her parents' ship had gone missing. She clung to him, fingers wound deep into his pelt, head resting on his shoulder against his neck, and sobbed. Holding her close, he returned with her to his own bed where he sat stroking her back rhythmically, making soothing noises.

"Hush, little one," he whispered, beginning to rock her gently. "I know. It's your Mamma again, isn't it? She'll be fine, don't you fret about her."

Gradually, the sobs stopped and she began to relax, sliding lower in his arms. He reached for the drawer in his night table, pulling out the small piece of her old blanket he kept there, and put it into her hands. It was grabbed instantly and she began to chew on it.

Yawning, Dzaka carefully edged his way into bed, cradling the drowsy cub till he could lay her down beside him. Curling protectively round her, he pulled the cover over them both and was almost instantly asleep.

* * *

Brynne woke more suddenly. Still caught by the dream of being attacked, he reached slowly under his pillow for the pistol he'd put there earlier. Keeza lay motionless beside him, deeply asleep. A movement against his other side sent fear racing through him till he realized it was Belle.

Mentally, he scanned the room. Empty apart from themselves. He ranged wider, to the rest of the house, then the garden beyond, but apart from Banner and Jurrel, nothing. He began to relax. No intruder was looking for Keeza.

He slid the pistol back, thinking through the dream, needing to be sure it wasn't more. It was the one he'd shared with Keeza, the one when she'd been attacked. There was something different about it this time, though, a flash of color where there'd been none before. Red. It had looked like red. He replayed it again in his mind, trying to remain detached, not get drawn into it. Yes, he had seen red, and more, a hand. If only it was like a vid and he could rewind and stop the images! Once more he endured it, watching this time for the image of a hand. It was there, and the sight of it burned into his mind, making him slide from the bed and grab his robe.

Stuffing his arms into the sleeves, he belted it as he ran down the stairs, heading for the den and his comm. Within moments, he was keying in the special code for Stronghold, the one reserved for the Brothers. He slid into his seat, waiting to be connected. The duty officer answered him.

"Brother Brynne. What can I do for you?"

"I need to speak urgently to Father Lijou."

The officer frowned. "It's early morning here, Brother. Father Lijou is likely eating right now, with Tutor Kha'Qwa. Is it that urgent? Perhaps his aide could help instead?"

"He'll want to hear what I've got to tell him," said Brynne grimly. "I'm under orders to report to him personally."

As soon as he was connected to the Guild Master, Brynne gave him his news. "The Valtegans have got them," he said. "I saw it. Another dream, vision, call it what you want, it's them."

"Are you sure?" demanded Lijou, ears pricking forward to catch every word.

"My Leska saw them on Keiss, Father. I know exactly what they look like. It's them, and they've at least got Carrie, probably Kusac and the others."

"Record the vision now, before you forget any details. I don't want to discuss this further over the comm. I'll join you tomorrow or the day after. Get Garras to sort some quarters out for me." The screen went black.

* * *

Kusac heard the door to his cell hiss open. The chill of the steel floor under him had sapped what strength he'd had left, leaving him too stiff to move. A strange mixture of scents wafted over to him, teasing his nose with their unfamiliarity as he tried to identify them. A pattering sound was coming toward him. He tried to open eyes that were gritty and swollen. Jerkily, he pulled his arm up and pawed at his face, hearing the pattering stop then hastily retreat.

A thrumming hum became audible, quickly turning into a burst of sound that was instantly recognizable as speech. He raised his head to look, catching sight of a cloud of strips of gauzy cloth amid which he could glimpse spindly bronze-colored legs.

"What the . . ."

A rifle coughed and something hit him hard at the juncture of his neck and shoulder. Before he could yelp in pain, his vision faded and his head hit the floor again.

"Conscious not you said!" the being hummed angrily, limbs and draperies moving continuously in agitation. "Place not again me at risk!"

"You should have waited," said the Seniormost's translator.

He made a sound of disapproval, mandibles making a small rattling noise as they quivered, but he began to settle down to stillness again. "Look now I will." Three-toed feet pattering on the floor, he stalked into the room, folding himself down to peer at the Sholan. Dark pupils swirling in the center of large oval eyes, he shifted his field of vision to the lower lens.

Three reed thin fingers touched Kusac's face, gently prodding at the swellings and cuts before moving lower to check the rest of his body. It was accomplished quickly, and finished, he stood up.

"Blame not this me for. Warned you I did of your priest. Not stable. Listen you didn't, results now here." He pointed to Kusac's still form.

"I did not ask you to implant him, Kzizysus. The experiment with the priest is terminated. He's being implanted now, Commander's orders."

"For Sholans not intended this device. Medical center

delivered have him." With that, the being stalked out in a swirl of draperies and scents.

Behind it, the Seniormost signed to the guards to pick up the body.

* * *

Day 33

"You asked for proof, Commander Chuz. It's there, in your hands," said Rhyaz.

"I didn't ask for proof, Rhyaz, what I said was if Shola faces a threat of that magnitude, the Forces will deal with it." He waved the piece of paper at Rhyaz. "I accept that finding this debris proves there is now a threat. What I need is the coordinates of your destination and this damned message of yours withholds it!"

"Obviously I'm aware of the location, Commander, but as I've said already, this is a Brotherhood matter and I will not divulge it."

"You seriously expect me to believe that your handful of people are capable of dealing with a ship able to not only disable the *Profit*, but remove it from that sector of space? Don't make me laugh!" snorted Chuz, slamming the message back on his desk.

"You're missing the point, Commander," said Rhyaz, beginning to get irritated. "We don't intend to stop it, except as a last resort. The point of us being there is to try to engage it in talks."

Chuz got to his feet. "Rhyaz, this whole conversation is ridiculous in the extreme," he said angrily. "You have neither the people, the craft, nor the experience to conduct such an undertaking. You're just a fancy version of the Warrior Guild with ideas beyond your capabilities. Now, I order you to give me the location immediately, or face charges of treason."

"I must refuse. This is a Brotherhood matter, Commander, and will remain one. We have the people, and the constitutional right to deal with it. I suggest you speak to the captains of your fleet in the immediate future to find out just how many operatives we have."

"Then you leave me no option but to arrest you for treason."

"I wouldn't do that, Chuz," said General Raiban softly. "Not a good idea at all."

Chuz glowered at her. "I just have. I'd have expected more support from you, Raiban! Dammit, we can't have unrecognized pseudo-military groups holding Shola and its appointed Forces to ransom!"

"Are you prepared to withdraw your accusations, Commander?" asked Rhyaz quietly, remaining seated.

"Not unless you're prepared to give me that location right now!"

"This is not wise, not wise at all, Rhyaz," said Raiban frowning. "You should have told Commander Chuz of your appointment first."

"It shouldn't make any difference, Raiban," said Rhyaz. "That's my point. Chuz, I'll ask you one last time, do you withdraw your accusations?"

"What appointment?" demanded Chuz, leaning toward him across his desk.

"Commander Rhyaz," she said, emphasizing his rank, "was appointed to the High Command last night by the decision of the World Council."

"Impossible! And he's not a commander! Self-conferred ranks don't mean anything here!"

"Chuz, for the Gods' sake, sit down and shut up before you dig yourself into a deeper pit," snapped Raiban. "Rhyaz, don't you . . ."

"Consider yourself Challenged as unfit to lead the High Command," said Rhyaz, drowning out Raiban. "On the grounds of your inability to assess the situation without a personal bias. Jorto, you've witnessed this."

In his corner at the rear of the room, the elderly Truthsayer stirred. "Witnessed, Commander Rhyaz."

"What?" Stunned, Chuz sat down. "You can't."

Raiban growled. "I warned you, Chuz. Rhyaz, you set this up, damn you!"

"Me, General? When you yourself warned Chuz to be careful of what he was saying, and I gave him two chances to retract it? I think not. Jorto, tell them about the World Council decision, if you please."

"The matter was first brought to the Council's attention

some two months ago at the request of Governor Nesul, to bring the Brotherhood in line with the other recognized military bodies on Shola and in space. The final discussion was scheduled for next week, but in view of the impending situation with the missing En'Shalla Brotherhood members, it was decided to reschedule it for last night. It was passed with an almost unanimous vote."

"As a High Command member, I have the right as an equal to Challenge you. And I have," said Rhyaz quietly. "However, I will give you an option. You may face a Brother of my choosing, of the same age as yourself, or you may step down voluntarily as President. The choice is yours. Either way, you will not ever repeat your allegations against myself or the En'Shalla Brotherhood."

"You can't do this," repeated Chuz, looking from one to the other of them.

"I'm afraid he can," said Raiban. "You knew he already had the backing of Konis, myself, and Naika at the last meeting, if he could produce proof. With his own vote he now has a majority. Before that, you had an even split on the Council, a clear indication his request should be taken seriously. You dug that pit yourself, and compounded it with allegations of treason and personal insults, Chuz."

"The Brotherhood was set up specifically to protect our people during the Cataclysm, a time of great civil unrest. We existed before even the Warrior Guild. We were the military backbone of Shola then," said Rhyaz. "Our constitutional role was to protect those deemed important to Shola. It's still our role. I told you this at our last meeting, showed you the entry pertaining to the Brotherhood in the transcripts of those first meetings setting up the guild system. You chose to ignore them. What's your choice, Chuz? The Challenge circle, or retirement as President?"

"You know there's no real choice," he growled. "I'll step down, dammit! I wondered what you were doing here, Raiban, now I know. You've gotten what you wanted, Rhyaz. Just remember, you'd better not fail, because if you do . . ."

"Chuz!" warned Raiban, thoroughly exasperated.

Rhyaz began to relax. He'd come prepared for anything from an armed takeover to his own rescue. Chuz had been President for many years, but they were facing less peaceful times. They needed someone younger and with a greater depth of vision to head the Council now.

"Your retirement as President is noted, Commander Chuz," said Jorto quietly. "As Second, all powers vested in the position of President are yours until a duly appointed successor has been elected, General Raiban."

Raiban got to her feet. "We've got work to do, Rhyaz. Chuz, I'll see you later," she said, heading for the door.

As they made their way down the corridor to Raiban's office, she glanced at him and at his escort of four Brothers and Jorto. "You came prepared. Just as well," she sighed.

"Had Chuz seen sense there would have been no need to force him to retire, Raiban," he said quietly. "As you said, he dug his own pit."

"So you're a commander, are you?"

"As head of the Warrior side of the Order, yes. Apart from the teaching staff, we don't hold a rank unless on a mission. We are only Brothers and Sisters, and the juniors in training."

She grunted. "Strange way to do things. Anyway, what is it you need?"

"A fighter carrier and three hundred fighters," he said, "plus the use of some troop transporters to get the Brothers to their ships. We've got everything else."

"Those decommissioned ships you've been buying up?" She shook her head. "If you won't give us the location, at least give me an idea of what sector you're in so I know how to plan our defense."

Rhyaz had always been prepared to give that information. "Between the Chemerian and Jalnian sectors. Far enough out from Shola to give you plenty of time and space," he said, mouth opening in a faint smile. "Should we fail."

"You can have the craft, and the crew to fly them because I know you don't have that many pilots," said Raiban, opening her office door. "I expect to be kept informed, Rhyaz. If you find them, you have two people empowered to negotiate at this preliminary level—Kaid Tallinu and Kusac Aldatan." She shut the door firmly on Jorto and Rhyaz's escort.

Rhyaz smiled gently to himself as he took a seat at Raiban's desk. "We'll be happy to take the crew we need,

Raiban," he said, knowing full well he had all the resources he needed. Once his people took charge of the craft, they'd be gone, leaving Raiban's crew behind them. Let Raiban think she would have spies in his camp, it would keep her quiet for now.

"I take it you'll have Kaid doing most of the talking."

"That's the plan," agreed Rhyaz. "Kusac will be consulted, as he is a member of AlRel."

Raiban raised an eye ridge as she activated her comm link to the main fleet. "He's qualified already?"

"Let's face it, Raiban, he has had a lot of experience in the field, so to say, with several different alien species. That was taken into account when the board examined him before he went to Jalna."

"Hmm. Well, let's hope you find them and manage to negotiate their release," she said.

* * *

Day 34

"I tell you, I'm going back there tonight!" The soldier slammed the blade of the spade into the grass, stamped on the edge and lifted out the clump of earth, flinging it on the small pile that lay behind him.

"Shut up, Fayal. The sergeant's around somewhere. He catches you talking like that and we'll all be grounded for the next month, never mind the next week!"

Fayal growled, standing back from the hole and leaning on his spade. "Let him! Think I'm going to let someone else move in on that little female I've been sweetening up for myself? Forget it, Vryal! You want to stay on the estate, your choice. Rraysa, what about you? You coming with me?"

Rraysa jammed the new post into the hole, then held his hand out for the hammer. Vryal passed it to him.

"I asked you if you were coming," repeated Fayal.

"No. This is my last day of this duty. I plan to keep it that way." He waited for Vryal to grab the post then began swinging the hammer, knocking it into the ground.

"Spineless, that's what you are," Fayal snorted derisively. "You change your minds, I'll be here at fourteenth hour."

"No way, not with those ferals you been feeding!" said Vryal. "Where are they, anyway? Thought they'd be out to complain at the noise we're making."

"They're there, all right," said Fayal. "Watching us from behind those bushes on the other side. Won't bother us when there's so many of us."

Rraysa glanced over the low fence before giving the hammer a final swing. "One day, those cats are going to get you for walking all over their territory."

"Not while I'm throwing them a nice chunk or three of raw meat," laughed Fayal, scooping a spadeful of soil up from his pile and dumping it round the base of the post.

"Hurry up, Fayal," said Rraysa, sticking his hammer through his belt. "I want to get back to the base as soon as we're through here."

"What for? To sit in the mess and drink c'shar? Spend the night watching vid comm?" He laughed again as he shoveled the remainder of the soil into the hole, then stamped on it to firm it down. "There," he said, moving out of the way. "Get on with it, then. Don't want that c'shar to get cold, do we?"

Vryal began hauling the mesh back across the gap to the new post while Rraysa dug in one of his pockets for the staples to secure it. Within minutes they were finished and heading along the cleared area around the fence to the old gate track that led to the main estate.

* * *

Brynne was waiting with Garras and Vanna when Father Lijou arrived. He'd left Banner and Jurrel keeping Keeza company. Half an hour later, they were entering Brynne's home.

"I want to know all the details," said Lijou, as he and Vanna were ushered into the den at the rear of the house to join Jurrel.

Upstairs, Keeza heard their voices and felt a stir of memory. Excusing herself from Banner's company, she returned to her own room where she lay down on the bed.

She'd heard the voice before, but where, and when? Fear that her new world, still so very fragile, was under threat again, filled her. She curled up, closing her eyes, wondering how much longer she'd have to endure the slow drip of returning memories.

"A red-robed Valtegan," said Vanna thoughtfully. "We saw none like that. Most wore the one-piece fatigues like the Humans. Green ones. Red robes, though. Suggests someone important, some officer."

"Priest?" asked Jurrel. "Priests always wear robes when on official duties."

"Trouble is, we've got all our Valtegan experts off-world," said Lijou. "This must never happen again. Can you remember anything more, Vanna?"

She shook her head. "Father Lijou, you're asking me to go back a long time."

"They probably weren't on Keiss when you were there," said Brynne. "They were off killing the settlers on our two colony worlds."

"That's true. If this one went with General M'ezozakk, then he's definitely someone of importance. What did you say he was doing in this vision?" she asked.

"I didn't. He was attacking Carrie," said Brynne.

"Attacking her? How?"

"Sexually," said Brynne grimly. "He knew her as far as I could tell."

"Oh, Gods! Not that!" said Vanna, shocked. "Didn't anyone stop him?"

"I didn't see enough for that," said Brynne, putting his hand over hers. "Just think. Who among the Valtegans knew her?"

"No one! Her sister was another matter . . . That's it! He must have known her sister, Elise!"

"Elise?" asked Jurrel.

"Her twin. She worked undercover for the Human guerrillas in the city of Geshader as a prostitute to the Valtegan officers."

"Wasn't she caught and tortured?" asked Lijou. "I seem to remember reading it in some files not long after Carrie arrived here."

"Yes. She was. Can you access those files from here? Perhaps what we need is in them," said Vanna.

"The comm is over there," said Brynne, pointing to his desk. "Please, help yourself."

It took only some ten minutes before Lijou found what

they wanted. "The red-robed priest was the torturer," he said, turning back to them. "May Vartra protect them if they're with him. Now we know the nature of the threat."

"Hold on," said Vanna. "Not so fast. We're forgetting something here. Carrie was put into cryo with a serious injury. How can she possibly be in any fit state for even a Valtegan to rape her? I didn't see any evidence on Keiss that the Valtegans were capable of performing that kind of surgery on Humans, let alone had drugs like fastheal to accelerate healing."

"You're right," said Brynne, thinking it through. "That's what the dreams of the tiled room and the bright lights were. But the priest was definitely present last night."

"If not the Valtegans, then who?" asked Jurrel. "Who would let one of them have access to her?"

"More Valtegans," said Lijou, feeling a chill run through him as he remembered what Rhyaz had said about the wreckage that had been found and the traces of ships' signatures. There had been two others as well as those of the *Profit.*

"More?" asked Vanna.

"We have confidential information to that effect."

"How many more? More ships? Their world? What?"

"I'm not at liberty to say," said Lijou, tight-lipped. "I want to go through all your dreams again, Brynne. Vanna, nothing you hear in this room, or pick up from Brynne, is to go any further. I need a Leska pair working for the Brotherhood at Stronghold for the foreseeable future. They must leave immediately. Can you get Garras to allocate us a team? Reliable, stable people, those with the longest mental reach."

"Tamghi and Kora," she said instantly. "What's up with Vriuzu? Is he ill?"

"He has duties elsewhere," said Lijou. "Please see to it immediately."

"You're on alert as of now," he said to Brynne and Jurrel once she'd gone. "I'd hoped to avoid involving you, Brynne, but it seems we may have no choice. Whatever took the *Rryuk's Profit,* and it looks likely that it involves Valtegans, has Brothers and Sisters capable of giving them the location of Shola. We could be facing a Valtegan invasion."

"Have you told High Command?" asked Jurrel.

"High Command has given us the authority to deal with aspects of the situation," said Lijou carefully. "As of yesterday, the Brotherhood is now a member of that council. Vartra warned us to mobilize our people, and we have done so."

"I thought the halls were a little empty of late," murmured Jurrel.

"Your visions are our best source of information, Brynne. More, you have an open invitation to visit Vartra. I need you to dream-walk to His realm today to see what more He can tell you."

Brynne nodded. "I forgot to mention Dzaka told me Kashini woke again the same night I had my dream."

"Let's pray the cub is only aware of danger and not actually seeing what's happening to her parents. I need to contact Master Rhyaz and update him," Lijou said, turning back to the comm.

* * *

Crouched on the tree branch, Kezule could see the fence for twenty feet on either side of the disused gate. The night was hot, the air alive with the chirring of insects. Nearby, the ferals roamed, leaping over the low fence at will yet never triggering an alarm from the sensor grid.

Earlier in the evening, after he saw the one called Fayal jump the fence and leave for the town, he'd tried throwing a stone through. No response. It was as if there existed a dead spot that the alarm system couldn't—or wouldn't—pick up. Having watched the ferals, he thought knew why. For most species, they were deterrent enough. Not for him. All he had to do was emit the right scent and they'd be gone. He'd had to use it before when he'd disturbed a nesting pair with young. Fear of them had given way to anger at the thought he'd come all this way, survived the Sholans' hunt, only to be torn to pieces by feral cats! His anger scent had had them squalling in terror and running for cover.

He looked up at the moon overhead. Only one tonight, and that on the wane. By his reckoning, it had been six hours since Fayal had gone out. Soon he should be back.

Though almost convinced the sensors were permanently disabled at this point, he wasn't prepared to take the risk. Far safer to wait for this Fayal to return and enter just behind him. And if the Sholan did sense him, then who would wonder at the ferals turning on him? Shifting uncomfortably, he eased his limbs a fraction, then settled down again, watching and waiting. He was going in tonight, one way or another. Two days he'd been sitting watching this place, ever since he'd seen the ferals leaping in and out without setting off the alarms. Now, at last, it had paid off.

When Fayal finally came, the noise of his approach was audible for several minutes. A soldier of this caliber disgusted Kezule. This was not a warrior, merely a drunk dressed up in a uniform. Had one of his troops behaved in such a way, he'd have been terminated immediately. But then, he reminded himself, this one was a lesser being, not worthy of recognition as a person.

Fayal emerged staggering from the overgrown pathway. Seeing the fence, he pulled himself upright, took a deep breath, and began to advance toward it more carefully.

"Mustn't forget the ferries," he muttered, stopping almost beneath Kezule's hiding place to dig deep in his uniform jacket pocket. "Where did I put it? Wouldn't think you could lose bits of chiddoe in a pocket! Ah, there you are," he said cheerfully, pulling a sealed container out. With great deliberation, he began to open it.

Kezule was also keeping an eye on the ferals. Unnoticed by Fayal, the larger female had been laying in wait for him and was now cautiously emerging from the undergrowth. Belly flat to the ground, tail extended behind her flicking lazily at the tip, she inched her way toward the drunken Sholan.

Fayal, meanwhile, had pulled one of the bloody gobbets of meat from his container and was peering around, looking for the ferals.

"Here, ferrie, ferrie," he chanted, waving the piece of meat in the air.

The scent of the blood was enough for the large feline. It leaped at the Sholan, hitting him square in the chest and bringing him down to the ground.

Fayal's cry of terror was drowned out by the cat's snarl as, dodging his flailing arms, it lunged for the meat. Its jaws closed on Fayal's arm instead and suddenly, both were fighting for their lives.

The commotion brought the male and the two half-grown cubs running to join in the fray. Within moments, the fight was over and the feeding frenzy had begun.

The feral's leap had thrown Fayal some six feet from the tree trunk. Now the cats were pulling and tugging the body around, snarling and snapping at each other. The sight sickened Kezule. His people eliminated any predator likely to threaten them as a matter of policy. To see a sentient being devoured by such animals, even if there was a rough justice to it, was not pleasant.

He remembered why he was there. Now, while the ferals were occupied, would be the safest time to go—he hoped. He stood up, and gripping the trunk with his claws, stepped onto the next thick branch, taking himself farther from the felines. If he crawled along it to the middle before dropping to the ground, it gave him the shortest distance to the fence. Once there, he could make for the tree he'd spotted during daylight. It had several limbs low enough for him to leap up and grab hold of. The ferals could climb trees, but he doubted they'd be willing to leave that much meat to come after him.

Cautiously he edged along the branch, squatting at the farthest point that would bear his weight. He waited for his moment, eyes never leaving the ferals as they ripped and tore at what to them was only a carcass. He sprang, jumping outward, landing only a few feet from the fence. Clearing it in one bound, he raced for the tree, having a moment's panic as he briefly lost his bearings. Then he was jumping for the branch, legs swinging in midair as he scrabbled with his claws for a hold. He could feel their hot breath on his legs, he knew he could, then he was up and clutching tightly to the branch.

Heart pounding, he looked over the edge. The ferals were where he'd left them, though the female was looking in his direction, sniffing the air and snarling. He shivered, then very slowly, edged back along the branch till he reached the bole of the tree. Leaning back against the trunk, he paused to catch his breath. He was in, and he was alive. Now he had to move on, just in case the alarm had been triggered.

* * *

Day 35

Master Rhyaz got to his feet as L'Seuli entered his office. The younger male looked tired and drawn.

"Master Rhyaz," he said, touching his right fist to his left shoulder in salute. "You asked me to report as soon as I got back."

"Finished so soon, L'Seuli? I really didn't expect you for another two days at the earliest."

"I knew the matter was urgent, Master Rhyaz. The outpost jump points are far faster than the normal routes, especially in *Striker.*"

"Sit down and make your report, then, Commander," he said, gesturing to the chair by his desk.

"Thank you," said L'Seuli, accepting the seat gratefully. "All four outposts are fully manned and ready, with provision made to accept the extra designated craft when the time comes. Training missions for flight and gunnery crews have already been implemented and morale is high. The commanders are aware of the possibility of incoming signals or telepathic messages from our missing personnel, and the likelihood of pursuit. Or possibly, of invasion."

Rhyaz nodded. "Well done. I've had similar reports in from our agents in the Forces. Those Brothers and Sisters who could not be recalled under some pretext are ready to leave immediately they get the word. Transport will be arranged from each sector to take them to Refuge, ready to crew the *Va'Khoi.* What's her current status?"

"My visit to Refuge took an extra day," said L'Seuli. "I took the time to inspect the *Va'Khoi* thoroughly. They're still working on the main drive problem but as for the rest, the ship's up and running. As you know, the refit should have been completed by your predecessor, Ghezu, but he decided to scale down the work. Our people have done extremely well in the short time they've had."

"Let's hope Ghezu's delay doesn't cost us dearly," said Rhyaz. "How long till she's fully operational?"

L'Seuli consulted his wrist comm. "Should be ready in a day or two if she isn't ready now," he said. "Captain

T'Chaku said if she had a Toubian swarm, she'd have been ready two weeks ago."

"You know we couldn't reveal we have these resources," said Rhyaz with a sigh. "If we'd been able to call in a swarm, we'd have been ready four years ago! When do they plan to test the *Va'Khoi*?"

"As soon as the drive is on-line and they get the go ahead from you. They have enough of a crew to man her for that, thankfully. The comp simulations looked good."

"I'll contact Captain T'Chaku tonight. Thank you, L'Seuli. Go and rouse the kitchen for something to eat, then get some rest. I'll hear the remainder of your report tomorrow."

L'Seuli began unfastening the gold commander's insignia as he got to his feet.

Rhyaz frowned as he realized what his aide was doing. "Keep the rank for now, L'Seuli. When this finally breaks, I want you out there organizing security for the exchange of hostages."

"As you wish, Master Rhyaz," murmured L'Seuli, taking his leave.

* * *

Day 36

It was late afternoon of the next day before Brynne and Father Lijou were ensconced in one of the rooms at the Shrine with the meditation lamp.

"I'll watch you as before," said Lijou, arranging himself comfortably on the prayer mat.

Brynne nodded and began to recite the litanies that would allow him to slip into a light trance. He was still somewhat nervous and Lijou picked it up.

"There is nothing for you to fear, Brynne. As I've told you, you have Vartra's invitation to travel to His realm."

Vartra was not alone. Noni was with him, but it wasn't the Noni Brynne knew. This one was younger. The pelt and long, braided hair were no longer snow white but a rich brown; her back was straighter and she had no need of the stick.

"What you doing here, boy?" she demanded of him as Vartra let him into his cottage. She turned on the Entity, who, totally unperturbed, went for the jug of water and mugs on the sideboard. "He shouldn't be here!"

"I told you not to interfere, Noni," Vartra said, returning to the table. "Sit, Brynne. You're welcome here. Noni was leaving."

She frowned. "I was, was I?"

"You were. Our business is concluded, Grandmother."

"Who brought him to you? Was it that tree-climbing, good for nothing Dhaika?"

As Brynne took a seat as far from her as possible, he could tell that though her outward form might have changed, she had not.

"I did. You asked for the price to be paid, Noni," said Vartra, holding her gaze with his. "It will be. Our way. And he is part of it."

Muttering under her breath, Noni got to her feet and turned to leave. As she went through the door, she looked back, fixing a steely glare on Brynne. "You, boy, did not see me here." Then she was gone.

"A strong female," said Vartra as the door closed behind her. "I will miss her when her time comes." He looked up at Brynne. "No, it's not soon," he said, mouth opening in a slight smile. "She stands for the old, wild ways of Shola, before the days of the guilds. Soon she will bring Teusi, the next generation, to me—a male for a female." He sighed, then picked up the jug to pour water into the two mugs.

"What brings you to my realm, Brynne Stevens? I see you have found Keeza Lassah." He pushed a mug toward Brynne, picking up his own. "And a cub on the way, too." He raised his mug to the Human before drinking.

Brynne picked up his drink. "You know about her?" He sipped the water. "Stupid question, really."

"She has her part to play."

"Did you send her to me? She said she followed a dream of Noni's garden and the smell of her nung tree."

"Not me. Perhaps Ghyakulla had a little to do with it."

"Tell me how come I feel her in my mind when I already have a Leska and a third," Brynne asked abruptly. "Garras is no telepath, is that why Keeza and I have a bond?" He took another drink from the mug, a larger one this time.

"There are no set groupings for you En'Shallans. What you are experiencing is the beginnings of something new. A community of people, all bound together by their Talents, be they great or small. Not in your lifetime, Brynne, but it'll be there for your children. You haven't told me yet why you came," he said gently.

Brynne blinked owlishly at him. He was finding it difficult to focus on his surroundings and was beginning to feel a little light-headed. He took another drink, then stopped, looking suspiciously at the mug before carefully putting it down. "Father Lijou sent me to ask what's going on," he said. "We know the Valtegans have got them, but we don't know why or which ones."

"Then you know more than I do. My knowledge is limited outside my realm, Brynne, as is the help I can give."

"What is your realm?"

"Look around you," invited Vartra. "What do you see?"

Gazing around the room, he peered through the haze gathering in front of his eyes. Images of gray-clad Sholans, weapons drawn, facing off an unseen enemy flicked into being: the blackness of space, sounds of conflict, and the scent of ozone in the air after energy weapons had been discharged.

"Then you've seen what's coming for yourself," he heard Vartra say as the scenes faded to darkness. "Danger lurks closer to home for some. You have to solve your own problems, Brynne. Use the skills Derwent taught you, then you can see without drinking the water from Ghyakulla's well."

The voice was fading now, leaving Brynne in darkness and silence as his head slumped down to hit the table.

With a gasp, Brynne came to and found himself back in the Shrine with Father Lijou helping him sit up. There was a mug of water in the priest's hand for him. He groaned, pushing the proffered drink aside as, inside his mind, he heard the faint sound of laughter.

"I hate it when He does that," muttered Brynne, putting his hand up to rub his head.

"What?" asked Lijou.

"Laughs like that."

"Kaid always said it was the most disconcerting thing about his visions," agreed the priest.

"That is only water, isn't it?"

Lijou frowned. "Of course."

"Good," he said, taking the mug from him and draining it. "Because I just got slipped a spiked drink by Vartra."

"You saw something then?"

"Yes. Armed Brothers in space."

"Where? Could you see where?"

"I don't know anything about space, Father Lijou. I wouldn't recognize the inside of a starship from a space station. It didn't look like all-out war, though. They were in a ship or a station, not fighting in small craft."

"Contact."

"Yeah, you could say that," he agreed, considering it for a moment. "He told me to use the stuff Derwent taught me rather than go drinking water from His well again."

Lijou looked at him expectantly.

"Maybe it's time I told you what Derwent taught me," Brynne said with a sigh. "One of the things I can do is go and look at a distant place, provided either there is someone there I know, or I have some information about where I'm going. It's as if I'm actually there."

"How far can you travel like this?" This wasn't new. Carrie and Kusac had done it before.

He shrugged. "Distance didn't seem to matter when we tried it. I could visit places back on Earth."

Lijou stared at him. "You could travel to where Kusac and Carrie are," he said. "Find out what's happening. Can you talk to people? Affect your surroundings at all?"

"I'm just an observer as far as I know."

Lijou's wrist comm buzzed, alerting him to an incoming call. He pressed receive and found Rhyaz' face looking at him.

"I'm with Brynne at the Shrine," he said.

"Call me back," said Rhyaz, signing off abruptly.

Lijou looked up at Brynne. "You'll have to excuse me. I'll meet you back at your house. You're fit to return on your own?"

Brynne nodded, getting to his feet. "Just tired," he said.

CHAPTER 14

Kaid had woken early, relieved, despite the Prime's assurances, to find Carrie curled against him still asleep. In the three nights she'd been back, this was her first restful sleep without nightmares. He hadn't been sure how best to help her. With T'Chebbi, it had been easier. She'd been kept prisoner by the Claws for several months before he was able to escape Stronghold and go back to Ranz for her. Then they were running for their lives; there was no time to stop and worry about anything else. He'd taken her to Noni, where the Brothers had been waiting for him. The repercussions of his illicit leave of absence had seen him incarcerated for several weeks before he was allowed to visit Noni again to see her.

His own experiences at the hands of his foster father weren't much help either, except he'd once been where she now was.

When he'd finally been allowed back into his room, Carrie had been sitting in his bed, wearing his gray tunic. She'd looked up as he'd entered.

"Before you ask, I'm all right," she said, but despite the fierce determination in her voice and mind, he could tell she wasn't.

He came closer, sitting on the edge of T'Chebbi's bed. "I'm not much of a bodyguard, am I?" he said, reaching out to touch her bruised cheek with gentile fingertips.

She flinched, then forced herself to remain still, but he dropped his hand without touching her.

"I tried to make them come for me but we rarely see the Primes. I'm sorry."

"It wasn't your fault," she said, hands clutching at the blanket wrapped over her legs. "It was because of Elise. She laughed at him."

He was at a loss to know what to do or say, and couldn't sense much from their Link as she was blocking her emotions from him—just as he was from her. "Can I do anything?" he asked. "Get you anything?"

She looked at him, eyes glittering too brightly in the artificial light. "Yes. You can hold me. I'm not made of glass."

"I didn't want to touch you without knowing I could," he said, going down on his knees to wrap his arms carefully round her. She was so fragile and brittle right now, he was afraid she'd break.

He felt her begin to shake and held her closer as sobs began to wrack her. "It's over," he said awkwardly, pulling her head down onto his shoulder.

"Just tell me you still love me," she wept. "That you don't hate me. I need to hear you say it, even if it's a lie!"

"Gods, no!" He was shocked she could even think that. "How could I ever hate you?" He turned her tear-soaked face to his. "I love you, Carrie. You're my life." He touched his lips to hers, meaning it to be only a gentle kiss, but she returned it frantically, her hands reaching for his face, twining themselves in his long hair. Her mental barriers broke then, and he felt her fear of his rejection, the beginnings of self-loathing that she'd let this happen to her.

It wasn't your fault, he sent. *How could you have stopped him? He's physically stronger even than us. And how could I ever reject you because of it? You mustn't blame or hate yourself.* He broke the kiss then, climbing into the bed beside her.

She leaned against him, rubbing her eyes as the sobs began to diminish. "Just hold me," she whispered, wrapping her arms around his chest. "I need to feel you close. I don't want to be alone."

He did, holding her close even when she drifted off

to sleep, remembering the first time he'd held her, pregnant and sobbing then with fear of the alien cub she carried. A short time later, she'd woken with a cry of horror at the first of the nightmares.

Reaching out, he gently touched the skin around the livid bruises on her side. Anger filled him, and a desire to rip J'koshuk limb from limb with his bare hands. His mind was suddenly made up. If they were all here this morning, they were leaving.

She stirred, turning round till she faced him. "We have to find Kusac first," she said, opening her eyes and looking up at him. "I felt him, Tallinu. Felt his mind and yours when I used the gestalt."

"He's not here, Carrie," he said in Highland, stroking her face. "They only found you."

"They lied about me, they're lying about Kusac. I smelled his scent on J'koshuk."

"I didn't feel him, Dzinae," he said gently. "As for his scent, the mind can play funny tricks on you at times like that. I know."

A puzzled look crossed her face, followed by one of understanding. "Oh, no, not you," she said, catching hold of his hand. "Yet you still sent your child-self forward to our time. How could you do it, knowing what you faced?"

"It happens," he said. "I did it because I knew the future held you. Memories of what we'd share made me stronger, helped me survive those years."

"Like you've helped me so many times," she said, kissing his fingers. "But I did sense Kusac. He's here and he's alive. I know he's not dead."

"I felt your mind when they woke you, Carrie. I'd have felt him, too. How could you and I be Leska Linked if he was alive and out of cryo?"

She closed her eyes, leaning her forehead against his chest. "I don't know. Maybe we Linked because you were there and he wasn't."

"We can't stay here any longer, Carrie. They keep taking us, in pairs, when we're asleep. Jo's pregnant, you are, and Kate will be soon, if she isn't already. We have to go now before they separate us again."

"You think they're breeding us? Why? Why would they want to do that?"

"You know why. They've been studying our Talent. Giyesh heard them saying they implanted the Valtegans from M'ezozakk's crew to make them more docile. Think what a troop of tame telepaths could do for them. I won't live in slavery, Carrie, and I don't want our child born into it." He tried not to sound forceful, but he was determined that they wouldn't remain any longer. "We've got to get home and warn them."

"You and Tirak are prepared to have us die rather than live in captivity, aren't you?"

"Do you want to live here and have your mind controlled and your body abused again?" This time he was being almost brutal. He had to make her realize that remaining wasn't an option.

"But he's here," she whispered, clutching the long fur on his chest. "We can't leave without him!"

"Then you'll have to choose, Carrie," he said, his voice becoming tight. "Are you willing to risk your life, our cub's, and mine, on the faint chance that Kusac is on this vessel? What about Kashini and your fears she's in danger? More people than Kusac depend on you right now. If you stay, then I've no choice but to remain. If that happens, the others probably won't make it, and Shola itself will be in danger."

"That's not fair, Tallinu." Her eyes began to fill with tears.

"What you're doing isn't fair," he said, holding her closer. "You're working on emotions here, not logic. You know how much I love Kusac. Gods, if I believed he was here, I'd do my utmost to find him!"

She was silent for a minute, remembering Khuushoi's warning. "I don't have a choice. I'll go with you," she said quietly.

"Remember Winter's kiss," whispered Kaid, sharing her memory. "When they woke you the second time, I heard that in my mind. Vartra told me the Entities couldn't come this far from Shola."

"Khuushoi said it was because I was in Her realm." She shivered.

"I know how afraid of cryo you are, but we had no

choice," said Kaid, wrapping himself and the covers round her to warm her. "You would have died of your wounds before we could reach the rendezvous."

"I'm not afraid of it, exactly. It's because I'm aware when I shouldn't be. My mind was still functioning on some strange level. At one point it was as if I was floating over Shola. That's when I saw the danger to Kashini."

"The greenness creeping toward the estate."

"I've seen that green before. It was a sharp, bright color, like the la'quo resin. And like J'koshuk's skin," she said slowly, "when he touched me."

"Why green? It isn't the color of danger, unless . . ."

"Unless it's to do with the Valtegans," finished Carrie, pushing him back to see his face clearly. "Kezule. He's the threat."

"How? He's at Shanagi, under the tightest security."

"He's gotten out, I know he has!"

"That's impossible," he said. "And even if he had, why would he head for the estate? He'd be more likely to go for the spaceport and try to get off Shola."

"No, he'd want to go back to his own time. He'd head for us, not knowing we're off-world."

He could feel the rising hysteria in her mind. "Enough Carrie. He doesn't know where we live."

"If he escaped, he could easily find out! When he finds we're missing, he's going to take Kashini! We've got to get back, Tallinu! Now! That's the choice Khuushoi meant!" She tried to push him aside in an effort to get up from the bed but he held her tight, preventing her.

"No. Calm down," he said firmly. "You're overreacting. First, we're leaving today, remember? I was the one persuading you of that. Second, if you're not calm and focused on what we're doing, it'll affect me and we'll fail. I'm dependent on you now, Carrie. I can't do my job if you're there, in my mind, panicking. Remember what you are, a Sister in the Brotherhood. Don't let me down."

He felt her stop and face the fear. As it began to recede, she nodded slowly. "You're right. We've one chance. Worrying about what's happening back home won't get us there any sooner."

He stroked her cheek, wondering if they'd see another night together. Now came the really hard part. "We've planned this escape during the weeks we've been here. I need to include you now, tell you what to do. We work well with the U'Churians, but when it comes to this, I know I can rely on you and T'Chebbi. We've got to get at least one person off this ship. If the rest of us don't make it, we have to survive long enough to kill our own people. There's another Leska pair, Kate and Taynar, and Rezac's formed a Triad with Jo. We only need to kill one of each group and the others will die. Same with us." He waited, hoping that she'd be strong enough to know this had to be faced and discussed.

"I'll make sure I dodge the enemy better this time," she said with a lopsided grin. "Don't let anyone else but you—do it—if the time comes."

"I won't," he said, gripping her tightly and kissing her, letting her feel how much he needed and loved her, and prayed they'd survive.

Introductions over, under the cover of first meal, Kaid and Tirak briefed them all again on what they planned to do.

"We're going to try and escape using bits of broken furniture against those armored Primes?" asked Zashou, looking from Tirak to Kaid. "We'll be like bugs against them!"

"We only need one guard, then we've got two weapons," said Kaid. "They each have a rifle and a sidearm."

"Manesh, round up the knives you've been adapting," said Tirak in a low voice. "Sheeowl, you and Giyesh loosen the faucet taps. I'll tell you when to disconnect them."

"Taynar, help Kate. Jo and Zashou dismantle drawer units for planks. T'Chebbi, you and Jeran get all the liquid soap containers."

"We get ours," said Annuur through his translator. "Also berry stones. Lots of them. On ground, make Primes fall."

Kaid grinned and reached out to pat the Cabbaran leader on the shoulder. "Well thought out. Keep some back for throwing at their heads, too. It'll distract them just long enough for us to get in close."

Annuur's prehensile lip wrinkled back in a grin. "They fall hard. We jump on them and chew through armor. Already spotted places."

"Guns first," reminded Kaid. "With them we can keep those guards down. Helmets next to stop them communicating with each other."

"Soap?" asked Carrie.

"Cover faceplates," said T'Chebbi. "Squirt in breather grilles. Stops them communicating with each other." She grinned evilly, showing her teeth. "Makes them feel sick!"

"Put some water in the containers first," Carrie advised. "More suds."

T'Chebbi continued grinning. "Know that, don't worry."

"What am I doing?" asked Rezac.

"Helping me dig a hole through the wall to the door controls," said Kaid, getting up. "I want you to try using some of those psi tricks you showed me. Annuur, can your people grip the door when we're ready to try pulling it open?"

The Cabbaran nodded, the crest of hair on his head bobbing with enthusiasm. He held his hands up, showing his long, thick claws. "Can dig into door, too."

"The rest of you can gather round us, hiding us from any surveillance devices," said Tirak.

"Let's move it. The longer we take, the more chance of them noticing what we're doing," said Kaid.

"What can I do?" asked Carrie, catching hold of his hand and drawing his attention to her.

"Help us with the wall," said Kaid, gripping her hand briefly. "Just use whatever psi abilities you think will work. You've done amazing things in the past."

"Don't know that I've any rabbits left to pull out," she murmured, getting to her feet.

Kaid's brow wrinkled in thought over her reference, then the meaning came to him. "You never know till you try," he said.

The wall, being a partition rather than one of the structural ones, was made of some lightweight plastic compound. Using a fork with all but one tine bent back, they were quickly able to stab their way into it, then use a knife to snap out larger chunks. Underneath the thin outer skin they discovered a softer expanded foam center. In the midst of this nestled the metal casing for the door mechanism.

"The back plate's riveted on," said Tirak in disgust.

"Let me." Rezac pushed forward to see it. "I'm not as good as Jaisa was, but I can try shaking it free," he offered.

"Try," ordered Kaid, glancing at his comm unit. Ten minutes they'd taken so far. Too long.

Rezac reached inside, putting his fingers on three of the rivets, and closed his eyes in concentration. Within moments, Carrie laid her hand on his shoulder, making him start and turn round.

I can help, she sent.

He nodded and began again.

Kaid watched with interest, feeling it for himself because of his Link with her, adding a little to the help Carrie was giving Rezac. Slowly Rezac began to draw his fingers back and as he did, the plate suddenly pivoted down, hanging from one rivet.

Rezac let go, leaning against the wall for support while Carrie continued to hold his shoulder. Gradually the paleness around his nose faded and he nodded his thanks, moving out from under her hand. "Don't weaken yourself," he warned her.

Meanwhile Tirak had grasped the plate, carefully easing it free to expose the tangle of wires and circuits.

Kaid took Tirak's place. He was seeing the mechanism in reverse. What he had to decide now was whether to try and pull the whole unit inside and betray the fact that they were tampering with it, or try to activate it from this angle.

As he looked at it, a small light began to glow, flicking from point to point, across the access side of the panel. "Someone's coming!" he hissed, turning round and pushing Carrie behind him.

The group providing cover scattered, leaving Rezac at the other side as the door slid open.

Knowing the Primes stood just at the edge of the doorway, Kaid reached round and grabbed hold of an armor-clad arm. Using his weight as a pivot, he hauled the person into the room. Tirak grabbed hold as well, added his strength and weight, and the Prime was dragged in to smack, faceplate first, against the wall. As Kaid reached for the sidearm, Annuur and his fellow Cabbarans leaped on the staggering Prime, bearing him to the ground.

Kaid spun round and pointed the gun at the other Primes as Rezac and Tirak raced for the nearest guard. Surprise gave them the precious seconds needed to wrench the rifle from his unsuspecting hands and pull him into the room, where T'Chebbi, Mrowbay and Sayuk jumped on him, grabbing his sidearm.

Rezac muttered an oath and demanded the handgun. As he was given it, he passed the rifle back to T'Chebbi.

Rifles are trank darts far as I can tell, he sent. *I'll check the pistol.* A moment later he sent again. *They're live.* Pistol aimed at the remaining Seniormost and guard, he advanced on them.

Jeran shot past him, diving for the Seniormost's legs. A shot barked out, the trank pellet just missing Jeran as he knocked the Seniormost into the guard, tumbling them all to the ground.

The rest of Tirak's crew erupted into the corridor, and within seconds, the Primes were pinned down and their weapons taken.

An alarm began to blare out, echoing throughout the corridors.

"Get them inside," Kaid roared over the noise. He'd heard no sounds of combat from behind him. That bothered him until he sensed from Carrie what was happening.

This one's wearing a gold tabard, she sent. *A leader or senior officer at least. His faceplate's cracked. The Cabbarans are trying to get the helmet off. He's struggling a little but it's under control. Same with the guard.*

Hauled to their feet, the other two captives were dragged into the room.

"Release the Seniormost," said a translator. "There is no need for this. We were coming to free you."

"Which one spoke?" demanded Giyesh, looking at the two that were on their feet.

I can read them, sent Carrie. *The gray one spoke. It's the gold one, he's their leader, and they're afraid for his safety.*

Kaid sensed her uncertainty. Something was bothering her, but there wasn't time for him to concern himself with that now.

"Get their helmets off," said Tirak, taking the pistol from Nayash and stepping forward to help cover the door.

Abruptly, the alarm stopped, the silence sounding deafening by comparison.

"Watch the corridor," ordered Kaid, walking over to see

the gold Prime for himself. "Strip them of all their armor. I want them as vulnerable as us."

The gold-robed Prime lay stunned, one hand moving slightly, as Sheeowl helped the Cabbarans to unlock the helmet. The faceplate was cracked but not enough for him to see the occupant. He turned back to the other captives. The first guard was still on the floor with Mrowbay and Sayuk crawling over him.

"This is unnecessary," repeated the gray Seniormost. "You are to be released."

"We *are* leaving, with you as insurance. Tell your people that," said Kaid, gesturing to Manesh and Taynar to remove his helmet.

"Leave our helmets. You will gain nothing by removing them," said the Seniormost, struggling between Manesh and Taynar. "You have not been harmed. Why do you attack us?"

"Break his faceplate if he keeps struggling," ordered Kaid, turning to watch as the gold's helmet was finally lifted off. He blinked, not trusting his eyes, then moved closer till he was standing over the unconscious Prime. "Vartra's bones! Valtegans!" He spun around to watch as the others' helmets were removed.

The gray Seniormost turned to look at him, large green eyes blinking rapidly in the unaccustomed brightness.

From the doorway, Rezac looked back as he heard Kaid's voice. His gun swung round to aim at the Seniormost but Tirak grabbed him.

"Eyes front!" he snarled. "You're on duty now!"

Growling, Rezac turned back to watch the corridor.

"We are releasing you," said the Seniormost in Sholan. "There was no need for this attack."

"You attacked us!" said Zashou from where she was helping to pull the second guard's helmet off.

"We did not attack your craft. We took the *M'ijikk*. We found you on board their ship."

"You took us from our companions and examined us against our wills!" she shouted, dropping what she was doing to start to her feet.

"Enough, Zashou!" ordered Kaid, striding into the center of the room. "Get back to work! We're not discussing this now!" He looked over to Sheeowl and the gold Prime.

"Get him out of that armor and on his feet, conscious or not. I want us out of here as soon as possible. And put his gold tabard back on him so they know who we have. You," he said, turning back to the Seniormost, "Tell your people that you are our hostages and we want safe passage down to the flight deck and onto our ship. Jo, over here and make sure he tells them what I said."

"I need my helmet for that," the Valtegan said.

"Give it to him," Kaid ordered Jo.

"Kaid, this Prime's got an implant on his head," said Mrowbay from where he knelt by the prone guard. "Just like Giyesh said."

"This one's also got an implant," said Jeran, tossing the helmet to the floor.

"Tell the guards to obey us, then send the message," said Kaid.

They waited while the Seniormost spoke to the guards, then to his commanders. Listening to the guttural speech, Kaid was acutely aware of Carrie's distress at being in their presence again.

You're doing fine, he sent to her. *They can't touch you, remember that.*

The gold Prime was being held in a sitting position, being stripped of his armor. He'd come round but was looking decidedly groggy.

"He's different," said Carrie, watching him. "They all are. Not the same as those on Keiss. For a start, three of them have crests. And the Seniormost, he's smaller, with rainbow colors round the eyes. Same with the gold. I've never seen one that pale yellowish color before."

"Later, Carrie," said Kaid, looking round at the other two Primes. "Get something to tie their wrists with, please. Get that armor off fast, people! I want to get out of here today! Those with rifles, they're trank darts. Use them only on unarmored targets. I reckon we'll see a lot more of them outside this area."

"You will have your safe conduct," said the gray Prime as the helmet was taken away from him. "You had it anyway, I told you. But you must . . ."

"We must nothing!" said Kaid harshly. "You're the prisoners now, remember that! Strip him quickly," Kaid said to Manesh and Nayash. "Don't bother with fastenings, cut through them if you can."

"We could use the armor," said Jeran, hefting a breast-plate up and examining it. "We're about the same size."

"Tie him up," said Carrie, handing him one of the strips she was ripping off a sheet.

"Legs are different," said Rezac from the door. "Theirs' are like the Humans. Suits won't fit us."

"Done," said Sheeowl, tossing aside the last piece of the gold's armor.

"Me, too," said Mrowbay, dragging his captive closer to the door.

"Almost there," said Manesh, hauling the final leg protector off as Taynar bound the gray Seniormost. "Ready!"

"Let's get going," said Kaid, heading for the door. "T'Chebbi, you at the rear with one guard, the gold in the middle with the civilians and the Cabbarans. Get the other two at the front near Rezac."

They began to assemble in the corridor, Rezac to the front, Tirak to the rear, until they were in position.

Kaid picked up a helmet, handing to Jeran. "Hang onto that for as long as is practical, in case we need it," he said before going to the front with Tirak.

"There's no damper out here," said Carrie. "I can sense the way ahead of us."

"Do it. You, too, Rezac. Zashou and Jo, check our rear," he said, leading them up the corridor to the junction on their right. A short distance, then they were heading down the corridor to the elevator. It was deserted, like a ghost ship.

"I reckon this gold Prime is important," said Tirak quietly as they waited for the elevator to come up. "It's as quiet as the grave here. Too quiet."

Kaid merely grunted, watching to make sure the elevator was empty as it came into view.

"How many do you want on?" asked Tirak.

"All of us. It's large enough," replied Kaid, gesturing to the others to leave their cover in the corridor. "Check out the fight deck, Carrie, Rezac."

"Done, said Carrie. "Two groups of ten about two hundred yards from here. More, farther in two largish groups and a smaller one."

"Agreed," said Rezac.

"Yell down the shaft and get them to move," Kaid ordered the Seniormost.

"If you'll listen to me first," the Seniormost began.

"No deals," interrupted Kaid. "Just do it."

"We want a treaty with you," said the Seniormost, speaking in a rush. "You were to be released. Your ship is ready. All you have to do is . . ."

Kaid pushed him toward the elevator cage. "Enough! Tell them to move!"

The Valtegan shouted down in his own language. Beside him, Jo translated.

This is so strange, sent Carrie. *I sense none of the usual fear or aggression from any of our prisoners. The gold and the Seniormost are terrified of us, the guards are just waiting for new commands.*

That's not a male, sent Rezac, staring the gray Prime full in the face. *That's a female! The Gods know what she's doing here, but it's a female.*

Focus on what we're doing, Kaid reminded them.

"She says it's clear," said Jo.

"They've backed off," agreed Rezac.

"Keep alert, people," said Kaid as they filed on and he pressed the control.

Whining and creaking under the weight, the elevator began to descend. T'Chebbi and Tirak crouched down so they could see the flight deck as soon as the cage cleared their floor. Kaid kept his hand poised over the stop button.

"They're clear," said T'Chebbi, standing up.

With a jolt, they came to rest. A hundred yards away, the *Profit* stood facing the bay doors, engines already running.

"As I said, your craft is waiting for you," said the gray Prime. "Proof of our good intentions."

"Cool heads, people. We take our time," said Kaid, opening the gate. "Same order as before. If you have to fire, make every shot count."

Those with the guns joined Kaid, forming a shield in front of the others and their captives as they filed out onto the flight deck. While he waited, he looked around, gauging their surroundings and assessing the numbers of Valtegans present.

Behind them and to their right—some hundred and fifty

yards away—were maintenance areas with twenty or so mechanics. Two large vehicles berthed there were obviously being worked on. Beyond them, half a dozen fatigue-clad soldiers stood beside another cage elevator.

On their left, barely ten yards from them, was the *M'ijikk* with two shuttle craft berthed beyond her. From that direction he caught the whiff of volatile lubricants. Though he couldn't see anyone from this position, there was plenty of opportunity for soldiers to hide between the vehicles. Level with the *Profit,* near the starboard bulkhead, were another two large craft and some thirty people.

"Remind them we have safe passage," said Kaid to the Seniormost. "Tell them if they shoot at us, we'll shoot you."

She yelled the message out, her voice echoing strangely as it bounced off the walls and high ceiling.

"Those with guns, fan out, cover us on all sides," said Kaid.

Slowly, very slowly, they made their way across the open hangar deck toward the *Profit.* Round the edges, the groups of Valtegans stood in tight knots, keeping very still. Here and there they spotted the odd armored guard.

"Don't like this. Still too easy," muttered T'Chebbi, maintaining her grip on the pistol she carried.

"They're scared, T'Chebbi, terrified of anything happening to the hostages," said Carrie from behind her. "Particularly the gold one. Many of them are terrified even to be seeing him."

"He's the Enlightened One I heard them speaking about," said Giyesh suddenly.

"Later," snapped Kaid, constantly scanning with mind and eyes. "Keep focused."

With only a few yards to go, Kaid caught the sudden movement by the leg of the *M'ijikk* out of the corner of his eye. A cry of pain, quickly stifled, came from the rear of his group before he could get his shot off. The armored marksman fell without a sound.

Kaid grasped the Prime guard from Giyesh. "Keep moving," he said tersely to her as he put the gun to the side of the Valtegan's head.

The Valtegan began to struggle, letting out a shriek of terror as Kaid pulled the trigger. The cry was cut short as his body began to sag. Kaid flung him aside and reached for the gray Seniormost.

"That's one gone!" yelled Kaid, pulling her in front of him.

A scuffle from the rear of the group, then the second guard made a break for freedom.

Kaid was about to fire on the fleeing Valtegan as a shot rang out, hitting the guard square in the upper back, felling him instantly.

Got him, sent Rezac.

Good shot. "She's next!" Kaid yelled, putting the gun to her head as he kept moving slowly toward the *Profit.* "Tell them that," he snarled in her ear. "You're next, then the gold one."

Green skin almost white with terror, the Seniormost shrieked out the warning as, stumbling, she was dragged closer and closer to the *Profit.*

They were in the lee of their ship now, protected from the Primes behind them.

"Take it easy. We're not out of here yet," Kaid warned them as Giyesh began to move a little faster.

At last he felt the *Profit*'s ramp under his feet. Dragging his captive with him, he backed up a few feet before stopping. "Rezac, bring the gold. Use him as a shield. Those with weapons, up front with me now. The rest of you, board! Tirak, get her fired up, ready to go!"

Carrie, Jo, and Jeran joined him, giving cover to the others as they scrambled for the safety of the *Profit.* As soon as he saw her, he knew T'Chebbi had been hit.

She's fine, sent Carrie. *Flesh wound, upper arm.*

Before his eyes, an old vision briefly exploded, showing him T'Chebbi, her upper arm wrapped in a blood-soaked bandage. It hadn't happened on Jalna, but it had happened.

"All on board," reported Rezac. "Our turn."

"We want a treaty with you," said the Seniormost urgently as Kaid hauled her up the ramp with him. "We must talk of this now!"

I'm picking up someone out there, sent Carrie as she ducked inside the *Profit*'s cargo bay. *If we don't agree, they plan to wait until we've left, then put that beam on us to bring us back unconscious. They'll keep several of us as hostages and release the others with the offer of a treaty.*

"Why?" demanded Kaid, tightening his grip on the Seniormost's arm. "Against whom?"

"The Valtegans from the *M'ijikk* and others. We're threatened by them. We need allies who can fight for us."

"Your people couldn't even keep the safe passage agreement! Do you really expect us to want an alliance with you?" Kaid stopped at the edge of the *Profit*'s cargo bay, standing behind the Seniormost.

"He was a bodyguard and unstable! We're not responsible for them! We treated you well! We examined you only to find out how much you'd changed since the fall of our Empire."

"What's your world called?" demanded Rezac, rejoining Kaid.

"K'oish'ik."

He let out a hiss. "The world we were on. The Emperor's world."

"We have no warriors now. Those from M'zull and J'kirtikk will find us soon. They have an ancient prototype weapon of ours. It's the one they used to destroy your two worlds. It must be retrieved and destroyed. You're as much at risk from them as we are. They hate you more," she added.

There was truth in that. But an alliance with less hostile Valtegans to fight a war not of their making? Vartra's words about a pact with the Liege of Hell came back to him. Shola had to be warned.

"We'll take this Enlightened One of yours back with us to plead your cause. He does talk, doesn't he?"

"Take me," she said anxiously. "I can put our case better."

"I will go," said the gold-robed Prime from where he stood with Jeran and Jo inside the cargo bay. "I came to present our arguments to you in the first place. I had documents . . ."

"Don't need documents," interrupted Kaid. "Tell your people we've listened to you and that the gold one can put your case to our leaders. Tell them not to bother using that beam weapon of yours on us again. If you do, he dies."

"How will we know your decision?"

"Stay here. We'll send a message," he said, pushing her down the ramp and ducking out of sight inside as Carrie shut the bay door. He hit the communicator control set into the bulkhead. "Tirak, Kaid here. On our way up. Get us out of here immediately."

"Taking off in two minutes," came the captain's reply. "To the bridge, on the double."

They raced across the *Profit*'s hold toward the elevator, feeling the ship begin to vibrate as the sound of the engines changed. They made it, but only just. T'Chebbi was sitting at the nav console, arm being dressed by Mrowbay as she worked.

Tirak turned his chair to look at them as they entered. "Take him to the mess and watch him," he ordered, pointing to their hostage. "Need you to tell us where we're heading," he said to Kaid.

"T'Chebbi, you coping?" Kaid asked.

"Almost done." He could hear the pain in her voice, see it in the set of her ears and the way she held her head.

Mrowbay looked up at him as he fastened off the bandage. "I want her in sick bay the moment she's through. This is only temporary."

"She will be," Kaid promised, flicking the safety on the pistol before sticking it in his belt.

"I'll go with her," Carrie said to Kaid.

"How fast you want to be there?" asked Annuur's voice through the comm.

Tirak raised an eyebrow at him. "I'd say as soon as possible."

"Shortest possible time," agreed Kaid.

"Can do five days," said Annuur. "But risky. Margin for error much less. Leave us exhausted. Ship need overhaul."

"Do it," said Kaid. "I want as much distance between us and them as possible. I've got to get a message out to Haven and our ship at Jalna immediately. It's ready encoded in with the nav data."

"Route it to Giyesh's board," said Tirak. "She'll send it."

"Done," sighed T'Chebbi, falling back in her seat. "Nav comp back on-line for Haven."

"Dorsal turret on-line," reported Sheeowl. "Ventral turret on-line. Batteries armed and ready. Waiting instructions, Captain."

"Five days it is, Annuur," said Tirak, turning back to his console. "Start powering the jump drives, Sheeowl. Sit in on nav, Kaid. Nayash will help you if you need it. Where we heading for?"

Kaid moved to the front to take Sayuk's vacant seat. "A Brotherhood outpost called Haven," he said. "It's in the outer reaches of the Chemerian sector."

"The Primes haven't opened the landing bay doors, Captain," said Nayash. "Switching to forward view."

"I figured there might be a delay," Tirak said as the screen changed to show the roof of the hangar. "Nayash, I'll take her out. Ventral turret, fire rearward on my command. Dorsal, fire at will: aim for the bay doors. I want a hole big enough to get out through."

"Understood." Manesh's voice sounded remote through the ship's speaker.

The engine noise increased until Kaid felt the *Profit* start to lift. He began to smile. "We're going to leave here like a cork out of a bottle," he said.

"That's the idea," agreed Tirak. "And do some serious damage in the process. Brace yourselves. Ventral turret, fire!"

The kickback from the missiles hurled the *Profit* toward the closed bay doors as simultaneously, blossoms of red began to mushroom across them filling the interior with smoke. Then the vacuum outside started sucking at them, pulling everything inside the hangar toward the hole Manesh was still blasting in the hull.

"I can't see for the smoke," said Giyesh, a tremor in her voice as they hurtled toward the center of the vortex they'd created.

"Don't need to," said Sheeowl calmly as the ship was buffeted from side to side. "We'll be pulled through the hole whatever we do."

Suddenly the buffeting stopped and they were floating free in the blackness of space.

"By Kathan, that looks good to me," said Tirak with feeling as he switched his controls to the pilot. "Full speed, Nayash. I want to jump as soon as we can. Rear view, Mrowbay."

"Aye, Captain," Nayash said, turning his head briefly to grin at everyone.

This was their first view of the Primes' ship. It was large, very large; a flattened diamond shape, with a gaping hole in the hull near the nose, around which floated a large mass of assorted debris and dead bodies.

"They won't be trying to take us back on board in a hurry," observed Tirak. "Or follow us."

"They don't appear to be powering up their weapons, Captain," said Mrowbay.

Kaid began punching details into the nav comp as Sheeowl continued to run the pre-jump checks with Nayash.

"Ready to jump, Captain," he said a few minutes later.

"Engage jump," said Tirak.

* * *

"You read the messages?" asked Rhyaz.

"Yes. Thank Vartra they escaped!"

"My feelings entirely. The first arrived this morning, the second several hours later. Our Brothers have been mobilized and are on their way to Haven. I've put Kheal in command of the forces gathered there. L'Seuli is taking charge of our negotiators' escort, and I'm remaining at Stronghold to coordinate. General Raiban is already complaining at the lack of our personnel, and the fact that we took her ships and left her crews." He opened his mouth in a wide grin. "She won't be bothering us, though. The arrival of the messages has given her more than enough to do. Maybe next time they'll listen to us. Couldn't get in touch with you sooner, I've been up to my ears in complaints and protocol, among other things."

"Your plan worked well, then. Are they finally increasing planetary defenses?" Lijou asked.

"Yes, and sending an Alliance presence to Jalna. The Chemerians are screaming that they're most at risk, as usual, and as usual no one's taking the slightest notice of them. The *M'Zekko* is still there, after all. One surprise. Kishasayzar, captain of the *Hkariyash*, which is still berthed on Jalna, requested coordinates for Haven. Says he wants to help his Sholan and Human friends. Not like the Sumaan to desert their Chemerian merchants."

"Most unusual. What did you do?"

"Gave him coordinates to meet up with an escort ship to take him there. Worth keeping an eye on that captain. He's not far from completing his indenture to the Chemerians. If it's not too much, we might be able to buy him out. Wouldn't do any harm to have an independent Sumaan ship and crew as our own allies."

Lijou flicked his ears in agreement. "A useful, if unexpected, ally. When do you expect the *Profit* to arrive? Is this Prime ship likely to be following them?"

"Message said five days. I'd believe them, they've got Cabbaran navigators. And, yes, I'd be surprised if the Prime ship wasn't following them."

"Warn our people to be careful, Rhyaz. Remember Brynne's vision of conflict. No news of Kusac yet?"

"At best, he's dead. At worst, he's still on the Prime ship," said Rhyaz, ears dipping in regret. "Kaid does have a bargaining point, though. A Valtegan, an officer or something. If Kusac's still alive, then perhaps an exchange can be arranged. As you saw, the second message was brief. We'll have to wait till they reach Haven for a full debriefing. Meanwhile, we prepare for the worst."

"I take it you've contacted the Chief Instructor."

"Yes, I have. I've apprised him of how many we need to crew our vessels. I need you to confirm the request. Do it when I sign off. This line is secure."

Lijou nodded. "How many are you requesting?"

"We need to more than double our current number, that's all you need to know."

"Do you need me to return?"

"No, stay where you are for now. Brynne might come up with something new. Don't say anything to Clan Lord Konis till we've spoken to Kaid personally. The Leska telepaths arrived an hour ago. All sworn in and signed up to the Brotherhood now. Pleasant couple. They're in touch with Haven on the comm link. Seems they can sense Vriuzu and Jiosha while they're using it. Useful."

"Very," agreed Lijou. "While I'm here, do you want me to recruit the gene-altered telepaths on the estate? They're all En'Shallans and so are ours by right."

Rhyaz hesitated. "Do it," he said. "Vartra forbid we need to call them up because of their telepathic Talents, but we can if they're Brothers."

"What about Kezule? Any sign of him yet?" asked Lijou. "They had a scare out here ten days ago. Someone briefly picked up a strange mental pattern. They sent a couple of units out to search the land around the main gatehouse but found nothing."

"We've found nothing either. Raiban finally gave up on the spaceport idea, though we still have a small presence there, and I've had to reassign those at Chezy. I'm afraid we've got larger problems right now. If the estate's secure, Lijou, that's the best we can hope for. I have to go. Raiban's baying for me again on another line. I'll be in touch."

"I may move up to the main house when we have concrete news on Kusac."

"Very well."

Lijou sat looking at the blank comm for a few minutes before mentally shaking himself and getting up. It wasn't fair to keep Ghyan out of his office for much longer. Kusac dead but Carrie still alive? He knew that the three of them had shared a full Link. The Gods knew they were all Level One telepaths, but had Kaid been able to step in as her Leska? It had happened with Josh and Mara. He sighed. Things were changing fast these days. It would be a tragedy to lose Kusac, but at least there were still two of them alive.

He realized he hadn't told Rhyaz that Brynne could see distant places. It could wait now until he'd gotten him to try his skill out properly. Maybe he could reach Haven. Was there anyone there he knew? Not yet, but he could request an image of the station interior, perhaps the area where Vriuzu worked. Maybe just seeing and talking to Vriuzu on the comm link would be enough. It would be a good test for him.

On his way out, he thanked Ghyan, and with a heavy heart, headed back to Vanna's and Garras' home.

* * *

It was some time later before Kaid was able to go to sick bay to check on T'Chebbi for himself. Mrowbay had already been in to find Carrie had redone his quick dressing from their own medikit and had given her the appropriate shots.

T'Chebbi, however, refused to lie down and rest, and had remained sitting on the bed with Carrie beside her.

"I'm fine," she said testily as Kaid came over to her.

"Only a scratch. Bloody fuss over nothing. Will heal in a few days."

Carrie got up. "I'll catch you later in the mess," she said to Kaid.

"No need for you to go," said T'Chebbi.

"I'll see you later, too," she said, firmly, leaning forward to brush her cheek against T'Chebbi's.

Kaid sent her a grateful thought as she left. He took her place. "I was concerned for you," he said awkwardly. "I had to see to locking our guest safely away from Rezac before I could come."

"Wise."

Tentatively, he put an arm around her shoulder, urging her closer till she leaned against him.

She scowled up at him. "You're going soft," she muttered. "You treat all your operatives like this?"

"No, only those who're my lovers," he grinned, ruffling her ears, glad she'd lightened a difficult moment for him. "You should rest, sleep if possible. Do you want me to take you to our room?"

She sighed, but it was with contentment at being asked, and for this time alone with him. "No, you need your privacy with Carrie. I'll be fine here."

"You'd not be intruding," he said.

"Not for you, but she's not used to our ways, only what telepaths do. She's not at ease yet with your new relationship, and if she isn't still having nightmares of J'koshuk, I'd be surprised." Her voice was getting drowsier. "Dammit, she gave me too strong a dose," she muttered, trying to sit up, but Kaid prevented her.

"You need me, too," he said, scooping her carefully into his arms and standing up. "No need for you to give up your bed. Carrie agrees with me." Not strictly true, she did, but she had a few concerns about their lack of privacy, despite the movable partitions between the beds.

Standing up, he carried her to the room opposite that they'd shared with Jeran and Tesha. "Only Jeran here now, and I reckon he'll be trying to arrange something with Giyesh."

"Kaid, these new Valtegans, the Primes. They're not so strong out of their armor. Or as violent. Very different from what you said Kezule was like."

"You're right," he said thoughtfully as he pulled back the blankets on her bed and sat her down. "I'd noticed it, even told J'koshuk he was different, but I couldn't put my finger on it till now."

He watched her fumbling with her belt and gave her a hand to strip, then covered her up. "You sleep," he said. "I'll wake you at mealtime." He reached inside the covers and pulled her long plait free. He knew she hated getting caught up when she lay on it.

"Got no option thanks to Carrie," she grumbled, turning on her side.

"She gave you the right dose," he said, leaning down to run his tongue across her cheek.

* * *

Day 37

Tirak's off-duty crew had been conducting a minute search of the ship for any sabotage or tracking devices but had turned up nothing.

"They even put the cryo unit back," said Mrowbay, helping himself to a drink at the galley. "And patched the hull breach in the workshop. Nothing special, just a good, temporary repair."

"Well, they had us long enough," said Giyesh. "Manesh wants us to move our stuff. He and you, Sayuk, are on the passenger deck opposite the hostage. Rezac, would you and Jo, Zashou, too, if she doesn't mind, move down to the cabin next to them." She looked over to Carrie. "You know where you and Kaid are."

"Where are you? And Jeran, I presume," asked Sayuk.

"Where Rezac was, with Sheeowl and Nayash."

"Cozy," said Mrowbay, checking out the cupboards above the sink for nibbles. "And what does the captain think of that arrangement?"

Giyesh gave him a withering look. "I'm not going to mention it unless I'm asked. Kate, you and Taynar stay where you are." She looked from one to the other of her crewmates. "Well, go on, get shifting your stuff. Mrowbay, you and I can move Sheeowl's and Nayash's kit and pack up the camp beds. Jeran can help."

They disappeared, leaving Carrie with Kate and Taynar until Kaid joined them. He looked around the deserted mess.

"Where's everyone?" he asked, nodding to Kate and Taynar as he went to help himself from the drinks unit.

"Changing cabins," said Carrie, taking another mouthful from her mug.

"Any idea what our guest would drink?" he asked as he waited for his beverage. "I'm going down to question him now. Coming?"

"Why take him a drink?"

"Because so far he's been cooperative. It's worthwhile fostering that attitude. I suppose water's as good as anything till we know."

"There's a galley on the passenger deck," offered Kate. "You can get him what he likes from there."

Taynar began to grin. "There's an entertainment console in the lounge down there! I'd forgotten about that! Coming, Kate?" he asked, getting to his feet.

The two younglings disappeared, leaving them alone. Kaid joined her at the table. "Didn't get the chance to tell you earlier that you did a good job back there in the hangar when you took over from T'Chebbi."

"I only did what I was trained for."

He reached across the table, stroking her cheek with the back of his hand. "Then you learned it well." He let his hand drop to the table beside hers, turning it palm side up as she took hold of his. "Is it always like this?" he asked, voice low. "When you're with me I want to touch you. It's like a physical need, almost a pain, if I can't."

"In the beginning," she said, feeling a bittersweet love for him flow through her. She slipped her fingers between his, lacing them with his as he responded. "You get used to it eventually." She could feel his heartbeat increase as she saw his eyes begin to glow. "It's strong now because tomorrow's our Link day."

"I will never get used to it," he said, voice roughened with intensity. He took his hand away reluctantly. "Let's go before I get too distracted." Finishing his drink, he got to his feet.

*   *   *

As they went past the passenger lounge, they could hear Kate and Taynar playing on the entertainment console.

"That's all those younglings should have to worry about," said Kaid. "Instead of which, they've suddenly been thrust into an adult world."

"They seem remarkably untouched by it," said Carrie.

"The damage is there, just pushed deep down for now. It'll surface in time."

They could see Manesh sitting on a chair outside the cabin door, one of the Prime trank rifles held across her knees.

"You've come to interrogate him," she said. "Captain said you'd be along."

"I want to take him to the galley," said Kaid. "We need you as the guard."

"You still armed?" Manesh asked.

Carrie nodded, patting the pistol she wore in the belt of her one-piece fatigues.

"If he makes a break for it, and I can't get him with the trank, hit him somewhere non-lethal. I'm not having him loose on my ship," said Manesh, getting up.

Aware of Carrie's hesitation, he grasped her shoulder briefly. *You can cope. He isn't like J'koshuk.*

I know. It's their scent, it reminds me of . . .

J'koshuk's was that of a rutting male. His mental tone was harsh. *This one's will be fear. Break that association, conquer the fear now, or it conquers you.*

She nodded as Manesh unlocked the door.

Their hostage was still sitting where Kaid had left him. His gold tabard lay discarded on the bed beside him. He looked up as the door opened.

"You hungry? Want a drink?" asked Kaid, standing in the doorway. He beckoned to him. "Come on. Let's go get something. What's your name?"

Surprised, the Valtegan got to his feet and slowly approached the door. "Zsurtul."

Kaid stood back, motioning him out. A few steps more and he saw Manesh standing with the rifle. He froze, looking from her to Kaid.

"A precaution," said Kaid. "No tricks, I assure you." *He's only a youngling, Carrie!*

I know. He can't be an officer, surely?

Hesitantly, Zsurtul stepped into the corridor. Kaid took him by the arm, drawing him past the storeroom to his right and right again into the main corridor.

"The food you served us, is it what you eat?" asked Kaid, "or do you prefer your meat raw?"

"Cooked. We have always eaten it cooked." His voice was light, the Sholan well spoken, as if it had been studied, with very little of the sibilance Carrie was used to hearing from Valtegans.

"The ones on Keiss ate their food raw," she said.

He looked sideways at her. "You met only the warrior caste, and from a different world."

They'd reached the galley. Kaid took him over to the food dispenser. As he turned to ask Manesh to translate the U'Churian script, Zsurtful pointed to an item, naming it in equally flawless U'Churian.

"You speak and read U'Churian, too," said Kaid in surprise. "How many more languages do you know?"

"A few more," he admitted, letting Kaid select the meal for him. "When you have dealings with a species, it makes sense to communicate with them in their own language if at all possible."

"You're the Valtegans that visit Jalna," said Carrie. "The science ship, was that the one we were on?"

"The *Kz'adul* hasn't called at Jalna, but her sister ship has," he said, picking up his plate of food. "I'd like a dish of maush to drink, if I may," he added, moving toward the long dining table.

Manesh got him the drink, keeping her eyes and gun trained on him all the while. Then, snagging a chair, she took up a post by the door.

We need Rezac, sent Carrie. *This Valtegan is so unlike any I've known.*

Ask him to join us. "Which world are you from?" asked Kaid.

"K'oish'ik. Ours was the world at the heart of the old Empire," he said, accepting the cutlery from Kaid. "We had four worlds of our own then. Those who destroyed your colonies and ruled Keiss are from M'zull. They are at war with another world called J'kirtikk. It's a war for dominance. That, after all, is what warriors want." He began cutting up the meat and eating it with obvious pleasure.

Can you read him? asked Kaid.

Yes, if I force the contact. The barrier natural to his kind is stronger in him. But then, everything about him is different.

Rezac came in and helped himself to a drink, sitting halfway down the table on the opposite side from Zsurtul. *I can read him.*

Not yet, Rezac—if at all, sent Kaid. "So. You're not warriors. What are you then?" he asked.

"Intellectuals and scientists. A curious people interested in learning about others."

"That's why you kept us prisoner and kidnapped us from our rooms to do experiments on," said Rezac, an angry rumble in his voice.

Startled, Zsurtul looked over at him, fork poised halfway between plate and mouth.

Go easy, Rezac, warned Kaid. *He's being cooperative.*

Too damned cooperative if you ask me! was the acerbic reply.

"We found you on the M'zullian vessel, I told you this. We studied you only to see how you'd changed in a millennium and a half, nothing more."

"You remember us from back then?" asked Carrie.

Zsurtul's eye ridges creased in confusion. "Not you, the Sholans."

"Genetic memory?" asked Kaid.

"And data banks," said Zsurtul. "The City of Light withstood the Empire's collapse, though those outside didn't fare well. We were self-sufficient and lost nothing during the years of the Fall. Ask him. He lived then."

"How do you know about me?" Rezac demanded. "Did you get the information from me under drugs when you took me from my companions?"

"You are named on our database. We were sent to Jalna because our previous ship received an ancient transmission from the planet as it left. It hadn't the authority to investigate, but we have."

Carrie frowned. "What signal?"

"The stasis cube," said Kaid. "When Jo and Kris opened it."

"Just so. It was an experimental device which you and

your Leska partner entered accidentally in your attempt to outrun the guards. It's thought M'zullian warriors must have taken it from the lab in the confusion."

"They worshipped it as a holy object," murmured Carrie, as shocked as the others by the depth of the Prime's knowledge.

"They probably used it as a deterrent at first," said Zsurtul. "After all, it contained the ultimate weapon against their enemies. Two Sholan telepaths. It would have given those who possessed it enormous power over the others on their world."

"And as time passed, they forgot what was inside it and why they had to be afraid of it," said Kaid. "It would become revered for itself—a holy object."

"As you say," agreed Zsurtul. He picked up the mug and attempted to drink from it but it was too narrow for his wide, almost beaked mouth. He put it down. "Do you have a wider container?" he asked hopefully.

Carrie got up to look in the galley cupboards under the sink. "The cups on the Prime ship," she said, turning round with a small bowl in her hand. "I saw them, I should have guessed!"

"You eat cooked food," said Rezac, suddenly noticing the remains of the meal.

"Our caste always have," said Zsurtul, accepting the bowl and pouring his herbal drink into it.

"But the raw meat!"

"Do you not feed your warriors on raw meat to make them fiercer?" he asked, then his mouth formed a lopsided smile. "I forget. You have telepaths. They are more formidable than warriors."

"I don't believe you," said Rezac. "I saw them eating raw meat at the city palace!"

"You saw only what it was intended you see. Don't you remember some took the meat from a central dish, while others were served plates already covered in the sauce of the laalquoi plant? They had the cooked meat."

Rezac growled low in his throat, dissatisfied. "That's so," he admitted.

"The laalquoi plant on Jalna. What happened?" asked Kaid.

"We over-farmed that world about a hundred years before the Fall. The plant interacted with a native mold and it mutated into a form that turned our people as well as theirs violent beyond reasoning. We had to pull out. There was nothing we could do to help the Jalnians until recently."

"Oh, yes. And what did you do for them, apart from call in every fifty years to take samples?" demanded Rezac.

"Why grow so much of this plant?" interrupted Carrie. "There are still resin stones found today on Shola."

"It was necessary to our diet. It had a calmative effect on those bearing the warrior blood. Worlds where the soil was right to farm it were rare."

"You just ate U'Churian vegetables," Carrie pointed out.

"After the Fall, there were few of us left in the City of Light. We had to employ our sciences to help us survive. We needed as large a gene pool as we could get, needed to eat what was available."

"The females. You socialized the females," said Carrie.

"Among other things."

"How?" asked Kaid. "I saw them. They were feral."

Zsurtul looked curiously at him. "So were you when deprived of your pregnant mate. Put yourself in a female's place. Stop giving her the laalquoi, give her no say in her life, and keep her in a breeding room with others like her. Then take her eggs away when they're due to hatch, knowing that her ravenous young will try to devour each other without her presence. See then how feral you would become."

"They did that to them?" asked Carrie, horrified. "You mean they were sentient all along? Gods, but your ancestors were barbaric!"

"What caste are you?" asked Rezac very quietly.

Zsurtul looked at him. "An Intellectual," he murmured

"You're lying. It's been bothering me since I first saw you, but I finally remembered what it was. Your color. You're not a breeding male, you're a drone, aren't you?"

"I'm not a drone, though there are drones in my ancestry," he admitted.

"Drones?" asked Carrie.

"Infertile females, almost asexual," said Rezac. "Used as servants and for sex because access to females was restricted. Jo says there were three on M'ezozakk's ship.

They were moved out of the room he put her in on the *M'ijikk*."

"I'm not a drone," said Zsurtul, his voice becoming lower as his sand-colored skin flushed a deeper shade.

Rezac got up and began to slowly stalk round the table to him. "There's a way to find out," he said. "Because if he's lying about this, then all the rest could be lies, too."

"Rezac!" warned Kaid, getting rapidly to his feet.

Rezac looked at him. *Trust me.*

Kaid watched as he slowly resumed his seat. Since Rezac had learned about their family relationship, the competitiveness and belligerence that had existed between them seemed to have disappeared.

Rezac stopped beside Zsurtul and reaching down, grabbed him by the front of his clothing, pulling him to his feet.

Zsurtul began talking rapidly in Valtegan, trying to dislodge his hands.

What's he saying? demanded Kaid. *Can you read him?*

Carrie was noticing for the first time how short Zsurtul's claws were, and that they were carved in intricate patterns. They were not the claws of anyone who might need to use them to defend himself—or was it herself?"

What's he saying? repeated Kaid.

He's babbling about being the Enlightened One, that this is an assault against his person.

Rezac transferred his grip to the neck of Zsurtul's garment, and fending off his scrabbling hands, ripped it open to mid-chest level. Then he froze. As he did, Zsurtul became still, his flushed skin paling to an almost deathly white.

What is it? asked Kaid anxiously.

His mind has gone still, I can't sense anything! replied Carrie.

"You're not going to believe who we're got here," Rezac said very quietly. He spun Zsurtul around, holding the garment open so they could see the markings on his chest. Tattooed there was a symbol Kaid had seen before.

"You're looking at the Prime Emperor's son and heir. The Enlightened One."

About three inches across, executed in iridescent colors,

was an open ovoid shape resembling an egg, with flames
coming from between the two halves.

"When he's Emperor, they'll add the symbols for his
name underneath," said Rezac. "Zashou saw Q'emgo'h's
when he tried to rape her." He released Zsurtul.

Carrie was no less stunned than anyone else present.
"They'll follow us," she said. "As soon as they can. The
Primes won't let us get away with their crown prince."

"I figured on that happening anyway," said Kaid, going
over to Zsurtul and pulling his clothing shut again. "My
apologies," he said. "We had to know. You understand
that, I'm sure."

Zsurtul was shaking with fear and shock. He tried to
move but was unable to do so. Kaid helped him return to
his seat then turned to Rezac, putting his hand on his shoulder reassuringly. *You did well. Was that what you were
looking for?*

*Not exactly. Breeding males have a tattoo on their chest.
A small sigil showing they're allowed access to the females,*
he replied as he went back to his seat.

"I said I was not a drone," Zsurtul said through
clenched teeth.

"So you used drones in your gene pool," said Kaid.
"How, if they're asexual?"

"Drones were inferior females' eggs kept too cool to
hatch as fertile offspring. Many of the eggs that hatched at
the time of the Fall were infertile—males and females both.
We were forced to utilize all the offspring that were born
to be able to survive." Still in shock, his voice was low
and remote.

Carrie got up and took his bowl to the dispenser to fetch
him another drink. He clutched it gratefully in both hands,
warming himself against it.

"And you have no warrior caste, only those who volun-
teer to be implanted with a device that does what?"

"I'm told it can be adjusted to control their moods by
shifting their hormone levels. It makes them quick to respond in a more aggressive way than we can."

"M'ezozakk's crew. What did you do with them?"
asked Kaid.

"Implanted them so they would be less violent. We need
their genetic material to breed our own warriors. Not like

them, though, we're adjusting their genetic memories so their hatred of the Sholans is removed. We only want to be able to defend ourselves effectively against the M'zullians and the J'kirtikkans."

"Two of your four worlds are locked in battle against each other, then there's you. What about the fourth?"

"It is harmless. They reverted to a level similar to that of the Jalnians. They are no danger to anyone."

"What's their setup?" asked Carrie. "Do they treat females as equals or shut them in breeding chambers?"

Zsurtul roused from his torpor. "Why should you care?" he asked. "Females are equal there. The castes are balanced. They are peaceful, there is plenty of laalquoi and they prosper. They are best left alone. We need your help to retrieve the ancient weapon that destroyed your two colonies, and to deal with the M'zullians and the J'kirtikkans who otherwise will wipe us out when they find us."

"Why didn't you tell us all this in the beginning, instead of treating us the way you did?" asked Kaid. "Why didn't you just ask us for help?"

"We did. When we took you telepaths, we asked you then. You refused us."

"We were never asked anything," said Kaid.

"It was done when we took you from your quarters. We couldn't let you know we were Valtegans, otherwise you would have refused us outright."

Rezac made a noise of extreme disgust. "We were drugged then. You expect that to make us change our minds?"

"You said you only found my cryo unit. Is that true?" asked Carrie suddenly.

He looked at her, hesitating, obviously weighing his answer. "We found the second unit," he admitted.

Hope leaped inside her. "And?"

"He lives. He's on the *Kz'adul*. But he's changed. You were found first. We operated on you as soon as we were able. He had seizures when we woke him. The doctors had to take desperate measures to ensure his survival."

"What measures? What have you done to him?" Her voice caught in her throat.

"I knew nothing about him until a few days ago," he said. "But I believe they had to permanently suppress his telepathic ability with an implant. I know he is your other mate and I wish I could tell you more, but I'm not a medic."

Carrie felt the surge of anger and grief from Kaid match hers. To go from knowing he was alive to this was just too much for her to accept right now. She forced it deep down inside, trying to distance herself from it.

"We want him back," she said, getting to her feet and leaning toward him. "If we don't get him, then they don't get you!"

Closing her mind to Kaid, she turned and left the mess. Too many emotions were fighting for dominance right now, and it could only affect what Kaid was doing, the decisions he had to make. She would have to deal with this alone.

CHAPTER 15

Commaner Q'ozoi looked up from his comp reader as Doctors Chy'qui and Zayshul entered.

"Chy'qui, what in the name of the God-King were you doing letting Prince Zsurtul conduct an experiment with J'koshuk? And why wasn't I informed first?" he demanded angrily. "Seems to me that since you took over Med Research, there's been a lot going on there that's been purposely kept from me."

"The Enlightened One insisted, Commander," said Chy'qui, taking a seat at the conference table opposite him. "He led me to believe you were aware of what was happening."

"Enlightened One be damned! He's still got shell between his toes!"

Zayshul winced at the blasphemy as she sat down beside Chy'qui.

"He isn't old enough to know what he's doing," the commander continued. "You should have refused him. You know that getting this treaty with the Sholans is our main objective. J'koshuk's gotten the one in the IC unit looking like a piece of raw meat! Which one of you authorized letting that damned M'zullian priest loose on the Sholan?"

"The Prince did, Commander," said Chy'qui. "Like yourself, I'd no idea J'koshuk was being so violent until almost too late. As for Prince Zsurtul, he is the heir to the throne, whether or not he's fully adult. You try reasoning with him when he says he'll inform the Emperor that we've been disrespectful of his orders. It makes my position as Head of Med Research and one of the God-King's counselors even more difficult."

"He's with us as the Emperor's personal representative,"

said Q'ozoi, pulling the comp reader in the center of the table over. "Not as a research scientist! And as for you, Zayshul, what possessed you to take him with you yesterday when you went to talk to our guests from the *Profit*? It's thanks to you he's been taken hostage by them!"

"He said the Emperor wanted him to have experience of the work we were doing with the M'zullians," interrupted Chy'qui.

"Commander, it isn't as easy for us to deal with Prince Zsurtul as it is for you," Zayshul said, shooting an angry look at Chy'qui. He invariably took every opportunity to remind the commander he was now in charge of Med Research. "I don't know about his interest in the M'zullians, but he's fascinated with our guests. It's difficult to turn him away when he has his own bodyguard. As for yesterday, he joined me at the last moment. I didn't take him with me."

The commander's forehead creased in a frown. "I suppose that does make sense. He was the one pushing for them to be released yesterday, to the extent of wanting to contact the Emperor if I wouldn't authorize it. Does he use his personal guards to threaten you?"

"No, not exactly," replied Zayshul. "He lets their presence intimidate. You know yourself that they're more likely to overreact than the regular guards because of their specialized implants. Normally, we aren't exposed to them, but they're wherever he is, and they're programmed to see everyone but the royal family as a potential threat. It's difficult not to feel intimidated by their very presence."

"If we get him back, what's left of his damned bodyguard gets shut down till we get home," hissed the commander angrily. "That incident in the landing bay nearly cost you and him your lives! Why didn't you tell me about this long before now?"

Chy'qui and Zayshul exchanged glances, for once in accord with each other.

"Point taken," sighed Q'ozoi. "Zayshul, how likely are the Sholans to harm Prince Zsurtul? I know you were doing most of the treatment to their injured personnel. After your experiences as their hostage, you probably know more about them than anyone on the *Kz'adul*."

"It depends on what he does," said Zayshul. "They did kill one of his guards and shoot the other when he ran."

A visible shudder ran through her at the memory of the murder. At that point, she'd been sure she was going to be next. "But they didn't harm me when they could easily have done so. And they worked as a team, all of them, despite the fact they belong to four different species."

"Damned overzealous bodyguard! The implant control room should have picked him up and neutralized him," said Q'ozoi. "I seem to remember from the reports that the only other time our guests offered violence to anyone was to the priest, J'koshuk."

Zayshul grimaced. "He's an animal. Why do we need the M'zullians' genetic material? The thought of hundreds of him running around is awful."

"Because the alternative is implanting volunteers, you know that," snapped Chy'qui. "We need reliable warriors who can breed. Implants become sterile. I disagree with Zayshul's opinion of the Sholans. I've viewed the log tapes of the incident in the hangar. There was no need to kill that guard just because he ran. They're killers as ferocious as the M'zullians. Look at the behavior of the one who mated with the injured female when he was returned to his companions. He ripped the room and its furnishings to shreds! He was looking for an opportunity for revenge on us because of what J'koshuk did. And he took it the first chance he got. By killing two guards and taking Prince Zsurtul."

"They don't know who he is," said Zayshul quietly. "They thought he was an officer. I don't think they'll harm the prince, Commander, because the one called Kaid saw him when he was brought to the stasis room to collect his mate."

"He'd no business being there," began Chy'qui but the commander waved him to silence.

"Why did you separate them, Zayshul? What was the point? If she'd been returned with him, then this regrettable incident couldn't have happened in the first place."

"I didn't separate them, Commander," said Zayshul. "I wanted her returned but Doctor Chy'qui overruled me. Said there were further tests he wanted to do. She was fit enough to be returned in my opinion."

Q'ozoi turned a questioning look on him.

"I wanted to be sure she wouldn't go into convulsions like the Sholan male."

"Highly unlikely, in my opinion. And not returning her was what made her mate, Kaid, trash the room, not a violent nature!" she said, thanking the spirits of past God-Kings that Chy'qui had been off-duty when the incident with J'koshuk had taken place. Had it not been for the Prince's backing in demanding the commander be involved immediately, she was sure the Human female wouldn't have been returned to her mate.

Q'ozoi had turned his attention to the reader again. "Chy'qui, have the M'zullians from the *M'ijikk* all been processed? Have you gotten all the genetic samples from them you need?"

"Yes," hissed Chy'qui. "They were handed over to Personnel for training assignments about a week ago."

Q'ozoi nodded, placing the reader back on the table. "Chy'qui, you were in charge of the Sholan male, Kusac. I see you had him implanted. Why? Surely the device is too specific to our own species to use on them? And why was he kept separate from the rest of his crew?"

"It's in the records, Commander. I had him implanted because when he was woken, he began to go into uncontrollable seizures. His very life was at risk. All I had left to try was the implant. Once it was in place, the seizures stopped. As well as saving his life, because he's been implanted, there are certain tests I'm able to run that are increasing our knowledge of their telepathic abilities. I couldn't do them if he'd been kept with the others."

"I see he's a telepath, one of a threesome with the Human female from the other cryogenic unit. Given the strong nature of their mental links to each other, they'll want him back. We can offer an exchange. Kusac for Prince Zsurtul and this General Kezule."

Chy'qui frowned. "Commander, if he's to be returned, then my research . . ."

"Will stop immediately," interrupted Q'ozoi. "Getting our Enlightened One back is more important."

Zayshul hid a smile behind a hastily raised hand.

"This implant, can you remove it now he's cured?"

"I'm afraid that isn't so easy," said Chy'qui. "The implants aren't intended to be removed, Commander. Once attached to the recipient, they bind themselves into the brain tissue."

Q'ozoi sat up in his seat, eyes narrowing as he glared at Chy'qui. "Why wasn't I informed about this matter before he was implanted? We could have returned him to a stasis unit and given him back to his own people to cure."

"I believe that was why he was in their cryo unit in the first place, Commander. And there wasn't time. We had no drugs we could use, and his condition had deteriorated too much for stasis to be an option. In the circumstances, an implant was worth trying."

Q'ozoi hissed angrily as he got to his feet. "I question your judgement, Doctor. The *Kz'adul*'s mission is to pursue a treaty with the Sholans. You may be a counselor to the Emperor, but your decisions over allowing Prince Zsurtul to experiment with J'koshuk and implanting the Sholan are flawed in the extreme. They could cost us our only useful potential allies! You're relieved of any responsibility for the Sholan. You will confine yourself to attending to the M'zullians. I had none of these problems when Doctor Zayshul was in charge of Med Research! You can be sure I'll lodge a complaint with the authorities when we return home."

He turned to look at Zayshul. "Doctor Zayshul, I'm putting you in charge of our Sholan's well-being. Get the TeLaxaudin onto it. Tell them they have to find a way to remove that implant. Once repairs to the hull have been completed, we'll be following the U'Churian ship. I want this Sholan fit to hand back to his people as soon as possible."

"Yes, Commander," said Zayshul.

"I'll expect a report from you within the next six hours," he said, heading for the door. He stopped, turning round to look at her one more time. "Glad you managed to survive the hull breech, Doctor. We lost too many people before we got the force field up."

* * *

Consciousness returned suddenly, bringing with it the smell of antiseptic and an awareness of paralysis as Kusac tried to move his head and found he couldn't.

"Don't be alarmed," said a voice nearby. "I am Commander Q'ozoi of the science ship *Kz'adul*. You were injured and have been sleeping in our medical center while your injuries healed. In a few days, we hope to rendezvous with your people and return you to them."

A voice, not a translator, speaking Sholan. It sounded like J'koshuk's but it wasn't. He took a deep breath, searching underneath the antiseptic for other scents. Valtegan, but not one he recognized. One of M'ezozakk's crew?

"I need some information from you."

He tried to laugh and found himself coughing and beginning to choke.

"Release the restraint field and get him some water."

A guttural reply was cut short by an explosive comment, then suddenly he could move again.

Immediately he rolled on his side, a task made difficult by the formfitting bed, and continued to cough. A bowl shaped cup was handed to him and he took it gratefully, gulping down all the water. His throat eased, he looked up. Standing by his bed, clad in a military style gray one-piece, stood a Valtegan. He looked unlike any Valtegan Kusac had seen before. The hairless skull wasn't smooth, it was crested with a knobbed rigid extrusion, like a continuation of its spine, running back from where his nose joined the forehead. Below it, dark green, slightly bulbous eyes regarded him.

Kusac pushed himself up into a sitting position. The bed seemed to relax around him, losing the configuration of his body and reverting to an oval shape.

He moved slowly and stiffly, finding he still hurt in many places, principally his head, ribs, and groin muscles.

"I thought J'koshuk had beaten everything you wanted to know out of me," he said.

"You have my apologies for that. He should not have been allowed near you. He has been dealt with."

Kusac stared at him. "Sure," he said, looking beyond the Seniormost to the armed guard standing behind him.

"You are probably wondering how you come to be on our ship. A signal was recently received from an ancient device of ours, one associated with the Sholans. The *Kz'adul* was sent to investigate and to make contact with your people. As we approached Jalna, we saw an enemy ship, the *M'ijikk,* attack and board your craft. We decided to intervene on your behalf. The crew of the *Rryuk's Profit* have been well treated, and the Human female was healed. You were taken ill when you were revived so we kept you separate."

"Why are you telling me this?" he asked, mildly curious as he continued looking round the room. It was large, well lit, with three more intensive care beds like his. All were empty. By the door stood another two armed guards.

"Because we have a common enemy and wish a treaty with you."

Kusac looked back at the Seniormost. He felt anger, but it was distant, as if not really part of him. "What common enemy?"

"The Valtegans from the *M'ijikk* whom you fought on the Human world of Keiss, and the J'kirtikkans with whom they're at war."

"You're from another Valtegan world?"

"We're from the home world, yes."

"The world that ruled your empire?" His interest was beginning to grow a little. Memories of Valtegans on Keiss were coming back to him, of their fear and psychotic hatred of Sholans.

"Our ancient empire, yes. These days, we only wish to defend ourselves against the M'zullians and the J'kirtikkians. Now that one ship has discovered Jalna, others will follow. All who trade there are at risk from the M'zullians' and J'kirtikkians' warlike nature. Our envoy explained this to your crew, but they chose to leave without taking the treaty papers. Why would they not agree to an alliance?"

He was having difficulty getting past the fact that he was having a rational conversation with a Valtegan. "I don't know. Perhaps they didn't think you were hospitable enough." This was confusing. Was he saying they'd escaped? If so, then his family were safe. The knowledge should please him, he knew it should, but again, he felt remote from it.

"We need your help. We can't be sure those on the *Rryuk's Profit* will present our petition accurately. The location of your home world, Shola, is known to us. We wish to go there but you have system defenses. We need you to take us through them so we can put our case to your leaders ourselves."

Shock reached through the indifference, but only just. He concentrated on what the Seniormost had just said. It sounded so logical that he began to wonder what was wrong with him. "I need to think about that," he said, lying down again. "I'm tired. Your priest hurt me too much and the drugs make it difficult to remember." Around him, the bed began to conform to his shape again.

There was a short silence. "As you wish, but the matter is urgent. I can give you an hour to consider your answer."

He heard the footsteps of the Seniormost and the guard recede in the distance. Turning his head, he saw the two at the door remained. They wore no armor now, only black fatigues, but they were still heavily armed. He looked at the ceiling, trying to marshal his thoughts. It was difficult to concentrate. Had they drugged him into complaisance? He remembered being controlled before, but not completely. They weren't able to force him, otherwise he'd have agreed to taking them into Sholan space.

Putting his hand up to his face, he felt the bruising and swelling on his cheeks and eye ridges. There was very little pain. How long had he been here? Reaching lower, he felt tentatively under his left ear. The implant was still there, he could feel the edges of it. He felt sick then, and his body begin to shake with reaction. Not drugs, it was the device controlling him. He checked his neck, feeling the warm metal of the collar. For all the commander's fine words, they hadn't removed that.

He let his arm fall back to his side. If they were telling him the truth, he was alone on this ship. There'd be no help for him. Kaid must think him dead, so must Carrie. Instinctively, he reached out for them, feeling the collar round his neck start to tingle and send a similar sensation down his back. He ignored it, pushing his mind harder, trying to find them mentally.

The tingling increased to a level of pain that threatened to break his concentration. Remembering what had happened to them on Jalna, he shifted mental wavelengths and immediately found that the pain began to recede and his head began to clear slightly.

Fear hit him. Now he realized fully just what they expected him to do. To betray his home world. If the Primes got a scent of the fact he could combat their implant at all, they could adjust it till he had no will of his own left. The commander might try to present the Primes as having been altruistic toward the rest of the crew, but he suspected the truth was quite different.

He remembered quite clearly a Seniormost bringing J'koshuk to him the first time, remembered the questions he'd been asked by him, and J'koshuk's torture. It wasn't possible that it had happened without the knowledge of their commander.

Somehow, he had to prevent the Primes from reaching Shola. If Kaid thought there was a possibility of being followed, he wouldn't head for home, he'd head somewhere farther away, somewhere capable of defending itself. Somewhere like Haven.

Some time later, Commander Q'ozoi returned, followed by an aide carrying a chair for him. It was placed beside Kusac's bed.

Kusac didn't wait for him to start talking. There were questions he wanted answered. "Why has a device been implanted in me?"

"When you were brought out of cryogenic sleep, you had violent seizures. They threatened your life. The implant was the only way of controlling them before they killed you."

He absorbed that for a minute. It was possible, depending on how long they'd had Carrie awake, but he'd never heard of seizures as a symptom of Link deprivation. In the brief moment he'd sensed them, he'd known that Carrie and Kaid had formed a Leska Link. At least she was safe. "Seizures?"

"Your body was suffering muscle spasms and you were choking. Between the seizures, you were violent. No other way to incapacitate you and control the fits without harming you could be found. It was an emergency measure, I'm afraid. The implants weren't designed for your species, they're for the M'zullian Valtegans. Our doctor did what he thought best at the time. I've answered your questions, now it's your turn, Kusac. Will you take us safely to Shola?"

He closed his eyes. He was tired, had no energy or interest in this or any conversation. "I can't. I don't know the codes you want. I can take you to the place where my people are going. Another of the Sholan crew is empowered to make Contact negotiations. You can show him your papers."

"Another, Kusac? Are you similarly empowered?"

It was said so softly that he almost didn't realize his mistake and the implications of the commander's question. "Not now," he said. "I was relieved of duty when I was put in cryo."

"But you're out now."

Kusac opened his eyes again. "You could make me, but anything I signed wouldn't be recognized by my people."

"Then give me the codes and coordinates for where they're going," Q'ozoi said, holding out a comp reader.

Kusac tiredly lifted his right arm and took it from him. Pushing himself up on his other elbow, he switched hands and punched in the figures before handing it back.

Q'ozoi took it from him, glanced at it, and stood up. His aide ran forward to remove the chair. "Thank you. Doctor Zayshul will be in presently to make you more comfortable," he said.

Kusac let himself fall back to the bed. Keeping his thoughts straight for this long had drained him. All he could do now was pray that he'd done the right thing.

* * *

It had taken Kezule that night and another to reach the first estate. By hiding high in the trees adjacent to it during daylight, he'd learned it was the Aldatan estate, and the one he wanted, Valsgarth, lay farther south. The route through the trees took longer but was safer than crossing the open fields and leaving his scent behind for them to smell.

Another night's travel had seen him in the woodland behind the small village. It was smaller than the other, consisting of only two main rows of wooden houses divided up by five short streets intersecting them at right angles. Construction work was still going on at the end farthest from the large house, but many of the buildings were occupied.

The inhabitants were a curious mixture of species, a fact he found baffling. Why would the Sholans want to share their private estates with aliens? He recognized one species, the Humans. The other, a brightly dressed, ungainly species, he had never seen before. A mixed group of all three species had left early that morning in several small aircars, heading for a distant hill topped by ruins. That intrigued him. Why were they going there? They'd had an air of purpose about them, as if going for a reason other than leisure. They returned just before dusk, their clothing stained and dusty. He deduced they were involved in some manual work, perhaps more construction.

Crouched as high in his tree as he could safely go, he'd watched their day unfold. It was essentially the same as the one on the other estate, with some Sholans heading out to work in the fields and others making themselves busy around the village with building, combat training, planting their gardens, and visiting the village store. The training had him confused. He'd understood from the telepath he'd killed and the female, Keeza, that this was the estate where the majority of telepaths lived. How could they be training when to fight made them physically sick? Then he remembered the two Sholan males who'd taken him had fought with others of their kind in the desert. Something about them had changed. Was it mixing with the Humans? He dismissed the puzzle for the time being. More important was his need to find out where the ones he wanted lived. So far, he'd seen no sign of them.

Darkness fell and streetlamps were lit as people retired to their homes for the evening. Overhead, the aerial patrol flew by at its usual time. He climbed lower, pulling on the dark robe again for better concealment. Still he waited, listening and watching for the night foot patrol he knew would come through the main street. He almost missed them, so quiet were they. Gray-clad, they blended in the shadows well. Not soldiers, these ones. They were more than that.

They were no sooner out of sight than he heard a noise from the building opposite. As he watched, the window was pulled quietly open and a head poked out, looking around. It ducked back in, then a knotted rope was thrown out.

Curious, he watched as, with much whispering and giggling, two small figures climbed down to the ground.

"Daira, shut up!" hissed the larger one. "If you keep up that noise, you'll wake my mum, then we'll never get to see the Touibans!"

"Sorry, Mandy," he whispered.

"Come on, let's get going," Mandy said, grabbing him by the hand and heading toward the back of their garden—and closer to Kezule.

He watched as they climbed over the low fence and crept round the rear of the gardens, heading for the end of the street. Keeping to the deep shadows, he followed them. At the last building, he stopped, watching as they scampered through the pools of light cast by the lamps to the buildings on the other side. Now he could see clearly what he'd suspected. One child was Sholan, the other Human.

He couldn't risk following them, and equally, couldn't afford to lose them. During the day, he'd seen others walking around the village wearing dark robes. Maybe if he pulled the hood up, he'd escape notice. It was his only option. He had to get across the roadway. Tipping his head down and pulling the hood well forward, he clasped his hands together, letting the wide mouths of the sleeves cover them. Stepping out into the open, he walked briskly across the street, making for the rear of the buildings opposite where the children had gone. Reaching the cover of the far corner, he slowed down, breathing again as he realized he'd made it.

Cautiously, he peered round the corner, catching sight of the two small forms scurrying down the back of the garden fences. He followed, once more keeping low, seeing them jump a fence near the far end. As he drew level with the house, he realized the reason for their illicit night outing was to spy on the household of garishly dressed aliens.

Easing his gun from his robe pocket and flicking the safety off, he stuck it through the tie belt. The night was still, what little movement of air there was came from the young ones toward him. If they saw him, his disguise should fool them long enough for him to get close. Maintaining his crouch, he inched his way slowly forward but they were too busy trying to peer through a window with partly open drapes to notice him. When he finally loomed over them, it was too late. A quick blow to the back of the neck of the young Sholan, then he grasped hold of the other one, hand over her mouth to stop her from yelling.

"Be very quiet or you and your friend will die," he hissed in her ear as she struggled to get free.

She stiffened and he felt her try to nod her head.

"I'm going to put you down and take my hand from your mouth. One sound and you know what I'll do." He set her down, removing his hand from her mouth and grasping her by the throat. "Don't try to pull away," he warned letting her feel the tips of his claws against her flesh. "One squeeze of my hand is all it takes. Understand?"

She nodded, putting her hand up to her mouth to stifle her cry of fear as she caught sight of him.

Pulling her with him, he reached down to pick up the Sholan child. Slinging him over his shoulder, he dragged the female back into the trees just beyond the end of the garden. When he could no longer see the lights of the village, he stopped, dropping the unconscious young male to the ground. He could forget about him, he wouldn't wake till dawn. He turned to the Human child.

"In which house does the Human called Carrie Aldatan live?" he demanded.

"I . . . I don't know," she said falteringly.

He shook her like a rag doll, claws causing tiny wounds in her neck. "Which house?" he demanded.

"The big one at the end," she whimpered, tears running down her face as she caught at his hand, trying to pull on his fingers. "But they're not there! They're not back from Jalna yet!"

He hissed with rage, hand tightening instinctively till he realized he was throttling her. He relaxed his grip. "Who stays there now? I saw people going in and out of it today."

"The doctor and his companion, Jiszoe, and Kashini, and Brother Dzaka. And the nurse."

"Who are they? Relations of the Aldatans?" He increased the pressure slightly. Relations would do, would force them to surrender to him when they returned.

"Their baby and Kaid's son. He guards her," she sobbed. "Please, don't hurt me! I haven't done anything!"

"You'll take me to this house." He needed somewhere to go, to hide out in safety with his hostages till the Aldatans returned. Then he remembered the hill and the ruins. "What are they doing at the ruins?"

"It's being excavated. There's tunnels in it where Sholans hid from the Valtegans in the past." She stopped, eyes widening even further in fear. "You're a Valtegan!"

He gave a short laugh. "Yes, I'm a Valtegan." He let his tongue flick out close to her face. "I have nothing to lose, so make no sound and you will be set free once I have the people I want." Reaching inside his robe, he pulled out the rope that was coiled round his waist. Turning her round, he quickly and efficiently bound her wrists behind her, cutting off the extra length with his teeth. He'd need that for the one called Dzaka.

Ten minutes later, Mandy stood at the back door waiting for someone to answer Kezule's knock. The light had already been on, and almost immediately, they heard footsteps making their way to the back door. It opened, casting a pool of golden light onto the path.

"Mandy! What on earth are you doing out at . . ." Jack fell silent as he found himself looking at the muzzle of an energy pistol held by a Valtegan.

Kezule waved him back into the house and, pulling Mandy with him, entered, shutting the door behind him.

"Sit," he ordered, pointing to the table where Jack had been working. He picked Mandy up and placed her on another chair as Jack resumed his seat. "Where is your mate?" he demanded.

"In bed asleep," said Jack quietly. "You must be Kezule. I had no idea you were free."

"Silence!" Kezule hissed, checking out the room thoroughly before looking cautiously through the doors to the adjacent main kitchen. Stuffing his pistol through his belt, he took a towel from the back of a chair and ripped it into strips. "The one called Dzaka, where is he?"

"In bed asleep," said Jack as his arms were pulled behind him and tied to the chair.

"I want him and the child down here, now. Call him."

"No need," said Jack as they heard a noise from the room next door.

Pulling his gun, Kezule dived for the door, standing to

one side as it burst open to admit a naked but armed Sholan male, a young child clutched to his chest.

"Jack, what . . ." Dzaka skidded to an abrupt stop as he took in the situation.

"Drop the gun," said Kezule, aiming directly at the child. "Slowly."

Dzaka lowered his weapon, dropping it to the floor near his feet.

"Kick it away," ordered Kezule. "Then sit down at the table, there." He pointed to the chair farthest from Jack and Mandy.

Dzaka sent the gun spinning across the floor, then moved toward the table and sat down. "What do you want, Kezule?" he asked, shifting Kashini so his body shielded her.

"You and the child. Put it on the table and place your hands behind your back," he ordered, readying another strip of towel.

Dzaka placed the unusually subdued Kashini on the table. "Leave the cub, Kezule," he said quietly, putting his hands behind his back. "You have me, you've no need of her. She'd only be a liability to you."

"Enough talk," said Kezule, binding his wrists individually, then together.

"The estate is crawling with guards. You can't possibly escape."

Kezule ignored him, unfastening Dzaka's wrist comm and turning up the psi damper field to maximum before putting it on him again. Pulling the remainder of his rope free, he placed it round Dzaka's neck, tying it in a noose with a rigid knot. He then tied a sliding knot at the other end. Turning to Kashini, who'd been watching the proceedings with curiosity, he scooped her up in one arm, tucking her inside his robe against his chest.

"Your guards are so good they couldn't keep me out," he said, going round to Jack. He grasped him by the chin, turning his head to face him. "I am taking them as hostages till the Aldatans return. Tell your people that. They can contact me on their wrist communicators." A blow to the back of his neck and Jack slumped unconscious to the table.

Mandy began to whimper as Kezule turned to her.

"Leave Mandy alone," said Dzaka, beginning to rise

from his chair. "There's no need to . . ." but already she was sliding bonelessly off her chair.

Grabbing Dzaka by an arm, Kezule pulled him to his feet, then slipped the other end of the noose round Kashini's neck.

"One sound and the child dies. There will not be a second warning. You are tethered to her. If you run, the loop will tighten and she will strangle. Do we understand each other?"

Dzaka nodded. Kezule switched off the light and opened the door.

The journey through the woods had been a nightmare one. Dzaka had been ordered to lead them to the tunnels under the ruins. That was bad news. If Kezule got holed up in the lab area, he could seal them in by closing the steel doors. They were blast proof and virtually impregnable.

The pace Kezule had set had been punishing and Dzaka hadn't time to watch where he put his feet. As he stumbled for perhaps the twentieth time, he suddenly felt his footing go completely from under him. With a yell of fear, he began sliding and rolling down the side of a small gully. He felt the rope round his neck tighten painfully, then suddenly go slack as he caromed off a tree trunk, stunning himself, before finally coming to rest at the bottom.

He lay there, head aching and spinning with the sick fear that Kashini was dead. Unable to get up, he had to lie there while Kezule slithered down to get him. Then he heard Kashini whimpering. Relief flooded through him.

Kezule stood over him, knife glinting in what little moonlight there was as he returned it to its sheath inside his robe.

"Lucky for the child I had that," he said, reaching down and hauling Dzaka to his feet.

Blood from Dzaka's cut brow was running into his eyes and he had to shake his head to clear them. He groaned as pain stabbed through his temples.

Grasping hold of the noose still round his neck, Kezule pulled him closer. "With one as clumsy as you, I cannot risk the child again. I want your oath of honor that you won't try to escape."

From the folds of Kezule's robe, Kashini reached out

for her bond-brother. Her fingers brushed his cheek before Kezule released him.

"I swear," Dzaka gasped. "Just don't harm her!"

They regained the path, Kezule holding him by the arm as they traveled parallel to it, keeping in the cover of the woods until they saw the opening to the tunnel ahead. It was in darkness. There wasn't the need for the archaeologists to work round the clock any more, so no one was on duty. As they entered, Kashini began to whimper again.

"Where are the torches or lights?" demanded Kezule, stopping just inside.

"There, to your left," said Dzaka, bobbing his head in the direction of the box on the wall. With any luck, someone would see the lights blazing out and come to investigate before Kezule got them holed up in the lab.

Kezule opened the box, looking carefully at the labeled switches. "What areas do they light?" he asked. "And can they be turned off from inside?"

"The top one is main lighting, the one below, emergency lights only. The others light individual caverns and tunnels."

Kezule's hand hesitated over the top switch, then flipped the one below. Above them, subdued lights flickered briefly then came on. Kezule rounded on Dzaka, hitting him once across the face, sending him staggering backward.

"Don't lie to me again," he hissed, crest rising briefly in anger. Grasping him by the arm again, they entered the tunnel.

Licking his split lip, Dzaka limped on, leading the way up the slope to the first chamber, then across to the next tunnel. When they came out in the main chamber, he heard Kezule's sharp intake of breath. There was a field kitchen here, complete with supplies, and even a couple of camp beds for their first aid station. It had just about everything he could need to stock up for a siege. Except raw meat.

Kezule made a quick tour of the room before leading him over to the lab. Again he hissed in pleasure as he saw the steel door. Surveying the room quickly, he dragged Dzaka to the ancient microscope, securing him firmly to its massive base. That done, Kezule returned to the main chamber to gather the bedding and stores.

Dzaka immediately began pulling at the bindings on his

wrists, trying to get free, but the harder he pulled, the tighter they got till his circulation was almost cut off.

Kezule returned for the final time. He'd located the kitchen generator and the feed for the lighting as well as several flashlights. Activating the flashlights, he stood them on the work surface nearest the door, then unplugged the lights and replugged them into the generator, switching it on. Heading for the entrance, he sealed the steel door. The sound of it sliding shut sent a shiver of fear through Dzaka.

"Now we wait for them to discover you're missing," said Kezule, pulling Kashini from his robe and coming toward him.

* * *

Day 38

Brynne awoke early to the knowledge that Dzaka and Kashini had been kidnapped and Father Lijou and Master Konis were on their way to see him. Banner was to report to Garras at the training hall as every able-bodied person was staking out the estate perimeter and the monastery hill itself.

The name Kezule filled Keeza with terror, but she didn't know why.

"Stay upstairs," said Brynne as he left their bedroom. "Between Father Lijou and Master Konis, very little happens on Shola that they don't know about. I don't want them recognizing you before we know more about your past."

She nodded, ears invisible in her halo of tabby hair.

Jurrel was letting them in as Brynne left, and their voices drifted up the stairs to her.

"Brynne, Father Lijou says you might be able to contact Dzaka. Something Derwent taught you. Would you try for me, please? I need to do something while we're waiting for Garras and Ni'Zulhu to report back to us."

"Of course, Master Konis. There was no need for you to even ask," replied Brynne.

"There's no guarantee it will work, Konis," warned Lijou as they left the hall for the den. "Brynne said he can see, that's all."

Keeza's senses began to spin as the voices triggered more images from her subconscious. She clutched the doorframe as colors, scents and images exploded in front of her eyes, transporting her back to the military facility at Shanagi.

> Tall, green-skinned, his oval head totally hairless, the Valtegan Kezule had gone to the feeding cage where a terrified chiddoe squealed frantically as it tried to dig its way out. She'd watched as he'd taken the helpless creature out and with a single, quick movement, snapped its neck. Then he'd turned to the concealed viewing window and begun to dismember it before returning to his table. She'd watched, fascinated and horrified, as he'd skinned and eaten it. She'd shuddered then, and she did so again.
> The Brother had taken her to another room, one where the males whose voices she'd just heard waited for her. They'd spoken softly to her, and done something to her mind.

Her head was pounding but the images didn't stop. She remembered Kezule's protuberant slitted eyes regarding her dispassionately as he handed her a plate of scraps.

> "You may eat," he'd said.
> She had, ravenously, her face and body still aching from the beating he'd given her the day before for trying to steal his leftover food. She could still smell the stench of the fresh blood and taste the raw flesh.

Memories were coming faster now, flashing before her eyes like a kaleidoscope of her life. Kezule taking her arm and sinking his teeth into it with great deliberation, telling her to watch him while he slept. Him waking, too weak to eat, needing her to feed him gobbets of raw meat. The blood had run down her arms, soaking into her pelt. The smell of the blood had made her hungry, but he needed the food more than she did now. In the shower, she'd sluiced the dead and flaking skin from his emaciated body, a body that was as smooth and hairless as his head. It was the first time she'd seen him unclothed. He was featureless, no sex, nothing. She'd lain with him then, after wrapping him in all their blankets for warmth. She'd felt the need to protect and care for him. He was hers, her male and beautiful in her eyes.

She moaned, slipping down to her knees, but it wasn't over yet. An alarm had gone off and the guards and medics had come. She'd crouched over his unconscious body, protecting him from her own kind. Then suddenly, he'd awakened, grabbing the male medic by the throat. Blood had fountained everywhere, spraying the female, the walls, the ceiling. She'd gone for the guards then, while they looked in horror at Kezule. One she kicked, hearing his neck snap, glad that he could no longer threaten her male. The other she'd shot, holding the neural stunner on him till he died in agony, his screams meaning nothing to her in her greater need to protect Kezule.

The race through the building with their hostages, the escape to the aircar, and the flight out of the city to the forest clearing where they landed, his killing of the telepath, all flashed before her eyes. Sick and feverish, convinced she was dying, she'd headed into the forest with him, then he'd turned on her. It had been him. The male she'd fought, who'd raped her, had been Kezule. And now he was here.

She pulled herself up, and returning to the bed, reached under Brynne's pillows for his pistol. The two males she'd heard talking, they were the ones who'd put her in with Kezule.

"I forget myself," said Konis, turning to Brynne and holding his hand out in greeting.

Brynne had no option but to reach forward, touching fingertips briefly with him, knowing the Clan Lord would notice his cut palm and know he was now life-bonded. He'd want to know who she was. He could feel how tight a rein Master Konis was keeping on his emotions; none of them needed this distraction right now.

"A marriage cut?" Konis held his hand, looking from the small healing wound to Brynne's face. "This is unexpected. You have my best wishes, Brynne. I thought I sensed a new presence on the estate. I wish it had been Kezule I'd sensed!"

"My congratulations, too, Brynne. Do I know her?"

Brynne was unable to answer. He stood there, swaying slightly, his eyes blank as his mind was flooded with Keeza's memories.

"Brynne?" asked Lijou, face creasing in concern as he put a hand out to steady him.

"She's been ill," stammered Brynne, putting a hand to his aching head as his mental link to Keeza abruptly ceased. "Later, you'll meet her later."

The door behind him opened and, as he was about to turn around, Konis spoke.

"Stay very still, Brynne," he said quietly.

He spun round, knowing it was Keeza. He hardly recognized her, everything about her was different, from the way her tail swayed lazily to the set of her ears, and the gun pointing directly at him.

"Get out of my way, Brynne," she said, her voice firm and determined.

"No," he said. "This isn't the way, Keeza. There must be a reason. Ask them."

"Oh, I intend to," she said with a small, mocking laugh. "Move aside!"

"No," he said, taking a step toward her.

She sidestepped him, aiming at Konis. "Don't interfere, Brynne. I don't want to hurt you if I can avoid it, but if I have to, I will. I want them to tell me why, what justification they have, for doing what they did to me."

She was on the edge of sanity now, Brynne could feel it, could see the hand that held the gun trembling slightly. It would take very little for her to kill again. He had to stop her, before Jurrel did.

Simultaneously, he reached out with his mind as he leaped at her, grabbing her arm and pulling it and the weapon down. From behind her, Jurrel launched himself forward, but before he contacted them, a single, muffled shot rang out.

For a frozen moment, Brynne and Keeza stood face-to-face, then Jurrel's attack felled them both. The gun went flying from Keeza's limp fingers to slither across the floor, landing at Lijou's feet. Stooping, he picked it up, training it on the three figures on the floor.

Brynne slowly sat up, gathering Keeza's still form into

his lap and looking over at Konis and Lijou. Jurrel rose, and meeting Lijou's gaze, left the room at a run, heading for the medikit in his room.

"I don't care what she's done, she's my life-mate!" Brynne said angrily. "Why? Why did you put her in with Kezule? What the hell were you thinking of?" He felt cold, was starting to shiver. Sweat was beginning to run down his back, soaking his robe. "She's a gene-altered telepath, dammit! How could you do that to her? You made her what she was, made her a killer!"

The room was beginning to spin, he was having difficulty staying conscious. "She's my life-mate and she's pregnant with our cub," he mumbled as he felt himself beginning to fall. "You can't take her from me."

* * *

The team, commanded by Garras and Ni'Zulhu, that entered the upper chamber was composed of those Brothers picked by Kaid as bodyguards.

"He's closed the blast door," said Rulla quietly into the mouthpiece of his headset from his forward position. "He's sealed in tight as a demon fish's arse."

"Fan out," said Ni'Zulhu. "Keep low. There's two-way vid cameras in the cavern, linked into the lab."

Keeping close to the far wall, Meral headed for the kitchen area. "He's taken the generator and emptied the food stores here," he whispered into his wrist comm.

"Sick bay's gone, and the heater," said Lasad.

"He's taken anything of use," said Ni'Zulhu. "At least they've got the basics."

"Not Kezule," said Garras, covering his mouthpiece. "He needs raw meat."

They exchanged looks as Garras' wrist comm began to buzz. "That's him," Ni'Zulhu nodded. "Answer him."

Moving his mouthpiece out of the way, Garras activated the tiny vid unit. "Release the hostages, Kezule, then we'll talk."

"This child has needs. Provide them or not, it matters little to me," the Valtegan said, then the line went dead.

A faint commotion came from downstairs, then the cavern and tunnel lights came full on, blinding them all.

"What the hell's going on down there?" Ni'Zulhu demanded of his people as the noise grew closer. "And who put the damned lights on?"

"It's the Clan Leader," came the reply. "She's on her way up."

Ni'Zulhu looked at Garras who shrugged. "Take cover and maintain your current positions," he ordered, signing off.

Her blue robe flaring out behind her, Rhyasha, followed by Mnesu, marched to the mouth of the tunnel where Ni'-Zulhu and Garras were crouched. "Why are you creeping around in the dark?" she demanded. "You're supposed to be rescuing my grandchild and Dzaka, not playing some childish game of Hide!"

Garras blinked, taken aback by her verbal attack. "Hide?"

She reached down and hauled him to his feet. "You know damned well what I mean!" she hissed. "Now, what does this—creature—want?" She punctuated her words by poking him repeatedly on the chest.

"Clan Leader, with respect, you're interfering with our . . ."

"Garras, find out what he wants! I will not risk Kashini's life, or Dzaka's!"

"Clan Leader, we can't negotiate with him . . ." began Ni'Zulhu.

"Can't?" she demanded, turning on him. "*Can't*? You will do what I tell you! If you don't, I will take charge myself!" She reached for his headset and only Garras' hand snaking out to catch hold of her prevented it being ripped off Ni'Zulhu's head.

"Your pardon, Clan Leader," said Garras, letting her go hastily as she turned a vitriolic look on him. "You'll break it if you pull it about like that."

"Find out what he wants!"

Ni'Zulhu activated his wrist comm this time. "What do you want, Kezule?"

"The three Aldatans who brought me to this time. When they come to me, then the child and the one called Dzaka will be released."

Ni'Zulhu glanced sideways at Rhyasha as he answered. "They're missing in action, Kezule. Their craft's disappeared. Likelihood is they're dead. Give yourself up now, before you make the situation worse."

A short silence. "You lie. I will wait for them. I wish to return to my time, that's all."

Rhyasha's ears had flattened in extreme distress. "My granddaughter for my son and bond-daughter?" she whispered, putting her hands to her face. "How can I trade one for the other?"

"They can't return you, Kezule," said Garras, activating his own comm. "They sealed the way back."

"Enough talking! I will wait for them. Meanwhile, this child has needs. You can hear her."

In the background, they could hear Kashini howling in distress.

Rhyasha grasped hold of Garras' arm, pulling his wrist unit up to her mouth. "If we gather what she needs, how will we get it in to you?"

They heard a hiss of anger. "Can you Sholans not control your females?" Kezule snarled. "Fetch me your leader, I will talk to him or no one!" Again the line went dead.

Stunned, Rhyasha let Garras' wrist fall from her grasp.

"Clan Leader, their females are feral, not sentient," he said gently, putting an arm round her shoulders. "When your son brought him to our time, he nearly killed a female medic for touching him. He won't deal with you. It has to be one of us. I'm sorry, but that's the way it is."

Dzaka had listened to the exchange anxiously. He knew the situation right now was volatile, so volatile that Kezule might kill either him or Kashini in anger. He had to get him to listen to Rhyasha.

"General, she's the one you want, the leader of the family," he began. The rest of what he was going to say was cut short as Kezule spun toward him, landing a blow on the side of his face.

"Be silent! You will speak only when told to do so!"

Dzaka's head rocked on his shoulders, pain lancing across his cheek as one of the Valtegan's claws grazed him.

"Females run the families on Shola," he said in a rush, lifting his head to look up at him. "She will give you what you want."

"Females should be kept in the breeding rooms, not allowed to meddle in the affairs of males!"

"We males are the warriors," said Dzaka, locking eyes with him as Kezule drew his hand back to hit him again. "We fight. Our females bear the cubs and tend the families, not us. Deal with her and you'll get what you want. She's the cub's grandmother. Or deal with our warriors."

The Valtegan hesitated.

"You heard her. She asked what you needed. The male refused to talk. Your choice, General."

Kezule let out a hiss of pure rage. "I will not deal with females!"

Dzaka shrugged and looked away as if it didn't matter to him. Inside was another matter. Fear gripped his heart and stomach with cold talons, making him think he'd black out. His life and Kashini's hung in the balance right now, and the cub wasn't helping as she squalled loudly in terror.

Kezule threw back his head and roared in rage. It was a sound so alien it sent shivers down Dzaka's spine and silenced Kashini.

"You will talk to her!" he snarled. "I will tell you what I need."

"Clan Leader?" The voice was quiet and almost went unnoticed as Garras was leading Rhyasha out of the upper chamber.

"Dzaka!" Rhyasha stopped dead and grabbed hold of Garras' wrist again. "What do you need?"

"Kashini's things—her old blanket that she chews, clothes—the nurse knows." He sounded tired and in pain. "Her food, too, and extra bedding."

"What about you?"

"Food for Kezule," he said in a rush. "Chiddoes, live and caged. At least four a day. For Vartra's sake, Rhyasha, don't let them stop his food supply!" His voice tailed off as the comm was taken away from him.

"Sholan female!" The voice was sibilant, the tone peremptory. "You will do as I say or I will kill this male, piece by piece. I can see the cavern on a display screen. Put the items on a wheeled pallet, with a rope at one end. Have one person where I can see him on the screen throw me the rope, then it will be pulled in. I am armed. If you try to shoot into the opening, the child or Dzaka will likely be hit, not me. Give me your word that you'll not attempt to attack me or force your way in."

Garras attempted to snatch his wrist away from her but she increased her grip, clamping her claws into his hide.

Ni'Zulhu grabbed for her, only to have his ear boxed severely by her other hand.

"Yes! You have our word!" she said.

"Rhyasha!" exclaimed Garras. "Dammit! You've no right to . . ."

"This is *my* estate, *my* Clan and *my* granddaughter, and you tell me I have no right? You will honor my oath, Garras Janagu!"

"You have given your word, Sholan Clan Leader," said Kezule. "Do not let your soldiers make a liar of you." The connection went dead.

Rhyasha looked at Garras. "Live chiddoes?"

"They eat freshly killed raw meat," said Garras. "Go and get the things you need, Rhyasha," he said gently, freeing his wrist from her unresisting hand. "We'll honor your oath, I promise. I'll see to rounding up a supply of chiddoes if you can get the grain for them organized."

She nodded, a glazed look coming over her face. "They'll need water. And Kashini's toys."

Garras gestured to Mnesu who came forward to take the Clan Leader by the arm and lead her back down the tunnel.

"We're not keeping it," stated Ni'Zulhu as soon as she was out of earshot.

Garras looked at him. "Oh, yes, we are," he said. "Does each one of us have to make a separate agreement with Kezule before it's honored? This is my Clan, too, and I'll not have us break our word, even to a Valtegan. Did you hear Dzaka's voice? Dammit, Ni'Zulhu! He's not that easily rattled, I know him! If you want to think of starving Kezule out, just remember, he's got quite a large supply of fresh meat in there with him, in the shape of a cub of three months and an adult Sholan. And as he said, he doesn't need to kill them to get it," he snarled.

Ni'Zulhu looked shocked.

"We play it straight, do you understand me? Let's just get through today safely."

* * *

Konis sat down abruptly as Lijou stuck the gun in his pocket and rushed over to Brynne. Pulling the Human's robe open, he looked up at the Clan Lord.

"Konis, give me the cloth on that table," he said. "I need to staunch this wound."

The Clan Lord stood as if carved in stone.

"Konis!"

As if in a dream, Konis reached for the small decorative cloth on the table in front of him and picked it up.

"Throw it to me!" ordered Lijou. "Dammit, Konis, pull yourself together! He's bleeding heavily!"

The Clan Lord shot out of his seat to the priest's side, handing him the cloth. "Is it clean enough?" he asked.

Lijou glanced at him as he folded the cloth into a pad. "Go sit down, Konis, I can manage," he said quietly as he pressed the pad over the wound in Brynne's side.

"I'm staying," Konis said. "What can I do?"

Lijou nodded to Keeza. "Check her. The shot could have hit her, too."

Konis moved round to check on Keeza. "I can't see any blood," he said after a moment. "I think she just hit her head when she fell."

"Thank the Gods! Now move her off him, please."

Konis eased Keeza's limp body off Brynne's lap onto the floor, getting up to fetch a couple of cushions. He put one under her head and handed the other to Lijou for Brynne. "He's right," he said abruptly. "We are responsible for her. Obviously what she's been through has broken our programming. We have to do something about her, Lijou."

"We will, my friend," said Lijou. "She was promised a new life. It looks like it's found her. She's En'Shalla now, my province. Raiban and her minions can yowl at the moons for all they'll get anywhere with me! But first, we have to see to Kezule."

Jurrel came running in. "How's Keeza?" he asked, handing the priest a couple of towels before opening his medikit.

"Only unconscious, we think," said Lijou, using one of them to replace the blood-soaked wad. "See to her first. I don't want her coming round and attacking us again. This looks like it's just a flesh wound."

Jurrel quickly checked Keeza, loading the hypo. "I'm putting her out for a couple of hours, Master Lijou," he said.

"I didn't know you had medic skills, Lijou," said Konis, making his way shakily back to his seat.

Lijou looked up at him, mouth opening in a smile. "You don't think I'm co-ruler of the Brotherhood without having been trained by them, do you, Konis? It was the first thing they did when I was elected to the post."

Jurrel took over from him. "Father Lijou, there's nezzu in the cabinet over there. I think the Clan Lord could tolerate a stiff drink." He lifted the makeshift pad to see the wound for himself.

"Good idea, Jurrel. Thank you," said Lijou, getting to his feet and wiping the blood from his hands on the other towel.

"You were right, thank Vartra," sighed Jurrel, getting out a pressure dressing. "Only a flesh wound. Deep enough, though. Can you contact Physician Kyjishi for me? He needs to get this properly treated."

"I don't think we'll need to," said Lijou, pouring out two drinks. "I sense Vanna on her way here now, in a full-scale panic."

Five minutes later, Vanna knocked on the den door, entering with a nurse towing a floater. She glanced over to the couch where Keeza lay, covered now by a blanket.

"I didn't even know he was mated!" she said as M'Zio and Jurrel lifted her Leska onto the floater. "What in the name of all the Gods was he thinking of, mating with a killer, putting all our lives at risk! I really thought he'd straightened himself out at last."

Jurrel looked up from packing his medikit. "You do both of them an injustice, Physician," he said. "You don't know what either of them suffered these past weeks when they shared memories and nightmares. Your mind would be as disturbed as hers if you'd been locked in with a Valtegan for two and a half months! You'd want answers from the two people who'd put you in with him, wouldn't you?"

Vanna looked from Jurrel over to Konis and Lijou, a stunned look on her face as ears dipped backward in shock.

"She was working undercover for us, Vanna," said Lijou. "She agreed to do it, but we had to wipe the memory of that from her mind before she went in with him. We never anticipated him escaping and taking her with him."

"Was going to tell you," Brynne mumbled as he came round. "Is she all right?" he asked Jurrel. "Was my fault. I pulled the gun the wrong way."

"She's fine," reassured Jurrel, taking his hand. "I gave her a sedative. She'll be out for a couple of hours."

Brynne clasped Jurrel's hand tighter. "Stay with her. Don't let them take her away," he said, trying to look up at him.

"I won't."

Lijou came over to stand beside him. "Thank you for what you did, Brynne." He put his hand on the young man's shoulder, gripping it firmly. "You have my word Keeza will remain here. She's En'Shalla, one of us. Take Jurrel with you. I'll explain everything later, but for now, be assured that Keeza did agree to go in with Kezule. When she made that decision, she knew what it entailed, I promise you. Rest easy, now."

Vanna stirred. "Once I've treated Brynne, I expect an explanation of this, Master Lijou," she said. "How you two could stoop to such depths—I can believe the Brotherhood would do it, but that you two would be a party to it . . ."

Lijou took her by the elbow, gently steering her toward the door. "You shall have it, my dear," he said. "Meanwhile, would you send another floater for Keeza? I'd like her kept under lock and key at the medical center for now, until Master Konis and I can talk to her and undo the conditioning we put there for her mission. She knows Kezule's here, I don't want her trying to run away from us. It's essential she remembers the whole truth, not just what we left her with."

Vanna allowed herself to be gently seen out. "Good job we didn't resort to firearms every time we had a row," she grumbled at Brynne as she and Jurrel followed the floater out.

"Don't scold me, Vanna," they heard Brynne say as the door shut. "She didn't mean to shoot me."

Lijou sighed with relief as the door closed behind them and went over to sit beside Keeza. Relaxing himself with an effort, he put his hand gently on her brow and began to match his mind to hers. After a couple of minutes, he sat back and looked over to Konis.

"The conditioning has broken down badly," he said. "She remembers most of what happened with Kezule, and some of her previous life. Nothing of her time at the Consortias, though she remembers being approached by L'Seuli, but not why, or more importantly, agreeing to spy on Kezule. We could restore the missing memories and erase those of her time with Kezule now, but we do owe her an explanation. And there's Brynne, of course. He'd still have them."

"We wait till she's conscious," said Konis, resting his elbow on the arm of the chair. "I'm afraid I wouldn't be much help to you right now, Lijou. With Kusac and Carrie missing, and now their daughter taken by Kezule . . ." He stopped in mid-sentence, resting his head tiredly on his hand. "Will Rhyaz cause a problem over Keeza?"

"No," said Lijou firmly. "As I told you, she's my concern as Head Priest, not his. Nothing connects Keeza to the murders of the two guards because legally she doesn't exist. The herb Kezule made her ingest, and the effects of his bite, affected the balance of her mind at the time of the incident. She wasn't capable of being responsible for her actions. As for this little episode . . ."

"Understandable," interrupted Konis. "The only person she injured was Brynne, and I don't think he'll want to press charges. I must admit to being surprised at his actions," he continued as Lijou left Keeza to rejoin him. "I hadn't realized he had it in him. He's always seemed more of a pacifist."

"It's the Sholan in him," said Lijou. "He's finally allowed himself to accept the two sides of his nature. Vanna was wrong, Konis, Brynne has changed. We alter the Humans almost as much as they alter us."

* * *

Kitra was already at the villa, packing Kashini's things, when her mother and Mnesu arrived. Within an hour, they were back at the site. Ni'Zulhu tried to take the bags from them, but Rhyasha came out of the semi-trance she'd been in since talking to Dzaka and resisted him fiercely, trying to push past him into the tunnel.

It was Rulla who came to her rescue, "Let her through, Sub-Lieutenant," he said to the security chief. "It gives her something to do, and she needs that right now," he added quietly.

"I don't like involving civilians," muttered Ni'Zulhu.

"Civilians are involved," said Kitra sharply. "My niece is one!"

He let them through, scowling at Rulla as the Brother escorted them in.

Upstairs, Garras had gotten an old jegget trap turned into a cage for eight terrified chiddoes. It sat on a wheeled pallet in the middle of the upper cavern. Beside it was an old metal collar and a bracelet, and two bright green la'quo resin stones. There were also several fuel packs for the heater and the lighting generator.

As Kitra and her mother began unpacking the bags of clothing, toys, and foodstuffs, she looked pointedly at the collar and bracelet.

"Kezule asked for them," said Garras. "They were found in the lab in one of the cabinets. The ancient Valtegans used them to collar telepaths. Kezule needs the stones to make them work, he says."

She shuddered visibly. "Why give them to him?" she asked.

"Because he's got Dzaka bound otherwise. This is more civilized," he growled. "I don't like it, but Kezule got Dzaka to ask for them and he managed to let me know it was what he preferred."

"How barbaric is Kezule?" she asked quietly so her mother couldn't hear.

Garras looked at her curiously. "In a way, he's not. I got hold of the Brotherhood files on him. He's got his own code of honor, strange as it may seem to us. So far, he's killed only when he needed to. The medic because he was about to give him a drug that would likely have killed him, and Zhyaf, because as a telepath, he was a threat to him. He spared the female hostages at Shanagi. I don't think he intends to harm Dzaka or Kashini, unless we make him."

"I'll push the pallet in," she said as she finished putting out clothing for Dzaka.

"No, absolutely not," he said firmly. "It's far too dangerous. I'm doing it. Now take your mother back to Rulla at the tunnel mouth."

Kitra stood back, watching while Garras spoke to Kezule. Minutes later, the steel door began to open just enough for the pallet to enter. Garras threw the coiled rope into the opening. It went taut and slowly, the pallet began to roll forward on its wheels.

She waited until it was almost inside then began to run for the gap, yelling loudly, "Don't shoot! *Please* don't shoot!"

Her mother screamed, and she was aware of angry shouts as she flung herself at the trolley, landing on top of it. Her sudden added weight made it shoot through the gap like an exploding bottle.

She and it hit a wooden workbench, sending her and the contents toppling to the floor. The chiddoes shrieked, the door shut with a reverberating clang, and clawed hands grasped her by the scruff, hauling her up in the air till her face was level with his.

She'd seen pictures of Valtegans, but it hadn't prepared her for actually meeting one. Yellow, slitted eyes glared angrily at her. The mouth was open, showing dozens of small, needle-sharp pointed teeth, and a forked tongue was flicking out at her face. Her vision faded as she passed out.

"Kitra!" said Dzaka hoarsely. "Don't hurt her! She's my Companion!"

Kezule hissed angrily at the limp form in his hand and turned to look at Dzaka. "Your female?" he asked, lowering her to the ground. "Why did she risk her life running in like that?" he demanded, stooping to retrieve the cage of squealing chiddoes and set them on the work surface. "Is she brain-damaged?" His wrist comm was buzzing but he ignored it.

"Must be," Dzaka muttered, relieved beyond measure that the Valtegan had apparently lost interest in her. "We looked after the cub together," he added on impulse. "She came because of her."

Kezule looked at him again, frowning. "We shall see." He returned to the unconscious young female, picking her up like she was a sack of grain, and carried her over to the camp bed on which Kashini was tethered.

The cub had been crying off and on since they'd arrived in the lab, but on seeing Kitra laid beside her, she stopped and began to purr a little, reaching out to pat her face. Dzaka breathed a sigh of relief as he tried to ease his aching shoulders and wrists.

"Pleasure noises," said Kezule, watching her for a moment before turning back to the overturned pallet.

The wrist comm continued to emit a low-key buzzing which he continued ignoring as he began to sort through the items. Dzaka saw him stop when he found the collar and bracelet. Picking them up, Kezule put the bracelet on the counter by the cage and began examining the collar.

Dzaka was still fastened by both wrists to the solid base of the microscope, but the bindings had been loosened a little once Kezule realized how tight they'd become. Going over to him, the Valtegan placed the collar round his neck, snapping it shut. It was cold, and when Kezule released it, heavy against his collarbone. A chill ran through him. This was the control collar used on the telepaths of Kezule's time.

Cold steel touched his wrists and his heart almost stopped until he felt the knife begin to cut through the towel bindings. Suddenly freed, his arms fell to his sides, sending shooting pains through his shoulder joints. Groaning, he slowly pulled them around in front of him and began to massage his wrists and rotate his shoulders, trying to return the circulation to them as they throbbed and prickled.

Kezule placed the tip of the knife under his chin, forcing it up. "Remember, I have your oath not to try and escape."

"You have," said Dzaka, aware he now had two people depending on him.

"I'm going to eat. You can see to your female, then sort through that mess," Kezule said, putting the knife away and pointing at the pile of assorted clothes and packs of food.

Dzaka pulled himself upright and staggered across to Kashini and Kitra. As he eased himself down onto the bed, the cub mewled uncertainly, leaving the unconscious Kitra to throw herself into his arms.

"Hey, it's all right, Kashini," he said, holding her with

one arm as she wound both hers around his neck, hugging him tightly. "Hush now, I'm here. Everything's going to be fine." With his other hand, he checked Kitra, pressing his hand to her neck for her pulse.

The chiddoes screeched their terror as Kezule opened the cage to take one out. Dzaka clearly heard the snap of its neck breaking. The wrist comm had finally stopped buzzing he realized in the silence that followed as Kezule went to one of the trestle tables to eat.

"She's the Clan Leader's daughter," he said carefully, aware how easily the Valtegan could be angered. "It would do no harm to tell her Kitra and Kashini are safe."

Kezule looked up from his meal. "When I wish your opinion, I will ask for it," he said mildly. "You will not venture it again. You will do only what you're told to do, nothing else. Your main task is to see to the child. I will not tell you this again."

Dzaka looked away, concentrating on the cub. The tone might have been mild, but Kezule's face wasn't. He'd been told to go through the goods sent in by Rhyasha. Kashini needed to be cleaned and clothed. Doing that would give her some feeling of security at least, and keep him busy.

Untying the tether round her waist, he took the cub with him, limping slowly down the aisle between the workbench and the steel shelving units that held the remains of the ancients' data processing equipment. He noticed irrelevancies, like the fact that one of the old monitors was still there. The other was in bits somewhere in the lab. Behind where Kezule sat were old store cupboards, their contents emptied for examination months ago. They would make an ideal place to keep the food and spare clothing.

He could feel the Valtegan watching him.

"You're a telepath," said Kezule. "Yet a soldier, too. How is this possible? I thought your kind couldn't stand the pain of others."

"I'm not a telepath," said Dzaka. "I'm an empath. I only feel other's emotions, not what they're thinking."

"Ah. And your female?"

He hesitated, and decided honesty would serve them better. "Yes, she's a telepath. So's the cub, but she's too young to be of any danger to you. She can't even talk yet."

"The device round her wrist, what is it?" Kezule asked

as, keeping to the other side of the workbench, he approached Dzaka to pick up the bracelet.

"It's called a damper. It prevents others picking her thoughts up. All children with a Talent wear it to protect the adults from their random thoughts. Kitra wears one, but hers is adjustable and can be taken off. The children's can't."

"Then we are private."

Dzaka nodded. "Yes." Suddenly he found himself being held by the throat.

Kezule slowly tightened the pressure, letting his claws prick into the back of Dzaka's neck for emphasis. "Don't ever lie to me," hissed Kezule. "If I discover you have lied, it will not be you I beat, it will be your female. Are we private in here?"

"Yes!" Dzaka could hardly speak. Then, just as suddenly, he was released. Massaging his throat, he began to back away from the Valtegan. How the hell had he moved so fast?

"You have nothing to fear if you are honest with me," said Kezule, going back up the lab to where a toolbox lay open. He sat down on the stool there and began to examine the collar's control bracelet more closely. "Bring me the female's damper now while she still sleeps," he ordered. "I will disable it, then she will not be tempted to turn it off. Once I have done that, I will tell this Clan leader she is safe."

* * *

Konis stiffened suddenly before leaping to his feet. "Kitra's gone in with Kezule!" he said, his voice barely above a whisper. "Rhyasha agreed to a truce and to give him supplies. Kitra ran in when Kezule was taking them. I've got to go there, Lijou, be with her!"

"Absolutely. We can drop Keeza off at the medical center on the way," Lijou said briskly. "Use your comm to call a vehicle for us." He strode to where Keeza lay on the couch and picked her up, slinging her over his shoulder.

CHAPTER 16

VANNA stroked Brynne's forehead gently with her fingertips. His breathing was light now, he'd be waking soon. She'd never considered the possibility of him being exposed to any danger before. Unlike Carrie and Kusac, he'd spent more time in Valsgarth town than on the estate. She'd gotten used to him leading an almost charmed life.

As she closed the door quietly behind her, she heard raised voices in the next room. Angrily she walked down the corridor and flung the door open.

"What the hell's going on?" she demanded. "This is a medical unit, people are trying to recover here!" She found herself facing the Head Priest of the Brotherhood. "Master Lijou!" she stammered.

"You're quite right," he said. "Sister Jissoh is just leaving."

The Sister, her jaw set in a hard line, briefly inclined her head in his direction before stalking out, tail flicking angrily.

"May I introduce . . ." he began, but was cut short by the female sitting on the bed.

"Keeza Lassah," she said, standing up. "And who are you?" She looked Vanna over with a manner the other found insulting.

Seeing Jurrel hovering to one side, she put two and two together. She could feel her pelt start to rise on her neck and shoulders. "I'm Brynne's Leska," she snarled, voice deepening with her underlying rumble of anger. "You're the one who shot him. Do you realize you put not only his life at risk, but mine and my unborn cub's, too? But then, I don't suppose that you'd care about that! Life is pretty cheap to someone like you!"

"Hold on a minute, Vanna," began Lijou, stepping toward her.

Keeza thrust herself in front of him. "Just what do you mean by that?"

"What's the count so far? Since the Pack Lord, two soldiers and almost my Leska! Pretty good going for someone who's officially dead, don't you think?"

Keeza began to growl deep in her throat as, around her face, her hair began to bush out in response.

Jurrel moved quickly, placing himself squarely between them, his back to Vanna. "Keeza, she's pregnant. The accident scared her, that's all," he said quietly, grasping her by the arm and shielding her from the physician.

"Damned right I'm scared," snapped Vanna, trying to push Jurrel aside. "Scared that this murderer tries it again! I want her out of here and off the estate, d'you hear me? Keep her away from my Leska!"

"Vanna, you're being unreasonable," said Lijou, putting an arm across her shoulders and forcing her away from them. "She cannot be held responsible for her actions at Shanagi. Jurrel told you she was being slowly poisoned by Kezule's bite and the herb he used on the food."

"Stop defending her, she's a killer, for the Gods' sake!" snarled the enraged Vanna, trying to twist free. "She was forcing you at gun point to tell her what you'd done! Nothing's changed! Even if she isn't responsible for the guards, she still killed the Pack Lord! Someone like her sees violence as the answer to everything!"

"Someone like what, Vanna?" asked Brynne quietly from the doorway. "You know nothing about her. You're making assumptions, just as the telepath at her trial did. Tell them, Keeza," he said, holding onto the doorframe for support. "You've got a reason to clear your name now. Our cub."

Jurrel abruptly let go of Keeza to go to Brynne's aid.

Vanna froze. "Your cub?"

"You shouldn't have gotten up," said Jurrel, slipping his shoulder under Brynne's.

Clutching his bandaged side, with his friend's help, Brynne limped across the room to Keeza's bed. "I heard these two squabbling like kits," he said, gasping in pain as Jurrel helped him sit down. "I had to come."

Blood was beginning to seep through his bandage as he reached for Keeza's hand. "I told you the truth, Jurrel," he said, as the Brother knelt to check his dressing. "She only killed in self-defense."

"Keeza? Is this true?" asked Lijou, steering the stunned Vanna toward the room's only chair.

"Let them think what they want of me," she said, her voice harsh. "It's done. They got what they wanted, a murder conviction. Only one person other than Brynne believed in me without proof, the Brother who came to the prison for me. That's enough."

"L'Seuli?" said Lijou in surprise. "He knows? Why did you offer no defense? You said nothing at your trial."

She returned his look with a steady one of her own but said nothing.

"I'll tell them," said Brynne, clasping Keeza's hand more tightly as his face began to turn pale.

"No!" said Keeza. "Let it be, Brynne. My name's dead anyway. I'll take your Clan's as is my right as your lifemate. I'll be Keeza Aldatan." Lifting her chin, she glowered challengingly across the room at Vanna.

"He's in shock," said Lijou, noticing Brynne's color. "You should be lying down, Brynne."

"I'll see to him," said Jurrel firmly, going round the other side of the bed to pull back the covers.

"Life-mate?" Vanna echoed. He'd taken her as his lifemate?

"Tell Master Sorli he needs to give the Court telepaths a shake-up, Father," said Brynne as Jurrel, with Keeza's help, eased him onto the bed. "They didn't even recognize a latent talent in her. She hid the truth from them."

"Enough, Brynne!" said Keeza, straightening up and trying to pull away from him, but he grasped her hand again and held it firm in his.

"You have Garras, Vanna, and his cub on the way. I've made my choices, accept them as I accepted your mate. Gratifying though it should be, I don't want the two of you fighting over me again. At least give Keeza a chance."

"Don't flatter yourself, Brynne Stevens," Vanna said sharply, but his words hit their mark and she couldn't meet his gaze.

"I'm going to look into this matter, Keeza," said Lijou.

"You were determined to keep your own identity a few minutes ago. If I can prove your innocence, will you let me clear your name?"

"Let him, for our cub if not for yourself," said Brynne quietly, tugging at her till she sat down beside him. "Keeza Lassah is who you are, not Ghaysa, or any other name the Brotherhood might give you."

"It could prevent another—next time perhaps fatal—injustice from happening," said Lijou.

Keeza closed her eyes and leaned back against Brynne, hiding her face against his chest. Even Vanna picked up her memories of that last terrifying night in her cell, when she'd faced the certainty of her execution. Then L'Seuli had come for her with his offer of a pardon. She understood now what had made Keeza accept the Brotherhood's terrible offer, and why they'd made it.

Brynne looked over to Lijou and nodded.

Vanna got to her feet. "Perhaps I judged her too quickly," she said, her voice low. "But I was afraid for you, Brynne, and angry with her for risking our lives."

He nodded again. "It's all right, Vanna. I understand." His voice was quiet, very quiet. "I'd like to rest now, if you don't mind."

* * *

"No wonder Konis was in no fit state to help you," said Rhyaz compassionately.

"I have restored all Keeza's memories, but it occurred to me that during this crisis, her knowledge of Kezule could be vital, so I asked her if she'd agree to wait till this is over. She agreed, and her help has already been of enormous value. General Kezule is first and foremost a soldier. He prides himself on meeting his responsibilities and being fair. Because Rhyasha gave her word to him, the cub and Kitra are now his responsibility. Provided Dzaka plays it straight and does nothing underhanded, they should all be safe—until Kezule realizes returning to his own time is impossible."

"Good thinking. I'll have Keeza's background thoroughly investigated, and pass on to Master Sorli Brynne's comments about the trial telepath, and speak to L'Seuli. Now that you mention it, I remember him being concerned about Keeza at the time, but he never said anything to me. If an injustice has been done, then thank the Gods it was Keeza we chose. At least she's still alive. Meanwhile, have Garras and Ni'Zulhu cut the estate off from all incoming and outgoing transmissions and visitors. Isolate yourselves, except from the Stronghold operational frequency," said Rhyaz. "We don't want Raiban getting wind of this and trying to march in and take over."

"Already done. Ni'Zulhu wants to force an entry to the lab but Garras has overruled him. For now, he wants to do it Kezule's way."

"Get Garras to try negotiating with Kezule. See if there's anything else he'll accept. I wish I felt confident enough to tell the Aldatans that Carrie's safe, but until the *Profit* arrives at Haven, I daren't risk raising their hopes. How are they coping?"

"Vanna's persuaded them to rest at the villa, even managed to get them to take a light sedative. They've spoken to Keeza about Kezule, and she managed to reassure them somewhat. What worries me is that Kezule has nothing left to lose any more. That makes him more dangerous than he was at Shanagi, when he had at least the hope of escape. He's got to know that's impossible this time."

"Tell him we're in negotiation with Valtegans and we'll give him safe passage to their ship," said Rhyaz. "He might just fall for it."

"We aren't in negotiation yet."

"I know that, Lijou, but we already know who they want, and we will be in a couple of days' time. Lie for now! Hell, even if we have to hand him over to save the hostages, it's worth it! We were getting damned little information out of him anyway."

"I'll tell Garras."

"Are you sure Keeza's no danger to you? She's not still protecting Kezule, is she?"

"Absolutely not. I told you how she and Brynne came to meet. There was no way it could have been planned, Rhyaz. Besides, Brynne would know about it by now."

"I'll take your word for it. Stay in touch, Lijou. And, well done."

"Rhyaz, I need to talk to Kha'Qwa," said Lijou awkwardly. "Our cub's due in just over three weeks."

"That soon? I'm sorry, Lijou. This is a bad time for you to be away from here. I saw Kha'Qwa a couple of hours ago, she's fine. I'll get her to call you in an hour, how's that?"

"I'd be grateful."

* * *

Day 39

The sound of pattering feet and a strange yet familiar scent drew Kusac's eyes to the door. Coming toward him was the alien he'd seen just before he'd been shot. Slightly over three feet tall, it wore an assortment of colored strips of transparent gauzy material that hung from a band above its broad hips. Its bronze-colored limbs were spindly, the joints large, and the three-toed feet wide and splayed. The stick-thin arms were bent across its body, hands held up near its face, the three long fingers moving restlessly.

Kusac looked higher, seeing the large eyes with their strange dual lenses. Below them, at the lower end of the oval head, was a small mouth with quivering mandibles. Round its neck it wore more of the bright strips, and as it drew closer, it brought with it a cloud of scented air.

Beside it walked a Valtegan, the skin a slightly darker green than that of the commander he'd seen earlier. This one's skull was totally smooth, but around the eyes and across the cheeks were bands of iridescent skin.

They stopped a few feet from his bedside, and he saw that the Valtegan carried a metal tray. Despite the many short periods of sleep he kept having, he was still exhausted, but he forced himself to concentrate on his visitors. This must be the treatment the commander had spoken about.

"I'm Doctor Zayshul and this is my colleague, Kzizysus. He's a TeLaxaudin, and our medical bio-engineer. We'll be looking after you until we reach our destination."

The species name was familiar. "One of the founders of the spaceport at Jalna," Kusac said.

"Yes," said Zayshul, her tone pleased. "We're going to

get you fit to rejoin your own people. The TeLaxaudin design and make the implants for us, so he'll be adjusting that for you under an anesthetic."

"You're different from the commander."

Her visible skin darkened, turning almost black. "Of course. You were on Keiss. You've only met M'zullian males. And Kezule. I'm one of the female members of our crew. How did you get hold of Kezule?"

"Our God gave him to us, in the temple in the plains." He could remember telling J'koshuk that. "It was ruined, there were ancient devices . . ." He let his voice trail off tiredly, hoping she'd not pursue it. A female Valtegan, sentient and almost friendly. He'd be past being surprised now, if he could feel any emotions at all.

She lifted a device from the tray and reached out to apply it to his neck. "This will relax you, make you sleep for a short time. The procedure isn't painful, but it is unpleasant, I'm afraid."

He reached up to stay her hand. "He said you put the implant in because I had seizures."

"I wasn't present when you were awakened, I'm afraid, but Doctor Chy'qui said that's what happened. You were a telepath, weren't you?"

Past tense. "Yes."

"The doctor tells me the implant has neutralized that ability because it was threatening your life. There's a lot to be grateful for, though. At least he saved your life."

Either she was lying, or telling what she thought to be the truth. When J'koshuk first took him, he could use his Talent, if he was willing to endure the pain. When he awoke after that first time, his mind had been quiet until J'koshuk had gone to Carrie. Then, for a brief moment, his Talent had returned. Even now, a tiny portion of it remained, but not telepathy.

A humming sound seemed to come from the TeLaxaudin. An electronic voice began to speak in Sholan. "Begin we cannot until hand remove. That shouldn't he be able doing."

Kusac let his hand fall back on his lap, realizing he might have given himself away. "I'm tired," he said, closing his eyes.

He felt the faint sting of the hypo, then the surge of the

drug rushing to his brain. Lassitude and nausea gripped him, and he knew immediately what he'd been given. La'quo. Shock made him fling his arms out, hands grasping the sides of the bed. Didn't they know what it did to Sholans? He couldn't tell them he knew what it was because it would betray a knowledge of their past that he'd been denying. He tried to remember more about the drug. It caused hallucinations, and the images seen depended on the state of mind at the time it was administered. Kaid had fought the stronger narcotic version Ghezu had given him. He'd only taken the weaker sap when they'd traveled back to the Fire Margins. This had to be the narcotic version.

The hypersensitivity began to build. He could feel every hair in his pelt, could hear the blood surging through his body. He focused on that, trying to slow it down, then realized it was futile. The drug had already reached his brain. Now he felt light-headed and disembodied, and the particles of the TeLaxaudin's scent hurt his nostrils—his lungs felt as if he were breathing in perfumed fire. It hadn't worked this fast with the plant extract.

A gray mist was beginning to fill the room, everything was losing its color. He felt lighter than air and utterly terrified.

Even though he was back home now, Brynne was bored. Though not confined to bed, he was expected to rest and, between them, Jurrel and Keeza were making sure he did. However, Father Lijou was in the next room talking to Keeza, Jurrel was busy downstairs, and he'd been left to his own devices. He remembered talking to Father Lijou several days earlier about his ability to travel mentally in space, and it had been suggested that he try to see if he could reach Kaid on the *Profit* when he felt up to it. Now would be as good a time as any to try.

He lay back against the pillows, and starting with his ankles, he began to relax each pair of muscle groups. Gradually, he felt himself growing heavier as his mind began to drift and reality began to fade. He let his mind roam, heading out into the darkness of space toward Jalna. As he began to think of Kaid, Kusac came to mind.

The sudden brightness of the white-tiled room almost blinded him. Blinking, he saw before him a bed, with two alien figures bending over the occupant. One was definitely a Valtegan; as for the other, he'd never seen its like before. Bronze in color, it most nearly resembled some outlandish humanoid grasshopper. This wasn't the *Profit,* he realized, it was the Prime ship. Why was he here? He thought they'd all escaped. Then he remembered Kusac was still missing.

He moved closer, needing to see the figure on the bed. The black pelt showed up starkly amid the white sheets. It was, indeed, Kusac, and the insectlike alien was doing something to the side of his neck.

Something nudged at his mind, but the scene in front of him was what he needed to focus on, so he ignored it. The nudging became more insistent, until he realized it was Kusac he was "hearing."

Everything moved more slowly when he was far-seeing, and it seemed an age before he could turn round, but there was nothing behind him save the other wall of the hospital room.

Brynne! In Vartra's name, listen to me, Brynne!

Kusac? Straining to hear him, he turned again, looking back at the still form lying in the bed. *What are they doing to you?*

I don't know. When the Primes woke me, they said I had had seizures, so they used an implant to stop them. They took our ship, and the Valtegan one from Keiss that attacked us. They want a treaty with us against those who destroyed our colonies.

I know. We had a message from Kaid. They're safe on their way to Haven.

Thank the Gods they're safe! We're heading for Haven. Warn Kaid. I don't trust them. They used one of them, a red-robed priest, to question me—the one who tortured Carrie's twin. They know about Kezule. I think they want him. I'm to be returned to you there, they say. The implant, they control it and me. They said it had neutralized my Talent. I can't send any more. Tell Kaid to be on his guard, even with me.

But you're sending now!

They gave me la'quo. It loosens your bonds in space and time. It's how we traveled back to Vartra, how Kaid visited and spoke to Carrie in our Shrine when he was imprisoned in Stronghold by Ghezu.

Your thoughts are beginning to fade, Kusac!
I must be waking. Warn them, Brynne.

Then he was gone, and as Brynne looked at the bed, he saw Kusac move, his body beginning to go into convulsions.

Shock sent him spinning backward, away from the room and Kusac, into the utter darkness of deep space. Fear filled him and he began to panic as he realized he hadn't returned to his body. He tried to turn round, to see what lay behind him, in the hope that at least he'd see some distant stars, but there was nothing: the darkness was so complete he couldn't even tell if he had turned round.

His panic grew as he tried to move and realized that here he had no body, there was only him, an awareness of identity and self. He tried to call out in the faint hope that someone would hear him, but if he made a sound, he could not hear it. Panic escalated to hysteria and fear to sheer terror as he realized he was utterly trapped in this dark prison.

"For him too much fast change. Keep sedate. Little by little we do. Implants not for Sholans. Dangerous is. Wrong Chy'qui insists," grumbled the small TeLaxaudin as, his patient finally properly sedated, he began again.

"Are you telling me Chy'qui insisted you fit the implant? He said it was one you'd adapted for the Sholan."

He looked up at her. "No adapting. All same."

"Can you remove it?" asked Zayshul, doubt about Chy'qui entering her mind for the first time.

"Maybe, not maybe. Never this asked. First try on him advise not. Weeks take. Try first on animals."

"That's no use. He has to go back in exchange for Prince Zsurtul in two or three days."

"Anyway do. Experiment useful. Worry not. Control himself by then." He stood up, looking at her, mandibles quivering. "Sleep tapes start you now."

"At least he's shown he's strong-minded, able to resist the implant. It should be easier to free him from it. Can we accelerate his healing? J'koshuk left him covered in bruises, deep cuts, and scratches. I want those gone before the exchange."

"Interferes not with work of mine."

"I'll go fetch something. Chy'qui isn't to be allowed near him, remember. Commander's orders, Kzizysus."

"Heard."

Satisfied, she left for the dispensary.

Jurrel scratched on the door to the den. A moment later, Father Lijou opened it.

"It's Brynne, Father," he said. "Can you come and look at him? There's something wrong with him. I can't wake him."

Lijou frowned. "You're a paramedic, Jurrel. Your knowledge of medical matters is far greater than mine."

"I don't think it's a medical problem, Father. When I touch him, I'm usually aware of him mentally. Now I feel nothing. It's as if he's in a very deep trance."

Lijou turned to speak to Keeza.

"I heard," she said, joining them. "I'm coming with you."

The darkness suddenly shattered into a thousand, thousand fragments, blinding Brynne with the brightness beyond it, sending him spiraling back into his own body. He gasped for air as he sat up, then moaned in pain as the staples in his wounded side pulled. He was back, and Jurrel was there.

Heart racing, still gasping for breath, he grabbed hold of Jurrel, holding onto him for dear life.

You're back safely with us, Brynne, sent Father Lijou.

The calming presence of the priest in his mind, and the familiar scent and feel of Jurrel holding him, helped fight back the fear that had overwhelmed him in the darkness. Keeza's hand touched his head, stroking back his hair. Gradually his breathing slowed and he was able to let go of Jurrel.

A towel was given to him, and he wiped his sweating face with it, discovering his hands were still far from steady.

"What happened, Brynne? What were you doing?" asked Lijou quietly, as Keeza took the towel from him and handed him a mug of water.

He accepted it gratefully, taking a long drink before handing it back to her. "I tried far-seeing to the *Profit*," he said. "And I got trapped. I couldn't get back." Keeza leaned against him, making soft, purring sounds of encouragement, as he began to shiver at the memory. "How did you get me back?" he asked. "Where was I?"

"Only within your own mind," said Lijou reassuringly. "What did you see that caused you such distress?"

He reached for Jurrel's hand, needing the extra reassurance that he was really back in his own home on Shola.

"I didn't go to the *Profit*," he said quietly. "I saw Kusac, on the Valtegan ship."

After talking to Brynne, Lijou borrowed the on-duty staff lounge to contact Rhyaz. He'd just activated the comm when a call came through from his co-leader.

"I know about them wanting Kezule," Lijou said, and proceeded to update him on what Brynne had seen and heard.

"I'll contact Kaid immediately," said Rhyaz. "You get Garras to put the Primes' offer to Kezule now, if he hasn't already. The Brotherhood needs Kusac back, Lijou. He and his Triad, they're figureheads for us, we can't afford to lose them. We have to get Kezule out of that lab as soon as possible."

"I know we need Kusac," said Lijou tiredly, trying not to think of what the young male must have gone through at the hands of the priest, or that he might be permanently mind-dead. "At least we have full confirmation of Brynne's visions now, enough even for you. Detailed down to the fact of the red robe of this J'koshuk."

"I need to be skeptical of visions, Lijou, just as you need to be susceptible to them. That's the difference between our roles in the Brotherhood," Rhyaz said quietly. "I didn't say that I personally doubted them. I'm giving Kaid the authority to decide whether or not to accept this treaty."

Surprised, Lijou asked, "Why?"

Rhyaz hesitated. "Let's just say I had a broad hint from the God that this was none of my concern."

* * *

Kitra stirred and, moaning, put her hand to her brow where a large lump had formed.

"How d'you feel?" asked Dzaka quietly, taking hold of her other hand reassuringly.

"My head aches," she said, opening her eyes and looking up at him. "What happened?"

"The trolley and you hit the wooden workbench. You took one look at Kezule and passed out. You've been out for some time. Kitra, you took a hell of a risk rushing in like that. Kezule could have shot you, thinking it was an attack."

"Your female's awake," observed Kezule, looking up from the workbench. "Good. I've finished the bracelet."

"Huh?" asked Kitra.

"Don't talk to him unless he asks you something," said Dzaka, keeping his voice low.

"Why not?" She reached up to touch the collar around his neck. "It was for you. Why?"

"It was what they used on telepaths in his time. It activates his bracelet and warns him if a telepath is trying to use his Talent. Then he can send a shock through the collar."

A horrified look crossed her face. "But you're not a telepath!"

"It's safer than the alternative. I know what he's capable of, Kitra."

"I'm going to test the bracelet," Kezule said. "It will be painful, but I will keep it short. Consider it only a taste of what you'll feel if either you or she disobey me."

As he spoke, a searing pain flowed through Dzaka's body. Crying out, he fell to the floor. As abruptly as it had started, it stopped, leaving him moaning and gasping for breath.

Kitra yowled in fear, leaping down to his side, trying to cradle him in her arms.

"Don't touch me," Dzaka gasped, flinching away from her. "It still hurts."

"Just a demonstration," said Kezule, slipping the bracelet on. "I can intensify the pain, and make it last as long as I wish. He will tell you the rules while you get food and drink for the three of you."

Dzaka could sense Kitra readying herself to shout her anger at Kezule. Despite the pain, he reached out, grasping her arm with his unsheathed claws, making her start. "No! He means what he says. I can't take that again, Kitra."

On the other camp bed, Kashini had awakened and was mewling in distress.

"Don't antagonize him, for Kashini's sake, if not mine,"

he whispered, trying to push himself up on his still shaking limbs.

Kitra steadied him as he got back onto the camp bed. "I'll see to Kashini. You're not up to it," she said as he collapsed on his side.

Going over to the cub, Kitra untied the rope and set her down on the floor, holding her hand as they walked slowly back to Dzaka. As Kashini climbed up to sit with him, Kezule spoke again.

"I said eat now. Unless you want to miss the meal altogether?"

Kitra shook her head in answer, not sure if this was an occasion when she could speak or not.

"The food's in the cupboards on the far wall, behind Kezule," said Dzaka, as Kashini cuddled up to him, making crooning noises as she stroked his face.

Giving Kezule a wide berth, she went over to the cupboards and dug around in them choosing three self- heating field ration meals. Finding a box of Kashini's cereal biscuits, she took it, too. Grabbing three spoons, she headed back to them.

A wrist comm buzzed and Kezule answered it.

"General, there's no point you sitting in there waiting for the Aldatans to return. They're lost, we don't know where they are. But we've made contact with a ship belonging to your people. They're from K'oish'ik, your Emperor's world, and they've offered to take you on board. Will you accept this? We guarantee you safe passage to them," said Garras.

"I don't believe you. I've told you, I wish to return to my own time. I'll wait for the Aldatans."

"They're missing, probably dead, Kezule. We couldn't return you to your own time, even if they weren't. The way back has been destroyed."

"Stop bothering me with your lies and fictitious offers," Kezule hissed. "I will wait, or I will get the two I have to take me back." Cutting the connection angrily, he glowered over at Kitra and Dzaka. "Is it true? Are they missing?"

"Yes," said Dzaka. "They failed to make a scheduled transmission five weeks ago. No one can find a trace of them."

Kezule picked up one of the green resin stones. "Then you will take me," he said.

"We can't take you," said Dzaka. "It took three powerful telepaths, my father and the Aldatans, to go back to your time. I'm not even a telepath, and Kitra's barely more than a child."

Kezule looked over at her. "She's your female, so she's of breeding age. That makes her an adult. As for you, what's the difference? You have a mind talent."

"I can't read minds! I only know how people feel," he said in desperation. "Telepaths are far more powerful than me."

Kezule bared his teeth and hissed in rage. "Again I must deal with females! What worm has eaten into the minds of your kind to allow them such freedom?"

"It's the way it is with us, General," said Dzaka. "Females are our equals, different from us but never inferior. We value their differences."

"The female takes charge then," snarled Kezule, getting up to go to the cupboards for a bowl. "I care not which of you does it, so long as it's done. I have the drug we need."

"But I can't do it," wailed Kitra. "I don't know how or where to go! Without that knowledge, we could all die."

"I know. I will tell you," said Kezule angrily. "No more discussion. I will make up the drug now. You'll eat and feed the child, then get ready to sleep."

* * *

Ruth had been in a flap since she'd awakened and discovered Mandy and Daira were gone. The fact they'd been found safe and well, apart from bumps on the head, half an hour later, had done little to ease her mood. She was still imagining all the things that could have happened to them at the hands of Kezule and giving both kids, in Mara and Josh's opinion, a really hard time.

Another loud spat had just died down when the doorbell buzzed. Relieved to have something to do, Mara went to answer it. It was Toueesut, accompanied by his swarm of males. At least, she assumed they were the males. She still couldn't tell the two sexes apart.

"Mara of the bright singing, we have heard of your troubles and come to you with offerings of help for you all," he said before she could open her mouth. "The small ones they were trying to see within our hive when they were apprehended by this most deceitful of persons, who now holds two of your people deep in the mountain of diggings. Our ladies have said they would wish to have the little ones and their mother come and see inside our hive, then their curiosity will not cause them to do foolish things again and put their safety at risk. This is not as a reward for getting caught by the deceitful one but as a help to their mother, who must be suffering greatly with the worries. This our ladies are fully understanding and would like to ease her burden of responsibility and remove a temptation from her little ones' lives."

Though the barrage of singsong words took her by surprise, out of habit, Mara was able to focus her mind almost instantly on what Toueesut was saying.

"You're inviting the children and Ruth over to visit?" she hazarded.

Six bristly whiskered heads bobbed in enthusiastic unison.

"That's very kind of you, but I don't know if . . ."

"Excuse us please, we will deliver our invitation," said one of the others, slipping past Mara into the house.

Too surprised to do anything but turn and stare, she saw the other four Touibans quickly surge past her, leaving her and Toueesut alone on the doorstep.

"Uh. Would you like to come in?" she said, realizing as she said it that it was a little late.

Toueesut grinned from ear to ear. "Of a certainty," he said, darting past her.

Aware that Josh was deriving great amusement from her surprised reactions, she shut the door, feeling the proverbial horse had not only bolted but taken its own tack with it for later.

Mara found Ruth surrounded by the swarm of Touibans, being verbally assaulted from all sides by trilling riffs of sound. She looked across to Mara with a totally bemused expression on her face.

"Mara, what are they saying?"

"It seems their wives have invited you and the kids over for a visit . . ."

"And much eating, drinking, and pleasure in each other's company," added one of the others.

". . . and a meal," added Mara. "They're doing this for

you because they understand how worried you are, and it will satisfy Daira's and Mandy's curiosity about them."

"That'll really scupper their plans to creep out at night and spy on the neighbors again once the fuss has died down," said Josh, picking up Ruth's cardigan and going over to hand it to her. "Think of it, Ruth. Where's the fun in sneaking out at night to see into a house you've already been invited to look around? I know you'll have a great time. Don't worry about us, we'll see to our own dinner tonight."

It sounded like a herd of elephants coming down the stairs but it was only Mandy and Daira.

"Woah! Touibans in our house! Wait till the others hear about this!" said Daira, claws gripping the carpet as he skidded to a halt.

"How many times have I told you not to do that?" demanded Ruth. "You're digging holes in my carpets, young man!"

"It's better than that," said Mara, grabbing hold of the young Sholan with one hand and Mandy with the other and pushing them toward the door. "You've been invited to visit them for dinner. Best behavior, mind, and don't give your mother any more grief, you hear me?"

"Yes, Mara," they chorused as two of the Touibans detached themselves from the group surrounding Ruth and headed for them.

Mara opened the door as the other two, fingers twined in Ruth's hand and in the cardigan that hung from her arm, began to shepherd her out. She ignored the pleading look Ruth gave her.

Think of the honor, Ruth. You're the only folk other than Rhyasha and me to be invited into their hive, and to dine with them. You're a family ambassador, paving the way for other such social gatherings.

Mara! How can you spout such claptrap? Ruth sent reprovingly.

Okay. You need the break, and frankly, so do we and the kids, sent Josh. *You've carried on at them too long, Ruth. Go enjoy yourselves. I wasn't joking about the visit removing the temptation for them to go nocturnal spying again.*

Mara gave a wave and shut the door firmly with a deep

sigh of relief, then turned to find that Toueesut was still there. "Oh, I'm sorry," she said, going to open it again.

"No, no. I have more help to give you," he said. "Understanding I am of these tellings off. When you have six mothers very intense it gets."

"Gods, six mothers!" said Mara, trying to imagine it. "I suppose you did. My mother and I never really got on," she said awkwardly.

"Ah, a sadness this is for you," he said, face creasing in sympathy as his hand took her free one and began to gently massage it in comfort. "More help we bring as I am saying. At the landing port we have our ship. Knowing I am that you will be needing one shortly, one of great speed and fastness. Augmented ours is by the Chemerians and one of the best around." He gave her a sly look, eyes twinkling. "Sholan craft good, as are Touiban, but Chemerians have tricks or six up their sleeves for civilian craft, and our hive can take advantage of them as we are in a financial position to do so. I sent for our craft a while ago, and now it is here but is not allowed access to your estate. Needing permission to land it is, then it and the pilot Captain Shaayi-yisis a Sumaan of friendly demeanor are at the disposal of your people."

She looked over to Josh and he nodded, going off to the lounge to call Father Lijou.

"Toueesut," she said slowly, "I'm sure your offer will be greatly appreciated, but how do you know so much about what's going on? We've not excluded you from information," she added hastily, "only tried to make sure you and your people haven't been put at any risk from this Valtegan."

He winked broadly. "Having our secrets we all are, sweet singer Mara, and I am not going to be letting you know what they are. Think only that we are allies on the same side as your family. We are part of your hive now. This means all to us." He pressed her hand firmly before releasing it. "Our resources are yours."

"I don't know what to say," she murmured, aware that the Touiban had just told her he considered himself and his swarm Sholan in all but shape.

"Then the matter is settled. Going home I must be lest I am the one getting the tellings off from six wives!" He pulled a wry face, mustache bristling, and tugging the door open, left. A gentle scent of flowers and desert springs remained behind him.

Josh returned to find her leaning against the door, a faraway look on her face. He touched her face in a Sholan gesture, bringing her back to reality. "They never cease to amaze us, do they?" he said. "Father Lijou is contacting the gatehouse to allow the ship to land—somewhere. We don't even know how big it is."

The air was filled with a deep whine and a shadow fell across the windows. Mara opened the door and looked up. "I don't think it's going to be landing," she said faintly.

Josh looked out. "No problem," he said, watching as the craft passed over the village toward the excavation site, its shadow gradually following. "One that size will just hover there till we need it."

* * *

Yesterday had been their Link day, but it had been a tense and awkward time for both of them as they tried to conceal from each other their deepest fears and emotions. By some stroke of luck, Carrie's damper, along with her other possessions that had been brought from the *Hkari-yash*, was still in the locker store where Kaid had left it. Their dampers had helped, a little. When Kaid woke that morning, he was almost grateful to find he was alone. Her mental presence was there, but not intruding.

He went to the mess, expecting to find her there, but apart from Rezac, it was empty. A faint disquiet began to stir within him then, but he pushed it aside. Carrie obviously wanted to be alone right now, and he'd respect her wishes.

Having chosen something from the food dispenser, he joined Rezac at the table.

"You look tired," said Rezac, pulling a stim twig from the pack in front of him. "I guess you had a bad day."

Kaid glanced up at him. "Bad day?"

Rezac nodded. "They happen from time to time. When you've had a fight to end all others, it can't be quickly put aside just because it's your Link day. It has to be resolved. And of course, everything's heightened then. This shorter jump's not helping anyone either. Tempers are getting frayed, even among Tirak's crew. Giyesh and Jeran just clawed some fur off each other." His mouth split in a slight grin. "It'll heal. They don't usually stay out of sorts for long."

Kaid grunted and began attacking his food.

"Zashou and I've been Linked for more than three years," Rezac continued, nibbling the end of his twig. "I might be able to help."

"Who says we have a problem?" Kaid said around his mouthful.

"I can feel it," he said quietly. "Look, I know as well as you that the situation between us is ridiculous. I must be half your age, but I'm your father. I can't ignore what I feel for you—the need to help you, to protect you. Hell," he grinned embarrassedly, "I should be feeling it for a cub, not someone like you who probably doesn't even want, let alone need me! But I'm stuck with it. And I reckon you're stuck at the other end of it, too, with the emotional bond of a son toward me. So, either we mess ourselves up trying to ignore it, or we find a way to live with it."

Kaid heard him out in silence. It had been on his mind for the last few days. "I used to wonder about you when I was a cub," he said, pushing some more food onto his fork. "About the father who was never there. I hardly remember my mother. She's just a shadowy figure who was ill, and who eventually sent me away." He stopped to put the fork-ful of food in his mouth and chew it. "I wasn't at the monastery for long before I met Carrie and my adult self."

"It must have been hard for you, growing up as an orphan, thinking yourself abandoned by both of us," said Rezac, lowering his ears. "I swear I didn't know you existed, Kaid. Your mother and I were together only a few months before the Claws started trying to recruit me. I had to leave her, for her own sake."

Kaid looked up, aware of Rezac's need to be believed.

"T'Chya. She was called T'Chya. She lived with her family in the center of Ranz. I can't honestly say if we'd have stayed together had my life been different. I know she wanted that, but I wasn't ready to settle down. She was a quiet person, but determined in her own way. Maybe that's why she conceived you," he added quietly.

Kaid remembered the fork poised in front of his mouth. He had a name for his mother at long last. "I appreciate you telling me," he said. "And your honesty."

"There's no point in lying after all this time," said Rezac. "So, what do we do about us, Kaid?"

It was difficult to suddenly turn around his beliefs and feelings toward the father he'd thought had abandoned him and his mother so long ago. But there was a blood connection between them that they couldn't ignore. For males, the natural emotional link to their cubs was strong: their family was everything to them. The solution he'd come up with would mean exposing his origins in the past, but it also meant that no one would try to walk the Fire Margins again.

"Brothers," said Kaid, pushing his empty plate aside. "If we think of ourselves as brothers, then it allows us to acknowledge the blood tie between us." He felt as well as heard the other's sigh of relief, and realized his father had expected to be rejected.

"Thank you," Rezac said with feeling. "Now, will you let me help you, if I can, with your Link problem? I've been where you are now."

Kaid felt the hairs on his neck and shoulders begin to stir and immediately forced his mind back to calmness. Letting anyone get involved with his intimate relationships wasn't going to come easily. He reached for his hot drink, nodding once.

Sticking the twig in a corner of his mouth, Rezac leaned his elbows on the table. "I was with the Claws for a good two years before the Telepath program picked me up. Like you, I was a fighter. I'm sure nothing much has changed in the Packs, so I don't need to tell you what that meant. I didn't want to be with the Claws and resented it and everyone around me for making me join, but I couldn't show it. So I cut myself off from them all, became good at what I did, just to survive. Then suddenly I was out of it, in the protected world of the University at Khalma, where I met Zashou." He fell silent for a minute, taking the twig out and reaching for his own drink.

"With the Claws, I'd quickly learned that I had to see everyone as a potential enemy, males and females both. To get emotionally involved with a female would alter how I reacted in the next fight. So when I found myself drawn to Zashou, I thought it a weakness, something that would take the edge off me as a warrior. When we Linked, that fear was even worse, especially because she hated what I was. I got the female I wanted—body and mind I got her—" he sighed, shaking his head. "And resented both it and her for the demands our Link put on me. How could I be a fighter when I had to spend every fifth day alone with her as her lover? What kind of fighter is that, for the God's sake, I'd ask myself."

Kaid stirred uncomfortably. Rezac had put his finger right on the pulse of his problem.

"But you couldn't fight after your Talent was boosted by Vartra."

"I could control my response better than the others because of my past," said Rezac. "It was only after the Valtegans took Zashou and me that we had to learn to cope better with each other. I learned to look for the advantages in our Link, rather than the disadvantages. Granted a lot of them were personal," he smiled, and Kaid could see the sadness in his eyes. "But there were those that enabled us to do our undercover work more efficiently. It's like learning to use a new weapon, Kaid. At first it can feel clumsy and a liability, but with time you get used to it, and eventually wonder how you'd managed without it before."

Even as Kaid frowned at the analogy, he remembered his objections to some of the old-fashioned weapons he'd been taught to use in his early days at Stronghold. "So you're saying just have patience." Though he found that advice odd coming from Rezac, he said nothing. It was at least reassuring to know it wasn't just him who'd felt like this about the female he loved.

Rezac nodded. "With yourself, and with her. Hell, you're a hundred percent better off than I was," he said, sitting up. "Carrie's like you in a lot of ways."

Kaid raised an eye ridge.

"A Sister in your Brotherhood, a warrior. Look at the way she handled herself when we escaped, and after J'koshuk."

"Yeah," he said, memories of the many times he'd been proud of her coming to mind.

"Another reason why yesterday was bad for you," added Rezac very quietly, "is what you found out about Kusac."

Kaid got to his feet abruptly. "I want to talk to everyone about this proposed treaty. Want to help me by rounding them up in here while I speak to Tirak about it?" He was not prepared to talk about his sword-brother to anyone right now.

"Sure, but, Kaid," said Rezac, getting up and reaching out to hold him back. "Deal with what you both feel about your Link and Kusac soon. It'll only fester the longer it's left."

"I hear you," he said. "I'll deal with it."

"So they're offering a nonaggression pact with the Sholan Alliance worlds and Kusac, in exchange for Kezule, this crown prince we've got, and help against the other two Valtegan worlds," said Tirak.

"Essentially, yes."

"And you're empowered to sign such a treaty."

"Theoretically, yes, but that was with the Free Traders. The Alliance wasn't aware of the existence of the Primes till now," replied Kaid.

"It's get into bed with less aggressive, more powerful Valtegans to defeat a bunch of psychotic, aggressive ones. A pact with the Liege of Hell," said T'Chebbi from her chair, looking across at Kaid.

"Yes, it is," he said, returning her gaze.

"All I can say is that they seem to have been no trouble at Jalna," said Tirak. "And this weapon the M'zullians used on your worlds, that should be retrieved and destroyed."

"But will they destroy it? Or will they use it against the other two worlds, then turn it on us?" asked Sheeowl.

"That's the question," said Kaid. "It could depend on who gets it first."

There was a knock on the door and Giyesh entered, holding out a printed message for Kaid. "Just come in. Said urgent."

Kaid took it from her, quickly scanning the coded page, then folded it and put it away. "From our HQ. The decision on the treaty is being left to me," he said. "And one of our telepaths has managed to contact Kusac. He is on the Prime ship and they are heading for Haven. J'koshuk had him in his claws for several days. He's in a medical unit now, being prepared for release to us. Zsurtul was right, he has been implanted with a device, but he doesn't trust their reason. Frankly, neither do I. He warns us to be careful of them."

"Sound advice. What do you intend to do?"

"I don't know. I want to hear what they have to say first. They know the location of Shola, they could have attacked us at any time after their Fall. They also know where Jalna is and visit there occasionally. They've caused no trouble for that world, or to your Free Traders. Perhaps they are as peaceful as they say. Maybe the risk is minimal and in our minds."

"When they're out to get you, being afraid isn't paranoid, it's caution," snorted Sheeowl. "Why didn't they ask us outright if they wanted our help? Why terrify us half to death by abducting us in ones and twos? Why not tell you they'd found Carrie? Why wait till now to tell us they have Kusac, and they've experiemented on him, and probably others of us?"

"How does a society of scientists and intellectuals behave?" asked T'Chebbi.

"Get wrapped up in their research and forget everything else," said Tirak. "They care about knowledge and proof of their pet theories, nothing else."

"Like the Primes," agreed T'Chebbi. "Fact they ask for treaty means they understand the concept. May be more dangerous as enemies than friends."

"I'll wait till I hear what they have to say," said Kaid patiently, "and take all you've said into account." He got up. "Thank you for your input. Captain Tirak, you'll see Annuur's kept up to date on this, won't you?"

He held Rezac back as the others left. "I want to talk to our guest again about some of the issues this message raises, and I want you with me. If I'm to decide on the treaty, I want to know a lot more about these Primes."

* * *

Kaid made use of the mess on the second deck again, but this time, Manesh sat outside in the passageway.

"Are you having enough to eat?" asked Kaid, sitting down with his drink.

"Yes. I am being fed adequately."

"What about leisure? Have you been given books?"

"I have. Your literature is interesting. Tales of battles and heroes, Gods and Goddesses. More exciting than what we have in our libraries," said Zsurtul, picking up his drinking bowl with both hands. "You wish to know more about us, don't you? Then you can tell your leaders. Will they make a treaty with us, do you think?"

"That depends," said Kaid. "Your record as a species isn't very good so far."

"You still hold the far past against us. I feared it might be so."

"I was actually speaking of your treatment of us on the *Kz'adul*. Without any explanation, we were taken off the *M'ijikk* at gunpoint by heavily armed soldiers and held captive for the Gods' alone know how long. Why?"

"I told you, we'd come for the purpose of meeting you and offering a treaty."

"Strange way to go about it," said Rezac. "I've seen the Court. Your people are—were—great on ceremony. Where were the senior officials to greet us, the tour of the ship, the banquet?"

"We couldn't greet you like that," said Zsurtul, putting his bowl down. "I told you why. As soon as you saw our true nature, you would have refused us."

"What is your true nature, Zsurtul?" asked Kaid quietly. "The armored guards, or what you claim, a planet of intellectuals incapable of defending themselves."

"You're twisting my words for a meaning I didn't intend," Zsurtul complained. "The armor is only to protect us, to hide our appearance from others. Our old empire made many enemies and, without our warriors, we are vulnerable. Because of the look of our ships and our armor, those species we've encountered see us as a powerful force to appease, not to make war on."

"You wear it to intimidate," said Kaid.

"Oh, it does that, all right," snorted Rezac, pulling his stim twig out from his pocket and sticking it in his mouth.

"You haven't answered my question about why we

weren't approached with a treaty offer much earlier than this," reminded Kaid.

"You were. I came with Doctor Zayshul to bring it to you, but you attacked us and took us hostage instead."

Rezac slammed the flat of his hand against the table. "And you took us from our rooms to examine us without our consent!" he snarled.

Zsurtul jumped nervously, his skin beginning to turn pale. "It was only for medical data," he began.

"It was not," corrected Kaid. "Only our telepaths were taken, and I at least was experimented on."

Zsurtul looked at him, the flesh round his eyes creasing in a frown. "Experimented on? How could you know that?"

"Gel marks on his temples," said Rezac. "I found them, and he was ill when they brought him back."

"Ill?"

Kaid noticed the sudden tensing of the Valtegan youth's body. This was news to him, news he wasn't pleased to hear.

"Feverlike symptoms with vomiting. We were even given drugs to treat him."

"No experiments were authorized, I'm sure of it," Zsurtul said. "You were only to be examined, nothing more."

"And J'koshuk? What about the experiments on him?" asked Kaid. "He wasn't implanted like the others, was he? Someone was using drugs on him instead."

Zsurtul looked from one to the other uncertainly. "I know little about that," he said.

"But you were there when I got my mate back, weren't you? I saw you, and you knew me by name. What is your position on the *Kz'adul*, Zsurtul? What do you do?"

"I'm no crew member," he said, his tone faintly offended. "I am the Emperor's heir. I was on the ship as his representative, to see that all went smoothly with you, especially . . ." He faltered to a stop.

"Go on," said Kaid quietly. "Especially as what?"

Zsurtul looked away to take hold of his drink again. "One of my Father's advisers was against the proposed treaty. When he asked to take up a position as Head of Med Research on the *Kz'adul*, it was thought wise for me to come, too. I don't like Chy'qui," he said in a rush, looking up at Kaid. "I was against him keeping you and your mate, Carrie, separate once you woke her, as was Doctor Zayshul, but Chy'qui's powerful back home and his people in Med Research obey him, not her. It wasn't till J'koshuk attacked the Human that I could do anything. Chy'qui was off duty, you see, and Doctor Zayshul wanted you fetched but his assistant refused. I was able to contact the commander and get him to give the orders."

"That's how you knew she wouldn't be taken again."

Zayshul nodded.

"I'd have thought the Enlightened One would easily outrank a mere counselor," said Rezac.

"I'd bet it's your age, isn't it, Zsurtul?" said Kaid. "This Chy'qui encourages others to see you as too young to be taken seriously."

The prince flushed. "I shall be ten in less than a year," he said defensively.

"Ten!" exclaimed Rezac, sitting up in surprise. "That's not even a youngling!"

"We mature earlier than your species," said Zsurtul stiffly. "We have much passed on to us genetically, we don't need as long a maturation time as you mammals."

"No wonder their empire was so large," Rezac muttered. "They breed like jeggets."

"How was this Chy'qui involved with us?" asked Kaid.

"Chy'qui took charge of you from the first, but he left treating the two injured ones and operating on your mate to Doctor Zayshul. He did treat the male who was in the other cryogenic unit."

"What about Kusac?" asked Kaid, forcing his voice to remain calm.

"I think he used him to test J'koshuk on. Chy'qui said he had new drugs he wanted to try out on the priest to control his aggression. It would be more reliable than the implants," said Zsurtul, faltering to a stop as he saw Kaid's ears turn sideward and his pelt start to rise.

"He did what?" demanded Kaid, as Rezac reached out to grasp his arm in a warning gesture.

Zsurtul cowered back in his seat, obviously trying to move as far from him as possible without actually getting up from his chair. "I didn't know anything about him until after we gave you back your mate! Doctor Zayshul had him treated immediately. I went to the commander and demanded you all be released once your time with your mind-mate was over and she was recovered enough to leave."

"You did that?" asked Rezac. "How could you demand anything if no one would listen to you?"

"The commander listened when I said if he didn't, I wished to speak to my father, because to delay you further could endanger the treaty," he said.

"What were they doing to Kusac?" demanded Kaid.

"I really know nothing about him other than what I've already told you."

This Chy'qui must have figured he was Carrie's Leska when they found them both in cryo units, sent Rezac. *I'll bet part of his experiment was seeing what would happen if he kept him and Carrie apart, then you started exhibiting Leska deprivation symptoms and they realized you were a Triad.*

"Had Kusac been beaten?" Kaid asked Zsurtul.

The Prince hesitated. "I believe so."

In my time, they knew if one of us was hurt, the other suffered the same symptoms. Kusac was being tortured to see what effect it would have on you and Carrie, sent Rezac.

Kaid took a deep breath and forced himself to relax. As his pelt and hair settled down again, he tried to remind himself that the Prince had not been responsible for their ill-treatment, quite the reverse in fact. How could Kusac have been harmed like that and neither he nor Carrie be aware of it?

"You said he'd been implanted because of having seizures. Who did this to him? Tell me more about this implant. What does it do?"

"It would have been Chy'qui who made the decision to use an implant. Your friend's was a special one, Doctor Zayshul said. Chy'qui had had it adapted to control his seizures."

"Do you think he lied about the seizures? Could he have made it up as an excuse to keep our friend separate so he could experiment on him?"

"I have no medical knowledge. I only know what Doctor Zayshul has told me," he said apologetically. "It's quite possible that Chy'qui tried to prevent the talks by delaying your release until you were so angry you refused to listen to us—and that almost happened. You were only supposed to be kept until your ship was repaired. Then we would have revealed who we were and asked for a meeting with your leaders. We'd have proved to you that we were different from the other Valtegans by our actions. Had you agreed to talk to us earlier, when you were taken for the medical tests, then we would have spoken to you sooner."

"Who did the tests and questioned us?" demanded Rezac.

"Chy'qui, of course." Zsurtul realized what he'd said and looked from Rezac to Kaid, eyes widening. "He could have lied about asking you."

"Like he lied about the tests and questioning us. Seems to me that this Chy'qui is playing his own game," said Kaid, his throat vibrating with a rumble of anger. "And an alliance with us doesn't fit into it at all."

Afterward, he went to find T'Chebbi. She was in their room, but once again there was no sign of Carrie. He began to pace, slowly at first, ears back and tail swaying. From T'Chebbi he didn't need to hide his feelings.

"How's Carrie taking this news of Kusac?" she asked eventually.

"I don't know, that's the problem. She's not only cut herself off, she's avoiding me. I didn't think she could do that!"

"You forget what she was like in the early days on Shola with Kusac. She knows what you've got to decide. It's Vartra's prophecy, Kaid. She understands. Could just be making it easier for you, giving you less distractions."

He stood still, tail lashing from side to side now. "Well, it doesn't," he growled. "It distracts me more not knowing where she is and how she's feeling."

"Why not go find her and tell her that," she suggested gently. "Must be going through hell right now, wondering if she's let Kusac down, wondering how he is, blaming herself for his state because of your Link. Is what you're doing."

He stared at her, then turned and left the room without saying a word.

The passenger lounge on the second deck had been empty so Carrie had gone there. Though she'd blocked his awareness of her through their Link flow, she was conscious of Kaid and sensed him approaching.

Closing the door behind him, he came and sat beside her. "Been looking for you."

"I needed some peace," she said, looking up at him. "And you needed to concentrate. You have to distance yourself from what we've been through if you're going to make the right decision on this proposed treaty."

His hand moved across the table to cover hers. "I understand why, but don't shut me out, Carrie. You don't make me weaker, you make me stronger—I admit, I didn't think you would, but you do. We're both experiencing the same feelings of guilt, and we shouldn't be. We did what was right."

"There's no right or wrong to it, Tallinu. We did the only thing there was to do. We survived and we escaped. The rest is—incidental." Her hand tightened on his as she relaxed her mind, letting his presence return fully, and hers flow back to him. There was still the void where Kusac should be, but it was less lonely when shared with Tallinu.

His eyes closed and she felt the tension leave him. He'd been afraid for her, that the knowledge they'd left Kusac alive on the Prime ship would drive her through guilt to do something to lose their cub.

"I wouldn't do that, Tallinu. Whatever happens, our cub is wanted by both of us. You've news of Kusac. Tell me."

He reached inside his jacket, took out the message, and handed it to her. "You'd better read it for yourself."

She read it twice before handing it back. "He tells us not to trust him, that he's being controlled by this implant. How?"

"All Zsurtul could tell us is that it's adapted to control his seizures. The good news is they intend to give him back."

"They've little choice when they want so much from us. He thinks his Talent is only suppressed, not destroyed."

"His judgment is flawed, Carrie. He's been tortured and drugged. He was full of la'quo when he spoke to Brynne. This says Brynne saw him having convulsions. It could be the la'quo. We know we're hypersensitive to it now. Or it could be as Zsurtul said—he went into convulsions when they woke him."

"There's a couple on the estate," she said, her voice low. "Nikuu and Dillon. She lost her Talent when their Leska Link formed. He supports her, makes sure she feels his mental presence. We can do the same if . . ."

"Don't say it!" said Kaid fiercely, his hand almost crushing hers as she felt his fear that her words would make it real. "We'll do anything, we both know that. Facing the possibility is one thing, talking about a solution now, that's—something else."

She nodded and fell silent, not wanting to air her deepest fear.

"Say it, Carrie," he said quietly. "Don't hold back from me. We're in this together, remember?"

"Is Kusac having seizures because we formed a Leska Link? Because I'm pregnant?"

"I've been asking myself that, but I honestly believe we couldn't have formed this stronger Link if Kusac had been awake and with us," he said, taking her hand between both of his. "If, and I do mean if, the seizures are because of his Talent, then it's because he was awakened after you. We are not to blame. If anyone is, it's the Primes. Our cub has nothing to do with it at all."

"How could they, or anyone, know we were Linked telepaths, though?

"I told them as soon as I knew you were awake," he said. "Told them about Kusac and asked if they'd found him, too," he said quietly.

"I know you did," she said, touching his cheek with her other hand. "You did everything you could, Tallinu. I wish we were able to talk to Brynne, ask him how Kusac felt and looked."

"I'm thankful this ship at least has the capability of sending and receiving messages in jump," said Kaid. "We can talk to him when we reach Haven."

She nodded. "It's going to be a long trip."

CHAPTER 17

WHILE they slept, Kezule worked, pounding the la'quo resin into a powder, then mixing it with water. He was concerned. This offer from others of his kind, it appealed to the Sholans for some reason. It was unlikely they were lying. He knew there were other Valtegans still in contact with the Sholans because of the modern things they'd given him while he was their captive. It seemed they wanted to hand him over more than they wanted the safety of his hostages. As yet, they might not realize it, but when they did, he'd be at risk, and he intended to be gone before that happened.

As he worked, he kept looking over at his three hostages, envying them their closeness. They'd pulled the two camp beds together and slept with the child between them. Neither his children, nor those of the Emperor that he'd have been bringing up, would have known the touch or sight of their mother. Nor would they have known such closeness as the child had with the male.

He'd seen it before in other species and had considered it a weakness, but now he was beginning to wonder. These Sholans were far from weak—his kind had been driven not only from Shola but from their sector of space—yet obviously they brought up their young with closeness and affection. Why did it work this way for them, but not for his people? Why was it different for Valtegans? Perhaps when he got back to his own time, he'd try an experiment. He could take one of the young and bring him up this way to see if he was different from the others.

A wave of tiredness washed over him: he needed to sleep. The drug had to soak for half a day at least before it was in a state he could use. He looked over at his hostages again. It was time to wake and tether them.

*   *   *

He came to suddenly, hearing the child begin to whimper and stir. He raised his head from the workbench, realizing he'd let his guard down just enough to doze off. Cursing under his breath, he looked toward the camp beds. Both adults were beginning to stir, and though not quite awake, they were already beginning to comfort the child.

How long had he been asleep? Looking at his wrist unit, he discovered he'd slept for six hours. What in the name of the God-King had possessed him? If the adults had awakened . . . He didn't complete the thought. Reaching for the container holding the la'quo, he glanced over at the door. Both were exactly as he'd left them. Looking round the room, he found everything else appeared unchanged.

"You can eat," he said, getting to his feet to stretch his cramped muscles. He checked the time again. Several hours still remained before the drug would be ready to use.

*   *   *

"We've got to get Kezule out of there," said Rhyaz. "We're running out of time. Has Garras contacted him again about the Primes' offer?"

"Twice more this morning," said Lijou. "He refused us both times. Keeza even offered to go in with him again if her presence could help matters."

"What did you say?"

"I thanked her and told her under no circumstances was I putting her at risk with him again," said Lijou firmly.

Rhyaz grunted. "Has anyone tried to reach Kezule's mind? Or his hostages?"

"Of course," said Lijou, a little offended. It had been one of the first things they'd attempted. "He's got a damper effect round him. Crude, but effective. I expect that's why no one picked him up when he entered the estate. The others are all wearing their personal dampers turned up to full."

"That scare you had a while back could actually have been him after all," said Rhyaz. "You figured out yet how he got in?"

"There's a portion of fence where the grid was turned off because of a family of ferals constantly going in and out and setting off the alarms. They were considered enough of a deterrent in themselves. One of the troopers on the estate was found there, half eaten, two days ago. Garras reckons Kezule saw the trooper go out that way and waited for him to come back. When he returned and was attacked by the ferals, Kezule took the opportunity to get in. The ferals have been captured and sent to the Taykui Forest reserve and the fence is back up again. The trooper's friends confirmed he used to go out that way, keeping the ferals occupied and in the area by regularly throwing them raw meat. Patrols round the perimeter have been stepped up and the troopers warned what will happen to anyone found leaving the estate without a pass."

"It comes down to the military again. They let Kezule escape in the first place," grumbled Rhyaz. "How's Ni'Zulhu's digging going?"

Lijou sighed. He understood all the reasons why they had to break the oath given by Rhyasha, but he didn't like it. "He's within fifteen yards of the back of the tunnel down into the lab," he said. "They're going slowly now, otherwise Kezule will hear them."

"When we get them out, I want Brynne going to Haven with Kezule. He's been able to contact Kusac once, he might be able to do it again. Thank the Gods that the Touibans have loaned us that ship of theirs. Saves us days. Rulla gave me a report on its specs. It's capable of going into jump from just outside Sholan orbit, with a hull strong enough to travel our route to Haven in three days."

"Banner and Jurrel have been up to the *Couana*, too. They're most recently familiar with some of the systems. They can crew for Captain Shaayiyisis."

"Good. Get Garras to keep asking Kezule to agree to the Primes' offer."

"We might annoy him into rash action," objected Lijou.

"I doubt it. He doesn't strike me as the suicidal type, and he knows that killing his hostages would result in his own death. Get back to me as soon as you have any news."

"I will," said Lijou and signed off.

* * *

J'koshuk's and Kusac's rooms were next to each other. As Chy'qui headed down the corridor toward them, he saw the guard posted outside Kusac's door. The commander was determined he shouldn't have access to him. However, given the nature of the guards, it was a sound bet that this one wouldn't have considered the possibility of there being an adjoining door between the rooms. At least he hadn't been prevented from working with J'koshuk, despite the interference of Prince Zsurtul. If all went well, that young male wouldn't be around much longer. The exchange of hostages would be the last time anyone would see the Enlightened One alive. The fool had only made his task easier by getting himself taken as a hostage!

He strolled into J'koshuk's room, stopping to examine him. The implant had taken, and the removal of the visible surface of the one at his neck had also been successful. Unless one knew to look for it, it would never be noticed. On the monitor by the bed, the display of J'koshuk's hormone levels showed it was working as expected. It was an inconvenience that he'd had to be implanted. With his own design of neck unit, J'koshuk had been unremarkable, but with this on his head, there was no way of hiding what he was. However, he could still complete his plan using the programming tapes he'd brought with him.

Bending down at the side of the bed, he took the one for J'koshuk out of his pocket, placed it in the player, activated it and pulled the viewer hood from its recess in the wall above. When his vital signs indicated that he was in a trance, he would hear a subliminal voice telling him to open his eyes. A holographic image would then be projected into the viewer, completing the programming, making J'koshuk totally his creature.

That done, he moved quietly over to the inner door, opening it slowly till he could see whether or not there was a guard in Kusac's room. Apart from the Sholan, it was empty, and the outer door was closed. He saw with pleasure that Zayshul had already activated his sleep tape.

He entered, making his way quietly over to Kusac's bed where he swapped the tapes. He knew which one Zayshul was using and had duplicated it, adding in his own subliminals and images. Now, instead of bland, soothing images, it would play him sequences of his torture at the hands of Prince Zsurtul, with J'koshuk pleading for him to stop. J'koshuk would cease to be his enemy, and Zsurtul would become the one responsible for all his pain and suffering. When he saw the Emperor's son at the exchange of hostages, he'd see an enemy. All it would take to make him turn on Prince Zsurtul and kill him would be J'koshuk using one of the small mobile control units to turn up the implant's production of the Sholan's own hormones. He'd become a killing machine. The minute he turned on the Prince, Zsurtul's remaining bodyguards would immediately cut the Sholan down with their guns, thus preventing anyone from finding out why the tragedy had happened. No one would even look at J'koshuk. And he'd be one step nearer creating the constitutional crisis that necessitated replacing the Emperor.

As quietly as he'd entered, he left. Minutes later, he was walking down the corridor with no one the wiser.

Awareness returned to Kusac, but it had an unreal quality to it. He could hear voices and see images but they were vague and confusing. He remembered the female telling him he'd be given an anesthetic, but that was before they gave him the la'quo. He must still be hallucinating, because they were very strange images.

The priest was there, the red-robed one, but it was another, one with sand-colored skin, who was tormenting him. That wasn't the way he remembered it. J'koshuk had been the only Valtegan present, apart from the armored Prime guard. Confused, he closed his eyes, trying to cut out the images, but the voice persisted. It began to irritate him, make him angry, and he began to move restlessly in the bed, setting off the alarm. The voice and the images stopped abruptly and the viewer retracted smoothly back into its wall niche.

The female doctor ran in, coming to his bedside and checking something on the wall above his head. "You're awake," she said.

"Obviously," he snapped. He tried to sit up, but something was preventing him. "What's going on? What are you doing to me?" There was a cannula in his arm, and a tube leading away from it. He tried to reach across himself and pull it out but again, he found his movements restricted. "Dammit, what the hell are you doing to me?"

"Everything's fine, Kusac," she said in soothing tones as

she reached up to touch a control. "You just woke a little too soon, that's all. You should get some more sleep."

"I don't want to sleep, I want to get . . ." His voice was slurring and lassitude was spreading through him again. He felt his consciousness slipping away.

Perplexed, Zayshul watched him until he was unconscious. He shouldn't have woken so soon, and he should definitely not have been aggressive. She moved to the other side of the room, checking his readings for the past couple of hours. There was a definite rise in the levels of his male hormones. Strange, since the implant's control over him had been reduced several times during the last day. It shouldn't be affecting him like this, if it was a specially adapted unit as Chy'qui claimed.

She went back to his bed and removed the tape from the unit. Maybe that had been the culprit, she certainly hoped so. It was unthinkable that Chy'qui could have lied to her—or was it? The tape had switched off automatically when the alarm sounded, but she wasn't taking any further chances. On her way out, she checked with the guard, but Doctor Chy'qui hadn't even approached him. Seeing the room next door was occupied, she checked to see who was there. J'koshuk, Chy'qui's patient. Her uneasiness began to grow. The guard told her the doctor had been in to see him a couple of hours before, but that didn't prove anything.

On impulse, she checked Kusac again, looking around the room till she spotted the connecting door. Had Chy'qui come in through there? It proved opportunity, nothing more. She still couldn't be sure any outside influence had caused the unnatural response in her Sholan. Calling the guard in, she told him to watch the patient from inside the room and to let no one but herself or the commander enter. If anyone tried, he was to contact his Control and have it reported to her immediately.

With an easier mind, she returned to her own office. Once there, she began to check the records of treatment for both J'koshuk and Kusac. She found nothing out of the ordinary, but she was still not satisfied. Chy'qui had complained that Prince Zsurtul had insisted J'koshuk not be implanted. She could find no evidence of that at all. Had it been Chy'qui who'd decided not to implant him, and if so, for what reason? And why blame the Prince? He wasn't a medic. This needed more of an investigation. She yawned, checking the time. It was late. It would have to wait till morning. The Prince had friends with him in his suite, perhaps one of them would be able to tell her what his interest had been in either Kusac or J'koshuk.

Turning off her terminal, she left her office for her own quarters. It wold be good to relax with her roommates. If she were right, this matter could touch on treason, especially since Chy'qui was one of the three counselors to the Emperor. The thought he was actually trying to discredit the Prince chilled her, and she was glad that she could warm herself against the bodies of her friends that night. The need to be careful occurred to her, as did the realization that she needed hard facts to put before the commander before he'd entertain any accusations against Counselor Chy'qui.

* * *

Kezule had tethered Kashini to the ancient microscope stand. Two sleeping bags formed a warm base for her to sit on and the female, Kitra, had given her the toys and scrap of old blanket as well as some cereal biscuits, dried meat strips, and a child's container of water to drink.

Now he turned his attention to them. Pulling a stool over to the camp beds on which they were sitting, he sat down.

"You will take me back to a time just after our cruiser hit Shola's moon," he said. "The location will be the desert settlement of Khezy'ipik. I have the drug necessary, and I have you. I want only myself returned, nothing more."

"I've told you we can't do it, General," said Dzaka quietly, reaching out to prevent Kitra from speaking. "My father was a Grade One Telepath, one of the most powerful, as were Kashini's parents. It took all three of them to do it. Only Kitra is a telepath and she's not yet fully developed because of her age."

"That matters not to me. They took themselves and me forward in time. I want only myself sent back to where I belong. You will do it. This is not a discussion, it is an order."

"You can't order us," Kitra burst out, obviously unable

to contain herself any longer. "Dzaka doesn't have the ability to do it! And there're only the two of us!"

"I am not concerned with that. I called Fyak, I can tell you how to take me back. I know where I'm going, after all," Kezule said. "The drug, in certain concentrations, loosens the mind, allowing one to reach beyond the here and now. You were right. All that's needed is a clear vision of where and when you want to go."

"Why can't you do it yourself if you brought Fyak back to your time?" demanded Kitra.

"I didn't bring him, I called him," he said, trying to remain patient. If he could get their cooperation, it would be better than forcing them. It was the female's he needed most, as she was the telepath. "He was trying to reach the temple at a time when I was experimenting with the drug. Why is no concern of yours. I was able to provide him with what he wanted to see, and he arrived there in person. We will do the same. You will picture the image I say and send me there. That is all."

"The drug's dangerous, Kezule," began Dzaka.

"I am even more dangerous," hissed Kezule, tongue flicking out in anger. "Do not try my patience any further!"

"No," said Dzaka. "You can't make us."

Kezule touched his bracelet, watching as Dzaka collapsed on the bed, crying out in pain. Kitra immediately reached for him, but her touch only made him howl and try to push her away. Releasing the control button, Kezule waited for Dzaka's spasms to subside.

"You're making it worse," he said at last. "Leave him. It will pass more quickly."

She jumped back, turning on him with all the fury she could muster. "You monster! How can you do that to him?"

"Do you agree to take the drug and send me back to my own time?" demanded Kezule.

Gasping for breath, Dzaka tried to reach out for her. "Don't agree!"

Kezule could see she was obviously torn between the desire to hurl herself at him and the knowledge her attack would only make it worse for Dzaka. Again he touched the control, keeping it down for slightly longer this time. Dzaka's back arched in pain, but slowly he raised his hands to the collar, grasping hold of it in a futile effort to tear it off. As his fingers touched it, he began to keen in agony. Kitra flung herself to her knees beside him, sobbing.

When Kezule finally released the control, Dzaka lay on the camp bed whimpering, his limbs still shaking as he forced his clenched hands to release the collar.

"Will you take me? If not, I will continue to hurt him." Doing this was distasteful to him. The young male's tenacity was worthy of his respect, and inflicting pain on him in this fashion was not honorable, but he had no option. He had to make them agree to this.

The male reached out once more to touch his mate. He wasn't going to give in easily. So be it. Since long bursts were not enough, he'd try several short ones. He wanted this over quickly. By the time he'd administered the third, Dzaka had fallen to the floor and lay curled in a ball of agony, making a low, mewling sound.

Kitra was distraught. "Yes!" she shrieked, turning a tear-streaked face to him. "Yes! Anything! Just leave him alone, damn you!"

"You swear you'll both take me back to where and when I want?" he demanded, hand still poised over the bracelet.

"Yes," she sobbed, "We'll do it. We'll take your drug and do our best to send you back!"

On her mat of sleeping bags, the child was also screaming and sobbing. He regretted having to let her see this happen, but it was his life and the future of his species on Shola that was at stake. "Silence the child," he said.

Getting up, he put the stool away and went to fetch the la'quo mixture. Taking three of the disposable cups he'd found in the room, he carefully poured an equal measure of the thick, bright green liquid into each. Picking up two of them, he went back to the adults.

The male was now beginning to sit up, wiping his face with a shaking hand. As Kitra returned from settling the child, Kezule handed the mixture to her first. Almost snatching it from him, she drank it down.

"Take it all," he said. Going round the other side of the camp bed, he reached down with his free hand to help Dzaka to his feet.

'I regret causing you pain," he said, guiding him onto the

bed. "You're a warrior. Were the positions reversed, you'd do the same to me."

Dzaka said nothing, merely accepted the cup without looking at him, drank the contents down and returned it.

"I will remove the collar now," said Kezule, reaching the fingers of his left hand inside the metal band. He let his claw tips find the slight indentations that marked the release mechanism and pressed. It came free in his hand. There was blood ringing Dzaka's neck where he'd cut himself on it while trying to pull it off.

"What do we do now?" asked Kitra in a very quiet voice as he took the now empty cup from her.

"Give me your wrist unit, then lie down. Look up at the ceiling of this cavern and imagine another like it," he said. Taking it from her, he walked back to place the collar and the wrist comm on the workbench and take off his own unit.

Picking up the last cup, he drank his own dose. "But there is a hole in the roof through which the sun shines down onto a stone altar directly below it. The walls are covered in murals of my people." He picked up the last of the sleeping bags and flung it down at the end of the workbench. Sitting down on it, he leaned back against the bench.

The drug took only a few minutes to work, then he felt himself becoming relaxed and slightly light-headed. He watched the two Sholans, seeing the female's eyes begin to droop. The male would take a little longer because he was still in pain.

"Think of the cavern roof with the hole in the center," he said, his voice low. "Sunlight is falling through it."

Kitra lay there, heart pounding as she felt the alien substance rushing from her stomach through her body. It had been vile to swallow; thick and almost viscous, it had oozed its way down her throat. She shuddered, feeling every hair on her pelt starting to rise. They hurt and prickled against her tabard, making her acutely uncomfortable. She could hear a pounding in her ears that grew louder and louder. Terrified, she glanced at Dzaka.

He lay on his side, hand reaching out for hers. She took it gratefully, feeling the sharpness of his claws as his fingers closed tightly over hers. His palm felt hard and leathery

against her now sensitive pelt, quite different from the feel
of his soft fingertips. Her senses began to swim and she
gasped for air, feeling the coolness of it hurting her nose
and lungs.

She felt sick as the room began to fade and swirl alter-
nately before her eyes, and in a panic, she reached mentally
for Dzaka, clutching his hand even more tightly.

"Think of the cavern roof with the hole in the center,
sunlight falling through it," she heard Kezule repeat from
a few feet away.

No, you mustn't! The thought filled her mind. *It'll be the
end of all of us!*

She felt herself drifting, being gently pulled away from
him.

Kitra! Stay here!

Panic in the thoughts this time, but they were growing
fainter as she seemed to float toward a brightness. His hand
felt as if it was slipping away from her as she was drawn
toward the glowing warmth. She was aware of Dzaka, and
of Kezule, but they felt remote. A memory nudged her.
They were supposed to be with her, not left behind.

Reaching mentally for them, she touched their minds as
the first searing heat of the flames touched her. Shock
jolted her from the lassitude, making her scream in agony.
She tried to retreat, but one mind held her firm.

Go through it! It is the way back, she heard Kezule say.

It burns me! she wailed, pushing back. Energy suddenly
surged through her, giving her the strength to resist the
pull of the flames and Kezule. Once more she could feel
Dzaka's hand holding hers, his claws pricking painfully into
her flesh.

Backlash him, Kitra! A new thought, a new presence,
intruded into her mind. *Send the power through him.*

How? I've never done anything like this before!

*Gather the power within you, youngling, then throw it like
the balls of energy you practiced with at your Guild. It's just
the same. Trust me. The result will please you.*

Conflicting energies swirled round her, trying to drag her
toward the flames, trying to drive her away. Trusting the
inner voice, she grasped them all, pulling them into herself,
feeling Dzaka suddenly there with her as she sent them
hurling toward the mind that was Kezule.

Flames erupted, the blast sending her flying back until she found herself lying sobbing in Dzaka's arms.

He was covering her face in kisses and tiny licks, frantic with relief that she was safe. *You did it, Gods you did it, Kitra! You managed to keep him here! He's unconscious now, we're safe!*

His thoughts were an almost incoherent jumble. It was difficult to make sense of them because images began to flash through her mind, images of Dzaka as a cub on the Arrazo estate in the Clan nursery, then being taken by a strange female out into the cold and left beside a gate to be found by two young males in dark robes.

Whimpering in confusion, she held him close, clutching his sides, breathing in his scent as he lowered himself onto her, whispering words of love in her ear.

Faster and faster the images came until they reached the present. Then they began to slow, finally stopping, leaving their minds and bodies Linked together as one.

But . . . How? Kitra sent, looking up at him as he stroked her hair back behind her ears.

Dzaka hadn't time to form an answer before a muffled explosion vibrated through the lab, sending pieces of rock falling from the ceiling overhead. Flattening Kitra under him, he prayed Kashini was safe. As the fall subsided to a rain of dust, he heard the steel door grating open a few inches. Looking up, he saw Garras squeezing through the gap.

"Well done!" the older male said, coming toward them, then stopped dead as he saw their compromising situation. He turned hurriedly to the gap, but already the door was being pushed aside. "Wait a moment, Master Konis," he said.

As Kitra shut her eyes, groaning in embarrassment, Dzaka sat up and reached for a blanket from the other bed, hauling it partially over them. He'd felt his pelt rising at the mention of her father's name. The Gods Themselves had joined them as one. This time, no one would stop him from making Kitra his life-mate.

Still poised astride her, he crouched down on all fours, looking up at the Clan Lord. All the anger he couldn't show before came to the surface now. "She's mine, Konis," he snarled. "My Leska, my life-mate. Neither you nor your Council will stop us marrying now!"

Konis stayed where he was, aware he was facing a dangerously enraged young male. "Thank the Gods," he said, the relief evident in his voice. "You've no idea how glad I am to hear you say that! Take her with my blessing, Dzaka."

Garras, meanwhile, had headed for Kezule. Finding him unconscious, he turned and picked up Kashini, who was crying lustily by this time.

Puzzled, Dzaka sat back on the bed while Kitra tried desperately to cover herself with the blanket. Belatedly, he helped her as Garras headed back to Konis with the cub.

Not Mother, too! I'm going to die of embarrassment! sent Kitra.

Blocking the doorway, Garras eyed Dzaka. "We need to get Kezule out," he said, trying not to grin. "If you don't mind."

Almost in shock, Dzaka just sat there till Garras came over and threw him another blanket.

"Take Kitra home to the villa, Dzaka." he said, grasping the young male by the shoulder affectionately. "The two of you have done very well indeed. Thanks to you we've gotten Kezule in plenty of time."

"In time for what?"

"Your father and Carrie have turned up safe. I'll come over later and tell you everything. For now, just go home with your Leska, Dzaka."

Konis had disappeared with Kashini, and now several Brothers stood in the room, waiting for Garras' instructions. He jerked his head in the direction of the unconscious Valtegan as Dzaka pulled the blanket round himself and got up off the camp bed.

"Who helped us?" asked Dzaka as he bent to help Kitra.

A strange look crossed Garras' face. "I'm not that religious, but if you asked Master Konis, I know he'd say Vartra. Whoever it was, he told your father it was safe to blow the door open, Kitra," he said.

"He said if I trusted him . . . ," began Kitra, then stopped. "He knew it would Link us."

"I'm glad it did," replied Dzaka, pulling one arm free of

the blanket and putting it around her as they walked to the door.

"Mother will definitely want a temple wedding," Kitra grumbled. "So much fuss and bother this will cause."

"I don't care," he said, hand tightening on her shoulder. "She can have a temple wedding at Stronghold if she wishes!"

"She can? *We* can? That sounds like fun," she said, grinning up at him as they went out into the main chamber.

Two hours later, Kezule's cryo unit loaded in the Touiban sick bay, the *Couana* left Shola for Haven. Keeza accompanied Brynne on the basis that when they arrived at Haven and resuscitated Kezule, should he come out of the comalike state he was in, a face he at least recognized was advisable. Jurrel and Banner were helping Captain Shaayiyisis crew the private craft, and planning to give Brynne some on-the-job training.

* * *

Day 40

After breakfasting in the mess, Zayshul had headed up to the royal suite. Under the pretext of carrying out routine health checks, she'd been able to exchange a few words with Prince Zsurtul's mistress.

"No, he didn't have any medical experiment in mind," M'ikkule said. "He was merely observing for his father. There was this huge argument between the Emperor and his counselors, you see. He wants this treaty with the Sholans, but one of them advised him against it. He overruled them, of course, but that's why Chy'qui came along. He's determined to be here when Emperor Cheu'ko'h is proved wrong."

A major split between the Emperor and his advisers over the Sholan treaty? This sounded reason enough for Chy'qui to be interfering with a Sholan captive.

"That's why Prince Zsurtul kept coming down to the medical research area?"

"Yes. Besides, he was curious about the aliens. He'd have gotten us in to meet them if he could, but he said

Chy'qui kept them isolated. You should know that, though. You were there." A suspicious tone crept into M'ikkule's voice as she watched Zayshul fiddling with her scanner keys. "Why are you so curious about what the Prince was doing?"

"Only on a professional level," she said hurriedly, picking up the female's own reader pad to transfer her data to it. "One of those we took from the M'zullian vessel wasn't implanted. Their priest, J'koshuk. I wondered if the Prince had heard why, that's all. The M'zullian caused quite a bit of trouble among our unexpected guests."

"Prince Zsurtul told us." She pulled a face. "He only goes to prove that we're better off without the warrior genes on K'oish'ik. The Prince said he feared Chy'qui wanted to find out the nature of the Sholans' telepathy and had been doing dreadful experiments on the male they found floating in space." She shuddered. "That's why he pushed for releasing them early with the treaty, rather than going to their home world."

"Prince Zsurtul was behind their release?" That surprised her, and explained why he'd joined her when she went to tell their guests they were to be released. The data now transferred, she'd given up any pretense of making idle conversation.

"Of course. He supports his father, naturally." M'ikkule held out her hand for the reader, making a small noise of annoyance when Zayshul failed to notice.

"Sorry," she said, handing it to her. "You're lacking some vitamins and minerals in your diet. I've listed some foods and the daily quantities you need to take to bring the levels back up to normal."

"If that's all?" M'ikkule asked politely, getting to her feet. "I've things to see to before the Prince returns." She hesitated as Zayshul rose. "You do think they'll give him safely back, don't you? What Chy'qui did to them won't affect the way they treat him, will it?"

"I hope not," Zayshul said with feeling. "M'ikkule, would you be willing to tell Commander Q'ozoi this?"

A horrified look crossed her face. "I absolutely refuse to get involved! I have to live in the Court in the City of Light. You've no idea what it can be like with all the infighting and arguments. No one in their right mind falls foul of Chy'qui, believe me! If you've any sense, you'll not ask any more questions about him.''

Thoughtfully, she made her way back down to her office. She'd have to be very careful indeed if Chy'qui wasn't to find out what she was doing. From the sound of it, he wasn't the kind of person to leave a provable trail. She needed information that probably only existed in the doctor's own personal secure files. This was beyond her now. She needed help.

Intrigue of one sort or another was a way of life on a ship like this. She had someone in mind to help her, but it would be better if she didn't go openly to him. Looking at the clock, she realized it was almost past lunchtime. If she hurried, she might catch him in the mess.

Disconsolately, she picked at her salad. She'd missed Kesh. Now she'd have to wait for him to come off duty in the evening and try to meet up with him inconspicuously in the recreation area. Was she being overly cautious, she wondered? Even if she was, breaking into private files was not her skill, it was Kesh's. He said he did it for amusement, to keep his hand in. Whatever the reason, she was thankful he did right now. It was only two days till they reached their destination, and she wanted to know exactly what Chy'qui had been up to before they arrived.

* * *

J'koshuk woke in his own room. He remembered something of the aftermath of his visit to the Human female, but not much. There'd been pain, and he'd been taken to the medical area, but beyond that, nothing. Glancing at the clock, he saw from the date that had been nine days ago.

Dread filled him, and getting up, he went to the cleansing area. He stopped at the mirror when he saw his reflection. Putting a shaking hand to his head, he touched the edge of the implant. Nausea welled up inside him and, hurriedly, he removed his hand. The sensation subsided, leaving him shaking.

Unsteadily, he headed for the lounge and something to drink. He gulped the herbal brew, feeling better as its warmth spread through him. Now he felt more able to con-

sider the situation rationally. Putting the cup down, he sat
back in his seat. He had an implant. He didn't feel different
in any way, it didn't affect the way he thought, so what
had been lost—or achieved for that matter—by implanting
him? He'd no idea right now, but he'd watch and see during
the next few days.

Round his neck, the metal collar vibrated, warning him
that he was needed, that someone would be coming for
him. Hurriedly he got to his feet and went to the food unit,
reading quickly down the varied menu, choosing a light
meal of eggs and three varieties of vegetables. He picked
his plate up, turning away from the unit and shoveling the
food into his mouth. It was good. He made a mental note
to remember the name of the meal for another time.

The door opened as he swallowed the last mouthful. A
Valtegan in gray fatigues, flanked by an armored guard,
stood there.

"I'm Doctor Chy'qui," he said. "A Prime Seniormost.
You've been my patient, J'koshuk, but now you're well
again. I've come to give you your new duties."

"Yes, Seniormost," he said, standing up.

"The crew of the *M'ijikk,* as you know, have been relo-
cated within the *Kz'adul* for several weeks. It's time you
were also given your permanent posting. I need an assistant
to help me carry out health checks on them from time to
time. When I do this, you will accompany me. Today is such
an occasion." He held out a small numeric pad mounted on
a wrist attachment. "Put this on and follow me."

They went first to the cargo area, where stores were
being redistributed throughout the ship. He could spot his
fellow crew members easily. They all wore fatigues of a
yellowish-green, and they all had implants like himself.

It was merely a matter of checking the readings for each
person on the tiny view screen, and if the red figures were
different from those in black, adjusting them using the keypad. It was repetitive and boring work, the only interesting
feature being that he got a tour of certain working areas
of the massive craft.

During lunch break, the doctor went to one end of the
mess hall, leaving J'koshuk to join those from the *M'ijikk.*
He was wary at first, wondering if they would want revenge

on him for carrying out the Seniormost's orders when he'd questioned them. The matter was resolved by them treating him with exactly the same level of contempt and avoidance as they had before. Consequently, he ate alone and was glad when his collar vibrated, calling him back to the doctor.

Their second location was the landing bay. As they came off the cargo elevator, J'koshuk could see suited figures working high above, finishing reinforcing the last section of a repair to what must have been a massive hull breach.

"What happened there?" he asked.

Chy'qui frowned, wondering if he'd allowed him to retain too much curiosity, but then, J'koshuk couldn't help him with these duties if he didn't have enough free will left to question the readings and make the necessary adjustments.

"The Sholans and their companions escaped through that hole," he said shortly, then remembered the task he was actually training him for. "Tomorrow, we reach our destination," he said quietly. "It's a rendezvous with the Sholans. They've taken one of our people captive and we're exchanging him for the Sholan male you were questioning. Do you remember him?"

J'koshuk nodded. Of course he remembered him.

"He is to be exchanged for their hostage. You will be accompanying me. Our guards will be out of range of their Control, therefore they must be monitored by us."

He nodded again. Made sense. His position hadn't suffered, despite the debacle with the Human female, and the implant. He only had to consider what the rest of the crew were doing to know that. Manual work, that was all they were worth, even his old enemy Mzayb'ik. That had made him laugh, but it had not seemed to bother Mzayb'ik at all when they'd come face-to-face.

"Come on, we've another twenty to do before we're finished," said the doctor.

Suddenly, they heard a commotion ahead of them. Someone had fallen to the ground and several tan-clad figures were converging on him, voices raised in obvious concern.

Chy'qui sighed. "There's always one or two," he muttered, gesturing J'koshuk to follow him as he headed toward the group.

J'koshuk glanced at the doctor, wondering why he wasn't
hurrying. It could be serious, a life could be at risk.

"Should we not hurry?"

"No point. They have him safe enough for now. When
his fit is over, I'll have him moved to Med Research, for
what good it will do."

"You know what's wrong with him?"

"Failed implant," said Chy'qui briefly. "He'll not be
much use to anyone in a few weeks' time."

The knot of people parted for them. J'koshuk could
barely see the figure being held down by three Prime docking hands. He could see he wore the same color of fatigues
as the rest of his crew.

"Failed in what way?" he asked, his mouth going dry in
fear at the thought of his own implant.

"Imperfect connections between the brain and the implant. He'll have to be terminated eventually."

As the crouching Prime moved aside, J'koshuk recognized the fallen male. It was his general, M'ezozakk. With
an effort, he managed to swallow the scream of fear that
rose from deep inside him.

* * *

Deep within the heart of an asteroid in the Haven belt,
the displays on six cryo units flicked to green. Lights came
on in the inner chambers, and with a faint hiss, the vacuum
seals were released. As the lids arched back into the units,
the sleepers within began to stir.

The Instructor for the facility waited patiently. He'd activated sleepers many times in the past, but only for retraining. Like the others he'd wakened earlier, he'd chosen this
group carefully, making sure there were none that would
be known to the present-day personnel who'd be at Haven.

He remembered the sensations of waking as he watched
them take their first deep breath. He'd experienced it himself several times over the years. The buzz of oxygen to
the brain, the feeling of hyper-alertness, of knowing that
you were still at the peak of fitness and health, and the
knowledge that you'd cheated time itself.

"Well come, Brothers and Sisters," he said, as the last
one made his way from his cryo unit to the chairs where

he and the others sat. "The year is 1551, and the reason you've been woken is to meet a clear and present threat to Shola."

He waited for the stir of interest to die down. "Background information plus the relevant Sholan and Alliance history to date has been provided for you through the usual sleep tapes as you were being revived. Your assignment is to guard the Sholan negotiators and facilitate the exchange of hostages between the Valtegan Primes and ourselves. You have all been fully briefed, again with the use of sleep tapes. If anyone has any questions on the situation, now is the time to ask." He looked round the two females and four males, but no questions were forthcoming.

"Lieutenant Dzaou, you are in charge of this unit. Your liaison will be Commander L'Seuli from Dzahai Stronghold. He will be here presently to meet you. You are now dismissed to refresh yourselves and get to know each other."

They filed out to the living area, beginning to talk among themselves.

His task done, he waited till they were out of earshot before heading for the adjacent sick bay. From there he passed through the secret entrance to the labyrinth of tunnels where the other sleepers lay. It was time to check the units, make sure all was well with them. As he walked slowly down the rows of darkened cryo units, all the panel lights showed their accustomed amber. They slept quiet and deep, those who came here, he saw to that. It was his task, his penance to the God and the Brotherhood, to be their guardian and Instructor for the next nine years.

* * *

This time, L'Seuli traveled up front beside the pilot as they began to make their final approach to Haven. It was on the outer edge of an asteroid belt circling the nearby gas giant. The largest asteroid was Haven itself. Inside the protective envelope of the belt, he could see smaller craft in parking orbits. A disk shaped trading vessel caught his attention.

"The *Hkariyash*," he said, pointing to it. "It's gotten busy here." The volume of craft there surprised him.

"Yes, Commander," said Chima. "It is the Brotherhood's first major turnout in three hundred years, and then we were only part of the combined Forces."

"Let's hope it remains peaceful. The Chemerian/Sholan wars cost a lot of lives on both sides."

"What's going on here, Commander?"

"Captain Kheal will have you briefed along with everyone else, Chima," said L'Seuli. Then the *Va'Khoi* came into view.

"Vartra's bones!" swore Chima, looking at the massive destroyer. "That's ours?"

"The command ship," said L'Seuli. "Captain Kheal will transfer there sometime today. There should be a fighter carrier around, too."

As Chima taxied the craft around into the refueling bay, L'Seuli saw one other Striker sitting ready. "General Raiban is going to be most unhappy. We've got half of High Command's new fighters," he murmured.

Ten minutes later, he was heading out of the elevator and along the busy corridor to Kheal's office. The station was quite different this time; there was an air of controlled urgency about the place.

"You'll find us a little busier this visit, Commander," said Kheal, dismissing his aide and standing up to greet him.

"Indeed I do, Captain," agreed L'Seuli, throwing his cloak over the back of the chair before sitting down. "I hadn't thought to be back so soon. When do you expect the *Rryuk's Profit*?"

"Tomorrow, with the Prime ship, *Kz'adul*, not far behind. My orders say you're in charge of the escort for the negotiators and the exchange of hostages. I'll have you ferried out to your unit as soon as you're ready."

"Thank you, Captain. They'll need to familiarize themselves with the layout of Haven. I'd like the exchange to take place on the landing deck here, if you've no objections."

"I'd rather it be here than on the *Kz'adul*," said Kheal frankly. "I've assigned you the office next to mine. One of my senior crew, Sub-Lieutenant Zhaddu, will assist you if you require anything. He'll be running this station, leaving you free for your primary task. I hope that's acceptable."

L'Seuli nodded. "I'll need an aide."

"Zhaddu will appoint one for you. Briefing is at the four-teenth hour and will be relayed from the *Va'Khoi* to Haven and all craft. I'm leaving within the next half hour."

"In that case, I won't delay you. If someone could show me my office and get my belongings stored in my quarters, I'd be grateful. I also need a shuttle to take me to join my unit."

"Certainly," said Kheal, summoning his aide. "I must admit, L'Seuli, I had no idea of the scale of this encounter when you last came," he said quietly. "Did you?"

"I knew what was coming, but not where," admitted L'Seuli. "I'd no idea we could field so many, though."

They exchanged glances, saying no more. Some matters were better not discussed, even among senior Brothers.

"Attention!" said Dzaou, jumping to his feet as he saw L'Seuli enter the small mess area.

"Good evening. At ease, Brothers, and Sisters," he said, taking the vacant chair at the top of the table. "I'm Commander L'Seuli. Introduce yourselves, please."

"Lieutenant Dzaou, Commander, and this is Brother Maikoi," he said, indicating the male on L'Seuli's right. "Sister Zhiko next to him, Sister Taeo, and Brothers Kholgou and Ngio," indicating those on his own left.

L'Seuli nodded to each of them in turn. They were of differing ages, but all were at least in their late forties. Seasoned warriors. He also knew what very few others did, that they'd been in cryo for an average of two hundred years, give or take the odd six months for retraining every thirty years.

"I believe you've all been *fully,*" he emphasized the fully, "briefed on the situation we are about to face here at Haven."

"Yes, Commander," said Dzaou.

"Our task is to ensure not only the safety of our negotiating party, but also that of the hostages. The first of ours is the Valtegan Prime, Prince Zsurtul. The other is a Valtegan general from a world called Kiju'iz. His name is Kezule, and like yourselves, he's from an earlier time than this. We hope he will be here before the Primes arrive in two days."

"Who are we getting in exchange?" asked Dzaou.

"A Sholan mixed Leska telepath named Kusac Aldatan.

He's the Clan Leader of the En'Shalla Aldatan Clan. Have you been told of the complications concerning him?''

"We've been briefed on the En'Shallans, Commander," said Dzaou. "Seems to me that even with the possibility of a treaty, this is an uneven exchange."

"The importance to Shola of the return of our Brother is immense," said L'Seuli carefully. He'd been well briefed himself on how to handle the sleepers. "And we have no option over the meeting with the Primes, not least because they know the location of Shola. I expect you to let his own Triad members deal with Kusac. They are telepaths and will be able to judge the situation quicker and more accurately than you can."

"When are we going over to Haven, Commander?" asked Taeo.

"As soon as we've finished here. I want you to familiarize yourselves thoroughly with the station. We hope the exchange will take place in the landing deck here, rather than on the Prime ship. The all-crew briefing is at the fourteenth hour tonight. My office is next to Captain Kheal's. He's handed over command of Haven to Sub-Lieutenant Zhaddu, who'll carry the rank of captain for the duration. My aide is Sister Lydda. You'll meet her on the shuttle when we leave. I'll meet you tomorrow in my office at the ninth hour, Lieutenant Dzaou, to discuss your plans for the deployment of personnel during Contact and the hostage exchange."

"Aye, Commander," he said.

L'Seuli got to his feet. "I suggest we waste no more time in getting over to Haven."

CHAPTER 18

Day 41

"Y'KNOW, I miss all this," said Zhiko, skinning an apple with her knife.

"What? The crappy food?" asked Ngio, pushing his plate away in disgust.

"No. The noise, the bustle. There's none of this at training."

"I can't believe I'm seeing this," said Maikoi, looking round the mess hall. "Humans and Sumaan at a Brother-hood outpost, when not even our own Forces know of its existence."

"There are several Human Brothers now we have mixed species Leskas," said Taeo. "What do you think, Dzaou?"

Dzaou took a sip from his mug before answering. "I think it'll get even more interesting when the *Rryuk's Profit* arrives tomorrow—if it does. Damned place'll be crawling with aliens. Not what I'd call security. I want all those off the *Profit* kept well out of the way during the exchange. Especially the female Human that's the Leska of the Primes' hostage."

"Alliance members, though. First time in a long while there've been new ones," said Zhiko, looking at a table nearby where two Human males sat with several Sumaan. "And we get to meet them."

"This is my last tour," said Kholgou, staring into his mug. "I stay out this time."

"Time's up, eh?" said Maikoi.

He nodded. "I only signed up for three awakenings. This is it."

"Tried it once," said Ngio. "Lasted three months before I beat down the door at Dzahai Stronghold asking to go back. Can't think why. Don't feed us properly, even now. Nothing changes, only the faces."

Dzaou listened to them with half an ear. They'd hung around for most of the day waiting for the *Profit* to arrive. Finally a message came saying they'd be a day late. Now they needed to let off some steam. Sleeping got to you like that. Right now, he was watching the same Sumaan traders and their Human companions as Zhiko. They seemed to be getting on well. Unusual for the Sumaan. They were usually taciturn and kept themselves to themselves. Was it something to do with the nature of the Humans? The sleep briefing had said the Humans were also a telepathic species, he remembered.

"Hey, boss, we getting leisure time tonight?" asked Zhiko.

He turned his attention back to them. "Yeah. You got four hours. I want everyone in their own beds—alone—by nineteenth hour. Don't drink much. Keep alert and see what you can find out, especially from the Humans."

"Funny that," purred Zhiko, getting to her feet. "Just what I had in mind." She walked away from their table, tail and hips swaying.

Maikoi and Ngio exchanged grins with each other, then looked at Dzaou. He shook his head, trying not to smile. "Get out of here," he growled. "Go find some amusement of your own."

* * *

Day 42

The next morning, Dzaou met L'Seuli. "I've had a good look round the landing deck, and I need an extra unit of ten people, Commander," he said in his slow, drawling accent. "We've not been in verbal communication with any of our people since they went missing. It's quite possible they could have been subverted to the Primes' way of thinking. I want the whole of the docking bay secured, all gun emplacements occupied and sealed, all vehicles out, and the two crews separated and taken under escort to debriefing rooms. I want to be sure this Kaid character is fit to be a negotiator."

"Brother Kaid is *the* negotiator," corrected L'Seuli automatically, as he considered the request. "I'll pass on your recommendations to Captain Zhaddu, but as for taking the people on the *Profit* into custody, I would remind you they are not criminals, Lieutenant, and should not be treated as such."

"They are a security risk, Commander, almost as great a one as the other aliens here. And there's the matter of the extra day."

L'Seuli could hear the condemnation in his voice. "The *Profit* arrived in this system on schedule. It's their journey from the gas giant that's delayed them. Remember, Dzaou, this is our time," he said, putting an underlying growl of annoyance into his voice. "You are merely passing through. Stronghold and Shola have to live with our decisions. I'm well aware of your reasons for choosing cryo, but Brothers should be capable of rising above their personal prejudices. If you cannot, I will report you to your Instructor and request your return to Stronghold. Do I make myself clear?"

Dzaou suppressed his anger with an effort. "My priority is the safety of our species."

"You'd do that best by not starting an incident through insulting our new allies. Agreed, our people could be a security risk, but the U'Churians and the Cabbarans will not be subjected to an inquisition style debriefing. Remember, had it not been for their help, we'd have lost Clan Leader Aldatan and his Leska."

"Very well, we can escort the crew of the *Profit* to safe quarters, but I insist our people be taken into custody until fully debriefed." Concessions had to be made, and if the aliens from the *Profit* were in guarded quarters, and kept there till this encounter was over, he'd be satisfied. Briefly, he wondered why their Instructor hadn't given him a larger unit.

"Maybe because he knew that with it you wouldn't be forced to make compromises," said a voice as the door opened. "Sorry to interrupt, Commander L'Seuli, but Master Rhyaz said to report to you immediately."

Flanked by Banner and Jurrel, Brynne stood just inside the room. Behind him stood Keeza and Shaayiyisis, the Sumaan captain of the *Couana*.

"We're to augment your unit. I presume this means we'll be working with Lieutenant Dzaou."

Dzaou had spun around in his chair as he heard the voice. A Human, wearing the Brotherhood active grays edged with purple. What the hell was he doing in that getup?

"Brother Brynne, I'm sure Master Rhyaz didn't envisage such a sudden entrance to my office," L'Seuli said coldly, while blessing him mentally for his interruption.

Dzaou couldn't believe what he was hearing. The Brotherhood had alien members?

No problem, came the reply. *Master Rhyaz said to tell you this fellow needs to lose some of his species prejudice or he'll not be returning to his unit, whatever that means. I came in because he was broadcasting his dislike so loudly I picked it up as we came past. At the moment, he's freaking out about alien Brothers.*

Several emotions flitted through L'Seuli's mind, as well as several thoughts. Foremost of those was that putting Brynne on Dzaou's team could be almost as much trouble as it was benefit. The wry face Brynne pulled wasn't lost on him.

He stood up, looking at Dzaou. "These three Brothers will be added to your unit, Dzaou," he said. "You must learn to work with Brynne and any of our other alien Brothers, or return to Stronghold at the end of this mission. As for your request, I'll make sure the additional ten Brothers are sent to the landing bay within the next half hour. And you may escort our people from the *Profit* to the debriefing room when they arrive. The U'Churians and the Cabbarans are to be quartered in dormitory one, the others in dorm seven."

Dzaou got to his feet, aware from the sleeping arrangements that the commander had already considered the potential risk posed by the returning Sholans and Humans. "Which room has been designated for debriefing, Commander?"

"The offices on the starboard side opposite the briefing room have been allocated to us. And, Lieutenant Dzaou," he said quietly. "I'm in charge of debriefing. Remember that. Brother Jurrel, your orders, if you please. Where have you left Kezule?"

Jurrel came forward to hand him the comp pad with their orders on it. "He's being revived from cryo in the sick bay, Commander. Master Rhyaz wants Brynne to be present with the negotiating party. He's the one who contacted Kusac a couple of days ago."

"Noted," said L'Seuli. "Dismissed."

Dzaou saluted sharply and turned to follow the other three Brothers into the corridor. Working with a Human did not please him at all. The fact he was a telepath was an extra annoyance. Unable to stomach violence, they had no business being out here in the front line.

Brynne turned round and blocked his way. "If you think working with you when you're broadcasting your dislike of me is any kind of a picnic, think again, mate," he said, making sure to show his teeth in an unfriendly grin. "En'-Shalla Brothers fight, and our training at Stronghold is as complete as anyone else's. I may have started later than you, and be a beginner, but don't underestimate me, or any other Humans."

"Brynne," said Banner warningly. "On a mission, we're given ranks, even though none exist otherwise. He's our lieutenant."

"Yeah, well, I have this problem with racists," said Brynne. "He should button his mind if he doesn't want me knowing what he's thinking!"

"Is he your pupil?" asked Dzaou coldly.

"Mine," said Jurrel. "And with respect, Lieutenant, he's right. If you haven't worked with En'Shallan telepaths before . . ."

"I'm aware of their level of Talent," he interrupted. "Stow your belongings in dorm eight and get down to the landing bay on the double!"

He watched them head off, then angrily made for the comms room, requesting a secure line to his unit Instructor.

"You set me up for this," Dzaou said.

"There are lessons you must learn if you wish to be part of Shola's future. It's not enough to condition you to accept the new species with whom we must work," said his Instructor placidly. "You must learn to accept them. See the strengths they bring to our world as well as our species."

"What I went through in the Chemerian wars . . ."

"Is known to us. You should use that to help you deal with our returning Brothers and Sisters with compassion. That is why you were chosen."

"When I volunteered to be a Sleeper, I thought . . ."

"That you were a perfect warrior because you were accepted." The Instructor nodded. "It's a common mistake, one usually rectified during the first awakening. You were unlucky that this didn't happen for you. Swallow your pride, Brother Dzaou. You are no better than any of the current day Brothers with whom you work."

"Will you let me finish talking, dammit!"

"I've listened to such arguments many times," his Instructor sighed. "Say something new and I will listen, Brother."

"Why was I chosen if I've got so many flaws?" he demanded.

"Vartra's reasons are sometimes known only by Him. You know what you must do, Brother Dzaou. I have confidence in your ability to succeed. Do not prove me wrong and have to return to Stronghold, unless that's what you wish."

Dzaou began to growl angrily. "What of our imperative to protect our species?"

"We do that best by listening to those who lead us. A briefing of the situation is only that, not a knowledge of it. They live now, they know their own time. Be guided by them, Brother Dzaou. And make use of the En'Shalla telepaths. They are a gift from Vartra Himself. The future will see their children come into their own for the benefit of all the Alliance."

"Their children?" he asked, startled.

"The hybrid cubs born of the mixed Leskas." The Instructor frowned. "This was in your briefing tapes. Don't you remember?"

"Yes, now you mention it. I hadn't realized that the cubs were actually hybrids of both species."

"Now, perhaps, you see the wisdom of learning to work with these Humans. They are our future, Dzaou. We either embrace them, or are overtaken by them. As for our new allies, the U'Churians and the Cabbarans have already shown their worth in the help they've given us during the past few weeks. Contrast them with the Chemerians of your own time. Doesn't the jegget in your den keep out the rodents who would otherwise inflict poisoned bites on your cubs? Strange times bring strange bedfellows, Dzaou. Try to open your mind to them, accept them for what they are, rather than what they're not."

"All very well for you to say, Instructor," he grumbled. "I'm the one who's got to do it, not you."

"Do you think I don't have my own lessons to learn?" He raised an eye ridge. "I assure you, I have. The higher we aspire, Dzaou, the harder the lessons, and the farther we can fall. Now go back to your unit, and welcome the new Brothers as comrades in arms. You're on the same side, after all, and the telepath Brynne has lately learned his own lessons concerning our people."

Dzaou sighed. "Yes, Instructor,"

* * *

As the *Profit* settled down gently on the landing deck, Kaid began the power-down sequence, then transferred the board over to Sheeowl. The journey back had been a tremendous strain on everyone. They'd lived with the constant fear of the Prime ship following them and the worry that the repair would not stand up to the pressures of the journey. That was in addition to their fears for Kusac.

Tirak had asked him to handle the emergence and landing at Haven, since he'd been there before. In order to cut the time from their journey, they'd had to emerge as close to the gas giant as possible, taking into account that he'd no real idea of where the craft that would inevitably be there would be deployed. But they'd made it, and been escorted in to Haven itself.

"Got a reception committee for us here, too," said Tirak, indicating the forward view screen.

Kaid looked up. A group of gray-clad Sholans was running forward to surround the craft. One of them was Human. A lone figure stood off to one side by the elevator. L'Seuli.

Hello, there, Kaid, Carrie, came Brynne's thought. *Commander L'Seuli says he knows you'll understand the need for the security.*

He sounds bouncy, Carrie commented.

I see you joined up, sent Kaid.

Done a lot of things recently. How you all doing? Anyone hurt?

T'Chebbi's injured. Arm wound, not serious, but we're all exhausted.

Brace yourselves. Dzaou, the tan one, he's in charge. He wants our lot all debriefed immediately. Not the Profit *crew, just your group. He's got an Attitude problem with us Humans and telepaths.*

Figures. We'll be out shortly. Middle cargo air lock, port side.

Gotcha.

"They'll want to debrief us," said Kaid to Tirak as he got to his feet. "Not you, though. See they put you somewhere comfortable and feed you. I said we'd exit from the cargo bay."

Tirak nodded. "I want to have a word with you about Jeran. He's asked to join my crew. All his friends and family are dead. Says he's got nothing to go back for."

"Wants to stay with Giyesh."

"I'm a military ship, Kaid, so are my people," he said awkwardly. "If I were a trading vessel, it might be different. I shouldn't have let Giyesh take up with him, but she's the youngest and she needed someone during our captivity. If it becomes general knowledge on Home, she'll find herself compromised when it comes to finding a mate."

"Then why not let them stay together? Tell Home you need him as an ambassador. Because of the time he spent on Jalna, he's got a good working knowledge of the Free Traders, and he's Sholan. Perfect for the job," he said, knowing if he wasn't so tired, he'd be amused. "Request him from the one called L'Seuli. Tell him, if he asks, I said yes."

Tirak nodded. "You make a good argument for him, one I think even our people will accept."

Kaid patted him on the shoulder as he went past. "Got something to see to before we debark," he said.

Carrie and the others had gathered in the mess with their belongings. "You go on down to the cargo bay and wait for me," he said as they got onto the elevator. "I want to catch Rezac on his own. We'll bring Zsurtul."

As Kaid and Rezac, with Zsurtul between them, came across from the elevator, Tirak opened the outer hatch and extended the ramp. Cold air surged in around them, making him shiver as he joined Carrie.

"Well come back," called out Brynne as they began to walk down the ramp onto Haven.

"Good to be back," said Kaid, watching as the Sholan wearing the insignia of a lieutenant stepped forward.

"Well come to Haven," Dzaou said to them. He gestured two males forward. "Prince Zsurtul, my people will escort you to your new quarters. The commander of this facility will be along to see you shortly."

"Lieutenant Dzaou," said Kaid as their hostage was led away, "Prince Zsurtul has been cooperative with us. May I recommend you bear this in mind?"

Dzaou barely looked at him before turning to the U'Churians and Cabbarans. "Captain Tirak, my people will escort you and your crew to your quarters, where a meal awaits you."

At least they're treating Tirak decently, sent Carrie, eyeing the group of Brothers and Sisters that were moving to surround them.

As Tirak and the others were led to the elevator and L'Seuli, Dzaou finally turned to them.

"We're taking you up to level two for debriefing, then you'll be shown to your quarters."

"My people are exhausted, Lieutenant Dzaou," said Kaid. "Can't this wait? We need food and sleep, and clean clothes. We've got civilians and younglings with us."

"All that will have to wait, Brother Kaid. You know the protocol as well as anyone. The Prime ship is only a day behind you. We have very little time."

"What's your gift, Lieutenant?" asked Carrie.

Startled, Dzaou looked at her. "Excuse me?"

"Gift. All Brothers have a psi gift. What's yours? Or do you have anyone capable of receiving telepathic communications, apart from Brynne?"

The seven guards looked at each other, then Zhiko spoke. "I can receive a little. Why?"

Carrie stepped toward her and instantly six rifles came up to bear on her. The only one that didn't was Brynne's. She ignored Kaid's mental warning as she stared at the Brothers ringing them.

"Don't be ridiculous," she said. "Do you think we escaped from the Primes to come here and kill you?" She looked round them. "You do! Of all the damned foolish ideas! I'm too damned tired to be bothered with your games of soldiers."

Dzaou stepped forward. "Let's get moving," he said, indicating the elevator with his gun barrel.

"Is there a problem?" asked L'Seuli as he strolled over. "Well come back, Kaid, Carrie. T'Chebbi, I didn't realize you were injured," he said, gesturing toward the medics still standing by the elevator. "Or that there was a pregnant female with you. Jo, isn't it? Lieutenant Dzaou, see these two females are taken straight to the sick bay," he said.

"I'm going with her," said Rezac. "So's Zashou. We're Linked as a Triad."

"Take them as well," said L'Seuli to the medics. "And for the Gods' sake, see they're fed."

"I want a Brother to accompany them," said Dzaou.

"I'm a Brother," said Rezac. "No need for anyone else."

"That's not sufficient!"

"They're hardly going to cause any trouble, Lieutenant," said L'Seuli dryly. "They're so exhausted they can barely stand."

"Take them to sick bay," ordered Dzaou through clenched teeth.

"The younglings, Commander L'Seuli, do they have to be debriefed right now? Can't it wait?" asked Kaid quietly.

L'Seuli looked at them. The male was only about sixteen, the female he couldn't guess, not having any experience of Humans.

"She's sixteen, too," said Carrie.

"Kate and Taynar, isn't it?" L'Seuli asked, getting tired nods in reply from them. "Taeo, take them to the dorm. They should be in their beds at this time of night."

"That just leaves the three of us," said Kaid.

L'Seuli looked at Kaid. "Never straightforward when you're involved, is it, Kaid?"

"I do my best, Commander," he murmured, letting his tail sway gently.

"No, I want you three debriefed. Jeran was with M'ezozakk's ship until Jalna. His information is invaluable to us. I'll debrief you myself, and see you're fed, but it will be done tonight," he said firmly.

Carrie stepped up to him and linked an arm through his. "In that case, since you insist so nicely, Commander L'Seuli," she said, smiling up at him as she began walking him toward the elevator.

Dzaou looked on speechless, then powered down his gun and, slinging it over his shoulder, gestured Kaid and Jeran to follow them.

Quite put him off his stride, we did, Carrie sent to Kaid.

"Master Lijou warned me about you," said L'Seuli in an undertone to Carrie. "I take it Brynne updated you as you landed."

"Forewarned is forearmed. You don't really think we've been brainwashed, do you?"

"It's a possibility."

"All you have to do is ask Vriuzu to read us. He knows us, and he'll be able to tell you right away. He says he'd be happy to do it."

L'Seuli stopped in his tracks. "You've contacted him already? Of course you have. Why didn't I think of that?" He shook his head and started moving again. "I should have. I'll get him to join us in the debriefing room."

"Already done. Another problem solved," she said. "You're just not used to having the resources of us telepaths at your command, that's all."

Dzaou was too taken aback to be angry at the partial collapse of his plan. As he walked in the rear of their small party, he analyzed what had happened. The commander had been right. The pregnant Human and the injured Sister should have been sent to the sick bay. As for the other two, well, he sighed inwardly, if he thought of a Triad as being Leska partners plus one, then there was a justification for sending them, too. He hadn't been aware that the male, Rezac, was a Brother. He and his original Leska were the two from the stasis cube and therefore from the past. How could he be a Brother?

"He became one when he and Jo became Linked," said Kaid at his elbow. "And I recruited him and his partners, as is my right."

Startled, he looked at him, actually noticing him for the first time. "You're a telepath, too."

"The first Triad," agreed Kaid.

Dzaou looked from him to Carrie and the commander.

"With her," Kaid confirmed as they waited for the elevator to return.

"You've been an active Brother for years. How can you be a telepath?" Dzaou demanded.

"It's a long story, and not relevant right now," said Kaid. "What is important is that I'm well enough rested for tomorrow. So let's get this debriefing over as quickly as possible, shall we?"

Dzaou bristled at the implicit order.

"We're En'Shalla, we don't need a rank," said Carrie, her voice a silky purr as she turned round to look at him. "Do we, Commander?"

"As negotiator, Kaid carries the rank of Ambassador," L'Seuli said smoothly as the elevator doors slid open.

As good as his word, L'Seuli had provided the three of them with hot food during their debriefing. Vriuzu had let Carrie send the information to him, which had helped keep the session as short as possible. He'd then gone to check on the others and pronounced them all of sound mind.

After a short consultation between L'Seuli and Dzaou, they'd been told they were free to go where they wished on the station.

"Commander, a word in private, if you please," said Kaid as they prepared to leave.

L'Seuli glanced at Dzaou, who nodded and left with Jeran. "What is it, Kaid?"

"We need our own room, L'Seuli," said Carrie, idly toying with the paper and stylus that lay in front of her.

"The situation between us is a little more complex than I said," Kaid began as he walked over to stand beside her.

"I did wonder," said L'Seuli, watching them. "Brynne told me it happened with him and Keeza."

Carrie looked up. "Keeza?"

"You haven't had a chance to talk to him yet. He's life-bonded to a Sholan called Keeza, a gene-altered telepath like yourselves. He's found that with Vanna so pregnant, he's formed an almost Leska-like Link with her."

"Brynne, married? Good grief."

"I take it she's here with him," said Kaid. "That explains his good humor."

"I'll arrange a private room immediately for you," said L'Seuli, reaching for his desk comm.

"Thank you," said Kaid as Carrie's hand came up to touch his where it lay on her shoulder.

"Is everything fine at home?" she asked. "I had disturbing dreams while I was in cryo."

"We had a crisis while you were away, but it's over now," said L'Seuli. "Kezule escaped."

Carrie's hand tightened her grip on him and he could feel her sudden anxiety. "I knew he had! Kashini, is she safe? Nothing's happened to her, has it?"

"Kashini is fine," reassured L'Seuli. "No one was hurt."

"What happened?" asked Kaid.

"He got onto the estate and managed to take Dzaka, Kitra, and Kashini hostage. Thanks to Kitra, however, we managed to recapture him. He's in sick bay right now, still in a coma."

Carrie shut her eyes as visions of what could have happened flashed through her mind.

But they didn't, she's fine, sent Kaid. "Why take them?"

"He wanted to be returned to his own time."

"But that's impossible without at least two telepaths and the la'quo." He looked at L'Seuli. "Tell me he didn't have the la'quo." Fears for his son filled him. He knew what the drug could do.

"Kezule was given some la'quo resin and did force them to take it, but as I said, Kitra was able to deal with the situation. She mentally knocked out Kezule and we were able to get in and get them out."

"What about the effects of the drug on them?"

"None, except . . ."

"What?" demanded Kaid, hands clenching inadvertently on Carrie's shoulders. "Tell me!"

"He and Kitra are Leska-bonded," said L'Seuli with a smile.

"Is that all?" asked Carrie in a faint voice.

"That's all," said L'Seuli. "Apparently the effects of their bonding burned out the drug from their systems. Vanna checked them over thoroughly." He reached in his pocket and handed Carrie a crystal cube. "They knew you'd be worried, so they sent this for you with Brynne. We got it yesterday."

Almost sick with relief, Kaid sat down again as L'Seuli pushed his comm over to them.

"Brynne said that Kitra and Dzaka plan to life-bond as soon as this is over," he added as Carrie inserted the cube into the reader slot.

"I told you she'd have Dzaka," Carrie said.

Zashou couldn't sleep. Getting up, she left the dorm quietly, going to the mess and recreation halls. Getting herself a drink, she headed for an empty table. At this time of night, there were quite a few of them.

She sat there, looking around her, finding the Sholan surroundings almost alien. In her time, they'd had nothing like this. No space travel even. She watched a couple get up from another table and head in her direction. The Human she recognized immediately, Kris, but the female was unknown to her.

"Can we join you?" Kris asked. "This is Zhiko. She was among the Brothers who met you earlier."

She nodded, remembering her now.

"Can't sleep?" asked Kris sympathetically, slipping into the seat opposite.

"No."

"How's Jo and Rezac? I hear Carrie's fine now."

"Jo's pregnant," she said abruptly, lifting her glass to take a drink. Her hand shook and she put it down again hurriedly.

Kris nodded. "I had a feeling she was before you left. How are you coping?"

"What's to cope with?" she asked. "He's delirious about it. She's all he could want—a fighter like him! I even messed up between him and his son!"

"His son?" asked Kris.

"Kaid! Kaid's his son." Something wet landed on her hand. She brushed it away. "I accused him of trying to start an affair with him, so T'Chebbi told me he was his father."

"Rezac is Kaid's father? How?"

"When he went back to the Fire Margins, he sent himself forward in time." A damp spot appeared between her hands this time and she realized it was tears. Hurriedly she put her hands to her face, trying to scrub them away, but they wouldn't stop.

Kris' arms were suddenly round her, holding her close, hiding her face against his chest while she wept.

"It could have been me, Kris. It should have been, if only I hadn't been so blind and so frightened."

Another hand stroked her head; a soothing, feminine voice spoke. "What were you frightened of, kitling?"

"Of his fighting, of us dying because of it. We had no choice, the Valtegans were everywhere, taking us captive as their slaves and pets," she wept, clutching Kris' jacket. "Oh, Gods, why did I have to push him away because I was so afraid of losing him?"

"It happens all the time, kitling," Zhiko said gently, continuing to stroke her hair. "We make what we fear most happen because waiting for it is worse." She looked at Kris over Zashou's head. "Let me take her. You get help," she whispered.

"I'll get a medic," he mouthed back.

She shook her head, moving closer to the distraught female, putting her arms round her. "Get Rezac."

Carefully, Kris let her take Zashou from him.

"No male is worth all this crying, kitling," she said, guiding Zashou's head onto her shoulder. "There'll be others, you wait and see. Ones more appreciative of you."

"I love him! He's my Leska and I'm losing even that now she's carrying his cub."

"She's taking him away from you?"

"No, not like that. It's me. I've pushed him away for so long that he really believes I don't love him."

"Have you ever told him you do?" she asked.

"I couldn't! He's always so capable, so strong, and I'm nothing but scared. He despises me."

"Do you want him? If you do, you have to fight for him."

Zashou lifted her head, pulling back slightly to look at Zhiko. "Fight? I can't fight for him!" she said, wiping the tears away.

"Sure you can. You start by telling him the truth about how you feel. Face up to him like a warrior, then you'll start to earn his respect, and maybe get back his love." Zhiko saw Zashou's face change and knew Kris had returned with Rezac. "Remember, face him like a warrior, not a mewling kit," she said, getting up.

Rezac looked tired as he nodded his thanks to Zhiko and sat down opposite her.

"What's all this about, Zashou? Kris said, you were in a state and needed me."

"I didn't know he'd gone for you," she said, looking down at the table.

"You seem all right to me. You really pick your times, don't you?" he said, beginning to get up again.

"Don't go!" she said, reaching out to stop him. "I need to talk to you. I want to talk."

"What is it? I'm tired, Zashou. I don't have time for your jealous tirades."

This was probably her last chance. She had to tell him now. "Yes, I'm jealous," she said quietly. "When I see you and Jo together, I realize we could have had that if I hadn't been so scared of losing you." She watched the look of incredulity cross his face. "I lied to you," she said in a rush. "I pretended to myself and you that I didn't love you when I did. You were right when you said you felt it on our Link days."

"You were scared of losing me?"

She nodded. "You'd always been a fighter. Up in Ranz, and when the Valtegans came. It's what attracted me to you from the first, until we became Leskas." She looked back at the table, hardly aware she was clenching her claws into her own hands at the effort to tell him this. "I'm not like you, Rezac. I'm too scared of danger, and with our Link, every time you faced it, so did I. I didn't want you to be killed, or me. You don't know what it's like, when you're a coward, to be Linked to someone who looks danger in the eye and isn't afraid."

"You think I'm not afraid?" he asked after a moment's silence. "How wrong you are. I'm terrified, Zashou. I don't want to die either. I'm surprised you never felt my fear."

"Never."

"You must have thought it was your own." He reached across the table for her hands. "You're bleeding," he said, separating them. "You weren't a coward, you know. Like the time you turned on Q'emgo'h."

"That wasn't brave. He was repulsive." She shuddered at the memory. "I was terrified."

"But that's what courage is. Being afraid and still doing

it. You could have given in, agreed to pair with him, but you didn't, even though it could have cost you your life."

"That was for myself, though."

"What about all the times you worked on the minds of those Court guards, turning them against each other over several weeks? You were frightened of them realizing what you were doing, I know you were. And when we snuck out to the hatchery to make those eggs and the females sterile? I couldn't have done it alone, you know that."

She looked away again. They'd had to use the extra energy they created when they paired for that, and the memory both embarrassed and worried her.

"Why does it worry you?" he asked.

"Because we don't have Link days anymore, and I want them back, Rezac. I do love you, and I can't face the thought of not being connected to you again," she said, fresh tears springing to her eyes.

"Carrie says our Link days will likely return in a week or two, when Jo's Talent shuts down because of our cub."

She felt her hand lifted, then the touch of his tongue on the cuts she'd managed to give herself. She tightened her hand on his. "Don't leave me, Rezac. I've loved you for so long. I should have told you, I know."

"You've told me now, that's what matters," he said softly. "Come back to bed. With me. Now. Because you choose to."

"Because I love you?"

"Because we love each other."

* * *

Day 43

"Picking up emerging jump signal, Captain Zhaddu. Dead ahead. And incoming message," said the comm operator.

"Sound full alert. Target emergence point on the view screen," ordered Zhaddu, running to his command post. "Looks like they've arrived, Commander."

"Nothing on visual, Captain, but there's something out there," said comms.

"Keep tracking. Where's that signal?" he demanded.

"On audio now."

The speaker came to life. "This is *Kz'adul,* science ship of His Imperial Majesty the God-King, Emperor Cheu'-ko'h. Be advised, our purpose is peaceful. Request instructions." The message began to repeat itself.

"Still nothing on visual," said comms. "But it's out there, by the smaller moon."

"Open a reply channel," said Zhaddu.

"Channel open, Captain."

"Captain Zhaddu of the Allied Worlds here. Your request acknowledged and granted. Place yourselves in close orbit around the planetary body adjacent to your point of exit and remain there."

For several minutes, nothing was visible on the screen.

"Dead ahead," said L'Seuli quietly, as his eye caught a flicker amid the backdrop of stars. It became stronger, wavering slightly, until the diamond-shaped Prime ship *Kz'a-dul* was clearly visible.

In their room, Carrie and Kaid heard the alarm.

"The *Kz'adul,*" said Kaid. "It's arrived."

"I know," said Carrie, moving closer to him.

"We need to get up now."

"It's still our time. We've another few hours, surely."

"We have," he agreed, surprised as she began to slide her legs round his. Realization came to him as he sensed her need to feel herself encircled by his body. "You're afraid," he said softly. "Of what they've done to Kusac."

"I'm afraid for him," she whispered, wrapping her arms around his back as he held her tighter within his. "He's been a telepath since he was a youngling, he knows nothing else. If they've taken that from him, I don't know if he can cope, if he'll want to go on living."

"Whatever they've done, we'll find a way to manage, you know that. You mustn't be afraid, not even for him. He'll know if you are, even if he can't sense you. He'll see it in your eyes, your body." He reached for her chin, tilting it up till he could kiss her.

I'm afraid for him, too, Dzinae. Afraid of why they're controlling him, what they want him to do. Do what I do, lose the fear in your work. We have to be cold and calm if we're to be able to do what's right. Reluctantly, he broke the kiss.

"We'll have several hours before they've negotiated the exchange details. We need to use that time to get the landing bay ready the way I want it, never mind what Lieutenant Dzaou wants. We've got dampers, we can use them until the Primes actually arrive. Then I want you, Rezac, Brynne, and me picking up what color sheets each one of the Primes use."

She grinned at that.

"That's better."

"Arrange it so there are eight guards and eight negotiators on each side, Commander, plus a medical team, not to exceed a doctor and three medics. A total of twenty people each."

"The breakdown?" asked L'Seuli.

"A senior officer, the negotiator, three advisers, an interpreter, recorder, and in our case, an official telepath."

"Who are you taking?"

"Carrie, Rezac, Brynne, Jurrel, Banner, and T'Chebbi, with Jo, Zashou, and Keeza out of sight but nearby for backup." said Kaid. "Vriuzu with us, and Joisha with the backup."

"My unit's supposed to be providing security for you," said Dzaou. "You've too many vulnerable people there."

"I'm the negotiator, I want my team with me. All visible personnel but Brynne are seasoned fighters."

"Brynne's not in dispute," said Dzaou. "It's the others. For a start, I don't want some overemotional female there."

Kaid looked at him. "Just who do you mean?"

"You know I mean his Leska."

Kaid turned back to L'Seuli. "Then there's no problem. Kusac has no Leska right now, does he, Commander?"

L'Seuli tapped his claws on the table. "He has a point, Dzaou. She isn't technically Kusac's Leska, she's Kaid's right now. Nor have I seen her being overemotional."

Dzaou glared at the back of Kaid's head. "She will be when he's brought out."

"I don't tell you how to run the internal workings of your unit, despite the fact it's only been a few days since you left Winter. Don't try to tell me how to run mine, when

I've been working with them for nearly a year." Kaid's voice was very quiet. "I not only work for the good of Shola, but for Vartra, too."

While he spoke, he was watching L'Seuli's face. Only the slightest movement of one ear tip betrayed he'd struck a nerve without saying he had knowledge that was forbidden.

"Kaid uses his own team. You'll back him up," said L'Seuli abruptly. "He has experience of the Primes, and Kusac is his sword-brother. Work with him, Dzaou." As they got up to leave, L'Seuli said one more thing. "Full body armor, Kaid."

She couldn't wear it on Jalna, Commander. They were body searched before they were allowed out of the spaceport, he sent, as he acknowledged the order and left the room. *And they didn't have time after they teamed up with Ashay and the shuttle.*

L'Seuli began to wonder if Master Rhyaz was trying to teach him something very subtle by giving him this as his first major command.

A junior Brother came running up to Kaid with a note as he left the commander's office. "From the Physician, Ambassador," he said, thumping his chest in an enthusiastic salute.

Raising an eye ridge, Kaid took it from him. "At ease," he murmured, trying to remember being that young himself. He scanned the report and handed it back to him. "No reply," he said, then turned to Dzaou. "We need our own runner. Can you get us one?"

Dzaou beckoned Ngio over. "Get us allocated a runner from the duty officer," he said. "Meet us . . . ." He looked at Kaid.

"In the landing bay in fifteen minutes."

Ngio nodded and headed off.

"What have we got that the Primes don't have?" Kaid asked Dzaou as they headed back to the dorms. "Telepaths. We have nine on this station of two hundred souls. I'd lay odds the other outposts have one at most. Until now, Stronghold has only had those it's recruited. Telepaths are rare, Leska pairs, let alone Triads, even rarer. Four of mine have experience reading Valtegan minds, Dzaou. Do you know that training to read the minds of other species

normally takes years? My telepaths can pick up the Primes'
surface thoughts, know if they're planning any subversive
action before it actually happens. Think of the advantage
that gives us."

"Good point," he admitted grudgingly. "So long as the
Primes don't have personal dampers like you."

"Most of them didn't. Think of it as a way of getting
extra guards past the Primes," he said as they stopped at
the dorm doors. "I'll meet you with your people in the
landing bay in fifteen minutes."

"Captain Tirak and his crew are in the briefing room,
Commander," said Lydda, popping her head round his
door.

"Coming," said L'Seuli, getting up. "Have you laid on
adequate seating for our Cabbaran allies?"

"Yes, sir."

"What did you do?"

"Tables piled with blankets," she said with a grin, as they
walked down the corridor. "Annuur claims he's got the
best view."

"They're the official ambassadors for their worlds,
Lydda. They've a right to see what involves them. Thank
the Gods we don't have any more ambassadors!"

"From my experience, these people are easy to handle.
Not like the Chemerians."

"No one's like them," said L'Seuli as they went in.

Tirak rose to greet him. "Thank you for this courtesy,
Commander. I hope you don't mind, but I took the liberty
of inviting Jeran, as well as Kate and Taynar, in to watch.
As civilians, they'd be the last to know what was happening
to the people they lived with for so many weeks."

L'Seuli frowned, then decided there were far more pressing matters to worry about than three civilians. "In the
circumstances, I think we can overlook their presence," he
said. "I just came to see you were comfortable. There's a
drinks and snacks dispenser over there if you want anything. You may have a long wait, I'm afraid."

"I just wish we could be of help."

"You have been, Captain. Without you, none of our people would have escaped. Did you get your message sent?"

"Yes. The comms officer said it would be relayed to our home world as soon as the carrier left this sector."

L'Seuli nodded. "Good. I'm afraid you'll have to excuse me now, I've got things to attend to."

"Of course, Commander."

Laughter drew Kaid's glance over to the rear of the hangar, where Carrie and the others were being fitted with armored suits.

The smallest suits are too big for T'Chebbi and me, sent Carrie.

Where are they too big?

Leg length for a start.

What about torso?

You could get two of me in it! T'Chebbi at least has the body for it.

I'm on my way. He handed the list to his runner. "Get those items brought down here immediately," he said. "You know where I want them put, so set them up when they arrive. Conscript anyone you need to help you. The mess is a good place to go for off-duty personnel."

"Yes, sir," said the junior, disappearing at a run.

He headed down to the suiting area. Carrie stood there, swamped by the gray formed body armor. "Cut it down to size," he said, checking his wrist comm. "You've got an hour. She can wear a skin suit underneath to give her vacuum protection," he said to the engineer in charge.

"You're kidding! Sir."

"No, I'm not! Get to it immediately! And get someone else fixing the legs for T'Chebbi at the same time. Have you checked helmets?"

"Helmets fit fine," said Carrie.

T'Chebbi nodded, unconsciously giving her injured arm a rub.

"You up to this, T'Chebbi?" he asked.

"Sure. Just an ache, nothing more. Won't stop me thinking or shooting."

"Everyone else kitted out?" He looked round the others.

"No problems," said Rezac. "Do you want Zashou and Jo suited up, too?"

"No, the command office has air locks and is pressurized

in the event of an emergency. The four crew standing by to help won't be suited, but they're near the elevator."

"How long now?" asked Carrie as the engineer helped her out of the suit.

"Three hours," he said. "I'm getting some food and drink sent down for us in an hour and a half. Something light. It'll settle our stomachs."

"I didn't feel this bad before my Challenge," said Carrie.

Zhiko looked at her. "You fought a Challenge?"

"I challenged Kusac's betrothed for the right to marry him," she said.

"I'm impressed."

"What she isn't saying is it ended up a Blood-Rite to the death," said Brynne.

"You fought a Blood-Rite?" asked Dzaou.

Carrie shrugged. "Didn't have an option. She changed the rules in the middle of the fight. There wasn't time to stop it."

"You won," he said.

"Just. I'd rather not talk about it," she said, following the engineer into his workroom.

"Vartra was with her that day," said Kaid quietly. "She nearly died, and she did lose her first cub. Back to work, people," he said more loudly. "If you're finished, go help our junior bring down the tables and chairs, or the medics their equipment."

* * *

Chy'qui was working late in his lab, running through the data he'd acquired from J'koshuk before the TeLaxaudin had had to insert the main implant in him. He was correlating it to the answers J'koshuk had accepted from the Sholan, Kusac. There were certainly areas now where, judging from his previous sessions with the crew of the *M'ijikk,* he'd accepted answers from Kusac he'd previously have discounted as lies. And the *M'ijikk* sessions were before his neck implant was fully operational.

Had he been developing a form of telepathy because of the electromagnetic stimulation from the neck implant? Or had he been becoming unstable, as the TeLaxaud doctor, Kzizysus, had said? J'koshuk hadn't been unstable in the sense Kzizysus meant. The point of the experiment was to see if it was possible to turn a warrior into a telepath, and to do that, he couldn't suppress the priest's aggressive nature completely. It would have been interesting to see if the trend had continued, but that was no longer possible. Still, he would find how the impulse generator and the main implant interacted. That in itself was a worthwhile experiment.

A knock on the door made him cover his notes up before calling out.

"Seniormost," said Zhy'edd as he came in, making sure the door closed behind him. Approaching the desk, he held out a small container to Chy'qui. "The sample you asked for."

"She got it?" asked Chy'qui, taking it from him. "How old is it?"

"Fifteen, maybe twenty minutes. I waited for her in a room around the corner."

"Excellent. And the drug. She gave him the drug?"

Zhy'edd nodded. "On her skin, like you said. N'koshoh said he was no trouble. Within a couple of minutes, he was as docile and obliging as she could want."

Chy'qui handed the sample back to him. "Tell N'koshoh she did well. Prepare this immediately for storage in stasis with the others. Good work, Zhy'edd."

* * *

"There must be some clothes left in the suite they were in. They didn't take anything with them," he heard her saying. Her tone was sharp, she wasn't pleased with whoever it was.

He eyed the clock again. He'd been awake now for four hours. She'd fed him not so long ago, his first solid food in a week, she said. It had been something between a soup and a stew and quite pleasant. He'd begun to feel better after he'd eaten, but he still felt as if he was only half awake. Maybe getting up and walking around would help clear some of the fog from his mind.

Getting to his feet, he glanced around, wondering what to look at first. A day room, she'd called it. The walls were a warm gray, not particularly soothing though she'd said they were. A dining table with hard chairs, where he'd eaten, the soft chairs on which he'd been sitting. There was a unit with what looked like book tapes in it, and a large vid screen near the door. She'd said the vid screen was disabled right now, but then he remembered her saying a lot of things recently. Some of them hadn't made much sense.

He decided to head for the door, but as he got close, it slid open unexpectedly, making him jump back in surprise.

"You're looking around now, are you? That's good," she said, coming in with a gray tunic and a belt folded over her arm. "I've brought you some clothes. They were left behind by your friends." She held them out to him.

"Thank you," he said, taking them from her. This close, he could smell her scent. It was almost familiar. He sniffed again, trying to remember.

"Last night," he said, reaching out to feel her face with the fingertips of his other hand. Her skin was softer than it looked, faintly warm and pleasant to the touch. "Last night, someone came to my room. Was it you?"

She moved away from him, going farther into the room. "Not me. No one should have come near you except for your guard. You must have been dreaming."

He turned to keep her in sight, noticing she did the same. The skin around her eyes was creased.

"She said it was a dream." He returned to the chair, putting the belt over the back of it before pulling his tunic over his head. Taking up the belt, he fastened it on. "She put the light out as she came in, I think because she wanted me to think she was Human. She felt like one at first, but wasn't. She was one of you."

Zayshul came closer. "One of us, a female, came to you last night?" She couldn't believe what he was saying.

He nodded. "She wanted me physically."

"And did you?"

He gave her a slow, Human smile. "She was persuasive, for a dream."

"What did she look like? Did she give you a name?" Who could have gone to him? Only Med Research staff knew he was here, and she was the only female who had access to him.

"I thought it was you. It was only a dream, so how could I see her or know her name?"

She took his hand, leading him to a chair and making him sit, before crouching in front of him. Taking a scanner the size of a small comp pad out of her pocket, she put it close to the implant under his ear.

"Do you remember what I told you earlier, Kusac?" she asked quietly as she pressed several controls.

"About the experiments?" He was beginning to remember now.

Glancing at the door, she continued. "Yes, that's right. Someone wanting this treaty we're proposing to fail, did things to you they shouldn't have done. Experiments to do with your telepathy. You're feeling content and rather forgetful, aren't you? That's because your visitor last night drugged you. I've done what I can to counteract it, but you must fight it and try to remember what I told you. Tell your people they mustn't let this person win. We need this treaty with Shola!"

He frowned, touching her face again. "You're frightened. Why?"

"A friend trying to get more information for me has disappeared, and last night while I was out, my office was torn apart. They were looking for something, but I don't know what."

"You're taking me back to my people. Come with me," he said on impulse.

"I can't." She put the scanner back, then froze, pulling another container out of her pocket and looking at it before hastily stuffing it back in. He saw her skin had suddenly paled.

A siren sounded outside. Three short blasts. "We have to go now." She stood up, grasping his hand and pulling him to his feet. "You're not just some big, dumb creature, are you? You've been drugged all along. You've got to fight it, Kusac!"

The door slid open to admit two guards in armor.

"We're ready," Zayshul said.

They came over to him, each taking him by an arm, and led him out into the corridor.

When they reached the landing bay, a shuttle stood waiting for them. Boarding it were armor-clad Primes, several of them wearing the gray over-tabard of the Seniormost. As his guards led him toward it, he looked over his shoulder for her, seeing her being helped into her armor. Beyond her, he could see the red-robed priest emerging from the elevator cage.

Something stirred in his memory. He reached for it, teasing it, but it refused to surface.

CHAPTER 19

THEY stood against the wall by the elevator in the landing bay, watching as the Primes' shuttle maneuvered into the position drawn out for it on the deck. As it settled to the ground, the whine of the engines began to slow to a gradual stop.

Kaid glanced down the line at Carrie, Vriuzu, T'Chebbi, and L'Seuli, who, like himself, were helmetless. "You hear the siren, go for your helmets," he reminded them quietly. The rest, designated as guards, were fully armored.

Dzaou led his group forward, rifles at the ready as they formed a line forty yards from the shuttle's air lock. As the iris opened, the first of the Prime guards appeared. In quick succession, seven of them emerged, armed with energy pistols. They fanned out ten feet from their vehicle, giving cover to their negotiators as they came down the ramp. J'koshuk's unprotected body and red robes stood out visibly against the black-armored Primes.

Keep calm, Kaid sent to Carrie as he felt her stiffen beside him. *He can't get near you. If he tries, he's dead.*

Kaid led the rest of the group across the deck to take up their positions behind Dzaou. As L'Seuli, Vriuzu, and Lydda formed a third rank, Brynne neatly stepped past Kaid to stand behind Rezac.

"Open order," murmured Dzaou. The front rank parted, allowing Kaid and Carrie through. At the rear, L'Seuli moved forward to take their place, leaving Vriuzu and Lydda in the rear rank.

"Close order," said Dzaou, and the ranks closed up. Now they were ready.

From the other side, a figure wearing the gray tabard of a Seniormost stepped out from behind the guards. He wore no helmet, and Kaid noticed his tabard was edged with gold.

Link with me, he heard Carrie send to the other telepaths. He sensed the network build until she drew him into its web to complete it. Through it, he became more aware of those around him, and the Valtegan standing opposite.

"I am Commander Q'ozoi, of the *Kz'adul,*" the Valtegan said.

Kaid remained where he was. "I'm Kaid Tallinu. I speak for Commander Kheal of Haven, and the people of Shola. I believe we have hostages to exchange."

"We have, but that's only part of our purpose. We wish to negotiate a treaty with you. An alliance against a common foe."

"Hostages first," said Kaid firmly. "What better measure of good will can we show each other?"

"As you say. You have a member of my crew. Zsurtul."

"We have Prince Zsurtul," corrected Kaid. "And you have Kusac Aldatan."

Commander Q'ozoi made a gesture of embarrassment. "You indeed have our Prince. Let me see him and I'll have Kusac brought out."

Kaid raised his hand in a signal to the medics still standing by the elevator. They parted, revealing Prince Zsurtul standing in the charge of Banner. Leading him forward, Banner escorted the Prince toward the Sholan group, taking up a position with him at the end of the front line beside Maikoi.

"You can see that your Prince is safe and well," Kaid said. "Now Kusac."

Q'ozoi turned to a guard, issuing a guttural command, then waited while he ran to the shuttle, shouting up to someone inside. At the open air lock, two armored figures, one without a helmet, emerged holding a wrist-cuffed Kusac by the arms.

Kaid could hear Carrie sucking in a gasp as she saw him, felt her shock ripple through their web. Kusac looked dazed and confused, and at one side of his neck, the hair had been shaved back.

Cold and calm, he reminded her. *Can you pick him up at all?*

No. There's nothing, not even a sense of him being there.

Then he's either drugged or they've got a damper on him.

The air in this landing bay was chill and held familiar scents. The guard gave Kusac a shove, urging him out.

"Don't push him," Zayshul said angrily.

A shiver ran through him as he began to walk down the ramp. The lights were bright in comparison to what he was used to, making him blink rapidly, trying to ease the discomfort.

"You have seen Kusac," he heard someone say. "Now show us Kezule."

"After we have Kusac."

The voice sounded familiar. He tried to remember.

"That's not acceptable."

"My decision is non-negotiable."

It was Kaid.

"This is Haven," said Zayshul quietly as they came to a stop. "You remember Haven? You told us to bring you here."

He nodded. The chill air, coupled with the cold of the deck beneath his feet, was making him shiver after the warmth of the shuttle. He moved his hands, feeling the weight of the cuffs round them. "The collar. Do I still wear it?"

She looked at him closely, examining his face, then shook her head. "No, I removed it several days ago. It should never have been put on you. It's a punishment collar and rarely used."

He looked around, seeing only the wall of Seniormost and Prime guards. Then he saw the red robe in front of him.

"J'koshuk," he said quietly.

"Yes, the priest."

A figure to one side of them turned round and scowled. "Zayshul. You should be here with the commander," Chy'-qui said, trying to keep his voice low. "Leave the hostage with the guard."

"I have to go," she murmured as she left his side. "Remember what I told you."

The guard took him forward to stand in the open in front of the priest. Memories of his imprisonment were beginning to drift back. Hadn't J'koshuk tried to stop one of the Primes from beating him?

Frowning, he looked across the open space at the group
of armored figures opposite. Sholans. Some he knew. Was
that Carrie? It must be. She'd been on the ship with Kaid,
and he was here. He could see him now, talking to one of
the Primes. The priest had said Carrie and Kaid were safe,
but she hadn't been. Then he saw the sand-colored Valtegan at the end of their line. He recognized him instantly.
Zsurtul—the one who'd beaten and tortured him.

Slowly at first, his anger began to build. His pelt was
starting to rise, bushing out around his neck and shoulders,
making his hair stand away from his scalp. A draft of air
from behind brought a scent to him, a scent he knew only
too well. The priest's. J'koshuk had wanted information
about Carrie, information he'd tried to keep from him despite the beatings. He frowned as another memory contra-
dicted this one. How could it have been the priest? It was
the one standing with his people, Zsurtul, who'd done that.
Those memories of being repeatedly struck by Zsurtul's
hands were so clear. But scents didn't lie, and the scent
that filled his nostrils when he remembered the pain came
from behind him, not in front.

He was confused, and his head had begun to hurt. He
shook it, hearing her voice again. What had she said? Remember. Remember to . . . Fight. He was to fight. Fight
what? Or was it who? Frustrated, anger surged through
him again, and as the hair on his spine began to rise, he
began to sway his tail in short, infuriated arcs. As the guard
jerked him forward, pain lanced through his head, making
him shake it again.

He snarled, trying to pull away. He didn't want to move.
Fight what? That was what he wanted to know. A sudden
rush of energy flooded through him. He felt clearheaded
and stronger than he had in weeks. It was like a drug rush.
That was it. She'd said he'd been drugged. He was to fight
the drug he'd been given.

Stopping dead, he saw Zsurtul coming toward him, just
as he'd done many times before in his cell. Pain had always
accompanied him, and the priest. What was it about the
priest? Bracing his legs, he tried to sink his claws into the
deck, refusing to move any farther. He needed to work
this out right now. It had been the priest who'd demanded
information about Carrie, who'd known her sister. But the

voice had said the priest had tried to protect him—the same
voice that told him that Zsurtul had been his torturer.
Again the pain stabbed him, this time at the side of his
neck. He put his hand up to it, feeling the shaved area and
the edge of the implant. He began to growl deep down in
his throat.

"What the hell's up with Kusac?" muttered Rezac. "He
looks like he's ready for a Challenge."

"Something's gotten to him for sure," said T'Chebbi.
"That's no way to get free. He knows better."

"I'm getting nothing," said Carrie, clutching her rifle
tighter as Kusac began to growl. "What's wrong with his
neck? Why's he touching it?"

The implant, sent Brynne. *He's touching the implant.*

Dzaou's getting damned twitchy, sent Rezac.

Watch him. Don't let them interfere, ordered Kaid.
Brynne, see if you can reach Kusac. Find out what's wrong.

Kusac's arm was jerked again. This time, he turned on
the guard, tail lashing, snarling his fury. "Don't pull me!"

Zsurtul was getting closer. He could see his features now.
Hate and anger combined in Kusac in a deadly mixture.
He wanted to sink his claws in him, rip him to shreds.
Beyond the Valtegan he caught sight of Carrie, knew by
the way she stood she was afraid. The priest, she was afraid
of the priest. He looked back, searching for J'koshuk amid
the Primes, finding him standing on the edge of the Seniormosts. The memory of Carrie's cry for help echoed
through his mind, and he felt again his impotent hatred and
fear of what the priest was about to do to his mate.

"Carrie! Not Carrie!" he howled, twisting himself free
from the guard and flinging him aside. Stumbling, Kusac
caromed off the Prince, then staggered a few steps till he
righted himself. Zsurtul's scent was in his nostrils now. He
didn't know him, had never met him. It was J'koshuk he
wanted. He'd raped Carrie. Oblivious to the Valtegan pistols aimed at him, he spun round, his predator's instinct
finding the priest again instantly.

Chy'qui had watched Kusac become more and more agitated as he was led out for the exchange. Everything had

been going as planned: all eyes were on Kusac and the Prince, no one noticed J'koshuk surreptitiously using his wrist control.

The Sholan had suddenly called out the name of the Human female and broken free from the guard with such force he'd spun into the Prince. Then, instead of attacking Zsurtul, Kusac had turned away. Chy'qui knew his plan was beginning to go very wrong.

"You! It was you all along," Kusac snarled, raising his hands and reaching out for the priest.

J'koshuk began to back away from the Primes' group, fear written all over his face and scenting the air.

The memory of Carrie's mental cry was still there, as was Kaid's presence. And more—the gestalt. Kusac felt it whisper at the edges of his mind.

The priest had turned, was begining to run for the shuttle.

Kusac's vision narrowed as he targeted J'koshuk. He saw nothing but him, smelled only his scent. The blood roared in his ears, his head pounded with pain. Reaching within his mind, he grasped the memory of the Link and then beyond, finding not only the web of six, but the gestalt.

Behind him, the fallen guard rose, pulling out his sidearm.

Zayshul cried out in fear, clutching at Chy'qui, demanding he do something. Chy'qui pressed frantically at his control pad, trying to shut the guard down. He couldn't allow the Sholan to be shot in the back, not while there was still a chance he'd turn on Zsurtul. The guard stiffened, then dropped to the deck.

He's gone feral, Kaid! Carrie sent. *What the hell's happening to him?*

I don't know! He was on the verge of going kzu-shu, and the Prince was within feet of him. *Brynne?*

Nothing. He's too tightly blocked. Is he being controlled?

Then Kaid felt his mind grasped, whirled in with Carrie's and their web as, in front of his disbelieving eyes, the priest stopped dead in his tracks. The web shattered as energy was ripped from their minds, and later, Kaid swore he actually saw a bolt of pure energy hit the priest full in the back.

"Burn in hell, you nest-raiding lizard!" Kusac yelled.

J'koshuk fell like a stone and the air began to reek of scorched flesh. Above his body, a small cloud of smoke hung in the still air.

Somehow, Chy'qui realized, Kusac had managed to break through the drugs and conditioning. How? Had he forgotten something? In a flash of understanding it came to him. The female, he'd forgotten that J'koshuk had raped the female. That was what had angered the Sholan far more than the torture!

He heard Kusac shouting, then watched as a pulse of energy hit the priest's back, knocking him to the ground. How, in the name of all that was holy, had he done that? Had he gotten hold of a firearm from somewhere?

"The guards! Stop the guards!" Zayshul shouted.

"Do it!" Q'ozoi snapped. "We can't risk the Prince!"

Cursing, Chy'qui entered the override code that deactivated all the guards as Kusac took a staggering step toward the Prince. Now he was praying the Sholan wouldn't attack Zsurtul.

Still shocked by what had happened to the priest, Kaid watched disbelievingly as the Prime guards suddenly all fell to the deck. "What the hell's going on?" he demanded.

Too stunned to react, they all, Sholans and Valtegans, stood and watched as Kusac spun round to face the Prince. His hands went up to his neck, clawing at the implant as, snarling, he took a staggering step toward him.

Kusac looked straight at Carrie and Kaid as he took another lurching step toward the Prince. The mute appeal in his eyes was visible even from that distance. Nobody moved, and for the first time in his life, Kaid froze. Not just his body, but his mind. He knew what was at stake, but this was Kusac, his sword-brother, his Triad partner.

Kaid heard the whine of a single shot and Kusac suddenly collapsed at Prince Zsurtul's feet. The sound of a gun hitting the deck echoed through the landing bay, shattering the unnatural silence.

"Get the Prince back to his people now!" yelled Carrie, her voice breaking.

Banner was the first to move, running out to grasp hold
of the Prince. Dragging him forward, he thrust him into the
heart of the group of Valtegans. Then, with a glance at
J'koshuk's body, he sprinted back to the safety of his
own side.

Kaid could sense nothing from Carrie. Her mind had
gone as numb as he'd been moments earlier. He heard the
guns powering up around him and spun round. The Sholan
camp had split into two factions, with his people turning
their weapons on Dzaou's, and Dzaou's aimed at the
Primes.

"Hold fire!" he roared. "What the hell do you think
you're doing? We've a Brother down! Get the medics out
to him, fast! The rest of you, power down and about face!
Immediately!"

After a moment of hesitation, Dzaou dropped his rifle,
then the others of his unit followed. Satisfied, Kaid turned
back to the Valtegans.

The Seniormosts stood in a confused and vulnerable
clump, staring at the Sholans in fear. He needed to do
something now to retrieve the situation. "Take command,
T'Chebbi," he ordered. "Rezac, with me."

"Aye, sir," she said crisply.

Grasping Carrie's arm and pulling her close to his side,
he strode out across the open area toward the Primes. As
they passed where Kusac lay, hidden by medics, she tried
to stop, but he pulled her on, thanking Vartra that they'd
had the sense to surround him.

"I shot him," she moaned. "I can't believe I shot him!"

*You did what I couldn't do, you saved his life! We've got
work to do, Carrie,* he sent. *So have they. I need your help
to read the Primes.*

Zayshul slowly backed away from where her people were
huddled together. Everyone's attention was on the approaching Sholan and Human. With luck, her actions would
go unnoticed. A shiver of fear ran through her as she recognized the Sholan male. He was the one who'd almost shot
her when they were escaping. She prayed he wouldn't see
her now, but she had to get to J'koshuk's body.

She'd seen him backing off from the main group, just as
she was doing now, and fiddling with his wrist. There was

only one explanation for his behavior and Kusac's aggressiveness—he was using a control unit on the Sholan. And the person who'd shown him how to use one, whose assistant he was, was Chy'qui.

The Valtegans with sidearms pulled them out, aiming at them as they approached. Kaid ignored them, pushing them aside till he faced the commander.

"Who ordered Kusac to be implanted?" he demanded. "He's being controlled by one of you through that device on his neck!"

A female pushed forward to the front. "Not me," she said hastily as Kaid turned toward her. "Commander, I think I know who's behind this, and I believe I can prove it." She handed Q'ozoi a slim tape. "Someone searched my office last night. I believe it was for this. I took it from Kusac's room a couple of nights ago and didn't realize I still had it."

Q'ozoi took it from her. "What is it?" he demanded, turning the tape over in his hands.

"Kusac's sleep tape. I was called because his monitor alarm went off. His hormone levels were much higher than they should have been. I adjusted them and removed the tape. I think his tape was switched for this one."

"What's the purpose of the tape?" demanded Kaid. *Read them, Carrie!*

Zayshul turned to look at him. "We use them for healing. Soothing and uplifting sounds and images. They're used for learning as well."

"Are you saying he could have been programmed to kill the Prince?" asked Q'ozoi.

"It's possible, yes. The tape will prove it one way or another."

"Who do you think is responsible?"

"The only person in the area at the time was Doctor Chy'qui. He was treating J'koshuk in the next room, one with a door leading into Kusac's." She handed him something else. "And I found this on J'koshuk. A wrist control unit for the implants. Kusac was being controlled by him, that's why he was so aggressive."

She's telling the truth, sent Carrie. *The Prime backing off, near the shuttle, he's Chy'qui.*

Rezac, bring him here! ordered Kaid.

Aye!

"It's been melted," said Q'ozoi, looking at the control unit. "How did it get melted?"

"J'koshuk was killed with some kind of energy weapon," said Zayshul, aware that the truth was quite different. "I saw the priest wearing and using this. It's what we use to control the guards when they're off the *Kz'adul*, Commander. J'koshuk is Chy'qui's assistant. He was doing the rounds of our M'zullians with him a few days ago. Chy'qui is the only one supposed to be using a unit here."

They heard a scuffle breaking out by the shuttle and looked around to find Chy'qui being dragged toward them by Rezac.

"Does this tape hold evidence of a plot against my life?" Zsurtul asked, his voice deceptively quiet.

"I protest, Commander! This is a further Sholan violation of our neutrality!" said Chy'qui, trying to shake himself free of Rezac. "First they kill J'koshuk, and now they take violent hold of me."

"Does this tape incriminate you?" the commander demanded.

"It's nothing to do with me, Commander. Zayshul's been jealous since I came on board. The plot is hers to discredit me."

"You took charge of the Med Research unit when you boarded this vessel at K'oish'ik," said Q'ozoi. "You were responsible for the actions of the priest and, I believe, for this attempt on Prince Zsurtul."

"He's wearing a psi damper," Carrie said. "On his armor somewhere. Take it off him and I'll tell you if he's guilty."

"Strip him," ordered the commander. "Psi damper?"

"They suppress our telepathy," said Carrie.

Q'ozoi shook his head. "We don't have anything like that."

Carrie traded glances with Kaid. *Chy'qui. He's the one who separated us.*

"While we were with you, our telepathic abilities were limited by a damper field outside the room, and on an individual basis," said Kaid. "I know I was given psi-inhibiting drugs and their antidotes several times."

"Chy'qui ordered the drugs," said Zayshul. "I know nothing about the dampers."

"When you get back to your ship, I suggested you look around the suite we were in. You'll find a damper unit somewhere," said Kaid.

Chy'qui brazened it out, continuing to protest his innocence, but once he stood clad only in his fatigues, Carrie was able to get the information she wanted.

"He's guilty. The tape has the evidence you need. He's also responsible for the death of someone in your computer section. Something to do with locked files."

The commander handed Chy'qui's control unit to Zayshul. "Reactivate the guards, Doctor. Counselor Chy'qui has committed treason against your person, Prince Zsurtul. He'll be questioned tomorrow, but he must be returned to the City of Light to face Emperor Cheu'ko'h."

Around them, the guards began to stir, getting to their feet. The sight unnerved Kaid. It was like watching toys receive new energy cells. They stood motionless, guns ready, waiting for fresh orders.

"Secure Counselor Chy'qui so he doesn't escape," Q'ozoi ordered the nearest one. "Return him to the shuttle and remain with him."

Rezac handed him over to the guard.

"Fire!" yelled someone, pointing to the now thick cloud of smoke hanging above J'koshuk's body.

As the Primes scattered, Kaid saw flames begin to lick at the edges of J'koshuk's clothing. The air began to reek with the stench of burning flesh. "I don't believe it," he murmured. "Kusac must have fried him from the inside out."

Sholans with extinguishers rushed past them.

"I need to see Kusac," said Carrie, beginning to move away from him.

"No," he said, grasping hold of her wrist. "When he's been seen by the medics, I'll come with you."

"Let me go," she said, squirming in his grip. "I need to see how badly I hurt him."

"Dammit, I can't come with you now!"

She broke free and headed off across the bay at a lope, slowed down by the weight of her armor.

He turned to the nearest Prime. "Go back to your shuttle

till we've cleared this mess up," he said, indicating the smoldering body of J'koshuk and the fire-fighting team. "We'll meet again in half an hour."

Zayshul nodded, and Kaid took off after Carrie.

The physician looked up briefly as Carrie lumbered over. "Good shot. Took the head right off this little device and disabled it. You only just grazed his neck."

Kusac was on a floater now, a drip attached to his arm. His tunic was spattered with blood. One medic was carefully swabbing more off the side of his neck while another—Jurrel—was checking the implant, making sure the circuits weren't shorting.

"How is he?" she asked the physician, trying to crouch down beside him.

"Unconscious. He's high as a kite on epinephrin, but we're bringing him down now. For the rest, I won't know until I do a detailed analysis in sick bay, especially because of this implant. I don't even know what the hell it does." He stood up, taking her by the elbow and drawing her aside. "Get him ready to move," he said to Jurrel over his shoulder.

She turned back, seeing Jurrel begin to fasten the restraints. "What are you doing?" she demanded. "Why are you tying him down like that? He's no danger to us!"

Kaid arrived, taking in the situation immediately. He placed himself firmly between her and the floater as it rose up to a comfortable towing height. "Let them get on with their job, Carrie. We know he's had at least one set of seizures. If he has another on the way up to the sick bay, he could fall off the floater."

How can you stay so calm about it all? she demanded.

Because I have to. The situation's too explosive, Carrie. All our lives are at risk. This could still end in war.

"He's waking," said Jurrel, looking over to Carrie.

She pushed past the two males to Kusac's side. Pressing the release on the nearest wrist restraint, she took hold of his hand.

"Lo, cub." His voice was a barely audible murmur. "Your aim's improved. Say thanks to T'Chebbi for me."

"Kusac." Her voice broke and she couldn't continue. Instead she lifted his hand to her lips.

"I've missed you so much," he whispered, his voice growing a little stronger. "My mind's been empty without you." The he saw Kaid. "Codes. You had to know if you gave him the codes."

Kaid looked puzzled, then put his hand to Kusac's face, stroking the edge of his jawline with his thumb. "You just rest," he said. "You're safe with us now."

"Asked me to tell you when I knew. Worked it out while I was with them. Ghezu."

"That! Gods, it's not important now, Kusac."

"Wanted Sholan approach codes. Gave them Haven's instead. Guess I got it right since you're here." He moved his hand, drawing Carrie's to his mouth, licking her palm gently.

"You did it right, Kusac. Followed exactly what I told you," said Kaid.

"There's a female doctor in danger . . ." Kusac began, trying to turn his head but Jurrel reached out and stopped him.

"Don't move your head, Kusac. The implant's still live and unstable."

"She's fine," said Kaid. "You got used in a plot to kill their prince, but they got the one responsible."

"I've got to get him up to sick bay now," interrupted the physician. "This can wait, surely."

Kusac flicked his ears in assent, squeezing Carrie's hand gently before letting it go and reaching for Kaid's. "Look after her. At least I got J'koshuk." His speech was becoming slurred now, and his eyes began to flicker upward.

Kaid pulled Carrie back. "Let them take him now," he said, swinging her well away from him.

"What is it?" she asked, panic in her voice as she tried to look over her shoulder.

He prevented her. "He's having a seizure. You do not want to see it, and you'd only be in the way."

She looked at him, eyes wide with fear. "I've got to go with him."

He took her by the shoulders, looking into her face. "If you go up to the sick bay, you'll have to go alone. I can't spare anyone from here. They'll leave you sitting outside, on your own, possibly for hours. You'll worry, and I'll worry for both of you when I should be concentrating on these Primes. Or you can stay and help me. You're not the only one capable of reading a Valtegan mind, Rezac can, but I'd rather it were you, no offense to Rezac. We can lose ourselves in our work and support each other while we wait for news. Now, what are you going to do?"

"I'll stay," she said quietly, knowing he was right. Kaid was all that had kept her going since she'd first thought that Kusac was dead. She needed him no less now they knew he was alive. And she could feel that Kaid needed her just as much.

He held her close, lowering his head so he could rest his cheek against hers. "Well done. I'm proud of you, and so will Kusac be when he wakes."

Footsteps made them turn round. Approaching them was the female doctor they'd talked to a few minutes earlier.

"The commander asked me to come and see how Kusac is," she said.

There was a familiarity about her voice and scent that they both recognized. "You're the one we took along with Zsurtul," said Kaid. "Why did you lie to your commander about the energy pistol?"

"I didn't want to cause trouble for Kusac," she said, looking away from him for a moment. "However he managed to do that, I know he wouldn't use it indiscriminately."

"He's convulsing, maybe because I shot the implant," said Carrie abruptly.

Zayshul paled, turning several shades lighter. "The implant controls his hormone production and the seizures," she said. "The TeLaxaudin physician has offered his help. They designed the implant, no one knows its workings better."

"Why use a device meant for your people on him in the first place?" demanded Carrie.

"It was all we had left to try. We don't know enough about your species to use much in the way of our drugs. We could have caused permanent damage."

"What the hell do you call that thing on his neck?" she asked angrily.

The female took a step back in shock at the anger directed at her. "It was not my decision, it was Chy'qui's, but it was, we think, done for the best reasons. I don't understand your anger."

"I'm his mate, and his Leska—or was, till Chy'qui started experimenting on him!" She felt Kaid's restraining hand on her arm.

She's not to blame, Carrie, he sent. "You said TeLaxaudin. You work with them?" asked Kaid.

"They're our allies."

"I'll pass your kind offer on to our medical section," said Kaid. "I must consult with my advisers now. We'll meet again in about half an hour, as I said." *Call sick bay on your comm and tell the medic on duty to pass their offer of help on to the physician when they arrive.*

Carrie did as he asked while he excused them. They headed for the negotiating table, where the other Sholans on their team had taken up a position, realizing they'd been constantly shadowed by T'Chebbi, Rezac, and Dzaou. Kaid began unfastening his armor as soon as they reached it.

"I'd prefer you suited," said L'Seuli from his chair. "One casualty is enough. How is Kusac?"

"Send for some drinks for us," Kaid ordered a passing Brother. "I don't know," he said shortly. "L'Seuli, do you honestly think that if they didn't shoot us during that chaos, they're going to shoot us now?"

L'Seuli looked round the others, waving them away with an abrupt gesture. A muted chorus of grumbles met his command but they complied, stopping out of earshot.

"Kaid, Father Lijou gave me advice about dealing with you. I wish to the Gods someone had given you some about dealing with me!"

"What did I do?" he asked, looking up from the lock he was unfastening on his side. "Oh, chain of command and all that. Sorry. Got a lot on my mind right now." He sniffed the air. "Gods, but it stinks of burnt lizard!"

Carrie pulled off her gloves, then reached out to help him.

"They're going to flush the hangar's air supply as soon as the Primes have allowed us to dispose of the body. You'll remain in your suit, Carrie," L'Seuli warned her with a frown.

Do it, Dzinae, he's right, sent Kaid as she supported the chest pieces till he got his arms pulled free. He sat down carefully, pulling first his tail then his leg out. "Glad you sent them off, L'Seuli. I've got news for you. How well briefed are you on the Jalna treaties?"

"Fully. Why?"

Kaid pulled his other leg free, dropping the suit on the floor with relief. "Never could stand suits. The spaceport on Jalna was built mainly by the efforts of the Jalnians and three alien species, we were told. I'm betting there were four, and that the original idea came from the fourth un-mentioned species."

"The Primes," said Carrie, pulling up a seat. "Zsurtul said they'd done something for the Jalnians but refused to go into any details." She was trying hard to keep her mind off what was happening to Kusac.

"What draws you to that conclusion?"

"Need. Who needed the spaceport? Not the U'Churians or the Cabbarans, or even the elusive TeLaxaud; they'd all been trading in space for some time already. Nor the Jalni-ans. They didn't even know there was anything beyond their atmosphere. It was the Primes. They call in every fifty years to collect soil and plant samples. Much easier to do it openly at a spaceport as the Jalnian population expanded. Not just that, if the Primes are as secretive as they seem to be from the Free Traders' viewpoint, then by helping fund such a venture, the Primes can get their good friends and allies, the TeLaxaudin, to collect trade goods for them without any need for them to expose their weaknesses to any other species."

"Their lack of a warrior line," said L'Seuli. "You're tell-ing me that the TeLaxaudin are allied with the Primes?"

"Yes. Had we realized it, Giyesh, from Tirak's crew, ac-tually saw one when she was abducted with Jeran. Their doctor has just offered us TeLaxaudin help for Kusac. They designed the implant for the Valtegans."

"We could already be allied to the TeLaxaudin," said L'Seuli thoughtfully. "I need to call Stronghold as soon as possible. It doesn't mean we're allies of the Primes, though."

"No, but it could frighten them. Here we are, the only species to have ever beaten them, and suddenly we turn up in their private little trading post in pursuit of Valtegans who have destroyed two of our colony worlds. Valtegans that scare them spitless because they aren't capable of defending themselves."

"Then you believe this story about needing warriors."

"I do. Did you see them out there? The minute they thought their guards were about to shoot Kusac, they dropped them to the deck. They've no idea of tactics, either defensive or offensive. And that's the crew of a vessel knowing it's coming to make a treaty with us, the fearsome telepathic warriors."

"That's why they want Kezule and the M'zullians. To breed their own warriors," said Carrie.

"Exactly. With what Vanna knows about our genetics, if we do get involved with the Primes, we could possibly guide them, influence them so they don't end up with psychotic warriors like the M'zullians."

"A pact with the devil," murmured Carrie.

"Why say that?" asked Kaid sharply.

"We have a saying, better the devil you know, than the devil you don't. Seems to me that we're forgetting just what the Primes did to us, especially to Kusac." *And your conviction they're breeding us,* she added mentally.

"I'm not. I think Kusac's treatment was an exception, due to Chy'qui and J'koshuk. As for the rest, we may never know the full truth of the matter, unless they let us probe Chy'qui. At least we can sit down and talk to these Valtegans, Carrie," said Kaid. "The others were too busy trying to tear us limb from limb or commit suicide. That's a hell of a big difference. We need someone between us and them, someone the M'zullians will listen to, and so do the Primes. Given the right breeding and training, in time we could have a group of soldiers who can infiltrate M'zull, fight them from within as we did in the past."

"If that assassination attempt's anything to go by, then not all of the Primes are in favor of a treaty," said L'Seuli.

"Chy'qui is one of three advisers to the Emperor," said Carrie. "He disagreed with the treaty idea. I picked that up when we went over to find out about J'koshuk."

"We're no better concerning internal disagreements. Look at the case of Esken. A treaty with Keiss wasn't a popular decision at the time, but it didn't stop it being made and working," said Kaid, spying the Brother returning with a tray of c'shar and mugs. He beckoned him over. "Find out if we have signed a treaty with the TeLaxaudin yet, L'Seuli. Get Captain Zhaddu on it. It won't affect my decision, but I'd like to know."

The Brother put the tray down and left. Kaid grabbed three mugs and began pouring. "I'm finished with my say. The others can come back unless you've anything more to add," he said, passing him the first mug.

L'Seuli accepted it. "I know why Master Rhyaz appointed you and me to this mission," he said, sipping his c'shar.

"Why's that?" asked Carrie, accepting her mug gratefully.

"So I could learn that by the book is a good rule of thumb, but not necessarily useful when matters descend into chaos."

"Depends on the book," said Kaid, sending to Brynne to tell them they could come back.

"If it had been done by the book, I have a feeling this would have degenerated into a firefight."

As the others settled around the table again and helped themselves to drinks, Kaid's wrist comm buzzed.

"Get the TeLaxaudin up here if you can," was all the medic said.

He looked at Carrie. "They want the TeLaxaudin," he said. "You stay here with Brynne. T'Chebbi, you're with me." Then he looked over at Dzaou. "You come, too."

Carrie watched them head for the Prime shuttle. In her hands the mug of c'shar began to shake slightly as reaction set in.

"Kusac will pull through, I'm sure of it," said Brynne, wincing as he leaned forward to pat her shoulder. "He managed to link into our mental web and take energy from us, as well as control the gestalt. His mind's obviously Okay and the wound was minimal."

"I don't have any experience of this gestalt," said Vriuzu, "but to take so much power into himself, there could be a backlash effect. He could have burned himself out."

"I really needed to hear that," said Carrie, putting the mug down. "We've done it before. At least," she amended, "I have. Back on the *Khalossa*. And what I know, he knows."

"He looks a strong male," said Zhiko encouragingly.

"That helps a lot in recovery. Don't listen to him, he knows nothing of Leskas and Triads, only you do. They've got more chance of helping him now the people who designed the implant are involved. I think this is good news, not bad."

Carrie smiled over at her. "Thanks. I hope you're right." She turned back to watch the shuttle. As she did, she felt something damp and furry nuzzle her hand. With an exclamation of shock, she looked round to find Belle crouched on the table. "A jegget!"

"Not another," said Rezac.

"Another?" asked Brynne, as his pet began to twine herself round Carrie's hands. "I thought she was the only tame one."

"Kris has one. Better keep them apart, his is male. We'll be snowed under by the damned animals in a couple of months if you don't!"

Picking her up, Carrie turned back to watch Kaid, taking comfort from holding the small, purring creature.

Kaid spoke to the guard outside, then waited. A few minutes later, a bronze-limbed TeLaxaudin, resplendent in pastel-colored gauze strips emerged. In an almost hesitant, rocking gait, it stalked beside the Sholans as they headed back toward them. Before they reached it, however, the elevator opened to disgorge a Cabbaran moving at a speed she'd not thought possible.

Past the end of their table he went, making the Sholans leap up in an effort to stop him. Dodging them nimbly, he came to an abrupt stop in front of the TeLaxaudin. Rearing up on his hind legs, he burst into rapid speech which his translator began to render in U'Churian as Kaid ordered his people to leave Annuur alone.

"You come to aid the injured ally. New, they are. Good ones. We help you."

The TeLaxaudin cocked its oval head on one side, mandibles flicking as it listened carefully. Then it made a gesture with its hands and resumed walking.

"Useful is Cabbaran helping always. Come," he said.

Kaid ordered T'Chebbi and Dzaou to accompany them up to the sick bay and returned to the table. He could feel Dzaou's resentment and anger simmering just below the surface, and his fear that the telepaths would pick up his reluctance and report him to the commander. Kaid sighed. It wasn't so much what Dzaou thought but what he did that mattered. He needed to stay out of sleep for longer this tour and really get to understand both the Sholan and Human telepaths.

"Today is just full of surprises," murmured L'Seuli.

"Female doctor's on her way over again," said Ngio, ears flicking in the direction of the shuttle.

Zayshul was, indeed, running toward them. She stopped a few feet away. "Let the Cabbarans help Kzizysus. If I'd thought about it, I could maybe have done more, and Kusac's injury wouldn't have had to happen."

"Excuse me?" said Kaid.

"The Cabbarans are the only species that can understand the TeLaxaudin properly. Something to do with their language being more versatile. Trying to explain exactly what you want to them can be a problem. If they can even neutralize the unit, remove the surface panel, this would be very good. Then his own system would take over again, I think."

"Thank you," said Carrie.

She smiled, then saw the jegget in Carrie's arms. "Oh!" she said, impulsively reaching out to touch her. "How lovely!"

Belle stretched out her long neck, offering it to be stroked as she continued to purr gently.

"Would you like a drink?" asked Kaid, indicating the mugs and the jug. "It's safe. Kezule has had some and survived it."

Zayshul hesitated, glancing back to the shuttle. "Yes, I would," she said firmly.

Just before the half hour was up, Kaid escorted Zayshul over to the elevator to wait for Dzaou and Zhiko to bring Kezule down from sick bay.

"How, exactly, was the general injured?" she asked.

"He took powdered la'quo resin in an attempt to return to his own time," said Kaid.

"Time traveling." She shook her head. "And killing J'koshuk from a distance. It's hardly credible. Your people have very strange mental abilities."

"Kezule's the one who discovered the trick. He stirred

up one of the desert nomads in our time until he believed Kezule was his deity and his mission was to destroy all telepaths."

The elevator doors opened, and Zhiko emerged, towing a floater bearing the still unconscious form of Kezule. They stopped just in front of the Valtegan Prime physician.

Quickly and efficiently, Zayshul examined him with her hand scanner, finally checking the fluid drip attached to him.

"He's been in that coma state for four days," said Kaid. "We've given him no treatment but the fluids. Like you, we don't know enough about your species to do much more." He was seeing Kezule through her eyes, giving him a unique perspective of the person he'd known briefly only as an adversary.

Kezule was not as old as they'd thought, but he was just past his physical prime. Kaid could see the marks and lines of age on his face and hands, see the features that characterized him as an individual, subtleties a Sholan would take time to notice—the angle of the jaw, the breadth of bone around the eye sockets, the shape of the mouth.

Zayshul looked up at him. "He is, indeed, General Kezule. He was a junior member of the royal line of the late— very late—Emperor Q'emgo'h."

"Another lost royal?" he murmured. "A little careless, aren't they, of their safety?"

"You make a joke?" she asked, her wide mouth twitching at the corners. "He may not be injured. This state is like a laalgo trance."

"He did that a couple of times in captivity," said Kaid. "What is it?"

"Warriors are different from us, you must understand. They evolved to fight, therefore they have the capacity to heal themselves faster than us, and to take a long sleep— to let much time pass until the danger is gone."

"Useful, but surely you all have that ability?"

She hesitated briefly. "That's true, but not the same ability to heal that the warriors had. He will be an interesting person to study. His line was a combination of the best of the warriors and the intellectuals of his day."

As she said this, he was aware that her interest was not purely professional. "Be careful in your research," he said.

"He's also from a time when females were thought feral and never seen outside the breeding grounds. One of our female medics was almost killed by him when he arrived. He doesn't tolerate females easily."

"I'll be careful," she said, beckoning to the Prime guards waiting a little distance away. "Take him to the shuttle and guard him closely. Don't let Chy'qui near him," she added. "Then return the floater." She began to follow them. "I'll tell Commander Q'ozoi we're ready to begin the talks."

Kaid reached out to detain her. "You plan to breed from the M'zullians and Kezule," he said. "Could Chy'qui have been trying to do that with us?"

"No, absolutely not," she said, obviously startled by his question. "Why would you think that?"

"Only the telepaths were taken from our quarters to be medically examined and tested."

"Yes, we tested you, but nothing was taken that could be used for breeding! For that we'd need females of your kind living with us."

"Just check, if you will. I don't trust anything that Chy'qui did to us or Kusac. My feelings are that part of the reason he implanted him was he hoped to keep him on the *Kz'adul.*"

"The commander wouldn't have allowed it," she said firmly. "I have said I'll check, and I will. You have my word."

"Thank you," he said.

Aware that Carrie couldn't settle down, he decided to send her up to the mess with Brynne as company.

"His side is hurting," said Kaid. "He could do with the rest. So could you."

"What about these talks?" she asked tiredly, rubbing the back of her neck.

"Let me," he said, turning her around. He reached his thumbs down inside the neck of her armor, beginning on what he could reach of her shoulders.

He could feel her start to relax almost immediately. "Rezac can read them for me. You need to unwind."

"You always could turn me to mush," she murmured, leaning back against him. "I used to look forward to the massages you gave me back when I was recovering after the Challenge."

"I viewed them with more mixed feelings," he said quietly, remembering those sessions for himself. "I can't tell you how many times I almost told you how I felt about you. And you lay there, purring and reciting relaxation litanies." He shook his head. "I needed all my self-control, believe me."

"What makes you think I didn't know?" she asked. "I used to tease you. Remember?"

On her neck, his touch stilled briefly, then became a caress. "So you did," he said as he resumed his massage.

"That's when I decided to choose you as our Third."

"Because of my massages?" he asked lightly, turning her round again while keeping one hand against her neck.

"No. Because when you touched me, I knew you didn't just want me, you really cared."

"My touch gave me away?"

"It still does," she smiled, putting her hand over his.

"S'cuse me, boss," said Brynne, from where he waited by the table. "But it's time for us to leave. The Primes are on their way over."

Kaid nodded. "Send to me as soon as there's any news about Kusac," he said to Carrie. "When you've eaten, try and get some rest. Our room's almost opposite sick bay, they'll come and wake you." *Brynne, you and Keeza look after her till I send a relief up.*

Of course, replied Brynne, putting an arm round Carrie's shoulder as he walked her to the elevator.

Kaid watched until the doors closed behind them, then took his place beside L'Seuli at the negotiating table. He remained standing as the Prime commander and his party approached.

"Have you made a decision yet?" asked L'Seuli in an undertone.

"I want to hear what they propose first," said Kaid. "But if we do make this treaty, we need to make it one of the conditions that the outposts remain our property, and the undisputed boundaries of our territory."

"You believe they were Valtegan?"

"I know they were."

*   *   *

Someone was shaking her.

"Carrie, wake up. Kusac's awake. He's asking for you."

It was Banner. "Kusac's awake?" she asked, sitting up and rubbing her eyes.

"Yes. He wants to see you."

"I'm coming." Someone had put a blanket over her, she realized. Throwing it back, she swung her legs to the floor, searching for her shoes. Slipping them on, she got to her feet, stumbling as she tried to navigate the darkened room. Banner caught hold of her.

"I'm Okay. Just sleepy. Where's Kaid?" she asked, steadying herself against him for a moment.

"Still talking to the Primes. They should be stopping for the night soon, though. Even they've got to sleep some time."

Looking like he was still asleep, Kusac lay propped up in bed by a couple of pillows, the upper area of his neck swathed in bandages. Carrie could see from the bald patch just above the edge of the dressing that the physician had cut back even more of his hair.

As the door closed behind her, he opened his eyes, mouth widening in a slow smile as he saw her.

"How are you?" she asked, moving over to stand by his bed.

"Better," he said, taking her hand.

His voice sounded stronger, but she noticed he kept his eyes hooded, not looking directly at her. She sat on the edge of the bed beside him. "The implant?"

"The unit's gone. Said when it heals, there'll hardly even be a scar."

She could feel his fingers moving restlessly against her palm as he tried to link them between hers. "I had to . . ." she began in a rush, but he cut her short.

"Thank you for stopping me," he said, his hand clenching over hers. "For saving my life. I'd have killed the Prince, too."

"I didn't want to . . ."

"Hush." His other arm reached round her waist, drawing her down till she lay against his chest. "You don't know how good it is to just hold you and breathe in your scent again," he said, his voice catching as he released her hand to hold her close within the circle of his arms. "I was afraid I'd never . . ." He stopped, unable to continue.

"So was I," she whispered, sliding her hands under his back. "So very afraid." She felt light-headed with relief as she rubbed her cheek against his, feeling the softness of his pelt against her skin.

His tongue touched her cheek in the way she remembered so well that instinctively she reached for his mind to share her pleasure. There was no response. It was as if he was mind-dead—unTalented.

She started in shock, lifting her head to look at him. Catching his eyes this time, she could see the pain and fear in them.

"Kiss me," he whispered, his arms tightening round her. He returned her kiss frantically, cupping the back of her head and neck in his hand, trying to hold her even closer.

She could sense him, feel his fear that his Talent would never return, and that its loss would cost him her. Tears she was unable to stop ran down her cheeks as she pulled her hands free and held his face. "Never that! I can't live without you beside me!" she wept between kisses as frantic as his.

He broke the kiss, taking her hands in his, urging her to rest her head on his shoulder. As he fought for self-control, she could feel him shaking, his heartbeat racing beneath her. "I have to tell you something," he whispered, his voice finally breaking.

"Don't you know by now how much I love you?" she asked, desperate to reassure him.

"Yes! I just can't *feel* you any more!" The words sounded like they'd been ripped from his soul.

"It's not gone! You used it when you killed J'koshuk— we all felt you!" she said, trying to sit up.

He held her tightly, keeping her where she was. "*Listen* to me! The implant's gone, but not what it's done to me. It's embedded bits of itself in me," he whispered, the words coming out singly between ragged breaths. "It was done purposely to isolate us from each other, to see what would happen. Then he realized we were a Triad. She, Zayshul, didn't know about me. Only you and Kaid. She and Zsurtul brought Kaid to you, saved your lives." He stopped, resting his head against hers as he tried to slow his breathing.

"How do you know all this?"

"Kaid told me."

"You've spoken to Kaid already?"

His arms tightened round her again. "He was here when I first woke. I know what's happened between you . . ."

"Then you know we *are* a Triad, no matter what!" she said, pushing herself up against him till she could see his face. "Chy'qui didn't succeed in isolating us, Kusac, can't you see that? If he had, you'd be dead—maybe all of us would. But you're not." She touched his cheek, wiping away the tears they'd both shed. "Gods, Kusac, your Talent's still there somewhere, so's our Link, I know it is! Just give yourself time to heal."

He searched her face and she could feel some of his fears begin to recede, replaced by a glimmer of hope. "Stay with me tonight. I don't want . . . I can't bear to be . . . alone." he said as she leaned forward to kiss him.

"I promise I'll never leave you alone," she whispered, her heart breaking for him.

EPILOGUE

IN his cabin on the shuttle, Chy'qui heard a noise outside the door. As it slid open, he heard his steward exchanging pleasantries with the guard outside.

"You're late," he snapped, sitting up and leaning against the wall behind his bed as the male entered carrying a tray of food. "It's bad enough that I've been locked in here for the last four hours without the food being delayed, too."

"All in good time, Doctor," said the steward, walking toward the desk and putting the tray down. "Too much haste causes situations such as you find yourself in now. Your job was to procure samples from the telepaths, nothing more. Your experiments on the Sholan have put not only those, but all of us at risk." He turned round to face Chy'qui. "As for your ambitious personal attempt on Prince Zsurtul, what can I say? The Directorate is most displeased."

Chy'qui frowned. "The samples as you call them, will enable the Directorate to breed these new hybrid telepaths. How else could they have been obtained? Perhaps it was naive of me to think I could keep the adult male, but the data I obtained from him is as unique as they are."

"Granted, but you took unauthorized risks, Chy'qui. Time is still on our side. Once we've brought them to maturation, we will have years to study and experiment with these hybrids in the security and privacy of the City. There was no need to risk everything by putting an implant in the male and keeping him separate from his partners. And allowing the priest to question him was sheer folly."

"I had to find out if I'd managed to suppress his telepathic ability and isolate him totally from the other two. For that I needed J'koshuk. You know that the telepath Leska pairs have a physical transference of injuries and symptoms between them. How else could I test my work? As for the plot against Zsurtul, that was none of my doing, as I've already said. It was Doctor Zayshul. Her resentment of me is well known."

"That's why she's at the treaty table and you're in here?" The tone was rich with sarcasm.

"My staff will back me up," said Chy'qui. "If the Directorate think I'm going to resign, they're mistaken."

"Oh, the Directorate don't want you to resign," said the steward softly, reaching into the top pocket of his white coveralls. "They expect you to terminate yourself before the commander calls on the Sholan telepaths to probe your mind for evidence of your assassination attempt on the Prince. You know too much about us, Chy'qui. You're a security risk."

Chy'qui laughed nervously. "Q'ozoi wouldn't authorize that! It would be their word against mine."

"He's already taken their word against yours. That's why you're here." The steward held out his hand, opening it to display the three gel capsules lying in his palm. "Quick-acting and painless."

"You're joking!" Chy'qui said, getting up from the bed to stand as far away from the steward as possible. "I've no intention of taking them. I can prove my innocence easily!"

"You have until I return for the tray to take them." He put the capsules down on the bed. "If you have not . . ." He shrugged.

"But the work I've done for the Directorate! You said yourself that the specimens were valuable! That surely counts for something!" blustered Chy'qui.

"You're quite right. I forgot to thank you. How remiss of me." He turned away toward the door but Chy'qui lunged forward to grab him by the arm.

"You can intercede for me! Tell them I'm innocent of the charges and can prove it!"

The steward brushed Chy'qui's hands away. "I think not. You've caused us to be responsible for the deaths of two of the crew already. Making sure the blame for that lies at your door wasn't easy. We haven't the stomach for taking any more innocent lives. We're trying to protect our species."

Chy'qui felt a sudden sharp prick on his hand. Surprised, he stood looking at it as his sight began to blur.

"You've become an embarrassment to us, Chy'qui," he heard the steward say, as if from a great distance. "And don't bother with the pills, they won't be necessary now."

Lisanne Norman

The *Sholan Alliance* Series

"Will hold you spellbound"—*Romantic Times*

The seventh novel takes readers into the heart of a secret Prime base—where Kusac must make an alliance with an enemy general to save his son's life.

To Order Call: 1-800-788-6262
www.dawbooks.com

DAW 29

CJ Cherryh
Complete Classic Novels in Omnibus Editions

To Order Call: 1-800-788-6262
www.dawbooks.com